S0-AFN-348

COULD YOU,
WOULD YOU,
RISK ALL
FOR SOMEONE
YOU LOVED?

One thing stands between a passionate man and a woman on the other side of freedom— the Berlin Wall! But alone, no man can challenge the wall. So a brazen group, driven by conflicting desires, defy the symbol of two worlds' hatred. Beneath the Wall, they dig for something more important than their lives.

*There are many secret tunnels
beneath the city of Berlin.
This is the story
of one of them.*

"IT'S A MIGHTY CLIFF-HANGER . . .
an adventure story of such sustained tension it has the power of immediacy."
Publishers Weekly

BERLIN TUNNEL 21

DONALD LINDQUIST

AVON
PUBLISHERS OF BARD, CAMELOT AND DISCUS BOOKS

This book is dedicated to my mother,
MARTHA RIETH LINDQUIST,
whose life exemplifies
the strength, courage, and determination
of those who refused to accept defeat and repression
and who escaped to freedom
over, under, and through the Berlin Wall.
Sie ist ganz bestimmt eine Berlinerin!

BERLIN TUNNEL 21 is an original publication of
Avon Books. This work has never before appeared in book form.

AVON BOOKS
A division of
The Hearst Corporation
959 Eighth Avenue
New York, New York 10019

Copyright © 1978 by Donald Lindquist
Published by arrangement with the author.
Library of Congress Catalog Card Number: 77-95094
ISBN: 0-380-01843-8

First Avon Printing, March, 1978

AVON TRADEMARK REG. U.S. PAT. OFF. AND IN
OTHER COUNTRIES, MARCA REGISTRADA,
HECHO EN U.S.A.

Printed in the U.S.A.

PART I

THE TROOP

᠎᠎᠎᠎᠎᠎᠎᠎᠎᠎᠎᠎᠎᠎᠎᠎᠎᠎᠎᠎᠎᠎᠎᠎᠎᠎᠎᠎᠎᠎᠎᠎᠎

THE old Army truck rumbled over the cobbles, shaking every bolt and nut in its body. The arched wooden stays holding up the canvas covering the bed of the truck creaked and groaned like an old man complaining about his arthritis. On the long, worn wooden benches along both sides of the bed of the truck, twenty-two men of the Second Regiment, Fourth Defense Brigade, sat shoulder to shoulder, each with one hand on the sling of his submachine gun, the other up over his shoulder, gripping the top rib of the siding to keep from being thrown to the floor. They endured the bouncing and tossing in silence, staring ahead or down between their legs, averting their eyes whenever they met one another's, glancing occasionally out the back at the gray buildings, caught naked by the bright afternoon sun, to see where they were. Most of them were not Berliners and did not know the city. Only easily identifiable landmarks—a *Platz,* a church, a park, a government building—told them where they were.

Konrad Möss was a Berliner. He had the fierce pride in his city that all Berliners had—East or West, it didn't matter—a pride that dated back generations to Frederick the Great. To say *"Ich bin ein Berliner"* was to say everything. Everything except "I am free." Only West Berliners could say that now. Konrad had watched The Wall go up, making an ugly scar across the face of his beloved city. He had felt the shame, the humiliation, the anger of an unjustly punished man, emotions he dared not show, let alone speak of. And he understood the

3

disgrace The Wall had brought to the memory of all those proud Berliners who had gone before him.

But these pig sloppers imported from the country to guard The Wall had no pride in the city, no sense of its history, not even a longing to be free. They stank of lime and manure. They were crude, witless, and sullen, and talked about nothing but getting back to the farm. They hoarded their pittance of pay, unwilling to join him in a night on the town—as if he would want their company, anyway—and sold him their cigarette ration at an exorbitant price. He could not count the times they had driven him to the point where he wanted to clout one of them—anyone, it wouldn't have mattered—but they were uniformly thick-chested and broad-shouldered, with biceps as big as his calf and hands like iron. He found it prudent to hold his temper.

At the moment, he especially despised the truck driver. Konrad was trying to light a cigarette, and each time he got two hands free to strike a match, the truck would hit a pothole or go careening around a corner, and he would have to catch hold of the rib to keep his seat.

"Stupid, ignorant pig slopper," he muttered to himself. He kept all his grievances to himself. Right now, he wanted a cigarette badly. He did not know whether or not the next time the truck stopped he would be called out. Then it would be too late. It was forbidden to smoke on guard duty, and it would be just his luck to be caught and reported by some zealous citizen hoping to ingratiate himself with the authorities.

The truck came to a screeching, jarring halt. The men went flying forward, falling against one another like a row of dominoes on end. Growls of protest arose from those in the front near the cab who received the full weight of the others. The cab door banged open, and the sergeant's voice rattled on the fragile pane Konrad had erected between him and those in authority. He was relieved to find the sergeant's invective directed at the driver. "I told you to get them brakes fixed! I told you, didn't I? *Didn't I?*"

The driver muttered a reply, inarticulately trying to defend himself against the merciless lash of the sergeant's tongue. Konrad took the opportunity to light up a cigarette, inhaling it deeply and fast on the assumption that he might be called out next. They never knew in advance which post they were going to man. Konrad sat there with the cigarette cupped in his hand between his knees, listening to the sergeant giving it to the driver. It pleased him to hear one of those peasants getting it from the sergeant, even though he had no use for him, either.

The cab door slammed shut, shaking the old truck to its bones. Konrad could hear the sound of the sergeant's boots outside on the cobbles. Then his stony face appeared over the tailgate, a crooked ridge line of a nose rising from a flat gray plain. He held up a clipboard and called out, "Poldiek! Möss! Out!"

Konrad sighed. He put his head down between his knees, drew long on the cigarette, dropped it to the bed of the truck, and inhaled. The others all looked at him, then looked away as if he were infected. It was always that way—the air inside the truck heavy with incipient hatred, the smell of gun oil and sweat, the silence of momentary relief.

"All right, let's go! Get a move on! Come on, out you go!"

Poldiek moved out first. In the street behind the sergeant, the two guards being relieved approached the truck like cattle at feeding time. Konrad picked up the cigarette, took a last hasty puff, and dropped it again. He got up and stepped gingerly between the two rows of feet toward the back.

"How about dropping the tailgate?" he said to the sergeant. It was something he knew he could say without getting into serious trouble, something that demonstrated his independence but was not insubordinate.

"I'll drop *your* tailgate, sonny. Get your ass down here."

Someone in the truck snickered. Konrad put his hand behind his back and made an obscene sign. He put his other hand on top of the tailgate and vaulted into the street beside the sergeant.

"Private Möss, is it?"

Konrad did not answer. The sergeant looked him up and down. "Got your poncho?" Konrad showed it to him, folded over his belt in the small of his back. The sergeant turned on Poldiek. "Where's yours?"

"I didn't bring it, Sergeant."

"And what if it rains, sonny? What'll you do then? Go to sleep in a cozy corner somewheres, I suppose?"

One of the men being relieved stepped forward, pulling his poncho out of his belt. "He can use mine, Sergeant."

The sergeant put his thick hands on his hips and cocked his head to one side. "Now ain't that sweet. Look here, Private Poldiek, your comrade wants to help you keep your pants dry. Ain't that touching? Ain't that just too thoughtful?" Abruptly, his manner changed. He turned on the Good Samaritan, snarling through his yellow, serrated teeth, "Get up in that truck before I boot your ass up without you attached!"

The private's face went white with fear. He scrambled up the tailgate, his weapon banging against the metal, and went sailing into the dark pit of the truck bed head first. His partner clambered after him. Konrad laughed.

"You think that's funny, Möss?"

Konrad swallowed his laugh and did not answer. He had learned that answers got you into trouble. The sergeant glared at him until he felt satisfied that his authority had been reestablished. He drew a mechanical pencil from his blouse pocket and made a mark on the clipboard he was carrying. "This is post forty-one. Either one of you had this post before?"

"I had it a couple of days ago," Konrad said.

"I had it two weeks ago or so," Poldiek said. He was short and stout and spoke with a high, chirping voice.

"Okay. So you should know what to do. Report in every hour on the hour. There's a phone up at the corner." He gestured up the street where an unlighted street lamp hung in lonely solitude against the backdrop of blue sky. "Any questions?"

The two privates had none. The sergeant stuck the pencil back into his pocket, turned on his heel, and called out to the men in the truck, "Okay, hang on! We're off!" The cab door opened and slammed shut, the engine turned over, and with a grinding of gears the truck was off, staggering down the street, wavering from one side to the other as it took on speed. The old man was drunk as well.

Konrad looked around. On the east side of the street, old apartment houses rose to four and five stories. The windows presented an irregular pattern of light and dark, according to whether the shades were drawn or not. The only relief in the block of flat-faced gray stucco was the sign of the Gasthaus Edelweiss jutting out over the sidewalk. At night, he remembered, it cast an elongated rhombus glow on the pavement below. Konrad thought of the comfort of the place and longed to be in there with his feet up, drinking a light beer, reading a book, waiting. . . .

The buildings along the west side of the street rose up like a weathered cliff of basalt on a desolate shore. They had been evacuated when The Wall went up. The area behind them had been cleared as far as The Wall and was laid with barbed wire, tank traps, antipersonnel mines, and gun emplacements. At night, light from the floodlights playing on the cleared area—the Death Zone —flickered over the rooftops like distant shooting stars.

Post forty-one extended for six blocks along the western side of the street. One sentry was to walk north three blocks and return, the other south three blocks, meeting each time at the corner where the telephone box had been installed. Their duty was to keep people off the western side of the street, out of the vacant buildings, and out of the Death Zone. In case of an attempted escape, they were to assist the guards patrolling along The Wall.

Konrad hated this duty. Along The Wall the guards walked in pairs to lessen the chances of the soldiers themselves attempting escape. Time passed faster with someone to talk to, even if it was about crops and pigs and the evils of the city. The guards had to walk eight hours without a break, and each succeeding day the hours seemed longer and longer, the conversation duller and duller. Today, on post forty-one, not even the drone of a stupid peasant would be there to console him.

But the worst thing about post forty-one was that it was not at The Wall. Konrad had hopes of getting over, under, or through The Wall into West Berlin. Ever since his regiment had been reassigned to border patrol duty, he had been looking for an opportunity to escape. Back this far, on the fringe of the Death Zone, he had no way to look for possible escape routes. It was to be another day wasted, another day restricted to his own bitterness.

Poldiek was inspecting the uniform of the blue sky. "It's supposed to rain tonight."

"So?"

"Do you think it will?"

"Definitely."

"What will I do? He could have let me borrow that fellow's poncho."

"Serves you right, dumbhead. I hope it pours." Konrad spit into the dry gutter and slung his weapon upside down in anticipation of the rain. He had never fired the weapon and never expected to. He certainly would never try to hit anyone if he did have to fire it. "I'll walk south, you take the other way." He wanted the three blocks that included the Edelweiss so that he could keep in periodic touch with humanity. He started off before Poldiek had a chance to argue.

He walked slowly—the "border patrol gallop," they called it, a pace just fast enough to keep one's balance—focusing his mind on escape. He thought about it constantly, especially about what it would be like once he was across. *If I was over there, I'd be having a great time right now. I'd have money in my pocket and a girl to spend it on, a bright-eyed girl with thoughts only for me. If it rained, who'd care? We'd snuggle up in a cozy bed and make love—mad, passionate love—and she'd bring me tea and light me a cigarette. She'd light it in her lips and put it between my lips and snuggle up while I smoked and drank my tea and thought about how good it had been between us. And we'd let the thunder break the sky apart. Ah, how good it would be, how good. . . .*

At the end of the three-block stretch, Konrad paused and gazed past the end of the last building, down where the street used to cross into West Berlin. The macadam was still there, except at the very end, at The Wall, where it was rolled back like a carpet. The face of The Wall was painted white so that at night, with the lights on it, anyone trying to make an escape would make a good target.

So near and yet so far. He'd never get past that first row of barbed wire. He thought of the Bible story his mother had told him, of the way the Red Sea had parted for the Jews when they were fleeing from Egypt. Too bad I'm not a Jew—they have all the luck. He laughed at his own irony and started back.

At least over there he wouldn't be bored. Even if he didn't have a girl like that, he wouldn't have the ever-lasting, boring routine in the barracks—up at dawn, make your bed, sweep your area, wash, shave, brush your teeth, comb your hair, get dressed, listen to the same stupid complaints, calisthenics, breakfast, drill, target prac-tice, lesson on ideology, lesson on duties of the border police, lesson on hygiene (it never sinks into those pig-slopping peasants), sit, sit, sit, listen, listen, listen, yak, yak, yak. It's all so boring. "It's so *boring!*"

His words rattled down the empty street. He looked around, expecting someone to be there watching him, expecting something to happen. Nothing moved. No one was in sight except Poldiek plodding slowly up the street toward him.

Nothing will ever happen here. Nothing. Nothing will change, ever. I'll go on walking guard duty forever, on and on into infinity, and nothing will ever happen. Noth-ing.

╳╳╳╳╳╳╳╳╳╳╳╳╳╳╳╳╳╳╳╳╳╳╳╳╳╳╳╳

O N the other side of The Wall, in the borough of Kreuz-berg, Sepp Bauer sat in the window seat in his room, waiting to see if Emerich Weber would come. From his window he could see down the length of the narrow street, where the old shops and houses stood hunched together like old friends gossiping in the sun. The shop windows were bright with their wares, and the windows of the apartments on the south side of the street were dotted with colored curtains drawn against the heat. Sepp liked these buildings with their elaborate cornices, ornate entryways, colonnaded facades, and rooftop gargoyle rainspouts, which during rainstorms spewed aesthetically pleasing, albeit inconsiderate, fountains of water down onto the pedestrians below. And he liked the easy pace of the inhabitants as they shopped from store to store, called to one another from window to window, and sat on their stoops at night to smoke and while away the twilight.

The sun stood a quarter of the way down the sky, peer-ing through the lacework of the church steeple across the street like a hungry vagrant peering through the win-dow of an elegant restaurant. There were boys playing soccer in the churchyard. Their shouts and the thump of their feet against the leather ball echoed up the narrow street. A young priest was sitting in the sun on the church steps, reading. He held the book in one hand and, in the other, the end of an attached red ribbon bookmark, poised, ready to lay it between the pages and close the book if he had to. Occasionally he would glance up at the boys, then down the street, then up at Sepp. When their eyes met, the priest would smile shyly and quickly return to his reading. Sepp would have liked to talk to him, not because he was particularly attracted to the priest's shy personality but because he felt sorry for him. He was not sure why, but he did. He made a mental note to do so someday.

The gold-painted hands of the church clock read twenty-five past one. Emerich was late. Or wasn't coming. Sepp looked up the street again toward the subway stop. No sign of him. The street lay shimmering in the heat.

Emerich would come. He knew it, he was sure of his man. Just because he was late did not mean he was not coming. Emerich had more reason than any of the others. He had to come.

An argument broke out among the boys. The priest marked his page, closed the book, and got to his feet. The boys were shouting, some in strident soprano, others in surprisingly deep baritone. The priest took a hesitant step toward them and said something. No one paid any attention to him. One boy pushed another. The boy holding the ball flung it against the fence. It bounded back, and the boy who had been pushed caught it with his foot in midair and sent it sailing over the wrought-iron fence into a garden beyond. Everyone, including the priest, stopped to watch it; then, as if by unanimous agreement, they all turned on the boy who had booted it. He raced past them, past the priest, out of the yard down the steps, and up the street with the pack close behind, the priest waving at them and shouting ineffectually. Emerich Weber came around the corner and had to jump aside to avoid being trampled. He stood in the street shaking his fist, cursing after them.

Sepp hooted in victory, and hopped off the window seat, got two bottles of beer from the small refrigerator in the closet, snapped them open, and set them on the table. From below came the sound of the door opening and closing and Emerich taking the steps two at a time. Sepp opened the door, and Emerich came in.

"I'm late."

Sepp waved it away. He was too happy to be angry. "People shouldn't be late. My hair falls out if I have to wait." He was carrying a battered briefcase. He set it on the floor against the wall by the door. Emerich was an agronomy student at the Free University, and during the summer recess he was working the night shift at the Siemens Electric Company. He always had about him the odor of oil and pitch and grease, much as some men smell of too much cologne. "You live in a dangerous neighborhood," he said.

Sepp handed him a beer. The bottle was already covered with condensed moisture. Emerich took it and drank half of it straight down. He belched and wiped his mouth on his sleeve and set the bottle on the table and wiped his hands on his trousers. The shirt and trousers he wore were old U.S. Army khakis he had picked up somewhere. They were too big for him: The shirt hung down over his thin shoulders, and he had had to turn back the cuffs; the trousers bunched at the waist, and the bottoms flapped over his shoes. Even the belt was too long. The end dangled down on one side like a dog's tongue hanging out on a hot day.

Emerich was thin, sinewy, and hard, made of twine, leather, and wood. His Adam's apple protruded from his long neck like the node left where a branch had been sawed from a tree. A misshapen nose was stuck onto his face and, bent a little to one side, resembled a piece of unfinished wood carving. His long black hair stuck out in all directions. It was never combed. He always had a day or two's growth of beard, a sparse, patchy sprawl of whiskers that rose to high points on his white cheeks and descended deep down the escarpment of his long neck.

In combination, the disheveled black hair, scraggly beard, and whitewashed skin might have given him a sickly appearance had it not been for his eyes. As tiny as pebbles, as black as carbon, they were set far apart, as if by such wide dispersion they could make up for their size. Though small, they missed nothing, taking everything in with quick, intent glances, not so much looking, observing, or seeing, as questioning, evaluating, challenging.

As his eyes saved his face from a false impression of weakness, so his hands served the rest of his body. Dirt was encrusted under his chipped and broken, deeply fluted fingernails, and grease was embedded underneath and around the cuticles, in the lines of his fingers, and in the leathery wrinkles of skin around his knuckles. They were strong, competent, quick hands that knew hard work. But they could turn a figure in air with disarming grace, giving the intimation, even before he spoke, that there was much more to Emerich Weber than his appearance suggested.

Sepp was waiting for his decision. Emerich looked at him, then out the window. The evasion gave Sepp an intimation of rejection, and the joy of victory began to wane. "What about it?" he said finally, too anxious to let Emerich answer in his own time.

Emerich finished the beer in one go. "Let me see the plan," he said cautiously.

Emerich's answer did little to reverse the trend of Sepp's feelings. "Your enthusiasm is overwhelming."

Emerich turned on him half in anger, half in a plea for understanding. "How can you expect me to be enthusiastic? If I go through with this, I'll be taking the lives of my entire family into my hands. That's nothing to get enthusiastic about."

Sepp was taken aback. He had lived with that fear for Ilse for so long now that it had become commonplace. Once he had made the decision for the tunnel, he had let it drop out of his thoughts. Either you accepted the responsibility or you lived with the consequences of not accepting it. With Emerich, there were more people involved, but Sepp could not believe there was more love or that numbers alone made any difference. He gave Emerich his beer and got another bottle for himself from the refrigerator. Then he took a rolled-up sheet of draft paper from a wardrobe drawer and spread it out on the table, laying books on the corners to hold it in place. The paper was a diagram of the area of a tunnel under The Wall, carefully drawn to scale in India ink. Emerich pulled up his chair alongside Sepp's and looked it over, waiting for Sepp to begin. He sipped the beer absently.

"The warehouse, here, at Forty-seven Koenigstrasse, is where we start."

"I know the street. In Wedding."

"It belongs to a man by the name of Komanski who lives in Frankfurt. He's in construction equipment. He has a big plant down there."

"How did you find that out?"

"From the owner of the plastics company next door to the warehouse. I inquired there, saying I was interested in buying the property. He told me he had tried to buy the building himself last year to expand his operations, but the price was too high. It's an old building, but the foundation, walls, and roof are in good shape."

"How many floors are there?"

"Three, besides the cellar."

"What did you do, break in?"

"It wasn't hard; there was only a padlock on the back door. I sawed it off one night and installed a snap lock. We'll enter and leave only by the back door, using the alley to Margstrasse. It's a dead-end alley. There are no windows in the plastics factory overlooking the alley, but there are in the machine shop, and they're always open during the day in the summer."

"What happens if those people get nosy?"

"We're going to pose as construction workers—masons, carpenters, painters—reconditioning the inside of the warehouse. We'll dress and act the part."

"Somebody might want to take a look inside."

"The door has to be kept locked at all times. That's essential." Sepp took a brass key from his shirt pocket and gave it to Emerich. "Whenever you enter or leave, be sure to lock the door. If anybody asks to see inside, tell them it's too dangerous, that we're not covered by liability insurance."

Emerich turned the key in his bony fingers, then laid it aside; he was not yet prepared to make any definite gesture of commitment. He traced the distance from the warehouse to the escape house in East Berlin. "Seventy-five meters." He grunted. "A long tunnel."

"We'll have to shore it as we go."

Emerich nodded. "A tunnel that long has to be shored. How do you know the distance is correct? If you're wrong we could come up short in the Death Zone."

That he had said "we" did not escape Sepp's notice. "I used triangulation. I checked it three times."

Emerich looked skeptical.

"I was in the Corps of Engineers in the Army. We learned how to survey."

"All right."

"I'm just as concerned as you are that it's right."

Emerich had accepted it. "What about the cellar? Is it big enough to store the earth, or do we have to truck it away?"

"The tunnel will be one meter square. That's seventy-five cubic meters of earth we'll remove as we dig. The cellar measures more than three hundred and thirty cubic meters. We won't be able to make use of all that space just to pile up earth. We'll have to have a working area, so we may be cramped toward the end."

"Seventy-five cubic meters is one mountain of earth. How long do you expect it will take to finish it?"

"Two weeks, maybe three. It depends on how often and how much it rains, and whether or not the tunnel drains well if it does. Rain could be our biggest problem, but we'll be three meters underground. That will be to our advantage."

"I'll pray for clear skies," Emerich said, as if that took care of the rain. "What's the soil like?"

"At that depth, clay—at least in the warehouse cellar it is. It will be heavy digging, but the compactness of the clay ought to reduce the danger of a cave-in."

Emerich made a dark face. "Don't even talk about a cave-in."

"It can happen."

"Not if we do a good job of shoring." He had dismissed the possibility, either because he really believed a cave-in was unlikely or because he dreaded thinking about it. "What do we use for shoring?"

"The lumber in the flooring—three floors of it. It's all heavy planking."

Emerich brightened. He rubbed his hands together. "A juicy piece of thievery. Maybe you have some peasant blood in you. Where did you say your father came from?"

"Frankfurt, and he's a stockbroker."

Emerich searched Sepp's face, perhaps seeking out a telltale feature which would betray peasant ancestry, but found none. "You have too much class to have come from peasants."

Sepp suspected Emerich's compliment was a bit inverted. Emerich would have felt better if Sepp had had some peasant stock in his background.

"What do we do for lights? Are there leads into the warehouse?"

"Yes, but—"

"We can tap them."

"The electric company meters the lines. I looked into it."

Emerich was disappointed. "So what about lights?"

"I've bought a generator."

"Do you know motors? You should have taken me along. I know motors." Emerich's admonition was more a personal concern than a criticism: He was projecting himself into a commitment without having given it.

Sepp reassured him, "I know motors. The generator is in good shape."

"Motors are like oxen. You have to know when to pamper them and when to kick them to get the most work out of them."

"I'd just as soon you didn't kick this one."

"If it's in good shape, it won't hurt it." Emerich bent his long, narrow head over the diagram. "What is the work plan? Do you have one?"

"We'll work from seven in the morning until six at night. One man will be digging at all times, one removing the earth, two shoring up behind the digging, two preparing lumber for the shoring."

"You'll want a lookout."

"I don't think it's necessary. Besides, we can't afford a man to sit and do nothing all day."

"They may be stupid, but they aren't deaf. They'll be able to hear us."

"There's plenty of noise in the area from traffic and the factories during the day. Remember, we'll be three meters underground. That's a lot of insulation. You're right about noise at night. We can't work at night; it's quiet as a graveyard then."

Emerich was unimpressed. "I think we should have a lookout."

"There are only six of us. We can't afford it."

Emerich looked at him for a while, considering whether the point was critical. He took a drink of beer and went to the window. The sun came into his black eyes, and they narrowed. "Who are the others?"

Sepp had been expecting the question; now that it was out, he was apprehensive. He knew that the site for the tunnel was the best he could find, and the plan he had made was a good one. He could defend both with confidence. He was not, however, so confident about the people in the troop—even Emerich, he realized—but they were ready and willing. Whether or not they were able as well had to remain a question mark until they had been tested. "Joachim Lentz," he said at length, "his brother, Wolf, Georg Knauer, and Bruno Balderbach."

"The artist?"

"Yes."

Emerich leaned against the window frame and looked down into the street. The sun had dropped lower, coming through the ornamentation of the church steeple.

"What do you think?"

"I know Joachim Lentz only by reputation."

"He's intelligent and strong."

"True." Emerich sat back on the window seat and ran his hands through his hair, which simply rearranged itself in different but equal disarray. "Joachim Lentz is intelligent and strong. He has a family in the *Sektor,* true. But Joachim Lentz is for Joachim Lentz—and no one but Joachim Lentz—and if digging the tunnel interferes with his career or his love life, *auf Wiedersehen,* Joachim Lentz. His little brother I don't know anything about. If he has muscles, good. We have enough brains. I know Georg Knauer only slightly. He's a little high-strung, I hear, a loner, not very sociable, but this is not going to be a tea party." He looked down at the patterns the grease and dirt had made on his work shoes. "Why the artist, for God's sake? How did he ever get involved with something like this?"

"He wants to do it, Emerich."

"How old is he?"

"Forty-five. Fifty, maybe."

Emerich sniffed. "It's crazy."

"He'll do his share."

Emerich gave him a look that said he thought otherwise. He got up, stuck his hands deep into his pockets, and went back to the table. He stood over it staring down at the diagram. "What about the Vopos?"

"We'll probably have to take the one who passes the house."

"That shouldn't be too hard. We'll need a gun."

"I have one."

Emerich jabbed a finger at the rectangle representing the escape house in East Berlin. "Can we get in? Does it have a cellar?"

"Good question."

"Of course it's a good question. Don't you know?"

"No."

Emerich sat back and renewed his search of Sepp's face. His own reflected his puzzlement.

"I'm going in there," Sepp said. "It's an evacuated house—that whole side of the street has been evacuated."

"And you're just going to walk in and take a look around."

Sepp smiled. "In a manner of speaking, yes."

"More insanity."

"It won't be so hard. I've been going into East Berlin every night for the past month, ever since I got out of the Army. Ilse and I spend our time in a little *Gasthaus*"—he indicated the Edelweiss on the diagram—"here. We've studied the layout carefully. It can be done."

"You can also be shot."

"I won't be shot."

"Isn't there an easier way to find out?"

"Can you suggest one?"

Emerich gave in. "When is this insane operation to be executed?"

"Tonight."

"Crazy, man," Emerich said in English. He grew solemn. "Have you made arrangements—in case?"

"Joachim will contact a friend of mine in the American Army if I'm not back by midnight."

"You're the only one who can cross over?"

"I'll make it. I'm not going to get caught."

"You haven't lived there; you don't know what they're really like." He turned his black eyes on Sepp in more a threatening than a pleading voice. "If they catch you, don't mention my name. The bastards will take it out on my family."

Sepp flushed with sudden anger. "You don't have to tell me that."

Emerich looked at him and closed his eyes in dismay, on the defensive for the first time. "Misery, I am a stupid peasant with a clod of dung for a brain."

"I'm not going to be caught," Sepp said flatly. He felt confident. The risks were considerable, but it would be foolish to dig the tunnel without knowing if they would be able to use the house. He got up and went to the window. The sky was still a brittle blue, free of clouds. The heat displaced the air with its weight, like a rock set in a pail of water. Below, the street lay silent and empty. He felt his anger draining away. He had too much on his mind to find room for anger long.

Emerich said, "We always expect you Americans to be innocent of our barbarity."

"You Germans all think we're as naive as children."

"Do you forgive me?"

"I've forgotten it."

Emerich slammed his hand down on the table. "You see, you are naive! You don't even know how to take advantage of an insult."

Sepp waved him off. "You're mad, Emerich, you're wholly mad." The humor he had meant to put in it did not materialize.

"In more ways than you'll ever know. When do we begin this tunnel?"

Sepp turned to him, smiling. "Tomorrow morning."

"I have to be at work every day at three."

"Yes."

"We go on vacation next week. The place will be closed down for two weeks."

"That's good."

"Am I the only one with a job? Ah, no, Lentz is a fashion model, isn't he? Or has he become a movie star? I've heard he expects to become a movie star. He says it, doesn't he?"

"He may do it someday."

"That he may, that he may. He has just the personality for it." Emerich's tone said he did not mean it as a compliment.

Sepp was becoming annoyed. "What is it, Emerich?"

He feigned innocence. "What is what?"

"I didn't expect you to be ecstatic about everybody I picked, but I didn't know there was something personal between you and Joachim."

"Personal? There's nothing personal. I hardly know the *Mensch*. But I know the type."

"I didn't know Joachim was a 'type.' "

"Come off it, Sepp. The bugger is so in love with himself, he believes everybody else is, too. He'd faint if he ever found out they weren't."

"It's all right if you don't love him, Emerich. And I don't think he'll faint when he finds out."

Emerich chose to take it personally. "Who would want love from a peasant like me, eh?"

Sepp was momentarily embarrassed. Emerich saw it. "*Ach,* don't pay any attention to me when I rant like that." He patted Sepp's arm consolingly and smiled. "Now tell me, what does the loner do for a living?"

"Georg?"

"The same."

Sepp did not know.

"And you've never asked him, of course."

Despite his sudden mellowness Emerich would now go to work on Georg if given the chance.

"Maybe Georg's a millionaire, or a thief. I couldn't care less."

Emerich bristled. "People who don't work are worthless parasites."

Sepp lost his patience. "I should have made you director of personnel."

"I could have come up with a better lot than you did."

"Fine. Let's go get them. All I want is a tunnel dug. I don't give a damn who digs it."

Emerich backed off. "I'm being too critical, eh?"

"You are."

"I don't know if *I'll* be any good at this."

Sepp was not deceived this time by Emerich's chameleon change of mood. He purposely understated the expected response. "You'll do."

If Emerich was miffed, he showed no sign of it. He drained the second bottle of beer and set the empty next to the first.

Sepp asked him if he had thought about how they could get his family to East Berlin.

"I have an aunt living over there, my father's sister. She took me in when I was working out my escape. She married a salesman and left our village years ago. She's a widow now, living on a pension, drinks a lot; but she's got a soft spot in her, and she hates the Communists. My idea is that if she were to get sick, if she were dying, they would let my family come to East Berlin to pay their respects. But we'd need a doctor to certify that she was really on the verge."

"Ilse would know some doctors in the *Sektor*."

"Knowing doctors and knowing one who would take the risk are two different things. No one left over there has any guts."

Sepp suddenly remembered, "Joachim's father is a doctor. If he knew he could get out, he might do it."

Emerich seemed reluctant.

"What's wrong? It wouldn't hurt to try."

"I don't want to end up owing Joachim Lentz a damned thing."

Sepp dismissed his objection. "The more I think about it, the better it sounds. I'll ask Ilse to talk to Dr. Lentz. Your aunt ought to start getting sick soon if it's to look authentic."

"My family should be told what we're up to. They'd never go packing off to Berlin just to bid old Aunt Magda good-bye, not in a thousand years. The story is she *had* to get married to that salesman. She's been sort of a black sheep. My father would spit and cross himself and say good riddance."

"I'll pose the problem to Ilse."

"Is she going to do the contact work over there?"

"Yes."

Emerich eyed Sepp openly, without a trace of inhibition. "She's really worth all this, eh?"

"She's really worth it."

"You're a lucky man."

"I am."

"I hope she's the cautious type. Tell her to make sure she's not being followed, tell her—"

"Emerich, Emerich, she's lived over there all her life, too. She knows how to handle this sort of thing."

Emerich made a face. "*Ach*, I get carried away. But it's better to be too cautious than too confident." He smiled in a distracted way. "I'd love to see how she handles Aunt Magda."

"You'd better give me her name and address. And I'll need a note from you. She's not apt to trust Ilse on just her word."

"Magda Halzapfel. Eighty-seven Baunallee, Prenzlauer-berg."

Sepp repeated it to himself, committing it to memory. He gave Emerich pen and paper to write a note.

"What should I say?"

"Tell her that Ilse is a friend of yours. Tell her you hope she'll do Ilse the favor she's asking."

He wrote it out.

"You should put in something so she'll know the note is from you. She probably won't recognize your handwriting."

Emerich thought for a moment. "How about if I say I still have the pocketknife she gave me when I stayed with her?"

"That should do it if she remembers."

"She'll remember. She knows how she spent her first pfennig." He finished the note and gave it to Sepp. Sepp looked it over to make sure he had not used surnames. Emerich knew better.

Emerich gave the diagram a final scrutiny. "There are probably a dozen more questions I could ask, but I have to get to work." He looked up. "What time should I be at the warehouse?"

"Joachim and I will pick you up in his car at six forty-five tomorrow morning."

"I'll get there on my own."

Sepp shrugged. "Suit yourself."

Emerich picked up his briefcase. "How did you ever get involved with Bruno Balderbach?"

"We're old friends, in a manner of speaking."

"Does he have people in the *Sektor?*"

"No. He just wants to help."

"I've never known any famous people. What's he like?"

"He's not very different from other men."

"He's doing this, isn't he?"

"So are you."

"I'm not fifty—and famous." He held Sepp's bottle of beer up to the light. "You didn't touch it."

"It's all yours."

Emerich grinned. He recapped the bottle and caressed it affectionately. "Maybe we could just telephone my father at the tractor station." He rolled his eyes. "The Reds are so suspicious, they might not suspect anyone would be as stupid as that."

Sepp laughed. "And you were just giving me a lecture on the need for caution. We'll think of a way. First we have to see what reaction Ilse gets from your aunt and Dr. Lentz." Sepp put his hand on Emerich's bony shoulder. "Don't worry, we won't let anybody through the tunnel until all of them are ready—your family, the Lentzes, Georg's parents, Ilse. They all come, or none."

Emerich nodded. He glanced at the clock on Sepp's night table. "I can't be late for work."

Sepp shook his hand. "Thanks, Emerich."

"No, Sepp. I thank you. It means . . . much to me . . . to my family." He might have said more. His face was becoming flushed with the bitterness his own words were generating. He made a gesture of resignation. "I'll take that ride tomorrow morning," he said. "It will save me the bus fare."

Sepp nodded. "At six forty-five."

"I'll be ready." He tucked the bottle of beer into his briefcase. "Where's that key?"

Sepp got it from the table and gave it to him.

"So we're going to do it."

"Yes."

Emerich stuck the key in his pocket. "Be careful tonight."

"I will."

They shook hands.

" 'Wiedersehen, Sepp."

" 'Wiedersehen, Emerich."

Sepp watched him jog down the steps, the loose clothes bouncing away from his bony body this way and that as if looking for some warm flesh upon which to light. Like his Aunt Magda, Emerich, too, had a soft spot, and all his bristling antagonism and sarcasm could not hide it. "You'll do," Sepp said to himself. "You'll do just fine."

After Emerich had gone, Sepp rolled up the diagram of the tunnel and put it back in the wardrobe drawer. When he did, he moved a pile of shirts, uncovering his revolver. He took it out, felt its heft, and wondered if he would have to use it. He had considered taking it with him tonight, but he never knew if this would be the night Lieutenant Geller would decide to search him. He put it back and closed the wardrobe door. He put the empty beer bottles with the others in the wooden case in the hall.

Sepp's room had not changed much in a year. There were still the bottles in the hall. Bruno's painting of the white deer still hung over his desk. The room was still in a state of disarray he had never learned to care enough about to change. Even the calendar on the wall was the same—still turned to August 1961. Sepp had taken the room a month after arriving in Berlin to have a place to stay away from the barracks. He probably could have found a better room in a better neighborhood at a cheaper rent, but he was taken with the old street that gave some intimation of what Berlin had been in the days before the war.

It was a week after he had rented the room that he had met Ilse. Afterward he thought about it and decided that fate had been at work, anticipating her coming into his life. He had wanted the room for those occasions when the girl he picked up had no place of her own for them to go to, and just to get away from military life from time to time. He wondered if he would have associated any girl who attracted him with the room, or only Ilse. He was never to find out.

He had met her on a brilliant Saturday afternoon in May, a day that pronounced winter dead once and for all. The outdoor cafés in the Kurfurstendamm were back in business, crowded with Berliners taking in the full breath of spring. The laughter and music that had been holed up for six months had moved out into the streets. Sepp was out, too, moving with the crowds, feeling as if he had been holed up along with the laughter and music. He felt alive and gay and full of determination to make something of the day. He was thinking about his determination when he saw her sitting alone at a table with coffee and cake, watching the people go by.

He stopped by the canopy that walled the café off from the sidewalk and stood watching her, waiting to catch her eye, wondering what approach he should use. She either did not see him or chose to ignore him, and he decided to use a do-or-die tactic that had worked in the past. He went in under the canvas and, zigzagging through the tables to hers, pulled out a chair and sat down across from her, smiling as cheerfully as he knew how.

She had watched his approach calmly. So, she had noticed him after all.

He looked her straight in the eye. "Yes or no?"

She had gotten a piece of cake onto her fork, but it rested on the plate, the handle still in her hand, the only sign he had momentarily overwhelmed her. At the same time she let the fork go, a smile broke across her lips. Then she began to laugh. She laughed harder and harder and had to stifle it with her napkin. She looked at him, holding her napkin over her mouth, and started laughing again, a muffled, tremulous laugh. He laughed a little, too, but he began to wonder if she were ever going to stop. Suddenly a waiter was at his elbow.

"Coffee."

The waiter enunciated each word as he wrote it down. "One. Coffee. Anything else?"

"No." Sepp turned back to her. She had stopped laughing and was sitting in her chair studying him with a lack of inhibition uncommon in a woman. The way she was looking at him made him uncomfortable, and he wanted to say something—anything—but the tactic required that she answer his question in some fashion.

"Has anyone ever said yes?"

"Of course."

"I don't believe it."

"Why not?"

"It's insane."

"Not when it works."

"You should be locked up."

"On a day like this?"

She smiled. "Tomorrow, then."

The waiter came with the coffee. "Separate checks?"

"Yes," she said.

"No."

The waiter glanced from one to the other. "If you

don't mind, Fräulein, I will take the easy way out."
He made out one check.

"Your buying me coffee and cake doesn't mean yes."

"I didn't expect it to."

"And if you are seriously waiting for an answer, it's
no."

He shrugged. "Win some, lose some." He knew that
she really meant maybe, and it was not until later that
he was glad she had not said yes.

When he walked her to the subway station, she told
him she lived in the *Sektor*. "I work in the Ministry of
Education. I want to teach, but they must know I come
over here to West Berlin a lot, so they are unsure of my
political reliability. To be a teacher, you must be politically reliable."

"And are you politically reliable?" She hesitated a moment, and he knew he had given her reason to suspect
him. "I'm sorry," he said. "I don't give a damn about
your politics. Can I see you tomorrow night?"

"Yes."

"So you can say yes after all."

She laughed and waved good-bye and boarded the
train.

Going home, he thought about her and looked forward
to seeing her again. He called her at work the next day.
"Am I damaging your political reliability?"

"Irreparably."

"I'll hang up."

"No."

"You're always saying no."

"I think you're a sex fiend."

"I wasn't until I met you."

"Perhaps I shouldn't see you tonight—for your own
good."

"No."

She laughed. "Yes and no will never be the same. I
have to get back to work."

"What are you doing?"

"Shuffling papers."

"They won't blow away."

"We have to keep them moving from desk to desk
to justify our jobs. It's a kind of conspiracy."

"I've been conspiring, too."

half smile that hid her thoughts. He sipped some champagne; that still had some sparkle, as if holding out some hope.

"My father once told me that when I met the woman I loved I must take her to the Resi in Berlin, buy her champagne, dance all the slow, romantic dances, and then, on the way home, tell her I love her. We haven't danced any dances yet, and we're not on the way home, but I'm telling you that I love you, Ilse."

The half smile left her face, and she gazed at him as if she were uncertain she had heard him correctly. Then she smiled the warm, radiant smile he loved, and tears came to her eyes. "I don't even care if the story isn't true."

He held her hands across the table. "My father wouldn't lie."

Later, walking in the clear spring night through the quiet streets of the sleeping city, she said, "I think I've missed the last train." He held her and kissed her, and when they reached his room, it was as he had always wanted it to be.

Somewhere in that forgotten clutch of hours before dawn, a storm came up to waken them. He left the window open enough to keep out the rain, but so they could still hear it and smell it fresh in the room. They lay together watching the lightning open holes in the night, listening to the rain beating on the windowpanes.

"Did you know you would win?" she asked.

"I wasn't sure."

"Neither was I."

"When did you decide?"

"It crept up on me slowly. There was never any precise moment." She moved. "Do you really love me?"

"I love you. I've never been in love, but I know I love you."

"Yes. It's that way with me, too."

"I didn't think it could happen so fast."

"We don't really know each other."

"I know you."

"I mean we don't know much about each other."

"What do you want to know? I'll confess everything."

She persisted. "All I know about you is that you're an American, you live in New York, you're a lieutenant in the Army—"

"*First* lieutenant," he realized.

"Is there a difference."

"Not much, but I just became a first lieutenant."

"When?"

"Today is the fifteenth, isn't it?"

"I think so."

"Today I am a first lieutenant."

"Congratulations."

"Now you know everything." He tried to close off the inquiry by kissing her, but she would not let him off.

"Do you have something to hide?"

"Of course, don't you?"

"I'm serious, Sepp."

"All right." He lay back and put his hands under his head. "I was born on September 1, 1939, in Lying-In Hospital in New York City. I didn't like my nurse, who was a cranky old spinster, so I requested a change and got a beautiful redhead assigned to me."

"You were born a sex fiend."

"Until I was fifteen I really believed the war started because I was born. I could see Hitler reading about it and saying, 'This is the last straw.' Can you imagine going around for fifteen years with that guilt on your conscience? It affected me psychologically."

"I believe you."

"My parents were immigrants, from Frankfurt. They insisted I keep up my German. We spoke German at home. Sometimes, when I was daydreaming in school and the teacher asked me a question, I would answer in German. The whole class would yell out, 'English, Sepp, English!' It was very embarrassing." He turned on his side and looked at her. "I'm glad they made me keep up my German."

"My English is frightful. I'll have to practice."

He smiled at her and kissed her. "Let's practice something else."

"Not until you finish telling me about yourself."

"I went to college, went into the Army, and here I am. That's it."

She laughed. "What am I to do with you?"

"I have a suggestion."

"I thought you would."

The rain lasted until morning. At first light they went

out looking for a place to get breakfast. They found an open coffee shop near the subway stop.

"I can't stay nights," she said. "Last night was special."

"Oh?"

"I live with my mother. My father was killed in the war. My mother and I are very close. I don't want to hurt her."

"What about last night?"

"I told her when I left I would be staying with a friend." Sepp laughed. "Just in case?"

"Last night was grand," she said. "We'll work something out."

The spring turned to summer, and his love for her bloomed full and rich, an enduring flower different from the ephemeral blooms of spring. They spent summer weekends sailing and swimming at Wannsee. They lay on the beach and read. When the sun rose high and killed the breeze, they would go for a swim. They practiced swimming in unison and would swim far out and then race back to shore for lunch. They ate paprika schnitzel and boiled potatoes at the outdoor restaurant and talked about the people they saw. In the afternoons they would rest in the shade of the nearby woods, working crossword puzzles in a book he had bought at the post exchange. When there was a wind, they rented a boat and sailed out across the lake and back. Evenings they spent in his room, letting the silent joy of love seal their memories of the day. Then he would walk her to the subway station to catch the train back to East Berlin.

It seemed to Sepp that those times were as it must have been before the war, when *Schatz* meant "treasure" —before it became a slang word turned foul in the mouths of drunken GIs. Those were dream days served on a golden platter like champagne cocktails before the close of a play.

Whether it was because of the unusual heat or because of the situation in the city, the last Saturday he spent with Ilse at Wannsee, the beach was jammed. It seemed as if all of West Berlin were there. There were more boats out on the water than usual, and hungry bathers were standing in a long line for tables at the outdoor restaurant.

The events of the summer, particularly of the past few

days were ominous. Ever since the June meeting between Premier Khrushchev and President Kennedy in Vienna, the radio, television, and newspapers had carried stories about an impending separate peace treaty between the Soviet Union and the East German regime. Renewed Russian demands for the withdrawal of American, French, and British troops from West Berlin and the establishment of a "free city" there were flowing out of Moscow and Pankow. Rumors of an imminent sealing of the border between East and West Berlin were being spread on both sides of the Brandenburg Gate, and the flood of refugees from the Soviet sector to the West had reached almost two thousand a day.

A policy of harassment of the tens of thousands of East Berliners who crossed the border each day to work in West Berlin had added to the mounting tension. Workers were being pulled off subways at the border by Vopos—the *Volkspolizei,* or People's Police—and border guards. They were branded as "traitors," their West Berlin employers as "white slavers." Ilse told Sepp that a list of the names of those who lived in her apartment building and who worked in the West had been posted at her entryway door, and that everyone in the building was supposed to urge them to quit their jobs and find employment in East Berlin. They were being threatened with eviction from the building, confiscation of their identity cards, and curtailment of their children's schooling. "They'll all defect for good," she said. "It's stupid. Ulbricht is truly a goat."

That Saturday afternoon, the reports on the radio continued to be discouraging. The day before, Khruschev had given a saber-rattling speech in Moscow threatening atomic war over Berlin. Premier Ulbricht had returned from a meeting there, stirring up renewed rumors about closing the border, which sent thousands more East Berliners streaming to the West. Marshal Koniev, the highest-ranking Russian military commander, had turned up in East Berlin.

Sepp was worried and tried to get Ilse to face the situation realistically. "They are going to close the border. It's bound to come. Ulbricht can't lose any more people—he's being bled white."

She sat up and shook her hair and put on her

sunglasses. "That I would like to see—a white Ulbricht."

"It's no time for jokes."

"You made the joke, darling."

"What will happen if the border is closed?"

"They wouldn't dare. Your President Kennedy won't let them do it." Her face suddenly darkened as she paused to weigh the consequences of the impossible. "You would be in the thick of the fight, wouldn't you?" She stared at him from behind the glasses, then smiled abruptly. "Well, it's silly to think about it. *I'm* certainly not going to, not with this glorious weather to enjoy."

"But what if they do it and get away with it?"

"It is simply *not* going to happen."

"But what if it *should?*"

She sighed. "Darling, you're terribly exasperating at times. I've lived in Berlin all my life—we're used to this sort of thing. We have crises with our morning coffee. And it's never quite so bad as we thought it would be." She bent down and kissed his shoulder. "Don't fret about it. You'll see. In a week all this nonsense will be forgotten. There will be a war in Somaliland or an earthquake in Urkutsk, and that's what everyone will be talking about. They'll forget all about Berlin."

It was useless to try to convince her. And he thought perhaps she might be right. The Russians had been making intermittent threats about Berlin ever since the end of the war, and the half-city was still free, one moment intoxicated with its growing wealth, the next moment sober and frightened at the prospect of its new glamour's fading into the perpetual bleakness of its other half. He got up and took her hand. "Come on. If there's nothing to worry about, let's have some fun."

They stayed at the beach until dusk, had dinner at the outdoor restaurant, and took a taxi to Sepp's room.

"So you love me?" she asked.

"You know it."

She ran her hand over his chest. "Would you be able to get out if it came to a fight?"

"That's all arranged. They won't abandon us here."

"You're not just being kind, are you?"

"I thought we had decided nothing was going to happen."

"We had. But I was supposing. Let's not talk about it."

She kissed him and held him tightly, and he held her very close, and felt the desire rising again.

"What, again?"

"Um."

"Lovely."

Later, he walked her to the Bülowstrasse subway station. The night was clear and hot, and many people were still in the streets. The traffic was noisy, the pulse of the city beating faster and louder than on other Saturday nights.

"Do you feel it, too?" he asked her.

"Yes," she said. "The city is nervous."

He looked down at her and saw the anxiety in her eyes. "Please stay, just tonight."

She shook her head. "If it doesn't happen tonight, then it will mean staying tomorrow night, just in case; then the next night, just in case. I'm not going to live 'just in case.' "

Ahead of them the spire of the Lutherkirke loomed up from the center of Dennewitz Platz. They entered the square and walked toward the station.

"It's a lovely church," she said. "Have you ever been in it?"

"Would you like to see it?"

"Tomorrow, perhaps. Churches are for Sunday."

They turned the corner and looked up the street toward Nallendorf Platz. There the subway ran above ground, and they could see the lights of the train coming toward them. She gave him a quick kiss. "Tomorrow at noon."

"At noon. Good night, Ilse."

She was off, running across the street for the train, her heels flying out to the side in the awkward way women run. He stood on the sidewalk watching to see that she made it all right, then returned to his room. When he arrived, the telephone was ringing.

"Hello."

"Lieutenant Bauer, this is Sergeant McCory, sir. Alert's on. Your jeep's on the way to pick you up."

"What's up?"

"I don't know, sir. I've got to go, sir—others to call. 'Bye."

Sepp hung up, knowing that what he had expected had happened. And at two o'clock the next morning,

August 13, 1961, the East Germans uncoiled the first roll of barbed wire that was to become The Wall dividing East and West Berlin.

Sepp kept the room, even though he knew Ilse would not be coming there anymore. At first he tried staying in his assigned room at the barracks, submerging his loneliness in the routine of Army life. There was always more than enough work to do during the day. Sepp drove his platoon hard, demanding high performance in every aspect of their training. As long as he kept busy, he could forget about Ilse and the nights ahead.

At first, he read at night and wrote letters to Ilse. After a while he began to go out on the town with his friend Lieutenant Wayne. The Wall had not affected the traditional gaiety of Berlin's nightlife, and there was plenty of drink and women to go around. He tried hard to enjoy it; he drank more than he should and went with any woman who gave him the chance. None of it mattered so long as the time passed. And the time did pass. From one training day to the next, from one night's oblivion to the next, it passed in a closed circle of utter futility.

Wayne brought it out into the open finally. "The cure isn't working, is it?" They were in one of their favorite cafés waiting for the night to begin its magic. There were no women around yet, and the piano player had not started his first set.

Sepp did not answer. He had vowed he would go along with the routine and not ruin his friend's good times. He had never talked about his loneliness, had never been able to formulate in his own mind a description of the nights when he lay in bed—whether alone or with a woman whose face he could not reconstruct in the darkness—when the physical pain of his longing for Ilse drained the strength from his body, so that he lay as if paralyzed in an iron lung, kept alive only by the vague hope for a miracle. Now he realized that he had not had to describe it, that he had been doing a bad job of concealing it.

"There's not going to be any miracle, Sepp. You'll have to make your own."

After they had been in the café an hour, a woman

came in and sat in the booth near the door. Sepp asked her to dance, and from there it was much like any other night, as if some religious ritual had to be followed. But the ritual always ended in a Black Mass for dead memories. And he knew that Wayne was right, that the age of thaumaturgy was past. Miracles had to be created by the hand and mind of man, and as a gesture of his determination to make his own miracle, he gave up the nightlife with his friend and moved back to the room in Kreuzberg.

The new year was measured out in letters from Ilse, and free nights and weekends used to seek out the friendship of students in the beer halls around the university. And to study The Wall.

As winter gave way to spring, Sepp intensified work on the plan he had devised. He had examined all the possible methods of escape he could think of or had heard of, and he kept coming back to the idea of a tunnel. A tunnel was unquestionably the most difficult possibility, but it held out the best hope of success. In a very short time, the Communists had found the leaks in their great dike and had plugged them with brutal effectiveness. An escape requiring deception of a border check was almost certain to fail.

There were formidable problems in a tunnel, chief among which were finding people able and willing to help, and locating a site in the West where work could be carried on in relative secrecy and which would connect to a hidden but accessible place on the other side of The Wall.

Sepp came to know the houses and streets along The Wall as well as he did his own. Week by week, he narrowed his selection from twenty possibilities to ten, to five, and finally to one in Wedding, with another in Kreuzberg as a less desirable alternative. He waited for the day of his discharge in June, when he could cross over into East Berlin to investigate the other end of each site—and see Ilse again for the first time in almost a year.

Nights he haunted the beer halls and wine cellars of the students' quarters. At first he was a novelty, an *Ami* who spoke fluent German and who seemed sincerely interested in making friends. He learned to distinguish between the talkers and the doers, which was no small achievement among German students. He knew there were so-called troops—secret groups—engaged in arranging escapes and carrying out sabotage. Each week stories of bizarre and ingenious escapes appeared in the newspapers, and it was clear that Berlin's students were behind most of them. Everyone knew that so-and-so was in a troop; however, so-and-so denied it but knew for certain that some other so-and-so was most assuredly in a troop.

But the security of the student troops was impregnable; he could not gain the confidence of the members, if indeed, he began to wonder, there actually were any. In desperation, he decided to form his own troop and sought out students who had relatives in the East and who had professed an interest in getting them out.

And now, with Emerich, he had his troop—three university students, a high school boy, and a famous, but middle-aged, artist. He had no idea how they would work together, whether they had it in them to do the job. He would have liked to have known them better, to have been prepared for their weaknesses, their idiosyncrasies, their strengths. But there was no time to get to know them. They were committed, they were all he had, and he was grateful for them.

As he sat in his room watching clouds gather in the western sky and savoring the contentment of his accomplishment, he felt the first intimation of a fear that everything had gone too well, that it had all been too easy. And now that the real work was to begin and the real danger was upon them, he felt that unknown forces were gathering, much like those rain clouds, to begin their conspiracy against him.

ༀ⅏⅏⅏⅏⅏⅏⅏⅏⅏⅏⅏⅏⅏⅏⅏⅏⅏⅏⅏⅏⅏⅏⅏⅏

J OACHIM LENTZ stood on the platform under the glare of the klieg lights, straining to look casual in ski togs. Karl danced around him clicking away with his camera like a bee trying to decide which flower promised the sweetest nectar. Suddenly he stopped, letting the camera drop on its strap. "You're supposed to look *casual*."

Joachim broke his pose. "I need a rest."

"You just had a rest." Karl tapped his wristwatch. "We're working forty minutes past quitting time already."

Joachim hated Karl. He hated his prissy meticulousness, his wide hips, his flaccid buttocks, his baby lips that caressed his words with obscene suggestiveness, his waspishness. But Karl Buhlen was the best fashion photographer in Berlin, he was Joachim's employer and agent, and Joachim loved that. He loved the money he earned, and he loved the reputation he was slowly achieving. So he did what Karl told him.

"All right." He wiped the perspiration from his face and tried again. He picked up the ski poles and assured the pose of a happy skier lounging against a rustic fence with a cardboard snowcapped Zugspitz rising majestically in the background.

"Turn your right hand inward a little."

Joachim did as he was told.

"More."

He turned it in more.

"Head up."

He raised his head.

"Let's see the pearlies."

Joachim smiled.

Karl threw up his hands. "That's a smile? If I had teeth like yours, I'd smile at my enemies. Now, let's see them."

Joachim forced his face to brighten.

"Better." Karl adjusted a ski pole and stood back. He examined every detail, then brought the camera up. "All set? Big smile. Think happiness. Think joy, the thrill of being in the cold mountain air." *Click, click, click, click.* Joachim's mouth went dry. The muscles of his face began to ache. Perspiration ran down his ribs and back and started his skin itching. Karl adjusted the light and studied the new effect. "Turn your head to the right. There. Good." He hopped up on the platform and pulled a lock of Joachim's hair down onto his forehead. His fingers felt cold. "Let's try a little insouciance." Down from the platform he raced, a rabbit running to its hole. "Set!" *Click, click, click, click. "Benissimo!* That's it."

Joachim let the ski poles clatter to the floor, leaped down off the platform, and bolted for the dressing room, peeling the hot jacket off as he went.

"Careful! Careful!"

He slammed the door behind him, dropped the ski jacket in a heap on the floor, and slumped into a chair. He let his body go limp. The glare of the lights had left multicolored fish swimming across the sea of his eyelids. They came unceasingly, floating out from the shore, wiggling across the expanse of dark water, disappearing behind the sheltered beach on the other side. Joachim opened and closed his eyes, hoping to exorcise the images, but they persisted. He gave it up and tried to think about his date with Rita tonight. He'd take her to the Resi for dinner and dancing, later for a drive along the Havelchausee, then, presto, into bed. He smiled, and fondled his genitals and felt his depression slowly sinking into the soft down of imagination.

Karl came in, a ski pole in each hand. Joachim looked at him in the cracked mirror. Karl set the poles in a corner and picked up the ski jacket, brushed it, and hung it in the wardrobe. Joachim watched him in the mirror, waiting. He came over and stood behind the chair.

"I have to pay for those things."

Joachim closed his eyes and waited. The hands touched his shoulders, lightly at first, then with strength. They squeezed and kneaded with a force of which Joachim wouldn't have believed Karl capable. He felt Karl's breath on the back of his neck and looked up into his eyes reflected in the mirror. "Not tonight, Karl."

Karl smiled.

"Not tonight."

"Tonight."

"No."

"Yes, my dear, dear Joachim." There was command, not affection, in his voice.

Joachim sat forward, and the hands dropped away. "Your dear, dear Joachim has a dear, dear date with a dear, dear lady." His hands trembled as he unlaced the ski boots. It was always that way when he tested Karl's determination. He pulled off the ski boots and let them drop. From behind, he could hear Karl walk away and begin getting ready to leave. He massaged his feet, conscious of the strength and beauty of his long fingers.

He gazed with weary satisfaction at his reflection in the long wall mirror, a reflection of youthful vigor and masculine beauty. Every feature of his face commanded attention on its own merit. His face, in fact, was so perfect as to distract attention from his fine body, a body that was muscular, yet gave the impression of plumpness, as if, once the flesh had been worked to muscle around the bones, the bones had been removed.

He was tall and broad-shouldered—although not uncommonly so, like his brother, Wolf—and he moved with the seemingly effortless grace of an athlete. His dark brown, almost black hair tended to wave if he let it grow. He combed it with care from a part on the right side and had it trimmed once a week.

From beneath a wide, slightly protruding forehead crested by straight, thick black eyebrows and from behind long, dark lashes, his pale blue eyes gazed out with deceptively cheerful innocence, like two fragile little rich girls used to constant protection and loving care. His eyes might well have intimated femininity had it not been for his wide, firm lips set in an expression of gently mockery, yielding easily to a generous smile, revealing shallow dimples along the lines of his long, square-chinned jaw. But even at its most engaging, accentuated by a brightening of his eyes, his smile suggested an imperiousness that no one could begrudge. The mockery, the imperiousness were not studied. They were as much a part of his smile as his lips and teeth, and even if he had wanted to do something about them, he did not believe he could have. They were too much a natural expression of the way he felt.

Joachim could not recall when he was not aware of his own beauty. When he was a toddler, his mother's friends cooed over him and stared at him, wondering why this child of parents marked by unexceptional beauty should have turned out so well, when their own offspring were so ordinary. A bright, alert child, he listened to their compliments, caught the stares of admiration and cruel envy, and accepted them as his due. In a kind of childish *noblesse oblige* he held court and passed out the favor of his attention to one and all.

Unlike many babies, he did not lose his beauty as he grew older. Even during the last years of the war and in its desperate aftermath, when food of any kind was scarce, his body grew strong and his beauty became transformed at an early age to that combination of virility and feminine delicacy that reflects the most attractive characteristics of each sex. It prospered on a meager diet of roots, scrawny chickens, occasional eggs, and precious milk his father received as payment from his patients.

In school, teachers took pride in him and excused his mistakes—but then he made so few. Schoolmates looked to him for leadership, and he did not disappoint them, whether serving up justice in the summary fashion children instinctively expect or plotting mischief designed to titillate his peers and harass authority. No one ever noticed that Joachim always arranged it so that he went undetected and unpunished. To Joachim, life was a most marvelous invention. Each day he sprang from his bed to make certain it persisted. It was as if the idea of life had been dreamed up especially for him, and in no way did it disappoint him.

The birth of his brother corroborated his belief. Life

had sent him a toy to play with. When he was in danger of becoming bored, he held Wolf up and coaxed him to walk; he taught him to tie his shoes, dribble a soccer ball, comb his hair. From Joachim, Wolf learned all the rudimentary skills of boyhood, and in speech and gesture he was a mirror of his older brother. Joachim's attentions to Wolf, his unusual solicitude for one who should have presented a challenge to his position in the family, did not go unnoticed. His mother's friends oohed and aahed over such sweetness in a boy. Joachim heard and smiled to himself.

When he was fifteen he had his first sexual experience. He had gone with the Free German Youth members from his school to Silesia to help with the wheat harvest on a state farm. One of the party youth leaders, a girl of eighteen, led him off into the woods, and when the harvest was in and it was time for the students to return to Berlin, he instinctively knew that she had taught him everything she knew. It was enough for a start.

Back at school, he realized that his life had taken a new turn, that a secret realm had been opened to him, one that for his schoolmates was but a faint hope. He told them nothing. He felt like a boy who was reluctant to share his bag of candy; instead, he decided to find out if candy were really so hard to come by.

Joachim kept count. He carried with him a long piece of string, and each time he made a conquest, he tied a knot in the string. By Christmas he had added eighteen knots to the first seven. He learned quickly to be alert to the sidelong glance, the half-hidden look of interest, the obvious stare. He had long ago become accustomed to being noticed. People looked at him just as the sun shined on him—it was in the natural order of things. Now he began to differentiate among the looks, to sort out those that told him they wanted him now from those who would someday, when they got up the nerve.

Each rendezvous became an adventure. He enticed girls into the cellars of churches, into abandoned buildings, bombed-out ruins, unlocked cars parked in dark side streets (which often took hours of tramping through the cold night air to find), and into an unused storeroom he had discovered in the bowels of the Bode Museum,

where courtiers of the Renaissance looked down in sub-
lime detachment from within their ornate frames.

By the time Joachim was sixteen, he could pass for
eighteen or nineteen, emotionally as well as physically.
He found himself becoming increasingly bored by his
schoolmates. Although he still liked to play soccer and
hockey and to swim, he did not share the same enthusiasm
in a team victory as did his friends. For them, it was the
locus of their existence; for Joachim, only peripheral
amusement. It was satisfying to improve his footwork in
soccer, his stickwork in hockey, to see his time steadily
drop in the hundred-meter freestyle, the swimming race in
which he excelled. But their outbursts of joy in victory
were alien to him.

His friends' ineffectual attempts to enter the secret
realm amused him at first. When they described with bra-
vado the awkward pawings they foisted on their girl
friends, he had to hold back his laughter. He eventually
became disgusted with their hyperbole, their outright lies.
Not one of them had the faintest notion about how to
make love to a girl, and would have been petrified if the
opportunity had actually presented itself. He listened,
watched, evaluated, and discovered—wistfully—that he
had left his friends behind.

On his eighteenth birthday he started a new system of
accounting. The strings—by now he had gone through
four lengths—did not take care of a statistic he had been
able to keep in his head but which now was becoming
muddled—that of the number of times he had had girls
he had had. He bought a small bound book with a lock
and entered not only the count but the names of the girls,
brief descriptions of each, and dates. When he made the
transfer from strings to book, he had conquered twenty-
eight or twenty-nine girls—he was not certain which—a
total of two hundred and forty-three times.

In the spring of his eighteenth year, he applied for admission to the Free University of Berlin. It had always
been understood that he would go on to higher education; his father took it for granted that Joachim would become a physician like himself. But being the son of a
doctor, Joachim could not hope to be admitted to an East
German university. Only sons and daughters of workers,
peasants, and party officials were accepted—on the pre-

mise that children of the bourgeoisie already had a head start in life. Everyone knew, of course, that the policy was purely political, spiked with vindictiveness.

After he was accepted, he began to dream of life as a student in the West. Even though he would still be expected to live at home and commute to the university, he would enjoy greater freedom, he would be on his own for entire days at a time, at liberty to harvest the fruit of a vast new orchard. The prospect was dazzling.

He was not disappointed. Life in West Berlin exhilarated him. The stale recital of political ritual, which invariably was chinked into the structure of any discussion in the *Sektor*, was replaced by an intellectual free-for-all. No subject was immune to scathing invective, no position too extreme to be defended, too sacred to be attacked. Art and politics, theater and morality, religion and sex—whatever endeavor or abstraction invented by man—was a fit topic of inquiry. Joachim found himself well equipped to dabble in most subjects, and in the coterie of friends he made he was the standard reference on communism and the East. Being naturally outgoing, he did not hesitate to join in the discussions. He was an effective, articulate speaker and made a diligent effort to be an attentive listener. At night, closing his books after long hours of study, he would take the subway back into West Berlin to join his friends in the cafés, *Gasthaüser* and *Weinstuben* that proliferated in the university quarter in Dahlem. He enjoyed the camaraderie that came naturally to a group of young people who shared the same hopes and dreams, uncluttered by the paraphernalia of caution and prudence that experience accumulates.

Like a convert, he tended to expansiveness, especially whenever the discussion turned to the division of Germany, which it often did. At first it was because he honestly wanted to impress his friends from the West with the luxuriousness of their own life compared with his own, and later because he discovered they wanted to hear the worst about the Communists and were enthralled by his narrative, nodding and exclaiming that the Reds were indeed the monsters they had always believed them to be. Describing living conditions in the *Sektor*, he was apt to overstate food and fuel shortages, exaggerate the disaffection of the people from the Ulbricht government. He invented terrifying night raids on his neighbors by the secret police, embroidered with all the savage trappings he had seen in films of the Nazi era. He spoke of official arrogance, hinted at an operative underground, and ended up swearing that he would one day take out his personal revenge on the *"Sektor* scum."

So jealously did he guard his evening hours with his fellow students that he came to arrange his times with his girl friends in the afternoons. In his student social life it was not necessary to spend money on a girl except for an occasional coffee or beer. He sought out women who lived alone, and soon was forced to buy a second notebook.

In all, Joachim led a full, rich life and continued to believe that it was, as he had originally thought it to be, a Ptolemaic world with himself at the center. So situated, he naturally scorned conventional ethics as too restrictive and adopted a code so flexible that any action directed toward his own pleasure, immediate or future, was easily justified. Any decision which resulted from accumulated circumstances he had not been able to control and which did not enhance his pleasure—or detracted from it—he ascribed to fate. One such was his decision to join Sepp in digging the tunnel.

He could trace it to that day in July 1961 when his father announced that the Lentz family should look forward to a two-week vacation in August on the Black Sea in Bulgaria. Joachim's excitement was unbounded. He struggled through his examinations, casting aside visions of bikini-clad beauties lying languidly on the white sands of the Black Sea. He had rarely been out of Berlin; he had never seen the sea—any sea. It held a romantic fascination for him. Wolf talked of nothing but sailing and fishing. Joachim made plans with him to rent a boat, explore the Roman ruins in old Varma, and strike out for deep-sea fish, all the while dreaming of new faces— dark Bulgarians renowned for their passion.

The Lentzes left Berlin in the frenzy of those days of early August, when more than fifteen hundred East Berliners were crossing the *Sektor* boundary to the West daily, when the radio and television of both East and West were blaring out provocative charges and counter-charges. But Berliners had become numb to crisis, and although there were rumors that the boundary between the two sectors of the city might be closed, Dr. Lentz gave it little credence. Joachim gave it none at all.

The family was having Sunday breakfast on the terrace of the hotel overlooking the Black Sea when a man at the next table, a garment salesman from Munich whom they had come to know during the week, leaned across toward them and asked, "Have you heard the news?"

Dr. Lentz looked down over his pince-nez. "What news?" He did not like the Bavarian.

"Why, I thought you'd be the first to know. They've closed the border between East and West Berlin. They're putting up barbed wire, a fence of barbed wire."

Joachim dropped his knife. It clattered onto his plate and to the floor. He picked it up and stared at the man, unconsciously holding the knife as if he were going to stab him with it. "A fence?"

"And they've brought up tanks and troops. We heard it on the radio just this morning. No one is getting across at all."

Dr. Lentz wiped his lips with the white linen napkin. "But surely they cannot build a fence along the entire border."

The salesman shrugged, looked around, and whispered, "Who knows what the crazy bastards—excuse me" —he nodded apologetically to Frau Lentz—"who knows what the *Communists* will do? They're not rational like other men. They don't believe in God. They have no hearts, no souls." He screwed up his nose in a grimace hinting of secret knowledge. "I do not for an instant doubt that they will build a *wall* all *around* Berlin if they are so inclined. A wall of *stone,* meters high."

Joachim's mother sought some assurance. "But surely the Americans—"

"Pah! The Americans will send a note of protest. A scribble of words is all you'll see from our *Ami* friends."

"Will there be a war?" Wolf asked.

"No, no," Dr. Lentz assured him.

"War?" The salesman from Munich laughed. "Who is to fight, my boy? Who is to fight? Ha! Ha! A war indeed!"

The Lentz family glanced apprehensively at one another. Only one question stood, like a giant Tiger tank, in the path of Joachim's thoughts: Would he be able to return to the Free University in the fall?

"We must not become alarmed until we know more about the situation," Dr. Lentz intoned.

"What more do we need to know?" Joachim demanded, finding it hard to keep his voice to a whisper.

"You must learn to be more patient in your judgment, Joachim. When we have finished our breakfast, we will listen to the news. Then we will have more information with which to make a decision."

"A decision about what, Papa?" Wolf asked.

"Whether we're going back to Berlin or not," Joachim snapped, preempting any attempt by his father to delude him. He had spoken aloud, and the four of them looked around defensively at the other guests to see if anyone had heard, but no one was paying any attention to them.

Joachim turned away and gazed out over the beach at the sea lying shimmering in the early sun. Its indolence served only to intensify his growing agitation. He knew better than to accept his father's placebo. Wasn't it Dr. Lentz himself who in his hatred of the Communists had taught Joachim to believe the regime capable of any outrage? Were they now to sit back and placidly refuse to accept reality? Contempt for his father's well-controlled serenity competed with his agitation. As he watched a gull lift off from a rock near the shore and take flight eastward, he wondered how far it was to the Turkish coast. Maybe they could sail there. The sea was calm; there was no sign of a storm. "It never rains here in August," the desk clerk had assured them on their arrival.

They returned to their suite and tried to raise Munich or Vienna on the radio, but all they could receive was the incomprehensible jumble of Balkan tongues. They could pick out familiar names—Berlin, Ulbricht, Kennedy —which only added to their frustration. As if tacitly hoping among themselves that somehow a report in German would come over, they let the radio drone on. Dr. Lentz stood by the window staring out over the brightly colored umbrellas lined up on the beach like Swiss guards in formation. Wolf sat with his chin in his hands, hunched forward, looking bored. Frau Lentz sat on the bed, two pillows propped behind her, gazing at the back of her husband's head. Joachim paced the floor, taking measured steps between the radio and the door, as if undecided whether to stay—and in a kind of defiant masochism stand like a prisoner in the dock hearing his sentence repeated over and over again—or to make a dash out the door toward—who knew where?

"Must you pace?" his mother pleaded.

"Why are we just *sitting* here?"

"What shall we do?" Wolf asked. "Do you want to go for a swim?" His face brightened, and Joachim couldn't decide whether his fifteen-year-old brother was stupid or of good heart, trying to console him.

"Well, Papa? Have we been patient long enough?"

Frau Lentz rebuked him. "Do not use that tone of voice with your father."

Joachim ignored her. "Papa?"

He did not answer. He removed his glasses and held them behind him with one hand, rubbing his eyes with the other.

"We're not going back there, are we?"

"Don't pester your father, Joachim." She said it perfunctorily, seeing that her husband was not inclined to join her in her rebuke.

"Everything we have is there," his father said quietly, "our home, our friends, my practice. . . ."

"You can start a new practice somewhere else."

His father said nothing. The radio kept up its incomprehensible staccato reports, undoubtedly giving a minute-by-minute account of the events taking place in Berlin. Even without being able to understand his words, Joachim felt the urgency in the broadcaster's voice, and it reaffirmed his own sense of urgency. "We should plan an escape."

Dr. Lentz turned slowly to face them. He set his pince-nez on his nose and squinted through the unrimmed lenses. They caught the sun and reflected it in two roving spots of light on the wall. "Our visas are good only for Bulgaria."

"We can sail down to Turkey. I've been thinking about it."

"Don't be ridiculous."

His mother gasped. "Turkey? They're not even Christians!"

"We don't have to stay there, Mama," Joachim said impatiently. "We can get back to West Germany once we're there."

"I'd like to visit Turkey," Wolf offered.

"We are going back to Berlin," his father said with impregnable authority. Joachim recognized the tone. It was a pronouncement that countenanced no argument. Further words would bring his father's quiet wrath into the open.

Joachim suddenly noticed that his father was trembling. The doctor directed his words to his older son, his voice cold with fury. "You know how I despise them, how I have taught you to learn their ways, to know them for what they are. Do you believe for a moment that I would not prefer even your Turkey to that madhouse back there?" He paused, trying to bring his anger under control. "Why have I remained in East Berlin? Why did I not move us all out to the West years ago? For the same reason we must go back even now, when it appears we will be cut off entirely: *I will not leave my patients.* Already hundreds of physicians have fled. I can name fifty at random—some of the best specialists in the city."

"Would one more make any difference?"

"It would make a difference to *me.* I cannot desert those poor people. They need me now more than ever."

And so, after a desultory second week of vacation, the Lentzes returned to Berlin. Joachim spent the remainder of August and September working on a cooperative farm in Mecklenburg. When he returned home, he took a job in his father's clinic, helping with the paperwork.

He was miserable. His missed his friends in the West, the evenings in the cafés, the girls he had so carefully cultivated. After two years of freedom, he found it very difficult to guard his words, and he grew quieter, went out in the evenings less frequently, and slowly withdrew into brooding bitterness.

After three months, he decided to act. He spent hours after work each day wandering along the edge of the Death Zone. He came to know the area along The Wall better than he knew any other part of Berlin, and in the middle of December, when he had found what he was looking for, he announced his decision to his family. "I'm crossing over."

His father lowered his newspaper and took off his glasses. His mother, who was knitting, began to knit faster, her needles setting up a clacking like the sound of a distant machine gun. Wolf, doing a jigsaw puzzle at a table in the corner, asked, "How?" and put in a piece of sky.

"Yes, how?" his father asked, obviously skeptical.

"I'm going to swim the Spree, in Friedrichshalle, where it forms the border with Kreuzburg. Other's have done it."

His father folded the newspaper in his lap. "Has it occurred to you that it is below freezing outside."

"That's to my advantage, Papa. They won't be expecting anyone to swim the river in this weather."

"Of course not, because it can't be done. You will perish from exposure."

"Perhaps it can be done, Karl," Frau Lentz said, taking her eyes from her knitting. Joachim was surprised to hear any sign of support from his mother. He had not considered her feelings one way or the other; only his father's acquiescence to his plan had concerned him.

Dr. Lentz adjusted his pince-nez on his formidable nose and glanced over them at his wife. "Just what do you mean by that cryptic remark, Mama?"

"I recall reading that those people who used to swim the English Channel"—she looked up from her knitting and pursed her lips firmly to show she knew what she was talking about—"covered their bodies with grease to keep warm. Why can't Joachim do the same?"

His father grunted. "This is not sport. This is life and death. The Sprecht boy tried the same thing only two weeks ago—without the benefit of *grease*—and was badly wounded. Only God knows why he was not killed like the others who tried the same idiotic thing." He warmed to his argument. "And where will he spend the next ten years of his life—or who knows how long? In Brandenburg Prison, that's where." Dr. Lentz turned from his wife to Joachim. "Is that what you want? A grave in the Spree? Or, worse yet, a rat-infested cell in a Communist prison?"

Joachim was so determined to make the attempt that his father's arguments only fired his temper. "It was you who taught me to hate them, and now you cringe in fear behind their Wall while they make a mockery of the so-called German nation! I refuse to live here any longer!

What am I to do the rest of my life? Sit in that antiseptic clinic and fill out forms? Is that to be my future, Papa? Is it? I'd rather die!" Joachim was surprised at the vehemence of his words, especially when they were not an expression of his true reasons for wanting to get across The Wall to West Berlin.

His father was unimpressed. "Sophomoric nonsense. If you want to do something else, get a different job." He turned again on his wife. "And you would encourage him. *Grease,* indeed!"

She put aside her knitting and folded her hands in her lap. Her face showed hardly any emotion, much as if she were only an objective witness to the dispute; but her dark eyes seemed unusually bright, and there was a slight flush in her cheeks. "It is not fair to them, Papa, to teach them one idea, then forbid them to carry that idea to its logical conclusion. It was you who put the notion of becoming a doctor in Joachim's head. It was you who taught them what they believe. What Joachim says is true. They will wither here and become twisted, torn between their love for you and the high standards you have set for them, and the need to conform to the Communists' standards in order to succeed. We must not only encourage them to excape. We must *insist* that they do."

Dr. Lentz stared at his wife, speechless. Joachim felt a spring of pride well up within him. He beamed at his mother. Wolf gaped. She looked from one to the other, a smile playing at the corners of her mouth. Her eyes came to rest on Joachim's, and behind the smile he saw the pain and suddenly felt confused.

"I forbid it," his father said. "I forbid it." His impregnable dignity collapsed in a shout. "I forbid it, do you hear!" He closed off further communication by snapping the newspaper in front of his face.

Joachim had never heard his father raise his voice. It was totally inconsistent with this man of gentle hands, this man of science whose faith lay equally with God and reason. He had handled it poorly; the lines had been assigned to the wrong actor and were too contrived for the scene. The result was hollow and unconvincing, and Joachim knew that he had won.

The next morning, as his father was pulling on his heavy woolen overcoat, he gave his consent. "If you are determined to go, plan it carefully. You will be responsible for Wolfgang, you know. It is not only your own life that will be in the drink."

Joachim nodded, suddenly caught in a drift of fear, now that his father's blessing had removed any excuse for not making the attempt.

"And not a word to anyone, do you understand? Not even to your best friends. Trust no one."

"I understand, Papa." He wanted somehow to express the mixture of fear, love, gratitude, excitement, and relief he felt, but he could not find the words.

Dr. Lentz adjusted his scarf and took his hat from the shelf. He looked at Joachim and there was a twinkle in his eye. He started to say something, but, like a flock of birds which seems to be headed toward a landing and as if of one mind swiftly veers off in continued flight, the words were gone.

Joachim got out the wire cutter. He crossed his fingers to Wolf and, taking a deep breath, engaged the lower wire in the jaws of the cutter. Wolf held the wire on each side of the cutter to prevent it from springing away and clattering against the other wires or the walls of the buildings between which it was strung. Joachim felt the wire giving under his pressure. He put his gloved hand over the cutter jaws to muffle the sound. The wire separated with a barely audible snap. They stopped to listen. Nothing. Working quickly, they cut the other wires and passed through the hole into the passageway between the buildings.

While Wolf waited, Joachim went ahead to reconnoiter the river. There was little snow on the ground between the buildings. A pile of lumber and another of bricks blocking the way had to be navigated. It took him ten minutes to get to the retaining wall at the river's edge.

The waves lapping gently in the darkness made a deceptively comforting sound. The water was visible for only a few meters out; then it dissolved into impenetrable darkness. Beyond, the lights of West Berlin spread out in a glaucous glow like a subdued aurora borealis. Here and there, pools of light from the lamps that stood on the promenade along the riverbank spread from the far shore out onto the water.

Joachim peered around the corner of the upstream building and stared into the darkness, listening intently. He could see nothing moving, hear nothing. Downstream, the darkness rose like a great concave wall to the gray ceiling of cloud. He waited, watching and listening, loath to commit himself until he was certain they had not been detected. When he decided there was nothing to be gained by waiting any longer, he signaled Wolf to join him.

The boy moved noiselessly and reached Joachim's side with the agility of a cat. Joachim grinned and squeezed his arm. They began to undress, removing their clothing with great care. They stripped to their underwear and socks. The lard, warmed by their bodies, had melted and saturated their underwear. The smell was heavy on the cold air. Lord, Joachim thought, they don't need to see us, they'll smell us. Gathering his clothes into a bundle, he once more checked the river upstream and down and, nodding to Wolf, slipped over the side into the water.

At first contact, the water was not so cold as he had expected. He glided away from the retaining wall, using the scissors kick, clutching the bundle of clothes to his chest. Wolf followed in his wake. Gradually, the coldness of the water began to penetrate his body and generated a pain that spread from his ankles and wrists to the center of the chest. He could feel his skin tightening as if being drawn up on a rack from within.

Not far out, he felt the force of the current and let himself be taken with it. A few strokes later, he remembered the clothes and let them go, watching to see that they were swept away in the current. The boots sank immediately, and in a few seconds the rest of it disappeared into the dark water. Taking a last look behind him, he saw Wolf let his bundle loose and switch over to the breast stroke.

His impulse was to swim fast, to put the east bank far behind him as quickly as possible. But they had thought about this moment too long, had anticipated it, and had resolved to control the impulse, to maintain a steady, slow, silent stroke.

He judged that they were about halfaway across when he heard Wolf swimming. The pain of the cold was subsiding, turning into a numbness that began to fill his body with deceptive warmth. Wolf was up alongside him now, swimming fast. Too fast. The water was breaking around his hands, as in his haste he was bringing them up through the surface instead of keeping them under the water. His head was bobbing rapidly, indicating the short, fast strokes he was taking

Joachim became alarmed. He glanced back over his shoulder, but only the dim silhouettes of the warehouses were visible. Ahead, he could see the promenade lights clearly, the grillework of the wrought-iron fence, the water shimmering under the street lamps as if in moonlight.

The shell of the night cracked open. A single shot rang out. A series of shots ripped into the water around him. His body responded instantly. His arms flailed the water ahead of him. His legs contracted and sprang out in swift, coordinated convulsions. A second rattle of shots. A third. A fourth. If they had struck near him, he did not know it. His body surged through the water, instinctively using the faster crawl. He could feel the speed of his stroke, hear the roar of the water flowing past his ears. His brain was inundated by the flood of purely sensory perceptions.

As his body had responded instinctively to the peril, so had his mind abruptly signaled the anomaly. Something was out of place. The alarm brought him up short. He stopped swimming. He was startled to find how close he had come to the western bank. Two men were leaning over the railing. They were clearly visible—one tall, the other short; one with a peaked cap, the other bareheaded. The tall one was shouting and pointing out to the river. Shots rang out from across the river, and the men instantly dropped down. To the left, shots came from the western side, and the two men were up again, shouting and gesturing frantically.

Then he understood. *Wolf! Where was Wolf?*

He turned in the water. The boy was nowhere in sight. Terror sent out a second trembling rush of adrenaline. He dove back across his settling wake, swimming with all the strength he could summon. God. Dear God. Please, please, pleasepleaseplease. Dear, sweet God! Please, pleeeeeease . . . His fingers struck the cold flesh, the congealed lard, and before he could stop swimming, he was on top of him. He grappled in the dark water, found Wolf's head, his chin, and raised his face to the surface.

With one hand holding up his head, Joachim rolled him onto his back and, getting as firm a grip as he could across his chest with one arm, started swimming the side-stroke. The current had carried them both downstream. He headed toward the shore, swimming diagonally across and into the current. Now he could see the east bank. There was no shooting. The night was silent except for the sound of his swimming.

Suddenly, brilliant light obliterated the darkness. Its beam found the river and began darting about like a water spider. A fusillade broke out on the western side, and the light was gone as abruptly as it had come on. Shots raked the retaining wall ahead and ricocheted through the air. From somewhere in the distance came the undulating wail of a siren horn.

Joachim felt oddly calm. The panic was gone. He was taking inordinate care to keep Wolf's face above the water. He swam with a strong, steady stroke, barely breaking the surface of the water, feeling it glide by as it would past the hull of a slow-moving boat. As he neared the western embankment, two men climbed over the railing and held out their hands. They got hold of Wolf, one under each arm, and raised him out of the water. In unison, they each threw a leg over the railing to brace themselves, and with both hands free, they drew him up into the air and over the barrier into other outstretched arms in one effortless motion. Without losing their timing, they had hold of Joachim. He felt the water slip away as he floated up into the air. He felt the rough texture of tweedy wool against his skin, a muttering of confused commands, hot breath on his cheek, then nothing.

"Feeling better, are we?" The nurse slipped the thermometer into his mouth and began taking his pulse. She smiled cheerfully in the bright sunlight of the white room.

He took the thermometer out. "Where is my brother?"

Her smile stubbornly in place, she snatched the thermometer away from him and wagged a finger at him. "We mustn't do that."

"Where is he? Is he all right?"

"He's fine. He's still asleep. He'll be quite all right."

"You're not lying to me?"

"We don't lie about such things, do we? Now let's put

this back." She slipped the thermometer under his tongue expertly and began counting his pulse again. He looked her over as she stared at the watch. She was tall, with short, dark hair, glasses, a long nose, a wide, sloping mouth, and a cleft chin. There was a lively light in her brown eyes, and self-confidence in her manner. She was probably in her late thirties. She finished with the pulse, recorded it on his chart, and took out the thermometer.

"How am I?"

"We're disgustingly normal."

"Why 'disgustingly'?"

"After what we did, we should be dead. D-E-A-D." Through it, she smiled and smiled. It's wired from behind, he decided. "There's someone here to see you."

His face must have betrayed his sudden fear. "He's been cleared," she assured him. "We clear all visitors in cases like ours, we do. He's from a newspaper. Do we want to see him?"

"Who is he?"

"He's such a nice boy, and he's been waiting for over an hour. Let's see him, shall we?"

Joachim hesitated. He was curious. "All right."

With springy little steps she went to the door, opened it, and beckoned the caller in. He was a young man with a deliberate smile.

"We'll leave ourselves to our own devices," she said, and with her sugary smile still stuck to her long, thin lips, she skipped out, closing the door behind her.

"She's something else," the caller said.

"Aren't we, though."

The visitor gave Joachim a look and a shrug that said he didn't understand. He drew up a straight chair and sat in it backward, leaning his chin on his hands on the back. He was a thin blond with small blue eyes, a short rabbit nose whose point moved up and down when he spoke, and a full, somehow cynical mouth. He had a boyish quality about him, an air of perpetual youth, although Joachim judged him to be somewhere between twenty-five and thirty. He extended his hand. "I'm Dieter Brim. I'm with the *Berliner Zeitung*."

Joachim took the hand, felt its brittleness, and was careful not to squeeze it too hard. "What can I do for you, Herr Brim?"

"First of all, let me take a load off your mind. The East Berlin authorities don't know who you are yet. None of the West Berlin newspapers—and I mean literally none of them—will use your name, or your brother's, if it will jeopardize anyone in the *Sektor*."

"I'm afraid it will."

Brim nodded. "That's usually the case. Of course, they'll find out who you are, anyway."

Joachim nodded. "I suppose so."

"But it's easier on the family over there if you don't get a lot of ballyhoo in the press." Brim offered him a cigarette.

"I don't smoke."

"Do you mind?"

"No."

As he lighted the cigarette, Brim eyed Joachim in a way that made him feel uneasy. The newspaperman blew out a long trail of smoke and grinned. "You're wondering what the hell I want."

"I suppose I am."

"I was there last night when they fished you two out of the Spree. You're a bit of a hero, you know. That was a damned brave stunt you pulled off."

"I passed out."

"Little wonder, I'd say." He stuck the cigarette in the center of his mouth and let the smoke curl up around his nose and into his eyes so that he had to squint, and up through the tight curls of his hair. It struck Joachim as an affected pose, one designed to suggest a roguishness that wasn't really there. "What are your plans, Lentz? Need a job?"

"Maybe."

"I have a friend, a professional photographer—I'm a photographer, too, by the way, not a reporter. My friend does commercial stuff—you know, magazine and newspaper ads, trade journals, that sort of thing."

Joachim did not understand. "I don't know anything about photography."

Brim chuckled. "You don't need to know anything about photography. I'm talking about modeling."

"I don't know anything about modeling, either."

"You'll learn. I've already spoken to my friend—his name is Karl Buhlen. He has a studio in Wilmersdorf."

Joachim didn't know what to say. The idea was strange.
"He pays big money, Lentz." Brim smiled, this time
with a peculiarly malicious expression. "Of course, it's
worth every pfennig."

Now Joachim understood. "Thank you for the suggestion, Herr Brim," he said coldly.

He saluted with one finger. "Any time," he said. He
dropped the cigarette on the floor with ostentatious unconcern and got up. "Remember the name: Karl Buhlen."

I remembered, Herr Brim, Joachim thought with a
mixture of bitterness and satisfaction. After two weeks
of job hunting, he had discovered that he was classified
as an unskilled worker. The best wages were in the factories, and the noise and dirt of a factory were not for
Joachim Lentz. The few marks the West Berlin government had given him were almost gone. Wolf was recovering quickly, and the hospital had subtly suggested
that the bed he was occupying would soon be needed.
Joachim decided that it would not hurt to go and see
Karl Buhlen. Perhaps he had misconstrued Brim's message.

As soon as he stepped through the door of Karl's
studio, he wondered why he had wasted two weeks, why
he had resisted the obvious. The job, the money became
everything—food and clothes, the apartment in Dahlem,
the car, his education, and Wolf's to follow. It was Mosel
wine at the Resi; an orchestra seat at the concert hall; a
bracelet for Rita, for the others before Rita, for those
to follow Rita; cuff links to curry a photographer's favor.
The money was a way of life—Joachim's way of life—and
he was not going to give it up for anything. And certainly not for a tunnel.

Until today the tunnel had been only a vague commitment due sometime in the future. Not even Wolf's
continuous and burgeoning enthusiasm had brought it
home to him. It was only today at breakfast, when Wolf
had spoken of it again, that he had realized his note to
Sepp had come due, that tomorrow he was expected
to be there in that rat's nest in Wedding, ready to go to
work.

He had met Sepp one night shortly after he and Wolf
had escaped. Joachim had become a celebrity among his

old friends from the university. He was in a café where Sepp was one of a dozen faces around a long table, faces all turned to his as he answered their questions about his life in the *Sektor* and recounted his escape across the Spree. The others were excited and avid for every detail he could provide. Sepp sat back listening, watching, never taking his eyes off Joachim.

After several rounds of beer, when the conversation came around to a more general discussion of The Wall and the division of Germany, Joachim became expansive. He spoke deprecatingly of American timidity in not having prevented the erection of The Wall. He disparaged the complacency of the West Germans and West Berliners and compared their indifference to the plight of the East Germans with that of the indifference to the persecution of the Jews under Hitler. He called upon his colleagues to throw off their apathy and fight the Communists in every way possible.

He only halfheartedly believed what he was saying. The admiration of his fellow students and the stimulation of the beer seemed to draw from him far nobler ideas than he had any notion of putting into practice.

"You're for storming the barricades, are you?"

It was the first time the American had spoken to him all night. Joachim's mind was too hazy from the beer to discern whether Sepp was baiting him or not. "You Americans think only of the obvious, the violent."

"A while ago you were denouncing us because we didn't do the obvious and the violent when the Communists put up The Wall."

The others laughed. "Score one for the Americans."

Joachim bristled. "There are other ways of fighting, now that the Americans have let us down."

"For instance?" Sepp asked.

Joachim was momentarily flustered. A friend came to his rescue. "Some fellows have arranged escapes. We're not all apathetic and smug, you know."

"I hear that just as many are escaping now as before The Wall went up."

"You're always hearing about tunnels. The Wall ought to collapse any day now, just from being undermined by tunnels."

"Is that the sort of thing you have in mind?" Sepp asked.

"Yes, yes, that sort of thing."

And so it was that a week later, when Sepp approached him about the tunnel, he had little choice but to agree. In one respect, he liked the idea: After the tunnel was completed, after the escapes had been made, the word of the daring feat would get around, and his hero image would be enhanced. Among the students this sort of political commitment, as had already been demonstrated by Joachim's dash across the Spree, inspired respect and, with some, even awe. Women were particularly impressed by daring, and Joachim was delighted with the prospect of solidifying the reputation his escape had established with them.

In other respects, however, the tunnel presented problems. For one, it would interfere with his work. He had hoped to work longer hours during the summer recess, and had, in fact, promised Karl that he would. Helping with the tunnel, even for two weeks, would cost him at least six hundred marks in earnings that he had been counting on. Also, there was the danger of injury. Even the smallest scratch, a broken fingernail, a bruise could render him useless for jobs requiring close-up shots. He would have to be extremely careful, and he worried that being too careful would court disaster.

The second problem was more serious: He did not want his parents living in West Berlin. He liked the way his life was arranged. He was jealous of his freedom to come and go as he pleased, answering to no one. If his parents were to escape, he and Wolf would be expected to live with them as before, and his freedom would be severely restricted.

He consoled himself with the conviction that his father would not change his mind about leaving the *Sektor*. He would have everything his way in the end, and pay very little for it.

"You're pensive today, dear Joachim." Karl seemed uncommonly solicitous.

"I *do* think sometimes," he said.

"I have no doubt you think too much about too many

things. It's not good for you, you know—it causes wrinkles and gray hair."

Joachim had to laugh. Karl's single-minded devotion to his work could be outrageously inane. He got up, stripped off his underwear, and headed for the shower.

"Come along, Karl. You may scrub my back."

"TOMORROW. Tomorrow."

Wolf pronounced the word over and over, forming it elaborately on his lips until it began to sound silly, a non-word sound that lost its meaning in repetition. He lay on his bed in his room watching the shadows lengthen, waiting for Rheinhardt, thinking about the tunnel. From the living room came the tick of the cuckoo clock, and from below the singing of Frau Meizner's canaries.

"Tomorrow. Tomorrow. Tomorrow never comes." That isn't true. Tomorrow will come. When I wake up in the morning, I'll know it's tomorrow.

He turned on his side to look at the clothes laid out on the chair—tan dungarees, blue cotton shirt, gray socks, fresh underwear, heavy leather gloves—and on the floor under the chair, ankle-high boots made of light, soft cowhide with thick, treaded rubber soles. Except for the gloves they were not new clothes; Joachim had bought them for him when he was released from the hospital. He had worn them for a week until Joachim got paid and could buy him school clothes, and he wore them painting the apartment, working on Joachim's car, shoveling snow from the walk, playing soccer. Though spotted with grease and paint, they were washed and ironed and looked almost as good as new.

Ever since Joachim had told him about the tunnel, Wolf had been preparing for it. It would be hard work, Joachim had warned him, harder work than he had ever done before. So the next day he had started getting up at six o'clock. He ran in the Grunewald forest for half an hour and spent another half hour in his room doing calisthenics. He repeated the same routine at night before going to bed. Sometimes Joachim would be just getting back from a date in the morning and would join him for the run.

"You'll turn to steel," Joachim would tease him.

"I want to be able to do my share."

"Don't worry about that. Just because the others are older doesn't mean they're stronger."

"Do you think I'll do all right, Joachim?"

"Of course you will. You'll be the toughest of the lot."

He trained harder and longer than ever. The tunnel promised to be the greatest adventure of his life, more exciting than the escape across the Spree, and he did not want to fail, he did not want to let Joachim down a second time.

He bought a book on diet and followed it religiously, counting calories after each meal. He did the shopping and cooking for the two of them, and prepared meals high in protein, minerals, and vitamins, and low in carbohydrates and fats. Joachim found his dieting amusing, too. "You're just like a woman with that diet."

"Don't you think it's a good idea?"

"It's a very good idea. But can't we have a piece of cake now and then? Just a *little* piece?"

Wolf felt he had been selfish. The next day he bought a cake at the bakery, but Joachim was not home for meals for three days running, and the cake went stale.

He got out his old clothes and took them to the laundry. His boots had rips in the top seams, so he had them sewn. When his clothes came back, he tried them on to make sure they still fit. Joachim came in and looked him over. "You'd think you were getting ready for your first date."

"Will these do?"

"They'll do. You had better get some gloves—good, strong ones with double leather in the palms."

He took great care in selecting the gloves, shopping in six stores, comparing quality and price before he made a purchase. Joachim liked them. Wolf was pleased.

Then the day came when he went with Joachim to meet Sepp Bauer and learn the details of the tunnel. He liked

Sepp at once. Sepp treated him as an equal and answered
his questions patiently. Coming away, Wolf said to
Joachim, "Is he really an American?"

"From fingernails to toenails. Don't let his perfect German fool you. Like all Americans, he is an excellent salesman, especially at selling himself."

Wolf was surprised at his brother's hostility. He had
gotten the impression that Joachim and Sepp were good
friends and were working closely together on plans for the
tunnel. He decided to ask him about it. "Are you mad at
Sepp about something?"

"Mad at Sepp?" Joachim laughed. "Whatever gave you
that idea? Let's stop on the Kudamm for some cake and
coffee."

As the day to begin the tunnel drew nearer, Joachim
talked about it less and less. He was spending more time
away from the apartment, cramming for exams at the university library and putting in long hours at photographic
studios around the city. Whenever Wolf saw him, he was
tired and irritable.

One morning at breakfast, Wolf began talking about the
tunnel. "What do you think Mama and Papa will say when
they hear about it?"

Joachim shrugged. "You know Papa."

"I think he'll come over, I really do."

Joachim rubbed his eyes. "Maybe."

"I sure hope so. It would be good to see them again,
wouldn't it? It would be good to . . . have them around."

Joachim looked at him, pulling apart a roll. "You'd like
that, wouldn't you?"

Joachim's tone perplexed him. "Wouldn't you?"

Joachim drew an arc around the room. "This isn't good
enough for you." He was suddenly on the verge of rage;
his words cracked like a whip across the table. "You want
to live in Charlottenburg Palace, maybe. Or . . . or Schloss
Belvedere! You want servants and . . . and gold-plated
dishes!"

Wolf was dumbfounded. "I didn't mean that. I . . ."

Joachim's mood changed abruptly. He waved his hands
over the table between them. "Forget it. Just . . . *forget* it."
He was fighting to control his temper. "Don't say . . .
anything. I'm sorry. I apologize." He rubbed his eyes and
drew his hands down his unshaven face. "I'm tired. I

haven't been sleeping well. I'm . . . it was stupid of me. I didn't mean what I said." He smiled wearily. "Just forget it, okay?"

But Wolf could not forget it, and whenever he thought about the tunnel, when his imagination played out the scenes of joyful reunion with his mother and father, the memory of Joachim's anger broke in and distorted the vision. How different we are, he thought.

Wolf was different from Joachim physically as well. He was slightly taller than his older brother, and his shoulders were unusually broad, which made his coats and jackets seem too small for him. Blond like his father's, his hair grew thick over his head and down the back of his neck. He had their mother's dark blue eyes set close together on either side of a narrow-bridged nose under blond eyebrows. Surrounded by light, delicate skin, ruddy at the cheekbones, they dominated his face disproportionately to their size or beauty. While Joachim's eyes seemed always alert, ready to join in the formulation of the expression of an emotion, Wolf's were brooding, reticent, noncommital. He did not have Joachim's generous mouth, although his lips were full and firm and seemed suited to his narrower face. He had never been quick to smile. When he did, there had always been the intimation of a lingering sadness that tempered whatever joy lay behind the smile. It was as if he had not dared to be too happy and was sad that he dared not.

The prospect of the tunnel, however, was changing all that. Tomorrow was almost upon them, and not even Joachim's words could detract from his excitement. It was a growth in his body, a fetus kicking, impatient to be born. The tunnel would be the beginning for him. He knew it. His life would never be the same again. He had no picture of just what would be different, but he had a feeling, a sense of urgency which commanded his every resource. The anticipation of the change stirred him to an uneasy evaluation of his present life. He would pause at odd moments to contemplate a restive longing he had for something he was unable to identify, a longing which, like a siren's wail in the night, informed him that something was amiss, but what or where he didn't know. Only tomorrow, only the tunnel would provide the answers.

Rheinhardt's low whistle ruffled the hot silence of the

room. Wolf got up and leaned out the window. Rheinhardt
was in the street, straddling his bicycle, looking up. A
white towel was lodged under the spring on the carrier.

"I'll be right down."

"Bring a towel. We're going swimming."

Rheinhardt was a year older than Wolf and took it upon
himself to make plans for their times together. Wolf didn't
mind, and, being new to the school, to the neighborhood,
and to the boys there, he felt obliged to go along with
them. Rheinhardt was the most Procrustean of the lot, but
he was inventive and adventurous. Wolf always had a
good time with Rheinhardt. He took a towel from the pile
in the bathroom and, on his way out the door, took two
apples from the bowl on the dining table.

In the street the sun was raising bubbles on the
tar. Wolf walked his bicycle to the curb and handed
Rheinhardt an apple.

"Thanks." Rheinhardt rubbed the apple on his trouser
leg and bit into it.

"Where are we going?"

"I've got a surprise for you."

Wolf got on his bicycle. "Good. I like surprises."

"We're going swimming with girls. In the raw!"

Wolf looked at his friend, not knowing whether he was
joking or not.

"I'm not kidding."

"But . . . how? Where?"

"You don't look so keen about it." Rheinhardt took a
big bite out of the apple and eyed Wolf suspiciously.

"Yes. Yes, I am. It sounds . . . great."

"There are these two girls, really hot stuff, sort of crazy
and brainy, but hot stuff. I was swimming with them day
before yesterday." Rheinhardt wiped his mouth on his
arm. "I don't know about yours, but mine does it." He
finished off the apple and dropped the core into the gutter.
He fished a pack of American cigarettes out of his pocket
and offered one to Wolf. "Smoke?"

"No, thanks."

"I won these from an *Ami* in a game of craps." He
lighted one and flicked the match into the gutter.

Wolf looked at him, wondering if he were only boasting
or telling the truth—about the cigarettes and the girls. He
couldn't tell, and he felt fear growing larger than excite-

ment, outpacing it on the scale of his emotions. He attached his towel to the carrier of his bicycle.

Rheinhardt watched him, squinting against the sun. "You don't have to go, you know."

Wolf's temper erupted. "Who says I don't want to go?" Rheinhardt started to say something but only shrugged. Wolf bit into his apple and with one hand on the handlebars started off. "If we're going, let's go."

They stood their bicycles in among the trees off the Havelchausee and went down through the underbrush to a grassy clearing on the riverbank. The trees were thick with foliage, and with the underbrush the river could not be seen from the road. It was not yet twilight. Across the river the sun clung to the edge of the horizon, reluctant to give up the field to the night. The dark, turbid water glimmered in the sun's glow, casting the far shore in a copper relief of boathouses, docks, sailboats with their sails luffed lying serenely in the water, and beyond, an unending sweep of wood up and down the river as far as they could see. The gables of resort hotels rose above the branches of trees. The air was filled with the lush smell of the woods, still and heavy with the day's heat.

Wolf shaded his eyes and looked up the shoreline. "I don't see anyone."

"They'll be along. They said they'd be here."

"Maybe they can't come."

Rheinhardt made a sneering noise in his throat. "They'll come." He got undressed, dropping his clothes in a pile at his feet. He went to the water's edge, looked up and down the river, then waded in and stretched out his arms to balance himself. He dove and came up spurting water.

"Come on in! It's wonderful! Be careful of the rocks near the shore!"

Wolf watched Rheinhardt swim out toward the middle, heading diagonally upstream, fighting the current. Ten meters out, he stopped and waved for Wolf to come in.

Wolf took off his shirt, folded it neatly, and laid it in the grass. He took off his shoes and socks, tucked the socks in the shoes, and put them under the shirt. He took off his trousers and, tucking the cuffs under his chin, aligned the creases and folded them in quarters and laid them on top of the shirt. He thought of swimming in his shorts, but he knew Rheinhardt would ridicule him, and maybe the girls would, too—if they came. He had the momentary feeling that he was forever doing things he had not planned to do, did not want to do. He stepped out of his shorts, folded them, and placed them neatly on top of his trousers. Then he decided to put them under the trousers.

Stepping quickly into the water, almost slipping once on the rocks, he swam out toward Rheinhardt. He swam well, taking long strokes, kicking his legs fast and rhythmically. As he came up alongside Rheinhardt, his friend dashed a spray of water in his face and laughed and swam away. Wolf welcomed the horseplay and swam after him, reaching him easily. He caught hold of his foot and, with a quick twist, turned him on his back and pushed him under. Rheinhardt came up laughing. Wolf dunked him again and held him under for a full minute. Rheinhardt began to struggle violently, and Wolf let him go. He bobbed up through the surface like a cork and fell back gasping.

"You . . . bastard!"

Wolf laughed.

"You . . . damn near . . . drowned me!"

"You started it."

"I didn't . . . try to . . . drown you."

"You're not hurt."

"Just that . . . my lungs . . . are punctured!"

They were interrupted by a call from the shore.

"Here they are!" Miraculously recovering his wind, Rheinhardt began to swim toward the bank, where two girls stood beside their bicycles much like cast-iron figures set out to decorate a lawn, one yellow, one pink. Wolf treaded water, staring at them. The one in pink waved and leaned her bicycle against a tree.

Slowly he forced himself to begin the swim back to shore. Halfway there, he stopped. The girl in pink was already undressed and was stepping gingerly into the water, making squealing noises. Rheinhardt was laughing and shouting for her to hurry. Wolf floated on his stomach and stared at her. He had never seen a girl naked before. She went in up to her knees and stood there, her arms across her breasts, afraid to venture farther. Rheinhardt urged her on, but she would not move. Wolf heard her say something about the rocks. Rheinhardt waded in toward shore and took her by the arm.

Wolf watched the indifference of his friend to exposing his body; he moved just as if he and the girl were fully clothed, neither shy nor swaggering. And the girl seemed not at all concerned, either. They laughed together as he maneuvered her across the rocky bottom out into the water, both oblivious of Wolf and the girl in yellow. They reminded Wolf of a painting he had seen in a book, of naked men and women on a picnic, lolling about on the grass in the woods. What had struck him was the natural-ness of their expressions, the nonchalance of their de-meanor. They seemed almost bored. He had thought that it would be impossible to be with a naked woman without being sexually excited and had considered the painting an aberration of the truth. As Rheinhardt and the girl dog-paddled out into the river, he wondered where the truth lay.

Wolf watched them swim away, letting the current take them downstream. Their heads and arms flashed in the sun-streaked water as they stroked in unison. He looked at the girl on shore. She, too, was watching them. Then she turned toward him, and though he was not close enough to see her eyes, he knew that she was gazing at him, waiting for him. He started swimming.

When he was close enough to shore to touch bottom, he looked up at the girl. She had set her bicycle against her friend's. A Lufthansa flight bag was slung on the handle-bars. The pink girl's clothes were strewn over the branches of a bush like laundry laid out to dry.

He stood in water up to his waist, balancing precariously on a slippery rock. She leaned against a tree and took off her shoes. She glanced at him and asked him his name. It was a simple, reasonable question. But he was afraid that it was going to be the same as it always had been: She would dominate the relationship. Her words came out on parade, confident that they were properly attired, assured that they would evoke the desired response. They were not words meant to intimidate. But then, it was never the words that sent him racing for refuge; rather, it was the aura of the world beyond them, the years in which he and girls—all girls—had developed in their separate ways. The words were but the immediate manifestation of those years, that accumulation of strangeness that he feared.

The strangeness invariably represented the strength and composure that he lacked.

Riding out to the river with Rheinhardt, his resentment had slowly blossomed into a determination that this time it would be different. He had visualized himself making casual, witty remarks, handling the situation as he would Joachim's car, with ease and mastery. It would only be a matter of recognizing that the girl was no older than he, had no monopoly on intelligence, charm, or common sense. Oddly, he had not thought of the unusual nature of their meeting. Rather what he had visualized was riding side by side on their bicycles or having cake and coffee at a *Konditorei*. These were the familiar benchmarks of his previous experiences with girls, and though he knew very well the purpose of Rheinhardt's arrangements, that they would meet here at the Havel, that they would come face-to-face naked, that they would, indeed, if the girls were willing, "do it," he had not given that any thought. He realized he had purposely refused to accept what he knew to be the truth, because it frightened him. Now, as he stood there mute, lost in recrimination for not having prepared for yet another humiliation, the idyll of the painting corroborated by Rheinhardt's attitude which had provided him a temporary refuge forgotten, she repeated her question.

"Wolf," he answered with a trace of belligerence. "Wolf Lentz."

"Is that short for Wolfgang?"

"Yes, but I go by Wolf." His own name sounded ridiculous, and he hoped he would not have to say it again. The sound of laughter and water splashing came from out on the river. What did Rheinhardt know that he didn't? What was the secret?

"Aren't you going to ask my name?"

"I was just going to."

"It's Uschi Myer. Myer's a terribly common name. I wish I had a more interesting name, something more glamorous, but there's nothing I can do about it, is there?"

Wolf shook his head.

"Are you a friend of Rheinhardt's?"

"Yes."

"He's crude."

"What do you mean?" Wolf now began to hope that she

would just stand there and talk until it became dark. The shadows were climbing higher up the trees. He wanted to turn around to see how far the sun had gone down, but he was afraid he would give himself away.

"You do know what crude means."

"Of course."

"He's crude. C-R-U-D-E. Crude."

Wolf's hopes vanished as the girl began to undress. As she removed each garment, she folded it carefully and placed it in the flight bag. He was glad she was neat.

"You've never done this before, have you?"

"Oh, yes. Lots of times."

She did not say anything, but he could tell that she did not believe him.

"I think it's rather silly, myself. For one thing, the water here is filthy dirty. The mosquitoes will be out as soon as the sun goes down. It's such a bother, when all you want to do is fornicate, anyway."

He gasped mentally. He had never heard a girl talk like that before. "I didn't plan to . . . I didn't say anything . . . about . . . that."

In two quick motions she was out of her underwear. She turned to face him. "Do you like me?"

She seemed much smaller, almost childlike, without her clothes. He gazed at the plump flesh that seemed so incredibly soft it would bruise if he touched it. How he wanted to touch it, to scramble out of the water and explore every part of her.

"Do you?"

"Yes." His voice came in a hoarse whisper, and he said it again, too loudly. "Yes."

She threw back her head and laughed. It was a wild, raucous laugh that skittered across the river like a flat stone thrown across its surface. Suddenly she was in the water beside him. She took his hand. "Come on. We'll swim. It's all right."

Confused, not knowing whether he was glad of it or not, he swam out into the river with her.

Later, in the remnant of the day when the lights were coming on in the resort hotels in the woods across the river, they came out of the water, and he was all right. She babbled on about her daily life, as girls always do, and there was no embarrassment, even when she paused once while they were drying themselves and said, "You're very well developed."

"So are you."

"I started young. I was only eleven when I first menstruated. Did you have an early puberty?"

"I . . . don't remember." He remembered well his thirteenth year when his body began to change, when his father explained explicitly why it was changing, but he was not about to discuss it with a girl.

"Boys never pay much attention to that sort of thing. They're less analytical than girls, don't you think?"

"I guess they are."

She continued dressing. "I'd like to fornicate with you sometime, but properly, in a bed. Is that all right?"

He swallowed audibly, but she did not seem to notice. "That's the only way to do it."

"I'm glad you agree."

He didn't know what to say next. "I wonder where Rheinhardt and Lotte are."

"Oh, off somewhere in the rushes, being devoured by passion and mosquitoes."

The image of his friend "doing it" with Lotte formed vividly in his mind, and he now wished that he, too, were doing it with Uschi. He watched her finish dressing and realized that if he suggested it now, she would be annoyed, since she had just gotten all her clothes on.

"Would you like to do something tomorrow night?" he asked.

"All right." She seemed indifferent. She was folding her towel and tucking it away in the Lufthansa bag. He wondered if she had actually flown, or if she had only bought the bag for show.

"I flew to Bulgaria and back last summer," he said.

She didn't seem to be listening. She was combing her long blond hair, hanging her head to one side, tugging the comb through the snarls.

He watched her and wondered if Joachim had ever gone swimming like this with a girl. He supposed he had, probably hundreds of times. Joachim's private life began to seem less mysterious. Wolf reflected on all the nights he had lain in the darkness of his room, longing for relief from the ache that throbbed throughout his body, an ache aggravated by the knowledge that beyond his door, across the living room behind another door, Joachim was at that moment alleviating his own, similar ache. As he thought about it, he felt the familiar excitement stirring. He cursed his timidity.

Lightning flashed in the west. He paused to look out across the river, listening for the thunder, but it was too far away to be heard. "We had better go," he said. "It's going to rain."

Wheeling his bicycle through the undergrowth up onto the road, he realized that he had not thought of the tunnel once all evening.

5

THE ghost army invaded from the west, firing battery upon battery of artillery. Making certain he had the screwdriver, pencil flashlight, and a supply of East German marks, Sepp put on his raincoat and went out.

The army was deploying ahead of its artillery in a broad skirmish line across the night sky, moving forward at the quick march, an irresistible thunderhead of firepower. The wind made a flanking armored attack down the street, setting the trees to swaying and moaning like old women in mourning, their black arms rising in supplication to an indifferent God. The artillery thundered, its flashes illuminating the western front, where the steel bayonets of the infantry could be seen in the light of distant street lamps moving steadily onward, occupying the city at terrifying speed.

Berliners pulled their heads down into their upturned collars and scattered. A young woman, defying the onslaught, brandished a flimsy red-and-white polka-dot umbrella and charged forward, smug at her foresightedness. The rain came down in a torrent, spattering noisily on the cobbles. The wind picked it up on the rebound and threw it in all directions. Within a block, Sepp's trousers were drenched, and by the time he reached Checkpoint Charlie, his shoes were soaked through. But he was glad for the rain, if only it lasted long enough for him to make use of it.

Eddie Doyle, a sergeant Sepp had come to know while

in the Army, had the duty at the checkpoint. When he saw
Sepp, he came out of the shack under the overhang and
waited for him. He wore the white helmet liner of the
Military Police and a black-and-white MP armband.

"How's business?" Sepp asked.

He gave Sepp a salute for old times' sake. "Evenin',
Lieutenant. Lousy. There's nothin' movin' either way,
only the Russkies changin' the guard at the War Memorial." He nodded toward another MP in the shack. "My
biggest job is keepin' Armstrong in line."

"He's new?"

"He acts like he's had the duty ever' night for a year.
Punk kid, but I'll straighten him out." Doyle spoke loudly
enough for Armstrong to hear, but there was no response
of any kind from inside the shack, where the young corporal sat tilted back in a chair absorbed in a comic book.

Sepp gazed down the street to the *Sektor* barrier,
where the parking area and customs shack lay bleak
and deserted under the rain-streaked glare of the floodlights. The only sign of life was the occasional movement
of the guard at the barrier.

"They been real quiet ever since that last bombing. Who
you figure done that, Lieutenant?"

Sepp shrugged. A few nights earlier, a charge of explo-
sives had been detonated near Potsdamer Platz, blowing a
sizable hole in The Wall. It was the third blast in recent
days and had stirred up a propaganda storm in the East.

"You think they're up to somethin' new?"

"They're always up to something new."

"All day they're workin' like moles in them holes
they're diggin', and stringin' more barbed wire'n U.S.
Steel makes in a year. I even hear they're pullin' down
some houses up around Bernauerstrasse. But come night,
they turn on the lights and nestle in real quiet." He turned
back. "You goin' over?"

Sepp nodded.

Doyle did not say anything. The rain drums beat a
stentorian cadence on the roof, and occasional rumbling
thunder, now from the east, played an atonal bass viol
solo. The sergeant seemed to be listening for something, as
if deciphering from the sound a message meant especially
for him.

"What is it?"

Doyle shrugged. "Nothin'. Sometimes I think I hear things." He made a face to suggest that he was perhaps a bit loony, but what more could you expect from an old soldier? Then he said, "I know it ain't none of my business, and if you was still in the service I wouldn't say it, you can be sure, but since you're a no-account civilian now"—he grinned—"I just wonder out loud if you ain't feedin' a ghost. I been here watchin' you goin' over and comin' back for . . . nearly a month, ain't it? And ever' time it eats my heart out, Lieutenant. You just can't keep plowin' the same furrow without plantin' no seed. You're either gonna do somethin' desperate or go outa your mind."

Doyle's unexpected expression of concern—more, its incisiveness—caught Sepp by surprise. He knew that the MPs must have talked about him, speculated on the purposes of his nightly trips to the *Sektor,* and must have come up with the obvious conclusion. He winced to himself at times, imagining their conversations and the licentious embroidery with which they were undoubtedly trimmed. He had never thought, however, that they felt any compassion. He had not expected it. When it was expressed, he was shaken. The tension that had been building in him for a year, and acutely so during the past month, must have been more apparent than he had realized. The mixture of dread and excitement he felt each time he crossed into the *Sektor*—the dread of entering the concentration camp atmosphere of East Berlin, wondering each time if the unpredictable Communists would decide for some trumped-up reason to detain him there; the excitement of seeing Ilse, being with her, touching her, cheating time of each moment they shared—those competing emotions must have taken their toll without his realizing it. And now, when more than ever he was striving for anonymity to avoid suspicion, Doyle's words impressed him more deeply than they should have.

He tried to gloss it over. "Things aren't really that bad, Eddie. I haven't reached the desperate stage yet."

Doyle refused to let it go. "I been in too many wars, I seen too many guys with that look, Lieutenant. Just do me a favor—give it a good, hard think before you do whatever you're gonna do. Like the book says: Don't underestimate the enemy."

Sepp wanted to end it. "I'll go over my battle plan with you, Eddie, before H-Hour."

Doyle managed a grin. "You do that, Lieutenant."

"Sepp."

"You do that . . . Sepp."

Sepp pulled his raincoat collar up around his neck. "I'm late already."

They exchanged salutes. "Good luck, Lieutenant."

"Thanks. See you later, Sergeant."

As he began the short walk across no-man's-land, he suddenly saw himself a comic figure alone on a stage, unable to remember his lines, struck dumb so that even if he could remember them, he could not speak them. But then, the audience knew he was a clown and was waiting expectantly for the first laugh of the play. They were ready to laugh at anything.

At the Communist side, Lieutenant Geller greeted him with his usual sarcasm. "Ah, Herr Bauer. I was beginning to think we would not have the pleasure of your visit this evening. You are almost half an hour late." He swung his feet off the desk and got up. A cigarette dangled jauntily from the corner of his mouth. When he spoke, it bobbed up and down like a metronome with a broken spring.

Sepp wiped his hair dry and looked around. The two other Vopos in the shack, a sergeant and a private, were new. The government rotated the border guards often to discourage defection, but Geller must have been a trusted officer—he had been on duty regularly for the month Sepp had been crossing over. He was probably a party member. The Vopos looked Sepp over in their customarily dull, listless way, then went back to what they had been doing —the sergeant reading *Neues Deutschland,* the private typing at a desk.

"It's such a perfect night for provocations, Johann. A few of us were planting bombs along The Wall. It took us longer than we had planned."

Geller made a *tsk-tsk* sound. He removed the cigarette from his mouth and used it as a pointer. "I have warned you before, Herr Bauer. You must not address an officer of the People's Police by his Christian name."

Sepp raised his eyebrows. "His *Christian* name?"

Geller's face suddenly reddened. He glanced at his subordinates and, seeing that they showed no evidence of having heard, gave a nervous chuckle. "*Ach*, Herr Bauer, you do delight in taunting me, don't you. That's good, good. It demonstrates that there is still a little fire in your decadent imperialist spirit. I like that. Yes, I do." To get Sepp off the subject, he handed him the currency form to fill out.

"You can't just make a few carbons of this every so often, I suppose."

Geller laughed. "What would we do with Private Essenwein then, eh?" He turned to the private with a malicious twinkle in his eye. Essenwein looked up from his typewriter, gave them both a bored, contemptuous look, and went back to his work—hunting and pecking his way through the mysteries of another government form.

The Vopos Sepp had seen on duty in the customs shack had the suspicious, watery eyes of oxen. He had come to believe this characteristic was a prerequisite for the job. They plodded through their work looking as weary and bored as oxen in their traces drawing manure carts. Lieutenant Geller was an exception, and Sepp had assumed the offensive as the best defense against his quick mind. When he had completed the form, he handed it over to him and put the lieutenant's pen in his own packet.

Geller looked the form over carefully and put it in the wire basket on Essenwein's desk.

"Passport."

Sepp gave him his passport. "It's the same as last night."

"Yes, and as the night before, and the night before that." He perused it carefully, page by page, glancing up at Sepp occasionally with an expression of triumph, as if he had discovered an irregularity, only to let the expression fade when Sepp failed to respond. He came to the last page, closed it, then, as if remembering something, reopened it. "If we always assumed all was in order, we would not need to be here, would we, Herr Bauer?" He kept turning pages.

"If all were in order, Lieutenant, you wouldn't be here."

"Tsk, tsk. Someday you will catch me in a bad mood and I shall deny you entry."

"On what grounds?"

Geller looked thoughtful. "How would 'suspicion of espionage' strike you?"

The proximity to the truth, in their terms, put Sepp on guard, and he resorted again to the flippant. "Flattery."

"Oh, yes. But then, there is every reason to suspect you."

"I can't think of one."

"You are not so enamored of the German Democratic Republic that you visit us each night out of nostalgia."

Sepp decided to back off. This was one night he did not want to cause an altercation that would give the lieutenant an excuse to keep him out of East Berlin. "Lieutenant, you know perfectly well why I come over here every night."

Geller snapped the passport closed and handed it over. "Of course we know. You did not believe you could become such a frequent visitor without arousing our curiosity, did you? We are a curious people. It is part of our nature." His eyes twinkled again, and he made what could only be interpreted as a lewd gesture. "Ah, *l'amour!*"

It was suddenly all very French, and Sepp was prompted to laugh. Instead, he went along with him. He asked in a confidential way, "Do you think I'm making a fool of myself?"

"No. No." Geller came closer and spoke in low tones. "I only wish you would find someplace to *go*." He looked at Sepp knowingly. "You know what I mean? The reports on you are drearily the same. 'Met Fräulein Raab at the Schönhauser Allee subway station. Walked her to the Gasthaus Edelweiss. They drank beer and talked. Walked Fräulein Raab back to the subway station.'" He looked pained. "Where is it all to end?"

At first Sepp thought that Geller was merely being friendly; then he realized he was warning him that Ilse and he were indeed being watched and that, if they had only suspected it, their suspicions were being officially confirmed.

"The lady demurs."

Geller shrugged. "Naturally. Don't they all? You must make careful preparations, lead her into it as you would lead a tigress into a trap. She wants to, of course, but she is frightened. You must convince her that her fright is an illusion." His eyes glittered as he looked intently into Sepp's face to see the reaction to his advice. "Eh?"

Sepp thought of her true fright, and that was not an il-

lusion. It was as real as The Wall, as oppressive as the
musty air in the customs shack, as ordered and certain as
the Communist mentality was capable of making it.

"Perhaps you are right. I'll give it some thought." He
started to leave.

"Yes, Herr Bauer, give *it* some thought and *me* my
pen."

Sepp tried to look befuddled and failed, and they both
laughed with mock politeness as he handed it over.

Ilse was waiting at the subway station. When she saw
him coming, she ran out into the rain and into his arms.
He held her for a moment and felt her trembling. She
wouldn't look at him, and he knew she was crying.

"I'm sorry."

"You've never been late before."

"I'm sorry." He had been late before. He turned her
chin up to him.

She wiped away the tears. "It's only rain," she said
angrily, angry at herself for crying.

He kissed her and took the umbrella she had brought.
As they navigated the puddles and overflowing gutters on
the way to the Edelweiss, he told her about the meeting
with Emerich. "Everything is ready. We begin tomorrow."

"Tomorrow." She did not sound excited; awed, perhaps, or cautiously hopeful. They had talked about it so
much, made so many plans, changed them, resurrected so
many old ideas, and dreamed up so many new ones that
the realization of it all no longer had any more importance
than its expectation. He suspected they were much like
an engaged couple who, having planned their wedding for
months, are not apt to become excited in knowing that
everything has finally been taken care of.

"Then tonight is the night."

"Yes. Are you all right?"

She nodded.

"The rain is a blessing."

"You're soaking wet." She was suddenly scolding him.
"Look at your trousers. And why did you wear those
shoes?"

He had on some old khakis and a pair of sneakers. "I
wore them purposely—they're quiet, and I can run like
hell in them if I have to."

"Where would you run?"

He thought it a silly question and didn't answer. Besides, he did not intend to get into a situation where he would have to run. Everything was too well planned.

"Do you remember everything?" he asked her.

"Yes."

"Are you afraid?"

"A little."

"That's good. You'll do a better job if you're afraid. It's like stage fright. It's supposed to help an actor give a good performance."

"Do you still insist on doing it this way?"

"That's been settled." He had decided they were to stage a lover's quarrel at the Edelweiss. If he were caught, he reasoned, she would already have dissociated herself from him and from any implication in his plot. It was a flimsy alibi, but it was better than none at all. She had argued against it, insisting that she should take the same risks as he, but he had insisted on having his way, and he had won out.

They stopped at a yarn shop, ostensibly to look in the window. Sepp looked to see if they were being followed. Some nights he thought they were, some not. Of late, they had not been, and as far as he could see, tonight they were not. He was relieved—it would have made it more difficult.

"We're alone," he told her. She squeezed his hand. He decided not to tell her that Geller had said they were being watched. They always assumed they were, but it would still unnerve her to know their fears were justified.

As they walked, he explained his and Emerich's plan to get the Weber family to Berlin, using his aunt's illness as a ruse.

"Do you think Dr. Lentz will agree to it?" She wondered. "It's a big risk for him."

"He let Joachim and Wolf escape—that was a risk, too. From what Joachim has told me about him, he's ardently anti-Communist."

"I'll do my best," she said.

"Can you start tomorrow?"

"Yes, of course."

"Good."

They came around the corner into Vierickstrasse, the

street that formed the borderline between the city and the
Death Zone. It was a quiet, dark street, usually deserted
at night except for an occasional pedestrian going home or
going to or leaving the Edelweiss. The houses on the west
side of the street were dark and empty and in the rain
looked much like the relics of a ghost town. Boards had
been nailed up across the windows, and the doors were
locked, some with padlocks. The house he planned to use,
an old three-story gray stucco building, huddled between
two larger buildings in the middle of the block. Its heavy
oak door, set into a larger wooden framework, opened inward directly from the sidewalk. The entryway, set about
half a meter into the building, provided some protection
against being detected once he was there.

Each of the past three nights he had loosened the screws
of the latch a little more, so that tonight he would be able
to unscrew them quickly. He had found it was very easy
to get across to the house and back without being
observed.

For a month, since he had made the site selection for
the tunnel, Ilse and he had plotted the guard pattern of the
two Vopos assigned to the street. Each patrolled three
blocks of the six-block-long street. They would set out
from the corner near the Edelweiss, walking in opposite
directions—one north, one south—for three blocks, then
return. It took them approximately ten minutes to cover
three blocks, twenty for a round trip.

The Vopo patrolling the block including the Edelweiss
and the proposed escape house passed the *Gasthaus* at
intervals of three and seventeen minutes, and the escape
house every four and sixteen minutes. In all the times
Sepp had timed them, they had never been more than
thirty seconds early or late.

Every hour on the hour, they reported in on the telephone at the corner.

Sepp and Ilse had considered making it a point to greet
the guard each time they saw him to make themselves
known as regular visitors to the street, but here, too, the
guards were changed erratically and it was impossible to
know which man would be on duty tonight. Sepp sought
out the Vopo. He was far down the street, moving away
from them, a dark, lonely figure retreating in the rain.

The Edelweiss was situated on the east side of Vierickstrasse, across from the escape house, but closer to the corner. They went in, made their greetings, and sat at the table by the window. From there, they could clearly see the escape house and beyond, up the street, almost to the end of the third block, where the Vopo would turn to retrace his steps. There were a few couples, some tables of men talking quietly over beers, and the usual card players at a back table muttering oaths, slapping the cards on the rough wooden tabletop.

Adolf, the waiter, brought two steins of beer without their ordering, and made two pencil marks on one of the cardboard coasters. He was a short, thin man with thick gray hair and a hooked nose. His dark eyes lay deep in his head, brooding like two animals caged in a zoo. As usual, he commented on the weather and gave a forecast. "We need this rain. It will last all night."

"Tomorrow?"

"Tomorrow will be clear and hot again." He set his chin to support this piece of meterorological dogma. His expression gave no room for contradiction.

"I'm so sick of the heat," Ilse said in a convincing pout.

Sepp was suddenly aware that the first lines of the play had been spoken and that they were his cue.

"Marvelous, Adolf," he bubbled, purposely opposing her. "I'll go for a swim."

He reprimanded him. "Tomorrow is a workday."

"Then *I'll* be sick. *I* can be sick, too."

Adolf was embarrassed by their open bickering, but he was too much the busybody to leave them alone. "You can get into trouble malingering."

Sepp turned on him. "You forget, Adolf, I live in West Berlin. We are permitted to get sick." Adolf's expression told him he had gone beyond discretion, and he tried to recoup his losses. "Perhaps I'll go after work."

Adolf was relieved at this reasonable turn. "It's better that way. You won't get sunburned." Having imparted his measure of wisdom, he returned with his springy, tiptoe steps to the high stool behind the beer tap, where he sat eyeing the customers much like a vulture in a tree in the desert waiting patiently for the inevitable victim.

"He makes my flesh crawl," Ilse whispered.

"He's harmless."

Sepp held up his beer and offered to clink glasses. She

deliberately drank without touching his, and he gave her a contemptuous look. We're doing well, he thought.

He looked at his watch. It was nine fourteen. The Vopo would come into view. The card players were still at the muttering stage. Outside, the rain came down relentlessly, showing no sign of letting up. Occasionally a gust of wind came up and washed the windows with rain. The smell of it had settled in, much like the mustiness of the customs shack. It was a vaguely funereal smell, and he felt, as he had again and again, the tortured vacuity that hung like a great backdrop behind the meaning of every gesture, every spoken sentiment, every thought of the people.

Once, while walking Ilse back to the subway, he had been dreaming of making love to her again, thinking of each move he would make, unfolding her love as one unfolds a lace tablecloth laid out only for special occasions, and as they passed under the darkened windows of the houses along the street, he wondered if behind each one someone was realizing the moments of pleasure he ached for at that moment. How he envied them. Then, as they went along, they passed within sight of The Wall with its whitewashed facade dazzling in the bright glare of the lights, strewn with the grotesque shadows of the steel tank traps laid out in the Death Zone, and at that moment he realized that not even an East Berliner's conjugal bed held any but a fleeting glimpse of what love could be.

Now Sepp looked at Ilse and saw that she was having a hard time of it.

She turned away. "If I look at you, I won't be able to do it."

"Don't let me down, *Schatz*." A year ago she would have thought it a great joke, and he would not have had to worry about her ability to go through with it.

"It's just . . . so awful, even pretending." She looked at him, and sadness dwelt like an interloper in the secret shallows of her eyes. "If it doesn't work, if you get hurt, or . . . get caught, then this is what we'll have, and it's so ugly, so ugly."

"It *will* work. I *won't* get caught. Everything will be all right." He said it with vehemence, as if he could talk the dream into reality. He would have liked to have done this alone, without involving Ilse. But to go to Vierickstrasse or to the Edelweiss alone would have aroused suspicion.

Any change in routine, he knew, was cause for suspicion. And then, he admitted, she was going to be of some help after all, even though only in a passive way.

Since he had been seeing Ilse again this past month, after a year apart, he had come to see that their roles had been reversed. It was she who was the constant pessimist, he who had to reassure her. The sudden separation and the year behind The Wall had eroded her spirit. Despair had become so commonplace that she was hardly aware of its insidious effect. He had to combat it continually, to hold out the hope of escape as not only possible but probable. In this he had to be on guard to keep separate the truth he knew in his own mind, with its concomitant doubts, and the idyllic truth he urged on her.

Outwardly, Ilse had not changed very much in a year; if anything, she seemed to him more beautiful than ever, and he wondered if she were one of those chosen women whose beauty would never fade but would advance with age much like a flower whose petals each day give an intimation of first bloom.

Her face was wide for a woman—the breadth of a hand's span. Her high cheekbones protruded like polished stones reflecting the light from her brown eyes. There was a gentleness about her eyes, a disposition to look upon whatever they saw with understanding and compassion. But they showed her intelligence as well, a sensitive awareness that not all could be understood, not everyone deserved compassion. For him there was also love, an image of the intimacy she had known only with him.

She had lost weight in the past year. Her shoulders, which had been round and smooth, inviting his touch, were bony now, giving the impression that it was an effort for her to maintain good posture. Yet she always did, just as she would force a smile when she did not feel like smiling. Her eyes still held the glow of her love for him, assuring him that it was not dead, only dormant. Now that he needed her, was counting on her old spirit to rise above her despair to reach out for the hope he held out, he wanted to touch her hand, to reassure her of his love, but they had begun the play, and it was not in the script.

Through the window the Vopo came strolling into view, his cap set on his head at a jaunty angle in spite of the rain. His automatic submachine gun was slung on his thin shoulder with the bore down. A poncho that was much too big for him drooped down around his ankles, dripping with rain. Sepp thought about him and wondered if skinny people always had trouble getting clothes to fit. He looked at his watch: nine eighteen.

The Vopo was kicking a stone, and as he came directly across the street from them, he gave it a hard kick that sent it streaking up the sidewalk and out into the street. He stopped to watch it land. Sepp looked at him intently. He was slight in build, perhaps twenty years old but no more. Sepp recognized him as one of a dozen or more they had observed in the past month. He was relieved to see that without his weapon the fellow would be no match for him, but even more relieved to know that he was not particularly conscientious about his duty. As he ambled on, he glanced occasionally at the row of buildings on his side of the street, at the lighted windows of the *Gasthaus,* but not once, as they watched him pass up the street, did he look behind him.

"It's one of the young ones," she said softly.

"Yes."

"That's good, isn't it."

He nodded. "We'll wait until he comes back." He looked at his watch again. It was nine twenty. The Vopo met his comrade at the corner, said something, and started back on the long leg, the one they planned to make use of.

"You know I won't mean anything I say," she said.

"I know. Nor I."

She glanced out the window. "Is he coming back?"

"Yes."

She quickly drank some beer. "It still seems like a dream. Right now it's a nightmare. Oh, darling, be careful. Don't do anything foolish."

"There's nothing to worry about." There was much to worry about, but it would only make things worse to dwell on it. He began to feel that everyone in the *Gasthaus* knew what they were up to, that the Vopo out there knew and was waiting for him, that Lieutenant Geller knew and had a squad of People's Police hidden all around outside, that Sergeant Doyle knew and had tried to warn him. He could reason that it was all his imagination, but to control his fear was another thing. He glanced out and saw the Vopo passing again, right on time. The wind was blowing the rain up now, and he was hunched over, protecting his face from it. The windows rattled in protest against the beating they were taking.

"He's just passing."

"Oh." It was a plaintive sound, a plea for a last-minute reprieve. "Can't we let him go one more round?"

"It won't do any good."

She did not answer. She turned away and looked around the drab room. An old, crinkling picture of Premier Ulbricht was hanging askew on the wall behind the beer tap. Sepp thought, if Adolf knew, he would be mortified. But no one in the room would tell him; it would mean committing oneself one way or another.

"We have to start," he said. She looked back at him with that vacant, haunted look that said she knew what it could be like again, as it had been before when they were apart and life was reduced to a kind of somnambulism.

From all the canyons of his mind, the words began to flow, rushing like swollen streams after a rainstorm into the reservoir of his mouth. As though regulating the cocks on a dam, he let them out, slowly at first, later with terrifying speed and vigor. "You're being unfair. It's unreasonable and selfish of you."

She gave him a disgusted look. "Not that again, please."

He raised his voice a notch. "It's all right for you, it's easier for you, but I suffer."

"Suffering is good for the character, isn't it?" She could be marvelously snide. "And yours could use some development. I'd like another glass of beer, please."

He pushed the stein aside and leaned across the table. "Why? Just tell me why."

"Stop acting like a child."

"A child doesn't have this feeling. I'm a man, and a man needs love, he needs. . . ."

"There's no place to go."

"There are plenty of places to go."

"I won't go to a hotel." She was almost shouting now. "Why?"

"It's dirty, that's why."

"It's unbearable this way.'"

"You're oversexed, darling." She was so smug he thought for an instant she really believed it.

"I'm not oversexed, I'm undersatisfied."

"I can't help that." She folded her arms in a gesture of finality.

Sepp looked out the window. The Vopo was out of sight. He looked back at Ilse. She rubbed her nose, a signal that the Vopo was well up the block. He glanced around the room and saw that they were attracting attention. "You don't want to because you don't need to."

"What is that supposed to mean?"

"You know damned well what it's supposed to mean."

"How dare—"

"Don't hand me that outraged female bit. You're either frigid or someone else is making it with you. And you aren't frigid."

She pushed her chair back. "You're drunk!"

"Like hell I am! I'm cuckolded!"

Her hand made a wide, sweeping arc and came cracking against the side of his head. It was a sharper blow than he had expected. It stunned him for a moment. Ilse was up, pulling on her raincoat, heading for the door. Unexpectedly, she turned, strode back to the table, snapped up her umbrella, stared at him with fury, tears standing in her eyes, and gave him a second crack. That they had not rehearsed, and he sat dumbfounded as she fled out into the rain.

The room was silent. Even the card players had stopped, and he knew they were all staring at him. Adolf sat on his stool with his mouth open, looking every bit the school dunce. Behind, somebody started laughing. Sepp forced himself to sit for a full two minutes, staring numbly into his beer. The laughter died, then erupted again in response to a joke one of the card players made at his expense. He had to let it go. If Ilse did not return within two minutes, it was his signal that nothing unusual was happening in the street, that it was all clear and he could go ahead.

He waited five seconds longer than two minutes. He pulled himself together, got up, threw a five-mark piece on the table, grabbed his raincoat from the chair, and strode to the door. As he closed it behind him, the laughter renewed itself, and he had the momentary thought that here in East Berlin any excuse for laughter must be understood.

Up and down the street there was no one in sight. Ilse

was gone. The Vopo, up in the next block by now, was invisible in the heavy rain. He walked down the sidewalk out of the light of the café, staying close to the buildings. Once in the darkness, he stopped again to look and listen. Nothing. He took a deep breath and raced across the street.

At the doorway to the house, he pressed himself into the recess and looked and listened again. The sound of the rain overwhelmed the sound of his heart beating in his ears. Satisfied, he turned and went to work.

The door was a heavy oak door with a latch lock screwed onto the outside. There were three screws holding the receptacle for the bolt. He got out his screwdriver. Hurriedly, in the dim light from the apartments across the street, he found the screws on the latch and took them out. They came out easily. He put each one carefully in his coat pocket.

Slowly, gently, he pulled down on the handle, heard the catch click, and pushed the heavy door inward. At any instant he expected the hinges to cry out, but they made no sound. When it was open wide enough, he squeezed through and pushed it shut behind him. He stood in the darkness with his back against the door, listening in the eerie silence. Then the sound of the steady drum of the rain came, as if from far off.

He ran his fingers down the crack between the spine of the door and the jamb until they touched a bottom hinge. He felt it carefully. It was an ordinary strap hinge with a removable pin. He felt for a center hinge, but there was none, only a second near the top of the door.

He crouched down and played the pencil flashlight across the floor. The flooring was solid parqueted hardwood covered with a thin layer of dust. He was in a small vestibule. To the left, the first steps of a staircase going up were visible; to the right, a door which he assumed led to the first-floor apartment; directly in front of him, another door. He opened it. It squeaked loudly, once, complaining about being disturbed after a year's disuse. His heart fled and came out pounding in every part of his body. He stood frozen, listening. Nothing but the rain. He pulled the door open wider, wide enough to pass through, and shone the light beyond. It was the staircase to the cellar.

Sliding through the opening, he took each step as slowly

as he dared, testing each before he put his full weight on it.
The wood was old but solid. The top half of the staircase
was enclosed by walls, but the lower half descended into
the open, with handrails on each side. The steps were only
heavy slabs of wood spiked in from the sides, open at the
back. At the bottom, the floor was earthen.

The earth of the floor was hard and dusty. He probed
into it with the screwdriver. There was no concrete underneath. He shone the light on the wall ahead. It was covered
with plaster. Big pieces of it had dropped off, like scabs
from acned skin, exposing the red brick underneath. Other
sections of the plaster bulged out, with ugly cracks running
from the centers of the bulges and disappearing into the
healthier parts around them. The only object in the room
was an abandoned lamp standing in one corner, the frame
of its shade bent, the fabric ripped and spotted with
mold. The cord wound around its base was also green with
mold.

He went to the wall and reached up to get an estimate
of its height. His hands came within a palm's breadth of
touching the ceiling. That would make it about three meters. He had judged the height of the cellar foundation
wall on the outside to be a meter and a half above the
ground; thus, the cellar was half above ground level and
half below it. He probed around the base to see if he could
determine how far down the foundation began, but the
brick ran deeper than the length of the screwdriver blade.
He paced off the dimensions—seven paces in each direction. It was three paces from the front of the staircase to
the wall. Satisfied, he shone the flashlight on his watch. It
was nine thirty-nine. He couldn't believe so much time
had gone by. The Vopo would already have passed the
house on his way back to the corner. He was due to pass
the house going the other way in three minutes.

Sepp stood wondering if there was anything else that
had to be done. He would have to wait four or five minutes
until the Vopo passed the house again and was well up
the street before he could leave, so he decided to check
his measurements again.

He was finished and heading for the stairs when he
heard a noise overhead.

He froze and listened. It came again—a metallic click.
The wind? A rat? Then another sound. Rain. A draft came

in, and he knew the outer door was open. The sound of rain and the breeze subsided as quickly as they had come. The vision of the door opening and closing registered in his mind's eye. Again a foreign sound, this time different —scraping, like wood on wood. Or leather on wood! He found he had been holding his breath, and exhaled slowly, deliberately, silently. Somehow he thought to switch off the flashlight. The upper door creaked. He moved slowly, so slowly he thought he would never get there, under the stairs, back up against the wall. His heart was pounding wildly.

"Who's there?" It was a man's voice, thin and tenor— strangely more curious than demanding. He held his breath. Fear raced to the limits of his control. His mind played a fast motion picture of alternatives.

Don't move. Don't breathe.

Give yourself up—it's better than being shot.

Jump him if he comes down. Grab his legs from behind through the openings between the steps.

"Who's there?" More demanding now, insistently curious.

If he goes for help, get out and make a run for it.

A beam of light bounced down the stairs one at a time. It paused at the bottom, swinging back and forth in a narrow scan.

"Come up out of there." The voice sounded thinner than before. The young Vopo. The conclusion was like a minor victory, as if knowing it was the young Vopo made things not so bad as they had been.

A foot tested the stairs hesitantly. "You aren't permitted in here, you know."

The remark was motherly. Sepp almost laughed. Hysteria was building on the periphery of the tension, and recognizing it relaxed him a little.

Another step. "I know you're there, whoever you are. You've got to come out, you know."

It suddenly occurred to Sepp that he was *not* certain anyone was there, that he was as frightened as Sepp, that he was hoping that whoever had been there had gone. Sepp stood pressed against the wall, not moving, alert and ready now, waiting for him to take his initiative further or retreat.

He came down another step, stopped, waited, threw his

light about, took another step, stopped. He was no longer talking—a good sign. His light traversed fully three-fourths of the width of the room, and having found nothing, he might have begun to think his hopes were true, that no one was there any longer.

He took another step, this one the first without a back-board, and his boots showed clearly in the reflected light. Droplets of water shimmered on the smooth leather and dripped down on the step. If he goes farther, Sepp reasoned, he'll realize he can shine his light under the staircase.

Without giving himself time to think about the consequences, Sepp lunged for the boots, caught them around the ankles, and jerked them back with all his strength. The Vopo went crashing forward. A scream shattered the silence. Light did an erratic dance around the room and vanished. Metal clattered against the wall. Sepp was around the steps and on him, groping desperately for the flesh in the mass of wet clothing. Another cry—a screech more than a cry. His hands found the throat and surrounded it, his thumbs tight up under the Adam's apple. They began to tighten, hard, so hard he could feel the muscles in his arms straining to break through the skin. The body was writhing under him. The boy's hands found Sepp's and clawed at them frantically. He felt the boy's nails scraping the skin away from the tops of his hands and the thin legs flailing convulsively under him.

Sepp stopped. He tore his hands away and fell forward. His arms stiffened and caught his heaving body. He gasped for breath. The air was a hot wind in his throat. His eyes burned. His arms shook with the weight of his body. He sat back, straddling the boy's thin body, trembling. Sweat ran down over his eyebrows and to the edges of his lashes. He wiped it away and felt a throbbing ache in his fingers.

The boy's legs were still now; his chest heaved up and down, noisily inhaling the precious air. Sepp sat immobilized, awed by the ease with which his mind and body had almost seduced his soul. He raced his memory down a gigantic spiral to this moment, this place, four thousand miles from his home, in a dark cellar of an abandoned house in East Berlin, strangling the life out of another human being. The absurdity of it made him shudder and he

had to hold his hands tightly to keep them still. He felt the
warmth of his own blood on his hands and the pain of the
wounds the boy's fingernails had made. He sucked
the blood and tried to assemble his thoughts. Slowly he
came to his senses, and his mind was once again on the
alert.

Fumbling in his pocket, he got out the pencil flashlight
and shone it in the Vopo's face. He was younger than Sepp
had thought. He hardly had a beard. His long blond hair
was smudged with dirt, and there was a small cut on his
forehead. His cap was nowhere in sight. He kept his eyes
closed, intent only on massaging his throat.

Sepp shone his light around. The boy's weapon lay under a sprinkle of plaster chips it had shaken loose when it
struck the wall. His flashlight, an ordinary two-celled military light, lay close by. Sepp leaped up and had them both
in an instant. He turned his light back on the boy. He
hadn't moved. He was still rubbing his throat. He
coughed, a rasping, painful cough. He had given up. Sepp
put the bigger light on and turned it on his face. He
blinked and put a hand to his eyes.

"Get up."

He lay there, covering his eyes with his hands. Sepp
kept the light in his face. "Get up!"

The boy turned his head aside and sat up. He wiped a
hand on his uniform and brushed his hair back. "Are you
going to kill me?" He brushed his hair again. "If you're
going to kill me, I'm not going to get up."

Sepp kicked the sole of his boot. "On your feet."

"I'm not going to get up just to be murdered." He
rubbed his throat as though reminiscing about how close
he had come to death once already. His resignation to
death seemed to be reinforcing that reminder. He folded
his arms and, with his eyes closed tightly, sat there like a
pouting child.

Sepp kicked him again. "Get up, damn you." It became
a game of wits with no relation to the obvious peril Sepp
was in as the seconds passed. The boy was either insanely
brave, incapable of realizing his own peril, or just plain
insane. He must be a little stupid, too, Sepp thought, to
have come down into the cellar alone.

"There's no point in kicking me. I'm not getting up."

Sepp was exasperated. He slung the weapon over his

shoulder and with his free hand reached down, got hold of the front of his uniform, and jerked the boy to his feet. He was surprisingly heavy, and he let his legs go limp, so that it took all Sepp's strength to hold him up. "I'm not going to kill you."

"Is that a promise?"

He was insane, no doubt about it.

"That's a promise."

"How do I know you mean it?"

"I could have killed you before. I didn't, did I?"

The boy considered this. "That's true." He got his footing and put his weight down. He straightened himself out in a prim, fussy way and looked around for his hat. When he found it, he slapped it against his thigh twice and set it squarely on his head. Sepp kept the light on his face and backed off a few paces. The boy turned from the light. "Do you have to shine that in my eyes? It's very annoying."

"Turn around."

"You said you wouldn't kill me." A rivulet of fear spilled over the edge of his equanimity. "You promised."

"I'm not going to kill you." He would not budge. Sepp began to feel panic gnawing at his self-control. He did not know how to cope with the boy's idiotic behavior. "If you don't turn around, I *will* kill you."

The boy gave this some thought. "All right." He turned around slowly.

"Put your hands on your head."

He did as he was told. Sepp approached him cautiously.

"If you're going to use this place for a tunnel, I'd like to help you."

Sepp was startled. "What do you mean?"

"That's the only reason you'd be here, isn't it?"

"Maybe I'm hiding from the police."

"You wouldn't come *here,* not a place that's watched by the police." He shook his head. "No, you can only be thinking of a tunnel." He spoke with conviction.

Sepp gave him a cursory search, wondering what to do. Time was short. He had to get out, get away from that house, from that street. Nothing seemed to matter now but to reach safety, to survive. The instinct to survive was vaguely supported by the logic that unless he did, there was no hope of ever being with Ilse again. He decided to simply knock him over the head with his weapon and get out of there as fast as possible. But he clearly did not relish even this idea or why the insistence that the boy get to his feet? There was no need for that. He could have done it more easily while he sat there.

"I want to get to the West, too," the boy said. "I'll work with you. In my job, I can be of great help."

"You've got it all wrong."

"Please don't play games." Now he was condescending. "There isn't much time. I have to call in in a few minutes. If I don't, they'll be here looking for me. Then we'll both be in trouble."

"Both?"

"It won't look good for me, will it? I mean, I investigated without calling in first. I should have called in first. The sergeant will be furious with me."

"Why didn't you call in?"

"You are dense, aren't you?" Now he was exasperated. "If I had called in, I wouldn't be able to join you, would I?"

"How do I know I can trust you?"

"I trusted you, didn't I?"

"You had no choice. Besides, I had already demonstrated my trust."

He laughed. "By not killing me?" He shook his head sorrowfully. "Just look what we've come to." He rubbed his neck again as if the red marks of Sepp's fingers were the badge of a tenuous fidelity between them. "There's no time. Decide now. I'll go up with you, help you set the latch straight."

There was little choice. Whether he trusted him or not no longer mattered as far as the tunnel was concerned. In either case he would not know if the house had been compromised until they came to the end. The only question now was whether Sepp was to get out of East Berlin. Once outside and free, if the boy turned in an alarm, the checkpoint would be sealed and Sepp's fate as well. He made a hasty, wild decision. "Show me your identity card."

"Why?"

"If I'm going to go along with you, I want some hard proof of what happened here. If you turn me in before I cross over—"

"You're from the *other* side?" The boy was astounded.

"If I get held up at the checkpoint, I'm going to have proof that you came in here alone, against standing orders. I'd tell them the whole scheme."

He wasn't paying any attention to Sepp. "Lord, what luck! You're from *West* Berlin!"

"Listen, damn it! Get out your identity card." He got it out of his wallet and handed it over. Sepp held it up to the light. "Konrad Möss," he read aloud. The picture made him look even younger, like a schoolboy. He had a silly grin on his face, as if mocking the photographer. Sepp handed it back to him. He held the weapon up to the light and read the serial number on the stock. He repeated it to himself until he had it memorized. Then, as a last piece of insurance, he removed a cartridge from the magazine and put it in his pocket.

"What are you doing that for?"

"It proves you have lost possession of your weapon. That's a serious offense, at least in our Army it is."

"They'll catch me. I know it. They always check our weapons when we go off duty."

"You'll think of something."

"Some trust, I'll say."

"My neck is on the block."

"You needn't substitute mine for yours."

"Let's just say I want yours there with mine."

Konrad threw up his hands, resigned. "We'd better get out of here or Poldiek will be coming down."

"You go first." Sepp motioned him toward the steps. "What about my weapon?"

Sepp retracted the bolt to see that the chamber was clear, closed it, and handed it and the flashlight to him.

Konrad grunted. "Some trust, I'll say," he said again. He went up the steps.

Upstairs, they peered out the window to see if there was anyone in the street, but it was deserted. The rain had subsided, but the wind was still blowing strongly. Sepp could see the rain in the street light, coming down at a wide angle.

"How did you discover me?" Sepp asked.

"The latch was flapping in the wind like a flag. You really ought to be careful, you know." This came as an admonishment, much as if he were telling Sepp he expected better things of him in the future.

Sepp gave him the screwdriver and screws, but Konrad was nervous and kept letting the screws drop. Sepp took the screwdriver. "I'll do it. Keep your eyes open." Sepp realized he had crossed the barrier—they were fellow conspirators. He wondered at the insanity of it all. The boy was leaning in the corner of the building as nonchalantly as if he were on a street corner watching the girls go by.

"Done," Sepp said. He looked up and down the block, but there was no one in sight.

"Where's your sidekick?"

"Poldiek? The dumbhead didn't bring his poncho. He's probably curled up in a doorway somewhere."

"We'd better get away from here."

Konrad shrugged. "I can tell you're from the West. We're safe now. No one would dare question me. They're all sheep, willing to munch grass on the way to the slaughterhouse." He thumbed his nose at the million souls confined behind the rainstreaked facades of half a city. "When will I hear from you?"

"Not for several weeks."

"I'll give you two. If I haven't heard from you by then, you might just as well save your strength."

"It may take longer. How can I contact you?"

"Write me at Seventeen Schaumstrasse, Pankow. I'll get it there. The date you plan the escape, say you'll be celebrating your birthday. Put the time in it somewhere. Any excuse for a time will do. And for pity's sake, don't mail it in West Berlin."

Sepp was about to protest, but all he wanted was to get out of there.

"Seventeen Schaumstrasse, Pankow," Konrad said.

"All right."

"Repeat it."

"Seventeen Schaumstrasse, Pankow."

Konrad nodded. "I'll try to arrange to have this duty that night. I don't know how, but I'll try. I'll be here even if I have to desert. I can be a big help to you."

Sepp did not say anything. They stood looking at one another. Hesitantly, the boy put out his hand. Sepp took it, a thin, bony hand, but one which gripped his firmly.

"The Reds must be more hard up for manpower than I thought," Sepp said.

He grinned. "You noticed."

"I couldn't help but notice."

"No, I'm not cut out for this sort of thing. I'm more the scholar type, don't you think?" He did not wait for an answer. "My father's a party man—an *ambitious* party man. It looks good if his son is a trusted member of the People's Police. He's not a bad sort, he's just adaptable. 'We must adapt to the times,' " he said in a deep, authoritative voice, mimicking his father. "He adapted to the Nazis. Now he adapts to the Communists. I often wonder if he would ever be able to adapt to democracy." He sighed. "The whole business is so damned *boring*. You have no idea. It's not the shortages, the repression, or even the fear. It's the constant, unrelenting boredom." He drew out the last word to such a length that the last syllabel was garbled in a gasping yawn. He came out of it laughing. "Do you see what I mean?"

Sepp had to laugh with him. "Now I'd better go."

"And I." Konrad held his watch up to the street light. "Time to check in." He peered down the street through the rain, but his comrade was not in sight. "I'll have to dig Poldiek out of his hole. This rain is a filthy nuisance."

Sepp started to leave, but Konrad caught him by the arm. "My clip."

Sepp had forgotten it. He handed him the magazine.

"You won't change your mind about the cartridge? It will cause me no end of trouble."

"I can't very well."

Konrad stared at him, then shrugged. "I'll think of something."

"I'm sure you will. *'Wiedersehen*."

" *'Wiedersehen*," Konrad said, and as an afterthought, "Don't forget to write."

Sepp had to laugh again. The world he had come to know in Berlin had never been quite sane; it had always walked precariously along the shoreline, washed from time to time, when it was slow to react, by the dark waters of madness. On occasion a wave had surprised it, engulfed it, and sent it tumbling head over heels into the abrasive sand; but it had always righted itself and continued along its destined path, the perpetual beachcomber.

Before leaving the *Sektor*, he called Ilse's mother and told her to tell Ilse when she got home that he was all right and would see her again tomorrow night, as usual.

Back in West Berlin, he stopped at a telephone booth and called Joachim's number. Wolf answered.

"Wolf, this is Sepp. Let me speak with Joachim."

"He's not here, Sepp." Sepp was too stunned to say anything. "He called and said he wouldn't be in tonight."

"Are you sure he said he wouldn't be in at all?"

"I'm sure."

"Did he ask if I had called?"

"He didn't mention it. Is something wrong? Are we still going to start tomorrow?"

"There's nothing wrong, we'll start tomorrow."

"That's good. I'm really looking forward to it."

"Tell Joachim not to be late in the morning."

"He said he'd pick me up at six thirty."

"*'Wiedersehen*, Wolf."

"*'Wiedersehen*, Sepp."

Sepp hung up. He stood in the booth, the water dripping from his hair down his neck, dripping on the floor, and recalled Emerich's warning about Joachim. He wondered if Wolf had given him an accurate report of his conversation with his brother. Perhaps Joachim did plan to return before midnight. Or maybe he was planning to call Wolf again at midnight to see if Sepp had called. The thought brightened his mood, and he converted the possibility into probability. He opened the door and stepped out. It was still raining, a hard, fast, driving rain, and with the wind gone, it was coming straight down. That's the only explanation, he thought.

He started out for home, but the thought of going back to his empty room unnerved him. His memory of it turned to thoughts of Ilse behind The Wall. He could not go back to his room, not tonight, and he went back to the booth.

Her phone rang only twice before she answered.

"Hello."

"Sophie, this is Sepp."

"*Liebchen*." It was noncommittal; a little cold, perhaps. He realized he was excited. Ernst was not home.

"How are you, Sophie?"

"I'm fine, *Liebchen*. Are you calling me from New York? Or Chicago, maybe?"

He bit his lip. She was going to make it difficult. "I'm in Berlin, Sophie."

"Berlin? And here I've been pining away this past month for my *Liebchen* who was rotated to the United States, and all the time he was right here in Berlin."

There was a long silence.

"Sophie?"

"I'm tired, *Liebchen*." The parody had ended, and she was herself. "I have just come from the theater. It was a stinking bore of a play."

"Ah, Sophie, you never get tired."

"Like hell," she said in English.

"Don't be sore, Sophie. I couldn't call you. I couldn't see you. I'll tell you all about it."

"Some story, I'll bet."

"Let me come up?"

"Where are you?"

"In the phone booth at the corner."

There was another long silence.

"Sophie?"

"It had better be a good story, Josep Bauer."

"Like out of Maugham."

"Where's that?"

"I'll be right up. And run a tub of water for me. I'm frozen." He hung up quickly before she could refuse.

He hurried down the block to the big, elegant apartment house where Sophie lived. Ivy covered its walls, the leaves shimmering with rain. It was a dark stone and brick structure that had escaped the war's bombing and stood heroically, if eccentrically, among its newer Bauhaus challengers like a fencer in the midst of a gunfight.

As he was going up the walk, a short, fat man came out of the building. As they passed and their eyes met, the man paused almost imperceptibly, as if he had recognized Sepp. There was a peculiar warmth in his expression, the look one friend would give another under circumstances in which they could not give any outward sign of recognition. Oddly, Sepp reciprocated with the same expression and a slight nod. He knew he had never seen the man before. He was in his early forties, wore an expensive but aging raincoat, and despite the suggestion of a waddle, carried himself with an air of dignity and authority. Perhaps it was the way he held his head—to one side and back, his round chin protruding arrogantly. Class, Sepp decided, without money. Charm, intelligence, wit, some guile in those dark eyes—a man who knew his way around. Sophie was particular and, thinking of it, he felt a genuine empathy with the older man. They would understand each other. Then he realized he had assumed that the man had been Sophie's escort for the evening with little, if any, evidence for the assumption. He could have come from any of the dozen apartments in the building. He felt intuitively, though, that he was right.

Sophie opened the door of her apartment at his first knock. "God in Heaven! Don't you own an umbrella?"

"Hello, Sophie." He moved to give her a kiss, but she backed away. He entered the outer vestibule and closed the door behind them. "May I come in?"

"Heavens, no! Take those wet clothes off. I'll get a towel." She scurried off.

He leaned around the doorway. "This is one hell of a way to welcome back a long-lost lover!"

She said something that sounded like "Pfabhf!" He took off his clothes, and she returned with a bath towel. "You look like a blue baby."

"I'm cold, all right."

"There's a hot bath. What happened to your hands?"

He had forgotten about them. "A cat scratched me."
He wrapped the towel around him, and she let him kiss her on the cheek. "You're the best, Sophie."

"And you are the worst. Get into the tub."

While he soaked in the hot water, she sat in front of her big mirror brushing her hair. She had long blond hair that came down almost to her waist.

Sepp loved her bathroom. It was big and old-fashioned. There were big cracks in the marble of the bathtub that made interesting designs in the natural pattern of the stone. The faucet handles were gold-plated, and the spigot was a golden gargoyle. In one corner, a huge rubber plant grew from the floor to the ceiling. There were brightly colored stuffed birds singing ethereal melodies among its leaves. An elegant set of ornate gold lacework shelves containing bottles, jars, and boxes of fragrant perfumes, colognes, creams, and powders was hung on the wall in the corner near the dressing table. Sophie used several of these preparations when she was getting ready for bed. The blend of their fragrances filled the air and with the steam of hot bath water had an anesthetic effect on him.

Going to Sophie was like going home. She made him feel comfortable and warm; her affection for him was almost motherly. He needed to "go home" tonight, to touch base, to be reminded that despite the hell he had been living through, all was right with one corner of the world. Thinking all that, he felt a strong sense of loyalty and affection for her. "Ah, Sophie," he said, "you're a wonder."

"I'm counting." She was stroking her hair rhythmically, holding it gathered at the top and pulled around to the front, running the brush down its length with long, graceful sweeps. He loved to watch her brush her hair.

"Where is Ernst this time?"

"Amsterdam. Fifty-eight."

"When is he due home?"

"Tomorrow. Fifty-nine."

"Oh."

"Sixty."

He lathered his arms lazily. "Who was the man leaving when I came in?"

"Sixty-four. A friend from the old days. Sixty-five."

Aha! He had been right! He made a guess. "Nazi type."

"Sixty-six. Quite."

"What's his name?"

"Why do you want to know?"

"I don't know. Jealousy, maybe."

She laughed. "Sixty-eight. He goes by the name of Klaus Schoenemann."

"Schoenemann? Unfortunate name in his case."

"Sixty-nine. *Ach,* you young people are so addicted to superficial beauty." She paused in her brushing and looked at him in the mirror. "He *is* a beautiful man. He has intelligence, charm, sophistication, and good breeding—things no one cares about anymore. These things make a man attractive." She smiled cagily. "He's even more attractive than you, *Liebchen.*"

"I didn't think it was possible."

Her smile changed to one of amusement. She had a gay smile, and with her head tilted to one side and her long hair down, shining in the light, she was much as he imagined she had been twenty years before. He held her gently in his heart at that moment and embraced her with the tenderness of the man he hoped to be. He thought of Ilse and wondered if she would be like Sophie in twenty years. She set the brush down and spoke to his image in the mirror. "He *was* a Nazi, but in those days there was nothing wrong with that, you know."

"So I've heard."

"He was kind to me when I needed kindness. That's all I care about. The rest was all politics."

"How did he get through the great net?"

She took up her brushing again, but she was not counting. "It was quite simple. He became a Communist. Toward the end, he saw that he would lose. He helped a few of the Communists who were beginning to poke their noses out of their holes. They put in a good word for him, and abracadabra! he was a functionary in the German Democratic Republic." She made a small space between her finger and thumb. "Only a petty functionary, but a functionary just the same."

"Why did he defect?"

She smiled benignly. "But he didn't defect."

"He's working for them? Over here?"

"Please don't tell anyone, will you? He's such a charming man. And I'm sure he's not harming anyone."

He stared at her in disbelief, then burst into laughter. "You're serious."

"Of course I'm serious."

"But—"

"None of your buts, *Liebchen*. You're a darling lover, a lion in a den of fat muskrats, but Klaus is not a muskrat. Don't stick your nose in *his* den."

Sepp slid down in the water up to his chin. "Yow, what a woman!" he said in English.

She winked at him. "No more questions, *Liebchen*. I don't think I can trust you. Men do such damned silly things when it comes to politics."

He made the Boy Scout's sign. "I promise not to turn him in."

"You're a sweetie."

He looked to see if she was teasing him, but her attention was on her hair. She was a middle-aged Rapunzel with her long, golden hair. She was counting again, and he could not tell whether or not she was teasing. He thought of the dark, round face that had passed him on the steps of the building. The man fascinated him, and he felt the same affinity for him as he had before, when he had responded only to his intuition.

"Will you introduce us sometime?"

"Why? You have nothing in common." She turned on her stool and looked him over with new curiosity. Then she turned back and resumed her brushing. "No, I don't think so. Let's not talk about him anymore." Her tone was final, and he knew he should not pursue it.

"Do you want to hear my story?"

"Of course. I love fiction."

"I was on a special assignment. In northern Norway. The Russkies shot down one of our planes. It was all very hush-hush."

"Pfabhf!"

Later, going back to his room in the rain, he put together a wonderfully fantastic yarn, and he felt a little disappointed that he would never be able to use it.

6

GEORG Knauer sat alone at a table in the empty out-door café. The rain pounded the canopy overhead. Water was pouring down over its scalloped edge, spatter-ing noisily onto the sidewalk. Georg could judge the in-tensity of the rain by the sound—intermittently it grew as loud as a kettledrum roll, as soft as brushes on a snare. Water gushed in the gutters, carrying debris in swirling eddies toward the sewer at the corner. He breathed deeply and felt the cool, fresh air chill his lungs. He exhaled and gulped down some beer. On the Formica tabletop, he made an Olympic design of rings with the water clinging to the bottom of the glass. The waiter appeared from in-side and stood in the doorway watching it rain. He was a tall, thin man with rounded shoulders. His hairline had receded to the middle of his head, and the bald part of his head gleamed in the light.

"What time is it?" Georg asked him.

"What do you care? You're not going anywhere in this weather."

"I'd like to know just the same—if you don't mind."

The waiter held his watch to the light. "Half past ten."

In return for his impudence, Georg made it a point not to thank him; however, the waiter was unmoved, and Georg felt cheated. He finished off his beer. "Bring me an-other, please." He had not meant to add the "please." He could do without the man's insolence—he was in a bad enough mood as it was. The waiter scooped up the stein and loped off, indifferent to Georg's mood. The tempo of the rain increased. Georg stared down the street into the rain-glittered darkness, looking for Klaus, but no one was in sight.

He didn't like it. Klaus had never been late before. Perhaps the rain had held him up. But Georg knew better. Nothing would detain Klaus. His tardiness was intentional, a calculated ploy. But for what purpose? Georg curled his toes and felt the water dribble out of his wet socks. His trousers clung to his calves, and his collar was wet where the water had run down from his hair. He let his self-pity run its course from his physical discomfort to the fifty-four marks he had lost in a card game that afternoon, to his ridiculous fight with Elsbeth, and back to Klaus's tardiness. All in all, a terrible day. The only consolation was the prospect of the tunnel. "Tomorrow," he reassured himself, as if in the next day the tunnel would be completed as well as begun.

But Georg knew that there would be days, perhaps even weeks, of hard work, torturous work, before the tunnel would be finished. Then there was the danger of the escape. Anything could happen—other tunnels had been discovered, people shot or captured and sent to prison. People had been killed trying to escape. . . . The memory of Greta came to him again, as it did more than once every day, and he fled from it in terror.

The waiter rescued him, sliding a stein of beer across the table, letting some slop over the side. He made a second pencil mark next to the first on the cardboard coaster and sauntered off. Georg was about to complain when he caught sight of Klaus's silhouette against the corner street light, an enormous black blob bulging here and there like spilled ink sliding across glass, undergoing constant transformation as it moved. Georg felt his stomach go tight, and he tried to relax.

Klaus came into clear view, puffing the stump of a cigar under the shelter of his thick hand. Rainwater clung to the long black hair that, much like Klaus himself in its hardy resiliency, stood in high, arrogant arches across the back of his hand. He lumbered in under the canopy, shedding his raincoat as he came, slapping his battered hat against the back of a chair. His muttered "Good evening" came from deep in his cavernous chest, and Georg believed he could actually feel the vibrations of the sound. He noted how solicitously the waiter bowed and took Klaus's coat and hat, as if he were his personal valet. He came over, beaming as usual, and Georg knocked over his chair getting up to greet him.

"Please pardon me for being late, my friend. Ah, you're ahead of me," he noticed, scraping a chair out while Georg reclaimed his own from the floor. The smell of Klaus's cheap cigar invaded the air, scented with talcum powder gone stale at the end of the day. Klaus had on the same frayed gray suit he always wore, with the tiny Iron Cross emblem in the lapel bottonhole, the same blue-and-silver foulard tie, tied in a long, slim knot and hanging slightly askew. His shirt, with the collar tips curling upward like two daggers taking aim at the rolls of flesh ringing his thick neck, might have been the same, except that it had obviously been laundered. It shone where spots of excess starch had been ironed.

"Do you believe in poltergeists?" His query was typically not to the point. It was as if he detested his business and took pains to avoid it as long as possible, being forced to do it at last only when time had begun to run out. There was an air of distracted amusement about him. Every moment seemed a parody of life around him. All men were fools. Life was an absurdity, and the only way to make it bearable was to distill from its pitiful mash a supply of slightly intoxicating humor. His manner irritated Georg, who combated it by coming directly to the point, asking a question in reply: "Did you bring my money?"

A slight twitch of Klaus's head, as if to rout a fly, shook off Georg's impertinence. "A poltergeist visited me tonight —that is the reason for my tardiness." His speech was deliberate, each word carefully selected from among a vast variety at his disposal. There was always the flavor of the archaic, as if he had a preference for it. Georg suspected he was the last of an old line of Junkers who through mismanagement, dissipation, and indolence had lost their land, their money, and their position, and were left finally with only a sense of *noblesse oblige* inbred over fifty generations, a little pride, and a family name forgotten to all but a handful of other similarly reduced

members of the aristocracy. Georg's sense of humor was
aroused when he considered the spectacle of Junker
turned Communist bagman. The thought gave him a little confidence.

"You're always digressing."

"My boy, you are impatient. You run so hard and so
fast that the luscious taste of the zephyr is burned out
upon your hot lips before it can reach your tongue."

What was he talking about? Georg fidgeted in his chair,
decided to drink some beer to give himself time to think.
The waiter appeared with a glass of wine held high, as if
it were the sacred flame of an Olympic torchbearer. With
grace of which Georg had thought him incapable, he
gave the table in front of Klaus a swab with his towel
and in a great swirling motion glided the green-and-amber
glass into place before him. Making a slight bow, he retreated as if from the presence of royalty. The swine. If he
only knew whom he was serving, he'd pour the stuff
down the back of his neck!

Klaus caressed the bowl of the glass and lifted it to the
light in both hands. "Ah, Mosel wine. Is there another like
it in the world? The most blessed juice of the grape.
Prosit!" He filled his mouth and swished it around, pursing
his lips as he lingered over the taste. He swallowed and
sighed. "Not even my poltergeist has the power to dimin-
ish such pleasure."

As though to contradict him, the rain suddenly came on
hard again, beating out its strident chords on the canvas
overhead. The wind sang a mournful tune to the rooftops.
Spray blew in from the edge of the canopy and fell across
the top of the adjacent table.

"A conspiratorial setting, eh? 'When shall we three meet
again,' " he quoted, leaning forward, hunching his round
head down into his massive shoulders, squinting his dark
eyes, making his voice crack in a querulous falsetto, " 'in
thunder, lightning, or in rain? When the hurlyburly's done,
when the battle's lost and won.' " He leaned back and
laughed so uproariously that his stomach shook and the
rolls of fat under his jowls quivered. As suddenly as he
had begun, he finished, and with a touch of wistfulness,
added, "But then, there are only two of us, aren't there?"

"You can always count your poltergeist."

His face brightened, and he laughed again. "So, my

friend, you are not totally devoid of humor. Good for you!" And then, solemnly: "Do you believe in them?"

"Not especially."

"Pity. They exist, you know." He held up his hand, not yet disenchanted with the power of Shakespeare, and swore, "God's blood. One did visit upon me tonight. He hid my necktie, the devil, and stole a button from my shirt." He caught a shirt button between his thick fingers and turned it, a piece of evidence for the jury to consider. "I'm not much for sewing. It took me half an hour to get the needle threaded. Going out, he sent the wind into my umbrella, turning it inside out, ripping out the spokes, rending the material to uselessness."

"He didn't make you forget my money, did he?"

The humor faded into the shadows of sadness that fell across his face. "Perhaps you've had a poltergeist about you all along."

Georg was afraid he'd gone too far. He pleaded, "Can't we get to business?"

"You've a young lady waiting?"

"I'm tired."

"Worked so hard for us today, did you?"

"I work hard for you every day," Georg muttered.

"Of course you do, my boy. I'm impressed with your diligence, your dedication. Each week, after our little get-together, I return home, my head fairly bursting with the choice tidbits of information you've given me."

"It's hard—"

"Of course it's hard. If it were easy, we wouldn't have to pay you so well, would we?"

"I told you about the Bernauerstrasse tunnel."

"Which never materialized."

"I can't help it if they gave it up." Georg was pleading now, all the pretense of defiance dissolved in the solution of annoyance and anxiety.

"Fortunate for them."

"And what about the Ziglers?"

"We had already heard of that."

"My information confirmed it."

Klaus waved his hand in front of Georg's face. "You've given us nothing but hints, possibilities, glimmerings. Not one escape attempt has materialized; not one solid shred of evidence have we received on which to arrest anyone. Nothing. Nothing."

Klaus was exasperated, not angry. Georg watched him sip the wine, obviously relishing its taste, as if he had forgotten what he had just said; however, he immediately pursued it. "Each week, I hand over fifty West German marks. In return, you hand over ten pfenning's worth of information. So far, I have been willing to accept your ineptitude as that of a beginner. But it is seven months now that you've been at it, seven months, my boy, and the scales are woefully unbalanced." He turned inward, lost, it seemed, in another thought. "Woefully," he murmured. He looked into the palm of his left hand and began rubbing it with the thumb of his right. "Perhaps the carrot has spoiled you. Perhaps an application of the stick is required, eh?"

Georg's hatred was ignited spontaneously. "I'll kill you."

Klaus grinned, unmoved. "Oh, yes, you've said as much before. I'd forgotten how brave you are."

"I mean it."

"Of course you do, my boy. You needn't emphasize the point. A threat of that sort is never taken lightly, especially by one in my position. And particularly from one whose courage has been so amply demonstrated in the past." The words were laden with vicious sarcasm.

Hatred and humiliation pounded at Georg's temples. Tears forced his eyes shut. He took the stein in both hands and gulped down the remainder of the beer. Some of it dribbled down his chin, and he wiped it with his sleeve. He stared across the table at the eyes which showed no sign of emotion. He clasped his hands between his legs to keep them from trembling.

"You go too far." The hoarseness of his voice betrayed the collapse of his control. He fought to exorcise the nightmare crowding the vision of his mind, and failed. The terrified shriek pierced the thin membrane of his memory and entered his consciousness, rebounding inside his skull like a laser seeking its target, burning away everything else in its compulsive path. *Gee-orrg!!!* The memory threatened to possess him. He shook it off and looked across the table at Klaus, knowing there was nothing left within him with which to fight.

"What would they do to them?"

Klaus's black eyes narrowed, and he shrugged his heavy shoulders. "Arrest them, of course. Your father would lose his job, probably go to prison."

"You know he had nothing to do with my escaping. You know that."

Klaus swirled the wine, eyeing its circular motion through the tinted glass. "And *you* know quite well that that is of no consequence whatever."

Georg knew it. It was useless even to discuss it. When Klaus had first approached him seven months before, he had known it, and nothing had changed, nothing would change until his mother and father were safely out of East Berlin.

So far, they had used the carrot of money with him, and he had been able to satisfy them with unimportant information about student-planned escapes. But their patience was running out. He would have to come up with some hard information or they would indeed use the stick. They would arrest his parents and hold them hostage in prison in exchange for information. Up to now, Klaus had been willing to pay without resorting to that threat, but it was clear that his indulgence was near an end.

"I know of a tunnel," Georg said.

The fat man's face lighted up. "Where?"

Georg shook his head. "I don't know yet. I only know that one is being planned."

"When are they to begin?"

"I don't know, I don't know. I need some time."

"But, my boy, how much time?"

"A few days, maybe a week. I'm trying to get into the troop myself. I think I have a chance."

Klaus gazed out into the rain, turning the bowl of the wineglass slowly in his thick hands. "You have, perhaps, thought of rescuing your parents, eh? Of snatching them from under our noses?" He smiled benignly. "Then you would be free of me, would you not?"

Georg's mind clutched at his tongue, holding back the incriminating protest that was all but spoken. He smiled slyly. "I like the money, Klaus."

His adversary paused in drinking his wine and stared into his eyes. Georg fixed his own on the dark, unrelenting gaze and, summoning all his willpower, held it there. At last, Klaus's broad face slowly relaxed into a smile. His body shook with quiet laughter. "Incorruptible youth!" He laughed aloud. *"Ach,* it is a delightful comedy, a masterpiece of villainy. I am to be congratulated." He drank down the remainder of his wine.

How much he enjoys it, Georg thought. He enjoys the good things, the high life of days lost when he lived among kings. There's no glitter in drab communism.

"I will give you four days," Klaus said. "Meet me here again at ten o'clock Friday night."

"That may be too soon."

"Perhaps we should arrest your father as an insurance policy. After all, how do I know I can trust you?"

Georg felt the hand of fear again and the anger it generated. He had no escape from it or from the power Klaus represented. "All right. Friday night."

Klaus smiled. His tone was mockingly suppliant. "Try to bring me some hard information for a change, my friend." He looked into his empty glass and sighed. He took two marks from a small change purse he carried in his jacket pocket and placed them on the table.

"Aren't you going to pay me?" Georg asked.

"Friday," Klaus said, and with surprising agility he was on his feet. "Oh!" He raised a finger, remembering something, and taking out the purse, said, "Under the circumstances, I should pay the . . . ah . . . expenses."

"Two beers," Georg said.

"I don't drink beer."

"Two marks will do it."

He fished out two more mark pieces, set them next to Georg's glass, and returned the purse to his pocket. He looked out at the rain and said, "This weather is not propitious for tunneling. I do hope your friends are not discouraged by it. We do so love to uncover a tunnel now and again."

When Klaus had gone, Georg remained behind, nursing his beer. The rain hammered on the canopy. The waiter stayed inside where it was warm, content to ignore Georg now that Klaus had left. Georg shuddered and wrapped his arms around his body. Again that haunting cry reverberated through his head. He closed his eyes, pressing the lids tight, squinting to keep out the memories, but they were too strong for him. What he had become, what had brought him to this night, to this desperate moment, had sprung from the highest he had ever reached, the lowest he had fallen.

He had never been much before he met Greta Dohr. He had never been someone someone else loved, someone who was different enough to be loved. He had been exceedingly ordinary, a man of mass man, a perfect member of the group, never an individual or a distinct being or a soul apart. Greta Dohr had changed all that

They had met in the Pergamon Museum in front of the famous altar. She was very much involved in examining reliefs, taking notes, and referring to a cumbersome text she had brought along. Georg stood a few steps back, watching her, amused by the intensity of her concentration and the difficulty she was having hanging onto the book while trying to take notes. He waited for her books, paper, and pencil to go flying.

From behind she seemed an attractive little thing. She had on Roman sandals, so her feet showed. She had painted her toenails bright red. He wondered if she had worn those particular shoes with the idea of capturing the mood of the ancient world the altar evoked. It was a rather nice touch, he thought. Her legs, though thin, were shapely and slightly bowed. He liked them—a hint of calf muscle with a light blond down covering the smooth tanned skin. At the angle from which he was viewing her, he could not see her face, except for an occasional partial profile. Her body, though, excited him. The smallness of her bones—thin ankles, shoulder blades arching outward gracefully, tiny wrists which seemed too weak to support even the long, delicate fingers of her hands—combined with the fullness of her buttocks and her breasts, which protruded proudly and got in the way of her work as she braced the spine of the book against her diaphragm, stimulated erotic fantasies in Georg's imagination.

Her blond hair hung down straight and long over her back and shoulders, and she would brush it back from her eyes when she lowered her head to her book. As he stared at her, she moved in such a way that the sunlight streaming from the windows illuminated the rest of her legs under the thin material of her yellow dress. He caught his breath. As he did, the expected happened. Her book slipped from her grasp, slithered down the front of her dress, evading her desperate, futile efforts to grab it, and landed with a thump on the floor. In the high-ceilinged chamber of the exhibit hall, the sound was like distant cannon fire. Her pencil flew in a great arc, striking the already disfigured nose of a Greek goddess; her notes scattered like snowflakes all around her. She made abortive, awkward little lunges at them, trying to catch them in midair, but they sailed capriciously out of her reach.

Georg retrieved the book and pencil and stooped to help her gather up the papers. There were a dozen or more, and as she snatched them, looking much like a canary pecking at grain, she noticed him, and blushed with embarrassment. She rose, shuffling the papers, trying to restore them to order. Georg stood staring at her, allowing his amusement to show. She looked up at him, the embarrassment transformed to anger. "Is it really *that* funny?"

He was too sobered by her beauty to answer at once. Hers was a classic beauty, mirrored in the exquisitely sculpted faces on the stone relief of the ancient altar. Her eyes were blue and, in her anger, bright with the film of tears. In her determination to hold back, her lips were pursed in the semblance of a pout or, as Georg preferred to imagine, an invitation to be kissed. Her nostrils were flared and quivering, undoubtedly in chagrin and anger, but in Georg's rapidly building fantasy, in restrained passion.

"I'll take my things, thank you," she said coldly.

He handed them back to her, but she had not got a firm hold on the book and it slipped again. He followed it down, trying to reach it, but it dropped flat on the floor with an echoing bang. He retrieved it and wedged it into the crook of her arm, folding her fingers tightly around the spine. He tucked the pencil behind the book and, taking the papers she had picked up, added them to his, aligned the edges, and gently folded her other hand around them and pressed the hand to her breast. Gingerly withdrawing his hands, holding them outstretched in midair, he backed off as he would from a delicately balanced house of cards. She gave in to a smile, then a laugh. Her laughter soared high in the big hall and came swooping down into his ears like a chorus of angels.

He implored her, "Please don't come apart again, I'm

only the son of a poor worker, not all the king's horses and all the king's men."

She was still smiling, looking him over ingenuously. "You have big ears."

"Better to hear you with, my dear."

"And you are addicted to fairy tales."

"Aren't you Snow White?"

"Humpty Dumpty, remember?"

They both laughed. The pencil popped out of its niche, and with an exaggerated leap, he caught it, which sent them deeper into laughter.

Georg cherished that encounter, holding it close to his heart as she had held her book, bringing it out to look at and linger over at his leisure. It was the first time in his life he had handled himself with any competence around a girl, the first time a pretty girl, a girl he could really care about, had not rejected him out of hand.

It was August 1961. He had graduated from high school that summer and had managed to get a job at a plating factory in West Berlin inspecting the quality of chrome plating on hinges and cabinet handles. The work was dreary and monotonous, and in the summer the fumes of the electrolyte hung in the hot air, biting his nose and throat. But the wages were much higher than he could have earned in East Berlin.

Lately, East Berliners working in the West had been submitted to increasing harassment. Once, Georg's train had been stopped at the border at Bornholmerstrasse and everyone had been ordered off. He had got out and walked across to the next station in West Berlin. At the border, the guards were very slow in checking them through, and there were crowds of Free German Youth baiting them, shouting insults, waving placards reading: "Border Crossers Are Traitors," "Stop the Slave Trade," "Close the Border to Capitalists," "Down with the Revanchists," and one which he read twice and still could not figure out: "Kick Out the Greek Warmongers." When he arrived home that night, his name was among four on a list of border crossers posted in the entryway of his apartment house.

His mother wanted him to quit his job and get one in the *Sektor*. "They have arrested the families of border crossers. They will arrest us. You must not go back."

"But I earn five times as much over there as I could here," he argued. "This nonsense will pass, Mama."

When his father arrived home from work, Georg hesitantly asked his advice. Herr Knauer was a practical man and gave him a curt, practical answer. "The first thing they will do is threaten my job. If that happens, you will quit. Until then, continue working."

And so Georg had stayed on. He took pride in his ability to earn money, to pay his parents for his board and room, to provide his own spending money, and to save.

And now, with Greta, life was full. As much as Georg might dwell on the real and imagined reasons why someone like Greta Dohr could not, should not care for him, there was convincing evidence that she did, evidence that could not be brushed off into the sweepings of his past.

Since that first encounter last Sunday, he had seen her every day. When he had finished work on Monday, she had been waiting for him at the gate of the factory. "Are you surprised?" she had asked. He had tentatively put his arm around her, and when she had moved closer to him, accepting it, he had given her a squeeze and felt a surge of joy that he could not hold back. He had laughed for no reason, and she had laughed with him. "You're not angry I came?"

"It's wonderful!"

"You look different in work clothes."

"You still look the same."

"I don't feel the same."

"You're . . . beautiful." He, ordinary Georg Nobody Knauer, had said it—just right!

"And you're handsome—more handsome in work clothes, I think."

"I have big ears," he had reminded her.

"You do, you know, but they're handsome, too. You wouldn't be Georg without them."

She had met him every day—Monday, Tuesday, Wednesday, Thursday, Friday, Saturday—he enumerated them, the names singing through his mind like verse. Each day held a memory of its own. They became fused in her lively smile, the way her eyes grew bright when she caught sight of him in the crowd of workers coming through the gate, the bright colors of her dresses, and, most of all, the headiness he felt, the sense of anticipation with which he awakened every morning and which kept him in a state of nervous excitement all day long.

When she met him on Friday, she had her father's car, a little Skoda. "Papa's gone off to Moscow," she explained laconically.

Georg got in beside her and watched her manipulate the gearshift and steering wheel. She handled the car well, as if she had been driving a long time. He looked at her curiously, for the first time seeing her not only as a genie who appeared only to him at his call and returned to her hiding place when he left her. She, like him, had a family, a home, other friends.

"Why are you looking at me like that?" she asked. "Do you think I'll seduce you with my affluence?"

"I never thought of you as belonging to anybody—having a mother and father."

"No mother—she died four years ago."

"I'm sorry."

"Papa is all the family I have. There are aunts and uncles and cousins, of course, but they're all over there." She nodded vaguely toward the West.

"And Papa is in Moscow."

"Yes."

"Very impressive. Just like a party bigwig." As he was saying it, it came to him. *"Dohr!* Not August Dohr, *the* August Dohr of the Ministry of Defense?"

She glanced at him with the first sign of anxiety she had shown. "Does that make a difference to you?"

He was bewildered. "If . . . it's so . . . I didn't have any idea. . . ."

"Some people are awfully opinionated about that sort of thing."

He was not certain what she meant. The fact that she was the daughter of a high official in the government was difficult to assimilate. He had never developed political acuity, and it suddenly seemed a terrible handicap. He was afraid she was about to lead him down a treacherous ideological path. He decided there was no point in trying to fool her. "Maybe it'll seem awfully bourgeois to you, but I don't care much about politics."

She did not accept that. "But how is that possible? It's like saying you don't care about breathing. Life itself is political."

"Only in the DDR, or so I understand. Did you know that there are people in the West who don't even vote?"

She looked at him to make certain he was teasing her. He smiled to reassure her, but he felt uneasy for the first time since they had met. It seemed as though her bringing the car was meant to serve as the introduction to the second stage of their relationship. They were now to test one another, to probe for defects as a soldier probes the soil of an idyllic meadow for the presence of landmines buried just below the surface. He resented the maneuver and wondered if this were but the beginning of an iconoclasm he had dreaded, one which he was afraid was inevitable, but one which he had imagined would arrive in different guise, under other circumstances. It would be ironic, he mused, if my inadequacy were turn out to be political.

They had been driving in the fast traffic on the Goerderlerdamm and now passed into Seestrasse, onto the bridge over the Westhafen Canal, heading for the Böse Bridge over the railroad tracks which separated Berlin West from East. It was impossible not to notice the difference between the two parts of the city. In West Berlin, the streets were always jammed with cars and people bustling home, hurrying to work, shopping, or simply standing around gossiping. Everywhere the city vibrated with life. Entering East Berlin was like passing into early Sunday morning. The streets were jammed only with heat and silence. The clutches of people they saw, on bicycles or walking, kept their eyes straight ahead, their mouths shut tightly in a universal conspiracy of mute insensitivity.

"Do you notice the difference?" he asked her.

"The frivolousness of the West compared with the industry of the East?"

"That's not exactly the way I see it."

She turned sarcastic. "My eyes do not wear political glasses, the man said."

He laughed. "Ouch. Maybe it's subconscious."

"Just as dangerous."

"Just as dangerous as what?"

"Not what, whom. As dangerous as the Fascist and imperialist enemies of socialism."

She turned the car into Blankenfelderstrasse, heading toward Georg's home. She stared ahead, refusing to look at him. He could tell she was angry now, perhaps hurt as well. He had learned long ago that those who had no sense of humor about their politics were usually fanatics. Greta would be, of course, he realized sadly. With a father who was not only a party member but a deputy minister as well, there was no other possibility. All her life she must have been subjected only to the Communist view of life, at home as well as at school. Questions had been posed in terms of the dialectic, and neatly answered in the dialectic. As in religion, there was a parable for each situation, a gospel from which to fashion the solution to any problem. Even though he had always lived with the parables and gospel, and recited them as effortlessly and automatically as Greta just had, they had remained words totally devoid of meaning. They were words he spouted to please authority, not ideas. It was the first time he had ever been close to anyone who actually believed in the ideas, and he found it difficult to understand.

"I was going to ask you to have supper with me," she said. "I was going to cook it myself." She was cold and distant, like the words of the dialectic.

"I'd like that," he said, unable to hide his sadness.

"Shall I drop you and wait, or come back for you?"

"Just drop me. I'll take a train."

She nodded. They turned into Georg's street. There were new apartments here, tall, cream-colored stucco buildings decorated with glazed tile, where the bombed-out buildings of his childhood used to stand. They had been up only five years, but much of the tile had fallen away. The pieces that were left looked like blue-and-red teeth scattered here and there in an old man's mouth. All the buildings were monotonously identical.

As they neared his building, he sought words to heal the wound that had unexpectedly erupted as from a latent disease which had hitherto lain dormant under the skin of their short relationship. But again it was she who took the initiative. When she pulled the car to the curb and stopped, she turned to him and said, "We have a maid, a kind of housekeeper, but she finishes work at six."

His first impulse was to ride her about the inconsistency of exploiting a worker for one's personal benefit in a Socialist society. But then he recognized the concession she had made not only to her pride but to her political intransigence.

He nodded. "What time should I be there?"

"Eight?"

He nodded. "All right."

"I promise not to talk about politics."

"It can't be helped, I suppose."

She shook her head. "It's been so nice. I don't like it this way. It was my fault."

Objectively, Georg had to agree, but he was eager to please her. "I guess my political consciousness could use some development."

She gave him a quizzical look and started to say something, but bit her lip. He had the idea it would have been an admonishment, but about what, he did not know.

He opened the door and got out. "Eight on the dot," he promised. As he stood watching her drive away, he wondered if the wound could be healed so easily. He doubted it. All they had done was hide it under the bandage of mutual desire.

If Greta's earlier reservations about his political respectability had affected her feeling for him, she was adept at concealing it that evening. Only once, after they had eaten and she was showing him around the roomy but sparely furnished house, did she mention politics. It was when he commented on a photograph of her father she kept in her bedroom.

"He's a good-looking man. Impressive."

"Papa's really very nice. You'll like him—despite politics. You know, he doesn't agree with everything that's done. He argues with the others all the time."

"Oh, yes, of course, such as how many ounces of butter shall we let the people have this week?"

She had to smile. "You're a scandal."

"Do they really argue?" he asked seriously.

"Of course they do. They don't all lie down like dogs at Uncle Walter's feet."

Georg was dazzled. "Uncle Walter, is it?"

She laughed and snubbed her nose at him, and he took her in his arms and kissed her. Perhaps she was not so fanatical as he had thought; perhaps it was only her disappointment in his lack of Socialist zeal and the bad impression it would have on her father that had made her so aggressive. Whatever the reason, the joy of their first days returned, and when he took her to his heart, he felt his love for her returned with a fervor unmatched by any he had imagined in his unfulfilled dreams.

On Sunday morning he awakened with a smile at the picture of Greta's beautiful face in mind. In a torpor of memory he lay stretched out on his bed, reliving the gaiety and excitement she had brought to his life during the past week. Rousing himself from sweet reveries, he remembered that they were going on a picnic together in the Eichwalde on the outskirts of the city. He had promised to take her fishing. Charged with the energy of anticipation, he leaped out of bed and went into the bathroom.

"Good morning," his mother sang out from the kitchen. The fragrances of breakfast filled his head. He smiled and called back a greeting. As he washed and shaved, he heard his mother rousting his father out of bed, using a mixture of threats and promises, a recipe perfected over the years and guaranteed to produce results.

Georg felt full of love—for his parents, his home, his Greta, himself. He looked at his image in the mirror, washing away some tufts of lather left after shaving, and said it aloud. "I love you, Georg Somebody Knauer. Yes, I do." Then, to himself: I love you, too, Greta Dohr. He believed it. But did she love him? Doubting it, he frowned and felt suddenly like a nobody again.

His mother's campaign was in the final stages. "Papa, the rolls are on the table! Georg, come right away! Papa, I'm pouring the coffee! *Ach,* such a smell, it makes me faint!"

Georg combed his hair and, after one last self-appraisal in the mirror, adjusted his robe and went into the kitchen. His mother kissed his cheek and poured his coffee. "Papa! The coffee is poured."

"Coming, coming. Turn on the radio." Georg reached behind him and turned it on. When his father asked for the radio to be turned on, the battle was over. He was getting up.

"It will be a beautiful day," his mother said. "Not too hot."

"I'm going on a picnic with Greta."

"You're seeing a lot of that girl," she said with a note of disapproval.

His father came in yawning and wiping the sleep from his eyes.

Not even on Sunday can a man sleep—Georg predicted him.

"Not even on Sunday can a man sleep," his father grumbled, pulling out a chair.

Georg laughed.

"Did I miss a joke?" his father asked sullenly.

The radio blurted out static. Georg turned it to RIAS. ". . . have been called into urgent session. It is reliably reported that whatever action they take will. . . ."

"What did you say her last name is?" his mother asked. She was pouring coffee for his father.

"Dohr, Mama. Greta Dohr."

His father turned the radio up. "Meanwhile, in East Berlin, the sealing of the border continued. Friedrichstrasse . . ."

"God in Heaven!"

"They've done it!"

"They've sealed the border!"

". . . the barbed wire. Thousands of East Berliners have assembled around the Brandenburg Gate, and the Pankow regime has brought up reinforcements. West Berliners on this side of the gate have. . . ."

Georg jumped up and raced into the bedroom.

"Where are you going?" his mother called.

He did not answer. He had to see it with his own eyes to believe it. He began to dress. His father came into the room.

"You didn't answer your mother, Georg."

"I'm going to see for myself."

"Do you doubt that they've done it?"

Georg shook his head. "No, I don't doubt it, but I want to see for myself."

Outside, the street was empty. It surprised him. He had expected people to be out. As he was hurrying down the street, a car came around the corner, and he recognized Greta at the wheel. He stepped to the curb and hailed her. When she stopped, he leaned in through the window. "You've heard?"

She nodded. Her face was drawn and pale. She looked

frightened. He got in beside her. "I was headed for the Brandenburg Gate. Do you want to come along?"

She looked at him as if she had not heard what he had said. "They've arrested Papa."

He was dumbfounded. "Arrested him! But why?"

"A friend of his, a man in the SSD, came and told me this morning. He said . . . he said . . . I should get out . . . defect to the West." She was having trouble holding herself together. "I don't know what to do, Georg. *I don't know what to do.*" He looked at her, unable to assimilate what she was telling him. Things were happening so fast he was overwhelmed. He rubbed his face and tried to think.

"Are you sure?" he asked her.

"Yes, yes. This man wouldn't lie to me. He's a good friend."

"You can't help your father. You realize that, don't you?"

She nodded. "He told me it could happen. He warned me. But it's impossible to believe. It's . . . impossible."

"If only . . . if only it were yesterday."

"Will you help me?"

"Get across the border?"

She looked at him strangely. "Are you afraid?"

"Afraid?" He thought about it. "I don't know." He suddenly became furious. The bastards! In one stroke, they had ruined everything—taken his job, arrested Greta's father, and put him on the spot.

She started crying, sobbing into her hands. He breathed deeply and closed his eyes, trying to think. He had never been asked to think for himself about so grave a matter. He listened to her sobbing, and the love he had for her displaced the anger. He put his arms around her and held her. He held her for a long time, until she was cried out. He held her face up to his and said, "We'll both go. We'll go now. The longer we wait, the harder it will be." She stared at him without responding. Her eyes were red and swollen from the crying. He kissed them and dredged up a smile. "Of course I'll help you."

They drove to the Brandenburg Gate. Huge crowds had assembled on both sides of the border. Most of the people were young men and boys. Greta parked the car two blocks away, just off Unter den Linden, and they hurried together down the boulevard under the shade of the young lime trees. At the gate, tanks were drawn up, their guns pointed menacingly toward the West. A half dozen armored cars stood in seeming disarray around the columns of the great memorial. Hundreds of militiamen, some with submachine guns at the ready, others with rifles fixed with bayonets, formed a human wall across the pavement in front of the giant columns. As Georg and Greta entered the crowd, they saw that many of the East Berliners were arguing with the guards and shouting at them.

"Let us go through!"

"Lay down your guns!"

"Would you shoot your own countrymen?"

"Go shoot old Goatbeard!"

Their faces were distorted with their anger and the humiliation of their impotence. The guards were frightened and nervous but stood their ground. On the other side, a mass of West Berliners milled about, shouting curses at the guards and tussling with their own police, who were holding them back. An occasional rock came hurtling through the air, landing with a spray of splinters against one of the great columns of the gate.

"We'll never get through here," Georg said. But they remained in the crowd, overcome by the drama. Up in front, a scuffle broke out, and the crowd surged back, driven by militia bayonets. Georg caught Greta around the waist and worked his way out of the crowd. They trudged back to the car in solemn silence. Georg glanced back over his shoulder at the huge six-columned monument, at the triumphant quadriga high at the top, and, in the distance, the golden Goddess of Victory shimmering in the sun, beckoning from the heart of West Berlin. The contrast between these magnificent monuments and the mobs at the border, between man's ingenious achievement and his insanities, saddened Georg in a way he had never felt sadness before. Oddly, he thought of his father. He wanted to talk to him then, to ask him how it was possible for men to span the spectrum from glory to depravity. But he and his father had never spoken of such things, and he doubted, even if he were to have the opportunity, that they could begin now. It was too late, too late for Georg.

face in the sideview mirror, pale and frightened—Georg
Nobody Knauer again. He knew that if he did not rise,
did not act, he would be Georg Nobody Knauer the rest
of his life. Did he want to *live*, to be *alive* as he had been
for the past week, or did he want to go on in the half
death he had been living before he met her? Now, *now*
was the moment to decide.

He threw open the door, scrambled out, raced around
to the driver's side, and jerked open the door.

"Move over!"

She stared at him, the helplessness transformed to
fear of her own.

"Move!" He got in, pushing her with his body. "Get
down on the floor!"

She stared, not moving.

"Do as I say!"

She was suddenly terrified of him. She did as he commanded, crouching down in the narrow space in front of
the seat.

"Stay there! No matter what happens, stay there!"

He started the car, shifted into gear, and, jamming the
accelerator to the floor, roared off. The buildings passed
in a blur. At the corner he did not slow as he turned. The
car rose up on his side, taking the corner on two wheels,
screeching, and came down with a loud *wham* as the
springs collapsed under the impact. Greta screamed. She
raised her face to him. Terror trembled on her lips. The
car swayed from side to side, then gradually regained its
balance. On the periphery of his vision he was vaguely
conscious of the color of flowers, buildings flowing by,
people stopping to stare. Greta raised her body.

"Stay down!"

Ahead, the bridge over the canal rushed toward him.
A gray form lounged against the concrete railing near the
center of the span. Another strolled in a leisurely way
across the pavement to his side. Beyond them, the wire lay
coiled like a great spring from one side of the roadway
to the other. As they came closer and closer, the engine
roaring in his ears, Georg could see the sun on the Vopos'
weapons slung crisscross on their backs, now the sun on
their glossy boots, now on the barbs of the steel wire.
They heard the car and turned slowly, curiously. For an
instant they stood staring, immobilized. Then, quickly,

they had their hands over their shoulders, going for their guns. The car reached the incline of the bridge. The last thing Georg saw as he ducked his head down below the dashboard was the glint of the sun off the pointed, star-shaped barbs of the wire.

The sound of the guns and the sputter of the bullets came a split second before the cannon burst of the tire blowing. Greta's scream rose with him, rose with the car. He was floating, floating outward and down, a bird soaring indolently, effortlessly with the high wind. The earth met him with a clangorous, deafening crash. His body tumbled back up into the air and came slamming down with immediate, searing pain. Silence.

"Gee-orrg!!"

He opened his eyes; bumpy, pebbled concrete. Shouting.

He lifted his head. The car lay on its side, a gaping hole in its side. The door lay in the street, gleaming black, a street lamp reflected in its surface.

"Gee-orrg!!!"

He got up on his knees. Wire insinuated itself around a slowly turning wheel. Two men were running toward the car, two men carrying guns.

"Gee-orrg!"

His feet found the pavement. He was up and running, running, stumbling, falling.

Shouting from behind. The rattle, the loud, deathly rattle, the whine of death in the air.

"Gee-orrg . . ."

So far back, so far, far away. Hands and arms helping him. Grim faces. Hands lifting him off the ground, racing farther and farther away, away from the rattle of death.

"Gee-orrg . . ."

7

〰〰〰〰〰〰〰〰〰〰〰〰〰〰〰〰〰〰〰〰〰〰〰〰

SEPP answered Emerich's first knock. He stuck his head out into the dimly lighted hallway, blinking, rubbing the sleep from his eyes. "It's you, Emerich."

"I wanted to know if you had made it."

He opened the door into the dark room. Sepp found a lamp and turned it on. A pair of wet trousers was hanging on the bathroom door. His raincoat clung to a wire hanger suspended from the ceiling light fixture, dripping onto a layer of old newspapers spread out on the floor. Standing in his shorts in the midst of the clutter, yawning, Sepp looked like a child awakened from his nap.

There was much innocence about Sepp. On balance, his face reflected more of the ingenuous than the cynical. He had large brown eyes set deep behind long, thick lashes and under thick black eyebrows growing like lush hedges at the base of the steep slope of his forehead. There was an imperturbable serenity about his eyes, as if they assumed that much of what they looked out on shared their comfortable security.

His hair, a dark, earth-colored brown, was in need of cutting and curled around his ears and the nape of his neck. His nose was narrow, with barely flared nostrils, and was made to seem even narrower by the wide, full mouth under it. His lips were thin and curved delicately into the classically elongated heart shape that suggests an incipient smile.

Emerich thought Sepp's smile was as kind as he had

ever known. He had been attracted to the genuine expression of friendliness it offered, committed to the belief that anyone who could smile like that had to be honest. Honest, he reminded himself, but not necessarily clever or bright.

Emerich looked into Sepp's sleepy eyes, eyes that were serene even when aroused from sleep. He and the American were the same height, but Sepp was broader, more heavily muscled. He had the well-fed, city look that suggests dexterity and agility developed from sports, not the crude strength of a body grown lean and tough from hard work. That Sepp was stronger than he, Emerich had no doubt. He outweighed him by thirty or forty pounds. Nor did Emerich doubt that, proportionately, pound for pound, he could outmatch him.

Sepp returned his gaze with another yawn. Emerich felt awkward.

"Everything went just as I planned it. No trouble at all."

"Good, good. What time did you get back?"

"About eleven o'clock. It went very well." Sepp yawned loudly and gave Emerich an expectant look. "Did you just get off work?"

Emerich nodded. He knew he should leave and let Sepp reclaim his sleep. He was not sure why he had come in the first place. He allowed the possibility that subconsciously he was jealous of Sepp's daring and that by coming here tonight he would somehow be sharing his danger. If this was the case, he had not succeeded. Instead, he felt more detached from it than before, when he had vicariously carried out the exploit in the safety of his imagination. Perhaps his disappointment was caused by Sepp's casualness. He acted as if what he had accomplished was of no particular consequence, nothing more than a successfully completed business transaction, one of many past and many more to come. There was no exhibition of triumph, not even a genuine satisfaction that Emerich could share. He felt cheated and, clumsily, he realized, was persisting in trying to extract from Sepp some emotional reaction which would serve to renew the sense of identification of purpose he had felt earlier in the day.

"So we start tomorrow."

"Yes."

"Well, I just wanted to know. I wouldn't have slept, not knowing whether you had made it or not."

"It was good of you."

"I shouldn't have awakened you."

"I'll go right back to sleep."

"I'd better get some sleep myself."

"Good night, Emerich."

"Good night, Sepp. See you in the morning."

As Emerich was closing the door behind him, Sepp caught hold of it. "I gave your note to Ilse. She'll be working on it first thing in the morning."

Emerich recognized it as a condescending token and accepted it as justly deserved. He nodded and left, reduced to ridiculousness.

He did not want to go straight home. He would lie awake, cursing his stupidity. He decided to walk, hoping that by the time he arrived home he would be able to induce sleep quickly. He walked north, taking the side streets, avoiding Potsdamerstrasse. He crossed the canal at Hafen Platz, where The Wall juts out like the broken-off blade of a knife, and went around the tip to Linkstrasse.

Along the west side of the street a row of apartment houses stood at the edge of an expanse of vacant land. Because it was so close to Potsdamer Platz, he supposed that before the war this must have been a fashionable area of Berlin, filled with elegant shops, government buildings, and fine apartments. Now it was bleak and desolate, left to the wind talking to itself behind the shutters of the crumbling buildings which, like forward sentries sent out long ago to guard the border, had been abandoned and presumed dead.

The Wall marked the border along the opposite side of the street. Here it was three meters high, constructed of three thicknesses of building brick with a capstone of concrete into which pieces of jagged glass had been fixed. Its course to the Potsdamer Platz was interrupted only by an occasional building whose windows had been bricked in. At one point, a set of wooden steps with a platform, weathered gray and splintered, had been erected to permit tourists a glimpse over The Wall into East Berlin. Although Emerich could not see them, he could sense

the presence of the charred skeletons of the Haus Vater-
land and the Luftwaffe headquartters just beyond The
Wall, grotesque reminders of German disgrace and human stupidity.

He passed the turn in The Wall into what once was
Berlin's most famous intersection, Potsdamer Platz. The
stand where postcards and soda pop were sold to tourists
was boarded up for the night. A lone police car stood at
the curb. Two policemen sat in the front seat, smoking.
Here, there was a larger observation platform. He
climbed up and looked out over The Wall into the
Sektor.

Instead of glass, barbed wire strung on steel Y frames
had been cemented into the top of The Wall. The frames
were rusted and bent in places, and the wire sagged
from the thousands of arms that had leaned on it during
the past year. In the distance the lights of East Berlin
huddled diffidently under the overcast. The Death Zone,
the quarter-mile area cleared between The Wall and the
first building of the *Sektor,* was illuminated here by floodlights from the eastern side. Rows of steel tank obstacles
were set out like giant jacks, as if to tempt a race of
giant children to play in the strip. A wooden tower,
where the Vopos kept the West under constant surveil-
lance through binoculars, loomed up into the night sky
like a giant recreation director. In the darkness the Vopos
were not visible, but Emerich knew they were there.

He leaned on the wire, taking care to avoid the barbs.
"Papa. We're coming for you, Papa," he whispered.
"We're coming to get you out, Papa."

He stopped to listen, but the only sound was the dull,
muted hum of the city around him. He turned his eyes
on the dark outline of the tower and considered the men
who occupied it, their purpose, their resolve. His hatred,
born ten years before in the little church of his village,
nurtured by the years of growing awareness of the evil
intent the Communists had for his village, his family,
himself, and perfected not long ago—was it almost a year
now?—when they had consummated their intent, swelled
the joints of his emotions like a recurrence of excruciatingly painful arthritis.

For him it had started that first day of plowing when
he was ten years old. There was excitement in the air.

The peasants in Überdreibrücken were up earlier than usual. Emerich was awakened in the dark by the sound of his father honing the plowshare for the hundredth time that week. The high-pitched scrape of whetstone on tempered steel came like Oriental music on the frosty air of the morning. He bounded out of bed, unperturbed by the cold of the earthen floor, and dressed by starlight, breathing deeply the smell of the virgin spring—the manure pile in the yard, warmed by yesterday's sun, steaming in the darkness; the spicy fragrance of arbutus blooming along the wall under his window; the ever-present, pervasive odor of the oxen, pigs, chickens, cats, their milk cow, Püppchen, the elusive rats in the barn —now more pungent with the growing warmth of the days.

In the kitchen, his mother was lighting the stove. "God's greeting," he said.

"God's greeting." She was dark, like his father, and unsmiling. Her long black hair was twisted into a big knot at the back of her head, held there by a curved comb made of hickory. Emerich's brother Ulrich had carved it for her last Christmas, and she had worn it every day since. "Fetch some milk," she said, handing him the pail. Her hands were thick and hard, like old leather. Dirt lay impacted under the long, thick nails, but Emerich did not think that unusual. They had always been that way.

"That's Ulrich's job," he complained.

"Ulrich is with the minister."

Too excited to grumble, he took the pail and went into the barn. The barn was but a larger room in the same building as the house. All the animals were kept there in the winter, and it was there that the plow, the tools, the horses, and the wagon were stored. His father, sharpening the plow, did not look up when he entered.

"God's greeting, Papa."

"God's greeting. Go about your work."

Emerich wanted to watch his father, to idle about, talking out the excitement within him, but he knew better than to disobey. He took the milking stool down from the nail on the stall post and set about milking the cow.

"Why is Ulrich with the minister?" he asked.

"The Lukens boy is sick."

"Albert?"

"He is the Lukens boy, is he not?" His father ran his
fingers along the shiny edge of the blade. The cow lowed
and moved. Emerich changed teats and continued to milk,
absently directing the streams of milk into the pail.

"How much will we plow today, Papa?"

"As much as God gives us light to plow."

"I'll bet we plow more than the Lukenses do."

"Our land is closer to the village; our oxen are younger
and stronger. There is no special grace on us if we do."

"I'll bet we do, though." He thought of the plowing,
walking beside the oxen, leading them by the headstall.
He remembered it from last year, remembered how he
had ached to guide the plow, to feel the share cutting into
the rich soil, turning it upon itself, uncovering the rotted
treasures of two hundred generations of Webers who had
plowed this land. Occasionally his father would stop, scoop
up a handful of soil, fondle it, squeeze it gently, sniff it.
It was a mystical rite, as sacred as the Eucharist. It was as
if in this act, too, God's blessing were bestowed on the
land and its keepers.

The Weber family had worked the same soil under
Charlemagne, Magyars, the Augustin kings, Frederick the
Great, Kaiser Wilhelm, and Hitler. They had pledged al-
legiance to lords, dukes, kings, and dictators. They had
known the cruelties of empty granaries and hungry bellies,
the tax collector's avarice, the gamekeeper's whip. They
had known, too, the destructive power of the archer, the
rifleman, the artilleryman, the bombardier. A hundred
armies had trampled their grain in the course of a thousand years. They had fought in their lords', dukes', and
kings' legions, died in their battles, and had their names
duly inscribed in the records of Europe's long and bloody
history. Ten thousand schemes had been devised to rob
them of their crops, their homes, their lands, their sons
and daughters. They had endured plague and locusts; ty-
phoid and wheat rust; smallpox and weevil; influenza and
lice, rats, mice, and fleas. Intimidated, insulted, spat upon,
kicked, beaten, raped, plundered, mutilated, and murdered
—through it all, they had always held their land.

Land. The soil. The sacred, coveted earth. It could not
be wrested from them. Nothing had succeeded—no
scheme, no army, no insect, no drought or flood or frost,

neither inflation nor depression, no duke, no king, no invention of God or man.

From father to son, from mother to daughter, the holy law of the land had been passed down as a priceless heirloom: "Never give up the land!" And for a thousand years the Webers had held the land—almost fifty hectares of it.

The land was more than the physical security it afforded, more than the tradition of ownership it bore. There was a mystique about it, an irrational compulsion to hold it at all costs, as if the land had been entrusted to the Weber family in perpetuity by Wotan and later confirmed by Jupiter and Christ, and losing it would bring on a cataclysm.

At ten, Emerich already understood the inheritance. He loved the land as naturally and completely as he loved his mother and father, his brothers, and Püppchen, the cow. He yearned to consummate his love behind the plow. "I'm pretty strong now, Papa."

"You're as strong as ought."

"Strong enough to plow, I think."

His father paused and looked at him, his dark eyes shielded under the brim of his black hat, immune to emotion. "It may be so."

He had not said no! Emerich's hands worked faster, hurrying to empty the cow's udder, as if his getting the milk to his mother would speed the dawn. Just as he was finishing, the church bells began to peal.

In the kitchen Ernestine, his older brother Dietrich's wife, was up nursing the baby by the stove. Dietrich was with the Army near Leipzig and got home on leave only twice a year. His mother took the milk and set it up by the window. "God's greeting, Ernestine."

She nodded sleepily. "God's greeting, Emerich." The baby's sucking sounded like a motor missing. Emerich stared, fascinated. The room was filled with the smells of cooking. There would be a special breakfast today—fried eggs and fresh trout. Later, they would drop the trout bones into freshly turned furrows for luck. Emerich did not know why trout bones were supposed to bring luck. It had always been that way.

When the baby had had its fill, the family joined the rest of the village going to church. Even Emerich's old grandfather, his father's father, went to church on the first day of plowing. He was eighty-two and had no teeth. Emerich could never understand what he said. The old man kept to his room in the back of the house, reading the big family Bible, mumbling prayers, slowly dying. Each year he was expected to die, and each year he persisted and, like the perennial arbutus, showed his mettle at the first sign of spring. He smelled of schnapps and manure.

From all the houses of the village came the people. No one would miss church that morning, not if he expected a good year. There were no atheists in Überdreibrücken, and there were no Communists. Everyone was Lutheran. Their ancestors had all been Lutherans since the Reformation. Once, in 1783, a Calvinist from Bohemia had purchased the Müller farm, but the villagers of Überdreibrücken had made life miserable for him, and he had sold out to a Saxon Lutheran the same year. The villagers spoke of "the Calvinist" as if he had lived only yesterday.

Even the sick would be in church, carried in the beds of rickety wagons, in the arms of the strong. They followed the winding village street, exchanging greetings muted by the solemnity of the occasion, by the darkness, and by the age-old foreboding every peasant felt at the beginning of a new season. Harvest was a time for celebration, plowing, a time for prayer.

The little church was crowded. The Weber family filed into its pew near the front. Emerich's great-great-great-grandfather, Richard Ulrich Weber, had contributed the money when the church was built in 1729, and the Webers had occupied that pew ever since. Around the alter, candles flickered in the wind that came down the aisle from the open door. There were candles burning under the Stations of the Cross, seven along each wall, illuminating the somber, faded colors of the frescoed figures. This Christ was no frail mystic of the Middle East, no shimmering, plastic-muscled perfection of man of the Italian Baroque; rather, he was a squat, thick-chested, broad-shouldered, dark-haired peasant. His agony the peasant of Überdreibrücken, eighteenth or twentieth century, could understand: an inward agony, stoically accepted, an agony which was known to be inevitable and which must be endured, an agony that slowly gnawed away the fiber of the spirit without ever totally devouring it, but which, over the life span of a man, kept just ahead of all his efforts to repair the damage it wreaked until, ultimately, in death it savored its final victory. Christ on the walls of their church confirmed the validity and the necessity of the peasants' suffering, real and imaginary, and gave them the strength to persevere.

As soon as the Webers were installed in their pew, Emerich knew that something was wrong. His father did not bow his head in prayer, as was his invariable habit. His mother's face went pale, and her lips formed an inaudible prayer. Throughout the church, people were whispering, leaning over the pews, speaking to one another behind their hands. Emerich looked to his father for the answer, but he was staring ahead, not speaking, his jaw set so tightly that the muscles quivered under his freshly shaved skin. Emerich would not have dared to ask. He had always been forbidden to speak in church. He looked to his sister-in-law, but she seemed unaware of anything different, absorbed in her baby, who slept peacefully in her arms. Emerich's mother handed him a hymnal. He opened it to the hymn number posted and waited for the first chord of the organ. The whispering continued, rising to a sibilant crescendo behind him.

Emerich gazed at the simple altar, at the dark stained-glass windows through which during Sunday worship the sun poured, casting rods of red, amber, and blue light into the corners of the choir. Now, in the darkness of early morning, lighted only by the altar candles, the choir lay in shadow, a corner here, a projecting piece of woodwork there occasionally and momentarily illuminated by the flame of the candles bent by the shifting wind.

From the door to the vestry on the right, Emerich's brother Ulrich entered, carrying the Holy Bible in his outstretched hands. He carried it reverently, holding it as far from his body as his short arms could get it, his head tilted back. Albert Lukens's white surplice was too long for him, and it flapped around the tops of his boots and down over his hands. He had to stand on tiptoe to get the big book up onto the pulpit. Emerich wanted to laugh, but laughing in church was unthinkable and would guarantee a licking from his father.

Ulrich's entrance silenced the whispering. In a moment

the organ sounded and the congregation rose to sing the opening hymn. Emerich loved to sing, even though he sang badly. He stood beside Ernestine, who remained seated with the baby, sharing the hymnal with her, singing at the top of his voice. When he sang in church, he felt the eyes of God on him and imagined Him to be cocking His ear toward that spot on earth where Emerich stood. Emerich sang loudly to be certain God heard him singing His praises.

As he sang, he looked up at the altar where, in a glass-enclosed cubicle, a relic of the leg bone of Saint John, the patron saint of the church and of the village, was enshrined. Emerich knew the story well, how in 1262 the villagers had contributed money to buy the relic for the old church which had stood on the same foundation as the present one. The church was Roman Catholic then, of course, and it was deemed essential to have at least one sacred relic, no matter how poor the parish was. When Saxony joined the Protestants in the early years of the Reformation, there was some agitation to have the relic removed, as it symbolized for many the old ways of Rome so recently cast off. But the villagers could not bring themselves to reject Saint John as readily as they had Rome, and the relic remained. In the fire of 1727 which destroyed the old church, only the relic, sealed in its glass case, miraculously survived, dug from the ashes totally intact. In solemn ceremony, it was cemented into the new altar of the new church two years later, where it had rested ever since.

As Emerich gazed over the one pew in front of him, past the head of August Steigler, the richest peasant in the village and president of the village council, he noticed the bald head of a man sitting in a chair in front of the Steigler pew. He did not recognize the man and wondered why he was sitting there and how he dared to remain seated during the singing of the opening hymn. Emerich saw that his father was also looking at the bald man and not singing. There was a strange expression on his face.

As the last note of the hymn took flight into the rafters in the high arches of the nave, the minister entered. In his black cassock with the purple stole of Lent draped carefully around his neck, his white, bony fingers clasped to his breast, his long, thin head with its crop of shiny black hair cast down in silent prayer, he looked as majestic and holy as Saint John himself. Emerich feared the minister and dreaded the day he would have to attend his classes to learn the catechism for confirmation.

"Let us pray. Almighty God, we are gathered here today in Thy presence to ask Thy blessing on us and our work. We beseech Thee in Christ's name to grant us Thy blessing as we once again turn our hands to the plow, as we reverently turn Thy bounteous earth to our use. . . ."

In the darkness of his closed-eyes world, Emerich's mind wandered from the minister's words to thoughts of plowing. The vision he had had countless times of himself behind the plow returned once again. So vivid was it that he could feel his muscles drawing taut as he put his strength into it, holding the share in a straight furrow; so strong that he could smell the oxen, see the steam curling up from the overturned earth. His dream ended with the intrusion of the recollection that something was wrong. His father's face appeared as it had been moments before, and Emerich realized it was fear he had seen there. He opened his eyes and looked around. His father's eyes were open, too, still staring at the back of the bald head, and Emerich knew then that whatever was wrong, that man was responsible.

Suddenly everyone was sitting down and the minister was entering the pulpit to read the Epistle. When the congregation was quiet, he began to speak in a firm, quiet voice, not reading the Epistle as he should, but delivering a sermon.

"Each year at this time we gather here in the Lord's house to ask His blessing on us and our work. It is an age-old custom, dating back into history beyond written recall. We in this little village in the valley of the Mulde have for ten centuries put our trust in Almighty God, and He has favored us with good land, enough food for ourselves, and some left over to sell to those who do not work the land. This is all we have asked, and He has seen fit to give it to us.

"We in this small village have ever been free men. Not even in the darkest of the Dark Ages, when a handful of the aristocracy ruled over the earth, when dukes and lords came and went as fleetingly as storms from the mountains, bent on deluging us with their evil power, were our ancestors serfs or vassals. The land has always been ours to plow, to sow, to reap as God meant for us to do. Saint John, our beloved patron, protector of free men, has watched over our lands and kept us free. We have indeed been blessed."

"That will be quite enough, Minister." The bald man was on his feet. The congregation gasped in unison, a Greek chorus in a drama they never dreamed would be presented on their rustic stage. The minister gazed at the man for a moment and then, as if he had been interrupted by the outcry of an unruly child, returned his eyes to the congregation and resumed his sermon, his voice now louder, stronger, echoing from the beams and rafters overhead.

"A new Dark Age threatens to descend upon us! A sinister evil has captured power, a power more menacing, more vicious, more destructive than the legions of the Devil himself!"

"I forbid it! Silence! I demand silence!" The bald man had not stirred from the stand he had taken in front of the pulpit. His pate gleamed in the candlelight. The muscles of his neck bulged like taut ropes when he spoke, and Emerich's heart was pounding out a beat of fear and wonderment. No one—ever—had interrupted the minister! Not even Herr Steigler, not even to ask a question.

The congregation broke into a flurry of whispering. Herr Weber leaned forward and whispered into the ear of Herr Steigler. Emerich's mother clutched a hymnal to her breast and lowered her head to pray. Ernestine gaped, frozen in astonishment, as if for the first time realizing something unusual was happening.

"They are going to take your land!" the minister shouted.

"I forbid you!"

"*God* forbids *you!*" The minister's wrath turned his face even whiter. The veins at his temples stood out like moraines at the edge of the great glacier of his forehead.

Little Ulrich raced past the altar and, skirting wide around the bald man, pushed through the transept gate and ran to his father's side. He stood there clutching his father's rough hand, his eyes wide with fear. The whispering of the congregation rose to a muted drone.

A shrill voice from the back rose over the sound. "Throw the Communist scum out!"

Others took up the cry:

"Throw him out!"

"Out with the swine!"

"Down with Goatbeard!"

"Feed him to the pigs!"

"Down with the collectives!"

Suddenly the bald man leaped up the steps to the altar and whirled about, his face twisted with rage, his eyes blazing defiance. "Silence!"

His voice boomed out over the heads of the peasants like a cannon shot. For a moment, everyone did as he commanded. The church became deathly still. It was the kind of silence his mother called "the voice of God." Emerich could hear his heart beating in his ears. He moved closer to his mother. She put a reassuring hand on his shoulder. The bald man's eyes swept the faces before him. For an instant they met Emerich's, and he felt as if the Devil himself had come to claim his soul. His body began to tremble in fear. God save me. God forgive me. God save me. God forgive me. God save me, forgive me, save me. . . .

"I have not come to take your land!" the bald man cried. He pointed an accusing finger. "The minister lies!"

Herr Steigler was suddenly on his feet, facing the congregation from his pew. "If this man had any claim on our attention up to now, he has just lost it! No man shall defile the house of God by insulting His minister on earth!"

"The truth is only in Christ!" the minister shouted. "And Christ is not in *you!*"

"Let the people judge the truth! If they are free and just men, they will know the truth when they hear it!" The bald man's appeal set up a murmuring among the peasants.

"Do not listen to him," the minister shouted. "Council President Steigler is right! This man's words will drip from his lips like honey, but it is poisoned honey. Do not taste of his words, or you shall be condemned just as Adam was condemned when he tasted of the apple."

Emerich did not understand what was happening. He knew there had been talk of the land being taken away by the Communists. But in school the teacher had said this was not so. On cold winter nights his father had sat talking with Herr Steigler and Herr Lukens about the Communists taking the land, and it had always been the same. If they came to take it, the villagers would fight. If they lost the fight, they would refuse to work the land under the collective organization. "They can't shoot us all," his father had always said.

"I have come only to wish you well with the plowing," the bald man said reassuringly. "The party is for the peasants, not against them. The party has given land to peasants who had none before, to those whose land was stolen by the capitalist Junkers and the Nazi bigwigs."

Herr Steigler moved out into the aisle and set himself there like a tree with roots meters deep. His silver hair glistened in the candlelight, and when he spoke, his big white teeth gleamed like polished ivory. "Those lands he speaks of! They were collectivized! The peasants were put to work on them like common laborers."

The minister's long white hand crashed down on the pulpit. "He means to form a collective here in our village!" One of his fingers jabbed the air in the bald man's direction. "He means to convert our beloved church to a *tractor station!*"

"With what tractors?" someone interjected.

Nervous, compulsive laughter tumbled from pew to pew, relieving the tension. "Yes! With what tractors?!" Whether with an ulterior motive or not, even the district secretary laughed. Herr Steigler took advantage of the pause to confer with the minister at the pulpit. When the laughter died away, Herr Steigler turned to the district secretary.

"If you will consent to answer one question, District Secretary, we will let you speak."

The man had not become district party secretary because he was stupid. "What is the question?" he asked warily.

"Will you answer it?"

The bald man looked perplexed for the first time. He sucked his upper lip thoughtfully and did not return the villagers' gaze as confidently as before. At last he gave a little shrug of one shoulder. "If I answer your question, you will permit me to speak?"

"You may speak then."

"Very well. What is your question?"

Herr Steigler turned to the villagers as he posed the question, as if he were asking it more of them than of the district secretary. There was a glint of his dark eyes, the hint of a smile on his lips as his deep voice boomed out the words. "Will you guarantee us, here and now, in writing, signed by your own hand, that the lands belonging to the people of the village of Überdreibrücken will not be collectivized, nationalized, seized, or in any way changed from their present legal status at any time for so long as your government is in power?"

A hush fell over the church. Not a sound could be heard. All eyes turned from the village leader to the district secretary. Herr Steigler's question could not have been more to the point. It expressed the thoughts and wishes of every man and woman there. Even Emerich understood the essence of the question. But he was confused on the point of the collective. He understood what a collective farm was—he had studied about the great collectives in the Soviet Union. There, all the land belonged to all the people, but only the peasants living on the collective worked the land. In school he had learned that the peasants were very happy with this arrangement. If the peasants of Überdreibrücken—his father, Herr Steigler, Herr Lukens, and the other heads of families—would not be happy, why did this man want them to have a collective? And why did this man and the others who lived in the cities want the peasants' land if they were not going to work it? Emerich knew that even if they owned it they would not profit from it, because to profit from another man's labor was a crime against socialism. He made it a point to remember to ask his father these questions later.

"Well?" Herr Steigler cried, turning on the bald man.

"You know I cannot give you such a guarantee. My authority is limited. Besides, such an action would reflect a kulak attitude"—and here he paused, eyeing the villagers with renewed confidence, with the power of the state, its threats of deprivation and force of arms, its ability to give and withhold privileges and torture, standing behind the man like a ventriloquist manipulating his gestures and words—"which I am confident none of *you* wants to be found guilty of."

Whether or not fully aware of the implications of the district secretary's answer, Herr Steigler pressed his temporary advantage to a final conclusion. "Your answer is no, then."

"I can give no other answer."

Herr Steigler turned back to the congregation, an expression of deep sadness sunk into the lines of his leathery peasant face. He passed through the gate and, taking his hat from the pew bench, motioned his wife and three sons out.

"Council President," the bald man called out, "you gave me your word that if I answered your question, I could speak."

Herr Steigler looked back absently. "Go ahead. Speak. Talk your head off, District Secretary." He spat out the title as he would a bite of rotten apple. "You may talk until your lips peel and your tongue turns black. We do not have to listen!" And with that he took his wife's arm and strode up the aisle. The villagers broke into cheers and applause. Men rushed to the aisle to shake their leader's hand, to clap him on the back. And to a man they followed him out of the church, the minister included, leaving the district secretary standing alone in his fury in front of the altar containing a relic of the leg bone of Saint John, the patron saint of free men.

The victory, as they were to learn later, was pyrrhic. The villagers cheered their leader's mastery of peasant guile, not the substance of the issue. For indeed the issue had been lost. The land in Überdreibrücken was not to be collectivized for another decade, but collectivized it was. Herr Steigler's resistance had only delayed the inevitable.

Later, when the first dull light of the sun raised the mountains in the south and set the cicadas droning, Emerich stood behind the plow, grasping with his too-small hands the wooden plow handles turned to gloss with use. As the oxen began to pull and the razor-sharp edge of the share cut into the black soil, it uncovered a chorus singing a hymn of indescribable beauty. The earth sang to him and him alone, and all thoughts of the battle in Saint John's church were forgotten.

The best in paperbacks *and* hardcovers.

Collectivization had a slow beginning. Villages where the peasants worked someone else's land welcomed it; others, where resistance was disorganized, succumbed. Gradually, it spread, like the first signs of the coming of the locust, the news received with relief that it had struck someone else's land. Then, like the locust, its swarm grown too enormous, too fearful to resist, it swept the country, laying waste the last vestiges of private property.

Überdreibrücken in the valley of the Mulde was one of the last to go, but it went, its destiny decided long before. The battle led by the minister and Herr Steigler ten years before had been but a skirmish. When the real battle came, they had been gone for years, imprisoned martyrs of a cause most of the villagers had forgotten. It was only when the cause was resurrected, when the threat of imminent disaster once again hovered on the perimeter of their lands, that the two men were remembered; and when the memory of their defiance might at least have instilled a sense of honor in their followers, it was the memory of their fate that the village of Überdreibrücken recalled most clearly, and its inhabitants surrendered without a fight.

The day after it happened, Emerich's father called him out to the barn. It was a cold, rainy day in October 1961. The rain dribbling forlornly down the small windowpanes gave testimony to the pervasive melancholy that had settled in the village and in Emerich's father's house. His father's face reflected the defeat that had ravaged his spirit. As if drawn to the sad sound of the rain, the drabness of the gray sky, the countryside lying fallow below, he stood at the window looking out, his calloused hands clasped loosely behind him, the fingers too hardened to intertwine comfortably.

"It has come," he said.

Emerich nodded, not knowing what to say. There were no words of comfort or defiance left that did not sound hollow or ridiculously inane.

"Two hundred generations . . . and it falls on me to—"

"What could you do, Papa?"

"Fight," he answered distractedly.

It was true. In the past the Webers had fought—and

won. No one had ever taken the land. No one. It was too
enormous a calamity to accept.

"I have decided," his father began, "you will leave here.
You will go to the West. You will become educated, learn
the new methods of farming. You will make a new beginning. The Webers will again have their own land."

Emerich did not know whether or not his father understood the risks. In East Germany there was a great abyss
between the desire and its fulfillment. And Emerich was
ambivalent about the desire. The prospect of toiling in the
fields as an employee of the Communist government did
not appeal to him in the least, no more than it did to his
father or his two brothers, but his family was all he knew,
all he cared about. Überdreibrücken had been the center
of his universe for all of his twenty years.

If anything tipped the scales in favor of flight, it was
the opportunity to study. He had always had a yearning
to go on to the university, but no Weber—not one in a
thousand years—had ever done it. Even when his teachers
in school encouraged him—for it was easy for a peasant
to gain admittance to the university—he dared not broach
the subject to his father. Hands were needed on the land.
He had been sired to work the land, not to fritter away
his time with books. And so he had forgotten about it. In
the two years since he had graduated from high school,
he had worked the farm with his father and brothers and
had been content. Interest in the university dwindled away
like a fascination for a childish game; he would from time
to time wonder how it had ever appealed to him. However, draped now in the irony of despair and unveiled
before a maturer eye, the prospect of an education looked
more enticing, especially an education free of Communist
dogma and bound to a definite purpose. Whether he
wanted to go or not did not matter.

"You will leave tonight," his father said, his tone per-
mitting no argument.

"But how do I go, Papa? Where?"

"Berlin. That is still the best door to the West."

"There is The Wall. . . ."

"You will find a way. My sister—your aunt—Magda
Weber Halzapfel, lives in Berlin. You remember her. She
will help you."

He had not remembered her. He remembered her now, though, with both fondness and pity.

As his father ordered, he left that night, saying good-bye only to his family. It was hard to accept the fact that he dared not say farewell to his life-long friends in the village for fear that someone might inform on him.

He ate his last supper with the family crowded around the big table in the kitchen where he had eaten every supper of his life. His father, aged beyond his years, his hair more gray than black, the weathered lines on his neck turned to the telltale cross-hatching of old age, his thick, bony shoulders stooped from too much work and worry, sat at one end of the table. At the other, his mother, no different, Emerich thought, from that morning ten years before when he had first been allowed to set his hand to the plow. If she was sad to see her second son leaving, she did not show it. But then, she rarely showed any sign of emotion; in this respect, she and her husband were well matched.

Arrayed along one side of the table were Dietrich and his family: his wife, Ernestine, and their children—the oldest, Roslyn, named for her grandmother, the second, Konstanz, named for his grandfather, the third, Emerich, named for his uncle. Beside Emerich sat his younger brother, Ulrich, and the baby, Dietrich, whom Emerich's mother fed from her own plate, chewing the food herself first, just as she had fed her own children, just as she had been fed.

Only old Grandfather Weber was not at the table. Too stubborn and independent to eat at appointed times—which didn't matter much, because he rarely ate—he passed the time in his room at the back of the house, unaware of what was happening in the world around him, lost in blissful memories of his youth and the occasional solace of passages from the Bible that Ernestine read to him, or which he recited aloud to himself or to whoever would listen.

Even though Emerich had been indoctrinated all his life with the hallowed tradition of the land, its full weight had never made itself felt as it did this night. The burden had suddenly been shifted to him, and in the long march of the Weber family down through the gener-ations, he saw himself at the front of the line with no one

ahead of him to pass it on to. It rested with him. The
realization reduced him to solemn silence.

Nor did the others have much to say. After grace,
adding a footnote asking God's blessing on Emerich's
mission, his father offered only occasional laconic pieces
of advice.

"Do not travel the main road." This because Emerich
had no travel permit and would not have been able to get
one if he had applied. Only exceedingly well-documented
reasons for travel were being accepted by the authorities.

"Take your Aunt Magda a present. She puts store in
pretty things.

"When you are across, send us a letter. Don't write
anything—the West Berlin postmark will tell us that you
are safe." This, Emerich thought, was extending the
bounds of caution too far, but he would abide by his
father's command to prevent him any unnecessary anxiety.

"Think before you act. You have a good brain. Use
it."

With these injunctions in mind, Emerich left Überdreibrücken. As he felt his father's hands clasp his between them in an unusual gesture of love, Emerich made
his vow. "I'll get you out, Papa. I will get you all to the
West. I don't know how, but I promise you, I will."

Berlin lay two hundred and fifty kilometers away. He
made it in six days, traveling only at night, not once
stopping in a town, eating food he carried in his briefcase, drinking water from streams while the mountains
were still in view, then from springs when he could find
them. He arrived in the capital with an empty briefcase
and fifty East German marks, not one less than he had
when he left home.

Contrary to what his father had assured him, Aunt
Magda was less than prepared to help him, despite the
gift of a bracelet which had cost him a fifth of his stake.
Crowded into one room on the fifth floor of a decrepit
building in a back street of the borough of Prenzlauerberg,
she had neither the space nor the inclination to put him
up. Her meager pension, she complained, was barely
enough to put food in her mouth and a roof over her
head. She set her short, flaccid body astride a wooden

box in the center of the room, her legs spread, a dirty, tattered dress drooping down between them, her hose rolled down around her ankles. She had cut holes in her dilapidated shoes to permit her corn-afflicted toes to stick out.

"And why should I stick my neck out for one of Konstanz's brats? He's never had a word, kind or otherwise, for me these thirty years. Pah!" She spit the invective through her toothless gums—her dentures lay magnified to the size of horse's teeth in a glass of water standing amid the clutter on a table beside her bed. The bed was as sunken as her cheeks without the teeth. "Never wear the damn things. They bite me better'n they do the little food I put in my mouth. Communist teeth!"

"I could sleep on the floor," he offered.

"Going to try to get across, I suppose."

"Yes."

She shook her thin gray head. "Won't make it, never make it. They'll kill you. Catch you, anyway, and be knocking at my door soon's they do. I don't want no part in it, no sir, no part at all." She twirled the bracelet on her arm, admiring it. "Nice bracelet. Buy it yourself?"

He nodded.

"How much money you got?"

He hesitated. "Twenty marks."

She made a face. "Better go back home. Your father always was a fool. Worse fool'n I thought, letting you come all this way with only twenty marks. I suppose he told me I'd put you up till you figured out how to get out of this concentration camp."

"He didn't say. He just gave me your address. I only want a place to sleep. I'll pay you for whatever food I eat."

"Pay? You think I'd take money from my own flesh and blood? That's the Communist way. They'll take your money and then turn you in. Swine! Pigs! Goats! Pah!"

The conversation traveled up and down the elevator of her emotions, at one time teeming with disdain for her family, at another with vehement hatred for the Communists—a hatred, Emerich discovered, based not at all on philosophic grounds but solely on her belief that they had cheated her out of her full due from her late husband's pension. Her antipathy toward "old Goatbeard's gangsters" finally outweighed her scorn for the "whole damned mendacious Weber clan," and she let him stay.

In three days he had his plans drawn. "You won't have to feed me anymore after tonight," he told her.

"Already? What did you do, find a hole in The Wall?"

"I wish it were that easy."

She seemed a little disappointed. "I thought it would take you a couple of weeks."

"Aren't you glad I'm leaving?"

"Of course I am. Don't think this piece of junk jewelry you gave me makes up for all the food you've taken out of my mouth." She fingered the bracelet carelessly; she had worn it every day since he had given it to her. She had also cleaned up her room, put on a fresh dress, lipstick and powder, and combed her hair.

"You know, Aunt Magda, you're a good-looking woman."

"All the Weber women are good-looking," she said indifferently, but he could tell she was pleased. While she was clearing the dishes from the little table, she glanced at herself in the small, cracked mirror over her night table. She had to follow a round-about route from the table to the washstand in order to do it, and she made up little excuses to do so, pretending once to be searching for a hairpin, juggling the dishes in one hand as she rummaged through the tiny drawer in the night table, and another time stopping to straighten a crucifix hanging next to the mirror. Her subterfuges were so transparent Emerich would have laughed were they not so pathetic. He was seeing for the first time the occasionally desperate grasp middle-aged women make for a lost youth which, even while they are grasping, they know is forever beyond their reach.

He dried the dishes for her. As a farewell treat, she got out a bottle of kümmel and sent him out for cigarettes. They sat in the untidy comfort of the little room sipping the kümmel, she smoking one cigarette after the other, talking, waiting until it was time for him to go.

"What do you suppose you'll do, once you're over there —*if* you get over there?"

"I'll get over, all right."

She made a skeptical rattle in her throat. "Those Vopos

ain't stupid. You've got to be stupid—or a genius—to try it in the first place."

He grinned. "Do you think I'm stupid?"

"Most of the Webers are, always has been. Potato diggers, the whole mendacious lot of 'em, back to as far as anybody'd bother to look. Ones that wasn't stupid was cracked. Anybody'd go cracked spending their whole life feeding swill to the pigs, trying to grow something on that dead land. Roast in the summer, freeze in the winter, with them mountains staring down at you all the time like they was watching every move you made and laughing at you all the time. Anybody'd live like that for a thousand years has got to be stupid or cracked."

Upheld by the evidence that she did not live as well as the Webers in Überdreibrücken, Emerich was tempted to refute her opinion. He blamed the kümmel for mellowing him; besides, there was no point in showing her up for what she undoubtedly knew she had come to. Whatever glories she had imagined for her life when she ran off to Berlin with the salesman Halzapfel, she had had to suffer the gradual, bitter realization that they were not to be—not tomorrow, not next month, not next year, not ever.

"We lived in the West End, on the other side, Heinrich and me. Did you know that?"

He confessed he hadn't known it.

"We had a big house—three stories—a garden, tennis court, servants. Ah, we had it good in those days. . . ."

She went on, adding row upon row of embroidery, crocheting dreams of what might have been into what at moments must have become confused with what was. The line between dreams and reality had become too thin to bear the force of heartbreak. It was the war, of course, that had destroyed it all—literally and figuratively. It was the first, but not the last, Emerich was to hear of how the war had destroyed wealth, position, future.

As he listened to her pitiable voice drone out the story of her rise and fall, a nova in the heavens of Berlin, the time to leave pressed in upon him. "I have to go now."

She stopped in mid-sentence, stared at him as if she had just remembered he was still there, downed the kümmel in her glass, and pushed herself to her feet with great effort. Her hair had come down on one side, and in the

course of the evening she had slipped off her shoes. She
pulled up the loose strands of hair and tucked them into
a clump on top of her head. They fell back down.

"Maybe you'll send me some coffee. Coffee's so hard
to come by."

He said he would.

Remembering something, she scurried to the night table,
pulled open the drawer, and dug something out. "Here!"
She held up an old mother-of-pearl pocketknife. "It was
Heinrich's." She pressed it into his hand. "Sharp as a razor.
He used to sit honing it by the hour. 'Man's knife has got
to be sharp as a razor,' he used to say."

Emerich took the knife and left. In the early morning
the city slept, a sprawl of silence lying like a great comforter over the incarcerated masses whose only certain
moments of privacy could be found in sleep. He doubted
the wisdom of waiting so long; he would have been less
conspicuous at an earlier hour when there were more
people in the streets. He had a long way to go—all the
way across the center of East Berlin from Prenzlauerberg
in the north to Treptow in the south. His destination was
a five-block stretch of The Wall along Heidelbergerstrasse.

An hour and half later, he was crossing the footbridge
over the Spree, six blocks back from The Wall. Here the
river was pinched close together, land jutting out from
either bank. The lights were on along the Osthafen quay
on the right, and river barges tied up alongside were being
unloaded. The cry of men giving orders and cursing, the
eerie creak of the cranes, the lap of the waves against the
hulls of the barges rebounded from the surface of the tumid
water. Looking down onto the scene, Emerich felt as if
he had come upon a great hole in the earth where, not
having been told the sun had long been down, men continued to labor, deceived by their bosses. It was the only
sign of activity Emerich had seen in his long trek across the
city, and he felt compelled to read some meaning into it.
Perhaps because he had no choice, or because the bustle
was a welcome change from the ghostly quiet of the dark
streets through which he had journeyed, he decided it was
a good omen and went forward.

At the head of Elsenstrasse he could look straight ahead
to The Wall, which severed the street from its other half
in the West. Along here were stands of new apartment

buidings put up since the war. He held to the sidewalk,
passing under their protruding balconies, their black,
shaded windows until he was within a block of The Wall.
Between him and it stood a five-story building like the
others, set back about twenty-five meters from The Wall.
Here The Wall was constructed of precast concrete slabs,
held in place by concrete buttresses and capped with Y
frames of barbed wire. It was, in all, three meters high.

Emerich had counted on two factors in selecting this
place to make his escape: the buttresses, somewhat inclined, provided a relatively easy means of attaining the
top of The Wall; and the border guards were required to
patrol two blocks of its length, providing an opportunity to
make a dash for it.

He reached the near side of the building and peered
around the corner, waiting for the Vopos to pass. The
sounds from the quay had almost vanished now; only an
occasional grinding creak penetrated the night air. A car
horn sounded beyond The Wall, jolting his nerves. He
caught his breath and let it out slowly, surprised by the
noise taking it in had made. From the left, behind the
apartment house across the street, came the unmistakable
scraping sound of leather against macadam. A single figure
came into view.

Only one! At first he was elated. On second thought,
he realized that they always patrolled in pairs. Where
was his partner? The figure became clearly outlined against
the gray-white concrete of The Wall—a tall, angular man,
his billed cap stuck jauntily on the back of his head, his
hands stuck into his trouser pockets, blousing his jacket
at the sides. A submachine gun was slung diagonally across
his chest. He was strolling languidly, scuffing his boots
against the pavement. In a few seconds he passed from
view behind the apartment building concealing Emerich.

He did not know what to do. If there were only one
Vopo on duty tonight, his chances of getting across undetected, or if detected, unharmed, were doubled. But if
there was a second, where was he now? Emerich waited.
In less than ten minutes, the lone Vopo returned, shuffling
idly back over the ground he had covered. When he had
passed from view, Emerich made his move. He rounded
the corner and crept forward, holding to the shadows
along the building. Just short of the street he stopped. To

his right he could see The Wall running straight off into the dark distance. Above and beyond it rose the upper portions of houses on the West Berlin side. A clump of young trees intefered with their regular geometry. The Vopo was almost a block away. He had another block to go before he would turn to retrace his steps.

Just as Emerich was about to make a dash for the closest buttress, a door on The Wall side of the building opened and into the street came the second Vopo, buttoning the fly of his trousers. He stood there gazing down the street after his partner, fumbling with the buttons. The man was only a few meters away.

Emerich did not dare to breathe. He had to have a weapon of some kind. The brittle grass surrounding the new apartments was Germanically neat, barren even of twigs. Then he remembered the pocketknife Aunt Magda had given him. Slowly, carefully, he got it out of his pocket and opened the larger blade. He ran his thumb along the edge. In one thing at least, she had spoken the truth. It was razor sharp.

Glancing quickly down the street, he glimpsed the obscure outline of the first Vopo. He had the impression that he was still moving away. The second Vopo, his trousers buttoned, ambled over to a utility pole a few paces to the left and leaned against it, awaiting his companion's return.

Emerich clutched the knife in his hand—so hard his fingers hurt. He leaped.

"What are you up to there?"

The policeman's light caught his eyes, and he averted them. The policeman came closer, peering up at him, trying to focus the light on Emerich's face. "This is closed," he said.

"Did you think I wanted to jump over?"

The policeman laughed and switched off his light. "Go ahead if you're crazy." He was a big man with a big stomach bulging out against the belt of his white raincoat. West Berlin police wore white uniforms and scurried about the city in little Volkswagens. Berliners referred to them affectionately as "White Mice." But Emerich had no affection for them. He distrusted all policemen, regardless of their political affiliations. They liked to order people around, using their power indiscriminately. Policemen were bullies at heart, and he hated bullies as much as he hated Communists.

"I'm not crazy."

"Come down now. They'll shoot for any reason. They like to shoot, you know. They're trigger-happy. You don't want them to shoot you, do you?"

Emerich stepped down. The policeman had a long, drooping moustache. It was heavily waxed and shone in the dull light. "No, I don't want to get shot."

The policeman looked him over. "You look worn out. Why not go home and get some sleep. You'll feel better tomorrow."

"I'm not drunk."

"I didn't say you were drunk. I said you looked tired."

"I was on the other side when they put this up."

"You crossed over, eh? Afterward?"

"Yes."

The policeman looked impressed. He pulled on one end of his long moustache. "That took nerve."

Emerich shrugged. "A little."

"How did you do it?"

"That's none of your business."

The policeman smiled knowingly. He was not offended by Emerich's tone. "I wouldn't tell anyone, you know. But it doesn't matter." He remembered his job. "It's not healthy around here at night. You never know when someone's going to make a run for it, and then the bullets fly!"

"Both ways, I hope," Emerich said.

"Both ways. We always give them something to break their teeth on."

The policeman turned toward the car. "Do you live far from here?"

"Not far."

"Which way are you headed?"

"Toward Wedding."

"That's a hike."

"I'll be all right."

The policeman stood there, pulling on the ends of his moustache. Emerich gave him an offhand salute and left. When he passed by the car again, he could hear the radio crackling with static and an occasional cryptic transmission.

He started out toward home, thinking about the tunnel, repeating the vow he had just made to his father over The Wall. Nothing was going to prevent him from fulfilling that vow. Nothing.

THE heat came, an unclassified creature, rattling cumbrously through the shutters and down the wall, groping its way across the floor, its antennae quivering, eyes glowing. In the middle of the room it paused to reconnoiter, to search out a lurking breeze, and detecting none, moved on, clattering across the hardwood floor to the edge of the bed where a sheet thrown off in the night hung down. It tested the sheet with a horny claw. The sheet held. Awkwardly, it began its ascent, one claw over the other, slowly, intently, insistently driven by the primordial force that had created it, nurtured it, and set it loose upon the day. At last, on top of the bed, gasping, exuding a noxious perspiration that dribbled from its oily, pulsating body, it sought out its objective. With a final spasm of effort it scaled the wall of heavy thighs, let itself tumble down the other side, and, finding itself safe in the hollow of its destiny, retracted its antennae, closed its eyes, and went to sleep.

Bruno Balderbach awoke and found it there. He lay still, considering its unwelcome insinuation. He closed his eyes and viewed his dark cavern, where the air was cool and moisture clung to the moss hanging from the high, vaulted ceiling. There, in the dank chamber where the light and heat of the sun never entered, where the distant gushing of an underground river created an intricate fugue whose notes were transfigured into infinite variations on the voices, he painted by the light of the million

157

gleaming eyes of the hydras clinging to the walls, staring at him.

There is cold melon from Spain in the refrigerator.

And an elegantly designed fork to eat it with. She would not have chosen clumsy silverware.

He let an arm drop over the edge of the bed. His fingers touched the hard, rubbery waxed surface of the floor.

We'll roll the carpet for the summer and store it in the attic. It's so much cooler with the floor bare.

What do I paint there? If I could only feel the design of the brush strokes, see for one instant the colors, recall —no, hold fast, *fix*—the form.

She was there in bed beside him, her low-pitched, muffled snore greeting the drift of time across the threshold of the day. Gingerly, so not to disturb her, he got up, tiptoed across the cold floor, and closed the door silently behind him. The living room was dark with the curtains closed, and cool. He found the pull rope and drew them open on the garden side. The light rushed in rudely, like a crowd of customers awaiting the opening of a store on the first day of a sale. He rubbed his eyes and picked the sleep from the corners.

It was a small walled-in garden with a circular pebbled walk. Flowers grew in tidy beds around the walk, and roses rambled up the brick wall and along its top. In the center grew a great oak tree. It was at least a hundred years old, perhaps even two hundred. He didn't know but liked to speculate. He loved this tree. He had painted it a score of times, in all seasons, at all times of day. The best of the twenty was of Frieda picking roses from the bed along the wall under its reaching branches. The tree dominated the painting, its burly trunk a massive black presence in the center, surrounded by the colorful trivia of lesser life—the flowers, the pebbled walk, the sunburned arms of the frail woman absorbed in insignificant, transient thought.

Although he loved the tree, he was jealous of its immutable strength, its apparent immortality. Gazing at it standing in shadow, a giant ridiculously set down in the tiny enclosure of the garden wall, he admired it with all the innocence he could summon. It was a ritual he had repeated every morning of the eight years he had awakened in the house, and the experience had rarely failed to stir in him the desire to translate that sense of strength, of immortality, to his painting. It was as if the contemplation of the tree provided the narcotic needed to stimulate his artistic imagination.

Today, he waited for that feeling to come to him again. For six months it had failed to materialize, much as if the god of the ritual had deserted him. Every morning he had reluctantly abandoned the view of the garden and entered his studio, only to confirm what he knew was true: He could not paint that day.

He went there now, a spacious two-storied room on the north side of the house. In the center of the room stood his easel with a large canvas in place. The same canvas had stood there for six months, vacant, a tabula rasa. Each day, he came to the studio, stared at the empty white canvas, turned away, and left.

He could not paint anymore. What he had learned, he had already set down in oil. He knew that whatever he did now would be redundant—the same thing, perhaps in different colors, different forms, but its essential statement would be no different from that of the last painting he had done. And he was no modern faddist, content to exploit the market while it was his. He had always painted for himself—in innocence and in maturity—and this he would not change. He closed the door on the studio and crossed the living room to the bedroom.

She awoke while he was dressing. She lay there watching him, in the heat and half-light. "You're going through with it."

"Surely we're not going to discuss it again."

She did not change her expression. It was as if she had not heard him. "You'll make a fool of yourself."

He shrugged. "Perhaps."

"And what's to become of me?"

This was a new tactic. "Of you?"

"Of this." Her thin hand inscribed an arc across the room. "We're not rich, no matter what people may believe. You know we're not rich. We've had no income for six months. Are we to lose this house?"

"You're talking nonsense." He adjusted the straps on his overalls. "There is still plenty of money in the bank."

"New painters come into vogue. They'll push you out

of the limelight, Bruno. We've suffered too long to lose it all now."

The "we" did not escape him—she had not meant it to. It was strange that his success had ended her suffering —the material deprivation—and had been the beginning of his. Before, he had been happy painting; he could work for days without giving food or bodily comfort a thought. It was only when she suffered in silence—God, how he longed to hear her scream out her bitterness—that he thought of it and felt guilty. Her investment in him had paid off, and she could not bear having the dividends stop coming in.

"You look ridiculous," she said.

"I don't feel ridiculous," he lied.

She turned her head toward the wall. "A man of your age—of your stature—digging in the ground like an animal. It's *revolting*." The grating texture of her voice lent an onomatopoetic effect to the word. He winced involuntarily as if the word had mass and she had flung it at him. He put on the cloth cap and looked at himself in the mirror. A most improbable imitation of a laborer, he thought. No one would be fooled.

"Aren't you *pleased* with yourself."

He caught her face in the edge of the mirror. She smirked expertly. Yes, he thought, I am pleased with myself, pleased that I have the courage to feel ridiculous and the faith to think I'll overcome the necessity of feeling so.

"What am I to do with myself all day?"

"What you do any other day."

"What *do* I do any other day, Bruno?"

He had not the slightest notion. He fetched his battered black briefcase from the top shelf of the wardrobe. That, at least, looked authentic. He'd have to have something in it—beer, he supposed, some bread, wurst, cheese. Lord knows what workmen eat for lunch. Would he dare take a napkin? He held out the briefcase. It flopped open. "I'll need some lunch."

Her anger turned to tears that came to the corners of her eyes. "Please don't do this, Bruno."

He couldn't look at her. He went to the windows and looked out. The tranquility of the day did not impress him. Nature was too much like man; he knew that behind that facade of peace, frogs were snapping up flies, beetles were devouring begonia bulbs, dead flowers were rotting in the earth. Only the big oak was true, ingenuously grand, serene, untouched.

"Grupmann called again yesterday." She was calm now, resigned to the knowledge that he had become immune to her tears.

"Grupmann always calls." He wondered if there were worms nesting in the upper reaches of its branches. He knew he would not accept it if he found them there. It would be too much to bear.

"He has your interest at heart—and mine."

"He has his percentage at heart."

"That's ridiculous."

He had to abort his sortie into irrationality. Grupmann was his friend. Grupmann did not give a damn for his percentage. He had more than half the first-rate German artists in his stable; he had all the money he needed. "I'll call him," he said, conceding more than he had meant to. Grupmann had seen him through the bad times and the good.

"If it hadn't been for the Frankfurt show . . ."

"I said I'd call him." The Frankfurt show. It had made a saint of Grupmann. Damn the Frankfurt show. Damn Grupmann. Damn success. He turned his thoughts to the days before Frankfurt and Grupmann and success.

He had had shows before Grupmann's Frankfurt show —all in small, unimportant galleries in small, out-of-the-way towns in West Germany. What little notice the critics took of him was devastating. "Old-fashioned objectivism," they sneered. "Photographic." "Regressive." "Reactionary." "Fifty years behind the times." "Hopelessly out of date."

His painting *was* objective and in a way it *was* photographic, but it was not old-fashioned, regressive, or reactionary. Bruno selected commonplace details from nature and arranged them on canvas in such a way that they seemed to have been deracinated from their natural environment and transplanted to a world unknown to nature, one in which their characteristics were amplified in color and texture, intensified in form. Yet upon close examination, each was not unusual in itself. The repre-

sentation was almost photographic in its realism. Only in
the total composition, in the way in which the elements of
the painting were arranged in relation to one another, did
the other-world atmosphere take hold. The effect on the
viewer was much like *déjà vu* in reverse—he felt as if he
had been *there* before, but the experience was vaguely
hallucinatory, as if what he was seeing he had seen in
consciousness, and now he was seeing it again in a dream.

The critics always infuriated him, but they never de-
pressed him and they never convinced him to paint the
way they wanted him to paint. He continued to do what
satisfied his own aesthetic sensibilities and, because of it,
continued to be excluded from the mainstream of
the art world until, to a small one-man show in a tiny gallery in Wiesbaden, came Alfred Grupmann.

Grupmann was not successful because he went with the
times; his success came from his knowing art history better
than most professors of the subject, from his ability to
recognize great painting when he saw it, and from his
unerring nose that could scent the smell of change in the
blustery winds of the fickle art world. He spent his time
with artists, not dealers. He knew hundreds of them in-
timately. He listened to their clumsy, passionate yearnings
(for artists are peculiarly inarticulate, especially about
their own work. "You produce your work," he told Bruno
again and again, "let me talk about it"), and he foresaw
that the days of the monopoly of nonobjective and ab-
stract painting were numbered. Artists wanted to return
to objective art, but only a few had the nerve to defy the
cult of 1913. In America, Andrew Wyeth was just gaining
recognition; in Germany, Bruno Balderbach was not
worth more than a line of type every six months in the
critics' columns.

But Alfred Grupmann knew. He gave Bruno his
chance—a one-man show in his elegant new gallery in
Frankfurt. The critics hated him for it; they despised
Bruno's work, but they had to hedge in their condemna-
tion, for no sane critic dared challenge Alfred Grupmann's judgment entirely. They suggested that perhaps
if the great Grupmann liked his work, there was a small
corner in the house of modern art where they might allow Bruno to dabble. With a collective shrug, they left it at
that.

But not for long. Art collectors of the highest repute bought out his Frankfurt show to the last painting and clamored for more. Bruno gasped. Alfred Grupmann smiled his cat smile and took in the money. Frieda sat down and sobbed with incredulous joy. The critics gnawed their manicured fingernails.

Grupmann arranged a show in Munich the following year. Bruno worked feverishly and produced twenty-one paintings in ten months. In those ten months he learned the price of success—he did not enjoy painting anymore. He felt like a foreman trying to meet a production schedule. Grupmann had asked for thirty paintings. Bruno rebelled, gave him the twenty-one on time, and refused to attend the opening. Again, the show was a financial success. Bruno earned more than double the fifty thousand marks he had received in Frankfurt. This time the critics had to concede—they paid him reluctant tribute and wrote of the "winds of change," "the shifting sands of taste," "the first mutterings of discontent with the recent extremism of the nonobjectivists."

Grupmann nodded knowingly. "After Kandinsky and de Kooning and Kline, where was there to go? I sometimes marvel that anything happened to nonobjective art after Malevich's *White on White.* Come to think of it, not much did. Both Dali and Picasso had enough sense to avoid it—rather successfully, I'd say. They and our German Expressionists have given us the only respite since. And now we have Balderbach to make a revolution."

But Bruno did not want to make a revolution. He wanted to be left alone, to paint when he wanted to paint. Each new show Grupmann planned for him had to be postponed because Bruno could not produce fast enough to meet the deadlines. His third show, in Paris, came two years after Munich; the fourth, in New York, thirty months later. He did not show again for three and a half years, and then only twenty-seven paintings, in Berlin's Twentieth Century Gallery. Every show sold out. He could have sold twenty times the work he produced. He had to admit Grupmann had been patient, understanding, flexible. "My dear Bruno, God Himself cannot force a man to do the impossible; who am I to insist? We will postpone again."

It was six months now since the last show, in Venice.

His paintings hung in the permanent collection of two dozen major museums of modern art. Grupmann had had to hire a secretary to handle Bruno's mail. Critics were now comparing newcomers to his work. At forty-six, he was taking on the aura of an Old Master. He was rich and famous. And discontent.

Frieda had prepared a lunch for him. He sat in the sun in the garden waiting for her, listening to the cicadas testing their shrill instruments, staring at the dripping branches of the tree reflected in a puddle left from the night's rain. He often sat there of late for hours at a time, letting time pass drop by drop like water dripping from the leaves, absorbed in torporous dreams never recalled. He would search his hands, turning them over and back, seeking there a reason for their idleness, as if they had a will of their own. In the chair in the sun in the garden he knew moments of peace, moments without earthly dimensions measurable by word or concept.

He was thinking now of the tunnel. With the fact at hand, he wondered if he were not indeed ridiculous, not only in act but in motive, and he had doubts that he could transcend his ridiculousness. Perhaps, if he were indeed *great*, that greatness was restricted only to his ability to apply paint to canvas, was but an electrical circuit, an intricately developed reticulum between his brain and his right hand, nothing more. Perhaps it had nothing to do with the moral fiber and the intellect of the man Bruno Balderbach.

He did not like thinking about it. He did not need, he mused, to be great, in the true, forgotten sense of the word, to escape ridicule; he needed only to be good, good enough to do his share of the work. The motive for working would serve its use if he were great, and if he were not, only he would suffer—and, of course, Frieda.

She came with the briefcase and a change of clothes, holding her robe closed at the neck. Her hair, streaked with gray, was hanging loose down her back. Later she would put it up in braids and wind it like earmuffs over her ears. He felt a welling of compassion for her. Love had gone long ago. Love that had endured the years of frustration, poverty, failure, could not succeed with success. It was a fragile flower, nurtured in deficient soil, and had not been able to survive the transplanting. In its place grew a variety of flowers, none beautiful, none rare, but collectively, like those in the garden, enough to fill the void. She ventured a smile when he took the briefcase and the clothes.

"There was some cheese," she said, "only *Bierkäse*, though, and liverwurst. The bread may be a little dry."

"It's all right."

"There's some Mosel. I put in a glass. You won't break it, will you? It's my good crystal."

"No, no."

"And an orange."

"Yes, I like oranges."

She gave an abortive laugh. "Do you remember the time you came home with the oranges in 1947?"

He remembered well. "That was a feast. We ate the rinds and all. Oranges never tasted so good." Unaccountably, he touched her cheek. "It's good of you to remember the good things."

She shrugged and turned away, gathering her robe about her neck. He wondered what she was keeping in—or keeping out. "I remember the other, but there's no good in talking about it. I remember it like a nightmare, and it frightens me."

He wanted to promise it would never be that way again. In one sense, he knew he could; yet he would not. The commitment would be too grievous, too complete; and compassion, born of pity, was tinged with enough hate to prevent him from assuaging her fear. He wondered if, after all, it would finally come to a kind of tolerant acceptance of one another. As he walked to the car, he realized that the next two weeks could decide.

PART II

THE TUNNEL

╒╤╒

9

JOACHIM stopped the car at the end of the alley, got out, yawned, and stretched. Sepp, Wolf, and Emerich got out the other side. He still felt tired and was having trouble shaking himself out of his early-morning lethargy. He could not get the thought of his stupidity of having forgotten to be home when Sepp called the night before out of his mind. When he had arrived at the apartment this morning, Wolf's casually delivered message, "Sepp called last night," came like an echoing call down a long canyon. So far, Sepp had not said anything. Joachim doubted that he would. Sepp was a gentleman.

He was vaguely irritated that the old warehouse looked the same as it had three weeks ago when he and Sepp had come to do their triangulations. If anything, it seemed more dilapidated than before. The dirty gray stucco was rain-streaked, looking much like the face of a tearful, pimply-faced urchin. Weeds grew high along the base of the wall, and spiderwebs, drawn tight from stem to stem, glistened with moisture in the early-morning sun.

The four of them stood there inert, as if too awed by the magnitude of their task to grapple with its initiation. Behind them, in the machine shop, someone was clattering about, clanking pieces of metal together. It sounded like a church bell calling the faithful to morning prayer.

"Misery, it's going to be hot," Emerich said.

Joachim rubbed his eyes and peered into the bright sky. At least it will be cool down there, he thought.

169

"You're wrong," Emerich said.

"About what?"

"It's not going to be any cooler in there."

Joachim did not appreciate having his mind read; more correctly, he was annoyed that he had let his emotions show. He had run into Emerich around the university a few times and had taken an immediate dislike to him. His original impression now seemed justified. "I don't mind the heat, peasant. You get used to it standing under klieg lights."

"Ah, yes, I'd almost forgotten. The famous cover boy." He bowed low, scraping the ground with his cap. "Forgive me for having spoken."

Joachim repressed a surge of contempt. So it was to be this way with him. He had known the face of jealousy before, both subtle and blunt, and he had learned that it must be dealt with at once—subtlety to match subtlety; bluntness for bluntness.

Sepp eyed them both judiciously. Joachim ignored him. He got out a mark piece and flipped it to Emerich. "Here you go, peasant." By bad luck, the coin caught in Emerich's hat, which was perfectly humiliating, reducing him to the status of beggar. Emerich was momentarily flustered. He tried to recover his ground by biting the coin to test its genuineness, but the gesture failed somehow.

Sepp intervened, "Let's get on with it." He inserted his key in the lock and opened the door. Joachim felt better. Life's little victories. He moved in behind Sepp, ahead of Emerich, scoring a second victory. He was beginning to feel positively euphoric.

His joy was short-lived. Inside, they closed the door, and Sepp turned on his flashlight. They stood close together, once again immobilized by the sight of the interior of the building. Entire sections of the walls had fallen in. Slabs of plaster looking like hardened cake frosting lay everywhere. Strewn among them were pieces of broken lath resembling chips of teeth lost in trying to eat the cake. The windows were boarded up. The panes were gone entirely; not even slivers remained stuck in the putty along the frames. It was as if someone had painstakingly removed the broken glass a piece at a time.

Everything was covered with a layer of dust. When they moved, it scattered, rising off the floor, drifting away, hovering in the air, settling again like flocks of birds taking wing at the first sign of danger, then returning to their nests when the danger had passed.

They went single file down the creaky steps to the cellar. A flurry of sound came up from below. Instinctively, they all halted.

"I'd forgotten about them," Joachim said.

"What is it?" Wolf asked.

"Rats."

"Misery," Emerich moaned.

"Scared of rats, peasant?"

"Only the kind down there."

Joachim did not answer. He was thinking about the rats. They had seen them before, he and Sepp. Some were as big as tomcats. They could hear them in the walls, squeaking, scraping, clattering. There were hundreds of them. There was nothing for them to eat in the cellar, but the warehouse to the south was loaded with emergency rations in the event of another blockade like the one of 1948–49. As a result, they were fat and happy. Joachim knew they would not bother them. They went on down into the cellar. Dust filtered down through the cracks from the floor above. It was thick in the cellar and quickly absorbed the dampness, lying like a covering of moss on the floor.

At the foot of the steps they stopped, and Sepp shone his flashlight about, now and then catching in its beam a rat frozen in its tracks, gazing dumbly into the light. From all around them the creatures peered out from the dark corners of the cellar, their eyes like lights burning in a remote village in the middle of the night. They darted about furtively, trying to avoid the light, seeking their holes, which dotted the perimeter of the cellar like a perforated border.

"Will they bite?" Wolf asked.

"Of course they'll bite," Emerich said. "I know rats. I grew up with them. They won't bother you as long as they're not hungry or scared. They'll stand and fight if they're scared."

Sepp shone the light on the generator. A huge brown rat was hunched atop the gas tank. He stared back at them in defiance, then silently loped off into the darkness.

"God in Heaven," Wolf muttered.

"If one bites you," Emerich said, "you can get rabies, or rabbit fever, or even the plague."

"Don't listen to his nonsense," Joachim said. They had been so concerned with the rats that he had forgotten about the stench of the place, a combination of rat dung and smoldering rock. It reminded him of the smell of old wine gone bad, and in the heat the odor was noxious. All Joachim could think of were the days of grueling toil that lay ahead of him, the awful monotony; and thinking about it, his muscles began to ache involuntarily. Now added to his vexation was the realization that Emerich Weber was as disagreeable as he was reputed to be.

Sepp thrust the flashlight into Emerich's hand. "Hold this." He went to the generator and, bracing himself against the armature housing, gave the starter cable a quick tug. The motor coughed, almost caught, and died. On the second try, it started and, like stage lights quickly brightening, two bulbs overhead came on. The cellar was clearly illuminated.

" 'And there was light,' " Joachim quoted.

"It works!" Emerich said.

"I said it was a good generator."

Sepp and Emerich were strangely enthusiastic about the generator, like boys with a new toy. Joachim could not understand Sepp's friendliness toward the peasant; it was incongruous. He turned his back on them and surveyed the room.

The walls were constructed of cut limestone, originally precisely fitted so that no mortar was required in their construction. Over the years earth had filtered into the cracks, giving rise to a growth of moss that outlined in neat geometric patterns the shape of the stone blocks. The blocks had weathered, so that the edges and corners were rounded. Here and there, the seams between the laminae in the rock had become enlarged and protruded from the face of the rock, looking like the cross section of a piece of French pastry. Four huge pillars, built in the same manner as the walls, were spaced symmetrically about the room.

An array of tools and equipment stood against the front wall. There were spades, picks, crowbars, one- and two-man crosscut saws, the two steel scoop-shaped sleds Sepp had fashioned, a big coil of black insulated wire, and a chest of smaller tools. The tools were both new and used, and all shone with a film of oil. Sepp had not been sparing with his money. Joachim felt a touch of envy at the ease with which Americans could spend money.

In the center of the room against the front wall stood a pile of earth beside a hole which Sepp had dug in order to examine the soil and to find out how far down the wall's foundation began. The hole was about half a meter deep. The tunnel would begin there.

"What's that smell?" Wolf asked.

"That's rat dung," Emerich said. "I'd know it anywhere."

"You get used to it," Sepp said.

Wolf looked skeptical. "Do you think the rats will go away after we start work?"

"They won't bother us," Sepp assured him.

Emerich was examining the equipment. "These are first class, Sepp. Your pockets must be empty."

From above came the noise of a key turning in the lock. The door opened and closed, and footsteps sounded on the stairs.

"Who's that?" Wolf whispered.

"Georg or Bruno," Sepp said. "You don't have to whisper."

The footsteps reached the bottom of the stairs, and a face peered around the doorjamb. "Am I in the right place?"

Sepp went forward. "Come in, Bruno, come in."

He came, a body heavier than the face would have suggested, a bulging of flesh at the neck, a long, bony nose sniffing the air. "Not exactly 4711." He grinned amiably, his gray eyes taking in the room and its contents with the quickness of a cat. He grasped Sepp's hand rather too eagerly, Joachim thought, and glanced around at them.

"Bruno, may I present the other members of our group: Joachim Lentz, Wolf Lentz . . ."

"Ah, yes, the brothers."

Joachim shook his hand. "I'm the older; Wolf is the better."

A laugh fluttered out of Bruno Balderbach's thick, sensitive lips. "Sibling loyalty is always touching."

"This is Emerich Weber."

Emerich took Bruno's hand, his face solemn, his manner hesitant. "A pleasure, Herr Balderbach."

"No, no, you must call me Bruno."

"I've admired your work tremendously," Joachim said.

The artist nodded and smiled. "Thank you. It pleases me to hear that. However, painters are notoriously gullible, so I urge you not to flatter me. It would be most unfair."

"I wasn't flattering you. I meant it as a true compliment." Joachim made a mental note to find out something about Bruno Balderbach's work.

The painter bowed very deeply, coming out of it with his hands folded across a small paunch. Joachim noted that his hands seemed rather ordinary, neither long nor short, neither fat nor thin. "I accept it as such," he said, and smiled in such a way that Joachim did not know whether he was really pleased or was making fun of him. There was no doubt that Bruno Balderbach was a man apart. Something about him was unearthly, as if, though he trod the same road as other men, he was of another world. Joachim believed that he would have left the same impression regardless of his fame. He had read of people who commanded attention the minute they entered the room; this was his first experience with one, and he was surprised to find that it was true. Even in those ridiculous overalls, in that stinkhole of a cellar, the man cast a spell. It was as if some sort of rays were emanating from his body, charging the air. One expected something to happen at any moment. Joachim wondered if Herr Balderbach was aware of the effect he was having on him; he wondered if the others felt it. He looked around at them and saw that they, too, were gazing expectantly at the artist, like schoolboys at a tea hanging on the words of the headmaster. But whether because he was unaware of his power or, being aware of it, chose not to exercise it, Bruno remained silent, looking toward Sepp with the same expression of anticipation that the others were directing toward him.

Upstairs, the door opened and closed. Georg Knauer came down, taking the steps two at a time. At the bottom he stopped, gave them a nod, and set his briefcase down against the doorjamb. "Sorry I'm late, Sepp."

Joachim barely knew Georg. They had had a chemistry

class together in the spring term and had exchanged a few pleasantries. Georg was always around the student cafés and beer halls, but he and Joachim had shared the same table only a few times. Georg had always struck Joachim as shy, uninteresting, and immature, and Joachim had never considered him worth cultivating.

Whether Joachim's impression of him was right or not, he had yet to learn, but about Georg's looks there was no question: He had little going for him. He was of medium height, well enough built—neither fat nor thin —but Joachim doubted he was as strong as his build suggested. His head was too small for his body, much like a child's head mistakenly screwed onto an adult's body. His eyes were hazel, sometimes more green than brown, sometimes more blue than green, never distinctive, never clearly any one color. They were rheumy eyes, rimmed with red, as though he rubbed them often. His nose was fairly well shaped, a narrow bridge flaring soon enough but in such a way that one nostril was considerably longer than the other, giving his face a slightly asymmetrical appearance.

Georg's least attractive feature, however, was his mouth. His lips were small and thick, perpetually set in a soft, fleshy pout. It was the sort of mouth one expected to see on a chubby adolescent, and only because his head was small did his mouth not seem entirely incongruous. He had small, even teeth, which, when he smiled—as he was doing nervously now, recognizing first Emerich and then Joachim—suggested a frantically ravenous chipmunk.

Sepp introduced him to Bruno. "This is Georg Knauer. Bruno Balderbach."

"How do you do, sir." His voice was surprisingly deep.

"Please call me Bruno."

"Certainly, sir."

Everyone laughed.

Emerich said, "He's a slow learner."

Sepp introduced Georg and Wolf. Then he turned to face them all. The feeling of expectation was still in the room, but now all eyes were diverted from Bruno Balderbach to Sepp. They were excited, but subdued by apprehension. Like a soccer team about to take the field, Joachim thought. He observed the mood but did not feel it himself; he felt more like a spectator than a player. He wondered if the others felt the same way. He looked at their faces and knew that they did not. Even Bruno Balderbach's expression reflected the intensity of his emotion.

"I know you are all as eager to get to work as I am, if for no other reason than to get the work behind us. You have been briefed on the overall plan, so I don't see any need to go into it again. Today will be a matter of getting adjusted to the idea, the pace of the work, the tools. I don't plan to go by a schedule today. We'll start with one tomorrow, if there are no objections." There were none. "Fine. I think the best way to proceed is to get a supply of shoring lumber piled up and cut while we're starting the tunnel itself. The first day of digging won't amount to much, so we probably won't get much shoring done. I suggest that Joachim and I start the digging while the rest of you are tearing up the flooring."

Joachim was pleased that Sepp had chosen him over the others. He disliked being one of the faceless herd, no matter what the situation.

"We'll pile earth here, on the left side, leaving the right half for lumber storage and working room. You should tear up the flooring at that end first so you can drop the lumber through the hole you make. It will lighten the work. But be careful. If the lumber cracks when you pull it up or when it drops, it won't be usable." He looked around. "Any questions?"

"If we tear out all the joists," Emerich said, "we may endanger the structural soundness of the building. I suggest we leave, say, every fifth one."

"All right," Sepp agreed. "We don't want the building to collapse."

Georg raised a hand hesitantly. "Who's in charge of the lumber gang?"

Sepp looked surprised. "I hadn't thought you would need anyone."

"No need, no need," Emerich agreed.

Georg shrugged. "People don't always work together harmoniously. I just thought—"

Sepp interrupted him. "I hope we can work harmoniously. We're all here for one common purpose. If there are any personal differences or if any develop, I hope

we're all mature enough to prevent them from interfering
with the successful completion of the tunnel."

"Well spoken," Bruno said.

"I didn't mean to start anything," Georg said defensively. "I only thought we'd work better with someone in
charge. *I* don't have any personal differences with anybody."

"Let's get started," Emerich implored him. "Time is
precious."

Eager zealot, Joachim thought. I wonder if the peasant
will take Sepp's little homily to heart. He's probably not
even intelligent enough to understand what he meant.

"Where do we change our clothes?" Wolf asked.

"There are some nails in the wall just inside the door
on the first floor. We can hang our things there."

They all headed up the stairs, saying little, constrained
by the strangeness of the new situation in which they
found themselves. It had been one thing to talk about it,
to envision what it would be like, but quite another
actually to be doing it. Joachim felt a little foolish, and
he could tell that the rest of them shared his feeling.

As each one undressed, Joachim filed away a brief
impression: The peasant was scrawny and dirty; Georg,
white-skinned and soft; the artist, agile for his age but
flaccid; Wolf, powerful but slightly awkward. Only Sepp
had the strength and grace Joachim himself had. He felt
distinctly out of his class, as if he were slumming, and
although committed to work with them, he found it difficult to take them seriously. He tried to imagine them
together at a cocktail party—it would have been an
unmitigated flop. He would never have sought out any
of them for a friend—with the exception, of course, of
Bruno Balderbach. A man of his stature was always
valuable to have as a friend.

"You look glum, Joachim," Sepp said in passing. He
went out the door and down the stairs without waiting
for a response.

"He's always glum in the morning," Wolf explained to
the others, as if it required an explanation. Joachim wondered if Wolf were embrassed by his ill-concealed discontent.

While the others began prying up the flooring, Sepp
and Joachim started the digging. In the hole Sepp had

dug, Joachim could see the bottom layer of rocks of the wall. From that point, which would be the ceiling of the tunnel, to ground level was just over three meters. The amount of work to do seemed overwhelming. Before they were finished, more than half the cellar would be filled with earth removed from the tunnel. Sepp's estimate of two weeks to complete it began to appear optimistic. As if to confirm Joachim's doubts, Sepp gave him a long-handled spade, saying, "We'd better get started."

From overhead came the first sounds of crowbars prying up the old planking, of rusty nails being pulled. The nails screeched out their resistance. Joachim thought of the four up there—Wolf, Emerich, Georg, Bruno—and laughed. It was a sad, incredulous laugh.

"What's so funny?"

Joachim pointed his shovel toward the ceiling. "Quite a crew."

Sepp was not amused. "They'll be all right." He drove his spade into the earth by the hole and rested his foot on it. "You agreed to all of them, you know."

Joachim did not want to get into an argument for fear that Sepp would bring up the matter of his over-sight last night. He began digging, taking out his annoyance on the compact earth of the cellar floor.

Their plan was to dig out an incline to the mouth of the tunnel up which the sleds filled with earth could be hauled more easily. The incline would extend from the middle of the floor to the base of the tunnel entrance. The digging began more easily than Joachim had expected. For the first half meter, the earth was fairly sandy, but he knew that when they got farther down, digging in the subsoil clay would be harder.

Overhead, the others had opened a small hole in the flooring and were dropping planks through it to the cellar floor. Dust filtered down through the hole and began to fill the air.

Emerich came down the stairs, his long face covered with sweat and dust. There was dust in his hair and on his clothes.

"You look like you've been shaken up in a bag of flour," Sepp said.

"The dust is hell," Emerich said, "but with that hole

in the floor, the fumes from the generator are worse. We have to do something about that."

Joachim suggested the obvious. "Open a window."

"No," Sepp said. He paused to wipe his face. Joachim let his spade drop and slouched down against the wall to rest.

"You're sitting on a rat hole, Lentz," Emerich warned him. Joachim jumped up, clutching his buttocks. Emerich hooted. As if conspiring with Emerich, a rat, hidden from view in his hole across the room, squeaked angrily.

"Filthy little bastard," Joachim snarled.

"He means the rat, not you," Sepp said to Emerich. He led him by the arm over to the generator.

Joachim eyed the rat hole and, taking up his shovel, scooped out a clod of earth, threw it on the hole, and tamped it down with his boots. Satisfied, he resumed his seat where the hole had been. Sepp and Emerich were discussing the problem of the fumes, but he could not make out what they were saying over the sound of the motor and the noise from above. He rubbed his arms and shoulders and speculated on whether the pain would get worse before it finally went away—*if* it went away. He had always been in excellent physical condition and had taken it for granted that whatever physical task he was confronted with he would perform well and without discomfort. He hadn't expected to have any aches and pains. It was annoying. He got up and went over to the generator. "Why not attach a hose to the exhaust and run it outside?" he suggested.

"We were considering that," Emerich said. When he spoke, the dust on his face continuously formed new designs.

"I can't think of any other way," Sepp said. "Measure it off." He got out his wallet and handed him a twenty-mark note. "See if you can get a used one."

Emerich nodded. "It may take a while. In the meantime, I think we ought to knock out at least one board in a window up there."

Sepp agreed reluctantly. "All right, but on the alley side, not the street side."

"Naturally."

"How is it going up there?"

"Some of the spikes are so rusty it's the Devil's work to get them out. But we're doing all right."

Sepp looked at Joachim expectantly. What did he want? He turned back to Emerich. "You'd better get going."

Emerich glanced at Joachim and, folding the bill carefully and stuffing it in his pocket, went to the tool kit and got out a tape measure. Then Joachim realized what they were after. "Do you drive, peasant?"

Emerich pulled out the tape and, pressing the button on the container, let it spin back in. His black eyes explored Joachim with mild contempt. "The Lord knows I am a peasant. He gave me life on the land of my father's father. He meant for me to till that land, to grow food for mouths that speak from ignorance and with arrogant sophistication against the peasants, and to give birth to my sons there." His eyes, sheltered under the dust-laden lashes, flickered like stars in patches of dark sky. "You may call me 'peasant.' However, understand that to me it is not a pejorative term but a fitting testament to God's wisdom that he chose me and not someone like you." The dust around his lips broke away into the lines of a sly grin. "Yes, Joachim, I drive."

Joachim looked from Emerich to Sepp and then back to Emerich, failing to hide his astonishment at Emerich's sudden eloquence.

Sepp said sympathetically, "It's downright unfair, isn't it." He shook his head and laughed. "Give him the keys, Joachim."

Joachim fished the car keys from his pocket and tossed them to Emerich. "Drive with care," he said, almost adding "peasant." Emerich pocketed the keys and set about measuring for the hose.

Joachim picked up his spade and went back to work, more confused than angry. "He started it, you know," he said to Sepp. Sepp nodded but said nothing. It bothered Joachim that he did not know whose side Sepp was on.

By the middle of the morning, they had finished the incline to the tunnel entrance, exposing a neatly trimmed square, one meter wide, below the base of the wall. At that depth, the earth was moist, heavy clay, the grayish-brown color of elephant hide. The amount of earth piled up from the excavation was surprisingly large. Joachim wondered if the cellar would be big enough to hold all the earth from the tunnel.

Sepp got down into the cut and, scooping up a handful, squeezed it and rubbed it between his fingers.

"What do you think?" Joachim asked.

"It's damp, but not as wet as I thought it might be."

A piece of planking came sliding down through the hole in the ceiling and clattered onto the small pile on the other side of the cellar, raising new dust. Georg stuck his head through the hole. "How's it coming?"

"So-so," Sepp said.

"We've got a dust storm up here. What do you think about bringing in some water to wet it down?"

Joachim said to Sepp, "There ought to be a water pipe coming into the building."

"There is. It's over in the southwest corner on the first floor where the toilet was. I don't know if we dare use it, though."

"Why not? The water isn't metered."

Georg called out, "And what about a toilet? We could all use one right now."

Sepp made a face. "Why didn't I think of *that?*" He went up the incline scratching his head. "I'll be up in a minute," he said to Georg.

Emerich came in, rattling noisily down the stairs, dragging a coil of black rubber hose. He had washed his face somewhere and brushed the dust from his hair. He still looked ugly, only less so. He was grinning with triumph. He held up the hose in one hand, Sepp's twenty-mark note in the other.

"You stole it," Sepp concluded.

"Um."

"Where?"

"From your friends at McNair Barracks."

Sepp groaned.

Joachim had to laugh.

Sepp reached out for his money, but Emerich held it back. "Please note that I could have kept the money, claiming I'd spent it on the hose."

"Duly noted."

"You see, you should have taken me with you when you bought all those tools."

"You would have saved me hundreds," Sepp conceded, "and landed us both in jail." Sepp snatched the bill away from him. "Hook it up, peasant." Emerich hooted and leaped across the room like a ballet dancer.

"Come on," Sepp said to Joachim, "let's look at that water pipe."

Upstairs, the dust was thick in the air. Wolf had tied a handkerchief over his nose and mouth. He looked like a teenage desperado from the old American West. All three of them were covered with the gray, powdery dust. Bruno's eyes were watering. Georg squeezed his nose and blew onto the floor. "It's not polite," he admitted, "but it works." Wolf pulled down his face mask. His face underneath was free of dust, while the top half was coated with it. He took off a glove and sucked a cut on his finger.

"There's a water pipe over here," Sepp said. They followed him to the corner where there were bolts in the flooring indicating where a toilet and washstand once stood. Two lead pipes with caps screwed over the ends stuck out from the wall; a third, larger one was set into the floor. "These are for the incoming water," Sepp said, indicating the pipes. "This one in the floor must be the drain to the sewer." The wall was still plastered over, so they could not tell whether the pipes came in directly from the outside or were installed inside the wall.

Bruno found a small door in the wall. "Here are the valves."

"Are they opened or closed?"

"They're closed, I believe."

"Try to open one," Sepp said.

Bruno got both hands on one of the round handles, but it would not budge.

"Let me try," Joachim said. Bruno moved away. Joachim gave the valve a hard twist, and the water came clattering into the pipe. He opened the second valve as well.

"Close one," Sepp said, "and leave one just barely open. Wolf, go get a wrench." He turned to the others. "I'm sorry I didn't think of toilet facilities."

"We could dig a hole in the cellar," Georg suggested.

"That's all right for urinating. . . ."

Georg nodded. "True. The gas fumes are bad enough."

"Maybe we can use the toilet in the factory," Joachim said. "There'd be no harm in asking."

"It's too risky," Sepp said.

"Aren't you going off the deep end with this cloak-and-dagger business?"

Sepp set his mouth in a narrow line of restrained impatience. "No, I don't think so."

"People get caught," Georg said quietly. "People get killed."

Joachim's anger flared. "I know that. No one has to remind *me* about that."

Bruno interceded. "As long as there is water in the pipes, why don't we simply purchase a toilet stool? I'll be happy to pay for it. It shouldn't cost much."

"Who knows how to connect it?" Georg asked.

"Emerich would know," Sepp said.

Wolf came back with a big monkey wrench. "Emerich wants to know if he should go acquire a toilet."

"You see?" Bruno said, pleased. "Our plumber has anticipated me."

Sepp smirked. "He means to steal it, Bruno."

"Oh." The artist looked befuddled. "Is he . . . a professional thief?"

"He's a peasant," Sepp said.

Bruno smiled. "And that explains it?"

"That explains it."

"What should I tell him?" Wolf asked.

"He wasn't serious," Joachim told him.

"He seemed serious," Wolf said.

"Tell him to fix the generator and forget about the toilet for now," Sepp said. "Let's see if we can get water out of this rock."

With difficulty, Sepp wrenched the cap loose from one pipe and unscrewed it. A dribble of rusty water spilled out onto the floor. They took handfuls of it and sprinkled it over the area where they were working, to keep the dust down. Eventually, the water ran free of rust.

Wolf asked, "Do you think it's drinkable?"

"I should think so," Bruno said. "Shall we try?"

"Let's."

They drank and washed the dust from their faces. Bruno looked at Wolf and made a face of mock surprise. "Ah, Herr Lentz, is it not?"

Wolf bowed. "At your service, sire."

"Would you care to join me in a bit of prying?"

"Prying into other people's business, sire?"

Bruno gave him a look of disappointment. "Unfortunately, nothing so fascinating, Herr Lentz. Prying up boards and pulling nails is what I had in mind."

"If I join you in prying, does that make me a prior?"

"Herr Lentz, with boards and nails we could make you a saint."

Laughing, the two of them returned to work.

Joachim observed the exchange with fascination. In the past, Wolf had always seemed shy with older people. With Bruno, it was as if they had been friends for years and understood one another perfectly. When Sepp called to Joachim, he followed him down the stairs, wondering if his brother's sudden facility were but a momentary spasm of wit or if it had always been there, needing only a man like Bruno Balderbach to draw it out.

In the cellar Emerich had attached the hose to the exhaust pipe of the generator and was up on the pile of boards, wiring it up along a beam near the ceiling to keep it out of the way.

"Do you think you can install a toilet?" Sepp asked him.

"I'm an old toilet man," he said. "I'll go get one as soon as I get this finished."

"Bruno will pay for it."

Emerich made a hissing noise. "God helps those who help themselves."

"Thou shalt not steal."

"Stolen waters are sweet." He tapped the flooring overhead with his hammer. "Are they not, my righteous friend?"

"Thou shalt not steal unnecessarily." Sepp turned to Joachim. "Let's get back to work before he talks me into it."

The earth they had excavated from the incline to the tunnel entrance stood in a heap to one side of the hole. While Sepp transferred that over against the wall where they intended to pile the earth, Joachim began work on the tunnel itself. At first it was only a matter of breaking the earth away from the face of the entrance and shoveling it up to Sepp. He worked the spade rhythmically, driving in the blade upside down, breaking away the earth in clumps, shoveling it up to the floor level. Within a short time, however, he was forced to squat down in order to get his spade into the opening he had made. His leg muscles began to ache and his toes hurt and he found it difficult to keep his balance.

"I guess I'll have to sit," he told Sepp.

"How do you feel?"

"Oh, I can go on for hours," he said airily. "This ground is damp, though. What's there to sit on?"

"There's a piece of tarpaulin over by the tools. You'll be on your back soon. I'll bring over the sled, too. We may as well try it out."

The heat of the day had begun to penetrate the old walls of the building. Joachim wiped the sweat from his forehead and discovered his shirt was soaked with sweat under his arms and down his back. The sound of work from the first floor had become normal background noise. They had expanded the hole in the ceiling to about four meters long by three meters wide. About ten planks lay piled atop one another like pick-up sticks on the cellar floor. Around the holes where the nails had been, the wood was starkly white against the dark, worn surfaces of the planks. The nail holes looked like the staring eyes of dead fish cast up on the beach by a storm. Through the hole in the floor above, broken into long rectangles of space by the joists still in place, Joachim could see their feet coming and going, and the occasional dark claws of a crowbar. The rhythmic *putt-putt* of the generator was muted now with the hose Emerich had installed siphoning off the exhaust. Joachim felt as if he had been in the cellar much longer than just a few hours. The odor of the moldering rocks and rat dung retreated before the vaguely pleasing smell of the freshly turned earth. The suspended pools of light around the bare lightbulbs cast a dull, melancholy aura over the center of the room, leaving the walls and corners in translucent shadow.

Sepp came back, pulling the sled by a knotted rope. He handed down the tarpaulin and a short-handled spade. "This will be easier to work with."

Joachim unfolded the tarpaulin to a double thickness and laid it out on the ground. He handed up the long spade. Sepp brought the sled down the incline into the tunnel, and they positioned it with the wider end opening up against the wall of earth to be dug out, the narrower end facing out. Joachim sat on the tarpaulin, his head still outside the shallow cut he had made into the tunnel, his legs bent and spread on either side of the sled. The sled was designed with the sides slanting up and outward to a width of exactly one meter. This would serve not only as a means of catching the earth dislodged by the spade but also as a way of maintaining the proper and constant width of the tunnel as they dug. The forward, wider end of the sled was open, and a narrow lip across the front slanted slightly downward from the bed of the sled so that the leading edge would lie flat across the floor of the tunnel. At its widest point, in front, a portion of each side was hinged so that it could be folded up and locked in place with a latch. This was necessary in order to clear the shoring struts when they were placed and the sled was being hauled in and out of the tunnel.

"How does it feel?" Sepp asked him.

"All right." He drove the spade into the earth and, twisting it, sent earth spilling into the sled. As he dug, he scraped the earth in the sled back toward him, filling the narrower end first. Ten minutes later, when the sled was filled, he looked up at Sepp. "Now what?"

"Move the sled back. I'll pull it out."

"When we're well inside the tunnel, there won't be enough headroom to climb over the sled."

"If we don't pile it so high, we'll be able to do it."

"The less we put in each sled, the longer it will take."

"If it's a choice between smaller sled loads and using only one sled, I'd opt for smaller loads, wouldn't you?"

Joachim had to agree. "Maybe we should make the tunnel bigger. There's going to be damned little space to turn around in there."

"We can't make it bigger. There won't be enough room down here to store the earth. Besides, don't forget that increasing the size of the tunnel by only half a meter means the extra work, and time, of hauling out thirty-seven and a half more cubic meters of earth. And it increases the requirements for shoring lumber. It also weakens the tunnel."

"All right, all right. But how are we going to use two sleds?"

"We can drag the second sled up over the loaded one."

"We can, but the thing will be damned heavy. We'll try it that way and see how it goes."

"Do you want me to work down there for a while?"

"I'll let you know when I've had it."

Sepp dragged out the loaded sled. It was very heavy when loaded, and with the rope over his shoulder, his body bent forward, his head down, his boots digging into the earth at each step, he looked like an ancient Egyptian slave hauling stone for the construction of a pyramid.

Joachim pulled the second sled down the incline and positioned it in the tunnel opening. He lifted it once and found it to be even heavier than he had expected. Sepp had been prudent in using steel plates in its construction, for no doubt the use it would be put to would soon wear out a weaker material. But he found that even with its weight he could maneuver it alone. He sat down and straddled the sled. His head was now just up to the tunnel entrance. He picked up the spade and drove it into the earthen wall. His knuckles scraped the rock at the top of the tunnel entrance. He dropped the spade in pain. "Damn!"

Sepp returned with the emptied sled. "What happened?"

Joachim took off his glove and examined his hand. "I jammed my knuckles on the damned rock." He shook his hand to relieve the pain. "Nothing broken. It just hurts like hell." He looked up at Sepp. He had stripped to the waist but was still sweating.

"I figured we'd have to work lying on our backs," Sepp said.

Joachim was disgusted. He was hot. His hand hurt and he felt dirty already. He hated being dirty. "What time is it?"

Sepp looked at his watch. "Ten fifteen."

"Is that all?"

Sepp laughed.

Joachim didn't see what was so funny. He pulled his shirttails out and tore his shirt and undershirt off over his head. "I thought it would be cool down here."

"It's not bad just standing still."

"That's for me, just standing still." (Or in between cool sheets with an air conditioner going full blast.) "All right, on my back it is." He put on his gloves, took up the spade, and lay back on the canvas. The ground felt cool on his back. In order to see what he was doing, however, he had to raise his head. He sat up again. "I have to have something under my head."

"I thought of that." Sepp went off toward the tool chest.

He thinks of everything, our *Ami* friend does, a most provident leader, thought Joachim. I wonder how he does with women. He looks as though he'd do all right. Probably the loyal type. Stupid to leave his girl in the *Sektor*, though. All this for a woman. She must be something.

Sepp returned with an improvised head support made of wood with cloth padding nailed to the top. "Try it."

Joachim lay back and placed the support under his head. *"Formidable."*

"It's a picnic," Sepp said.

"A picnic."

In the next hour, Joachim filled six sleds with earth, opening the tunnel to a depth of one meter. The walls and ceiling were still rough, however, not shaped level and smooth enough to accommodate the shoring. As he worked, loose bits of earth fell from overhead onto his face and over his body, and, dissolved in the sweat on his chest, stomach, and arms, the dirt turned to a thin coating of slime. At first he would wipe it off, but it was an endless task and finally he simply accepted it. Even now, working underground in the tunnel, he was hot and sweating profusely. The coolness of the tarpaulin under his back had long ago been dissipated, except at the beginning of each new sled load, when he moved the tarpaulin forward a little and the newly exposed ground under his buttocks felt cool. But that would last only a minute or two. Earth got into his nose and mouth. Mixed with the sweat from his forehead, it came oozing over his eyebrows and eyelids into his eyes. It was thick as gravel in his boots and gritty as sandpaper against his back and under his belt. His hair became sticky with sweat and earth. He was constantly blowing out his nose, and spitting, and blinking to make tears to wash out his eyes.

After filling the sixth sled, he lay back to rest. His arms felt as heavy and hard as rocks. Despite the head support, his neck ached, and his legs were stiff from the cramped position he had to keep them in.

He heard Sepp moving across the earthen floor. "Had enough?"

"I surrender."

Sepp was sweating heavily, too. He had tied a handkerchief around his forehead to keep the sweat out of his eyes. It was soaked through and smeared with dirt. "I'll give it a try," he offered.

"I don't know if I can move."

Sepp smiled sympathetically. "It won't be so bad tomorrow—I hope."

"It's not tomorrow I'm worried about. It's this afternoon."

Sepp pointed a thumb toward the ceiling. "There are four others eager to take your place."

Joachim grinned. "I'd forgotten about them." With an effort he got to his feet and stood surveying their work. Sepp had moved most of the earth over against the wall. There were shallow ruts in the soft surface of the floor where he had dragged the sled back and forth. The musty smell of the earth was strong in the air. The dent he had made in the tunnel seemed small. "Not much to show for a morning's work."

"You've dug out at least a meter in the past hour. At that rate, we'll be through in seventy-five hours. That's only eight or nine days of work."

"Do you think we'll be finished so soon?"

"Maybe."

"It's going to get crowded in there. When do we start shoring?"

"As soon as the tunnel is long enough—another couple of meters."

Joachim took off his gloves. His hands were cramped and stiff. He put a finger in his ear and brought out a fingernail full of dirt. He looked himself over. "People pay good money at spas for a mud bath like this."

"They say it's good for the skin."

"Do you mean to say I have skin under here?" Joachim drew designs in the mud on his stomach. "It's like finger painting. Maybe the women would go for that." He put on a French accent. "Ah, *chérie,* let me feengair-paint a peecture of my great love for you een zee mud on my baylee!" Sepp laughed. From above, came the sound of a toilet flushing. Joachim looked up. "Somebody doesn't think much of my humor."

"He's got it working." Sepp was excited. He headed for the stairs, taking them two at a time.

Joachim sighed. "Toilets. Who can get excited about toilets?" He slouched down against the wall, closed his eyes, and sighed. Every muscle of his body was aching. Two weeks of this? I'll never make it. Never.

10

"THEY'LL be haying at home," Emerich said. "A hot day like this is perfect for haying." He thought of the farm. He could see his father, his dark face screwed up in a squint under the old black felt hat he always wore, spreading the cut hay over the stubble with the long-tined pitchfork. "Now there's a dusty job. Lord, is that not the dustiest job You have set down for man to do?"

"We cut hay once," Wolf said. "Our Young Pioneer Club cut hay on a collective farm up in Mecklenburg."

They were eating lunch, sitting in the shade along the wall in the alley. It was quiet there. The machinery in the factory had been shut down, but none of the workers had come out to the alley to eat. They probably had a lunchroom in the factory.

They had each washed at the water pipe and combed their hair and put their shirts back on. Sitting in a row in the shade, they reminded Emerich of birds on a fence. You could pick us off—bang, bang—just like that. Not one would have the energy to fly. He knew his own fatigue was from lack of sleep. As he had expected, he had been unable to drop off and had lain for hours thinking about the tunnel, about the day when it would be finished and his family would be with him again, free.

"Do you think your people will get a farm over here, Emerich?" Wolf asked.

"You can stake your life on it."

Joachim stood up and stretched. "There are already too many farmers." Before Emerich could retort, Joachim said, "Oh, oh, here comes somebody."

Everyone started to get up.

"Sit down!" Sepp hissed. "You'll only arouse suspicion."

A man appeared from behind Bruno's car and came forward. He was dressed like a worker, and Emerich guessed he was from the factory. He gave them all a one-fingered salute and a toothless grin.

"What are you people up to in there?" He addressed his question to Joachim, apparently because he was standing. Without teeth, he lisped. Also adding to his difficulty in speaking was a cud of snuff stuffed behind his lower lip that he kept working on. He spit, speckling the side of the building with the juice.

"We're remodeling," Joachim answered.

"This old barn?" He shook his head and gazed up its stucco facade to the overhang of the tile roof. "Ain't worth it, I'd of thought."

"Nobody asked," Emerich said.

The fellow thought about that and grinned. "True." He spit again, sending the stream of brown juice in a great arc up against the building.

"What're *you* up to?" Emerich demanded curtly.

"Me?"

"It's you I'm looking at, isn't it?"

"I work in there," he said, pointing to the factory.

"What happened to your teeth?"

He put his hand to his mouth. "I had to leave 'em at the clinic. They're too tight, you know. They hurt my mouth. Supposed to get 'em tomorrow."

"In the meantime, you ought to keep your mouth shut."

The man's expression did not conceal his hurt feelings. Emerich was not chastened. He knew the type, the old factory hand who still had the same job he had started with thirty years ago because he was too stupid to learn anything else and spent too much time poking his nose into other people's business. Even now, the insult already forgotten, he was trying to peer through the cracks in the boards over the window.

"Do you see the rats?" Emerich asked him.

"Rats?" He backed off, his eyes growing big. "You got rats in there?"

"Some as big as dogs, with teeth as long as my finger."

At the mention of teeth again, the man put his hand to his mouth. He backed away farther, eyeing them all to see if it were true. No one denied it.

"Rats carry the plague, you know," Joachim said.

"The plague?"

"The Black Death."

"Your teeth fall out," Emerich said. "With you, it wouldn't be so bad. You wouldn't have to go through that before you bought it—only the black, blistering skin and the convulsions."

By now, the fellow had backed up all the way to the rear of Bruno's car, and it was a draw between him and the others as to who was more relieved to hear the factory bell ring, sounding the end of the lunch period. He bade them a hurried *"auf Wiedersehen"* and disappeared on the run around the corner of the building.

Once he was out of sight, they all laughed.

"Do you think he actually believed all that?" Bruno asked.

"He believed it," Emerich assured him. "There are people like him in every factory."

"You know," Joachim said, "everything we told him, except for the symptoms, was true."

"What do you mean?" Georg demanded, licking the last crumbs from a piece of bread from his small, plump lips. "There's no plague anymore."

"Of course there is," Emerich countered. "We had a case in our village a few years back. Fleas carry it, especially fleas from rats."

"Then you were serious this morning," Wolf said. He looked worried.

"Only partly," Emerich said. Wolf had struck him as a good sort, and Emerich did not want to take out on him any animosity he felt for his brother. "All those maladies are pretty rare nowadays."

"Practically nonexistent," Joachim put in. "Don't worry about it, Wolf."

"But stay away from the rats," Emerich warned him.

Sepp got up. "We'd better get back to it, rats or no rats."

The others got up slowly, reluctant to yield the last few minutes of rest. Wolf came over to Emerich, his expression still troubled. "Did someone in your village really get the plague?"

Emerich nodded. "It's true. He didn't die, though. They have a cure for it now. But he was very sick for days. Every so often we'd hear of a case in another village somewhere."

"He didn't die, though," Wolf repeated.

"He didn't die."

The boy looked relieved.

They filed into the old warehouse. Emerich thought of the man in his village who had gotten the plague. He hadn't thought of that in years. When the village came to mind, it was usually the pleasant things he remembered. He recalled the song of the plowshare, smelled the rough odor of the soil once again, and he suddenly felt alone, as isolated from the world as though he had been shipwrecked on an uncharted Pacific island. His yearning for the farm, for the village on the Mulde where he had left behind everyone and everything he loved became a physical ache. He caught up with Sepp going downstairs. "Let me dig now."

His friend explored his face and perhaps understood what he was feeling. "All right, Joachim can take your place upstairs."

Joachim agreed readily. "You ought to feel right at home in the hole." In his jibe he did not realize how close to the truth he had come, and went away looking puzzled by Emerich's smile. Sepp led the way down the steps. The rats had come out of hiding during the lunch hour and now set up a chorus of squeaking as they scurried back into their holes.

"I'm afraid we scared the youngster," Emerich said.

Sepp nodded. "He'll get over it. He's going to be all right." The way he said it, he meant that Wolf was going to be a good worker, was going to work out well in the group. Emerich had to agree that that, too, had been his initial impression.

Sepp explained the system of digging he and Joachim were using. The tunnel was about a meter and a half deep now, deep enough so that they had had to hook up the first light of the string that eventually would run through the entire length of the tunnel. The bulb hung from a long spike pushed up into the soft earth at the ceiling line of the tunnel. Emerich crawled in and positioned himself on his back, his legs straddling the sled, his head propped up on the makeshift support. The hole smelled of the damp earth. It was not the friendly, warm, sour smell of his Saxon soil, but the similarity was enough to bring joy to his spirit. He broke off a handful from the wall and pressed it through his fingers. It was clayey and gritty. Never grow even a turnip in this, he thought. Not even weeds. There's no humus at all, not a trace of it. You would think that after seven hundred years of living and dying, there would be some humus in the soil of Berlin, even this far down.

He drove the spade into the wall of earth before him and broke it loose. It fell into the sled in clods. Ah, that feels good, he thought. Again the spade pierced the earth. He worked hard and fast, whittling away the earth, filling the sled quickly. His arms and hands set up a steady beat to the music of the earth, which swelled to symphonic splendor in the tiny chamber. He listened to it as attentively and skillfully as would a critic to the Berlin Philharmonic. Two hundred generations of Webers stroked the violins and cellos. His father's thick arm drew the bow across the strings of the bass viol, and Council President Steigler sounded the brassy counterpoint of the trumpet. The minister conducted, of course, his baton slashing the air, counting the beat, the steady beat of Emerich's spade —*thunk . . . thunk . . . thunk*—driving into the earth.

Sweaty, filthy, tasting the dirt, blinking it out of his eyes, blowing it from his nose, fingering it out of his ears, he emerged an hour later invigorated, excited, too content to feel any pain from the work. He smiled gloriously.

"Joachim was right," Sepp said.

Emerich nodded, grinning, the joy of the work too much to contain.

"Right about what?" Joachim appeared at the foot of the stairwell, wiping the sweat from his chest, peering through the glare the naked bulbs made.

"He's a born mole," Sepp said. "He filled seven sleds in an hour."

"We ought to award him a medal of some kind."

Emerich was determined not to let Joachim bait him. At this moment he felt much too good to let anyone spoil it, least of all Joachim Lentz. He picked up his shirt and undershirt. "I'll have to be getting along," he said.

"From one hole to another, eh, peasant?"

Despite his determination, Emerich felt the joy draining away. Joachim worked a chemistry on him that he could not control. "The factory is not a hole. It's a clean place with good people working there, productive people."

Joachim, grinning, appraised him as he would a purchase he was about to make. "Come on, I'll give you a lift."

Emerich had forgotten that Joachim had to go to work, too. Now he did not know whether or not his pride would allow him to accept the offer. His consternation was compounded by Joachim's sudden departure. He had turned back up the steps without waiting for a reply.

"Now how do you figure that?"

Sepp shrugged.

"Should I take him up on it?"

"I don't see why not."

"I wish I had a good reason not to. He's not doing this out of simple generosity, you know."

Sepp gave him a weary look. "He's only giving you a ride, not offering you the car."

"Um, maybe." Emerich wondered if he were being too harsh in his judgment. But suspicion was too deeply fixed in his character to be dispelled easily. And more often than not, he had been right. However, he decided that he would only look foolish and petty if he refused Joachim's offer. Damn the man, anyway. He'd rather have him hostile than suddenly kind. At least he'd know how to handle him then.

He left, wondering what Joachim had in store for him. But he was disappointed. The ride to the factory was taken up with small talk about the tunnel, and Emerich had to consider the possibility that he had been wrong about Joachim Lentz. It would take a while, though. His feeling of suspicion was too strong to be ignored.

11

ꝋꝋꝋꝋꝋꝋꝋꝋꝋꝋꝋꝋꝋꝋꝋꝋꝋꝋꝋꝋꝋꝋꝋꝋꝋ

A S he approached the garden wall, Bruno could hear Frieda and Grupmann talking. It always amazed him how they chattered—like two birds. With what words did they fill the void for hours on end, drinking cup after cup of coffee at the table under the big oak? He paused at the gate, not to eavesdrop but to collect his thoughts. Grupmann could have only one purpose in coming—to implore him to produce. He would not scold or flatter or beg; Alfred Grupmann was too clever for such pedestrian tactics. But implore he would, in his own way. And there would have to be an answer, a promise of something. Bruno knew that he could not let Grupmann leave empty-handed.

Would Grupmann chide him about the tunnel? He inspected his dusty clothing, the scuffed, soiled boots, his scratched hands full of tiny black splinters—how ironic not to have thought of gloves to protect his hands.

Had Frieda called Grupmann and asked him to come? Probably. It was typical of her to connive in this way when her importunities and tears failed with him. Grupmann had always been as amenable an ally to Frieda as he had been Bruno's devoted friend. The roles complemented one another, and with the deftness of a master Grupmann would lay on his paint so as to bring about a composition of pleasing harmony. With a tired sigh, Bruno entered the garden.

The conversation stopped. They looked up—two birds

alert to the intrusion, dropped words scattered like crumbs around them.

"Look who is here, Bruno."

"What a pleasant surprise."

Grupmann got up. With his pointed ears, tufts of gray hair standing on end, tiny nose, and big eyes bright with the low sun reflected from them, he was every bit an owl. And Frieda? A sandpiper, with her nervous hands flickering about, her little mouth pecking at the moment. The two men shook hands.

"You're looking splendid, Bruno."

"And you, Alfred. You never change."

"Why should I change? I like me the way I am."

"The whole world likes you the way you are."

Bruno gave his wife a perfunctory kiss. "How gay you look, my dear."

"Alfred's visits always make me happy."

Ah, it begins. "You're staying for dinner?"

"Of course he's staying for dinner. I won't let him get away so easily."

Grupmann bowed floridly. "Madam, your cooking is challenged only by your graciousness."

"And your turn of words, Alfred," Bruno interposed, "only by my stink. If you'll excuse me, I'll clean up and join you for a drink."

"Must you use such words?" Frieda implored. And to Grupmann: "He has a penchant for the vulgar, I think."

Grupmann ignored her. "Take your time, Bruno. Take your time."

"I always do, don't I? By now I must have a reputation for it." Whatever quality of humor he might have hoped for was lacking.

In the shower, he let the water run as hot as he could bear it, and repented his hostility. Grupmann had never once given him cause to be rude. Perhaps it's only fatigue, he thought. How these old bones do ache, how my nerves stand on end, vibrating like a tuning fork. Two weeks of this? And I've yet to take my stint at the digging. Madness. For what purpose? What did I expect? A revelation? A vision? Catharsis? Will God reach down His bony finger to inscribe a message in the dust for me? How does it go? "Vanity of vanities, all is vanity." No, it wasn't that sort of thing I had in mind, not that at all.

It was over two years ago that he had met Sepp at his Berlin show. It was the second week after the elegant preopening reception to which West Berlin's social and political elite had come to pay him lavish homage, after the generous, often extravagant reviews had thrust him unchallenged to the pinnacle of German art, after the last painting had been sold at a price inflated by his fame and Grupmann's promotion that Bruno returned on a Thursday afternoon to take a last look at his work.

The gallery held only a few people strolling through as though they had been chased in out of the rain and were merely passing time, waiting for the chance to resume their usual activities. The American soldier caught his eye. He was so intent, as though he were actually enjoying the painting he was studying. It happened to be a boating scene on the Havel that Bruno had done in three days' time—very fast for him. He remembered that his intention had been to capture the archetypal impression he had had seeing the boats on the water. He had thought of all the boats men had paddled, poled, sailed, and propelled since the first crude hollow log; of their sense of pride in their ability to master the water. He had wanted to convey his feeling that those prosperous, civilized Berliners out on the Havel were not far removed from Paleolithic man, not far removed at all.

As he took up a position beside and a little behind the American, he was oddly pleased to see that the fellow gave him no ground, as if to say, "You can have it to yourself when I am done—but I am not yet done." Still, there was a connection established between them, that vibration which sets itself up between two people who experience an identity of purpose.

Bruno made his play. "Well, what do you suppose is so great about this one? Looks very ordinary to me."

The young man turned his eyes on Bruno's, and a smile broke slowly across his face. "Two sins in one: dishonesty and deceit, Herr Balderbach."

Bruno was mortified. His jaw dropped, and suddenly the two of them were laughing hilariously.

"Of all people to recognize me! An American! I'll never do that again!"

"But doing it must have brought you many moments of amusement."

"And anger, don't leave out the anger. But tell me, how did you know?"

"I bought one of your paintings when I was ten years old. It cost me twenty dollars."

"Twenty dollars—that's eighty marks. I hope you still have it; it's worth a hundred times that now. Ten years old. Precocious type, were you? Which painting is it?"

"It doesn't have a title and it's not catalogued. I call it *The White Deer*."

He thought a moment. "I know the one, I know it well." Bruno was becoming excited. "Yes, yes, I painted that centuries ago. I rather liked it then—I wonder if I still would."

"Would you like to see it? I have it with me here in Berlin."

"Here? In Berlin? Yes, yes, I'd love to see it. I wonder how that painting ever passed from my hands to yours."

"I found it in a curiosity shop on Third Avenue in New York. Do you know the story of Bambi? The children's story? I was crazy about that story, and when I saw your painting, the deer was Bambi to me. My father let me buy it. It took almost all my savings."

"But how unusual, how extraordinary!"

They chatted a while longer. They went out together for a drink that extended into dinner. Afterward, they went to Sepp's room in Kreuzberg to look at the painting.

"Not bad," Bruno mused, examining it critically, "not bad at all. It's more like some of my newer stuff than I might have hoped."

"It deserves a better frame," Sepp said. "This is the same one it had when I bought it."

Bruno had to agree. It was an old, cheap plaster frame, chipped here and there, painted a dirty gold. The ornate scrollwork and filigree detracted from the simplicity of the painting.

"I suspect," Bruno ventured, "the shopkeeper considered the frame worth more than the painting at the time. Do you suppose he ever found out what a dreadful mistake he'd made?"

"I was tempted more than once to go back and tell him about it," Sepp said, "but I never had the heart."

Ah, Bruno thought, a man of sensitivity.

In the year that followed, Sepp and Ilse came to dinner

on occasion. Sometimes they would have tickets to the Philharmonic or the opera, and they were fond of picnics in the Grunewald. They became friends, but they were never what you would call close.

Still, it was Sepp and Ilse they thought of first that Sunday morning when they heard about The Wall. "Oh, dear God," Frieda exclaimed, "do you suppose she's over there? Oh, Bruno, they're so much in love. Such a lovely couple. Oh, those swine, those horrid, horrid swine!" For four days she kept calling Sepp until at last he called them and told them what had happened. Ilse was indeed trapped behind The Wall, and he was helpless to do anything to save her. Frieda's anguish was genuine and surprising. "Bruno, we must *do* something. Isn't there anything we can do? Don't you know someone high up who could help?"

He was acquainted with many people in the Berlin municipal government, but he knew there was nothing they could do. To appease her anxiety, he had spoken to a few friends in Schöneberg, but it was, as he had expected, fruitless.

Gradually Sepp drifted out of their lives. By Christmas they had not seen him for three months. A card arrived two days late with a hastily scrawled note: *Have a joyous Christmas. I think of you often. Have been very busy. Affectionately, Sepp.* Busy doing what? Bruno wondered. He and Frieda were both disappointed at Sepp's curtness —Frieda particularly, since she had created in her mind a much closer relationship between them than had in fact existed.

It was April before Sepp turned up at the house again. Frieda was visiting her sister in Erlangen, and Bruno, idle, unable to work, welcomed the visit. He got out a bottle of Scotch and they sat in the garden. The tulips and hyacinths were in bloom, and the roses had sprouted their first leaves. The late-afternoon sun filtered through the newly leafed branches of the oak, casting lacework shadows on the pebbled walks.

"I always loved this spot," Sepp said. He had changed, yet he was the same. Somehow he looked older, although when he smiled, it was still the same friendly smile. His conversation was as lively and responsive as before, except that occasionally he would appear distracted, as if by some distant sound he could not be certain he was hearing. His hair was longer but neatly trimmed, and though he seemed as sturdy and vigorous as always, his face was thinner and paler. The winter, perhaps, Bruno thought. None of us looks our best at the end of a long winter, and for Sepp this has surely been a long one.

"Tell me what you have been doing. What news from Ilse?"

"I don't want to keep you from your work."

"My work? Ha! That's a good one. I haven't done any work in almost three months. It's what is known as an artistic hiatus, a euphemism for no inspiration. I think I'm supposed to be in transition from one period to another, you know, like Picasso from the blue period to the rose or from realism to cubism. The only trouble is, I don't know what period I've been in for twenty-five years, so I haven't the faintest notion where I'm expected to go!"

Sepp laughed. "I had no idea. I thought each painting was an entire unto itself, that style evolved from one to the next imperceptibly, albeit consciously."

"Oh, don't omit the unconscious. Some of today's foremost artists paint unconsciously, especially in your country!" Sepp laughed again. Bruno never fancied himself a wit. It seemed that Sepp drew it out of him. He felt voluble and keen when they talked, and he realized how much he had missed the fellow. "It's fortunate Frieda isn't here. She's terribly put out with you for having neglected us."

"Yes, yes . . . I imagine she is. . . ." He caught his thoughts drifting. "On the contrary, I wish she were here. I'd hoped to see her again as well, and to apologize."

"Waste no words on apologies. Instead, tell me about yourself. What have you been up to?"

Sepp took a long drink of his Scotch. "I'm going to try to get Ilse out of the *Sektor,* Bruno."

"Officially or unofficially?"

"If there were an official way, I'd use it."

"It's a dangerous idea."

"But worth the risk. I know. I've tried living without her for almost a year now. The voice commanding me to endure was becoming feebler every day—until I decided to do something about it."

"And what have you decided to do?"

"Dig a tunnel."

"Ah."

"I've considered everything else I could think of, every ruse, every trick I've ever heard of. A tunnel requires the most work, but it offers the best chance of success."

"What can I do to help?"

Sepp seemed surprised. "You? Why . . . nothing. I didn't come to ask for help." He searched Bruno's face as if seeking out the artist's intent. "It's good of you, Bruno. I appreciate the offer, but there really is nothing."

"I have two hands."

"Two hands to paint with."

"But I am not painting."

Sepp obviously had not expected Bruno's offer and was not certain whether it was genuine or merely a gesture he was supposed to have sense enough to reject. "I'm recruiting students, people . . . my age. The work will be hard and dirty and, as you said, a little dangerous. It is not the sort of thing for a man of your . . . stature."

"You were going to say a man of my age."

"There is that, too," Sepp admitted.

"Surely I don't seem so old to you."

"Bruno, Bruno, render unto Caesar the things which are Caesar's."

Bruno's offer to help had been impulsive. But the more he thought about it, the more inclined he was toward the idea. He needed to escape his daily lethargy, his useless contemplation of times past and the void of the future. And more, he needed to release himself from the process of involution which was slowly devouring his spirit and emasculating his talent. "At times," he said, "it is good for men, especially men of . . . what is properly modest?— men of note?—to retreat, to return to the beginning and renew their acquaintance with what they once were. Wasn't it Machiavelli who recommended that princes withdraw from affairs of state every so often to contemplate, to gather up new ideas, new energy in order to return to their pursuits refreshed? Perhaps this would be just the thing I need to get me back to work."

Yes, that was what it had been—a return to the beginning, a return to the innocence of hard physical labor, labor totally divorced from the intellect, but labor with a purpose. Sounds rather Communistic, somehow, he thought, like the time Russian students must put in on farms and in factories before they take up their intellectual careers. Maybe there's something to it. There are aches and pains to it, I can attest to that.

Out of the shower, he put on clean clothes and headed for the garden. He felt much better. The hot water had soothed his muscles, and his reflections had renewed his confidence in his new involvement. If he was wrong, if after two weeks nothing was solved and he still could not paint, then he would have the satisfaction of having helped those poor people escape from the *Sektor*.

Twilight had settled comfortably over the garden, where Bruno found Grupmann alone with the brandy. Bruno poured a glass and eased himself into a chair.

Grupmann raised his glass. "To you, Bruno. May you live to be a hundred and read about yourself in the art history books."

"I will be content to survive the day."

"Then you do care about survival."

Such crudeness was out of character for Grupmann. Bruno wondered if the man were actually worried. He doubted it. Grupmann had more sense. Bruno attributed the remark to his loyalty to Frieda, a commitment he had made earlier and was now delivering on. That was all it was, nothing serious.

"*Ach,* Alfred, don't fret." He patted his friend's arm. "I will paint again. Let me do this tunnel thing, let me make a fool of myself, then I will paint for you again."

"You have never painted for *me*." He actually looked hurt, and Bruno was astonished. Grupmann had stainless steel for skin. And gold for a heart.

"No, no, of course not. I apologize, Alfred. That was a careless remark."

"I have always been careful not to press you, Bruno. You know it's not the money. I have money to light cigars with if I choose." He chuckled, coming out of his momentary pout. "And you have not suffered in my care, Bruno, have you?"

"Suffered?"

"Financially."

"No, no, though I wouldn't consider lighting a cigar with a five-mark note—but then, I don't smoke."

Grupmann was suddenly his old solicitous self. "Bruno, Bruno, my friend, you are an artist in the true, great tradition of the word, in the way Leonardo, Dürer, Cézanne were artists. Painting is your heartbeat, your circulatory system. Not to paint is not to live."

"Hyperbole doesn't become you, Alfred. Besides, who says I have stopped painting? A six-month hiatus. What is six months in the life of a man? And if it goes to seven, or eight, or even a year?"

Grupmann looked away, up into the twilight gathering among the branches of the tree. "Artists come into vogue and go out. It has little to do with talent or quality. It is a matter of the public's fickleness."

The impact of Grupmann's observation angered Bruno. "Picasso endures," he snapped.

"You are not Picasso."

It came like a fist driving his stomach against his backbone. He caught his breath and gripped the arms of the chair. Once more he became conscious of the aches in his body, and he felt very tired and very old. He wanted to fight back, to return Grupmann's blow, to accuse, to defy, to . . . explain, but he no longer had the energy. Grupmann is right, of course, I am *not* Picasso. Perhaps I am deluding myself about the tunnel because I really no longer want to paint. But, oh, I *do* want to paint. God knows how I want to. But I have committed myself to the tunnel, to Sepp and the others, and I am stuck with it, as they say.

His anger mellowed. Grupmann had, after all, only spoken the truth. He knew better than anyone the fancies of the public, and Bruno understood that, as always, he only had Bruno's interest at heart. Why shouldn't a painter receive his due while still alive to enjoy it? The romantic notion of posthumous recognition had always infuriated Grupmann. The art historians loved to dig up old, unrecognized masters, to bring their work into vogue, to gloat over their success as if they themselves had painted the work they were hawking. Grupmann might be a hawker, too, but he at least benefited the artist himself, not simply his memory. Of that he was most proud.

Bruno filled their glasses and, lifting his, proposed a

toast: "To the next twelve years of our friendship. May they be as fruitful as the last twelve."

Grupmann worked a smile into his face. "Has it been twelve years, Bruno?"

"Twelve years and a hundred and fifty-seven paintings."

Grupmann raised his eyebrows. "That many? And I had always thought myself so lenient."

They laughed together, but Bruno was troubled and he knew that time was running out. He would have to start painting soon or he would be pushed off the mountain by the crowd of younger men scrambling toward the top.

But first there was the tunnel—he remembered he was to ask Frieda for some old nylons that they could use to make caps.

12

USCHI MYER talked. She talked and talked and talked, and Wolf listened, sometimes hearing what she said, making perfunctory responses, nodding, grunting; sometimes thinking about yesterday. Wolf thought he knew what was under the white dress she was wearing, had seen it all with his own eyes, and it gave him a feeling of superiority. He glanced around at the other couples in the *Konditorei,* all their age, some of whom he knew from school, and for the first time in his life he felt a little smug. He enjoyed the feeling immensely.

"My father is always telling me how different things were when he was a boy. And Mutti is no better. Sometimes you'd think they lived in the Dark Ages. Are your parents like that?"

Wolf had not been listening to the first part of what she was saying, and he was not quite certain what it was all about. "A little," he said noncommittally.

"I think Papa's being a banker has something to do with it. Everyone knows bankers are hopelessly stuffy. My Uncle Rainer says Papa was a septuagenarian at thirty. I can believe it. You'd love my Uncle Rainer. He's terribly intelligent and witty. What does your father do?"

"He's a doctor," Wolf said. "He lives in the *Sektor.* Both my parents live there."

"Gracious. They aren't Communists, are they?"

"No, they're not Communists."

"But what are you doing here if they're over there? How do you live? Oh, you live with relatives, I suppose. Don't you miss them? I'd miss my parents terribly. The filial tie is stronger for a woman, of course."

"Yes, I miss them. I—"

"Isn't it awful living with relatives? Oh, I wouldn't mind living with Uncle Rainer. That would be exciting, but I wouldn't want to be too far away from Papa and Mutti."

"I don't live with relatives—well . . . I mean . . . my brother, Joachim, and I live alone . . . together."

"You have a house all to yourselves?"

"An apartment."

"How exciting! And you take care of him?"

"He's the older."

"Then he takes care of you."

Wolf was mildly indignant. "I don't really need taking care of."

"Oh, *I* do. I'm just a child, really. Every once in a while I play at being an adult, but at the first teensy crisis I go flying back to Mutti. It's a very difficult period, don't you think? Of course, it's terribly adult of me to realize I'm still a child, which makes it quite confusing, not knowing whether I'm being a child acting like an adult or actually an adult even though I'm acting like a child."

Wolf blinked.

"You must know just everything about health and hygiene and first aid, being a physician's son."

"A little."

"It's no wonder you're so healthy. I've observed that children of physicians are always glowing with health. You don't smoke, do you? It stunts growth and causes impotence."

The merest allusion to sex made him nervous. He felt he had to say something to hide his nervousness, but he did not want to encourage her to keep talking about it, either. He knew he could not be so coldly analytical about it as she was.

"I've never heard it causes—"

"And pimples during adolescence. You see, you have no pimples."

"Well, I do have one."

"Neither do I. It's because we don't smoke. Look at

all those people smoking. They're all pimply. Nicotine is a depressant which restricts the diameter of the arteries and veins. The blood can't get through to the skin with its curative powers. Did you know that boys who smoke cannot achieve a complete erection? An erection is caused by the flow of blood in—"

"I know what causes—"

"Certainly if they knew that, they wouldn't smoke."

"I don't think smoking has anything to do with . . . that."

"Don't you? Perhaps it's drinking. Sometimes I get the two confused. You don't drink, do you?"

"Beer, sometimes."

She made a face. "How *can* you? It tastes so awful. Ugh!"

"It tastes all right."

"Men are physiologically adapted to the taste of beer. A man must have invented it. Are you interested in the origin of things? I'm utterly fascinated by stories of how things got started. Do you live by a schedule?"

"A schedule? What sort of schedule?" He felt as if he were in a plane doing loops, flips, and spins.

"I have a schedule. I know exactly what I'll be doing every minute of the day."

"Really?"

"Oh, yes. Name any time and I can tell you what I'll be doing at that time tomorrow. Go ahead. Just any time."

"Four minutes after eleven."

"Morning or night?"

"Morning."

"I'll be at the hairdresser's—ten thirty to eleven thirty. Mutti and I always go to the hairdresser's on Wednesdays."

"Two o'clock in the afternoon."

"Reading—one thirty to three. I'm reading Ortega y Gasset's *Revolt of the Masses*. Have you read it?"

"Ten o'clock at night." He was fascinated.

"I'll be with you."

"Oh?"

"Yes."

"Don't I have anything to say about it?"

"Don't you want to be with me?"

"Yes, of course, but . . . I don't know . . . what if I don't call you? What happens to your schedule then?"

"I've never had to change my schedule."

"Oh."

"You did promise me we would fornicate, and tomorrow will be the first safe day this month." She smiled secretly. "And Mutti is going to Stuttgart with Papa on a business trip. I'll be on my own for three days."

There she goes again, he thought, feeling the blood threatening to rise to his face. He could not get used to the nonchalant way she talked about sex. He assumed it was more adult to talk about it openly that way. His father had always answered his questions forthrightly, using the correct terms. When Wolf was thirteen, Dr. Lentz had given him a book explaining in great detail how babies are conceived and born. He had discussed this with his father at length and come to understand it thoroughly, and there was never any embarrassment between them. It was only recently that he had come to feel this way, and he chided himself for being so sensitive about it. It was clearly a manifestation of his inexperience, and when he blushed he felt like a child, which angered him and made him blush even more. But he still wished she wouldn't talk that way. Maybe I'll get used to it, he thought, but I doubt it. Maybe she's only joking about tomorrow night. She's so cuckoo she might be. Or might not be. He recalled the sight of her body—the breasts that turned up and out, as if they were snubbing one another, the slight bulge of her stomach that invited his touch, the way the rise of her plump thighs stood guard over the tuft of light matted hair between them. His nerves played havoc with his control, and he felt his desire swelling, responding to the involuntary pulsation. He quickly tried to think of something else.

"It's all right for tomorrow night, isn't it?" she was asking.

"Yes, of course."

"You're certain you want to."

"Of course I want to." She had no idea how much he wanted to or how scared he was. If only she would stop *talking* about it. He wondered if girls always talked about it this way. He tried to recall how it was when he talked so freely with his father about the book he had given him, and suddenly realized that Uschi could become pregnant, that what he longed for and what she promised him could end in disaster. His fright turned to terror. "Are you . . . are you sure tomorrow is safe?"

"Oh, definitely. I'm disgustingly regular. You don't think I'd take *that* kind of chance, do you?"

He reminded her that she had been willing to yesterday.

"You'd have had to use a contraceptive, silly."

"Oh."

"I don't like them, do you? It detracts somehow, and I know it makes all the difference in the man's pleasure. I suppose I ought to use pills, but they're quite impossible to get without a prescription, and I doubt dear Dr. Ficht would give me one. He's a sweet old man, but he simply wouldn't understand and he'd go blabbering to Mutti. I wish I had a brother. I'd adore having an older brother. Do you and Joachim get along?"

"We get along fine. He saved my life."

"How exciting! Tell me about it!"

"When we were escaping—"

"You escaped?"

"We swam the river."

"After they put up The Wall?"

"Yes."

"How thrilling!"

"Well, it wasn't exactly thrilling."

"But you must be terribly brave. How did you save his life?"

"*He* saved *my* life. They saw us, and I was shot, and—"

"With a gun?"

"Well . . . yes. I was shot, you see."

"It must have hurt terribly."

"Actually, it didn't hurt at all, I didn't feel it. I mean, there wasn't any pain."

She began to look very strange. She leaned her head on her hand and gazed into his eyes with an odd, faraway look. "Go on."

He told her about what had happened that December night in the Spree. As he talked about it, he realized that for the first time she was not interrupting him. She let him tell the whole story without once saying a word.

When he finished, she continued to gaze at him, then, with a slow, languid movement, she planted a light kiss on his cheek.

"Tomorrow night will be heavenly," she said. "Simply heavenly."

~~~~~~

13

I T was after nine o'clock by the time Joachim left Karl's
studio. He was exhausted. His arms ached, his eyes
burned, his feet hurt, and even though he had used
heavy gloves, he had raised a blister on each hand from
using the spade in the tunnel and the crowbar on the
flooring. Karl had noticed them, of course. His vulture's
eyes missed nothing. He had wanted to know how he'd
got them. Joachim had made up a tale about helping his
landlady put in some trees. Furious, Karl had thrown a
tantrum. He had accused Joachim of carelessness, professional negligence, stupidity, and personal disloyalty. In
his pique he had kept him under the lights in front of
the camera from three thirty until eight thirty without a
break.

Outside, the heat was staggering. Joachim leaned
against the door and closed his eyes. His body sought the
refuge of sleep.

He pulled together the last resources of his energy and
was starting for the car when a man called to him from
a Volkswagen parked across the street. The voice was
familiar, but he could not place it. The man was leaning
out the window, his face unclear in the darkness.

"Who is it?"

"Don't you remember me, Herr Hero?"

Joachim stood on the curb peering through the darkness, trying to make out the man's face. He vaguely
recognized his pale gray eyes, thick yellow curls, and rab-

bit nose. He had not given the news photographer a thought since he had gone to work for Karl—not until yesterday, that is. Joachim felt that thinking about the man must have brought him back into his life. "What brings you here, Herr Brim?"

"I see you found my advice useful."

"I'm very tired, Herr Brim."

"I warned you that Karl is a demanding fellow. He pays well, but he gets more in return—more than he deserves, the little fart." He delivered the epithet with surprising malevolence.

"I thought he was a friend of yours."

"He is, he is. One of my favorites." There was a pause. Joachim wanted to go, but he was curious to find out why Brim was there. "I have lots of friends," he went on. "In fact, I have a *very* good friend who wants to meet you, Herr Hero."

"What are you, Herr Brim, a matchmaker?"

He chuckled. "In a way, in a way. My friends are always on the lookout for talent like yours. Now, the one who wants to meet you is *very* special. You'll like him."

Clearly, Brim wanted Joachim to show an interest, but he was not in the mood to play guessing games. He stepped off the curb, getting out his keys.

"Hold on, Lentz."

"I told you—I'm exhausted, Herr Brim. I'm in no condition to match wits with you, and I'm certainly in no condition to meet any of your friends, not tonight, not even if I wanted to, which I don't."

"Supposing I told you that Walther Curzmann wants to see you? What would you say then, Herr Hero, eh?"

Joachim's thoughts took off like a squadron of jet interceptors. He struggled to recall them, to bring them to earth and reorder them. "The movie director?"

"The movie director."

Walther Curzmann. The name was magic. It stood for quality, innovation, excitement, success in German films. And for money and fame.

"Well?"

"I'd say—when, Herr Brim?"

"That's what I figured you'd say. Tomorrow night, eight o'clock."

"At night?"

"At his home. Do you know where he lives?"

"I can't say I do."

"Suppose I pick you up."

"All right. I live—"

"I know where you live. I've followed your career with interest, Herr Hero." He started the motor. "I'll pick you up at seven thirty. Don't be late."

"I'll be ready."

"*Auf Wiedersehen,* Herr Hero."

"*Auf Wiedersehen,* Herr Matchmaker."

Joachim sat behind the wheel of his car, stupefied. He couldn't believe it. Doubts crowded in and out among the fantasies that unreeled before him.

Walther Curzmann. It was unbelievable. It was. . . .
Walther Curzmann. And he wants to meet *me*.

14

EACH hour that passed brought Georg closer to the dreaded meeting with Klaus. But he came no closer to a solution to his problem. He simply could not figure out what to do, what to tell him. Unless he came up with some hard information, Klaus would have his father fired, perhaps even have his parents arrested and put in prison. Also, he would not pay up, and Georg was down to his last hundred marks.

At times he thought that they would not take action against his parents for fear that he would no longer co-operate with them. Then he would think that they *would*, and hold them for ransom, the ransom being information. It was a deadly game from which he could not withdraw. If only he could think of a way to stall Klaus until the tunnel was finished.

But the tunnel was far from being finished. It was barely begun. Just before noon today, Wednesday, the second day of digging, Sepp had emerged to announce that they were now beyond The Wall—past the ten-meter mark into East Berlin territory. Ten meters in a day and a half. At that rate they would be finished in twelve days—ten days from today. Could he stall Klaus for ten days? What if he couldn't? What if they arrested his parents? The tunnel would be worthless then. Worthless.

As they worked the tunnel, they realized that everything was not going to go as smoothly as they had hoped.

216

Sepp had drawn up a schedule whereby each of them worked an hour digging, an hour hauling out the loaded sleds and returning the empty one to the digger, and two hours on shoring and tearing up flooring and joists and cutting them for shoring. On average, they could fill six sleds an hour, which lengthened the tunnel one meter. The schedule worked out well; the digging rate was what they had anticipated; and they were able to prepare shoring lumber faster than they could use it. The bottleneck was the shoring.

Since a filled sled had to be hauled out every ten minutes and, once emptied, brought back in again, the shorers were constantly interrupted. When an empty sled was being returned to the digger, the shorers could manhandle it past them, but when a full sled was being hauled out, they had to leave the tunnel. Often they would just have gotten struts in place, ready to be pounded flush against the walls, and would have to take them out or delay the digging. It was a constant frustration.

Emerich proposed widening the tunnel by half a meter, which would give the shorers room enough to move aside when the sleds were being taken in and out.

"The shorers are getting nowhere," Emerich argued. It was true that the shoring was falling dangerously behind the digging. When the tunnel was ten meters long, only two meters of it had been shored. So far, there had been no signs of a cave-in, but it had not rained since they had begun digging, either. "If we get one good rain like we had two days ago, we'll be in real trouble. The shoring has got to keep pace with the digging."

Sepp was not in favor of widening the tunnel. "If we widen it, we increase the amount of earth we have to take out. That will take us fifty percent more time."

"Why don't we stop digging and work on the shoring until we catch up?" Wolf suggested.

"That will slow us down," Georg protested. The prospect of taking even longer than they had planned unnerved Georg. "We can't slow down, we just can't."

"The idea is to keep digging and shoring all the time," Emerich argued, "without these damned interruptions. What's going to happen once we're fifty or sixty meters in? It will take so long to get out of the tunnel that by the time we get back to work it will be time to haul out another sled."

"Emerich is probably right," Bruno said. "But if we can avoid widening the tunnel and still achieve the same results, that would be a better alternative."

"What do you have in mind?" Sepp asked.

"We have been thinking only whether it is necessary to widen the tunnel or not. I'm suggesting we think of other possibilities."

"What other possibilities?" Emerich demanded.

"The problem is," Bruno continued, "that the removal of the earth interrupts the shoring crew. The solution is to eliminate the interruption. Correct?"

"Correct."

"Then we should consider a way of reducing the number of times we must haul out the sled."

"If we had more sleds," Wolf offered, "we could fill them all before we hauled them out."

"Where would we put them?"

"Well, the shoring could stay a few meters behind the digging," Wolfe reasoned. "We could use that space— where the shoring hasn't been done—to store the filled sleds."

"What about the empty sleds?" Sepp asked. "Where would we put them?"

"We could hang them from the ceiling," Joachim suggested.

"Or set them up flush against the walls," Wolf said.

"Maybe it would work," Emerich agreed. "If we rigged up some way to hold them along the walls and hung the sleds on sheaves, the digger could just pull them forward as he needed them."

"We could line up four or five loaded sleds and then empty them all at once."

"While the digger was still working, filling another."

"It might work," Sepp agreed. "What do you think, Bruno?"

"How long would it take to make three or four more sleds? If it's going to take several days, it may not be worth the trouble."

"I could do it in a couple of days," Emerich said, "once I had the materials."

"We have enough lumber piled up for shoring," Sepp

said. "If two of us worked on them, we could get them done in one day."

Georg was all for the idea and wanted to get started on it right away, but they had to discuss it all again, elaborating on details, figuring out just how they would hang the empty sleds, what kind of materials they would use and how much they would cost. And then Sepp and Emerich went into the tunnel to take measurements.

"All these delays all the time," Georg complained. "Yesterday it was the generator . . . and the toilet. Today it's this business with the shoring."

"Do you want the thing to cave in?" Joachim demanded sarcastically.

"What difference does it make if we're never going to get it done?"

"You'll know the difference if it ever happens and you're in there."

Georg got up and squatted down at the entrance to the tunnel. Sepp and Emerich were on their knees using a measuring tape. Everybody can be so calm about it, he thought. They don't have somebody like Klaus to worry about. They don't have to wonder if their parents are going to be arrested. Georg looked up at the smoothly shaped ceiling ahead of the shoring. It doesn't look as if it would cave in. I wonder if we even need the shoring. Sepp should have thought about this; he should have realized this would happen. But what does he care? He can take a year to dig the tunnel if he wants to. *Two* years. It doesn't make any difference to him.

Georg picked up a loose clod of earth lying on the tunnel floor and went back up the incline. Bruno, Joachim, Wolf were sitting up against the wall. Bruno's eyes were closed. They were all dirty and sweaty and tired-looking. Bruno had brought some of his wife's old nylons, which they had pulled over their hair and tied in a knot on top. The makeshift caps kept the dirt out of their hair, but they made them look as if they were bald. Wolf had taken his off. He was not wearing gloves, either. This morning he had turned up with an old pair of short leather pants to work in. Georg wondered why it was that Wolf did not like to wear confining articles of clothing. He sat there picking at the blisters on his hands.

"We should have thought about this before we started," Georg said.

Joachim sniffed and gave him a quizzical look. *"We?"*

Bruno opened his eyes and looked up at him. "Did *you* think of it? Did *I?*"

Joachim regarded him out of the corner of his eye. "But *we* didn't plan the tunnel. Sepp did."

"He went over the plans with each of us. If we'd been omniscient"—Bruno enunciated the word with caustic precision—"we'd have recognized this situation at the time."

"I thought everything had been taken care of," Georg said defensively.

"Sepp gave us that impression," Joachim agreed. Georg was comforted having him on his side. Bruno could be overpowering.

"But we left it all to him," Bruno argued. "If he was unable to foresee every single difficulty, we are in no position to blame him."

"One man can't think of everything," Wolf said. He bit into a piece of loose skin on his finger.

"There will be other problems, other delays," Bruno said. "We may as well accept them philosophically."

Georg wanted to ask him what other delays he was talking about, but Sepp and Emerich came out of the tunnel.

"It ought to work," Sepp said.

"It *will* work," Emerich said. "Let's get on with it."

Georg was gratified that somebody else was interested in hurrying. Maybe the peasant wasn't such a bad fellow after all.

As they worked deeper under The Wall, they had to remember to talk as little as possible in the tunnel and then only in a whisper.

"It's crazy," Joachim complained to Georg. "We pound these struts into place with a sledgehammer, and Sepp tells us to whisper."

"But with the sledgehammer padded, it doesn't make much noise. And Sepp says talking is a different kind of sound. Voices carry farther."

"And what about the digging? Do you think that's not noisy?"

"That can't be helped. I think it's sensible. Why take any chances?"

"We're three meters underground. Who can hear us through three meters of earth?"

The rope attached to the sled Wolf was filling, extending out of the tunnel into the cellar, suddenly rose up in a wave between them, the sign that the sled was filled and ready to be hauled out. They picked up the sledgehammer and spade and crawled out into the cellar. Bruno was already at the rope, waiting for them to get out of the way before he started hauling. On the other side of the room, where Sepp and Emerich were fabricating the new sleds, the flame of the oxyacetylene torch sent their shadows undulating fluidly across the wall like ghostly dancers. Bruno slung the rope over his shoulder and began hauling, digging the sides of his boot soles into the earth. It was hard work, and the difficulty was compounded by the necessity of pulling in a straight line so the sled would not go askew and become lodged up against a strut.

"He's not strong enough for that kind of work," Georg whispered.

Joachim took off a glove and wiped the sweat from his face. His hand smeared the sweat and dirt together in a pattern of black and white finger marks. "Nobody's forcing him to be here," he said.

The sled emerged from the mouth of the tunnel. Georg took hold of the rope and helped Bruno drag it out and up the incline and over to the pile. They got hold of the narrow end and tipped the sled up to empty it. Bruno stood for a moment leaning on the upright sled, breathing fast and heavily.

"That's hard work," Georg said.

Bruno nodded. "I'll . . . have to . . . get . . . used to it."

"I'll take it back for you."

The artist nodded wearily. George dragged the empty sled back into the tunnel behind him. He felt good doing Bruno the favor. He hoped he could become friends with him. Ahead, in the glaring light of the naked bulb, Wolf was working, filling the other sled. When Georg reached him, he asked how it was going.

"All right." Wolf paused and wiped the slime from his face. "You know, it's cool when you first come in here, but it gets hot awfully fast."

Georg nodded. "The air is getting foul. We'll all come down with colds, especially if it gets wet in here."

"Maybe it won't rain," Wolf said.

"Maybe." Georg climbed over the empty sled and crawled back to where Joachim was. He had brought in the lumber for the next section of shoring.

"Through chatting, are you?"

"I was only a minute. Your brother's a good worker."

"A man of steel, Wolf is. A man of steel. Let's get this next section started before we have to move again."

They set about installing the shoring. While Georg held the crossbeam up in place, Joachim wedged the two struts under it. While he held the struts in place, Georg slid the planking up over the crossbeam and onto the next crossbeam nearer the entrance. When the planking was in place—three pieces were used, spaced a few centimeters apart—Georg took up the sledgehammer and pounded the base of the struts until they were upright, flush against the wall. They tested their rigidity by trying to jiggle the struts loose.

"Solid," Joachim said.

"That one was easy, wasn't it?"

"Um." Joachim gave him a peculiar look. "Fetch some more lumber."

Georg crawled out of the tunnel and went to the far side of the cellar where Sepp and Emerich were working. They were making a racket pounding the steel plates into shape before welding them together. The clangor hurt Georg's ears, and he put his hands over them. "How's it coming?" he shouted.

Sepp stopped hammering. "What?"

"I said, how's it coming?"

"Oh, fine, fine." He started hammering again. He looked like a blacksmith or an auto body repairman. Georg admired Sepp's and Emerich's ability to shape the sleds from flat sheets of steel. Whenever he saw others undertake work like that, he wondered where they had learned how to do it, or, if they had not learned, how they knew that what they were doing was right.

The hammering stopped. Emerich picked up the oxy-acetylene torch and slipped a pair of goggles down over his eyes. He adjusted the torch, and a bluish-white flame shot out of the nozzle.

Emerich looked up at Georg. "Don't you have anything to do?"

Fascinated, Georg had forgotten about the lumber. "I was just watching," he said. He went to the lumber pile, resenting Emerich. He had no reason to get so huffy, Georg thought. Of course, that's the way he is. Everyone knows he's huffy. And he's only a peasant. He gathered up two struts from the pile, a crossbeam and three pieces of planking. The load was very heavy, and when he carried it like firewood, the edges cut into his arms.

When he reached the tunnel entrance, Joachim was coming out. "Drop it there. Another sled's coming out."

Georg set the lumber down. "Your brother sure is a hard worker."

"You said that before."

"Well, he is."

Bruno started hauling on the rope. This time, Joachim helped him. When the sled was empty, Joachim pushed it back into the tunnel. Georg followed, dragging the lumber behind.

"It was good of you to help Bruno."

Joachim snorted. "I'd like to get this tunnel done sometime this year. Hand me the sledge."

Georg handed him the sledgehammer, wondering if there would ever again be someone like Greta, someone who would make him feel that he counted, someone who cared what he said and felt, who believed that he was worth caring about. He did not dare think about that golden week of happiness. He didn't even dare hold her face in his memory. Quickly he turned his mind to the work at hand.

When they had installed another section of shoring, it was time to change crews. Georg crawled forward to relieve Wolf. "I'll take over now," he whispered.

Wolf looked up at him and nodded. He drove the spade into the earth and sat up. With a grimy handkerchief, he wiped the sweat and dirt from his face. "It's getting a little gravelly," he said. "I'll tell Sepp about it."

"What difference does that make?"

"I don't know. It might mean something, though."

"All right." Georg took off his shirt and undershirt. "Take these back for me, will you?"

Wolf took the clothes and, edging around Georg,

started crawling back toward the cellar. Georg surveyed the work area. The sled Wolf had been filling was half-full. The earth was speckled with small chunks of gravel. In the face of the digging area the gravel was also apparent—yellow nuggets of sandstone strewn through the clay. He brushed off the tarpaulin drop cloth and got down into position. The cloth was cold against his bare back, and his skin turned to gooseflesh. He shivered and quickly got to work.

Georg hated digging. It was not so much the exhausting labor, or the earth dropping down into his eyes, ears, and mouth. The discomfort was secondary to the seclusion which gave him time to think and remember when he did not want to think or remember. He knew he had to think about Friday night, about what he was going to tell Klaus. But he did not have to remember, he did not have to dwell on the memory of the past year. . . .

They took him in a police car to the Marienfelde reception center for refugees, where they dressed his wounds—he had a bad cut on the forehead and had broken his left ring finger. It was strange to discover his injuries, because he had felt no pain. The pain came later, when they put a splint on the finger and taped it. All the time the doctor was working on him, he felt as though the wounds belonged to someone else and he was merely watching that someone else being treated.

Later, there were the questions and the forms to be filled out. Who was he? Why had he crossed over? How? What did he intend to do? Where were his parents? Was he a member of the Communist party. Questions and forms, forms and questions, and then he was given some money—he couldn't recall how much—and a list of places where he might find a room. The people were very kind and helpful and efficient and seemed particularly pleased that he already had a job at the plating factory. They suggested he return to work the next day as usual.

He found a furnished room with board in the home of a Frau Schneider, the widow of a factory worker, in the borough of Wedding. Everyone in the street worked in the factories in West Berlin. It was a drab, uninteresting street full of drab, uninteresting people. He would go to work in the morning, come home to the tiny room on the third floor at night for supper, watch television with Frau Schneider's daughter, Elsbeth, until ten o'clock, when the widow would come home from the neighborhood *Gasthaus* reeking of beer, and then the two women would go off to bed. Then Georg would walk.

He walked the streets with no purpose in mind except to get so tired he would fall asleep the minute he touched his head to the pillow. He would walk on the main streets where there were shops with things in the windows to look at and people to watch. He was careful never to go near The Wall.

Not only has he having trouble sleeping, but his mind would wander at work. Several times he had been reprimanded for inattention. He came to dread work, always wondering if he would be fired that day. The foreman was not interested in his personal problems—all he wanted was a high production record. Even the union steward was unsympathetic. "The union will stand behind you all the way when the company is in the wrong. But when you're in the wrong, my boy, there's nothing we can do for you."

He wrote long letters to his mother and father but never mailed them. He was afraid they would write back, telling him what had happened to Greta, and he dared not find out. Sometimes he could convince himself that she was all right, that the authorities had not done anything to her. Why should they have done anything to her? She was not a threat to them. It was her father they had arrested. She couldn't help it if her father had done something wrong.

But he knew she had been arrested. Undoubtedly she was in prison at that very moment. He would visualize her in a gray prison dress, her hair hanging straight and unwashed, without makeup, her skin sallow from a lack of sun and air. She would be standing in a long line with other women prisoners, shuffling slowly forward, on her face a blank, listless expression of hopelessness. Occasionally she would remember Georg, and then hate would come into her eyes, her lips would form his name— slowly, as if they had his soul clutched between them and were grinding it to oblivion—and then he would hear her screaming his name. *Gee-org!* Her cry would ring in his ears over and over and over until he thought he would go out of his mind.

He tried to reason with himself. What could he have done? It was only by chance that he had been thrown out of the car and she trapped in it. If he had tried to rescue her, surely they both would have been caught. What good would that have done? He might even have been killed, the way those crazy Vopos were firing their guns—it was a miracle he hadn't been. But his reasoning always failed him. He knew that it was only a balm for his conscience, and an ephemeral one at that. If he had really loved Greta, loved her the way that a man truly loves a woman—if he had been a *man*—he would instinctively have gone the other way, toward the car, toward her cry for help, and not away from it toward the safety of the western side of the bridge. For in those frantic moments after the car had crashed, he had acted on instinct and instinct alone. Saving his own skin had been the only thing that mattered. He'd had to run, to get away from the menacing black holes spitting out fire and death.

A whisper behind him broke into his remembrances. Sepp's face appeared, hovering over his. "Wolf told me about the gravel." He looked at the irregular wall before them and at the earth piled high in the sled. "You've loaded that a bit high, haven't you? You'll have a hard time crawling over it."

Georg had not noticed how much he had dug out. In fact, he had not even been aware that he was working. He suddenly felt his arms turn to lead, and he let the spade down on the pile of earth between his legs. "I'll manage all right," he said. Now Sepp was picking on him, too. He didn't want to lose Sepp's friendship. "You're not sore at me, are you?"

"Sore? For what?"

"I didn't mean to pile it too high. I was working faster than I realized, I guess."

Sepp shrugged it off and scooped up a handful of earth. "Is it getting worse?"

Georg hadn't noticed. "It's about the same."

"If it gets more gravelly, use a pointed spade. There's one in the cellar."

"Okay."

"Let me know if it gets worse." Sepp smiled and patted his shoulder. "You're doing fine, Georg, just fine." He left, climbing back over the empty sled behind.

Georg sat up. He was glad Sepp was their leader. He dragged the full sled back far enough to make room for the empty one, then, turning on his stomach, he pulled the empty sled with him up over the top of the full one and maneuvered it into place. He gave the rope attached to the full sled a snap, sending waves along its length. He watched until the rope went taut and the full sled began to move back along the tunnel toward the cellar. He began filling the empty sled.

It was in late September that he began to pay attention to Elsbeth Schneider. She was not a pretty girl. At eighteen she looked twenty-five. She wore too much makeup to cover up a pockmarked face. Her eyes were small and dull, so she tried to enlarge them with eye liner and brighten them with mascara. The effect was grotesque. She looked like a carnival kewpie doll. But her figure was not doll-like. She had enormous breasts, wide shoulders, and spindly legs. When she walked, it always seemed to Georg that she was about to topple over. And she was not very intelligent. Her sole interests were television, popular music, and boys.

But Elsbeth was there at hand, and it was inevitable that with her mother gone every night, leaving the two of them alone, they would end up in bed together. She yielded to his first advances without the slightest hesitation, as if she had been wondering what had taken him so long.

Elsbeth, Georg soon discovered, was a cow and considered him no more than a bull. She demanded no attentions and gave none, so long as each night they performed their sexual ritual, preferably timed so as not to miss the best television programs. After a month of it, Georg despised her—and himself even more.

At first he did not think of Greta. The physical gratification was exciting, and the first week he grew smug and complacent. Then the memory of Greta, frail, lovely, ethereal in her yellow dress, began to intrude. Finally, he saw her, mocking him, every time he looked at Elsbeth.

See what you have to settle for? she seemed to say. See what a cow you have instead of me? See what cowards end up with?

He considered moving out. He was about to many times, but each time he put it off until the next day. Instead, he would not return to the apartment after work until late at night, after the two women had gone to bed. The next evening, Elsbeth would be at him, no longer a cow but a snarling, bawling cat, upbraiding him, accusing him of cheating on her.

With the beginning of the fall term at the university, Georg made his escape. In order to attend lectures during the day, he changed over to the night shift at the factory, working a part-time, four-hour shift. At first Elsbeth was furious, but then he rarely saw her anymore and there was little chance for her to take out her fury on him. Sometimes, when he arrived home from the factory after midnight, she would be up, waiting for him. He would take her to bed, grateful for the release of his pent-up desire, but repelled by her stupid giggling, her cooing of hackneyed words of love and tenderness, her cheap perfume, which failed to hide the fetid smell of her body.

And smell she did, for as the winter came on she refused to budge outside. She sat around the apartment all day, eating and worrying, worrying and eating. She was getting fat. When he told her as much, she blamed him for it. She always ate when she worried, she said. And she was worried.

"What are you worried about?" He didn't care, but he asked it to fill a void.

"About us, naturally, silly. I don't think you love me anymore." She put on a childish, petulant expression.

"*Love* you? Whoever said I loved you?"

"There! You see?"

She was impossible but she was there, and he knew he needed the satisfaction she gave so readily.

By January, the strain of work and study had begun to wear him out. He caught cold easily, slept through lectures, made more mistakes at work. He would come home and collapse on his bed without undressing. If Elsbeth was there waiting, eager to make love, there would be a row because he was too exhausted to satisfy her. She would sit on the bed, pinching him to keep him awake, hissing insults one moment, cooing inanities the next. At last she would give up and leave him, clutching herself in her arms, moaning like the winter wind in the night.

It was the last week of January that he was fired. He'd known it was coming. If he had been the boss, he would have fired himself long ago. The shock was no easier to bear, however, because he had been expecting it. Without his job he could last a month, perhaps two, on his savings. The stipend from the university was not enough to cover his expenses. He thought of his savings in the bank in East Berlin and cursed his stupidity for not having withdrawn them before he fled. Now they were lost to him forever, confiscated by the state. He trudged through the snow, sniffling from his cold, weary to the bone, beaten.

As he approached the subway station, a man came out of the darkness and across the street toward him. When he reached the curb, he waited until Georg came up to him. "Good evening, Georg."

Georg stopped and stared into the man's face. He was quite certain he had never seen him before. In the half-light reflected from the dirty snow, the face struck him as extraordinarily kind and solicitous. "I'm sorry, I don't believe I know you."

"Oh, you don't. But I know you. Yes, indeed, I know you extremely well."

Georg suddenly felt endangered. The man was heavy-set and dark-featured, but he spoke in a cultured manner which was somewhat reassuring. "What is it you want?"

"Just a chat, Georg, just a friendly little chat. You need a friend, Georg, and I am here to befriend you."

"But who are you?"

"You may call me Klaus."

And now he had arrived at this time; after months of deception—clever deception sometimes, he liked to think—he had come to the end of the free ride. He had duped them out of thirteen hundred marks, but there was not to be another thirteen hundred to come. Not a hundred. Not even one. What was to come was as unbearable as the memory of what had passed. He had been the cause of the ruination of the life of one person he loved; he knew he would not survive the knowledge that he was responsible for the destruction of yet two more. If only they could get the tunnel completed quickly, before Klaus began—what was Sepp's saying?—breathing down his neck, the final victory would be his.

After an hour and five and a half sleds filled, Joachim came forward to take over the digging. "It's your turn to rest."

Georg nodded.

"Tell them we need another light in here."

"I'll hook one up."

"All right. Hurry it up. I don't know how you could see what you were doing here. The light is too far back."

"Sitting up, we're blocking it. There's still light when you're lying down."

"Hook up another one, anyway. We'll need it soon enough."

Georg crawled past him over the empty sled and back toward the cellar. Wolf and Bruno were in the tunnel working on a section of shoring.

"How is it coming?" he asked.

A strut on either side was wedged up under the crossbeam at a wide angle, indicating the struts were too long to be pounded into place. They would have to dig out under them.

"Slowly, slowly," Bruno replied. "These struts are like women: They're either too tall or too short, and being fully aware that we must have them, are contrary and willful, refusing to yield to force or supplication." Georg and Wolf laughed. Georg liked Bruno. He would have liked to stay there and talk with him and Wolf, but Joachim would be waiting for the lightbulb.

In the cellar, Sepp and Emerich were still working on the new sleds. A completed one was set to one side, looking much like the excavated jawbone of some giant prehistoric creature. Georg resisted the urge to stand watching them and got a lightbulb-fixture, pliers, screwdriver, and a length of insulated wire from the tool chest.

Bruno and Wolf were pounding away at a strut when he returned.

Ahead, Joachim's steady, slow, rhythmic spadework beat in syncopation with the pounding of the sledgehammer behind. Georg arrived at the second light fixture, at the ten-meter mark, and laid down his equipment.

At that moment, he saw Joachim's spade flash forward and bury itself in the earth; then, almost as if its impact had set off a silent explosion, the ceiling caved in, burying Joachim in an instant.

Instinctively, Georg leaped back, cracking his head. He fell forward and felt his knee come down on the lightbulb he had brought in. The pop it made sounded like a gunshot, and all at once the memory of the terror of the bridge came back like a film unreeled before his eyes. He knelt there, immobilized by the sound of gunfire, the running feet of the Vopos, and Greta's cry echoing through the great cavern of his mind. He relived every moment as if it were happening all over again. The smell of the river and the scorched rubber of the tires were thick in his nostrils; the blinding glare of the sun broke across his vision; and he felt the wind on his face as he ran. The hallucination mounted in intensity, repeating itself over and over, faster and faster.

He was thrust aside against the cool wall of earth. Wolf scrambled over the empty sled. His hands and arms sent earth flying behind him into Georg's face.

"Oh, God." It was Bruno's face, a ghastly mask of horror in the glaucous glare of the bare lightbulb. He was suddenly alongside Wolf, gouging out handfuls of earth, flinging it back over his shoulder. It rattled on the metal of the empty sled. Georg had the sudden thought that they would fill the sled and he would be the one who would have to haul it out. He knew they would expect him to do it. A chunk of gravel struck him under the eye. The shock brought tears to his eyes. He put his arm up to shield his face. He felt a pain in his knee, but he could not remember why it should hurt.

He crouched, staring, as Wolf uncovered Joachim's face. Joachim coughed and gasped. His eyes blinked. Wolf brushed the earth from his face with the tips of his fingers. He did it very gently, very carefully. Joachim spit out earth and moaned.

"You'll be all right, Joachim," Wolf said. "You'll be all right. We'll get you out. You'll be all right."

Wolf was talking out loud. Georg wanted to remind

him to whisper, but his body would not respond to his brain's command.

Suddenly, Sepp was there with Emerich. Sepp crawled forward. "Let me in, Bruno."

Bruno looked up and, nodding, squeezed by Sepp. Sepp took his place, his hands going at the gravelly earth like a machine. Bruno looked at Georg peculiarly, as if he were inquiring whether he was all right.

"Can you drag him out?" Emerich asked.

"We'll try," Sepp said. Joachim's shoulders were uncovered now, and they were trying to get a grip under his arms. "Joachim, can you free your arms?"

He was still gasping, his eyes wide, his head rolling from side to side. Blood oozed from a dozen places on his face. Sepp and Wolf kept up the steady pace, flinging back the earth. When they had his arms free, they tried dragging him out, but the weight of the earth was too great.

"Call an ambulance," Sepp snapped.

Emerich immediately turned around and headed for the cellar.

Georg began to think that they would blame him. He was not certain why, but he knew that they would. He remembered he was about to do something when the ceiling caved in, but he did not know what it was.

"It wasn't my fault," he told Bruno.

Bruno looked at him again in that curious way.

"It wasn't my fault."

"No one said it was your fault."

But they were blaming him. He could tell they were blaming him. Then he remembered, he remembered. "I was going to put in another lightbulb." Frantically, he dug around in the loose earth and found the screwdriver. "Here! You see! I was going to put in a lightbulb."

"Let's try now," Sepp said. They had uncovered Joachim down to the waist. He seemed to be breathing more easily. "We're going to try to drag you out, Joachim. See if you can help us. Try to move your legs."

That was it, Georg remembered. He had not tried to help him. They would blame him for not trying to help him. But it wasn't Joachim, it was Greta, and he couldn't have helped her. He would have been killed if he had tried to help her. They didn't understand that it was Greta, not Joachim. The vision of the bridge came back again, and he was running, running, with her scream chasing him down the long tunnel. . . .

AFTER fifteen minutes of digging, they got Joachim out from under the earth.

Sepp asked him how he felt. He looked groggy.

"I don't know . . . I'm not sure."

"Does it hurt anywhere?" Wolf asked.

"I don't think so."

"We'll haul you out on the sled," Sepp said.

"I think I can crawl."

"No, don't try. Emerich's gone for an ambulance."

They pulled him up onto the earth in the sled. Wolf got behind, to stay with his brother, while Sepp and Bruno crawled ahead to the cellar to haul the sled out. The door opened upstairs, and Emerich came down. "I called from the factory. It's on the way."

"Let's get him out of there." All three got hold of the rope and hauled the sled out of the tunnel and up into the cellar. Wolf came behind, not speaking, staring at his brother.

"Get some water," Sepp said to Emerich. He knelt knelt down beside Joachim. "How do you feel now? Any pain?"

"No."

"He's going to be all right," Wolf said.

Joachim's face and upper body were covered with tiny cuts and scratches in which bits of earth were imbedded. His eyebrows, hair, and ears were full of earth. He raised a hand to wipe his face, but Wolf caught it.

234

"What's wrong?"

"Don't rub your face, Joachim. It's all scratched. You'll make it worse."

Joachim gazed at him for a moment, then closed his eyes.

"They're superficial cuts," Sepp said. "They'll heal in a few days."

Joachim shook his head. "That's not soon enough . . . not soon enough."

"He won't be able to work until they're healed," Wolf explained.

Sepp nodded. "I know." Joachim seemed overly despondent about the loss of a week's work.

Emerich came with a glass of water. Bruno produced a clean handkerchief, and Wolf carefully washed Joachim's face. "We're even now, Wolf," he said. Wolf did not say anything. From the distance came the *hee-haw* of the ambulance horn.

"Where will they take me?"

"There's a hospital in Bernauerstrasse," Emerich said. "It's not far from here."

"I'm all right."

"Maybe you are, maybe you aren't."

The horn sounded close now.

"They'll want to take X rays," Bruno said.

"Where's Georg?" Wolf asked.

"You'd better get upstairs," Sepp told Emerich.

"Right." He ran up the stairs.

"Are you going to let them come down here?" Wolf asked.

"I can walk," Joachim said. He sat up and for the first time noticed how badly he was cut. Again he closed his eyes and gritted his teeth as if he were in great pain.

"Are you sure you can walk?"

The ambulance horn sounded in the alley. Emerich called down the stairs. "Here they come!"

Gingerly, with Wolf and Sepp helping him, Joachim got to his feet. "I'll walk up. Don't let them come down here."

"Be careful," Wolf said.

Joachim smiled weakly. "I will. I'm all right."

"You should go to the hospital for X rays," Bruno said. "There may be internal injuries."

Joachim nodded. "I'll go. Let me go upstairs, though."

They went upstairs, Joachim going slowly and carefully. Sepp began to wonder about the questions they would ask at the hospital. He knew they would want to know exactly what had happened. He supposed they would have to tell them the truth. Outside, the driver and the doctor were getting out of the ambulance. They came over to Joachim, and the doctor looked him over quickly. Men in the factory were crowded in the windows. "What happened?" one called.

"Nothing serious," Emerich told them. "I'll get his shirt," he said to Sepp.

The doctor asked the same question.

"He was excavating for a sewer line in the cellar," Bruno said. "Part of the wall of the trench fell in on him."

"How do you feel?" the doctor asked hm. He was a young man, probably an intern. There was a stethoscope sticking out of his jacket pocket.

"I don't feel any pain, except for these cuts."

"I think it best that you get off your feet. Climb in back there and lie down." The driver opened the rear doors, and Joachim got in.

Emerich came out with Joachim's shirt. He gave it to Wolf.

"I'm his brother. May I go along?"

"Certainly."

"I'll go, too," Bruno said. He glanced at Sepp, and Sepp understood. Bruno got in back with Joachim and Wolf, and the driver closed the doors.

"He's the boss," Sepp said. "He'll tell you whatever you need to know."

"Very well." The doctor and the driver got up into the cab, and the ambulance backed out of the alley. When it reached the street, the horn came on again like the high-low bray of a donkey, an eerie, foreboding sound Sepp had come to associate with movies about Nazis coming to arrest Jews in hiding.

"What happened?" another man from the factory asked.

"He fell," Emerich said. "He'll be all right."

"What are you fellows doing in there?"

"Remodeling," Sepp said.

"Did he break anything?"

Sepp knew the answer he was hoping for and ignored him. He and Emerich went back into the warehouse and closed the door.

"Not enough blood," Emerich said. "They're disappointed." He thumbed his nose at the door. "Now what?"

Sepp gave him a vacant look. "You're always asking good questions."

"How in God's name did it happen?"

"Georg was there. He'd know. I wonder where he went."

"He panicked. The creep."

The epithet irritated Sepp. "How do you know what you would have done under the circumstances?"

"I know what I would have done. Don't try to psychoanalyze Georg for me, and don't make excuses for him. He'll make enough of his own."

Sepp was not going to argue about something he could only speculate about. He left Emerich and headed down the steps to the cellar.

"Where are you going?"

"To take a look at the tunnel."

"Well, wait for me. The damned thing may cave in again. Joachim we can afford to lose, even Georg, but our *führer* is indispensable."

Sepp did not appreciate Emerich's humor. He jumped down into the incline.

"We'll need a flashlight," Emerich said.

"In the tool box." Sepp began crawling forward in the tunnel. Emerich came after him, the flashlight dangling by its ring from his mouth. When Sepp reached the end of the shored area, he stopped. Ahead, two lightbulbs illuminated the length of the unshored tunnel. As far ahead as the cave-in, the ceiling looked as solid as ever. There was no sign that whatever weakness had caused the earth to drop where Joachim had been digging extended back to the area of the ceiling still intact. Sepp proceeded slowly, thumping the earth overhead as he went.

"What are you doing that for?" Emerich whispered.

Sepp was not sure. It gave him a vague sense of safety to hear the solid report of his fist against the compact earth. When he reached the cave-in, he gazed up into the blackness of the gaping hole. There was not enough light to see far into it. Emerich came alongside and looked up. He turned on the flashlight and shone it up into the hole.

"There's a pipe up there, a big concrete pipe. Must be a sewer."

The hole extended up about a meter and a half. At the top they could see the curved bottom of a pipe crossing the tunnel diagonally. They could hear the water running through it.

"That's why it caved in here," Emerich said. "The earth came loose from around the bottom of the pipe."

"Shine the light around the sides."

The hole was the shape of a frustum, smaller at the top near the pipe, spreading outward toward the bottom.

"We'll have to shore up here before we dig anymore," Sepp said.

"Do you think we should fill it in?"

"I don't know."

"If it rains, we could be in for a lot of trouble. It might cause more earth to fall, even make the hole deeper."

Sepp realized that. "The whole damn thing could cave in, rain or no rain, and that would be the end of the tunnel."

"I think we ought to fill it in."

"Have you ever filled in an upside-down hole?"

Emerich made a face. "Good point. How would we do it?"

Sepp had no idea. They were not going to be able to do it just now, anyway. "Let's get the earth out of here first and worry about it later."

Emerich looked apologetic. "I hate to desert you, but the factory calls."

"I'd forgotten. You're probably late already."

"I have a good record. It won't matter if I'm a little late once."

They crawled back out of the tunnel. The heat was stagnant in the cellar. Even the sound of the generator seemed muted under its oppressiveness. They were covered with sweat and grime. Sepp's back and arms ached. He wondered how Emerich was going to take it, working at the factory for eight hours after putting in ten hours here. And with only five or six hours' sleep a night.

"We'll finish the sleds tomorrow," Emerich said. "I'd better wash up now."

"I'll go with you."

They went upstairs to the first floor. The dust was heavy in the air, and the heat was more intense. They skirted the big hole in the floor where the planking had been torn up.

"Do you think you'll ever get Joachim back into the tunnel?" Emerich asked.

"What do you think?"

Emerich shrugged. He turned on the water and put his shaggy head under the pipe. The water came out in a slow stream. Bruno had brought some soap and towels that morning. Emerich soaped himself well and splashed on water to rinse himself off. "It's hard to know what a fellow like Joachim will do. He could use this as an excuse to get out of the digging, even though he might not be afraid. But I doubt that he'll refuse to go back in. He's too proud to admit fear, even to himself."

"Would you be?"

"Afraid?"

"Yes."

"Tough question. I guess it has to happen to you before you know how you'll feel." He rubbed himself dry with a big white towel embroidered with roses. "Bruno must live high. I've never used a towel this thick before. Imagine, all that loot just for painting pictures." He moved out of the way so that Sepp could clean up. "I'd be more concerned about Georg."

"I am concerned about Georg."

"He's a creep, Sepp. Admit it. He's peculiar, messed up psychologically."

"He's been holding up his end."

Emerich did not answer. Sepp let the cold water run over his head. A big puddle was forming at his feet and running in rivulets around the toilet seat.

"I wonder if the old man has dreamed up a good story for the people at the hospital."

"He'll handle it all right."

"You think he's something special."

"Yes."

Emerich considered it. "Maybe."

Sepp dried himself, and they went to the door together.

Emerich took his shirt from a nail by the door and put it on. His briefcase was hanging on another nail.

"It's too bad it happened," he said, "but it happened. What are you going to do?"

"I'll haul the earth out. By the time I've finished, they should be back from the hospital."

"Do you think they'll keep Joachim awhile?"

"It depends on what they find."

"He'll be all right. He has to be. Think of the thousands of women who would suffer if anything should ever happen to Joachim Lentz. God is not so cruel." He grinned and took down his briefcase. "Those factory stiffs will be more curious about us now. We'll have to be on our guard."

Sepp was grateful that Emerich had not expressed the possibility that the tunnel was done for because of the cave-in.

"If Joachim is seriously injured, and if Georg won't come back . . ."

Emerich gave him a confident smile. "We'll still do it, Josep. We'll manage somehow, even if it's only you and I." He started to go. "Be careful down there, my friend. There's no one here to dig *you* out."

"I'll be careful."

After Emerich left, Sepp returned to the tunnel. He worked for two hours hauling out the earth from the cave-in. Then he measured the length of the tunnel, inspected the shoring, and took a compass reading. They were digging almost due east-northeast, at an angle of sixty-six degrees. Sepp set the compass on a box at the entrance to the tunnel and sighted on the flashlight he had placed in the center of the forward face of the tunnel. Taking care to line up the compass carefully with the tunnel entrance, he took a reading. The dial showed sixty-six degrees—they were headed in the right direction, straight for the escape house. He folded the sight and returned the compass to its case. He looked at his watch. It was five thirty.

He retrieved the flashlight and, back in the cellar, he sat down to rest and survey the situation.

The tunnel was thirteen meters, forty centimeters in length.

Four meters had been shored.

One man had almost been killed and was possibly seriously injured.

One had panicked and run off. Whether Georg would come back was anybody's guess.

Only two of the four new sleds had been completed.

And what about fear? What effect would the cave-in have on Joachim, on all of them? He wondered about himself. He knew that every second he had been in the tunnel with Emerich, and later by himself, removing the earth, he had been afraid. Fear drains the body as well as the spirit. Fear could ruin it for them.

And then there was the doubt about Konrad Möss. So far, he had been able to dismiss it as a necessary risk; now that his confidence had collapsed, the doubt became menacing. He imagined all the grotesque possibilities the enemy could pursue. He knew full well they would pursue the most deadly—they would wait until the troop had exhausted themselves in the tunnel, until all the would-be defectors had gathered in one place, filled with the fear and hope of the imminent escape, before they made a convenient mass arrest with the evidence at hand. Sepp had to accept the fact that he would not know whether the risk was warranted until it was too late to do anything about it.

He wondered what the others would think of him if they knew the secret, added danger in which he had placed them. He hated deception, but he was afraid that if he told them about Möss, they would give up the tunnel. That was a greater risk; he would not let it happen. He had told Ilse only so she would be aware of the added danger. But the others had no need to know. They were into it now, and like rats running a maze, they would have to exit at the other end before he would let them out of it. Nothing was going to stop him now—not if Joachim quit, not if Georg did not return, no cave-ins, no fear of his own, no risk, however great, was going to prevent him from completing this tunnel. Nothing.

"Nothing." His voice sounded weak in the dark, silent cellar. It shocked him, and he spoke more forcefully. "Nothing." A rat squeaked from somewhere, mocking his authority.

From above, he heard the sound of a key in the lock and the door opening. He got up and went to the bottom

of the stairs. Bruno, Wolf, and Joachim came in. Sepp
grinned. Joachim was all right, although he looked as if
he were diseased. His face was a panoply of cuts and
scratches, but none of them was bleeding and all seemed
to be minor.

"You're all right."

"Not a bone broken," Bruno said. "Not a bruise on his
innards."

"They said he'd be as good as new in a week," Wolf
said. "He's made of steel."

Joachim laughed, then made a face. "It hurts to laugh.

"Did they take X rays?"

"At least a hundred," Joachim said. "They turned me
ways I've never turned before." He looked around. "Where
are Emerich and Georg?"

"Emerich's gone to work. I don't know where Georg is."

Bruno looked concerned. "He hasn't been back?"

"No."

"Poor bastard," Joachim said. Sepp was surprised.
Joachim sounded as if he were sorry for Georg, rather
than angry at him. "What happened in there?"

"Do you want to take a look?"

Joachim hesitated. "I don't know. I've been thinking
about it ever since we left the hospital. I suppose the only
way to find out is by going in."

"I've been working in there ever since you left, if that
makes you feel any better."

Joachim shrugged. "A little, maybe. It came so fast,
though. Not a second of warning, no sound, no movement, nothing. One minute I was digging; the next I
couldn't breathe. Couldn't see, couldn't move. I don't even
remember seeing the stuff coming down at me."

"It's lucky Wolf and Bruno were in the tunnel at the
time."

Joachim laughed sardonically. "I wonder if Wolf and I
are destined to go through life rescuing each other from
certain death. It could become damned tiresome."

Sepp had to admire Joachim's spirit. Perhaps it was as
Emerich had said, only pride. Whatever it was, Sepp
was glad that he was taking it so well.

"Should we go back to work?" Wolf asked.

"Do you feel like it?"

Wolf did not seem to understand Sepp's question. He

glanced at his brother and then at Bruno. "Sure, I feel like it. We lost a lot of time, didn't we?"

"Now there's sibling sympathy for you!" Joachim put on a hurt look. "Here I am in one piece only by the grace of God, out of work for at least a week—and out of circulation, which is even more disastrous—and all my dear brother regrets is the time we've lost!"

Wolf looked shaken. "I didn't mean it that way, Joachim I—"

Joachim laughed and put his arm around his brother's shoulder. "I was kidding, Wolf, only kidding."

The boy broke away from Joachim's grasp. "It's not funny. You always try to make me feel. . . ." He clenched his teeth, unable to express what he felt.

Joachim was surprised. He stood back and contemplated his brother. "I said I was only kidding."

"All right." Wolf was only slightly mollified.

"What's got into you?"

Wolf shook his head and went off toward the tunnel. Joachim looked at Sepp and Bruno helplessly. Bruno followed Wolf into the tunnel.

"Maybe I ride him too much."

"Maybe."

"Do you think so?"

"It's none of my business. . . ."

"No, tell me, do you think I ride him too much?"

Sepp did not like to become involved in other people's personal affairs. He had learned that it often made things worse, and inevitably, being in the middle, he suffered the antagonism of both sides. "I don't know, Joachim. I don't know either of you well enough to have an idea."

"He's a problem sometimes. I have to be father and mother as well as big brother. In some ways he's still a child; in others, he's very adult. It's maddening—I never know which he'll be from one minute to the next."

"He's doing a good job here. He works hard, he takes it seriously. If all goes well, you'll be able to go back to being just a big brother in a couple of weeks."

Joachim nodded in a distracted way.

Sepp thought about the night before, when he had seen Ilse and gotten her report. Dr. Lentz had been cautious, suspicious, but she had had the feeling she would gain his confidence in time. The Knauers, on the other hand, had been hostile, terrified, and she wasn't hopeful about them at all. Aunt Magda had not been home. Ilse had asked Sepp to get another note, from both Joachim and Georg, and he reminded Joachim of it now. "Don't forget to write another note."

"For the good but cautious doctor?"

"We can't blame him, I suppose."

"When do you need it?"

"Before you leave."

"All right. What should I say this time?"

"Whatever you think will convince him that the note is really from you. Put in some personal item that only your family could possibly know about."

"I'll do it now. Do you have paper and a pencil?"

"In the tool chest."

Joachim started across the room, stopped and turned. "Maybe I'll wait until tomorrow to go back in there. It's almost quitting time now, anyway."

Sepp nodded. "Do it your own way."

"What are you going to do about Georg?"

"I don't know. What do you think?"

"He panicked. Wolf said he froze, looked like he was in a daze. Maybe we're better off without him."

"He was doing all right until this happened," Sepp said.

"He's so damned touchy and defensive. I can't say I like him much."

"Let's see if he comes back tomorrow."

"Why don't you go talk to him—if you can find him."

"Maybe I will," Sepp said halfheartedly.

"I'll talk to Wolf about it."

"What do you mean?"

"Wolf's ready to tear his head off."

"And you?"

"I'm not sure how I feel. I don't know if I would have panicked. I don't think I would have."

"You wouldn't have. You didn't in the Spree."

Joachim thought a minute and nodded. "Maybe *I* should go talk to Georg."

"Maybe you should."

"Okay, I will."

"Tonight?"

"I'm not having any dates with this face."

"Now you know how we uglies feel."

Joachim laughed. He grimaced with the pain, but then he laughed again.

Sepp left him writing the note and went down into the tunnel. Wolf and Bruno were working on the section of shoring they had been installing when the cave-in occurred. Wolf was using the sledgehammer to pound a strut into place. He stopped when Sepp arrived. He wiped the sweat from his face and eyed him expectantly. "Bruno's been lecturing me," he whispered sheepishly.

"Not lecturing, not lecturing at all."

"I suppose I acted childishly. But he got me sore."

"A display of anger is not necessarily childish," Bruno said. "It depends on the motive."

"I have no right to get sore at Joachim."

"Ah, but you have," Bruno countered. "You have a right to anger whenever it is justified, no matter who provokes you."

Wolf pondered this a moment. "Then I have a right to be sore at Georg. He would have let Joachim die. He just sat there in a stupor. He didn't lift a finger to help him. Joachim could have suffocated."

"Your rancor is clearly justifiable," Bruno said with conviction, "clearly justifiable."

Sepp was surprised at Bruno's attitude. He intervened. "Don't you think we ought to consider what made Georg act the way he did?"

"Cowardice has no defense."

"Well, I'm not so sure I agree with you on that, Bruno."

"If Wolf has as much gumption as I think he has, he'll go find Georg and give him a beating."

Sepp's surprise mounted to amazement. He scrutinized Bruno's face to see if he was serious. There was no sign of humor in the narrow, aesthetic face. "It seems to me that it's Joachim who has been injured, not Wolf. If anyone's going to give Georg a beating, it should be Joachim."

"But it is Wolf who is angry," Bruno insisted.

Sepp began to understand what Bruno was up to. He was trying to force Wolf to think through his anger, to understand it better so that he would not do anything rash.

"Maybe Sepp is right," Wolf said. "Joachim is the one who should be sore."

"And he's very sore," Bruno said.

"No, he isn't." Wolf looked thoroughly confused. "He didn't seem sore at all. He seemed . . . I don't know . . . sad."

Bruno's tone suddenly changed. "We like to believe that people will act as we would act, and of course we imagine ourselves to be heros at all times. Believe me, Wolf, each of us is a coward in one way or another. For some, the form of cowardice is the classic fear of death or physical pain, and is easily recognized."

"Like Georg's."

"Like Georg's. For others, cowardice is a subtle cancer that gnaws daily at the spirit. It doesn't manifest itself dramatically, but it is there nonetheless, just as real, just as insidious."

The three of them sat for a moment, not saying anything. Sepp had the feeling that Bruno had been speaking more to him than to Wolf, and he wondered what his friend had in mind. He couldn't recall anything that would have given Bruno reason to detect cowardice in him. He decided it was his imagination.

"I'll have to think about it," Wolf said.

Bruno smiled. "I can't conceive of a more mature attitude than that."

Wolf turned back to work, the pleasure Bruno's judgment had given him bright on his face.

WOLF came out of his room wearing his only suit. His hair was neatly combed, his shoes shined. A handkerchief was tucked carefully into the breast pocket of his jacket. He had on a shirt with French cuffs, and Joachim's best gold cuff links. He was cleaning his fingernails.

"She won't be able to resist you."

"That's what I'm afraid of."

Joachim laughed. It still hurt when he laughed. The cuts on his face were healing quickly and were drawing the skin tight around them.

"Are you going to be in tonight?" Wolf asked. He looked his fingernails over. "They'll never be clean again." There was a Band-Aid around each thumb.

"Why didn't you wear gloves?"

"It got too hot." He folded the blade and put the knife in his pocket. "Are you?"

"Am I what?"

"Going to be in tonight?"

"I have to go see Georg, but I'll be back before midnight."

Wolf looked disappointed. It occurred to Joachim that his question had not been an idle one. He scrutinized his brother's face and thought once again of his flare of temper at the tunnel that afternoon. He had thought about it several times since then—in the car coming home, at dinner, listening to Wolf clean up and dress. The incident

had disturbed him more than it should have. It was
strange that he had been more disturbed about Wolf's
anger than about almost being killed by the cave-in. It
was the first time Wolf had shown any outward sign of
defiance, and Joachim was still a little bewildered. He
thought that he had always been fair with Wolf. He had
let the boy live his own life with as little interference as
possible. He was rather proud of the way he had handled
him. Rarely had he had to demand obedience. Wolf had
been tractable, compliant. Whenever a difference of opinion had arisen between them about Wolf's activities, such
as the time he should be in at night, the diligence with
which he did his schoolwork, the amount of care he took
with his clothes, Joachim had made it a point to discuss it
with him, to explore the elements of their difference so
as to reach a reasonable and mutually acceptable resolution.

He had to admit that Wolf's habits had already been
well established by the time they had made their escape
and he really required very little supervision. His manners were always above reproach, and as far as Joachim
knew, his treatment of others was fair and honest.

Sometimes Joachim marveled at how well his parents
had done, and wished for their wisdom. With respect to
Wolf, he tried to think the way they would have thought
under similar circumstances. And it was not easy, for he
realized that his own code of behavior differed radically
from theirs. Now he wondered what his father would say.
It was obvious Wolf wanted to bring his girl friend home,
and his intentions were probably—what was that delight-
fully euphemistic phrase?—"other than honorable."

Joachim realized he was in a dilemma. Thinking like
his father, he should forbid it. What sort of girl would
agree to come up here to the apartment for the purpose
of having sexual intercourse with his little brother? He
envisioned a cheap little beatnik, a girl too advanced for
her years, smoking cigarettes, drinking cognac; an empty-
headed little slut who slept with everybody in pants who
looked her way. She's probably pimply, stupid, and diseased, he thought. The last possibility frightened him.

"Who's the lucky girl?" he ventured, trying to conceal
his concern.

"Oh, somebody I met." Wolf was straightening his tie in

the tiny oval mirror over the desk, picking nonexistent
lint from his trousers.

"What's her name?"

"Her name?"

"Yes, her name. She has a name, hasn't she?"

"Uschi Myer. She's just a girl I met."

"I'd like to meet her."

"She's just a girl, Joachim."

"I like girls, or haven't you noticed?"

He looked startled. "She's my age."

Joachim laughed. "I don't mean I'd be interested in
her for myself. I'd just like to meet your friends, that's
all. Have you met her family?"

"Her family?"

Joachim was becoming exasperated. "When did you
pick up the habit of answering questions with questions?"

"You never asked so many questions before."

"I ask questions when I think they need to be asked,"
Joachim answered sternly. "I repeat, have you met her
family?"

"No, but I know her father's a banker."

A banker's daughter. Joachim's vision disintegrated.
Banker's daughters are not tramps, he thought. Maybe
all he wants to do is bring her up here to play records
and dance. A banker's daughter. Well, how about that?
Little brother is doing all right for himself.

Now Joachim began to think like Joachim. Maybe it
was time Wolf got some experience. A boy should find out
about women at as early an age as possible. When he was
Wolf's age . . . But Wolf was different. Wolf was his little
brother, the baby whose bottle he had held, the little boy
whom he had taught to tie his shoes, part his hair, ride a
bicycle. The more Joachim tried to establish an attitude,
the more confused he became.

"Do you want to talk about this?"

Wolf shifted his weight and looked away. "About
what?"

"There's nothing to be embarrassed about."

"I'm not embarrassed."

"You want to bring this Uschi Myer up here, is that
right?"

"You have girls up here. All the time."

"Women, not girls. And I'm not sixteen. And I don't

have them up here 'all the time.'" He caught his temper before it got away from him. "Just what do you have in mind?" he asked evenly.

"Have in mind?"

"Is that a difficult question?"

Wolf looked away without answering.

"Let me be explicit. Do you plan to take this girl to bed with you?"

"It's her idea."

"*Her* idea?"

"Yes."

"You're not . . . you don't want to?"

"Sure I want to."

Now Joachim understood his problem. "But you're not sure how to go about it."

Wolf gave him a pained look. "It's hard to talk about it with you."

"With me? But I'm the best one to talk to. I'm your brother. I've had experience. I'm an expert. And I can tell you this: If she wants to do it, you have nothing to worry about. Except if she's a virgin. Do you know if she's a virgin?"

"I don't think she is. She sure doesn't talk like one."

"Well, then, it's easy. Just get undressed, hop into bed, and the rest comes naturally."

Wolf did not look reassured.

"I guarantee it. Once you've done it, you'll wonder what all the fuss was about. You'll laugh remembering how nervous you were."

"I suppose so."

"Have a couple of beers beforehand. It'll do wonders."

"Do you think so?"

"I know so. But brush your teeth. Beer breath in bed is not conducive to good sex."

Wolf nodded and breathed deeply. "Okay. I'd better go."

"Need some money?"

"I could use some."

Joachim got out his wallet and gave him twenty marks. "I wish I could let you have the car."

"I don't need it."

"You'll do fine. I know it. Think of the millions of

fellows who came before you. They all managed. So will you."

Wolf sighed. "I sure hope so." He went out looking as if he were on his way to a funeral.

Joachim sat back on the sofa and laughed. Maybe a father was supposed to discourage adventures like this, but not a brother. And no matter how much Joachim might pretend to the role of father, he was a brother by nature and by sentiment. He felt he had done the right thing. He only wished he could be here to watch. Two sixteen-year-olds! In bed! What a circus that ought to be!

Dieter Brim arrived at exactly seven thirty. When Joachim opened the door and invited him in, he stood there gaping, flustered, and finally sputteringly furious. Joachim acted mildly amused. "Your porcelain doll fell off the table and got chipped."

"Broken is the word. *Broken*. Damn you, Lentz, damn you! What happened?"

Joachim closed the door. "You can arrange another interview."

"You think it's so easy?"

"Isn't it?"

"No, it isn't. I had to use every favor owed me. I had to beg, cajole, argue, threaten." He stuck a cigarette into the center of his little mouth and lighted it, snapping the flint wheel of his lighter several times before the wick caught fire. With the cigarette dangling, he continued his harangue. "Walther Curzmann is a great director, but he is also a vicious, vindictive, petulant little queer. He loves golden boys, he's made a hell of a lot of them famous *and* wealthy. But he's a dictator—ruthless, demanding, exacting. If he expects you at eight o'clock on Wednesday night, you had better be there at eight o'clock on Wednesday night or never be expected again."

Joachim was shaken. "You mean you can't postpone?"

"I mean I can't postpone. Even if I could, the schedule the man keeps is insane. He may not be in Berlin again for months. Do you know when I started working on this appointment for you?"

"I have no idea."

"The day I met you at the hospital. That's how long

it's taken. And it wasn't until yesterday that I finally got the okay."

"Tell me, Herr Brim, just what do you expect to get out of all your efforts?"

"I'd be your agent. Ten percent of the gross."

"Oh."

"You don't like it?"

"It's academic, isn't it? I surely can't meet the illustrious Herr Curzmann with this face."

"The hell you can't."

Joachim was taken aback. "You're out of your mind."

"No, I'm not. I'm never out of my mind—never." He made certain Joachim understood that. "All we need is a story to go with it. Even with those hash marks, you're pretty." He stuck the cigarette back in his mouth and let the smoke curl up his nose and into his eyes. "You go get dressed. *Fast.* I'll think."

Joachim hesitated.

"Go on. Move, damn you." The little rabbit face was incongruously forceful. Joachim was impressed by the man for the first time. He admired perseverance, and Dieter Brim had it. He went to the bedroom to change.

"How did it happen?" Brim called out.

"I can't tell you."

"You'd damn well better."

Joachim dressed hurriedly. What could he tell him now? If he came up with a pedestrian story, such as Bruno had given the hospital authorities, Brim would wonder why he had said he couldn't tell him. It would seem pointless.

"Are you almost ready?" Brim came into the bedroom and looked him over critically. "The tie is too conservative. You need a little flash."

"I'm not the flashy type."

"You want to be an actor, don't you? No time like the present to start learning."

He took the liberty of rummaging through Joachim's ties. A long ash dropped from his cigarette onto a blue-and-red foulard Joachim favored.

"Watch what you're doing."

Brim ignored him. He came up with a red-and-silver flowered silk Joachim had bought in a weak moment and had never worn. It was too florid for his taste. He had thought of giving it to Wolf, but he did not want to encourage bad taste in him. For a moment he wondered how his brother was doing. He smiled to himself and wished him great success.

"This will have to do." Brim threw it to him. "Now tell me how it happened."

"Isn't it getting late?"

"Damned late."

"I thought we needed a romantic story. How about skydiving? We could say I landed through a skylight—right in a redhead's bedroom."

"And having nothing better to do, you screwed her on the spot." Brim grunted skeptically. "It's got to be something credible." He lighted a second cigarette from the first and jammed the stub into the soil of a potted philodendron. "You look okay—considering. Let's get going."

Brim's Volkswagen was old and rattling. He drove fast, not slowing for intersections, heading south on Clay Allee toward Zehlendorf. Joachim was neither excited nor indifferent; acquiescent, perhaps, much as if he were simply on a ride with destiny, a ride he had always known he would take someday. How he felt was of no consequence whatsoever, for he was no longer in control. Events would take their course regardless of how he felt, despite what he said or did.

He remembered that when Wolf had told him in the cellar that his face was cut up, his first thought had been of this interview tonight. The pain of disappointment and bitterness had overridden the physical pain. On the way to the hospital he had speculated on the reason for his having been the victim of the cave-in. Peraps it was fortune playing one of her tricks, coming through the back door disguised as her antithesis. She had done it before—The Wall had seemed like rotten luck at first but it had changed his life for the better. Even Wolf's getting shot—bad luck at the time—had turned to Joachim's advantage. Riding in the ambulance, he had not been able to perceive how that misfortune might be transformed into fortune. Now, as he and the curious, ambitious photographer raced through the hot night along the edge of the Grunewald, detached, it seemed, in time and space from the susurrous hum of life around them, he began to believe that once again a transfiguration might be in the making.

At Potsdamerstrasse, Brim turned west toward Wannsee. Far ahead, Joachim could see the clearance lights of the microwave tower on the Schaferberg. He glanced at his watch. They had only ten minutes left. Brim, too, looked at his watch and pressed harder on the accelerator. They had been exceeding the speed limit by thirty kilometers an hour. Brim raised it to forty. maneuvering the tiny car expertly through the light traffic. They crossed the narrow isthmus between the Grosser Wannsee and Kleiner Wannsee and turned south again down a dark, tree-lined street. Here the houses were invisible from the street. Occasionally they passed arched or pillared gateways beyond which a stretch of gravel or macadam roadway suggested the presence of life deep among the trees and shrubbery. The street was winding, now and then giving them a glimpse of the narrow arm of water that embraced the eastern shore.

"Have you thought of a story?" Joachim asked him.

"Ever done any racing?"

"In cars?"

"You could tell him you were racing in France or Italy—it doesn't matter where; dream up a race—and that you cracked up."

Joachim thought about it. Not a bad idea. Again he returned to the truth, and it suited him better. He was just not the auto racer type. A man like Curzmann would know it immediately. Yet perhaps it wouldn't matter to him; perhaps he wouldn't give a damn about the reason.

"How long will I be with him?"

"Not long. Ten, maybe fifteen minutes." He turned into a narrow opening in a line of fir trees, an opening barely wide enough to admit the car and which only a perceptive passerby would have noticed. "Here we are." Ahead of them stretched a gravel road, meandering among tall black firs. Brim was forced to go slowly.

"He'll try to unnerve you. He's notorious for that. Just keep your cool, don't let him browbeat you. Speak up, be firm, but do what he asks." He glanced at Joachim meaningfully. "*Whatever* he asks."

"You don't need to draw a picture."

The house was not overpowering—ten rooms, he

figured—a low, rambling English cottage type with a genuine thatched roof. Brim pulled up in front and stopped. He looked at his watch. "Two minutes to spare. Not bad." He peered into Joachim's face. "How do you feel?"

"Calm."

"Good."

He got out of the car, and Joachim followed his lead. The night air was calm, too, undisturbed by any wind. The smell of the river hovered about, and the call of field crickets emerged from the darkness beyond the house.

A short, thin man with a grizzled moustache answered the door.

"Herr Brim and Herr Lentz. We're expected."

The little man opened the screen door. "Come in quickly, please. Mosquitoes, you know."

They entered a small, dimly lighted vestibule. An antique coatrack inset with a mirror whose silver was peeling occupied one wall. Two black umbrellas stuck out of the umbrella ring, and a pair of rubbers stood toe-to-toe, heel-to-heel, perfectly aligned at the bottom of the rack. They were ushered into an equally dimly lighted sitting room, also furnished with antiques. The furniture was delicate and ornate. There were two matching easy chairs upholstered in a bright floral design. They reminded Joachim of his tie, and once again he was impressed, this time with Dieter Brim's perspicacity. A thick Oriental carpet covered the center of the parqueted floor. Although the room was elegant and rich, there was something precious about it, something fanciful that jarred Joachim's sense of proportion and taste. Perhaps it was the Dresden figurines, a set of delicately turned muscians—playing a Mozart divertimento, no doubt—or the profusion of other tiny, fragile knickknacks scattered about. The room was altogether un-German.

The old man spoke to Joachim, *"Herr Direktor* Curzmann is ready for you,"* and extending a frail, mottled hand toward a set of folding oak doors at the far end of the room, proceeded to open one quarter of them and stood there, waiting for him to enter. Joachim glanced once at Brim, whose face was already clouded with smoke from the perpetual cigarette, and, finding no last-minute suggestion of attitude there, passed by the little man and through the door into the next room. The door closed with a click behind him.

‹ The change in decor struck him at once. The room was large, much larger than the sitting room. A long, plump maroon leather couch occupied one wall like a phalanx of fat infantry. Two giant landscape canvases faced one another across the expanse of bare waxed flooring. Across one end, behind a massive mahogany desk cluttered with papers and illuminated by a single desk lamp, French doors gave a dim view of a garden. Reflected in the windows were Joachim and the back of the man sitting hunched over the desk, writing. In the reflection Joachim could see a round bald spot at the crown of the long, narrow head, an empty spot sharply in contrast to the growth of black hair surrounding it.

"Do you know any English?" Curzmann asked the question without looking up. The voice was surprisingly resonant, the words precisely enunciated, suggesting the speaker had had formal training.

"I was educated in the *Sektor*. We had to learn Russian."

"English is an impossible language. Nothing sounds as it is spelled or spelled as it sounds. Is Russian like that?" He looked up, his narrow face cast in half-shadow, half-light. Joachim noticed first the heavy eyebrows that bridged the long aquiline nose richly tufted with protruding hair. The eyebrows turned up at the ends like little horns, and Joachim thought in passing that they had been deliberately pulled and twisted for effect.

"Somewhat."

"I'm writing a letter to my niece in America. She doesn't read German. Apparently it is considered gauche to learn one's parent language in America, so I must write to her in the only language she understands." He sighed. "How she ever learned it is beyond my humble intellect. They don't even have the decency to place their verbs at the end of the sentence where they belong." Whether out of politeness, which Brim had given Joachim to believe was not in the man's nature, or because he had not yet noticed, or even possibly, Joachim thought, to corroborate his reputation for eccentricity, Herr Curz-

mann had not so much as blinked at the condition of
Joachim's face.

"Do sit down, Herr Lentz," the director said impatiently, as if annoyed that Joachim had not taken it upon
himself to do so from the start.

Joachim sat back on the center cushion of the heavy
couch. The air hissed out as the cushion sank slowly under
his weight. "Perhaps Herr Brim knows English," he offered.

"Brim?" Curzmann laughed derisively. "Don't be ridiculous. Brim is an uneducated pimp." He spit the word
from his thin, pursed lips with obvious distaste. "What
are you doing mixed up with his type? Low class," he
said contemptuously, "strictly low class."

And what, Joachim wondered, are you doing mixed up
with him? It works both days, *Herr Direktor*. "Sometimes
one can't be choosy," he said ineffectually.

"One must *always* be choosy." Curzmann's tone was
paternal, and Joachim expected a homily on the importance of one's associates. Instead, Curzmann took five
minutes to finish his letter, without once looking up or
speaking. When he had finished, he aligned the sheets by
tapping the edges on the desk, folded them carefully, pressing down the folds firmly with the heel of his palm, and
inserted them in an envelope. He appeared so concentrated
on what he was doing that Joachim began to feel annoyed at being ignored.

"You're wondering if I've forgotten you, eh? Not so,
Herr Lentz." He laughed. "How could I forget a face
like yours, eh?" He laughed again and clapped his hands.
He thought he was very funny indeed.

Joachim's ambition collided with his pride. It seemed
the two were always in conflict, and so far he had had
enough sense to subdue his pride in favor of ambition.
Maybe the bastard's testing me, he thought. Maybe he's
trying to see if he can provoke me. He remembered Brim's
warning that Curzmann would try something like this.
"You may laugh all you want, *Herr Direktor*," he replied
calmly. "When my face is healed, you'll cry with envy."

The laugh trailed off, as if through the French doors
into the night, seeking a more vulnerable target. Curzmann twisted his eyebrow horns thoughtfully. I was right,

Joachim mused, and failed to hold back a wry grin of satisfaction.

"Oh, I was young once, too. I was not exactly ugly then. How old are you, Herr Lentz?"

"Twenty."

He considered this reminiscently. "Twenty. When I was twenty I was in the army in Russia. You have not been in the Army?"

"No."

Curzmann did not seem interested in pursuing his memories. "What happened to you? I feel obligated to ask."

"Is it important?"

"To you, I presume, it is."

"*I* know what happened."

Curzmann smiled. "You are not afraid of me."

"Should I be?"

"Most people are. I frighten people. I take a delight in frightening people—they frighten so easily. Why? Because they are greedy for what I can give them." He left his eyebrows and picked up a pencil, which he began rolling between his palms. "It is what is known as power—the ability to get people to do things for one because they are afraid one will withhold a favor, a paycheck, a pat on the back, a kiss. Power is the ultimate goal of all men, Herr Lentz. Have you never figured that out?"

"In elementary school."

"Oh." Curzmann chuckled. "My profundity doesn't impress you."

"It might when I hear it."

The director laughed mirthlessly. "You're a cocky little shit, aren't you." The vulgar expression sounded cruder than it would have from someone else. It seemed to reveal his true nature more honestly than his previously well-articulated, cultivated speech and as a result, its genuine flavor, usually lost on the lips of any casual user, was intensified. Curzmann reclined in his chair, searching Joachim's blemished face. His eyes were peculiarly serene, almost empty of emotion. "Handsome, too. You're quite right about that, Herr Lentz, you have a face to bring out envy in men. Your beauty is apparent despite its unfortunate—but temporary, I trust—state. And there is your youth as well." He shook the pencil at him. "Oh, don't think that youth is so glorious. Only at moments when the discarded memories of lust wriggle their way out of the trash heap of the past—then and only then does the hungering after youth preempt more productive occupations."

"And how often does that happen?"

"Often enough to demand satisfaction—lest the memories become tyrannical."

Joachim felt uneasy for the first time since he had arrived. With Karl, at least, he did not have to talk about it. There was never a need to articulate, even subtly or indirectly, the substance of his surrender. It had been accepted and used, coldly, wholeheartedly, but unanalytically. Joachim had been able to regard it as part of the job.

"You are not attracted to this sort of discussion, are you." The man had an unsettling ability to read Joachim's mind.

"I don't think it's necessary."

Curzmann's anger bloomed in his cheeks and sent fibrils up into the wrinkles around his eyes. "*I* am the one who decides what is necessary and what is not. And you have managed with admirable skill to evade answering any question."

Joachim put on an innocent air. "What question was that?"

"What happened to your face?"

Brim's concern had been justified. The man's curiosity had a kind of puerile eagerness, as if he were begging for a fanciful story, regardless of whether it was true or not. Briefly Joachim considered the farfetched tale he had dreamed up about skydiving, but he concluded that so dramatic a fabrication would catch up with him, and decided against it. Instead, he embraced the truth as romantic enough stuff and safe with Curzmann. What possible harm could a man like Curzmann cause? He was certainly no Communist, nor was he likely to consort with any.

"I'm helping to dig a tunnel," he admitted with obvious reluctance.

"A tunnel? What sort of tunnel?"

"Under The Wall."

"Do you mean a tunnel through which people will escape?"

"Yes."

The tenebrous atmosphere Curzmann's sudden anger had created vanished, and his lifeless eyes showed a flicker of excitement. "But how were you injured? Tell me."

"I was digging at the time. When you're digging, you have to lie flat on your back. It's hard work, and hot."

"I can imagine."

"There I was, digging, and the next thing I knew, everything was black. I couldn't breathe. I couldn't see. I don't know what I thought at that moment. Then I could hear noises. They were loud, scratching noises. I think I was about to pass out, and I was becoming excruciatingly conscious of not being able to breathe. There was a tremendous pressure on his chest. I tried to breathe, but I sucked in nothing but earth. And of course I wasn't able to spit it out or blow it out of my nose."

"Horrible, horrible. What happened then?"

"Suddenly I felt air rushing into my lungs. A hand was brushing the earth away from my face, and I looked up into my brother's eyes."

"Your brother saved you!"

"Yes. It evened the score."

"Evened the score? What do you mean?"

Joachim told him about their escape across the Spree. The great film director sat there enthralled as a child, excitement glittering in his eyes. He licked his thin lips and kept raising his horned eyebrows at each turn of the story.

When Joachim finished, Curzmann sat back, his tension subsiding as evidently as a wave recedes from the shore. "You are a man of adventure," he concluded.

"Wasn't it Rilke who insisted that a life without risk is no life at all?"

Curzmann was not interested in literary allusions. "Tell me, Herr Lentz, have you done any acting?"

"No."

"I suspected as much." A gesture ruled it unimportant. "You will learn."

To Joachim the words were fateful. Dieter Brim had spoken them that day in the hospital when he had come to see Joachim and to suggest that he go to work for Karl as a model. He wondered if the way in which Curzmann had spoken them meant that he had already decided to

take Joachim into his—what would it be called?—retinue?
Stable, perhaps?

The director touched the tips of his fingers together.
"Well, let's see what a man of adventure looks like."

Joachim understood what he meant. He had been expecting it, but he was slow to react. Curzmann thought he
had not understood. "Strip, my boy, strip. And don't tell
me you think that is unnecessary, too, because I assure
you it is quite necessary. Yes, *quite*."

Once again, Joachim's pride got in the way of his ambition. The memory came to him—he had no idea from
where, or why it was this particular piece of information
rather than another, similar one—of how the Nazis had
stripped prisoners during interrogation, the theory being
that prisoners felt much less secure without their clothes
on. It was said that with women they had only to make
them go barefoot to humiliate them, to break down what
feeble defense they might put up. It struck Joachim that
this, rather than lust or—improbable as it might be—professional curiosity, was Curzmann's motive. He had
spoken of power and was now exercising it, blatantly and
without the slightest sign of emotion. Joachim was sure
that this same scene had been enacted in this room countless times before. How many of the others had made the
escape over the top, into unfettered fame and fortune—
and power—and how many had crawled out like whining
dogs with their injured tails between their legs, licking
unprofitable wounds? He had no illusions about how the
majority had exited. Rooms at the top were few and expensive.

"Surely you've been in this cage before." Curzmann
did not bother to display the self-satisfied smile that came
with the words, words carefully chosen to humiliate. "Or
are our moral scruples nibbling at our conscience?"

Perhaps to evade or postpone. Joachim seized on the
redundancy. It rattled around in his mind: *moral scruples,
moral scruples*. He wished he could throw it up to this
smug, unctuous egotist, to show him up on the ground
where he undoubtedly considered himself superior. But
the temptation dwindled, then disappeared altogether
under the pressure of the immediate need to decide what
to do. Perhaps his withholding of comment was but a

manifestation of a decision already made, for Joachim was on his feet taking off his jacket.

His commitment now given, he focused his mind on how to retrieve some advantage from it. Slowly, piece by piece—jacket, tie, one cuff link, the second cuff link, one shoe, one sock, second shoe, second sock, shirt, trousers, undershirt, shorts—he undressed, folding each article of clothing carefully, setting the shoes neatly side by side as he always had done (reminding him of the rubbers in the hallway, thinking his neatness would please him), until he stood naked before *Herr Direktor* Walther Curzmann. Now he expected anything and found himself calmly prepared for it. Curzmann was right—he had been in this cage before, and he was satisfied to discover once again that it did not bother him. Indeed, the same exhilarating satisfaction he experienced when he stood naked before a woman, confident that whatever degree of importance she ascribed to a man's physical beauty, his would measure up, he began to feel now. For the moment, Joachim held the power.

He purposely ran his fingertips over the tiny scratches and cuts on his chest, stomach, and arms, examining them with tender curiosity, conscious of the effect his calculated indifference would have on his adversary. Absently he scratched under his testicles and rubbed a buttock. Even to his own touch the flesh was invitingly firm and resilient.

The director was looking him over as he might a piece of art he was considering buying. There was surprisingly little emotion in the man's eyes; what was there was more akin to amusement than lust. "You look like a statue that some demented vandal has taken a knife to."

Again Joachim felt as though Curzmann had been reading his mind—or was it the other way around? "It will all heal in time."

"How long?"

"The doctors said a week to ten days."

Curzmann's eyes blinked under the dark hedgerows of his eyebrows and began a second, more detailed inspection of Joachim's body. "Turn around."

Joachim did as he was told. He felt the man's dull eyes on him and expected at any moment to feel his hands as well.

"All right. Get dressed." Relief swept over him, and he felt the tension subside, surprised to find that it had been there at all.

As he dressed, Curzmann talked. His tone was businesslike and to the point. Joachim found he had to admire the man for not having offered an explanation or an excuse for what he had required of him. "You have a contract with a photographer, one Karl Buhlen. I'll arrange to purchase it. You're not to return to his employ."

"What will I live on?"

"Otto will give you a check."

"Otto?"

"My manservant. He let you in."

Joachim nodded.

"You will join me as soon as you are entirely healed. I expect to be leaving Berlin in two, perhaps three weeks. You will be healed by then, isn't that so?"

"Yes."

"I'd have you move in now, but in your condition—"

"Do you mean I am to move in with you?"

Curzmann gave him a quizzical look. "Of course. What did you have in mind—remote control?"

Joachim buttoned his shirt and draped his tie around his neck. "What will my salary be?"

"You're making about two hundred and fifty a week now?"

"Five hundred."

"That's a lie. I'll pay you three hundred."

"I have a brother to support."

"How old is he?"

"Sixteen."

The workings of his mind were for once apparent on Curzmann's face. Joachim intercepted his thoughts before they had a chance to develop fully. "Never," he said emphatically.

The director looked at him and chuckled. "Ah. You are in truth your brother's keeper."

"Morally as well as financially."

The eyebrows shot up. "Morally?" He chuckled humorlessly. "I had no idea the word was in your vocabulary."

Joachim finished dressing. He was not going to indulge Curzmann's sarcasm. "I'd have to forget the whole thing for less than six hundred a week."

"Come now, Herr Lentz. I *know* what you earn working as a fashion model. Let's not try to blind me with a lot of horseshit about five hundred a week."

Joachim once again found himself debating, as he had so often with Karl, about how far he dared go. The ride with destiny had come to an abrupt halt. Until now he had had the sense, even when he was aware that pride and ambition were competing for his will, that whatever happened had already been plotted out beforehand and that any decision-making on his part that appeared real was purely illusory.

Now the power of decision had been returned to him. The alternatives had always been clear-cut and simple, just as they were now: He could either accept the three hundred marks a week Curzmann had offered—from which he had no doubt he could subtract enough for Wolf to live on—or gamble that Curzmann was taken enough with him to meet his price. There was no way of knowing which way Curzmann was leaning. He wanted him, yes, but did he want him six hundred marks' worth? Joachim recalled something Bruno had said about the price of paintings. Paintings, he had explained, were priced high—even those by unknown artists—because if they weren't, people would think they were not worth buying. Joachim had thought the psychology good at the time, and elected to apply it now.

"Herr Curzmann, horseshit or no horseshit, six hundred is the going price. Take it or shove it."

The director's mouth gaped for a split second, a slight weakening of his stage presence, but he was too accomplished an actor to lose control of the scene. He turned in the swivel chair to look out the window. His reflection showed no sign of his inclination, only a meditation as deep and impenetrable as the darkness beyond. "Four hundred."

"I'm not going to bargain."

"You're a fool."

"I doubt it. Yours isn't the only door to what I want."

"I could have you blacklisted. Not one director, not one producer would talk to you."

"Maybe I ought to strip again, just to remind you of the quality of the merchandise." The crudity of his own words shocked him, and he suddenly felt that whatever chance he had had was now destroyed. To his amazement, however, the face reflected in the window grew strangely serene.

"You will be a most difficult companion, Herr Lentz, most difficult. Perhaps I am losing my famous touch." Curzmann sighed and turned around, his expression one of childish petulance. "You, too, know how to use your power, eh? Well, we shall see who wins in the end. I am not indifferent to a little adventure—my personal life can be very dull at times, would you believe it?"

"No one is immune to boredom."

"True, true," the director said. "But let me warn you, Herr Lentz—"

"Joachim."

"Let me warn you, Joachim, when you are in my employ, you will do as I say, when I say it. There will be no more bargaining, no hesitation, no cajoling or finagling."

"And you will teach me how to act."

Curzmann made a gesture of vague promise. "*Ach,* anyone can act. It is the simplest art. Everyone acts a little all the time. Yes, yes, I will teach you the little tricks you need to know to satisfy the camera."

Joachim put out his hand. The director was startled, then slowly grasped it. Joachim felt the connection that was made, the difference that altered the clasp of their hands from a normal sign of agreement to an intimate recognition of mutual purpose.

"What about Brim?" Joachim asked. "He has delusions about being my agent."

"Have you signed anything?"

"No."

"Get rid of him. He has no legal claim on you. And if he has been stupid enough to go this far without some guarantee, would you want him for an agent? That is—" and he smiled coyly—"assuming you will ever need an agent."

Joachim returned the smile confidently. "I'll need an agent."

"Your type is *so* ambitious," Curzmann sighed. "So impatient."

"And you weren't."

Indignation fluttered across the director's face, leaving behind a smile of resignation. "Oh, Joachim, we shall

have an interesting time together. I wonder how long it
will last."

Brim said nothing until they had reached the seclusion
of his car. "Well?"

"I'll do," Joachim said.

Brim let out a victory whoop. "I knew it! I knew it
the minute I laid eyes on you in the hospital!" He was beside himself with joy.

All the way back to Joachim's apartment he pried the
details of the interview out of him. Joachim felt the least
he could do, considering it was to be the last he was to
see of Dieter Brim, was satisfy his curiosity.

"I'll talk to him about a salary," Brim said in his ignorance. "I think you ought to get at least three hundred to
start."

"At least," Joachim said.

"Maybe even four hundred."

"Who knows?" Joachim said.

Brim glanced at him quizzically. "You don't seem very
excited."

Joachim gave him his best smile. "Oh, I am. I assure
you I'm very excited, Herr Brim."

"Call me Dieter."

He smiled again. "Dieter."

From inside came the smell of cooked pork—a pungent
odor that filled the hallway with memories of his home
in East Berlin—and the sound of television. Joachim
knocked again, louder this time. It was a young woman
who answered the door, a plump, sallow, flat-faced woman
with her hair up in curlers. When she saw Joachim's face,
she gasped and clutched the front of her dress between
her heavy, protruding breasts.

"Does Georg Knauer live here?"

She stood there gawking, shrinking back into the refuge
of the room. The smell of pork came on strong. The television blared inanely with no one watching it.

"Is it really that bad?"

She tried to compose herself and put on a sheepish face.
"I'm sorry. You hurt yourself, huh? Was you in a fight
or something?"

"Does Georg Knauer live here?"

"He rooms here, if that's what you mean." She calmed herself and gave him a fresh appraisal. "You're kind of cute, even with that face like that, if you know what I mean."

"Is he in?"

She glanced contemptuously toward a closed door on the other side of the room. "He's in there, but I don't think he wants to see you. He don't want to see nobody."

Joachim grasped the situation quickly and looked her over again. So Georg comes home to this every night, he thought. She's probably good in bed, but who could stand to look at her or listen to her? "Would you tell him Joachim Lentz is here to see him?"

She shrugged. "Go tell him yourself. We ain't on speaking terms, if you know what I mean." She fished an apple out of a bowl on the table and bit into it. Deciding that Joachim was not interested in her, she slumped down into an easy chair drawn up in front of the television screen and became immediately immersed in its world.

At Georg's door, Joachim paused before knocking. He had not given much thought to this visit. When he had told Sepp he would speak to Georg, he had had the illusion that simply seeing him, saying a few solicitous words, would put everything right. That afternoon now seemed long ago; the passage of time had changed his perspective. The cave-in had faded quickly from his memory before the brilliance of his triumph over *Herr Direktor* Walther Curzmann—a new nova exploding into brilliance, obscuring the fading light of the older. He thought of the check in his jacket pocket—six hundred marks, as much as he had made in two weeks working for Karl. It gave him a heady feeling. And with it came the promise of fame and wealth; not Curzmann's vague promise—Joachim was too shrewd to believe he would be riding with destiny again— but his own promise to himself that, now committed to Curzmann's challenge, he would emerge the victor.

Engrossed in giddy dreams, it was hard for Joachim to concentrate on Georg and the tunnel. At one point, returning home from Curzmann's house in the car with Brim, he had considered forgetting about Georg altogether, even the tunnel. The only factor that bound him to his word was Wolf. He could easily have walked out on any of them, including Sepp. But not on Wolf. He tried to

reason out his loyalty to his brother, the need to keep up
a pretense of—what would it be considered: integrity?
honesty?—but the attempt was fruitless. Whatever sense
of obligation held him to his word, it was more than
reason was able to uncover. And then, there was every
thing to be gained by sticking with the pretense and the
tunnel. By the time his body was healed and Curzmann
was ready for him, the tunnel would be finished. His confidence in his father's intransigence about crossing over
was as firm as ever. The fact that he had been so suspicious
of Ilse that Sepp had had to ask for another note confirmed his belief that his father had not changed his mind.
Joachim would still be free to go his own way with Curzmann. Wolf would be more than adequately taken care
of financially and would learn to run his own life.

So went Joachim's thoughts as he knocked on Georg's
door, still undecided about what he was going to say. There
was no response to his knock.

"I told you he wasn't talking to nobody."

Joachim ignored her. He turned the doorknob. It was
unlocked, and the door creaked open. The room was in
darkness except for a shaft of light breaking across the
gray plaster ceiling from a small window.

"Georg? It's me, Joachim Lentz." As his eyes adjusted
to the dim light, he made out a lamp on a table in the corner. He turned it on and closed the door behind him.
Georg was curled up on his bed, facing the wall. "Georg."

"Leave me alone."

Joachim pulled up a flimsy straight-back chair and sat
down. The room was bare of pictures, knickknacks, or
any other indication of the personality of its occupant,
save a tortoiseshell comb stuck into the bristle of a chrome-
plated brush on top of the table. No clothing lay about,
no shoes stuck out from under the bed, no tie hung draped
over a doorknob. There were only three pieces of furniture in the room—a battered mahogany-veneer wardrobe,
the chair in which he was sitting, and the bed. A dry,
musty smell mingled unpleasantly with that of the pork.
The room reminded Joachim of a jail cell.

"I'd like to talk to you."

Georg made no movement and did not respond. The
cacophony of the television battered the door. Joachim
sighed, unable to summon any argument worthy of the

demands of the situation. He was not about to play amateur psychologist. He decided the only thing to do was state the facts.

"Look, Georg, what you did—or didn't do—was not particularly admirable, true. But Sepp wants you to come back, and I want you to come back. The others—Wolf, Bruno, and Emerich—want you to come back, if for no other reason than that we can't get anyone to take your place. We need you in order to get the damned tunnel finished as soon as possible."

No response.

"See here, if you're afraid of what we think of you or that we'll hound you about it, you can forget it right now. I promise you we've already forgotten it." As he made the promise, he knew he was not speaking for anyone but himself. But he doubted that any of the others would say anything if he were to return, except perhaps the peasant. Joachim reminded himself to talk to Emerich first thing when they picked him up in the car in the morning. "All we're thinking about is completing the tunnel," he concluded. "That's all, believe me."

Georg still did not reply.

"What do you say?"

Nothing.

Georg's silence began to annoy him. He had hoped to make his visit brief and get along to Rita's. He took a moment to contemplate Rita's reaction to his face. What would it be? Shock. Then sympathy. Then satisfaction at the revenge he had suffered for standing her up Monday night. Yes, he could predict the timing of her emotions, one crowding behind the other and straining to dominate her attitude. Satisfaction would triumph— smug satisfaction.

"Look, Georg, I came one hell of a long way from Dahlem to reason with you, to bring you . . . an amnesty. The least you can do is talk about it."

Silence.

Joachim's annoyance mounted to anger. He got up and, grabbing hold of Georg's shoulder, twisted him onto his back and held him there. Georg blinked and turned his head to the wall. Joachim seized his jaw and jerked his head around. Georg did not resist. He kept his eyes shut, his mouth clamped shut, his lips pressed tightly together.

"Now you listen to me, you jelly-boned twerp. I don't have the time to indulge your self-pity. I have more important things to do." He shook Georg's head as hard as he could. Georg took it without raising a hand to protect himself. "If I can forget the whole thing, so can you. Are you listening? Listen well, Georg. I'm going back into that tunnel tomorrow. I'm going to go in there, lie flat on my back, and dig. What do you imagine I'll be thinking about all that time? Don't you suppose I'll be scared hairless every second I'm in there?" He was shaking Georg's head in irregular beats to the flow of angry words that were being fired from his mouth like rockets from a battery of launchers.

"If I can do that, you can face Sepp and Wolf and Emerich and Bruno. You can, because if you don't, you won't ever be able to face yourself, just as you can't right now." He let go of Georg's chin. There were white marks on Georg's skin where Joachim's fingers had held him. Joachim stretched his fingers and felt pain throbbing through his badly cut hands. "You won't," he said, calm now, the anger worn away on the grindstone of his harangue. "You won't."

Georg opened his eyes tentatively, closed them, then opened them a crease. He stared up at Joachim for a full minute before he said anything. "Were you badly hurt?" His voice rose just above a whisper.

"No."

He closed his eyes. "I'm glad for that."

"So am I."

"Are you going to holler at me some more?"

Were it not for the pathetic tone of his voice, Joachim would have laughed. "I was hollering, wasn't I."

Georg looked up at Joachim, then away toward the tiny window, through which they could hear street voices. He sat up on the edge of the bed and breathed heavily. Although he was husky enough, he looked thin and wasted, as though he had been sick. "You don't have even the vaguest notion of what it's all about," he said, "not the vaguest." With considerable effort he got up and went to the window, pushing it wide open. A breeze brought in the summer's heat and the drone of automobiles passing in the street below. "I'm glad you weren't badly hurt."

"Are you going to be there in the morning?"

Georg hunched his shoulders as if he couldn't care less.

Joachim couldn't care less, either—about what happened to Georg. But he did want the tunnel to be finished as soon as possible, and without Georg it would take longer and mean more work for himself. He sought some simple truth that would at least push Georg's thoughts in the right direction. He had no real hope of getting a commitment from him tonight. "Getting hurt, dying—they come with the package."

Georg wrapped his arms around his chest as if he were cold. "What package?"

"Life, Georg, life. It doesn't come with a guarantee. There's no guarantee of any kind. At one instant it *is;* at another, it isn't. What happens in between is up to you, with luck and fate giving it a few little twists here and there."

Whether Georg was listening, let alone grasping what Joachim was trying to tell him, he had no idea. He remained mute, gazing out the window, his shoulders hunched forward as though he had not the strength to hold himself erect.

Joachim could think of nothing more to say. He wished now that he had not offered to come here. Sepp would probably have done a better job, or Bruno. He felt, however, that he had fulfilled his obligation.

"I have to go." He was again aware of the sound of the television and visualized the fat girl in curlers sitting in front of it, chewing on an apple. He left with a feeling of mild disgust, vaguely convinced that Georg had pretty much got what he deserved out of life.

More composed than Georg's low-class, fat girl friend, Rita Kleist nonetheless could not contain her immediate reaction of horror at the sight of Joachim's face. She, too, put her lovely hands to her mouth to stifle a cry. Joachim followed her retreating figure into the apartment, closing the door behind him.

"Twice in one night," he mused aloud to himself. "I'm beginning to feel like Frankenstein's monster."

"What *happened* to you?" She had backed into the middle of the room, her eyes still big from the shock, but she was gradually recovering her poise.

"It'll heal, you know. Do I really look that bad?"

She equivocated. "Darling, you could never look *bad*." She turned to the liquor cabinet. "It is temporary, isn't it?" She started making drinks. He saw that her hands were shaking.

"I went swimming," he decided to tell her. "I dove too deep and scraped the bottom."

With her back to him she had more nerve. "Somehow that sounds so appropriate."

"What's eating you?"

"We had a date the night before last."

"Monday night? No, we didn't."

She looked at him to see if he were lying. He held her gaze with considerable difficulty. "You're a terrible liar, Joachim." She turned back to the drinks she was making. "Maybe that's a good sign." She handed him his drink. "It's poisoned."

"I believe it." He took a long swallow and looked at her. She was dressed to go out. She was a marvelous woman, probably the best he had ever had, he conceded. He recalled the lush nights when they'd never had to struggle for the apt word, the consummate gesture, when her wit and charm had kept his intellect happy, when her body had satisfied his. He had found unusual contentment with her, devoid of the cloying stratagems that women so often insist upon. She was well-bred enough to let her primitive instincts prevail when they were most useful, then to grace them with civilized amenities in a way that made her seem almost regal. She looked regal now, glowing with beauty, slightly aloof.

"Why did you stand me up?"

"I didn't stand you up. You've got to believe me. I had to work. Karl had a rush order. We got all involved."

"You could have phoned."

"If we had a date, I forgot. I apologize."

She raised her glass. "I don't believe you, but I'll drop it. *Prosit*."

He smiled and drank with her. He had always been able to count on her good sense. She sat in the corner of the sofa where the light touched her hair, turning it to burnished copper, and eyed him across the room with an amused grin.

"What's so funny?"

"Seeing you this way. It's the first time you've ever apologized to me. You're like a little boy."

"Things are going well for me," he confided.

She shook her head incredulously. "You come here with your face covered with abrasions from ear to ear and say that things are going well for you? Blithe spirit! Perhaps that's part of why I love you."

He gazed at her intently and said thoughtfully, "You do love me, don't you."

"Yes." It was said evenly, without emotion.

With anyone else he would not have hesitated to swear his own love. He had done it hundreds of times. Even knowing that in a week or two she would be out of his life for good, he could not bring himself to deceive her. It was a new experience, one that made him wonder whether he cared too much for her or too little. He thought of Walther Curzmann's check in the envelope in his pocket, and for a moment he considered returning it to him; however, reason took hold of him again. There were other Rita Kleists in the world. He would miss her, but he would get over it. He took another long drink. He didn't usually drink much or fast, but he felt the need for it tonight. Nothing was going the way he had expected.

"I'm sorry," he admitted. "Besides, I'll be leaving Berlin soon."

She had been able to conceal whatever humiliation his failure to respond immediately had caused her, but not the shock of this piece of news. She caught her breath and bit down hard on her lip.

"I have a chance to work with Walther Curzmann. I've just come from seeing him." He had thought the telling of it would have been a joyful occasion, but there was only a feeling of wistful regret. He resented its being this way.

"The film director?"

"Yes."

"I'll try to be happy for you."

He nodded and finished his drink. There was too much

else to say to make anything worth beginning. He got up. "Are you going out?"

"A girlfriend from home is coming to visit for a few days. I'm going to meet her at Tempelhof."

"What time does the plane get in?"

"Eleven."

It was only nine thirty. He lifted his glass. "May I?"

"Of course. Fix me one, too."

He was oddly pleased that she was not going out with another man. But then she loved him, so she probably wouldn't have considered it.

"Is she going to stay here with you?"

"Yes."

"We can use my apartment," he said. He mixed the two drinks and gave her hers. *"Prosit."*

"Prosit." Her hand trembled slightly when she lifted the glass to her lips.

"We have time before you have to go," he said. "I'll drive you to the airport."

"Unconquerable spirit," she noted, dimly bitter.

"Don't you want to?"

"You know I want to, but there is some pride involved."

"Whoever had a problem choosing between pride and a good turn in bed?"

She looked at him with renewed curiosity. "You never have, have you."

He could see this approach could lead only to failure. "We've had good times, Rita," he said tenderly, "the best. I am sorry. Another time; another place, perhaps."

"Another girl."

"No." He meant it. "I couldn't want you as badly as I do right now if that were the case." He looked at her soulfully through his long eyelashes. She averted her eyes and drank her drink.

"You're despicable," she said without conviction.

"I hope you don't mean that."

She wouldn't look at him. He got up and went to her, holding out his hands. She looked up at them and caressed them with her fingertips. She held one to her cheek and kissed it. "Poor hand. Poor, poor hand."

He drew her up to him and kissed her. "You're beautiful. You know that, don't you."

She forced a smile. "It took me hours to get this way, and you'll ruin it all in a minute."

"Thirty seconds," he said, kissing her again, his passion progressing uncontrollably.

"Oh, God, Joachim, you are despicable."

᠎᠎᠎᠎᠎᠎᠎᠎᠎᠎᠎᠎᠎᠎᠎᠎᠎᠎᠎᠎᠎᠎᠎᠎᠎᠎᠎᠎᠎᠎᠎᠎᠎᠎᠎

THE cuckoo clock cuckoo cuckooed ten times. Wolf and Uschi paused in the doorway to watch it. When it finished and was safely ensconced behind the little door, they laughed together and continued into the bedroom. Wolf turned on his desk lamp. A light breeze lifted the window curtains.

"This is a nice room," she said, doing a pirouette. "You're very neat. I'm not surprised, of course. I could tell you were neat."

Wolf had taken Joachim's advice and had drunk not two but three bottles of beer. He felt a little giddy, a little ebullient, absolutely secure about everything he said and did. It was a marvelous feeling and a necessary one at the moment. He suddenly remembered about brushing his teeth. "Be right back." He strode quickly out of the room to the bathroom. By the time he had the toothpaste on the brush, she was there in the doorway watching him. He grinned and started brushing. For some elusive reason he felt very adult brushing his teeth with Uschi looking on. "You brush up and down. That's the proper way, isn't it."

"Brush the way your teeth grow, my father always says, . . . always *said*. Up and down," he sang, "up and down. Up and down." He spit and laughed and turned the water on so hard it spattered over his shirt and trousers. He jumped back. "It's all right. I'm going to take them off, anyway, right?"

276

She smiled and nodded.

"You're not so talkative tonight. Haven't changed your mind, have you?"

"You've been going on so much I haven't been able to get a pfennig's worth in. I think you're a little gaga."

"Gaga?"

"Gaga."

He turned to the mirror and eyed himself suspiciously. "Are you a little gaga, Wolfgang Lentz?"

She giggled.

"You don't *look* gaga," he decided.

"But you *act* gaga."

He turned on her, advancing. "Ga, ga, ga, ga, ga, ga," he babbled, and put his arms around her. She turned her face up to his, and he kissed her. He felt his body warming to her. She started to move away, but he held her and pressed himself against her. She let herself go, pressing back, kissing him long and relentlessly.

He started to undress her.

"No, not here. In the bedroom." She took his hand, and they ran across the living room into the bedroom. Wolf caught hold of the doorframe as they were passing through, poked his head back into the living room, and cuckooed at the clock. He giggled and, back in the bedroom, impulsively dove onto the bed. The springs complained loudly, but held.

She began undressing. "You're gaga, all right. You're very gaga."

He smiled so hard it hurt. He lay there watching her undress, smiling, feeling excitement breach the levee the beer had erected.

"Aren't you going to get undressed?"

"Oh!" He sprang off the bed. "I forgot about me."

He giggled again and started to undress. When he had his shirt and tie off, she was already naked. He stopped and gazed at her. She said something, but his heart was beating so loudly in his ears he didn't hear it. He stared, not taking his eyes off her as he finished undressing, letting his clothes drop in a heap at his feet.

Wolf lay studying the texture of the ceiling when the cuckoo sounded the quarter hour.

"What's his name?"

He turned his head on the pillow and looked at her. She was smiling with her eyes closed.

"The cuckoo's?"

"Um."

"Cuckoo."

"He ought to have a real name."

"What shall we call him?"

"We'll call him Wolfgang—because he's cuckoo."

He drew his laughter from a limitless reservoir of contentment. Not even in his most fantastic daydreams had he come close to imagining the ecstasy he had just experienced. Nothing had prepared him for such an exultant sense of freedom. He had flown like a bird no longer bound by the relentless gravity of inhibition, awkwardness, ineptitude.

"What are you thinking?"

He turned on his side and touched her face. It was not a beautiful face, true, but such a nice face, a pleasant face. He raised his head and planted a kiss on her cheek and, doing so, considered how naturally, how easily he did it, as if he had done it uncounted times before. She moved, taking in hand the source of her own contentment. Wolf was amazed to discover it responding to her touch. She fondled it gently, inquisitively. He reached for her and found that she reacted in kind. He took time to explore her breasts, the smoothness of their skin, the firm suppleness of the flesh. He moved his hands slowly, carefully over her body, pausing to assimilate fully the variety of its parts. His exploration gradually lost its deliberateness and gave way to a frenetic scrambling for a return to ecstasy.

The cuckoo informed them that three quarters of an hour had passed. Uschi lay diagonally across the bed with her head resting on his stomach. Whatever modesty they had had was now dissipated by the intimacy they had twice enjoyed. Wolf propped his head up on a doubled-over pillow and scanned her body. He caressed her shoulder, the soft plumpness of her arms. The relaxing effect of the beer had worn off, but the sense of release remained with him. "After the first time, I didn't think I'd ever need to do it again—or want to."

She traced the curve of his hipbone with her fingernail. "It was much better the second time."

"Oh? Why?"

"It just was."

"What do you mean, 'it just was'?"

"I don't like to analyze it. It detracts from it, somehow."

"But what did I do wrong the first time?"

"You didn't do anything *wrong*."

"Well, what did I do better the second time, then?"

"Really, Wolfgang, you are so. . . ."

For a moment the old defensive attitude returned, and he felt that she was right and he was wrong. But then his newfound freedom asserted itself. He decided that if he wanted to talk about it, he was going to, whether she liked it or not. "Was I as good as the others?"

She moved up, nestling her head in the hollow of his shoulder. "You were wonderful."

He smiled with satisfaction. It was good to hear her say it. He suddenly realized he had leaped from the need to have intercourse to the need to make a good job of it. "Please tell me why the second time was better."

"Are you going to nag me until I do?"

"Yes."

She sighed. "All right. It was slower, it lasted longer, you played with me more before. I almost reached a climax myself."

He was shocked. "You mean you didn't?"

"There's nothing so terrible about that. I hardly ever do."

"But I want you to enjoy it as much as I do."

"Perhaps tomorrow night . . ."

"Why not tonight?"

She raised her head and looked into his eyes. "Can you?"

"Look."

She looked and laughed and fell back into his arms.

The cuckoo reported the half hour, or was it only the quarter hour again? Wolf lay in a half sleep, his mind too full of questions and thoughts to yield to sleep, his body too wonderfully exhausted to fight it any longer. At one moment—or was it longer?—he was digging in the tunnel, rhythmically thrusting the spade into the soft earth while from overhead earth sprinkled down over him as from a sifter, slowly but inexorably burying him under its comfortable weight. In the next moment he was pedaling his bicycle across the surface of the Spree River, chatting amiably with Joachim, who was riding alongside in his car, while machine guns sputtered ineffectually behind them.

When he awoke he sat bolt upright. The room held the weak light of early morning. Heat hung in the air. Nothing stirred; not a sound touched the vacuum of time that held no recollection, no point of reference. Then, from below, one of Frau Meizner's canaries twittered tremulously, testing its voice on the day, and he remembered everything.

A corner of the sheet pulled up over her narrow shoulders, her head turned deep into the goosedown pillow, Uschi slept, hugging the far edge of the narrow bed. He rubbed his eyes and picked the sleep from their corners.

The room contained a new smell, a slightly sweet, pungent odor, making its subtle announcement that he no longer laid sole claim to this bed. He smiled to himself, reveling in the thought that this, too, this mixture of their odors, he now shared in common with other men.

The cuckoo clock sounded five thirty. He got up and went to the bathroom. He urinated, brushed his teeth, showered, and shaved quickly. "Same old face," he said to his image in the mirror. He turned his head this way and that and decided that he wasn't such a bad-looking fellow. Uschi had said he was not handsome, but attractive. He wondered exactly what she had meant. Again he was full of questions. He wanted to talk to her about last night. Three times they had fornicated. He repeated the word and it sounded . . . exciting, illicit, adult.

In the living room he paused by Joachim's door to listen. He could hear nothing. He opened the door a crack and peered in. Joachim slept, one arm wrapped tightly around a pillow, his face buried in it. The thought came to him that this was the first time in their lives that Joachim had slept alone while he had slept with a woman. Unaccountably, he felt sorry for the lonely figure stretched out on one side of the king-size bed. The goose-down comforter which he himself had fluffed up and laid neatly in place had not been touched. There was something forlorn about Joachim in sleep, as if all the strength and vitality he had during the day were shed with his clothes at night.

Wolf pulled the door closed and returned to his own room. Uschi had not stirred. He sat on the edge of the bed contemplating the strange sadness the sight of his brother had generated. Perhaps, he decided, it's only that he was injured. Or it's that he's alone, and it's so unusual for him to be alone. He looked lost lying alone in his big bed. He thought of all the nights Joachim had not slept alone while he himself had lain in bed, hungering for a girl, surviving vicariously on fantasy. The sadness slowly ebbed, giving way to a sense that finally a just balance had been struck between them.

The cuckoo announced five forty-five. Now the day came on insistently, its demands crowding his time. In three quarters of an hour he and Joachim would have to be on their way to pick up Sepp and Emerich. For the first time since he had heard about it, the prospect of the tunnel did not excite him. He would rather have spent the day here with Uschi. Fully awake, he relived the night, and memory became more insistent than the demands of the day. He tried hard to keep from becoming excited, but his thoughts worked a will of their own. He crawled into bed and roused Uschi with frantically tender caresses. She stirred, still half-asleep, and smiling with awakening desire of her own, yielded to him, languidly at first, then, under the relentless renewal of his energy, rose to meet him in full response. Once again, ecstasy reaffirmed its immutability.

Later, as he struggled to arouse himself from drowsy contentment, he wondered what to do next. He had to waken Joachim and get breakfast. What was he to do about Uschi? Should he just close the door and pretend she wasn't there? Should he tell her where he was going? He reprimanded himself for not contending with these practical problems yesterday, but they had not even occurred to him.

He sat up on the edge of the bed. She moved and he felt her fingers on his back.

"Does it hurt?"

"The scar?"

"Um."

"Sometimes, when it rains, it itches."

"Maybe that's because it happened in the water."

"Maybe." He doubted it.

"It's a lovely scar. It's like a medal of honor."

He felt uncomfortable talking about it. He got out of bed and stretched. "How do you feel?"

"Um, wonderful. I could just lie here vegetating—and fornicating—all day."

"What about your schedule? Don't you have things to do?"

She pulled the sheet up under her chin and folded her hands under her head. "My schedule today is Y-O-U."

"But . . . I can't . . . you'll have to change it."

She looked up at him quizzically. "Change it? Do you have something else planned?"

He nodded.

She did not try to hide her disappointment. "But I thought it was agreed that we'd spend the day together. I mean, after last night . . . and just now. . . ."

"I'm sure I didn't agree to spend the *day* with you. I couldn't have, because I knew I couldn't." He picked up the clothes he had left in a heap on the floor, put them away, and started getting dressed in his work clothes.

"Oh, you make me feel just awful! Cheap and . . . vulgar." Abruptly she turned away from him and pulled the sheet up over her head.

He continued dressing, wondering what to do. Any affection he had had for her was gone; she was just in the way, and he wanted to get rid of her. Yet, he thought, what about tonight? Though she did not appeal to him in the least now, he knew that tonight he would want her again. He sat on the edge of the bed to put on his socks and boots. "Will you listen to reason?"

"No," she said through the sheet.

"I thought you said, 'All emotion must yield to reason,' or something like that."

"That was when I was feeling reasonable."

She was completely frustrating. "But I *can't* spend the

day with you. I'd really like to, believe me. I'd love to,
but I just can't."

"You just don't want to."

Sepp's admonition to tell no one, absolutely no one,
about the tunnel prevented him from telling her at first.
But what harm could Uschi cause them? She was just
a girl with a schedule who was crazy about fornicating.
And Wolf was crazy enough about it now to take the
chance. "Can you keep a secret?"

She did not reply for a moment, then said warily,
"What kind of secret?"

"A very serious kind of secret, not a child's secret, an
important secret, a life-and-death secret."

She pulled the sheet down and turned toward him,
surveying his face carefully before she said, "It *is* serious,
isn't it."

"Yes."

"Is it why you can't spend the day with me?"

He nodded.

"All right."

"Listen carefully now. And don't ask any questions."
He waited for her acquiescent nod to make certain that
she was not taking lightly what he had to say. When she
obliged, he went on. "Some of us are digging a tunnel
under The Wall into the *Sektor*. We're going to help some
people escape, including my parents, I hope."

Her eyes grew large with amazement.

"That's why I can't spend the day with you. We've got
to keep working at it. But we quit at six, and I'll be home
by six thirty."

She stared at him, reexamining his eyes and his lips as
he spoke. Suddenly she put her arms around him and
hugged him. "I'm so proud. I'm so proud."

Wolf felt embarrassed and deeply touched. The affection he had had for her earlier returned, easing his way
to a gentleness he had not thought himself capable of.
He bent his head down and kissed her hair and warmed
to the particular odor she had, and he had the thought
that he would find it on his pillow long after he had forgotten her name. He let her hug him for a few moments,
then sat up again. "Promise not to say a word," he said
quickly but firmly, "not a single word, not to anyone."

She nodded her head vigorously, and inexplicably her

eyes filled with tears. She wiped them away with her delicate white fingers. "And I thought you were just a boy." She laughed and cried and wiped away the tears. She stopped and looked at him, smiling with joy through her tears. "I'm just—so *proud!*"

She kissed him quickly and got out of bed. "I'm going to make breakfast for you. You'll need a good breakfast. And what do you do for lunch? Do you carry it with you? I suppose you'll want some beer to take along." She made a face. "How on earth can you bear to drink the awful stuff?"

And she was his Uschi again, babbling on. He swept her up in his arms and twirled her around as she squealed with delight. He thought about throwing her onto the bed and himself on top of her, but there was the tunnel to finish.

18

W HEN Bruno arrived at the warehouse, Joachim's car was not yet there. However, the generator's exhaust hose, sticking out like an elephant's trunk through a chink cut in the window boards, was emitting fumes that rose in shimmering waves in the early-morning heat. At first he had the frightening thought that they had forgotten to turn off the generator when they left the day before. Then he remembered that he had done it himself.

Inside, yesterday's heat lingered, stale and musty, humidified by the evaporation of moisture from the pile of earth. Sweat broke out on his forehead and ran down his spine. From below came the lonely, mechanical beat of the generator. He hung his briefcase on a nail beside the door and looked around. There was no one there.

Downstairs, the heat was less intense, although later, when the sun rose higher and they were working, the difference would be imperceptible. No one was in the cellar, either. The tools stood against the wall shining dully with a thin coating of oil, just as they had left them. On the right, the generator vibrated erratically. The lumber they had ripped up from the flooring occupied a quarter of the floor space. Some of the wood was stacked in two neat piles: one pile comprised the flat, wide, oil-soaked floorboards; the other, the square support timbers. Thin, dark cross lines on the timbers indicated where the cracks between the floorboards had been. To one side stood the two new sleds Emerich and Sepp had finished before the

285

cave-in occurred. Two other partially completed sleds lay
beside the oxygen and acetylene tanks.

On the left rose the growing mound of earth. It seemed
much bigger than would have been expected from the
progress they had made in the tunnel in two days. Near
the beginning of the incline to the tunnel entrance, Bruno
saw a briefcase with a shirt and undershirt draped over it.
It was Georg's. He squatted down in the entrance and
saw him, his arms manipulating the spade casting short,
distorted shadows in the waxy glare of the naked bulb.
The sight of the boy working alone in the narrow con-
fines of the tunnel evoked a recollection of the terror in
his face the day before, and Bruno felt a heavy weight of
compassion settle within him.

He thought for a minute. He could see that the tunnel
had been extended what appeared to be about five meters
beyond the cave-in. That represented five or six hours of
digging, not including hauling out the earth. The full
import of the fact overwhelmed him. Georg must have
been working at least eight hours without rest.

It was so improbable, he looked for another explanation. Maybe Sepp, Joachim, or Wolf—or all four of them
—had worked through the night. That might explain why
Joachim's car was not there. And why the generator was
running. They might have gone off to get breakfast. But
why would they have left Georg behind?

Just as he was considering the possibility, he heard a
car in the alley. He went upstairs and saw the four of
them getting out Joachim's car. He closed the door behind
him. "Good morning, gentlemen."

They returned his greeting. Joachim's face looked better. He seemed to be in good spirits. "Sorry we're late,
boss," he quipped, using the low German vernacular. "I
had to drag the youngster from the arms of Aphrodite.
You'd better talk to him, boss."

Wolf, carrying his and Joachim's briefcases, made an
angry face and averted his eyes from Bruno's.

Emerich laughed. "When I was sixteen I still thought
the stork that had its nest on our chimney brought babies.
What's this younger generation coming to? Next thing you
know, they'll be expecting subsidies and pensions before
they even start to work."

"Just so they aren't expecting little bundles from

heaven," Joachim said, giving Wolf a meaningful glance.

The others laughed, but Wolf shot back a strange look at Joachim, not in anger this time, Bruno thought, but an esoteric kind of communication that was somehow too adult for Wolf's unlined face.

Bruno finally grasped what they were talking about and momentarily was diverted from his purpose. "I'm a man of nature," he told Joachim. "When a boy is old enough to walk, he will walk. When he is old enough to talk, he will talk. When he is old enough—"

"I get the message," Joachim said. "I think, if you don't mind, I'll get someone else to talk to him."

They all laughed, including Wolf. He slung the two briefcases up into Joachim's unsuspecting arms. "You'd better carry these, old man. I'm too weak."

"*Ach so!*" Emerich cried. "The revolt begins!"

"We won't get much work out of him today," Sepp said.

"Don't let him *near* the tunnel," Joachim said. "He'll dig us right into a Vopo tank trap."

"You know," Emerich said, making a tour of inspection around Wolf, "he does look different. Notice the dull glaze over the eyes, the slight wobble in the walk, the—"

Sepp broke in, "Before you get too carried away, peasant, may I suggest, at the risk of being branded a—"

"Ah, yes," Emerich interrupted in turn. "there's a time for play and a time for work, and this is the time for work."

"Good idea," Wolf agreed quickly.

Reluctantly, they gave up their baiting and started for the door. Bruno raised a hand to bar their way.

"Before you go in, there's something we ought to settle." He looked first at Joachim, then at Emerich. "Georg is down there." Their faces showed varying degrees of surprise. "Apparently he's been there all night. I think he's been digging steadily for eight hours, perhaps longer." Surprise escalated to amazement.

Only Emerich seemed unimpressed. "What's he trying to do, buy back his soul?"

"Perhaps that's just what he *is* trying to do."

"It doesn't change what happened yesterday," Emerich growled.

"It was Joachim who was injured," Wolf said. "He's the one who ought to decide."

Emerich gave him an annoyed glance. "You *are* getting cocky, aren't you, youngster."

Wolf retreated, looking to Bruno for help. "I only thought—"

"When you're old enough to think, I'll listen. Don't get the idea that just because you got laid you're suddenly a great thinker."

Bruno interceded. "We can do without this sort of personal attack, Emerich. The discussion is about Georg, not Wolf."

"Well, remind the kid we took him on for his muscle power, not his brain power."

Joachim took a menacing step toward Emerich. Sepp jumped between them. "Hold on, Joachim!" He turned on Emerich, his eyes narrow, his jaw set tight. "Let's get one thing straight right now, Emerich. Wolf is here as an equal. He has just as much right to express an opinion as you. If we're going to go by age, we should all shut up and let Bruno do our thinking for us."

Emerich was not so easily cowed as Wolf, but he took a less belligerent attitude. "I can do my own thinking without advice from youngsters." He glanced obliquely at Bruno, "Or oldsters."

"You're damned insulting," Joachim snarled.

Bruno would have liked to let Emerich's remark pass, but it affected him—more deeply than he would have suspected. The feeling of inadequacy he had experienced the first day, the fear of appearing ridiculous, returned. He could not help wondering if Emerich, the most candid, was merely verbalizing what the others thought—that he was too old, that he did not belong there, that he was, indeed, ridiculous. Momentarily, he was subdued.

Wisely, Bruno thought, Sepp decided not to indulge Emerich's talent for invective. Instead, he brought the argument back to the issue. "Emerich, it's as simple as this: We need Georg. Without him, the tunnel will take days longer. He's been a good worker, as good as any of us. And the fact that he came back shows a certain courage. It will be damned difficult for him to face us after what he did yesterday."

"What he *didn't* do, you mean."

Sepp sighed in exasperation. "All right. What he didn't do. Look here, Wolf has a point. Joachim has more reason than any of us to want Georg out of it. But he went to see him last night, to talk him into coming back." He turned to Joachim. "And it looks as though he did a good job of it."

Joachim demurred. "I doubt if it was anything I did."

Bruno, recovering from his disaffection, thought Emerich was wavering. "Whatever his motive, he is back. Don't you agree, Emerich, that it's a good thing that he has come back? As Sepp points out, we do need him. And are we all so perfect, so free of faults, that we can sit in judgment on him?"

Emerich surveyed the faces arrayed against him. "You're probably thinking that this peasant is too crude to make sophisticated distinctions. Maybe you're right. Maybe peasants are forced by circumstances to condemn quickly, to take sides unequivocally, to remain stubborn and hardheaded until they have the truth beaten into them. I wouldn't doubt it myself.

"But I know damned well that what troubled Georg yesterday will trouble him today and tomorrow and the next day. A coward doesn't become a hero overnight, except in fairytales. You may consider it unfortunate, I consider it reprehensible. That doesn't matter. What does matter is that someone like Georg can be dangerous in this situation.

"If the rest of you agree to take him back, I have two choices: I can accept your judgment and keep my mouth shut, or I can get out. Now, I'll tell you, I have no intention of getting out. I have as much at stake in this tunnel as any of you, maybe more.

"The last thing I want to say, and then I will keep my mouth shut, is this: We're working under Communist territory now. Each day increases our danger of being discovered. And as the danger increases, we're going to have to rely on each other more. Just be certain in your own minds that you can rely on Georg."

The implications of his argument brought silence. Bruno knew there was an element of truth in what Emerich had said.

Sepp looked around at them. When no one answered Emerich, he said, "Let's go to work." He unlocked the door, and they filed in behind him, hanging their briefcases on the nails beside the door, exchanging their street clothes for the mud-caked trousers that hung stiffly in a row along the wall.

As they were going down the stairs to the cellar, Emerich caught Bruno by the arm and held him back. "I'm sorry I made that crack. Sometimes the stupid peasant in me takes over." He shook his shaggy head sadly. "God knows, I can be stupid sometimes."

Bruno nodded. "I only hope you won't say anything to Georg."

Emerich looked confused. "But we have to say something. Oh, I won't make any cracks, don't worry about that. Not that I've changed my mind, but what I said goes. As long as the rest of you are willing, I'll go along."

"If you're concerned about amenities, I suggest you simply avoid him for a while."

Emerich thought it over for a moment and decided, "That's probably the best idea." His small black eyes stared into Bruno's inquiringly, as if to deracinate some secret they concealed, then he turned away abruptly. Bruno watched him go down the stairs, clumping his heavy, grease-soaked boots on the worn wooden treads, his thin, hunched shoulders seeming even thinner in the gray light than they actually were. His heart had room for compassion for Emerich, too.

In the cellar, Sepp approached Bruno with the day's work schedule. "Emerich and I are going to finish the sleds. The four of you work on shoring until it's caught up with the digging."

"Do you think it's necessary? Georg has already extended the tunnel five meters without incident."

"I'd rather not take the chance of another cave-in. The more we get shored up, the less we have to worry about." He gestured vaguely. "What Georg did was on his own initiative."

"Have you spoken to him yet?" Bruno asked.

Sepp looked apologetic. "I thought you might do a better job of it. Would you mind?"

"No."

Then he asked in a quiet, confidential tone, "Did you start the generator this morning?"

"It was going when I arrived."

Sepp bit his lip. "Ask him when he turned it on."

Bruno had wondered about that, too. But he doubted

that Georg would be so stupid as to make unnecessary noise. He didn't mind speaking to Georg. If Sepp wanted him to, he would. And though he questioned why Sepp, as their leader, had not chosen to take on the delicate responsibility himself, just as yesterday he had wished the job off on Joachim, Bruno was generous enough to believe Sepp's reasoning—he honestly thought Bruno could handle it better. Crawling forward toward Georg, he wondered if he could. He quickly searched his mind for an opening remark but had come up with nothing particularly apt when he reached the boy.

"Good morning, Georg," he whispered genially, trying to put on a light air.

Georg looked back without raising his head and nodded. He anticipated Bruno's question. "I just turned the generator on. I was using a flashlight before. Don't worry, I've been very quiet." He resumed his work.

Bruno saw that there was little strength left in the boy. The blade of the spade sank only halfway into the earth, and when he twisted the handle to loosen the earth, his arm shook with the effort and his breath came loud and shallow. His eyes were bloodshot from lack of sleep, and his body was thick with sweat and dirt. He raised the spade to drive it in again.

Bruno caught hold of it. "We're going to shore up what we've dug before we go any farther." Georg did not argue. Bruno was relieved. He had been concerned that the boy might carry his gesture too far, making a difficult situation impossible.

Georg sat up and closed his eyes, leaning back against the cool earthen wall. Bruno examined the progress he had made and was impressed. His earlier estimate of five meters was about right. And he had done a good job of shaping the sides and ceiling.

Georg's eyes opened but avoided meeting Bruno's. Bruno knew he had to say something to him before they left the tunnel, before Georg came face-to-face with the others. "You want to know what we think," he said.

Georg shook his head wearily. "It doesn't matter." The simple solemnity with which he said it convinced Bruno that it was not an idle judgment. What he and the others thought really did not matter to Georg, at least not at this moment. Apparently he had lived through the next few minutes many times over in the private agony of his imagination and was by now too numbed to care about their realization. Bruno's compassion for the boy slowly took a turn toward admiration. There was no need to say anything, and he was relieved. He doubted that he would have come up with anything startlingly profound, anything Georg did not already know.

Georg looked back down the stretch of tunnel toward the cellar and, as if wanting to get it over with, said, "I guess we may as well get to work."

"How do you feel—physically?"

Georg forced a grin. "That doesn't matter, either."

Bruno had had no specific idea of what he expected to happen when he and Georg entered the cellar, but whatever fears he had of an embarrassing scene were unfounded. Instead, a general impassiveness, an affected indifference conspired to leave the issue hanging like a choking man on a scaffold, neither dead nor alive. No one spoke to Georg, except about the work at hand, and he responded in kind. Whenever anyone approached Georg, Bruno could see in their eyes thoughts different from the perfunctory words they spoke to him. An uneasy tension gripped the cellar. It was as if a temporary truce had been called between enemies during which the two sides, secretly distrusting each other, were forced to work together.

At one point, while Bruno and Georg were cutting struts for the shoring, and Joachim and Wolf were working in the tunnel, Sepp came over and asked Georg to write another note to his parents. "You asked me for that yesterday, didn't you. I . . . forgot about it."

"It's important," Sepp said curtly.

"I'll do it now." Georg set down his saw and went to the tool chest for pencil and paper.

Sepp took the opportunity to quiz Bruno. "What do you think?"

"I think Georg is waging a battle within himself, the dimensions of which none of us can appreciate."

Sepp looked skeptical but let it go. "He looks tired."

"He's exhausted, but it would be a mistake to ask him to quit now."

"Has anyone said anything out of line?"

"Not even Emerich."

"We've been talking it over. I think he's not as hard-headed about it as he was before."

"He did have a point."

Sepp's face grew troubled. "I suppose I should have found out more about Georg before I asked him to join us. But what was I to do, ask him how he was on guts?"

"Don't start blaming yourself."

Sepp gave him an offended glance. "Don't worry, I'm not," he answered, and abruptly returned to work.

Bruno wanted to stop him and apologize for his patronizing attitude but thought better of it and let it go. Even Sepp was sensitive today, and Bruno wondered if perhaps for the good of the tunnel they would not have been wise to accept Emerich's reasoning.

He stood watching Sepp and Emerich working on the sleds. Sepp was bent over, hammering a fold into a sheet of steel plating that would serve as one side of the sled, while Emerich stood aside holding the oxyacetylene torch, waiting to weld the corner seam. The way the light from the torch fell across Sepp's arms and back, casting elongated shadows gyrating along the wall, created an eerie, unnatural quality that always attracted Bruno's aesthetic response.

In his mind's eye he stopped the motion as he would a film he was watching, holding a selected frame on the screen. He assimilated every detail and pondered the excitement he had not known for six months but which had been his benchmark on hundreds of previous occasions when he had perceived just the right combination of form, color, mood, and organization of subject to inspire a vision he cared enough to paint. The experience had always come at odd moments, when he least expected it. It was an almost painful insight, an exultation beyond the normal bounds of endurance and rooted in the knowledge that no one else could share what he had seen because no one else—even someone who had seen exactly the same thing—actually had perceived what he had. Only by transferring it to paint on canvas was Bruno able to share the dimensions of his vision.

"What's wrong?"

Georg's inquiry was an unwelcome intrusion, and Bruno was on the verge of making a vexed retort, but he answered, "Wrong, Georg? Nothing's wrong. Something is quite right for a change, quite right, indeed."

By noon, Sepp and Emerich had completed the four sleds. With all six of them concentrating on the shoring, they had finished the stretch up to the cave-in by two o'clock in the afternoon. Bruno, Sepp, and Emerich were crouched under the cave-in hole, considering what to do about it.

Emerich shook his head. "It's a bitch. I can't figure how to fill it, and I don't think we dare just leave it. A good rain could wash a ton of earth down here."

"And possibly cause a complete collapse," Bruno said.

"We'll have to shore it," Sepp said.

Bruno didn't understand. "What do you mean?"

"He means," Emerich said wearily, "that we'll have to shore up into the hole."

"And on all four sides."

"Are you certain that's necessary?"

Sepp gave him a slightly annoyed look. "Do you have a better idea?"

Bruno felt put in his place. "I didn't mean to sound critical. I was only wondering if there could be a simpler solution."

Emerich shone the light up into the hole again. "We can square it off on the sides, all right, but that pipe poses a problem."

"We can lay in planking on each side of the pipe until it comes down level with the bottom of the pipe," Sepp suggested, "then add another, final layer of planking across that."

"The planking will have to be cut to size," Emerich said. "I think we ought to remove the earth up to the top of the pipe and lay the shoring on top of it. The pipe will make a strong support."

Sepp disagreed. "The more earth we take out, the less there is between us and the Vopos."

"How do you propose to hold all this up?" Bruno asked. "We certainly don't dare do much hammering."

"Everything will have to be wedged in under stress, the same as we've done with the shoring so far."

Emerich looked resigned. "We're not going to get it done today. And I have to leave for work."

"It's not supposed to rain tonight," Sepp said.

Emerich made a scoffing rattle in his throat. "Those forecasts are wrong half the time."

Sepp smiled. "Pray, peasant, pray."

They accomplished very little shoring around the pipe. Shaping the sides presented no problem, but fitting in the overhead planking around the pipe was frustrating. The tallest of them, Sepp and Wolf, could just touch the pipe standing on tiptoe, so they had to pile up planking on the floor to serve as a platform to stand on.

Sepp's idea was to set the overhead planking in place on one side of the pipe, run a transverse beam across it, and wedge struts in under the beam, just as they had been doing so far in the tunnel. The problem was holding the pieces of planking—three across and three deep— in place while getting the beam under them. Two of them just did not have enough hands. So they took the precut pieces back into the tunnel, nailed them together, and toed the beam in with spikes. This worked, and they were able to get the struts up under the beam.

The other side of the pipe was completed more quickly, but that was as much as they got done by quitting time. The sides were still not shored up.

"I suppose the prudent thing would be to come back after supper and finish it," Bruno said. His suggestion was made with reluctance. He was very tired, and he had a notion that he might attempt to do a little sketching tonight.

Georg gave him a suppliant look. He was having trouble keeping his eyes open. His unshaven face had gone sallow.

"I don't want to run the generator at night," Sepp said. "And it gets awfully quiet around here after suppertime. With only two meters of earth left at this point between us and the Vopos, we'd be taking a big risk. Besides, Ilse is expecting me. I have to give her a note from Georg."

"I have . . . plans," Wolf admitted timidly. "But I'll cancel them if you want me to."

"So have I," Joachim said. Bruno noted that he did not offer to cancel them.

"Everybody's had enough for today," Sepp concluded. He smiled at Georg. "Am I right?"

Georg mustered a weak smile. It was the first time that

a semblance of concern for Georg had been expressed by anyone since Bruno had talked to him in the tunnel at the beginning of the day.

"I'll give you a ride home, Georg," Bruno offered.

He nodded his thanks, too tired to speak.

"What if it rains?" Wolf asked.

"We've got the ceiling shored," Sepp said. "That's the most critical part. It ought to hold."

"We had better get going," Joachim said. "It's almost six o'clock."

Sepp and Bruno ended the day's work by measuring the length of the tunnel while the others cleaned and oiled the tools. It was eighteen and six-tenths meters long, which meant that Georg had dug five and two-tenths meters during the night.

"That's an average of six meters a day," Sepp said. "At this rate, we have about ten more working days left."

"Perhaps it will work out just as we'd planned."

"If nothing else goes wrong," Sepp said glumly.

"I wonder how many times we'll say that before we're finished."

Sepp smiled bleakly. "I wonder."

It sounded like an animal groaning far off in the night. Bruno was only vaguely conscious of it, suspended between sleep and wakefulness, urging his mind to take the plunge into the sleep his body was demanding. A breeze came up, insinuating its foreboding fragrance through the window screen. Again the thunder sounded—unmistakably thunder this time—and Bruno abruptly abandoned the battle and came fully awake. Lightning opened his eyes. He listened for the thunder, watching the curtains blow back into the room, dancing with the capricious breeze.

Frieda drew her legs under her breasts. Bruno pulled the sheet up and covered her. Under the sheet, her body reminded him of a range of snow-covered hills seen from a great distance. He tucked the sheet close around her back and shoulders.

The lightning came more boldly, illuminating the room, followed close on by the thunder. He thought of the windows open in the house and got out of bed. Frieda awakened and turned her head on the pillow. "Bruno?"

"It's going to rain."

"What time is it?"

He held the alarm clock up to the light from the window. Lightning opened the darkness. "Ten after two." He put the clock back on the table. "I'm going to close the windows." She murmured and went back to sleep.

In the living room, the smell of the impending rain was driving out the stale heat that had accumulated during the day. Behind the French doors, the branches of the big oak argued with the wind. Bruno had too much faith in the old tree to have any doubt about which would win. He closed the windows, taking care to do so as quietly as he could so not to reawaken Frieda. Two he left partially open to admit the fresh wind. He stood watching the rain come on, the first drops spattering the pane noisily, rude visitors in the night. He thought of the tunnel and his halfhearted suggestion that they finish shoring the cave-in hole. He wished now that he had been more forceful about it.

Sepp had said that the rain would be their worst enemy. So far, the enemy had not chosen to put in an appearance. As if to assure him that the respite was over, a bolt of lightning illuminated the yard so that the hedge and the flowers along its roots were painted in vivid colors against the backdrop of gray sky. The thunder followed soon afterward, its crescendo of clamor but an anticlimax to the stupendous effects of the lightning. Bruno turned away, aware he preferred the lightning because he was more eye- than ear-oriented.

He had avoided his studio, perhaps consciously. He wasn't certain. There, tacked upon his easel, hung a sketch in charcoal on newsprint. If this were half a year ago, the fact would have been of no moment. Now, it was an enormously, frightening portent. When he had left the studio late that night, turning off the light, still standing in the doorway until his eyes became adjusted to the semi-darkness so that he could satisfy his desire to see the chiaroscuro without benefit of the lesser shadings, he had felt unexpectedly excited. The study was so good that he went to bed with the intention of moving from it directly to oils. Rarely had he been able to do so from only one sketch, even in his most productive years.

Now, hesitating, his hand on the door handle, he wondered if his reaction would be the same. Perhaps he had been carried away simply by the act of drawing again. Or he may have been too tired to make a fair judgment. Or worse, had he lost his critical acuity in six months of inactivity? If that were the case, he would be no better a judge now than he had been a few hours ago. He realized that this last fear was unrealistic. He could no more lose his ability to discern good art from bad than a swimmer could forget how to swim. It might be, as Grupmann said, that he was not much at articulating his judgment, but where his tongue might fail him, his eyes would not.

He flung open the door and strode in his bare feet across the linoleum floor to the easel. With exaggerated deliberation he placed himself in front of the sketch. Through the expanse of windows, the lightning spread an incandescence across the paper, embossing in its fleeting light the lines he had placed there. In the darkness he held them in his mind's eye. It was unnecessary to turn on the light. He would never lose the brief impression he had received. A smile came to his lips, touched his heart.

It was good. It was very good.

He went back to bed amid the tumult of the storm and slept a deep, gratified sleep.

19

GEORG awakened full of energy. He had gone to bed as soon as he arrived home and had slept a deep, dreamless sleep. He dressed in the meager light from the window. In the street below, puddles glistened here and there in the white, early sun, but the sidewalk and the streets were dry. If it had rained, it had probably been a light shower. Georg wondered if the tunnel had been affected. The newsstand at the corner was open for business, the morning papers displayed along the edge of the roof like clothes hung out to dry. A queue of people waited at the tram stop, reading, yawning, glancing from time to time up the street to see if the tram was coming. Georg lingered at the window, considering the dichotomy of the people in the line, each possessed by his own secret irretrievable past that had determined what he was at the moment, yet each at the moment bound to the others in a common cause—to get on the tram and find a seat.

Georg wondered what trouble each of them harbored behind the ostensibly serene breakwater of his or her face. Perhaps among them was someone like himself, one who would understand and forgive. Even as he thought of it, he remembered that the desire for understanding and forgiveness was from before he had returned to the tunnel, from before he had talked to Bruno, and was no longer important. Now what mattered was that he build on the first brick he had laid in place, regardless of its questionable strength.

The people in the queue began to fold their papers under their arms and to get out their fares. The tram was coming. They edged forward, drawing the line together with growing expectation. The tram nosed out from behind the corner building and came to a noisy, screeching stop. The doors flipped open, and the queue of people ascended in an orderly fashion through the door while a few descended from the center. The second person to emerge was Klaus.

There was no mistaking the round, plump face crowned by black hair, the enormous body poured into a shapeless mass that seemed to be collapsing to both sides while it juggled forward. It came to rest at the newsstand. Georg stared, fascinated, not yet connecting Klaus's appearance with himself. It was only when he glanced toward Georg's window—had he seen him?—and took up a vigil behind his newspaper near the newsstand that Georg made the association. He jumped back from the window and stood in the shadow, waiting for his terror to run its course. His heart was pounding everywhere in his body. Tears threatened his eyes. He put a finger to his teeth and bit hard.

He had to think. A score of questions fought for the first chance to be answered. He fought for control, sorting them out, selecting the most immediate to his concern. Why was Klaus there? If he only wanted to talk to him, he would have come up to the door, wouldn't he? Maybe not. He might not want to identify himself directly with Georg, he might not want anyone to be able to testify that he had come calling on him. The other possibility was that he intended to follow Georg.

That was it! He was going to follow him, hoping Georg would lead him to the tunnel. That had to be it.

What should he do? Should he stay there or get away? How could he get out of the building without Klaus's seeing him? There was only the one door to the street. The back of the building faced on a small courtyard, separated by a high wooden fence from other, similarly fenced-in courtyards that were entered from the backs of other buildings on the block. The only way out that way was to scale the fence and pass through one of the other buildings to the street behind.

He quickly decided to try it at once, letting the other

questions wait until he was safely away. He pulled on his socks and boots, laced them quickly, and, taking his briefcase, he entered the living room, closing his door quietly so as not to waken Elsbeth and Frau Schneider. But Elsbeth was already up, standing in the archway to the dining room in her bathrobe and slippers, her round, fleshy face gray in the morning light without makeup.

"Do you want some breakfast, Georg?" she asked.

"I don't have time."

She looked hurt. Her colorless eyes drew back behind the mounds of puffy flesh under them.

"Where you been goin' so early these last few days?"

"I don't have time now, Elsbeth."

"You sure you don't want no breakfast?"

He shook his head and left.

Once out the front door, he hurried down the steps to the courtyard. The small plot of ground had been sectioned off into eight equally smaller plots, one for each of the apartments in the building. Some contained flowers, others rows of vegetables—mostly green beans and tomatoes. Narrow pebbled walkways separated the plots, each of which had been tended with meticulous care. Not a weed anywhere.

The board fence was at least three meters high. He looked around for something to stand on, but in the tiny courtyard nothing had been left lying around. Then he remembered the garbage cans under the stairwell where he had many times, in his efforts to please Elsbeth and her mother when he first moved in, deposited their garbage for them. He lugged one out—they were heavy, made of sheet steel, like the sleds in the tunnel—and placed it at the end of a path at the base of the fence. He wondered in passing why people built fences, anyway.

As he made his way to the tunnel by way of side streets, constantly looking back to see if he were being followed, he tried to sort things out. Tonight he was supposed to meet Klaus at the café. If he didn't show up, Klaus's suspicions might be confirmed and he might decide to have action taken against Georg's mother and father. The thought of them in prison was unbearable. He would have to keep his appointment.

But what would Klaus say? Would he admit that he had planned to follow Georg? Would he demand to know

why he had not seen him come out of the apartment
building? He might even insist that Georg give concrete
evidence of the tunnel, that he take him there, right then
and there, or else. . . .

The terror began to build again. He knew that he
could not handle the situation alone anymore. He decided
to ask someone—anyone—for help. Bruno seemed the
most likely to understand. He would talk to Bruno—if
he could get up the nerve.

CLAD only in their undershorts, Sepp and Wolf crouched at the entrance to the tunnel. In the light of a flashlight, Wolf stuck a stick into the water standing in the tunnel and brought it out.

"About ten centimeters."

"Shine the light into the tunnel."

He pointed the light straight down the length of the shaft. Tumid water reflected the beam its entire length to where it fell in diminished power on the dark outlines of the four struts canted at different angles, like dead trees fallen in a swamp.

"You said it would hold," Wolf said, more in sadness than reproof.

"I thought it would."

From behind, where Emerich was trying to start the generator, came the sound of the motor sputtering, then dying. Emerich cursed.

"Let me give it a try," Joachim said.

Emerich growled, "You think I'm not strong enough?" The light passed from one hand to another.

"Let him try," Georg said.

Sepp motioned up the tunnel. "Let's go take a look."

Wolf inserted the metal ring at the end of his flashlight between his teeth and started forward. Sepp followed. The water was warm and added a new smell to the tunnel, a dank, putrescent odor that made the close air seem even closer.

"I hope this isn't sewer water," Wolf whispered. His voice sounded loud and hollow with the water to reflect it.

Along the way Sepp paused to feel around the struts to see if the water had loosened them. Those he checked were still solidly in place. He knew, however, that they would have to get the water out as soon as possible. The longer it stood in the tunnel, the greater was the risk of the struts being undermined.

As they approached the cave-in, he noticed the earth under his hands and knees was becoming softer. A layer of silt had accumulated under the muddy water.

Wolf started and squelched a cry. He rubbed a knee. "Watch out for gravel," he whispered over his shoulder.

Within a meter of the cave-in, the water became a thick sludge of silt and gravel. On both sides of the tunnel directly under the hole the walls had been eroded away, forming irregular concave recesses. The vein of gravel was clearly visible, reaching a half meter beyond the hole along the length of the tunnel, cutting across it at approximately the same angle as the pipe overhead. It extended up the sides of the tunnel into the hole. Water was seeping down the rough gravel faces of the recesses, carrying with it earth and gravel from above.

Under the hole, lodged in the sludge, lay the planking they had wedged around the pipe. One crossbeam, still held in place at one end by a strut, hung down like a broken arm. The other lay wedged between two struts that had fallen across one another, forming an X.

Wolf pointed the light up into the hole. Sepp had expected a serious situation, but not so serious as this. The concrete pipe was entirely exposed, the gravelly earth having been eroded away around it. Between the pipe and the earth above it was a gap of about a third of a meter, which meant that there was only about a meter of earth between them and the surface. Water continued to seep through from above, breaking off earth and gravel. They could hear the water and bits of gravel plinking onto the top of the pipe. The pipe sounded as if it were empty.

"Maybe there's a depression up there on the surface where the rainwater has accumulated," Wolf suggested.

"Most likely. It stopped raining three hours ago. The last of the water should have drained down by now."

"What are you going to do?"

"Shore this up as fast as we can. Come on."

While they were crawling back through the tunnel, the lights went on. A muted cheer came down the dank shaft to meet them. Sepp wondered if the noise could be heard through the thin layer of earth between them and the East Berlin Communists. They would have to be extremely careful about noise in the area of the cave-in.

In the cellar the others looked up expectantly when Sepp and Wolf emerged from the tunnel.

"Bad news," Emerich concluded from their expressions.

Sepp nodded. "The shoring in the hole is shot. The water's eroded a good meter of earth from the top."

"And it's still coming in," Wolf added. "There's a lot of water in the tunnel."

Sepp picked up his undershirt and wiped himself off. "We've got to put in new shoring as fast as we can. Joachim, you and Georg knock together a couple of ladders. Don't make them beautiful, just usable. And make it fast. Bruno, go upstairs and—"

Joachim and Georg were still standing there, listening. "Get going on those ladders," Sepp repeated. The two looked momentarily flustered, then, with deliberate haste, headed for the lumber pile, Joachim immediately assuming command, telling Georg to get hammers and nails.

"What do you want me to do upstairs?" Bruno asked. They were beginning to grasp the urgency of the situation.

"Take a look out the window at the area where the cave-in occurred—just beyond The Wall. You'll probably have to go up to the third floor to get a good view. See if there's water standing there."

Bruno left, moving in his peculiarly stiff manner, much as if his joints did not bend the way they were supposed to.

"Wolf, take a spade and start squaring off. But be careful—don't take any more earth off the top than you have to."

"Right."

"Clear the debris out of the way—put it farther up the tunnel."

"What about me?" Emerich asked. He looked very tired. His dark eyes were sunk deep in the sockets, the whites streaked with red from lack of sleep. His skin looked even more waxen than usual. He had not shaved that morning, and the dark stubble on his chin was spotted with grease and pimples. His speech, too, was slower, as if even speaking were an effort for him.

"You get the hard job."

"Sweet justice."

"Figure out how to get that water out of there. I don't care how you do it—or what it costs."

Emerich nodded. "I'll take care of it. Don't worry."

"I won't. That's why I gave you the job. But do it fast. As long as the water's in there, we can't continue the digging. And the shoring is in danger of being undermined."

"I guess a pump's the only answer."

"Don't forget that you've got to pump it someplace else—someplace where it won't arouse suspicion."

"I'll look it over." He headed for the tunnel.

Joachim and Georg were still going through the pile of planking, selecting pieces suitable for the ladder, discussing the merits of each in great detail. Sepp went over to them. "Just make it fast. Any planks will do."

"But it should be strong," Georg protested.

"If you don't hurry, it won't matter."

"Aren't you being a little dramatic?"

Joachim had tempered his inquiry with a smile, but Sepp recognized the derision behind it. His first reaction was to retort angrily. He realized that of late he found himself more and more forced to control his anger. "I wish I were," he said calmly, and went to the tool chest for the measuring tape and a spade.

Bruno returned. "There's a large collection of water, all right. It stretches from The Wall for about five meters in all directions."

"Could you guess how deep it is?"

"That's hard to say. Not more than a few centimeters." He eyed Sepp curiously. "What do you propose to do?"

"First of all, I want to get that hole shored up so the damned thing doesn't cave in entirely. Then we've got to get the water out of the tunnel."

"Even if we shore up the hole, won't the water continue to run down into the tunnel?"

"Maybe the sun will evaporate it."

"In a day or two—if it doesn't rain again."

"That's a lovely thought."

"Why not drain the water away? Drive a small pipe from the tunnel up to the surface."

"The Vopos would notice it."

Bruno sighed. "I think you give the enemy more credit than they deserve. If they were so clever, they'd never have needed to build that damnable Wall in the first place."

Emerich came out of the tunnel. "I've got the solution. I'll pump the water into the sewer pipe."

Sepp felt a nervous laugh break across the threshold of his control. "Bruno wants me to stick a pipe up under the noses of the Vopos. You want to pump the water out through their sewer system."

"Is there more water up there?"

"A small lake."

Emerich's face turned a darker shade of gray. "The gods are not with us, Josep." He scratched at a pimple. "What do you say?"

"You'll have to wait until we're finished shoring in there. Can you put a hole in the pipe without making noise?"

"With sulfuric acid. It will turn concrete to paste."

"All right. What about a pump?"

"A hand pump with some extra hose ought to do it."

Sepp got out his wallet. "How much do you think it will cost?"

"I'll try to scrounge one up secondhand."

Sepp gave him fifty marks.

"Take my car," Bruno said, handing him the keys.

Emerich's tired eyes turned bright at the idea of driving Bruno's Mercedes. "I hope you're well insured. I have to confess, I'm not the best driver in the world."

"I'm insured."

Emerich left, bounding up the stairs with renewed vigor.

"What is it between automobiles and young people?"

"Love."

Sepp turned to see how Joachim and Georg were doing

with the ladders. They had finally selected four planks for rails and were just beginning to saw pieces for rungs. "Give them a hand, will you, Bruno? And see if you can hurry them along."

Sepp joined Wolf in the tunnel. He had cleared away the debris into the forward part and was considering the job of squaring off the hole for the shoring. The hole was now almost two meters deep—three meters to the floor of the tunnel. Although still frustum in shape, considerably more earth had been washed down from around the top, so that the angle of the sides was less acute.

"At least it will be easier to shore without the pipe to worry about," Wolf said.

"Let's cut these walls as square as we can."

"Are you planning to shore the walls, too?"

"If we don't, the water will still wash the earth down the sides and gradually weaken the roof."

They set to work, cutting into the gravelly soil, making right angles in the corners, leveling the walls so that they could fit the planking flush against them. By the time they had done as much as they could reach, Joachim and Georg came in, dragging the makeshift ladders.

"Nice weather for ducks," Joachim whispered.

He was a sight—his stocking cap pulled tight under his ears and over his forehead, his upper body covered with dry scabs, his legs dripping with muddy water from the knees down.

Sepp suppressed a laugh. "If the roof should cave in, we'll just send you up through the hole. You'll scare the Vopos to death."

Joachim made a mock bow. "I stand ready to serve in any capacity, *mein Führer*."

They maneuvered the ladders up into the hole, one on either side, and Wolf and Sepp continued the squaring off. Joachim, Georg, and Bruno started hauling the earth out. It was a slow process because of the water. At one point, Bruno inadvertently struck his spade against the side of a sled. The sound seemed clangorous in the tunnel. They all instinctively stopped work to listen. Sepp thought of how wild animals grazing peacefully on a plain all stop to listen at the first sound of danger. Water began to run in the pipe again, and as if that sound were a camouflage for the echo of the other, they went back to work.

With five of them working in the tunnel in such close proximity, the air soon became foul with the stench of the water, the old wood and their sweat. Working so laboriously, they used up the oxygen in the air quickly. The heat became thick with humidity. Georg complained of a headache.

"We'll be finished here in a few minutes," Sepp assured him. "Then you can start cutting the lumber."

It was another fifteen minutes before Sepp was satisfied with the shape of the hole. His plan was to raise the struts under stress under overhead transverse beams and planking. The struts would be placed out from the walls just far enough to slide planking behind them. Once all the planking was in place—covering all the walls—they could pound the struts back against it to make sure it was in securely.

In two hours they had the ceiling shored. One strut was placed in each of the four corners. Along each transverse face, one strut was set on either side of the main tunnel shaft. "Now all we have to do is cut the planking, fit it in place, and knock the struts up tight against them," Sepp said.

Joachim poked his head into the hole. "Emerich's back."

"Did he get a pump?"

"So he says." Joachim looked at the work Sepp and Wolf had done. "It looks good—much better than yesterday's job."

"Tell Emerich I'll be right out. How are you coming with the planks?"

"We'll bring some in as soon as we have a load." He sniffed the air. "We're going to have to figure a way to bring some fresh air in here. It smells like a cesspool."

Sepp nodded. "It's not too bad now, but the longer the tunnel gets, the worse the air will be."

Joachim left, stirring the water behind him. Sepp gave Wolf a cursory inspection. "How do you feel?"

"I'm all right."

"If you start getting a headache, let me know, and we'll bring someone else in here for a while."

"I won't get a headache."

Sepp suspected that Wolf was flattered at being chosen to work with him on the shoring. Sepp had not done it out of kindness. After Emerich, Wolf was the most adept at doing this sort of work. He did not have to be told twice what to do, and often he grasped ideas before Sepp had expressed them completely. He worked fast, diligently, and without unnecessary comment. He remembered Emerich's remark that if Wolf had muscles, he wouldn't need brains, because they had enough brains. Sepp had come to realize that although muscles and brains were necessary in work like this, attitude was the paramount quality. Wolf had the right attitude—to get the job done as quickly and efficiently as possible.

"Let's go see what Emerich's come up with."

Emerich was coming down the stairs, into the cellar thumping a heavy contraption behind him, grinning through the effort. "Josep, not only have I found us a usable pump, but we can sell it later to an antiques dealer for a fortune!" He hauled the pump down onto the earthen floor and stood back so that Sepp could look at it.

If it was indeed a pump, it was like none Sepp had ever seen. A myriad pipes, valves, couplings, cams, levers, sockets, hoses, chambers, gearwheels, and bolts surrounded a tall, slender cylinder, at the top of which was fastened a crank of sorts. The whole thing was coated with peeling rust and a host of fungus, barnacles, and insect nests. In stark contrast to its thoroughly utilitarian appearance was a gargoyle spout protruding from what was apparently the front of the thing.

"What is it?"

"A pump!"

"A pump?"

"A pump."

"For once I hope you didn't pay."

"Five marks. He wanted ten, but I bargained with him."

"You lost."

"No, I didn't. It works. I tried it. And with the money left over, I got block and tackle."

"Is it really a pump?"

Bruno came over. "What in Heaven's name is *that?*"

"He says it's a pump."

"It *is* a pump."

"Do you believe him?"

"No."

"Neither do I."

Georg and Joachim came over.

"Looks like a doomsday machine," Joachim said dryly.

"He says it's a pump," Bruno said.

"It doesn't look like a pump," Georg said.

"Damn it all, it *is* a pump!"

"Who paid you to haul it away?" Joachim asked.

"I *bought* it."

"He paid money for it," Sepp said.

"Real money?"

"The poor boy is tired," Bruno said.

Emerich folded his long, leathery arms across his chest. "Carry on, gentlemen. When you're finished with your little jokes, my machine and I will make you eat your words."

If Sepp had allowed them, they would have gone on casting pearls of wit before this swine of a machine. But the job of shoring remained, and with some reluctance they returned to work, content to chatter about it among themselves.

They finished the shoring by lunchtime. Emerich couldn't wait to prove the worth of his purchase and went to work as soon as the tunnel was cleared. When he came out and announced that he had a hole cut in the pipe with the acid, Sepp went in and helped him move the pump through the tunnel into place below the pipe. It was heavy and they had a hard time getting it through the water.

Emerich removed two coils of rubber hose he had carried around his neck like a horse collar and dropped onto the lower rung of a ladder, panting. "The air is rotten in here."

"That's something you can think about when you get the water out."

"What are you going to do about the water on the surface?"

"Let it drain. The shoring will hold the earth in place. We may get some water in the tunnel, but I don't think it will be enough to interfere with the work."

"Well, if you do, I can always pump it out."

"If that thing works."

Emerich sat up. "It works." He attached one end of the hose to a pipe spout near the bottom of the machine.

The free end of the hose was covered with a piece of fine screening Emerich had bound to it. He carried the screened end down the tunnel beyond the area where the sludge had accumulated and laid it in the water. He fixed one end of the other hose onto a small pipe in the gargoyle's mouth and, taking the other end up the ladder, fed it into the hole in the side of the pipe. He came down, took his gloves out of his hip pocket, and put them on. They were heavy leather gloves, fraying at the seams and worn thin on the palms.

"I feel as if we should offer up a prayer," Sepp said.

"You are a man of little faith, my *Ami* friend."

"But of experience."

Emerich rested his hand on the crank and cocked his head. "Ready?"

"Ready."

He began turning the crank. It made a small creaking noise. At first it was the only noise to be heard in the tunnel, save for his heavy breathing. Sepp wondered if it were the sort of sound that would carry to the surface. Then the sound of gurgling water arose from the bottom of the apparatus, and, like the excruciating climb of a mountaineer over a rocky tor, the water struggled toward the top. Emerich beamed when the hose leading up to the pipe stiffened and jerked. From above came the unmistakable sound of water squirting from the hose against the inner wall of the pipe. The gurgle in the pump subsided as the water filled its array of fixtures.

"Congratulations," Sepp said. "How long do you think it will take?"

Emerich shrugged. "Two hours. I'll have to clean the screen every so often, and move the hose around."

As Sepp was about to leave, Emerich said, "All this is discouraging, isn't it."

Sepp studied his face before answering. He saw there, in the dark eyes watered from fatigue, a concern that not even his success with the pump could disguise. Sepp suddenly realized that what Bruno had said in jest was quite true. Emerich was tired, more tired than Sepp had been willing to admit. The long hours at the factory and in the tunnel had caught up with him. It was natural that his physical condition would be reflected in his attitude.

"I'm not discouraged," Sepp said as convincingly as he could.

"Tomorrow it will be something else."

"Maybe. And we'll lick that, too, whatever it is."

Emerich chuckled quietly, sardonically. "You Americans." He seemed about to say something else, but apparently decided that the two words were adequate for his thoughts.

Sepp grinned. "We dominate half the world, peasant. We must have something."

"True. A mystique is what you have, a groundless conviction that tomorrow will be better. And all the tomorrows far worse than today won't shake your faith in the mystique. It's amazing." He shook his head in mildly amused incredulity. "Amazing."

Sepp could not resist reminding him that he had just accused him of having little faith. For a moment, Emerich was chagrined, caught in a contradiction. He tried to extricate himself. "That was a small thing. I am speaking now of cosmology."

"Ah, cosmology. We descend to the depths to reach the heights."

"You sound like Bruno."

Sepp begged off. "I find it hard to carry on a philosophical discussion in my undershorts on my knees in ten centimeters of water, and having to whisper, besides." He turned to go but felt compelled not to end on a flippant note what Emerich had begun on a serious one. "Perhaps Americans used to be as you say, and there are probably plenty who still are. But we're changing." He pointed upward. "Things like The Wall make a difference."

Emerich smiled smugly. "The beginning of an education."

Emerich's remark revealed how little he knew about Americans, Sepp thought. "Someday I'll explain some things to you, peasant."

Emerich smiled. "I, too, am willing to be educated."

Taking turns at the pump, they had all but a thin film of water out of the tunnel at the end of three hours. During that time Emerich installed a block and tackle system to be used for hauling out the sleds. He attached a double block at the base of a stairway support timber and one at the top. The lead end of the rope was threaded through a single movable block and fixed to the base of the timber. The movable block had a hook which could be attached to the sleds. By having a block at the top of the stairway support, they could haul downward on the rope, which was easier than hauling horizontally.

"Hauling out six sleds, one after another," Emerich said, "we can have one man on the pulley rope, one taking the movable block back into the tunnel and guiding the sleds out, and one hauling the sleds from here to the pile. That still leaves a man digging and two working on shoring lumber."

"All that assumes the new system with the six sleds works," Joachim said.

It worked better than they had hoped. Sepp and Emerich had twisted steel rods into spiral hooks, three of which were screened into each side of the tunnel along the ceiling line. To pieces of straight rod they had welded little caps which fit over the ends of the protruding ends of the hooks. The rods served as rails on which the empty sleds were set, riding on sheaves welded to the top of the gunwales of the sleds. It was much like a short overhead railroad. When he had a sled filled, all the digger had to do was drag it back about six meters, then lift down an empty sled from the rails overhead. The sleds were heavy but not so heavy that they could not be lifted down by one man. When he had filled five of the six sleds, the shoring crew pitched in to help the hauler get the sleds out, empty them, and return them to the rails. Meanwhile, the digger continued to fill the sixth sled.

Since on average it took an hour to fill six sleds—Wolf and Sepp, the fastest, could each fill six in about fifty minutes; Bruno, the slowest, took about an hour and fifteen minutes—that much time was available for the shorers to work without interruption. The only work the hauler had to do, besides help haul out the earth once every hour —which took about fifteen minutes—was to shovel it from the base of the growing pile in the cellar, where it was dumped, up to the top—another ten minutes' work. This left him about half an hour to help either the shoring crew or the crew ripping up flooring and joists and sawing them to size, depending on where he was most needed.

It was going on six o'clock, and Sepp's spirits had been rising all afternoon. He felt he had good reason to feel buoyant.

They had made a good job of shoring the cave-in hole. It was a solid construction, and he was confident it would withstand even a torrential rain.

The new system was working well, even with only five men on the job. When he finished his digging stint, the tunnel would be three meters longer. It was true, he had to admit, that they were behind his original schedule. He had hoped that by this time—at the end of the fourth day—the tunnel would be about thirty meters long. Actually, it would be only twenty-one. He filled the last of six sleds, and while the others hauled them out, he sat on the tarpaulin, his back against the front of the tunnel, contemplating their work.

From his view, the tunnel ran straight and level toward the square of light that marked its entrance. The shoring jutted out from the walls at equal intervals, although in receding perspective they appeared closer together nearer the cellar. Spaced every five meters, the lightbulbs illuminated its entire length and evoked a dull gleam from the wooden struts, tranferring those surfaces on which the flooring had been laid, and thus had not been exposed to wear, to the texture of polished ivory. The smell of the wood had become strong, and even in the dead air at his end of the tunnel Sepp could appreciate its scent, a fragrance that called to mind spring days in the Grunewald.

He closed his eyes, for the first time that day feeling the ache in his body settling deep into the fiber of his muscles. It was the kind of ache that had no source, no single locus, but made itself felt in a hundred different places at the same time. In his closed-eyes darkness he listened to the sleds being hauled out, the hoarsely whispered exhortations, the scrape of the runners on the fine grit of the clay floor.

He sensed more than heard someone near him, and opened his eyes. Bruno was crouching in front of him, his eyes lost in the shadow his body made between Sepp and the last lightbulb.

"I thought you might be asleep." Bruno seemed uncommonly solicitous.

"Not that I wouldn't like to be." Sepp rubbed his eyes.

"I guess it's time to go home. It's been a long day." He started to get up.

Bruno put a restraining hand on his shoulder. "It's going to be longer." His face grew solemn and his voice anxious. "Georg has just confided a most distressing story to me."

Bruno was seated at a table at the opposite end of the outdoor café from Georg. Sepp exchanged a glance with Georg as he sat down next to Bruno. Only one other table was occupied—by two men arguing heatedly over cognac and Coca-Cola. It was a run-down café in a run-down section of Wedding. Sepp knew the type: The tables were cheap and wobbly, the chairs rickety, the waiter sullen and inattentive, the drinks of poor quality, the prices high. He wondered how places like this stayed in business.

He had had to leave Ilse earlier than usual in order to get to the café on time. Bruno had ordered a cognac for him. He sipped it and began to relax.

"How are things over there? How is Ilse?"

"She's fine. Has anything happened here?"

"We're still waiting. There's time yet."

"How has he been?" he asked.

"Georg?"

"Um."

"As well as could be expected. The boy is under a terrible strain."

Sepp said nothing.

"Has Ilse changed? You haven't spoken of her much recently."

"Changed? No, not really. The past year hasn't been easy for her, but she's in good spirits."

"And what of her progress?"

"Coming along." Actually, her progress was not "coming along" at all. In a second visit to Dr. Lentz, during which Ilse had presented the second note from Joachim, she had not moved the cautious doctor one bit. The only hope he had given her was an agreement to see Ilse again the next day.

Having failed with Frau Knauer the day before, Ilse had gone back at suppertime with the hope that Georg's father might prove less suspicious. Instead, he was sullen and unresponsive and in the end had virtually thrown her out of the house.

Emerich's aunt, who they had expected would pose the biggest problem, had turned out to be the most amenable of the lot. She had agreed at once to cooperate, not out of particular concern for her brother's family but because she hated Communists so vehemently that she was eager to do anything to cause them trouble, no matter how small it might be. However, her part was only a third of the plan—Dr. Lentz had to agree to cooperate, and the Webers had to be notified. Time was growing short.

Bruno glanced at his watch—ten minutes to go. "Georg said he's usually on time."

Sepp nodded.

"I still think it would be wise to turn the whole matter over to the police," Bruno urged. He was not as adamant as he had been earlier, but he was still reluctant enough to make Sepp wonder whether it was a good idea to have brought him along. He glanced at Georg. Seeing him sitting there alone, an ordinary-looking student, slightly hunched, his feet crossed under his chair, it was hard to believe he had got himself into such a mess. No wonder his nerves were shot.

"Do you think he'll manage?"

"He'd damned well better." Sepp recognized that he was just as angry with himself for having been taken in by Georg as he was with Georg's deception and stupidity. At the moment he was inclined to get rid of him once this business was taken care of.

"The whole thing still hasn't penetrated my brain," Bruno said. He sipped his cognac with uncommon fastidiousness. "Murder has always seemed so . . . remote. It's too horrible to comprehend." He seemed to shudder, whether from the effect of the raw cognac or the thought of murder, Sepp didn't know.

"You won't have to do it," Sepp reminded him.

"I am a party to it, however."

"We won't be caught. There's nothing to connect us to him."

Bruno gave him a quizzical glance. "It's not getting caught that bothers me."

Bruno's implication was not lost on Sepp. He did not, however, challenge it, partly because this was not the

time or place to do so, and partly because he recalled that
moment in the cellar in the house in East Berlin when he
had had to decide whether he could kill or not. He still
did not know, and it was not in him to feign indignation.
Sepp was not, however, in a mood to indulge Bruno's self-
righteousness. "You don't have the same stake in the tunnel as the rest of us. Knowing Georg, do you doubt that if
he had to choose between his parents and us, he'd hesitate
a second?"

"Yes, I do."

"That's foolish, and you know it."

"What do you expect to gain by eliminating this fellow?
They'll simply send another to take his place."

"But that will take time, and time is what we need. If
we can finish the tunnel and get Georg's parents out, he'll
be immune to their threats. Besides," Sepp remembered,
"maybe we won't have to do anything. Georg may be
able to stall him."

"You don't really believe that, do you?"

Sepp read deeper into Bruno's thought, and his anger
flared. "If you think I'm looking forward to taking a life,
you don't know me very well."

Bruno was surprised. "I wasn't even suggesting such a
thing. Surely you don't think I was."

Sepp was annoyed that despite his resolution he had
let himself be drawn into a discussion of conscience. He
decided to ignore Bruno's question and concentrate on the
problem at hand. He looked over at Georg, who was looking over at him. Like a schoolboy caught daydreaming,
he quickly averted his eyes. In that simple, brief movement, Sepp knew that Georg would fail, that he would not
be able to deceive Klaus again tonight. The momentum
would place the decision for action in Sepp's hand, much
as if he were the next man on a relay team.

Suddenly, Georg gave a start. Sepp followed his gaze
up the street and saw a man approaching.

"Here he comes."

Bruno started to turn.

"Don't look around." Sepp downed his cognac. The
glass was more than half-full, and the large dose burned
going down. The man came within range of the light of
the café, and as he passed along the sidewalk, across the
line of Sepp's vision, he glanced around the café, quickly

taking in Georg, the two men still arguing at the table near the door, and Bruno and Sepp. When Sepp saw his face clearly, he almost gasped. Swiftly he regained his composure and let his eyes meet those of his adversary with distant unconcern, then turned them on Bruno. "I got a good look at him. Don't even look his way, not for a second. It's very important."

"Is anything wrong?"

Sepp suddenly realized what a piece of luck he'd had. Klaus had come in under the awning and was handing his umbrella to the waiter. Sepp raised his hand to attract the waiter's attention and, in doing so, caught Klaus's as well. He gave Sepp a quick inspection, nodded perfunctorily, said "Good evening" to him and to the two arguing men as well. Sepp replied as if interrupted, and tried again to catch the waiter's eye. Klaus gave the waiter his order and headed for Georg's table. The waiter went back inside without answering Sepp's call.

Sepp smiled, sure that Klaus had not remembered from the night they had passed one another in the entrance to Sophie's apartment building. "I know who he is," he told Bruno.

Bruno's eyebrows rose.

Sepp smiled. "It will be very easy, much easier than we planned."

"Who is he?"

"A political prostitute. He was once a Nazi. Now he's a Communist. He's not the committed type, strictly a small-timer. I wouldn't be surprised if he were taking money from both sides."

"In that case," Bruno ventured, "perhaps we can buy him off."

"Oh, no doubt about it. And probably for only a few hundred marks. But we would never be able to trust him. If he took our money, he'd go on taking theirs, too."

The waiter appeared with a glass of wine for Klaus. When the waiter turned, Sepp caught his eye and he came over.

"Is there a telephone inside?"

"It's private."

"I'll pay for my call."

"Is it a local call? Only local calls."

Sepp got up. "It's a local call." And to Bruno: "I'll be right back."

Inside, the waiter directed him to the telephone resting on the Berlin directory near the beer taps. He opened the directory and found Klaus Schoenemann's name and address: 18 Muhlsteinstrasse, Tiergarten. He committed it to memory and returned to the table. The waiter stopped him on the way.

"I didn't make the call. The number wasn't in the book."

The waiter looked dubious but let him go.

He rejoined Bruno. "We can go now. I've got his address."

"Then we don't have to follow him."

"No."

"Thank God."

Sepp decided then that Bruno was not the one he needed to help him.

Georg arrived at Sepp's room an hour later. Sepp knew when he let him in that his supposition in the café had been correct.

"What happened?"

Georg slumped into a chair and ran his hand over his face. "I told him what you told me to, about a tunnel in Neukolln."

"And?"

"He didn't believe me," Georg said abjectly.

"Did you stick to the story?" Sepp demanded impatiently.

"Yes! Yes!"

"Be calm, Sepp," Bruno admonished him.

"I'm calm." And to Georg: "Well, what happened? What did he say?"

"He said for me to take him to the tunnel right then and there. I said I couldn't, I said I didn't know the exact location, only that it was somewhere near the canal." He sat back and stared ahead into the air. "If he doesn't know exactly where the tunnel begins and where it is to end by Sunday night, he'll have my father fired." He hung his head. "As a 'starter.'" He looked at Sepp blankly. "They'll put my father in prison. I know they will."

"Stop your whining."

Georg was not listening. "We should have done it to-night."

"If we had, his cohorts, whoever they are, would connect you with it. Then you'd have more than your parents to worry about."

Bruno got up. "There is another solution."

Sepp was thinking, and it was a minute before the import of Bruno's statement sank in. "What other solution?"

"We could kidnap him and hold him until the tunnel is finished."

"Which is how long?" Sepp asked sarcastically.

"A week or so, I thought."

"If everything goes well—which, up to now, it hasn't. I estimated we would be thirty meters in by now—and we've only done twenty-one. We'll be lucky if we're finished in another two weeks. Besides, we can't afford two men to stand guard over him night and day. It's altogether too risky. Anyway, where would we keep him that long?"

"I'm sure we could find a place."

"Well, I'm not so sure."

"How about the warehouse?" Georg suggested.

"The *warehouse?* Brilliant! We take the fox into the chicken coop and hope like hell he doesn't get out with a chicken—namely, Georg Knauer."

"It's not such a bad idea," Bruno said evenly.

"If the slightest thing goes wrong and he gets away, the tunnel *and* Georg's parents are *kaputt*. He'll have all day and night to watch us, study our movements. The chances are too great that he'd figure a way to escape. No. It won't do. We've got to get rid of him."

"And what if the very next day a new agent is assigned to Georg? What if that agent keeps this Klaus's appointment on Sunday night? What do we do then—murder him as well?"

Sepp found his irritation with Bruno growing. "Let's quit using that word, shall we? After all, we're in a kind of war, you know. It's a case of us or the enemy, and Comrade Klaus happens to be the enemy." Sepp felt very, very tired. "Bruno, this man . . . he's a cannibal, a savage."

"It's as simple as that, is it?"

"As simple as that."

Bruno turned away angrily. He stuck his hands into his

jacket pockets and strolled the short length of the room, pausing in front of his painting of the white deer. He gazed at it curiously for a long time, the anger subsiding from his face, as though the sight of the painting had worked as a chemical on his emotions.

"What *do* we do, then?" Georg demanded plaintively.

Sepp forced his attention away from Bruno and focused it on Georg. Like boulders tumbling down a slope one after the other, pity, consternation, disgust, and annoyance passed through Sepp's consciousness, leaving him insensitive.

"The best thing *you* can do is shut up."

Georg's immediate expression of humiliation didn't touch a nerve.

"Do you remember, Sepp," Bruno mused, "the day you brought me up here to see this painting?"

Sepp did not reply.

"Do you?"

He pleaded with him. "Bruno . . ."

"You were very special, Sepp, very special."

"What would you have me do? Give up the tunnel? I've lived that tunnel for a year. I've sunk all my savings into it. I've pounded the streets of Berlin, listened to the inane babble of hundreds of students. I've risked my neck going into the *Sektor* every night. And Ilse has risked hers." He shook his head vigorously. "No sir! No sir! I'll kill first if I have to. I don't want to, Bruno. Believe me, I don't want to, but I will."

Bruno looked at him sadly. "I'm sorry I ever got mixed up in this, Sepp—in the tunnel, I mean. Sorry for your sake, not mine."

"You asked me, remember?"

He nodded. "Yes, I remember." He chuckled acidly. "I begged you, as I recall. I thought . . ." He waved it away. "It doesn't matter what I thought."

Bruno seemed suddenly older, a tired, defeated old man who no longer had the energy to do battle. Sepp recalled the day he had shown Bruno the painting. He was like a boy then, a boy who had had his lost dog returned to him. How much he had admired Bruno's unashamed delight, his ability—no, his freedom—to express his delight so profoundly, so completely. In the glow of that memory, his affection for him returned. "I'll get Joachim. or Emerich."

Bruno nodded with consummate sadness.

"Will you continue to work in the tunnel?"

"Of course." He started to say something else, but let it go. He turned to Georg. "Come along, Georg. I'll drive you home."

Georg looked up at Sepp inquisitively.

"You may as well go."

He, too, started to say something, but thought better of it.

"Don't do anything foolish, Georg. Let us handle it from here."

"What . . . what if they do send another man on Sunday?"

"I don't think they will."

"What if they do?"

"Chances are a new man will have to start from scratch with you. That will give us time to finish the tunnel."

"Then I'll have to—"

"You'll have to keep doing what you've been doing for six months. And you'll do it."

Georg nodded weakly. He followed Bruno out of the door, too beaten to argue.

When they were gone, Sepp got on the telephone.

"Hello."

"Hello, Sophie, this is Sepp."

"*Liebchen,* how are you?" She was alone and glad to hear from him.

"Fine. Just fine. How are you?"

"I have a little summer cold, *Liebchen*. But it hasn't put me out of action."

"Good. I was hoping I might see you tomorrow night."

"Tomorrow night? Since when are you so solicitous? You've never given me a whole day's notice before."

"I've reformed."

"*Ach, Liebchen,* tomorrow night I am going to the theater."

"With your husband?"

She let out a raucous laugh. "*Liebchen,* you are wicked. Of course not with my husband."

"Oh, with your ex-Nazi friend. He's the theater lover, isn't he?"

"You musn't call him an ex-Nazi, *Liebchen*. It's so political. Can't you men leave politics out of anything?"

"It has a way of intruding."

"You might come around later, say, midnight. I do miss you, *Liebchen*."

"Maybe I will."

"Maybe?"

"Well, what am I to do with myself until midnight?"

"I thought you said you had reformed?"

"I lied."

"Call me again, *Liebchen*."

"You can count on it. *'Wiedersehen.*"

" *'Wiedersehen,* Sepp."

He hung up. The excitement made his hands tremble. He clasped them together and went to the window. A single light was burning in the bell tower of the church, casting eerie shadows through the concrete lacework. It had been only a hunch, a hope, but it had paid off. Now he had the luxury of knowing when Klaus would be where. That knowledge simplified the matter greatly. He mulled over the word *simplified* and wondered how it could have entered his head. What would be simple about killing this man? *Murder* was the word Bruno had used. Would it be murder? If he had choked Konrad Möss to death, would that have been murder? He considered the ease with which he had decided that Klaus Schoenemann must be killed. Murdered. More than ease—insistence, compulsion. He realized he did not want to consider any alternatives, that he wanted to commit this act in order to . . . yes, in order to make up for not killing Konrad Möss. That had been a failure of will.

How euphemistically you put it, he thought. No wonder you were so ardent in your plea to understand Georg —and so contemptuous of him when it suited you.

Was it . . . cowardice, then?

Aren't you intelligent enough to judge? And why haven't you told the others about Konrad Möss?

They would quit on me!

Would they? At least Georg had the courage to tell Bruno about Klaus.

But this is different. We can do something about it. With Konrad Möss, there is nothing we can do now.

Now.

Sepp wiped the sweat from his face and closed his eyes. He relived the struggle with Konrad Möss in the cellar of the escape house, trying to reconstruct each minute detail in the exact order in which it had occurred so that he could be certain of his motivation at the time. He came out of it convinced of two things: One, he had not killed the Vopo because he could not kill in cold blood. Two, it was good he hadn't because it would have rendered the house useless. He would have had to leave the body there, and it would have been found. He was satisfied with the second fact, but the first confronted him with a dilemma: If he had not been able to kill then, could he kill now? He could not answer the question.

He went to his wardrobe and opened the top drawer. From under his shorts in the back he took out his revolver, cracked it, and inspected the bore. It reminded him of the hundreds of times he had inspected the bores of his platoon's rifles at the barracks. He was chagrined to find that the revolver needed cleaning. He set about cleaning it right then, pondering whom to ask to help him: Joachim or Emerich.

⌐⌐⌐⌐⌐⌐⌐⌐⌐⌐⌐⌐⌐⌐⌐⌐⌐⌐⌐⌐⌐⌐⌐⌐⌐⌐⌐

P ROTECTED by an archway of oaks, the street lay serenely content in the night like an old man finally permitted a little peace after a hectic day. Only an occasional car had disturbed its tranquillity in the past quarter hour. It was a rich street, settled by modern, plush, glassed-in luxury apartments and a couple of old, prewar relics like Sepp's friend's building. Most of the cars parked in the street were Mercedeses, Porsches, and the higher-horse-powered Opels. In the Taunus Sepp had rented, Emerich felt conspicuously out of place.

They had parked about a hundred meters down the block from Sophie's apartment building. The lighted entryway was clearly visible to them. Klaus and Sophie had arrived in a taxi ten minutes ago, but he had not yet come out of the building.

"What if he goes the other way?" Emerich asked.

"We can just drive up alongside him."

"What do you suppose they're doing up there?"

"Having a nightcap. He won't be staying long."

"Are you sure?" Emerich yawned.

"I'm sure." He picked up the gun from the seat between them and fingered the safety.

"What if he won't get in the car?"

"He will."

"What if he won't? What if he starts running?"

Sepp leaned back and looked at him. The green luminescence of the dashboard instruments cast a ghostly glow on his face. "I guess I'll have to shoot him," he said.

"There may be somebody around just then."

"We'll have to take that chance."

Emerich accepted the rebuke and kept quiet. Ever since Sepp had told him about it that afternoon, he had thought of nothing else. The enormity of the act was then still anticipation, a distant reality. Now, when it was to be consummated within the hour, he had begun to have misgivings, not about the act itself or the justness of their cause, but about the chance of being caught. Emerich had no intention of getting caught, and it seemed to him now that the whole affair had been poorly planned, that Sepp had not taken into account any number of possibilities. The way Sepp had put it—"We'll just force him into the car, drive out to the Grunewald, find a quiet spot, and shoot him"—had made it seem simple. Too simple, Emerich had begun to fear.

"How do you feel?" Sepp asked.

"Fine."

Emerich remembered his escape again and thought about the Vopo he had. . . . "I killed a man." He did not know why he had said it. Perhaps it was to reduce the enormity of the act in Sepp's eyes, or perhaps to make himself equal to Sepp in manliness.

Sepp seemed unmoved. He only asked, "Whom did you kill?"

"A Vopo. It was when I crossed over."

"Um."

It was as he had expected. Emerich could not penetrate his coldness. Since Sepp had explained his plan that afternoon, he had displayed not one sign of emotion. He had turned into an automaton designed for one purpose alone —to dispose of Klaus Schoenemann.

"Did it bother you?"

"Afterward?"

"Yes."

"He stood between me and The Wall. He'd have shot me."

"How did you do it?"

"With a pocketknife. I cut his throat—so he wouldn't holler. I got away with his tommy gun."

"Do you still have it?"

"I still have it."

"We can use it when we bring the passengers through the tunnel."

Emerich was surprised to find that he was a little shocked that Sepp had shown as much interest in the gun as in the death of the Vopo. "Do you think we'll need it?"

Sepp shrugged and turned away, directing his attention up the street to the light of the entryway.

Emerich leaned forward against the wheel. He did not dare close his eyes. He would be asleep in seconds. The tranquillity of the street invited sleep. His mind began to wander, entertaining fragments of memory until the memory of his escape came to the fore. He tried to shake it off and would have failed had not Klaus Schoenemann appeared.

"Here he comes."

Emerich looked up and saw a man emerging from the entrance. "A fat man." He reached for the ignition.

"Wait." Sepp picked up the gun and held it in his lap.

The fat man turned right—away from them.

"All right."

Emerich started the engine. He backed up, turned the wheels away from the curb, and pulled out into the street. There was no one else around. The fat man was walking fast, faster than he would have thought him capable of doing.

"Slow down."

"I forgot the lights!" Emerich turned them on, catching Klaus in their path. The man glanced over his shoulder at the approaching car but kept walking. Emerich pulled up alongside of him. Sepp rolled down the window. "Excuse me, sir, I think we're lost."

Klaus paused, acted as if he were about to go without acknowledging them, then turned and came between two parked cars out into the street. Sepp opened his door and stuck the gun in his face. "Get in the back."

Emerich could not see their faces. There was an interminable silence. Sepp's arm made a forward jabbing motion. The man backstepped, opened the rear door, and got in. Emerich watched him move across the seat; he was uncommonly agile for his size. Sepp slammed the door.

Emerich drove off, heading northwest, taking side

streets until he came out on Bismarckstrasse at the Ernst Reuter Platz.

No one had said a word. Neither Sepp nor his victim had moved. Emerich glanced occasionally at the man's reflection dimly illuminated in his mirror. That he would be dead within a half hour was impossible to assimilate.

"Where have I seen you before?" For an instant Emerich thought Klaus was talking to him.

Sepp did not respond.

"Come now, if you're going to murder me, the very least you can do is inform me of my murderer's identity."

Emerich held to the pace of the traffic, concentrating on his driving. He knew Sepp would not reply, yet as each moment passed he expected him to. They had agreed not to say anything more than was necessary, in case something went wrong and Klaus got away.

"I know I've seen you before." A pause. "Now where could it have been?"

Emerich glimpsed him in the mirror, his fat chin in his fat hand, contemplating Sepp's face. His composure was remarkable, and Emerich began to wonder whether it stemmed from some hidden knowledge that what they intended to do was bound to be thwarted or whether it was sheer bluffing. They came up to Theodor Heuss Platz, where the flame which was to burn until Germany was reunited flickered in the spray of the big fountain behind it.

"Why are you doing this to me? Surely you can tell me that much."

There was not the slightest quality of anxiety in his voice; the man was merely curious. Emerich had to admire him. Free of Theodor Heuss Platz, the car picked up speed, heading due west along the continuation of Bismarckstrasse which was now called Kaiserdamm and shortly would become Herrstrasse, the highway that was once the route to Hamburg. They passed the old radio tower, its ironwork like great spiderwebs in the glare of the lights of the restaurant almost halfway up its summit. A strain of music came from somewhere, perhaps the restaurant. Emerich had never been up there, so he didn't know if they had entertainment.

Klaus began to hum, a different tune. It sounded like a march. Emerich glanced at him in the mirror. He was gazing straight ahead, humming softly to himself, much as if he were out for a Sunday drive, enjoying the scenery, distracted by a pleasant memory. After five minutes the humming unnerved Emerich.

"Shut up."

The humming ceased.

Emerich glanced in the mirror, saw Klaus looking at him, and averted his eyes.

"I admit I am not Caruso, but is it too much to grant a condemned man a little funeral music, eh?" Answering his own request, he took up the vaguely familiar martial tune again.

They passed under the railroad tracks at the edge of the Grunewald. Just short of the big apartments designed by Le Corbusier, Emerich turned into the wall of trees that formed the picket line of the forest that lay beyond. Here the roadway was still wide and fairly well traveled. He turned off at the first narrow side road.

The black trees overhung the road like the walls of a tunnel, through which they could see only so far as the headlights reached. In the sudden silence the engine sounded inordinately loud, and Klaus's humming even more annoying.

"Can't you make him shut up?"

"Turn into the next fire lane."

Emerich switched on the high beams and saw a break in the wall of trees on the left.

"Who would have dreamed it would end like this?"

Emerich slowed, passed over the culvert, and headed onto the grassy surface of the fire lane. Fifty meters in, Sepp told him to stop. He turned off the motor and the lights.

"Get out."

"Perhaps we can make an arrangement."

"Get out."

Emerich got out and opened Klaus's door. "Come on, comrade."

He wasn't budging. "I can pay you well. How much do you want?"

Sepp shoved the revolver into Klaus's ribs. His body jerked reflexively. He threw his heavy legs over the side and got out. Emerich smelled the fragrance of cologne. In the darkness Klaus's face was barely visible. He started humming again.

Sepp came out and closed the door behind him. Emerich's eyes were becoming adjusted to the meager light from the mass of crystalline stars in the black sky. Sepp was holding the gun close to his side, as if he needed his body to brace his arm. Klaus stood before them, his arms hanging at his sides. They seemed too short for his body, and because of his girth, his hands did not come down along his thighs but flapped out in the open, making him look like a fat penguin. He stopped humming and slowly turned his back to them.

Sepp glanced at Emerich, then leaped forward and got around in front of him. Emerich followed.

Again Klaus turned his back to them. Emerich looked at Sepp. He was standing there inert, staring at the back of the fat man's head. Slowly he turned to Emerich and shook his head. He offered him the revolver. Emerich took it. The grip was hot and wet with Sepp's sweat.

"Turn around, comrade."

Klaus did not move. He started humming again.

Emerich extended his arm until the muzzle of the piece was almost touching the fabric of Klaus's suit jacket. He pointed it where he thought the heart would be and pressed the trigger. It moved back a hair, but would go no farther. For an instant he grew frantic. He looked at Sepp in alarm. Sepp did not understand at first. Then he reached over and snapped off the safety. Emerich regained his control. His heart was beating fast, and his pulse was throbbing at his temples.

Klaus was still humming.

Emerich extended the gun again and fired. The kick threw his hand up in a high arc over his head. It surprised him. Klaus pitched forward and fell flat, his arms outspread, his face down, like a clown doing a belly flop.

Emerich brought the gun down and looked at it. The acrid smell of the expended powder tickled his nostrils. He blinked and sniffled. He looked down at the dark mound in the grass. It might have been a weathered extrusion of rock. He bent down and, with great effort, drawing one arm down along its side, rolled the body over. The suit coat was still neatly buttoned, the tie centered between the white collar wings. He did not look dead, only asleep. Emerich emptied the gun into his chest.

He looked up at Sepp, who had not moved. "Should we empty his pockets?"

"Why?"

"So they'll have trouble finding out who he is."

"It doesn't matter if they do, does it?"

"I guess not." He handed the gun to Sepp.

He took it, examined it a minute, and started to put it in his pocket. He withdrew it quickly. "It's still hot."

"Shall we go?"

Sepp nodded. "I'll drive."

"All right."

They got into the car. Sepp laid the gun on the seat between them.

"Don't turn on the lights until we're back on the road."

Sepp nodded and started the motor. He opened his door and leaned out to see where he was going.

In five minutes they were back on Herrstrasse, retracing their route into the center of the city. Emerich rolled down the window and let the wind rush into his face. He felt nothing. It was the same as the other time. Nothing. He thought he should feel something—if not remorse, then joy or exhilaration. It was as if it had never happened. One more Communist dead. Two down; how many millions left? As pointless as pissing in the ocean.

"I didn't plan it this way." Sepp's voice was dead.

It took a moment for Emerich to grasp his meaning. "I know."

"You believe me, don't you?"

"I believe you."

"I wouldn't want you to think I'd pull a trick like that."

"Look, I believe you."

Sepp took the rebuke in silence. Emerich watched the lights of the shops and houses flash by. They passed a Volkswagen driven by a fat man smoking a long, fat cigar. Emerich exchanged noncommittal looks with him. As the Volkswagen receded, losing to the superior power of the Taunus, the man made an obscene gesture with the cigar and laughed.

"What was that tune he kept humming?"

"Didn't you recognize it?"

"It was familiar, but I can't place it."

"It was 'The Horst Wessel Song.' "

Emerich looked at him to see if he were joking. He wasn't. "Are you sure?"

In answer, Sepp began singing the old Nazi marching song. It was the same tune, all right, a catchy march. The lyrics were gruesome, and he asked him to stop.

"You killed two birds with one stone—a Nazi and a Communist."

"How about that."

22

WOLF was getting dressed when the telephone rang. It rang again before Joachim answered it. In the street below, a car passed, its headlights throwing the tidy houses in fleeting relief, catching an unsuspecting couple, strolling in the heavy Sunday night heat, in an embrace. Wolf laughed at their surprise. He returned to the mirror to tie his tie, thinking of the night ahead. Whatever happened to him from now on would be forever framed in the picture of his life of the last four days. Nothing before that would have meaning for him any longer. It was as if he had always been locked up in solitary confinement and was now suddenly free, free to do what he wanted, with whom he wanted, and it would always be right.

His happiness had two sources: Uschi and the tunnel. In his conception they were root and branch of his flowering. Both had been vital, neither sufficient of itself. They worked together in harmony to feed him the nourishment on which his new life grew more hardy with the passing of each day. In the tunnel, he discovered confidence in his ability to share a burden equally with others whom before he would have considered his superiors. At times, as when Sepp had chosen him to help shore up the cave-in, he had felt that he was actually superior to the others. With Uschi, he had found his worth as a man. His physical pleasure had not diminished; if it had altered at all, it was heightened by the confidence he brought home from the tunnel.

But in addition to the pure joy of intercourse, he had discovered, in the times afterward when he lay in the darkness, awakened by what call from conscious life he did not know, the other joy of knowing that someone could care enough to seek his company in the most intimate of relationships a man could share. He had never felt that his mother, his father, Joachim, or his schoolmates had sought him out solely because it was he alone with whom they wanted to share something. Uschi made him feel that no one else would do—no one at all. Even the knowledge that he had not been the first with her could not change his feeling.

Joachim appeared in the doorway, an odd, wistful smile cracking the long, thin scabs around his mouth. "That was Sepp. He just returned from the *Sektor*. It's all arranged— Papa has agreed to come through the tunnel."

The conditioned reaction was out before the reasoned could stop it. "That's wonderful! Just wonderful!"

"Isn't it."

It was Joachim's unconcealed lack of enthusiasm that reminded him of the awful conclusion he had come to over the past four days: He no longer wanted his parents to escape to the West. He wanted everything to remain as it was. It was not actually something he had deduced; it was as if the conclusion, formed unconsciously from scattered pieces, had fallen together and, once there for him to behold, was forever indestructible.

He had first discovered the pieces were there three nights ago, when the rainstorm had awakened him. His first thought was to close the windows in the apartment.

In the living room the curtains were blowing wildly. He pulled the windows to and locked the latches. The wind had put a chill on the room, and he shivered. He looked in on Joachim. He was sleeping soundly, undisturbed by the approaching storm, confident that someone else would close the windows.

Wolf speculated that in every house, every apartment, there was someone who got up in the middle of the night to close the windows when it rained. He thought of them as a breed apart, not certain whether they were to be admired or pitied. He took comfort in recalling that it had always been his father who closed the windows. Perhaps he was up at this very moment, prowling the apartment in East Berlin, pulling all the open windows closed. The thought generated a strong sense of love for, and identity with, his father. He realized how much he missed him, but a second thought tested the edge of his consciousness. Trying to suppress it, he went back to bed, but he lay there unable to sleep, wondering if the shoring in the tunnel would hold.

The first drops of rain spattered against the side of the building. A bolt of lightning struck nearby, followed almost immediately by an explosion of thunder. Uschi awakened and sat up.

"It's all right," he told her. "It's only thunder."

"What are you doing?"

"Just thinking."

"About what?"

"The tunnel. The rain can raise hell with the tunnel." He did not curse much, and when he did, he always felt awkward afterward, as if he had tried a foreign language and mangled it. He pulled the sheet up and put his arm around her. She moved in close. He welcomed the warmth of her body.

"You're cold," she said.

"You're nice and warm."

"Do you like me here with you?"

"You bet."

"Tomorrow night is the last night."

"Will your folks go away again?"

"Not for a long time. Papa almost never takes Mutti along with him."

"When this tunnel is finished, my parents will be living over here."

"Will they stay in Berlin?"

"They've always lived here."

"Berliners are very loyal to this city. It's good they are. It wasn't fit to live in after the war."

"So I understand." The thought that had probed his consciousness and retreated before came forward again, this time in strength. It was too horrible to consider long, and he put it to flight, knowing that this time its memory would linger.

"Is your father strict?"

Wolf thought about it before answering. "He'd never approve of what I'm doing now."

"It's surprising you and Joachim would want them out."

"That's a terrible thing to say!"

"Is it?"

"Of course it is."

"Why?"

"Because you don't know what it's like to live over there."

She did not say anything for a minute. Then she snuggled as close to him as she could get. "I hope your old tunnel caves in. I hope it never gets finished. I don't care what you think of me, but I really hope it never does."

As if God Himself were sending down an instantaneous warning to Uschi—and to Wolf, who had failed to rebuke her—a bolt of lightning struck very close by, the thunder sounding a split second later like an exploding bomb that shook the house with terrifying force. Uschi clutched at Wolf, and he held her so tightly she complained. They lay together nursing thoughts they dared not voice anymore. Outside, the rain came in a pounding torrent now, as though the last bolt of lightning had ripped open a new source.

"I used to be afraid of thunder when I was a little girl," she said. "Were you ever afraid of it?"

"My father explained it. There was never any reason to be afraid."

"You love your father very much, don't you."

"Yes."

She moved away slightly. "I'm sorry I said what I did. I didn't really mean it."

"It's all right. I thought about it, too."

"Will the rain really damage your tunnel?"

"I hope not."

"I hope not, too."

Her mouth was close to his, and he kissed her. She responded with eagerness, and it was not long before Wolf had forgotten about his parents and the rain and the tunnel.

Now he knew that there was no use denying what he felt. It was there, wrong as he knew it was. It was there. Joachim spoke again. "Papa's going to help get

Emerich's family out. They need a reason to come to Berlin, so he's going to certify that an old aunt of Emerich's is dying." He made a face. "It looks as though Papa has located his guts in his old age."

Joachim's unexpected insult to their father seemed only to intensify Wolf's feeling of guilt. He had put his father down by his own rejection; Joachim had spit on him.

"Papa was never a coward."

"He was never quite a lion, either."

"What could he have done?"

Joachim shifted his weight and made a gesture of vague helplessness. "It's all past history. They're coming over—if we succeed with the tunnel." The last was delivered laden with anticipation. Wolf did not have it in him to satisfy him. He could not bring himself to speak the words both of them wanted spoken, to verbalize his feelings, setting them down in words of iron to be forever branded on his memory. He waited for Joachim to do it, but he refused the responsibility as well.

The opportunity passed, and Wolf sensed that, once lost, it would never return. He inspected his well-scrubbed, shaved face in the mirror. For the first time in his life he thought he looked very much like Joachim.

"Are you and Uschi planning to come back here?"

Wolf nodded, not because he could not look into his brother's eyes but because he did not want to. He was acutely aware of the difference.

"I thought her parents were back in the city."

"They are. I have to get her home by midnight."

"I hadn't planned to go out. I'm still not exactly socially acceptable."

"That's all right."

They looked at one another's image in the mirror.

"Amazing," Joachim said.

"What's amazing?"

"What it does for a man."

All at once Joachim's old luster was gone. He seemed petty and narrow of perception. The brass of Wolf's earlier contentment was suddenly heavily patinaed. "Isn't it," he said.

23

==

AS soon as Wolf was gone, Joachim telephoned Walther Curzmann. His servant, Otto, answered.

"*Herr Direktor* Curzmann does not receive calls on Sunday."

"I only want a minute of his time."

"I am sorry, but . . . one moment, please."

There was a muffled conversation.

"Lentz?" It was Curzmann. "What do you want?" He was curt, annoyed.

"I hadn't heard from you, and——"

"I said I'd let you know."

"Yes, I realize that, but——"

"Are you healed?"

"Not entirely, no."

"You'll hear from me." He hung up.

Joachim slammed down the receiver. He sat staring into space, thinking. He picked up the phone and dialed Rita's number.

"Hello."

"Are you alone?"

"No."

"Your girl friend is still there?"

"Unfortunately."

"When is she going to leave?"

"Who knows? Berlin is so *fascinating*."

"Damn."

"My exact sentiment."

339

"There's no chance you can get away?"

"None."

"I miss you."

"And I."

"Can't you steal away into the night?"

"I was taught not to steal."

"I'm in pain."

"Take an aspirin."

"You're a big help."

"I thought you were leaving Berlin."

"You sound almost eager to get rid of me."

"Your pain is contagious. If it's not around I may get well." She changed her tone. "How is your face?"

"Scabby."

"Just like your soul."

"Now that's not nice."

"Hold on." There was a prolonged silence, then she came back on. "Really, Joachim, you are the most wicked man I've ever known." He could tell that she had chased the girl friend out of the room.

"Is it wicked to want you?"

"For how long? Until you leave Berlin? No, thank you."

"If I could just see you—"

"And charm me into bed."

"That's not fair."

"It's fair, and it's true. The other night I weakened, but no more. You'll have to find a cure for your pain elsewhere." She was too serious.

"I thought you loved me."

"Your effrontery is equaled only by your charm. Good night and *auf Wiedersehen*."

"Hold on—" He was too late. She had hung up.

He dropped the receiver onto the cradle and sighed, " '*Wiedersehen*, Rita. *Auf Wiedersehen*."

He went to his bedroom and got out his most current notebook. Returning with it to the living room, he passed his mirror and stopped. He put his face up close and studied it. "Scabby. That's what it is, all right. Scabby. Damn!" He tossed the notebook onto the bed and went back into the living room.

The telephone rang. He leaped across the room, confident it was Rita calling back. He decided to let it ring twice more before answering.

"Hello."

"Hello, Herr Rat."

Joachim's excitement collapsed. The epithet told him that Brim, acting as his agent, had been to see Curzmann and had discovered he was no such thing.

"I suppose you're proud of yourself."

"I haven't thought about it one way or the other."

"You *used* me, Lentz."

Joachim had to laugh.

"That's funny?"

"Coming from you, that's funny."

He did not answer immediately, and Joachim knew that Brim realized there was nothing he could do about it.

"You owe me something." He said it with conviction, but Joachim could tell it was a plea, not a threat.

"How about 'Thanks'?"

"Won't do."

"That's it, comrade. Thanks. Thanks a lot." He hung up. It was gratifying to do the hanging up for a change.

He decided to have a cognac. He poured it, took it to the sofa, and sat down. A little music to soothe the savage breast. He got up, selected *Eine Kleine Nachtmusik,* put the record on the phonograph, and returned to the sofa. The excitement of the allegro was hardly soothing. He sipped the cognac, put his head back and closed his eyes, waiting for the sweetly melancholy *Romanze.* A quiet Sunday evening at home with Joachim Gottfried Lentz. See how he relaxes in his well-appointed Dahlem apartment, sipping French cognac, listening to Mozart, reflecting on the vagaries of man's fortune. See how content he is.

He got up and went to the window, taking the cognac with him. Twilight held the remnants of the day in its gentle hands. A barely perceptible breeze ran its fingers across his face. He stood staring down into the quiet street. From out of the past came the vision of his mother's face the night he had told them he was going to escape and she had taken his side. He saw it clearly, the pain her words had tried unsuccessfully to hide, a kind of pain he doubted he would ever know or fully comprehend.

The first cautious notes of the *Romanze* tested their welcome. He stood there a long time, drinking slowly, thinking, without coming to a decision.

24

BEHIND the church across from Sepp's room, an old coffeehouse stood squeezed between two new high-rise buildings like one old shoe between two new, highly polished boots. Here, Sepp took his breakfast every morning, fortified behind the parapet of the daily newspaper. Monday's paper contained the article he had expected to see.

Businessman Murdered
In Grunewald Forest

The bullet-riddled body of Klaus Schoenemann, Berlin sales representative for a number of textile firms in the Federal Republic, was discovered Sunday morning in the Grunewald. He had been shot six times in the heart and chest.

Police reported that a group of picknickers came across the body lying in a fire lane near the Trummerberg at the north end of the forest. He had been dead for about ten hours.

Although the police refused to comment, it was learned that robbery apparently was not the motive for the brutal killing. The victim's wallet, containing almost one hundred marks, was still in his pocket.

It appeared that Schoenemann had been "taken for a ride," American gangster style. Tire tracks leading from the nearby road up the fire lane indicated that Schoenemann had been brought to the isolated spot to be murdered; however, police could not be certain that there was a connection between the tire tracks and the murder. Preliminary reports showed that the cause of death was a bullet in the heart, fired from a .38-caliber revolver.

Schoenemann operated his business from his home at 18 Muhlsteinstrasse, Tiergarten, without assistance. No family is known to reside in West Berlin; however, Schoenemann escaped from the *Sektor* several years ago, and attempts are being made by the police to ascertain whether any family is living there.

Residents of his apartment building who knew Schoenemann could throw no light on the possible motive for the crime. "He was always cordial, always polite," a neighbor reported. "He was gone quite a bit of the time. His business called for a great deal of entertaining, I suppose, because he rarely came home before midnight. He was a good, kind man. This is ghastly news."

At this time, although they will not admit it, police are baffled.

Sepp read it a second time. The reference to an American-style gang killing unnerved him at first. He knew perfectly well that the reporter was not trying to suggest that an American had had anything to do with the murder, but the mere allusion was enough to worry him a little. The fact that the police were baffled was reassuring. He had heard that most murders were solved by detecting the motive. As far as the police knew, the motive was still a mystery.

He wondered about the tire tracks. It was unlikely, though, that they would be of much help. Tens of thousands of cars in West Berlin must have the same kind of tires as the Taunus.

He folded the paper and laid it aside. The tiny coffeehouse was crowded with people having breakfast, reading their morning newspapers. It was the same as every other morning, familiar faces all stealing the minutes before they had to leave for work so that they could find out what was going on in their world—here in Berlin and abroad. 'We have crises with our morning coffee," Berliners liked to boast. The people of no other city in the world could say that without appearing pompous. He finished his coffee, paid his check, bade *"Auf Wiedersehen"* to all, and left.

The day already promised continuing heat. Better heat than rain, he decided. He strolled slowly back toward his room trying to order his thoughts. It was a rare experience for Sepp to suffer confusion of the mind. He had always been able to deal with one idea, one memory, one problem at a time; he could line them up according to their priority. "A cluttered mind is worse than an empty one," his father liked to say. Sepp smiled, remembering it. His father had a passion for order. "Life is chaos. It is man's highest challenge to bring order to it." His father was given to clichés; perhaps that was why in retrospect his homilies seemed so unoriginal and uninspiring. Nevertheless, he smiled when his father came into his thoughts. He smiled a third time when he realized he was indulging in a fond memory to evade an unpleasant one.

He rounded the corner along the churchyard. Still in shadow, except for the top of the spire where the cross, painted gold, glittered like the real thing in the morning sun, the church reminded him of Trinity Church at the head of Wall Street in New York City. It was about the same size, of similar design, constructed of red sandstone which over the years had weathered to a dingy black. A hint of the original color still could be seen when the sun was on it, but now it looked black and singularly forlorn, as if it had been left by the awakening city to sleep on, with no one caring enough to rouse it. Unlike Trinity Church, though, it had no surrounding graveyard, only a yard on one side where patches of grass struggled to survive the daily onslaught of the parish boys who had made it their playground. By midday, dust would be rising high into the branches of the mottled sycamores that stood guard outside the line of black wrought-iron fence. Soon, Sepp realized, he would be back in New York, this time with Ilse, taking his place in his father's brokerage firm in Wall Street, where the only sycamores were those that took their chances on the side streets intersecting Wall. The prospect seemed so distant he let it slide away into its reserved corner in the back of his mind.

Crossing his street, he looked up at the church clock. It was six twenty-five. Joachim was due in fifteen minutes. He entered his building and climbed the steps to his room.

It was hot and, with the windows closed and the blinds drawn against the sun, foul with the smell of dirty clothes he had had no time to take to the laundry. He took up his briefcase, already packed for lunch, and went back down to the street to wait. The young priest he often saw came out of the church and stood on the steps. He gazed up into the sky, shading his eyes against a sun that had not yet risen above the rooftops. He saw Sepp and nodded.

"Good morning," Sepp called.

"Good morning." The priest smiled shyly, averting his eyes, glancing around the churchyard and up the street. He looked to be about the same age as Sepp. His blond hair was cropped short, and from a distance in the bright light he looked as though he had no hair at all.

"It's going to be hot again," Sepp said.

"Yes. Hot." The priest made a gesture of helplessness. He did not seem to want to talk—or perhaps he wanted to but did not know what to say. Sepp considered crossing over to talk with him. As he was making up his mind, the priest turned abruptly and retreated into the dark sanctuary of the church.

Sepp wondered what it was like to be a priest. The celibacy part had to be hard. He had heard that priests became drunkards, dope addicts, and homosexuals because of it. He supposed a few did, but he put little credence in those stories. People set apart, like priests, were bound to be subject to the gossip of more ordinary mortals. He wondered what the priest's reaction would have been if he had known he had just wished a good morning to an accomplice to murder.

An accomplice—not the murderer himself, only the accomplice. Only the accomplice.

How long had it been since he'd last thought about it? Ten minutes? How many times had that moment when he had stood in the dark thickness of the Grunewald and handed the revolver over to Emerich returned in memory? Two nights and one day had passed. He had endured them. He had accepted the fact, but he was not yet certain he had accepted the meaning of the fact, assuming the meaning was what he thought it was.

Afterward—after he had dropped Emerich off—he had gone to Georg's to tell him.

"Was it . . . difficult?"

"I didn't do it. Emerich did."

"Oh." He seemed disappointed.

Last night, it was different. Georg came to Sepp's room to tell him about the rendezvous at the café.

"No one showed up. I waited an hour, and no one showed up."

"Good." It seemed unimportant.

Georg nodded.

"Now just wait for them to contact you again. Chances are they won't, not before the tunnel is finished, anyway, and we've got your parents out."

"All right."

Sepp thought Georg would leave then, but he lingered. "I'm glad it wasn't you who did it—shot him, I mean."

Sepp had had enough. It hadn't left him all day, not even when he was with Ilse in the *Sektor,* not even when she told him the good news about the Lentzes.

"What difference does it make who did it?" He answered his own question to himself: It makes a difference to *me.* In *me.*

"I feel better knowing it wasn't you," Georg said.

"Do you know why I didn't do it?"

Georg was surprised the question needed asking. "You couldn't, could you."

"What do you mean by 'couldn't'? If you think it was a moral decision, you're wrong." He was suddenly angry with himself for having admitted it. As far as anyone else was concerned, including Emerich, it could have been a moral decision. And he would have appeared the better for it, he could have escaped not only with impunity but with an aura of righteousness.

Georg's reaction stunned him. "I wasn't talking about the morals of it at all. That never occurred to me. I meant that you just . . . couldn't."

Of course Georg was pleased to learn that Sepp "just . . . couldn't" kill Klaus. Now he had someone to share his cowardice, someone whom he had considered so far superior to him. If Sepp could act in a cowardly way, then Georg was not so different after all. He was no less a man than Sepp, and everyone knew that Sepp was quite a man.

Joachim's car came around the corner. Sepp welcomed the reprieve from his thoughts. Neither Joachim nor Wolf knew anything about the Klaus affair, and he hoped they would never have to be told. He trusted that Emerich and Georg would be discreet enough not to mention it. He knew he did not have to worry about Bruno.

The cellar was more stifling than ever.

"We've got to get some air in here," Joachim said. "Let's knock out some window boards on the alley side."

Sepp objected, "It's too risky."

"Take the risk," Emerich said.

It was a reflection of his morale that Sepp took it as a pointed remark. He immediately acceded. "All right. But on the second floor, where no one from the factory can see in."

"Naturally." Emerich was annoyed that Sepp would think he had to tell him that.

"I didn't mean—" Sepp caught himself, dismayed at how quickly he had turned obsequious. Emerich had not missed it. He gave Sepp a quizzical look and left to do the job. Sepp thought how typical it was of Emerich to do the work—once it was decided to do it. Joachim had suggested it, but it would never have occurred to him to carry out his own suggestion. Sepp wondered whether he would have had to do the killing if he had chosen Joachim instead of Emerich to help him with Klaus. This led him to wonder if he had unconsciously selected Emerich, knowing all along that he would not be able to do it and that Emerich would. How precisely you can machine a part. How carefully you measure, to the millionth of a centimeter. How you rub it to a high sheen.

"Shouldn't we get to work?"

That was part of the syndrome. Georg would not say "Let's get to work" or "What the hell are we standing around for?" The coward dare not be assertive.

From above came the sound of Emerich's hammering: insistent, strident, yet musically tintinnabulary—the peal of a victory bell. The rest were waiting for Sepp to give them instructions for the day, to assign them to their jobs as he had done every day.

And should I then presume?
And how should I begin?

Was it only a momentary aberration, or had he had an intimation of the time when he would have a bald spot in the middle of his hair? Would it come to that?

Bruno yawned.

Wolf picked up a spade. The oiled blade reflected the light. "It's my turn to dig."

"Yes, we should get started," Sepp began. He gave out the assignments and, while everyone was setting about getting ready for work, he went upstairs to where Emerich was unshuttering the window. He was just finishing up.

"The air feels good," Sepp said, "even if it is hot."

Emerich nodded.

"I wanted to talk to you alone."

"Is it still bothering you?"

"Yes, but that's not what I wanted to see you about. Dr. Lentz has agreed to do it."

A great smile broke across Emerich's face. He was clean shaven for a change. He looked much better than he had Saturday night. Apparantly he had had no trouble sleeping all day Sunday as he had planned. And he would be on vacation this week.

"I told Joachim about it yesterday on the telephone. The Lentzes are going to come through the tunnel, and he'll sign the necessary papers for your aunt."

"Now all we have to do is get the word to my father."

"Have you given it any thought?"

"I think a letter is the best way. There's a danger that it will be censored, but I know they don't censor all the mail."

"Ilse could telephone him. Calls within the *Sektor* aren't monitored—not ordinary civilian calls, anyway."

"I doubt that my father would believe her." Emerich grinned, assimilating it more completely. "This is really wonderful news. I have to admit I was skeptical. I didn't think any doctor over there would take the chance."

"Ilse is impressed with him. And with your aunt. Apparently the old lady has a lot of spunk."

Suddenly Emerich was beside himself with excitement. "Of course! Aunt Magda! Why didn't we think of her? She can telephone. She can convince him. My father sent me to her when I left. He must think something of her, even if she was disowned by the family."

It struck Sepp as a good idea.

Emerich laughed. "I've thought about the plan so much that I really had the old girl on her deathbed. It never occurred to me that she was available."

"I'll be seeing Ilse tonight. She can talk to your aunt tomorrow."

Emerich's exuberance was somewhat tempered. "So Joachim knows. Did he say anything?"

"He wasn't exactly delighted to hear that his parents had decided to come over."

Emerich gave Sepp a searching look. "Did you expect him to be?"

Sepp didn't understand. "Why shouldn't he be?"

"Consider his situation: He has a good job, an apartment virtually to himself, Wolf to keep house for him, a car, and half the women in Berlin lined up for their turn to jump into bed with him. If you were in his place, would you want your parents around?"

"Then why—"

"Why did he agree to work on the tunnel?" Emerich shrugged. "I confess I can't figure it out. I'll wager a week's wages he has a self-serving motive, though."

"Don't we all?"

Emerich considered this. "*Touché.*"

"I suppose it doesn't matter what his motive is. He's doing his share."

"True."

Sepp had nothing more to say. He started to go.

"Did you see this morning's paper?"

Sepp nodded.

"It looks good for us."

"Yes."

"Don't fret about it, Sepp. Everyone has his moments."

Sepp resented the attempt at consolation. "Sure they do."

"They do. God knows they do."

"I'm not 'everybody.' "

Emerich gave him a mildly admonitory look. "You'll have to learn to live with it—like the rest of us."

Sepp realized that Emerich had been telling him that he, too, had had his moments. This came as a surprise, and he recognized that he had fallen into the faulty logic that, because Emerich had been able to act when he himself could not, Emerich was immune to the same weakness.

Sepp felt a little better about it and began to think he
could, as Emerich had put it, learn to live with it.

Sepp and Georg were working together, sawing flooring
and joists. Although he would have preferred to work
with someone else, even Emerich, the schedule called for
Georg, and Sepp had no good excuse for changing it. Besides, he wanted everything to appear as normal as possible. It seemed very important that things look normal.

"Did you see the newspaper this morning?"

"I saw it." Sepp could not bring himself to be cordial.

"The police are baffled. That's what it said. They're
baffled." He was delighted.

"There's nothing for you to worry about anymore, is
there?"

"It's great, isn't it? Just great." He was ebullient. Sepp
wondered if he had thanked Emerich. Or doesn't one
thank a murderer?

"You saw Ilse yesterday, didn't you?"

"I saw her."

"Has she talked to my parents again?"

"They're being cautious. They were home, but they
wouldn't answer the door."

It didn't bother Georg. "They're simple people, you
know, suspicious and . . . afraid." He hurried on, as if the
mere mention of the word were an indiscretion. "They'll
come over. You'll see."

"If they won't talk to Ilse, how are they going to be convinced?"

"Oh, *you* can go talk to them," he said confidently.

"I can?"

"Can't you?"

"Don't you know that I'm usually followed when I cross
over?"

Georg's confidence collapsed. "But why?"

"Ask the Communists."

"You haven't . . . done anything wrong, have you?"

"For Christ's sake, Georg. You lived over there. You
know what they're like. Why ask such a stupid question?"

Georg was taken aback by his sudden hostility. He
started to apologize, to explain, but Sepp did not want to
listen. He picked up two sawn joists and headed for the

tunnel, surprised at his own vehemence but not regretting it.

It was not long after lunch. Sepp and Georg had taken over the digging and the hauling. Sepp was digging, filling his second sled, when Wolf appeared. He was obviously shaken, his boyish face drawn tight with unaccustomed anxiety.

"What's wrong?"

"You'd better come out. There's a man there who says he's the owner of the building."

Sepp was astonished. It was the last thing he had expected. He could see his own troubled expression mirrored on the boy's face. "It's all right," he said, knowing that he had no idea whether it was all right or not. "Is he alone?"

"There's another man with him."

"Police?"

"I don't know. I don't think so."

"Let's go talk to them."

As they crawled forward, Sepp asked him how they had gotten in. "They were pounding on the door like madmen. We had to let them in." Sepp was displeased but realized he probably would have done the same.

Georg and Bruno were waiting for him at the tunnel entrance. Bruno looked apprehensive; Georg, scared to death.

"Let me talk to him," Bruno said.

"No, I'll handle it."

Sepp started to leave, but Bruno held him back. "Tell him we'll pay for the damage we've done."

Sepp understood what Bruno was offering. "It will be in the thousands."

"I know."

"Let's hear what he has to say first."

Bruno nodded. "Very well."

"If he wants to pay, let him," Georg pleaded. His eyes were enormous with fear. He would do anything, sacrifice anybody except himself—to get rid of the fear. Sepp was puzzled because Georg had nothing to fear anymore.

"We'll talk to him," Sepp repeated.

"They'll put us out. We'll have to quit." Georg was gesturing frantically, hands trembling. "We'll have to give up the tunnel." Sepp listened and watched, the realization burgeoning within that the difference between him and Georg was enormous. One moment of weakness had not changed anything. He had no time to dwell on the notion, only to feel a sense of release.

"We'll talk to them," he said again and, leaving the tunnel, paused, wiping his face as best he could with his handkerchief. The two strangers were standing in the center of the room between the two stone columns, both with their hands clasped behind their backs, the younger one slightly behind the older. The older man was obviously impatient; the younger, mildly bored.

Bruno and Georg joined Joachim, Wolf, and Emerich in a huddle around the tool chest. They glanced apprehensively from Sepp to the two men, then back to Sepp. They looked like a gang of trapped criminals speculating on their fate. Their attitude was perhaps warranted by the circumstances, and the atmosphere of the cellar—the bare bulbs dropping pools of dull light among the shadows, the seemingly forbidding pulsation of the generator, the ominous, threatening attitude struck by the two strangers —contributed to the feeling of guilt that Sepp found he was in danger of sharing.

Sepp appraised the men quickly. The older one—a short, frail man with a thick mass of white hair, big ears, pale parchmentlike skin stretched tautly over the protruding bones of his face—dominated the pair. The younger one—a good-looking, well-dressed man in his thirties— appeared to find his surroundings distasteful. He made a point of examining his hands and cleaning a bit of imaginary dirt from his fingertips. The older man squinted at Sepp through thick glasses. The younger yawned. He was not a policeman.

"Are you the leader of this gang of vandals?" The old man's voice was high-pitched but firm.

Sepp walked slowly toward them.

"We are not vandals, Herr Komanski."

The man twitched his thin, bony nose and sniffled. As if by magic, a handkerchief appeared in the younger man's hand. Herr Komanski snatched it and blew into it noisily.

"So you know my name, do you? What's yours?"

"Bauer. Josep Bauer."

Komanski sniffled and wiped his nose. "Not vandals,

eh? What do you call yourselves, then? Look what you've done to my building." He waved a mottled hand around the room. He did not seem particularly angry, though. Sepp was not certain what his attitude was—annoyance, perhaps?

"We're digging a tunnel, Herr Komanski."

The older man waved the used handkerchief in Sepp's face. "I have eyes, I can see—not so well as I used to, but I'm not blind." He leaned forward and peered into Sepp's face. "What did you say your name was?"

"Josep Bauer."

"Humph. Probably an alias."

"It's my real name, all right."

"Why did you have to pick on me? Why couldn't you have dug your tunnel someplace else? Makes it difficult, you know, very difficult. Don't expect me to be honored— no, don't expect that. You've done thousands of marks' worth of damage here." His eyes, magnified behind the thick glasses, surveyed the cellar. "Yes, thousands."

"I doubt if it's that much, Herr Komanski."

The owner ignored him. He wagged a bony finger at the others. "Who're they?"

"Students, except for Herr Balderbach."

Komanski started to say something, but paused as if trying to remember something. "Balderbach?"—he looked inquiringly at his assistant—"Balderbach?"

The assistant leaned forward slightly. "There's a painter named Balderbach. Bruno Balderbach."

The old man remembered now and gave him an annoyed snort. "I know that. D'you think I'm a stupid old fool? I own some Balderbachs." He turned to Sepp. "Any relation?"

"One and the same."

Komanski's eyes did not flicker. He stared into Sepp's for a long moment, then slowly turned toward Bruno. "You there, Balderbach. Come over here."

Sepp's indignation erupted. "See here, you can't speak to him like that."

Bruno came forward. "It's all right, Sepp."

"I speak as I please."

"Not to Herr Balderbach, you don't."

"Forget it, Sepp," Bruno urged.

The younger man leaned forward, smiling a polite, patronizing smile. "We do not know that this is *the* Bruno Balderbach, do we?"

"Are you calling me a liar?"

"I am only suggesting—"

The old man waved him back. "Oh, shut up, Clemnitz." Clemnitz seemed unruffled, obviously used to that sort of thing. He gave Sepp a look as if to say, The money's good, so what do I care?

"I assure you," Bruno was saying, "that I am Bruno Balderbach."—and glancing with studied disdain at Clemnitz—"*the* Bruno Balderbach."

Komanski inspected him with deliberate care. "So you are. I met you once—yes, I did—at one of those ritzy gallery parties in Frankfurt. I never forget a face—right, Clemnitz?"

"You never do, sir."

"Never do. What are you doing with this gang of vandals?"

"As you can see, I am helping them with the tunnel."

"But that's ridiculous."

"Why?"

The old man thought for a moment, then said, "I can't think of a reason." He laughed at himself, a high, creaking laugh that broke brittlely on the rock walls. "No, I can't think of a single reason." He turned to his assistant. "Clemnitz?"

"Not a single reason, sir."

"Not a single reason."

"I was pleased to hear you own some of my work," Bruno said. "Which ones, may I ask?"

"I don't remember what you called them. Crazy titles, they were," he added scornfully, "so I forgot them. What's painting need a title for? You don't look at the title. It gets in the way, anyhow."

Bruno seemed amused. "You have no idea how hard it is for me to think them up."

"Then what do you do it for?" Komanski demanded irritably.

"The public expects it."

The old man stamped a tiny foot on the earthen floor, producing a minute noise. "Damn the public! The public are idiots, fools, and flunkies. One man in ten thousand resembles the meaning of the word."

"Perhaps," Bruno ventured with contrasting calmness, "that is why we had such a time finding six people willing to dig this tunnel."

The old man's owlish eyes flickered in confusion. Then a smile broke the corners of his thin mouth. He turned to Clemnitz. "What am I doing for dinner?"

"You are free this evening, sir."

To Bruno: "You must join me for dinner."

"I would be honored, but—"

"No buts, no buts. I'm staying at the Berlin Hilton. Be there at eight." As if that settled everything, he started to go. Bruno did not protest. Sepp took his cue from Bruno and said nothing.

Clemnitz, however, reminded the old man the reason for his coming. He had forgotten and looked momentarily confused. He surveyed Sepp, Bruno, the others, the damage to his building, the tunnel entrance, as if he were looking at them for the first time. His attention came to rest on Sepp. "You've got a lot of cheek—what did you say your name was?"

"Bauer."

"Yes, Bauer."

"Perhaps," Bruno suggested, "Herr Komanski and I can come to an agreement."

"Agreement? What kind of agreement?"

"A mutually beneficial agreement."

Clemnitz entered the discussion. "If you are hoping to inveigle Herr Komanski into disregarding the damage you have done to his building, I suggest you abandon the idea immediately."

Sepp's dislike of Clemnitz was increasing by the minute. "Herr Balderbach is no more an inveigler than I am a liar."

"Let it go, Sepp," Bruno said.

"Never let dignity interfere with your objective," the old man counseled.

Sepp did not want to let it go, but he did not want to jeopardize the tunnel, either. He decided to keep quiet.

"You were talking about an agreement," Herr Komanski said to Bruno.

"At dinner, perhaps."

"No, no," he said petulantly, "at dinner I want to talk

about painting. Let's settle this business now. Clemnitz, how much damage have they done?"

"They are not finished, sir. They will do more before they are finished."

"Well? Well? What's the price to be?"

Clemnitz looked around, yawned, and came up with a figure. "Five thousand marks."

Emerich gasped.

"That's absurd," Sepp said. "The whole building isn't worth five thousand marks."

"You are obviously unaware of the cost of lumber in Berlin," Clemnitz said imperiously. "Every stick of it has to be imported from West Germany, which in turn imports it from Scandinavia and Canada. Lumber is expensive."

Sepp knew the price of lumber very well. One of the reasons he had settled on the warehouse for the tunnel site was the availability of the flooring. Clemnitz was exaggerating the cost, but not by much.

"Forget about the price," Herr Komanski said. "I'll settle for a painting by Herr Balderbach here."

Before Sepp could protest, Bruno said, "Agreed."

Herr Komanski smiled and put out his frail hand. Bruno took it gingerly.

"It's not fair," Sepp said.

"To whom?" Herr Komanski demanded.

"To Bruno, naturally. His paintings sell for five times the value of the damage."

The old man squinted at Sepp through his thick glasses. He looked up at Clemnitz. "Is that true?"

"I doubt it, sir."

"Do you *know*?"

"Not *exactly*, sir."

"Then say so, damn it, say so. There's no law says you have to know everything."

"Why don't you ask Herr Balderbach?" Sepp said.

"I have made the agreement. I'll stand by it," Bruno interjected.

"There, you see? He is a man of his word."

"He didn't have much choice, did he?"

The old man thought about this, and a grin slowly spread over his face. "No, he didn't. But I'm paying for the dinner, aren't I?" He said it as if that made up the difference. He chuckled and rubbed his hands together. "Is it true, Herr Balderbach? Do your paintings sell for so much? I don't remember what I paid."

"The last ones I sold did, yes."

"Ah! Good, good." Grinning, he glanced around at the rest of them. We've done a good piece of business today, Clemnitz. A *good* piece of business. Come along, come along." He headed for the stairs, taking short, stiff steps. "Eight o'clock, Herr Balderbach. Don't be late. I don't like to be kept waiting."

They stood, watching the two men ascend the stairs. At the top, the old man paused and looked down at them. "What did you do with my padlock?" he demanded sternly.

"Threw it away," Sepp said.

"Cheeky thing to do—what did you say your name was, young man?"

"Bauer. Josep Bauer."

"Bauer, eh? You're a cheeky fellow, Bauer. I like that. Hum, yes, I like that." And with Clemnitz holding the door open for him, the owner started to leave.

"Herr Komanski?"

The little man turned around. "Yes what is it?"

"You won't tell anyone about this?"

He made a face. "What do you take me for, an informer? Cheeky fellow, damned cheeky." He went grumbling out the door, slamming it as he left.

A sigh went up in unison. They all laughed away the tension.

"Misery, that was unendurable."

"I thought we were done for," Wolf exclaimed.

"So did I," Sepp acknowledged. He turned to Bruno. "You're a great painter, Herr Balderbach, but a lousy businessman."

"Are you really going to give him a painting?" Wolf asked.

"Certainly."

"Why didn't you agree to pay him five thousand marks." Emerich asked, "if you can sell a painting for more than that?"

Sepp was wondering the same thing. Bruno gave them a peculiarly self-satisfied look. "Oh, I don't think I did as badly as you think. There is often more to a business transaction than the money involved."

"Such as?" Emerich asked.

"Yes," Joachim said, "such as?"

"Intangibles," Bruno answered cryptically. "Intangibles."

Georg stepped forward hesitantly. "I want to thank you for what you did," he said ceremoniously.

Bruno looked startled and a little embarrassed. The others looked at one another, realizing that they had forgotten the significance of Bruno's agreement. All at once they were around him, thanking him, shaking his hand.

"I guess to be a great painter," Wolf said, "you have to be a great man."

Bruno was quick to correct him. "No, no, do not believe that, Wolf." He was deeply serious, his long face grave with the effort to impress his meaning upon them. "I am not a great man. I'm not even certain I am a great painter. Greatness is not demonstrated by giving something that is so easily given. It is more, much more. . . ."

What more it was, Bruno either did not know or did not want to say. His words trailed off, and he turned away.

As they headed back to work, Joachim came up to Sepp. "It pays to have a celebrity around," he said. "Old Balderbach just proved his worth, eh?"

" 'Old Balderbach' proved his worth from the minute we started this thing," Sepp answered acidly.

Joachim was unmoved. "You know as well as I do that he hasn't been able to do as much as the rest of us. You don't need to protect him."

Sepp stopped and regarded Joachim carefully. What was it that made it so hard for Joachim to let someone else have a little glory? He recalled that after Wolf had virtually saved his life in the tunnel he had belittled his brother, too. In a way, Joachim had glory every day, he walked in glory—and not much of it was earned. It was like being born rich and acting miserly—there was no point to it unless he was so egomaniacal that he simply could not bear to accept the fact that anyone besides Joachim Lentz had genuine worth. Sepp resisted the analysis as unfair. He did not have enough evidence to support it.

"I haven't had complaints from anyone else about Bruno's work."

Joachim became indignant. "Oh, come off it. You know I'm not complaining about his work."

"What are you doing?"

"Stating facts. There's a difference."

"What's your purpose in telling me something you claim I already know?"

Joachim was nonplussed for a moment. He stared at Sepp, indignation giving way to anger. He started to say something, thought better of it, turned abruptly, and left.

Sepp stood staring after him, wishing that Joachim had let himself go. He was in the mood to have it out with someone—anyone. Joachim would have been his choice.

He headed down the incline and scrambled into the tunnel. Far up ahead, Bruno, Wolf, and Georg were back at work on the shoring. He hurried forward, eager to get digging, to take out his anger on the endless wall of earth. He realized his anger was not due to Joachim's disparagement of Bruno. That had been only the catalyst that had brought it to the surface. It was a frustrating, pervasive anger that had its origins in the affair with Klaus and culminated in his recognition of the exaggerated self-recrimination it had led to. Now if he could get it out, regurgitate it, he would be back to normal. Hard work was the answer.

He passed under the cave-in, noticing how deep the tunnel was becoming. The lightbulbs hung like markers for a swimmer along the side of a pool—five, ten, fifteen, twenty, twenty-five meters, the struts delineating the one-meter intervals between them. With luck they would reach the halfway point by the end of the day.

As he neared the shoring party, something registered in his mind, an anomaly which he could not place in time or character. He stopped, his sixth sense insisting that it was terribly important. For a few frantic seconds he searched the immediate past, trying to scavenge it from the clutter of impressions the mind takes in every instant and holds only long enough for the significant to be assimilated before casting the rest out forever.

He found it.

Quickly, he turned back and scrambled to the cave-in near the ten-meter point. It was well illuminated by the bulb fixed by a spike under the black insulated wire in the earth just beside one of the tall struts that held the planking in place above the pipe. There it was: Two of the struts were out of plumb.

He examined them carefully. The base of each had been knocked out of position—or had slipped out—not to the degree that they were in danger of falling, but enough to be of concern.

His first thought was to get them back into plumb. He braced himself in a sitting position with his back to the wall, his feet up against one strut, and gradually, with great effort, forced it back into place. He did the same with the other.

Wolf came crawling toward him. "What are you doing?" he whispered.

"These struts were out of plumb."

Wolf looked at them, following their height to the top beyond the pipe. "They're all right now."

Sepp nodded. He did not like to talk under the thin layer of earth between them and the surface overhead. He beckoned Wolf to go ahead out to the cellar, and he followed.

"Maybe a sled hit them," Wolf said.

Sepp got to his feet and, passing Wolf, went up the incline. "There's always somebody guiding the sleds. If one had hit the struts, whoever was there would have noticed it. He would have done something about it."

"Maybe the stress was weakened in some way. Maybe there's still some water up there seeping down and washing earth away from above."

"If that were the case, wouldn't the struts slip at the top instead of the bottom?"

"You're probably right," Wolf said, but he did not look convinced.

"I'll go upstairs and check it, anyway." He got a flashlight and crowbar from the tool chest.

Emerich and Joachim were sawing flooring. "What's up?" Emerich asked.

Wolf answered, "Sepp found a couple of struts out of plumb in the hole in the roof."

Sepp left them discussing it and climbed to the third floor. Here the heat was intense. The dark room had been collecting the rising heat all summer, with little means of dissipating it. He wiped the sweat from around his eyes and, selecting a window on the street side, pried a board loose from the bottom. The sunlight streamed in. Cautiously, he put his face to the opening. He could feel the hot air rushing out.

Below, the pavement reflected the heat, sending up undulating waves. The Wall stood stolid, mute, ugly, unchallenged, a memorial to the cowardice and indecision of others at another time. In the area just beyond it, where the water had accumulated after the storm, dust rose from the barren ground. Except for signs of rust on the lower strands of barbed wire in the first row of entanglements, no trace of the water was left.

A truck passed through the street, bouncing noisily on the old, rough cobblestones. In the distance across the expanse of wire, tank traps, and gun emplacements stood the blocks of empty apartment houses on Vierickstrasse. His eyes immediately sought out the narrow, three-story gray stucco building whose cellar was the object of their work. The sun glinted on the upper windows, which had not been boarded up, giving them the appearance of giant eyes peering back at him from their seclusion behind The Wall. He tried to judge where the tunnel reached at the moment, estimating it to be just beyond the last row of tank traps, where the open field began that extended to the rear of the apartment houses.

His eyes followed the great reach of the Death Zone down several blocks behind the row of buildings. A hastily constructed wooden observation tower rose up from the silence of the deserted strip like a deformed tree left behind as worthless by lumbermen who had laid waste the area. Just behind the tower, some men were working around a bombed-out building. A crane and a line of trucks stood in the adjacent street. As he watched with idle interest, a huge mushroom of dust rose from the center of the wreckage.

At first he did not understand what had caused it. Then, as the dust settled, he saw that a front wall that had been left standing had fallen in. Through the opening it gave to the street beyond, he saw another crane, this one with a demolition ball attached to a cable.

Suddenly, the meaning of what he had seen became clear. That building was one he and Ilse had passed on their way to the Edelweiss. It was not a bombed-out house. None of the buildings along Vierickstrasse had been bombed. The house, one of those evacuated along the Death Zone, was being razed.

When he went back down to the cellar, Joachim was standing at the bottom of the stairs, looking up expectantly, his recent altercation with Sepp apparently forgotten. "What did you find? Is there still some water over there?"

Sepp had forgotten about his reason for going up. "No, the water's gone."

Joachim perceived that he was troubled. "What's wrong?"

"They're tearing down a house on Vierickstrasse."

"Not *our* house."

"Not yet."

Slowly, understanding spread across Joachim's face. He wiped the sweat from his forehead and pulled off his stocking cap. His hair fell into disheveled clumps around his ears and over his eyes. He brushed it back and worked it into place, making a part with his fingertips. "This is decidedly not our day," he quipped humorlessly.

"Decidedly not."

"What are you going to do?"

"Try to find out if they are planning to tear down the whole street. May I use your car?"

"Where are you going?"

"To the nearest telephone."

"Sure." Joachim fished the keys out and handed them over. "Who are you going to call, Ulbricht?"

"The newspapers." He left. Going up the stairs, he felt old. Old and tired.

The first newspaper he called was *Die Welt,* the one he read every morning. The switchboard operator put him through to an editor.

"Hello, Schromm speaking."

"Herr Schromm, I'm calling to inquire about some buildings being razed in Vierickstrasse in the *Sektor.*"

"Hold on." The telephone was slammed onto a desktop. Sepp could hear teletype machines and typewriters in the background, and the editor talking to someone. The phone scraped across the desk.

"Hello?" It was a different voice.

"I was speaking with Herr Schromm."

"I'm writing the story. What do you want to know?"

"It's about the buildings in Vierickstrasse. . . ."

"Yes, they're tearing them down, the whole street. What about it?" He was a reporter in a hurry.

"The whole street?"

"The whole street."

"Do you know why?"

"Some poor souls were in one of them, digging a tunnel to the West. The Commies caught them. Seems they got hungry and came out for food. Uncle Walter ordered the street demolished. Sweet fellow, eh?"

"Are you sure?"

"Sure about what?"

"That they're going to raze all the buildings."

"Six blocks of them."

"May I ask where you got your information?" Sepp found he was having trouble speaking.

"That's no secret. It's in today's *Neues Deutschland*. And we have our own sources." He became curious. "What's it to you?"

Sepp grasped at the first thought that came to mind. "I used to live in one of those houses."

"Oh. Well, sorry, *Mensch*, but the old home is coming down."

"Yes, I guess it is."

"Anything else?"

"No . . . oh, yes. Do you know when they expect to be finished?"

"Finished? Haven't the slightest idea. Shouldn't take them too long. They're good at destroying things."

"Yes. Well, thank you for your help."

"My pleasure. Sorry about your house."

"Yes. Thank you. *Auf Wiedersehen.*"

"*'Wiedersehen.*"

Sepp stood leaning against the wall of the booth, the reporter's staccato voice hammering in his mind. *Yes, they're tearing them down, the whole street. Yes, they're tearing them down, the whole street.* What was it to him? Just another story, another float in the endless parade of barbarians Berliners had seen tramping through their streets for more than a quarter of a century. The bastards. The rotten bastards. The no-good, rotten, son-of-a-bitching bastards.

In a burst of rage he slammed his fist against the booth window. The glass broke. He was startled by the sound of it splintering on the sidewalk. Then he felt the pain. His hand was rapidly becoming covered with blood. It ran down his fingers and dripped onto the floor. He sucked his hand clean. It was a superficial cut. He got out his handkerchief. It was filthy, covered with the slime he had wiped from his face earlier.

He kicked open the booth door. The bright sun leaped into his eyes. A woman passing by stopped to stare at him. She looked from him to the broken window and back again. "Are you all right?"

He nodded and hurried to the car, sucking the blood from the cut.

Joachim was the only one in the cellar when he returned. "What's the verdict?"

He gave his answer by saying, "Go get the others."

Emerich emerged from the tunnel wiping the grime from his face. He saw Sepp. "You're back already?" He studied Sepp's face. "Bad news, eh?"

"Bad news."

Emerich stood for a moment, letting the weight of Sepp's words settle upon him, then ducked back into the hole to get the others.

"They're going to raze our house," Joachim concluded.

"The whole street," Sepp echoed. He crossed to the lumber pile and sat down. The floor was getting slippery from the mud their feet brought out of the tunnel. He would like to have taken the time to clean it up, but there would be no time for that now. He had forgotten how stifling it was in the cellar. He unbuttoned his shirt and wiped away the sweat that had already accumulated on his forehead. Joachim glanced at him but said nothing. Sepp couldn't tell what he was thinking. The generator sputtered. The lights dimmed, then came back brightly as the machine picked up its rhythmic pace.

Emerich came out of the tunnel, followed by Bruno, Wolf, and Georg. They all came over to the lumber pile, their faces reflecting the news Emerich had given them.

Emerich was angry.

Georg looked to Sepp supplicatingly, waiting for him to say it wasn't so.

Wolf was grim. It seemed to Sepp that he had aged a year in the past week.

Bruno was commiserative. Sepp felt his pity, an intimate expression for him alone. He resented it.

They arrayed themselves around him, waiting. Sepp looked them over, all uniformly sealed in the integument of their common labor—the gray slime of earth and sweat.

Bruno, the oldest, stood leaning against a pillar, his face as weathered, as gray as the stone. His denim overalls, fresh that morning—a reminder of Frieda's martyrlike devotion—were soaked with mud at the bagging knees. The flacid flesh hanging from the undersides of his upper arms seemed like an exaggeration of that sagging under his eyes. Except for the hard brightness of his eyes—eyes that had never surrendered the keenness of youth—he looked weary and beaten.

Wolf, the youngest, sprawled on the earthen floor at his feet. He might have been a pupil of Bruno's momentarily distracted. He was filthy from head to toe. Only a barely perceptible line denoted where the slime on his forehead ended and that on his stocking cap began. He perspired more than any of them, and his leather shorts were stained with sweat. Because he could not stand wearing gloves in the heat, his hands were covered with a reticulation of Band-Aids overlapping, flapping, wrinkled, and totally encrusted with dirt, offering questionable protection to the profusion of blisters that had formed, broken, healed, turned to calluses, and were in the process of forming all over again.

In a quiet, sympathetic voice laden with overtones of the depression that had come to occupy the cellar, Wolf asked Sepp how he had injured his hand.

"I punched out a window in the telephone booth."

No one made any comment. It didn't seem to matter. Gloom lay upon their spirits like the grime on their bodies.

Again, there was brooding, depressing silence. Sepp continued his survey.

Gaunt and wraithlike in the shadows along the wall stood Emerich, his black eyes shining in his sallow face. How fragile he seemed compared to the plumpness of Bruno, the brawn of Wolf. He still wore the same roomy khaki trousers, stiff with dirt, that exaggerated his spareness. Yet, like a fragile woman whose strength lay in her

spirit rather than in her body, he radiated power. Sepp
entertained a fleeting recollection of the facility with which
he had dispatched Klaus, and he realized that, more than
any of the others, the peasant possessed the kind of
strength that would be required in the next few days.

Seated on the edge of the tool chest, Georg looked
much like a fretful child awaiting punishment for something he was convinced he had not done. Even the arrangement of the dirt on his face suggested he had been
out playing in the mud. His soft red lips protruded from
the dirt like spring's first crocus expecting at any moment
to be watered from the overhanging pools of his eyes. If
Wolf had aged in the past week, Georg had regressed. He
seemed to have lost the tenuous grip he had had on himself and, like a manic-depressive, overreacted to each new
stimulus. Any hope that the removal of Klaus's threat
would stabilize him seemed vain.

In sharp contrast to the others and despite the profusion
of scabs which cropped up through the coating of dirt on
his skin, Joachim appeared the same as always. There was
an animal resiliency about him that defied subjugation.
With his hair in place, his primly manicured fingers forming a steeple of contemplation under his chin, his long
eyelashes fluttering to shake off bits of earth, he gave the
impression of transient involvement, as if he were a casual
visitor who had dropped in for the day to take a look and,
becoming intrigued, had taken a hand in the work. He had
been able to commit his body but not his spirit, and had
thus protected himself from the emotional strain the work
had wrought on the others. Sepp had ambivalent feelings
about him: He had to admire his ability to remain detached, but that very detachment raised constant suspicions in his mind.

Sepp had never felt anything for them as a group, but
now, when his own determination to succeed was near collapse, and despite his disenchantment with some of them,
he felt a strong bond with them. Their common purpose,
regardless of how deeply committed each might be to it,
had developed in him a sense of obligation to them as a
whole. He knew that, in varying degrees, they considered
him their leader and now expected him to lead.

But where was he to lead them? In the army, he had
learned enough about leadership to know that those who

THE TUNNEL

followed must have an attainable objective and a desire to reach it themselves.

"Emerich has told you," he began, "that I called *Die Welt*. It's true. They are going to tear down the buildings on the western side of Vierickstrasse—all of them, including our house. Some East Berliners were caught in one of them digging a tunnel to the West. They're not taking any chances that it will be tried again from any of those buildings."

"How about that," Joachim said. "Somebody else was coming toward us. If we'd gotten together with them, we could have met halfway."

No one was amused.

"Did the newspaper tell you how they had obtained their information?" Bruno asked.

"It's in today's *Neues Deutschland*."

Joachim chuckled sardonically. "I never believed a word I read in that yellow rag. Ironic, isn't it."

"Maybe it isn't true," Georg said. "Maybe they're lying."

"Why would they lie about this," Sepp reasoned, "when the evidence is there for everyone to see?"

Georg agreed with a solemn nod. "What are we going to do?"

"We'll just have to get to our house before they do," Wolf said calmly.

Sepp had expected this conclusion from Wolf or Emerich. He was gratified.

"And how do we do that?" Joachim demanded. "We're less than halfway across. There's at least another week of work left, and with one damned thing after another, we'll be lucky to make it in two weeks."

Emerich broke the shadowy silence. "Not if we work around the clock. We could do it in two, maybe three days."

"We *could* do it," Wolf said, sitting up, eager to elaborate on the idea. "We can lay some comforters on the floor upstairs to take naps—if we need to."

"We're used to the work now," Emerich said.

"You're out of your mind, both of you," Joachim protested. "We'd all collapse before we ever beat them to it."

"You should have exercised," Wolf said curtly.

"I'm damned if I'm going to quit now," Emerich said calmly. "I don't care what the rest of you do."

"I'm with you," Wolf said. He looked ready to go that instant.

"Can we work at night?" Bruno asked in his serenely reasonable tone. "We haven't been because of the noise of the generator and our own movement here in the building and in the tunnel. We must bear in mind that The Wall is just across the street."

"We can use flashlights," Wolf suggested.

"That doesn't eliminate the problem of noise."

"We'll just have to take that chance," Emerich said. "Maybe we'll have to post a lookout upstairs."

Joachim reminded him that that would reduce their working force.

"Let's take a vote," Georg said.

"To hell with votes," Emerich growled. "I'm going to keep going. Everybody else can do what they want."

Sepp decided it was time to commit himself. "I'm in favor of trying. Maybe it will take them days, even weeks, to get to our house. Maybe they'll raze it tomorrow. We don't know. But if we quit now, we'll never know whether or not we might have made it. I won't be satisfied with that." He turned to Bruno. "What do you say?"

"Of course I'll go along. There are problems, but then there always are."

"Georg?"

He breathed deeply and covered his face with his hands. "What else can I do?"

"Joachim?"

Unexpectedly, he grinned, his charm a resource that never failed him. "I will consider it a welcome relief. Even one night's respite from listening to my little brother making mad, passionate love in the next room is to be welcomed."

More as a form of release from anxiety than in response to his humor, everyone, including Wolf, laughed.

"I didn't know you were listening," Wolf said, uncommonly self-controlled.

"I never thought I'd see it," Emerich said. "Joachim Lentz jealous of somebody else making out."

"Life in the city is enlightening, eh, peasant?"

"Enlightening. I'll have to consult with the Lentzes on methods and means."

"At the risk of appearing uninterested in the subject,"

Bruno said, his eyes twinkling with a hint of mischief, "I suggest we consider methods and means, not of the pursuit of the fair sex but of continuing the tunnel by night."

"We know you're not that old," Joachim assured him.

Bruno bowed his head. "I thank you."

"There are problems," Sepp said. "Foremost, we'll need light. Emerich, can we soundproof the generator?"

He rubbed his chin. "How about digging a hole to set it in? We could cover it over with boards and maybe some comforters."

"That sounds good. We'll try it. That's your job—but nothing fancy, just whatever is needed to muffle the sound."

"Does anybody have comforters to donate to the cause?"

"I believe my wife may have some old ones," Bruno offered. And to Sepp: "I'm afraid I shall have to keep my appointment with Herr Komanski."

"I'm afraid so. We don't want any trouble from him."

"In that case, Emerich, I'll see what we have when I go home to change clothes. I'll drop them off on my way to the hotel."

"All right."

"Now, about other noise," Sepp went on, "we can't do any crowbar work or sawing. There's no way to muffle those sounds."

"Do you think sawing would be too loud?" Georg asked.

"When I came in before, I could hear it distinctly in the alley. At night this area is practically deserted. Sound will carry much farther. We have a good supply of pieces on hand, certainly enough to last through tonight. During the daylight hours we'll have to cut enough to make it through the night."

"Have you considered doing without shoring?" Joachim asked.

"There's no need to. Only one man can dig at a time, anyway, so the others might just as well shore. Those who normally would be cutting lumber can sleep. That way, everyone will get some sleep. It won't be much, but it will help."

"In the tunnel we've got to be extra quiet," Georg said.

"Right. Especially around the cave-in. Remember,

there's only a meter of earth up there between them and us. Make certain the burlap on the sledgehammer is thick and in good shape, and be sure it's tied on securely. And let's keep the talking to a minimum both in and out of the tunnel."

"No using the toilet or running water," Emerich added. He smiled dolefully at Bruno. "Sorry."

"A small sacrifice."

"We can dig a hole in the pile of earth."

"It's getting big," Emerich observed. It was getting big. Its base covered about a third of the floor area. "Let's hope it gets much bigger much faster."

"What about food?" Wolf asked.

"I thought you were living on love alone," Emerich said. No one followed up the razzing. They were too intent on the new plan of action.

"Can everyone provide his own?" Sepp asked.

They all agreed.

"Last, and as important as the tunnel, is the question of notifying our people in the *Sektor*. I am to meet Ilse at eight o'clock tonight. I'll tell her to tell your parents, Joachim and Wolf, to be ready to go in two or three nights —Wednesday or Thursday. That means that your father will have to sign the papers tomorrow to make it possible for Emerich's family to get travel permits."

"Do you think there's enough time for that?" Joachim asked.

"I don't know, but I do know this: No one is coming through the tunnel until everyone who wants to come is ready. Or until we know that we can't wait any longer. We're not going to take the chance of exposing it more than once."

He let that sink in before he went on. "Emerich, I'll tell Ilse to try to get to your aunt tonight. The sooner she makes her call, the longer we'll have to devise an alternative approach if she fails to convince your father."

The peasant nodded agreement, his dark face reflecting the sobering thoughts that he was having about the risk to which he was exposing his family.

Georg fidgeted on his perch on the tool chest. "What about my parents? What are you going to do about them? You ought to go see them yourself, convince them to come." It was embarrassing to everyone to listen to his quavering voice grasping for assurance.

"There's still time," Sepp consoled him, "there's still time. I think Ilse should try again. If she fails, I'll take a hand in it. But my usefulness is greater here just now."

"I'll write another letter," he said. "I'll explain it, how—"

"All right. That might help. It can't hurt."

Caught in mid-thought, Georg retreated into a search of the faces around him, all of which avoided his eyes. Sepp made a mental note to keep an eye on Georg for the duration of the work.

"I suggest, then, that we leave here at six as usual, go home for a good meal, pack some food, and plan to be back here around nine." He looked at his watch. It was almost four o'clock. "Emerich, you'd better get at that generator hole." He looked around. "Any questions? Comments?"

"We'll need water to drink," Joachim said.

"And to wash off," Bruno added. "A splash of water on the face is marvelous for morale." He looked around and found no supporters. "It is for *my* morale."

"Georg, how about going out and buying one of those big galvanized-steel containers. We ought to get it filled before quitting time."

"I don't drive," he said quickly. "I never learned."

"I'll get it," Joachim offered. "And you needn't get out your fat American wallet. I'll pay for it." As an afterthought, he grinned to let Sepp know he was joking.

"I was wondering when you were going to part with a little of your money," Sepp countered.

"*Touché.*"

"Have we forgotten anything?"

Emerich said, "We'd better park the cars in the street when we come back tonight. The police will get nosy if they see them in the alley."

"Good idea. Anything else?"

There was nothing else.

"Who was digging while I was gone?"

"I was," Wolf said. "I've had a rest, so I'll get back to it."

"All right. Bruno and Georg, you're shoring?"

"Yes."

While they were breaking up, returning to work, Emerich took Sepp aside. "What about those struts you found out of line?"

Although he had of necessity pushed the question to the back of his mind, he had not forgotten about it. He could tell by Emerich's tone that his peasant suspicion had been aroused. "You don't think it was done deliberately, do you?"

"Don't you?"

"We can't afford to think that—not now."

"We can't afford to think otherwise. Those struts didn't just walk out of line."

"A sled could have run up against them without whoever was guiding the sled realizing it."

Emerich would not accept that. "You don't believe that any more than I do. Somebody's determined to make sure the tunnel is discovered."

There was no doubt who Emerich's 'somebody' was. "If what you say is true, that somebody knows we've discovered his handiwork. I doubt he'll try it again."

Emerich snorted.

Sepp was annoyed. "What would you have me do, make an accusation I can't prove? All it would lead to is his leaving us, and just now we need everyone. *Everyone.* Besides, it may not have been the one you think."

Emerich sneered at what he considered Sepp's naiveté. "I'm not wrong about that."

"You are until you can prove it, and until then we're not going to say anything about it."

Emerich acquiesced. "All right. You're the boss."

Sepp started to leave.

"How bad is your hand?"

"It's just a scratch."

"You got mad, eh?"

"I got mad."

"Welcome to the club."

25

THEY'RE not going to make it, Emerich was thinking. They'll never get the travel permits soon enough. What do the Communists care about an old woman dying? It happens every day over there. That's all they have left —just old women. He drove the spade into the earth, forced it to the hilt with his booted foot, and laid the earth upon the pile. He was half-finished with the hole.

Make it deep, deep so the bastards can't hear a peep. They must be good at digging holes. All those damned trenches they've dug in the Death Zone. All the graves. How many? Thousands? Tens of thousands? Hundreds of thousands? If you count the Russians, it's tens of millions. He'd given them two graves to dig. That was some satisfaction. If everyone in West Berlin gave them two graves to dig, that would be four million graves. If everyone in the Republic . . . what's the population of the Republic? It must be fifty million, anyway. That would be a hundred million graves. Misery, they wouldn't have any land left to plow. Good, let them starve. The bastards deserve to starve. But not my family. Misery, they're not going to make it. God, let them make it. Is that asking so much, God? You know they hate it as it is. The land was everything. Why did they have to lose the land, God?

"How's it coming?" Georg hovered over him, grinning insipidly.

Emerich laid a spadeful of earth across his shoes. "Move your feet."

Georg jumped back, but too late. "What did you do that for?"

"I told you to move." Misery, I can't stand the little creep, he thought. He plunged the spade into the soft, moist earth.

Georg stood back at a safe distance. "Do you think we'll make it?"

"How the hell should I know?"

"Bruno thinks we will."

"Bruno's a great prophet. Listen to him." He shoveled up some earth so that some of it scattered across Georg's boots. He retreated farther.

"Why don't you like Bruno?"

Emerich stood the spade between his legs and leaned on it. "If you don't get your ass back to work, we *won't* make it."

Georg's face tightened. He blinked his eyes and rubbed them nervously. "I just stopped for a second," he said. "I guess it's all right to stop for a second. Besides, since when are you the boss around here?"

Emerich ignored him and went back to digging. When he came up with the next spadeful, Georg had gone to the lumber pile to gather pieces for another stretch of shoring.

Misery, what a mess that one is, Emerich thought. If he doesn't go berserk before we make it—if we make it—I'll go back to the church. He wiped his grimy face with an equally grimy hand. If it rained, we'd get some relief from this damned heat. But, God, don't let it rain. We'll take the heat, God. Heat and rain. Scylla and Charybdis. Georg and Joachim. Sepp can protect Joachim if he wants to, but not Emerich Weber. If I catch him so much as breathing hard in that tunnel . . .

Georg came back from the lumber pile. "I want to ask you something, Emerich."

"Ask away." He kept digging.

"Do you resent me because you had to kill Klaus Schoenemann?"

"I didn't *have* to kill him. And don't go blabbing it around. Not everyone here knows about it. And there is a law against that sort of thing. I'd just as soon we kept it among us three. Okay?"

"Bruno knows."

"Only that it was done. He doesn't know I did it."

Georg still stood there.

"Now what?"

"You didn't answer my question."

"I thought I had."

"Not really."

"No, I don't resent you," he said perfunctorily. "Satisfied?"

"I should think you would."

Emerich was becoming exasperated. "Look, if you want me to, I will. But as of now, I don't. I don't resent you for it. Do you want it in writing?"

Georg flushed and backed off. "You don't have to act that way."

"Yes, I do. I'm a peasant. I've got no manners. I was born that way, and I'll die that way. And I like it. Okay?" Misery, he'll drive me berserk before he goes berserk himself, he thought.

Georg went back to the lumber pile. Emerich continued digging. He had not associated Georg with the killing; he had been incidental to the whole affair. It had never occurred to him that Georg should do his own dirty work. The prospect was ridiculous. He couldn't imagine Georg talking back to a man like Klaus, let alone killing him. Now that he thought of it, it was amazing that Georg had even become involved with Klaus. He was the type who would have run as far and as fast as possible, regardless of the threat to his parents, to save his own skin. The more he thought about it, the more convinced he became that there had been more to it than either he or Sepp knew.

Emerich was climbing out of the hole when he heard the door upstairs open and close. Joachim came down the steps carrying the big container he had gone to fetch.

"Mission accomplished," he said. "How about you?"

"I just finished. Anyway, I think I'm finished. It's two meters deep."

"That ought to do it."

Sepp emerged from the tunnel. Joachim patted the container affectionately and set it at the foot of the stairs, sitting himself down on it. "Eighty liters," he announced. He pulled a package out of his pocket and held it up. "Dipper." He was pleased with himself.

"If you get it filled with beer," Emerich said, "I'll congratulate you."

"What's your favorite brand?"

He was in good spirits, which automatically upset Emerich. "Help me set the generator in the hole," he said irascibly.

Joachim didn't move.

"We'll have to turn it off and splice in longer wire," Sepp said.

"So we'll turn it off."

"Go tell the others, will you, Joachim?" Sepp asked.

"Sure." He got up and sauntered off toward the tunnel, whistling an airy tune.

"What's he so happy about?"

Sepp shrugged. "What are you so grouchy about?"

"Who's grouchy?"

"You're grouchy."

"I was born grouchy. Come on, give me a hand." He went to the tool chest and got out some wire cutters and a flashlight. He threw the flashlight to Sepp. He cut a length of wire from the roll, separated the double wires at the ends, and cleaned off the insulation. When he was finished, he turned off the generator. The lights slowly dimmed and went out as the motor ground to a stop. Sepp turned on the flashlight. Emerich worked quickly, making pigtail splices in the wires and attaching the ends to the posts on the generator. When that was done, they lowered the generator into the hole and Emerich started it. The lights came on again.

"If Bruno brings those comforters tonight, I'll lay them over it," Emerich said. "If it's still not quiet enough, we'll have to cover it with dirt as well. I'll connect a hose to the gas tank so that we can fill it from up here."

"What about the exhaust outside?"

"It's not very noisy."

"Maybe we ought to look for a place to divert it during the night."

"How about the factory?"

Sepp laughed. "You're not only grouchy, you're diabolical. I had in mind a sewer."

"There's a drain at the end of the alley by the plastics factory. We could run it down there."

"Do you have enough hose left over?"

"I think so. If not, I can use some from the pump."

"All right. I guess I'd better put in my hour of digging. Wolf must be down to his last ounce of energy."

Joachim emerged from the tunnel and came over to them. "Wolf said he had a dizzy spell. The air in there is really putrid."

Sepp sighed. "We spend so much time on these auxiliary things. We'll never get this tunnel finished."

"We've got to have air. Without good air—"

"I know, I know. I've just had it today, that's all. We have to have air. Any ideas?"

"A pump, I suppose," Emerich suggested.

Sepp managed a laugh. "With you, pumps solve all problems."

"How about a vacuum cleaner?" Joachim proposed. "You can run a hose down the tunnel and pull the old air out. New air will flow in to take its place."

Sepp wondered if a vacuum cleaner would be powerful enough.

"We'll experiment," said Emerich.

"What about the noise?" Sepp wanted to know.

"In the hole, with the generator."

"You'll have to get some more hose."

"Maybe we shouldn't buy the hose until we know it will work," Joachim interjected.

"How are you going to find out except by having the hose?" answered Emerich.

"True."

"Are vacuum cleaners available secondhand?" Sepp asked.

"Everything is available secondhand. I'll go see my junkman friend," Emerich said.

"You'd better get going. It's getting late." Sepp got out his wallet. Emerich did not like taking Sepp's money, but he had no choice. He compensated by doing his best to get the most for it. Before buying anything, he considered the feasibility of stealing it. Stealing was not wrong when your cause was just. He had no compunction whatever about stealing for the tunnel. He rationalized that whatever he stole was the least his victims could donate to the cause. Instead of sitting on their fat asses making fat profits, they should be working to help their fellow Germans out of the concentration camp. If they were too blind, too occupied, or too lazy to help, then, as in the old days when the wealthy man paid a substitute to serve in the Army for him, they had to pay those who were doing the dirty work against the Communists by suffering a little petty thievery. Since the first time, when he stole the exhaust hose from the *Amis* at McNair barracks, he hadn't said anything more to Sepp about stealing. Sepp was a nice fellow, but he was too scrupulous. He was too nice, that was his problem. If he'd had it in him to put away that swine, Klaus Schoenemann, he might have come out of it a better man. Some of the niceness would have been rubbed off.

Emerich took the money, a hundred marks, and went upstairs. The flooring on the first floor had been entirely stripped away, save for a walkway along the wall to the toilet and water pipe. The few remaining joists were separated by gaps a meter wide, so that the entire cellar was visible from there. They would have to start ripping up the second floor tomorrow, not for the flooring—they had enough of that—but for the joists. Emerich went along the narrow walkway toward the corner, where, leaning against the wall with his feet and arms crossed in a pose of complete nonchalance, whistling gaily, stood Joachim, waiting for the container to fill with water.

"What are you up to?" he asked Emerich.

Emerich stood over the toilet and urinated. "I have to run an errand."

"What are you out to steal this time?"

Emerich could not tell if he were serious or joking. "A vacuum cleaner. And some hose."

"Going to clean up the place?"

Emerich zipped his fly and flushed the toilet. He turned around to contemplate Joachim. With his face washed, his hair neatly combed, and only a trace of perspiration on his forehead, he might have been standing on a corner of the Kudamm waiting for the right girl to pass by. His face, though covered with tiny scabs, was as handsome as ever, and Emerich had to stifle an inward moan of envy. In the weeks they had worked together, his world and Joachim's had become even more distinctly disparate than before. The more he saw of him, the less he knew him. He was like a book with several levels of meaning, each level more obscure than the last. Without wanting to,

Emerich had developed a grudging admiration for him. Not that he could ever come to like him. Despite his admitted proclivity for sometimes strongly exaggerated feelings about people and their ideas, Emerich was capable of discrimination. He could admire Joachim's surprising capacity for work, his unruffled composure, his courage, his resiliency—above all, his resiliency. He had been trapped behnd The Wall and had escaped. He had landed in West Berlin without a pfennig, and in a few short months was financially well off and a hero of a sort on the campus. He had narrowly escaped death in the tunnel, and within a few hours was back at work as if nothing had happened. Not an hour ago he had lost his argument against working the tunnel around the clock, and here he was, whistling as if he had not a care in the world.

This last example rekindled the suspicion he had voiced to Sepp. Emerich was convinced that it was Joachim who had knocked those struts out of line with the intention of causing the shoring to collapse. He was convinced that Joachim did not want the tunnel to succeed because he did not want his parents living in West Berlin where they would interfere with his private bacchanalia. It was all too clear to be refuted, but impossible to prove. Joachim's present high spirits might be attributable to his resiliency, but more likely they reflected his confidence that, by either the hand of God or his own, the tunnel would fail.

"You're uncommonly jolly—considering."

"Good humor in adversity, that's my motto." Joachim turned off the water. They moved the can out from under the pipe so that Emerich could wash up. It was very heavy, and when they slid it along the floor, water slopped over the sides. While Emerich washed up, Joachim went down for some rope.

Emerich turned his attention to the vacuum cleaner. Where could he steal one? He ruled out small stores. There were never enough people in them to keep the clerks busy. The department stores were a better risk, except that if the vacuum cleaner department were deep inside, in the basement or on an upper floor, he would be taking the chance of being caught carrying it through the store to the street. And he didn't know anything about vacuum cleaners. If he was going to steal one, he might as well get a good one. He supposed he could tell by the prices—the higher, the better.

He was drying himself when Joachim came back, carrying a coil of rope over his shoulder. Emerich helped him lower the can of water to the cellar floor. Then he asked Joachim if he could use his car again. To his surprise, Joachim said he would go along.

"Where do you plan to get the vacuum cleaner?"

"At a secondhand store. There's a place in my neighborhood."

"Why not get a new one?"

"*Geld.*"

Joachim glanced at him. "I thought you were going to steal it."

So he had been serious after all. "I would if I could," he admitted.

Joachim thought awhile, then said, "I know where you can steal one."

"Without getting caught?"

"Without getting caught. And with some fun thrown in on the side."

"What kind of fun?"

"The best kind of fun."

Emerich scrutinized him to see if he was serious. He was.

"The store where I bought the can sells vacuum cleaners. There's only one clerk in the place, a girl. And what a girl. Ready, willing, and able. I almost had her when I got the water can, but a customer came in."

Emerich didn't know whether to believe him or not. "So what happens? Does she give us a vacuum cleaner just for the privilege of being screwed by the irresistible Joachim Lentz?"

Joachim grinned. "Now you're catching on."

Mockingly, Emerich leaned his head over the rafter.

"What are you doing?"

"Vomiting."

Joachim drove. Emerich felt the heat of the bright sun, but he welcomed the breeze blowing in the car window. It was always good to get out of the cellar.

"What about this girl? How can we use her to steal a vacuum cleaner?"

"It will be simple. As I say, she's ready, willing, and able. I'll give her some bull about needing a second container. We'll go into the back—that's where they're kept. By the time we come out, you'll have copped a vacuum cleaner and put it in the car."

"Just like that?"

"Why not?"

"What if there are other customers there?"

"We'll wait until they're gone." He slowed the car. Up ahead, stood a line of small stores—a butcher shop, a grocery, a yarn shop, and the housewares store. The parking space in front was vacant, and Joachim pulled into it. "It will be easy. Just walk out with it, put it behind the seat, and come back in."

"Where's the fun in it for me?"

"She's good for seconds."

The idea was less than appealing. "I'll settle for the free vacuum cleaner."

Joachim contemplated him for a moment and shrugged. "That's up to you."

"I may not shave every day, but I am a bit fussy about some things."

"If you change your mind, just say so."

They got out of the car. Emerich looked through the plate-glass window and saw the girl talking to a man.

"Let me do the talking," Joachim said.

Inside, the girl greeted them politely. "I'll be with you in a moment," she assured them and returned her attention to her customer.

Emerich looked around until he saw the vacuum cleaners. He wandered slowly toward them, looking at other articles as he went. When he came to the vacuum cleaners, he examined them quickly. There were three canister models and two uprights. The most expensive of the canister types was a blue-and-gray one. He passed on by. The cash register rang. The girl was making the concluding remarks of the sale. At last, the customer left. Emerich remained at the end of the aisle at a discreet distance, watching Joachim and the girl. She wasn't much to look at, he thought. A flat, uninteresting face, except perhaps for her eyes. They had a nice light in them. They might have been dark blue or brown—he couldn't tell from a distance. Flat-chested. Too skinny for his taste. She was laughing now. Joachim would have her laughing. Her eyes fell on Emerich. "Is he with you?"

Joachim turned his head. "He's my cellmate."

She laughed again.

"You don't believe me." He sounded hurt.

She shook her head. "You're crazy."

"That, too," he said.

"Come along. I'll get you another," she said. And to Emerich: "If someone comes in, tell them I'll be right out, will you?"

He said he would.

She headed toward the back room, with Joachim close behind. As he passed through the doorway, he turned and winked, grinning victoriously.

Emerich looked out at the street. There was no one there. Quickly he went to the vacuum cleaners, snatched up the blue-and-gray one, carried it to the door, realized he had not taken the attachments, which, he decided, he might as well have if the vacuum was to be of any use after the tunnel, and returned for them. They were conveniently displayed in a cardboard box under a clear plastic cover. He scooped it up with his free hand, returned to the door, managed to open it a crack without making any noise, caught it with his foot, pushed it open wide, backed out, let it close slowly, holding it with his foot until it quietly clicked shut. A woman walking a poodle passed on the sidewalk. He greeted her perfunctorily. As he was depositing his bundle in the back of the car, a man approached the door to the store. Emerich started.

"It's closed." He closed the car door behind him. The man stopped, looked at him and at the store. "It doesn't look closed." He was in his fifties, a dapper, mustachioed man wearing a straw hat set youthfully on one side of his head.

"Death in the family. I was in there when it happened."

The man's face became appropriately grave. "*Ach, so.* Her father?"

"She's very distraught, of course. She hasn't thought to lock up."

"Of course."

"It will be closed until after the funeral."

"Of course." He looked in as if hoping for a glimpse of

the deceased, then gave Emerich a solemn salute. "Please offer my condolences."

"I will."

"Hardenberg."

"Herr Hardenberg."

The man nodded and went off in the direction from which he had come. Emerich stood watching him until he was far down the street, then returned to the store as quietly as he had gone out.

He stood in the aisle, listening. There was no sound at all at first. He listened attentively and caught a faint rustle from the back. He could not tell what had caused it. He wandered aimlessly through the aisles, fingering some of the articles for sale. He was tempted to load his pockets with small items but decided not to tempt fate—until he came across a travel clock that folded into a compact, leather-covered case. He folded it up and stuck it in his pocket. The trousers were so baggy that it barely showed. A little frosting on the cake, he decided, makes it much more enjoyable.

Ten minutes passed, and still they had not come out. Emerich thought about what they were doing and tried not to think about it. Perhaps he was being overly fussy. After all, it had been a while. A while, hell. A long, long time. He ambled back up the aisle for the tenth time, wondering if he might not compensate by lifting another item, when he heard stirrings from the back, the sound of metal clanking against metal, and decided that they were finished with their "fun" and were back to "business." The bugger did it, all right. Once again, envy sent out its insidious pain.

As they came through the doorway, Joachim glanced at him inquiringly. He nodded slightly. Joachim seemed in no hurry to leave. A woman came into the store.

"Well, thank you, Fräulein. I'll come back when you have it in stock."

"I certainly hope so, sir. Thank you."

"You're very welcome." He bowed courteously. "Auf Wiedersehen."

"Auf Wiedersehen." And to the new customer: "May I help you?"

Emerich followed Joachim out the door. They said nothing until they were safely in the car.

"I see you got it." Joachim started the engine.

Emerich nodded. "And I see you got yours."

Joachim laughed and drove off. "You see how easy it was?" He was triumphant.

"Yes. Very easy."

They bought hose from the junkman. Emerich did not want to steal from the junkman, not that it wouldn't have been feasible and not because he was poor, which he wasn't, but because he liked the junkman.

Heading back to the warehouse, Joachim chided him about it. "If you're going to be any good at it, you can't allow yourself to become sentimental."

"I'm not considering it for a profession."

"You shouldn't allow sentiment to rule your actions at any time. It's foolish."

"Sentiment has its place," Emerich answered, although he fancied himself in agreement with the principle.

"Are you going to give Sepp his money back?"

"After it's all over. Don't tell him we stole the vacuum cleaner. He'll have a fit."

"What do you care?"

"I care."

It took him ten minutes to tape the hose to the nozzle and string it up on the spikes in the tunnel holding up the lights so it wouldn't be in the way. Georg was digging at the time. In the dull light his skin had a gray, sickly look, which, Emerich couldn't help thinking, was entirely appropriate.

"What are you doing?" Georg whispered.

"This is an air hose." Emerich held it up close to his face.

Georg grimaced. "It's a vacuum. I know you've got a vacuum cleaner on the other end. What good is that?"

"Wait and see." He was confident the idea would work.

Georg waited as he was told, sniffing the air.

"Keep digging. It's not a good test if you don't keep digging."

Georg started digging again. He was working on his first sled. The other sleds were hanging on the rails behind, waiting to be filled. He stopped. "I don't notice any difference," he said.

"Misery! It's only been fifteen seconds! Keep digging!"

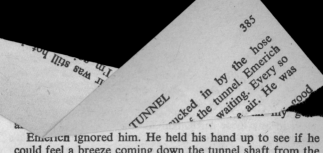

Emerich ignored him. He held his hand up to see if he could feel a breeze coming down the tunnel shaft from the cellar. He thought he could.

"It isn't going to do any good."

"You're too impatient."

"Why don't you go to work and come back later? I'll tell you if it's doing any good or not."

This was apparently the day for everyone to tell Emerich Weber what to do, what to think, what to feel. Even the little creep was getting in on the act. "I'll be back in five minutes."

Georg sniffled disdainfully. "Now who's impatient? Make it ten."

Emerich crawled back through the tunnel. Joachim and Wolf were installing shoring.

"How does it work?" Wolf asked.

"So-so. We'll have to wait awhile, give it time." He hurried past them so he would not have to answer any more questions. He was beginning to have his doubts.

When he reached the cellar he saw Sepp crouching over the machine. Sepp looked up as Emerich approached. "How is it?"

"Not so good."

"There's a blower on here. That ought to work better."

"A blower?"

"All you have to do is attach the nozzle to the other end."

Emerich was amazed. "That's great! Who ever thought of that?"

"Some American, no doubt."

Emerich laughed. "No doubt." Emerich attached the nozzle and hose to the blower end of the machine. When he went back into the tunnel to see how that worked, even Georg was impressed. He smiled.

"I could feel the difference right away. What did you do?"

386

Emerich to... ...going to get it

it was much ...with himself.

patented." ...loud as he had expected. Bruno

The m... it in the hole beside the generator. He

helped ... careful to set it up at an angle so the intake did not

was suck in any loose earth. He climbed out and brushed off
his hands. He still couldn't get over his delight. "That's
something, isn't it? A blower on a vacuum cleaner. That's
a perfect example of the difference between capitalism
and communism."

"How so?"

"It not only sucks in air, it blows out air. It's flexible.
The Communist mind would never think of it. They'd
make two machines, one for each function." He was giddy
with delight. "That's something, that blower, isn't it?"

Bruno smiled. "That's something."

By quitting time, the vacuum cleaner had proved itself,
the can of water was installed conveniently near the entrance to the tunnel, and the daily ritual of measuring was
taking place.

Sepp and Wolf were in the tunnel, measuring from the
mark made on Saturday—thirty-one and two-tenths meters. Crouched at the entrance, Emerich was watching
them, holding the compass, waiting for Sepp to turn on the
flashlight so that he could take a reading.

"What do you guess, Bruno?" Georg asked.

"Oh, forty meters."

"I say forty-one."

"Forty, forty-one," Joachim put in, "what's the difference? It's still just over halfway." He was slouched against
the wall, cleaning his fingernails with a penknife.

"An hour's work," Emerich said.

"What?"

"The difference is an hour's work."

In the tunnel they had finished measuring. The flashlight came on, and Emerich sighted the compass on it. He
read sixty-six degrees.

"Come and read this," he told Georg, handing up the
compass. Georg jumped down into the incline trench and
took the compass. He squatted down and sighted it. "Sixty-
six degrees."

"Check."

Emerich waved, and the light was turned off.

"At least it's straight," Georg said.

Joachim scratched his cheek, carefully avoiding the scabs. "I wonder how far they've gotten with their demolition work over yonder."

"Why don't you go find out?" Bruno suggested.

"Who? Me?"

"We'd all like to know."

Joachim made a poor job of concealing his annoyance. For a moment Emerich thought he was going to tell Bruno to go himself if he was so eager, but if he had the notion, he abandoned it. Without a word, he pushed himself up and ambled off to the steps, still cleaning his nails.

Sepp and Wolf reached the cellar. "Forty-point-four," Sepp said.

"That's nine-point-two for today," Wolf said. He looked around. "Where's Joachim?"

They told him. Emerich handed him the compass, and he took it and the measuring tape back to the tool chest.

"Thirty-five meters to go," Sepp said.

"About fifty hours' work," Bruno said, "including breaks."

"If nothing slows us down."

He nodded. "If nothing slows us down."

They were washing up and changing their clothes when Joachim reported back. "Someone is defying the gods."

Emerich had his head under the water, washing out the dirt and cooling off.

"They've brought up more equipment. It looks as though they're going to start on the block our house is on."

Emerich's heart turned over. He straightened up and reached for a towel.

"Have they quit for the day?" Sepp asked.

"Yes."

No one said anything. Emerich dried his face and his hair. The towel came away dirty. He wondered if he would ever get his hair clean again. God, God.

"We'll still do it," Wolf said.

"Sure we will," Joachim said sardonically.

Sepp left, heading for the stairs.

"He doesn't believe me," Joachim said. He came over

to the water pipe, peeling off his stocking cap. Bits of earth scattered around him. He looked at Emerich. "You believe me, don't you?"

"He doesn't want to believe you," Bruno said. "Nobody wants to."

Joachim shrugged and stuck his head under the water. "Fact is fact."

26

AFTER buying some sausage, bread, and fruit, Georg ate a leisurely supper in a neighborhood *Gasthaus*. It was seven thirty by the time he arrived home. Elsbeth met him at the door. "What have you got there?"

"None of your business." He brushed past her and headed for his room. She followed him.

"A couple of White Mice were here looking for you. What did you do, rob a bank?" She snickered.

Georg dropped the bag of groceries onto his bed. "Police?"

"Two of 'em." She came to the doorway and looked in, smug, curious. "What did you do, Gee-org?" She sang his name in a cooing, teasing strain.

He felt himself trembling and quickly sat down to hide it from her. "What did they say?"

"They wanted to see you."

"What did you tell them"

"I said you don't live here no more, you moved out a month ago. I don't tell White Mice nothin' never."

He didn't know whether that was smart of her, or stupid. The police. It could only be about Klaus. But how? What had only startled him before, now settled into immobilizing terror. He felt it tighten his stomach and chest. An ache began to throb behind his eyes. He put his hands to his face and fought for breath.

Her voice came through, no longer taunting now, but frightened, awed. "Hey, you really did somethin', huh?

What did you do, Georg? God in Heaven, Georg, what did you *do?*"

"Get out," he moaned. "Get out of here."

"But, Geeorg—"

He raised his head and screamed at her, "Get out, you pig! Get out!"

She backed off, then turned and fled in tears. He slammed the door and collapsed against it. The strength drained from his body, and slowly, without attempting to resist, he let himself slide down. He lay on the cool wooden floor, his arms wrapped around his knees.

From far in the distance came the sound of a braying police horn, playing the atonal theme behind the percussion of the submachine guns, the counterpoint of Greta's cry. Gradually, its volume grew louder and louder until it obliterated every other sensation. They were coming for him. They were coming now, in the street below, to take him. But I didn't do it. I didn't do it. I didn't do it! *"I didn't do it!"*

His own voice broke through the bray of the horn, and he heard it retreating down the street, passing on beyond the house. He stared in the direction of the sound, listening like an animal to the passing of a mortal enemy outside its lair. Slowly he brought himself to a sitting position. His fingers felt stiff. He rubbed them and wondered why they were stiff. The calluses, raised even under the protective covering of leather gloves, stood out in relief like weathered rock exposed on a desert. He picked at one, peeling away the tough, dead yellow skin.

Elsbeth knocked softly, hesitantly.

He did not move.

Again she knocked, more insistently this time. "Georg, are you all right?"

The pig. The stupid pig.

"Georg!" Angry now.

"Go away."

"Are you all right?"

"No!"

Silence.

She doesn't know what to do, what to think. Stupid pig, she expected me to say yes. He snickered under his breath.

"Geeorg." She was whining now, pleading with him. "Geeeeee-oooorg."

He slapped his hands over his ears. "No!" He clambered to his feet, breathing fast and hard. His hands dripped with sweat. He rubbed them against his trousers. He had to get away, away from all of them. He had to get back into the tunnel, where they couldn't find him. He snatched up the bag of groceries and flung open the door. Elsbeth backed off, startled. He ignored her and strode for the door.

"Are you gonna come back, Georg?"

Her timorous voice stopped him. He turned to look at her, at the pathetic gray lines deep around her fleshy mouth, the remnants of tears lying in the eaves of her dull eyes—dull even after tears—her sagging breasts squeezed together in a thousand wrinkles where they met above the line of the low-cut dress, pushed together by her fat arms drawn together by hands clasped in front of her genitalia in such a way as to suggest an invitation to enter. The sight of her anguish diminished his own.

"Do you want me to come back?"

"I don't care what you done. It don't make no difference to me."

"I didn't do"—his voice died with his conviction—"anything."

She shook her head and took a tentative step toward him. "I don't care. Honest, I don't." Her plump fingers scrawled a cross over her heart.

He held her love as he would an ugly but interesting worm that had crept mysteriously into his hand. Lying there, totally isolated from its ecological niche, exposed to his will, it lifted its head in one final supplication. "I never cared about nobody before."

Her simple confession aroused what pity he had not used up on himself. He could not bring himself to destroy the life she had created, no matter how ugly it was. And as he let it live, the moment engendered the realization that she was the only one who did care about him.

"I'll be coming back," he said.

A smile touched the corners of her lips. She nodded and tried to speak, but as if in fear that by doing so she would lose the momentum of the smile, she said nothing.

27

ﾉﾉﾉﾉﾉﾉﾉﾉﾉﾉﾉﾉﾉﾉﾉﾉﾉﾉﾉﾉﾉﾉﾉﾉ

"I'M sorry I'm late. I got here as soon as I could." She slid into the chair next to his and gave him a quick kiss on the cheek. Wolf had chosen a table in the corner. It was still early, and there were few people in the coffee-house. "What's this all about? You sounded so mysterious on the phone. I had to leave without eating dessert. Papa was distraught, to put it mildly. I've never done that before, left the table before everyone was finished. It just isn't done."

"I hope he won't give you any trouble."

"Oh, nothing I can't handle."

"What would you like?"

"What are you having?"

"Coffee."

"I'll have that, too."

"Would you like dessert? I didn't mean to deprive you of dessert."

"I'm getting too fat, anyway."

"You're not fat. You're as skinny as a wire."

"Oh, do you think I'm too skinny? Maybe I'd better eat desserts. I'll have two if you think I'm too skinny."

"You're not *too* skinny, you're just right, but if you want a dessert, why don't you have one?"

"When I said that, it wasn't because I *missed* having dessert. I mean, I don't *crave* dessert. Lots of girls just crave sweets, and you know why that is. Poor dears. If they had a man like you, they'd never have to eat another

392

dessert as long as they lived. Do you think it's affected of me to refer to you as a man. I suppose you aren't really, not until you're twenty-one, but age isn't really the determinant. I think you're more of a man than some real men —I mean, older men, even in their twenties."

The waitress came to the table.

"What have you decided?" he asked her.

"Perhaps I'll have a little dessert." And to the waitress: "Do you have punch torte?"

"One punch torte."

"And two coffees."

"Two coffees. Anything else?"

"Nothing else, thank you."

"One punch torte, two coffees." She left.

Wolf smiled. "I'm obviously not the man you say I am."

"Why do you say that?"

"You're having dessert. If I were the man you say I am, you wouldn't want it, like those other girls."

"I don't want it. I thought you wanted me to have it. I won't eat it."

"You ordered it; you'll eat it."

"Besides, you think I'm too skinny."

"I said you were just right."

"I'm as skinny as a wire. How much skinnier can one get than that?"

"You're not skinny where it matters."

"That's true. Objectively speaking, I can say that I'm not skinny where it matters. Some girls are terribly flat-chested. I'm awfully glad I'm not. You don't think I'm flat-chested, do you?"

"Good grief, no."

"Oh, do you think I'm overdeveloped?"

"I think you're just right. Why are you so sensitive to-night?"

"I didn't think I was being sensitive, although I suppose I am. It's because you were so mysterious on the phone, and now you won't tell me why you wanted to see me so fast, and I can only think that you're going to tell me it's all over, and if you are, I'm going to cry like a baby."

"I'm not going to tell you it's all over."

"Oh." She looked almost disappointed.

"If you'd rather have a good cry . . ."

"Now who's being sensitive?"

The waitress arrived with their order. As she was setting the coffee and cake out, Uschi said, "Tell me, Fräulein, do you think this boy is attractive?"

"God in Heaven, Uschi."

The waitress smiled. She looked him over in such a way as to make him blush. He could have strangled Uschi.

"Yes, I'd say he's very attractive. Give him a few years and I'd go for him myself," she laughed.

"Thank you," Uschi said brightly and dismissed her by digging into her cake.

The waitress leaned over to her and whispered loud enough for Wolf to hear, "He looks like the dangerous type. I'd keep my legs crossed if I were you," and with a shake of her ample head of hair and deliberately saucy laugh, she left.

Wolf was fuming. "What made you do a thing like that?"

"I wanted another woman's opinion."

"I felt like a dog being considered for stud."

"Oh, you loved it," she said airily. "This cake is delicious." She offered him a forkful. "Try it."

"No, thank you."

"Oh, don't be such a fuddy-duddy. It was all in fun."

Wolf was slowly getting over it. He supposed he would have to get used to her impulsiveness. Then he remembered that perhaps he wouldn't have a chance. He sipped his coffee. It was strong and hot, the way he liked it.

"I called you because I can't see you tonight, maybe for two or three nights. We have to work in the tunnel until it's finished." She went on eating the cake, glancing at him with her bright eyes, saying nothing. "They're going to tear down the house we're planning to come out in, so we have to speed things up."

She still did not say anything.

"I'm sorry. I want to see you, I want to very much." She nodded.

"When this is done, we'll see each other every night."

"Your parents will be here." She was acting very restrained.

"We'll work something out. Joachim will have some ideas. I'm going to talk to him about it."

"What will happen if your father decides not to stay in Berlin?"

"He's always lived in Berlin. Even during the war we lived in Berlin. I was born here, so was Joachim. He'd never leave Berlin."

She was listening, but she wouldn't look at him.

Her coldness angered him. "What do you expect me to do?"

"I hate that damned tunnel."

"You shouldn't swear."

"Damn, damn, damn, damn."

He was too angry and frustrated to speak. He drank his coffee and glared at her. She ignored him. She finished her cake, getting every last crumb by pressing the fork down on them. He could see that she was doing that purposely to give herself something to do so she would not have to look at him.

"Now you think I'm despicable," she said finally.

"Just because you swear?"

"No, silly, because I said that about your old tunnel."

His anger melted. "I don't think that, at all. You know I like you, I like you a lot."

"When will it be finished?"

"Two days, maybe three. I don't know. If it isn't finished soon, it never will be."

She worked up a weak smile. "I hope everything goes all right. I really do."

He nodded.

She drank her coffee.

"I tried to sabotage it," he said. "I tried, but I couldn't go through with it."

She stared at him, not fully grasping what he had said.

"It would have been like condemning all those people to life in prison—my parents, Sepp's girl, Emerich's family, Georg's parents. I would have hated myself the rest of my life." He was surprised at how calmly he had confessed it. Having said it, he felt better about it, as if simply telling her somehow absolved him. "Now it's your turn to think I'm despicable."

Tears brimmed in her eyes.

"What's wrong? I *didn't* go through with it. It was crazy to even think I could have done it. I thought of the great times we've had, and I just got carried away thinking about how it could go on, but it would have been terrible, living with that on my conscience. I don't think I'd have been able to touch you."

Nothing he had said had touched her. She stared at him with tears and a smile trembling on her lips. "Oh, Wolf. Dear, dear Wolf."

"Don't cry. Why are you crying? I told you I didn't do it."

She shook her head, trying to stop the tears. He would never understand her, he realized. Never.

28

"THE dinner was superb." Bruno puffed the Havana cigar with little pleasure. He did not smoke, never had, and undoubtedly never would. Somehow he had not been able to refuse it when Herr Komanski had offered it. He was careful to puff slowly and not to inhale.

The old man fluffed a bed pillow behind his head and turned his gaze on the spectacular view of the city afforded by the balcony of his hotel room. "I always eat well these days," he said. He patted his flat stomach. "Never gain a pound, not a pound. During the war I was as fat as a pig. Can you imagine it, my dear Balderbach? Me, fat as a pig?"

Bruno allowed he could not imagine it. Off to the left, the parabolic line of lights of the Kongresshalle stood out in the darkness of the Tiergarten like a distorted rainbow in the night.

"How do you like the view?"

"Magnificent."

"I always get a room facing the East. I used to live over there, in Pankow, in one of those dingy tenements. And I like our 'pregnant oyster.' It has a certain charm despite its modern design."

"I prefer the Schloss Bellevue, but then I've been accused of being old-fashioned."

"And aloof, I suppose."

Bruno glanced at his host's tiny face, conveniently masked by shadow. Komanski puffed his cigar, a ridiculously big one for such a small man, and the glow of the ash lighted up his face. He was smiling.

"That's all right, that's all right. Why should you be cordial to me? After all, I've beaten you out of a few thousand marks. No one likes that." He leaned forward to the tray of liqueurs on the table before him. "Some brandy? You are a brandy man, aren't you?"

"Thank you."

Komanski poured them each a glass, his hands trembling with the weight of the full decanter. He handed Bruno his glass. *"Prosit."*

"Prosit."

Komanski drank and sighed. "Ah, nothing like a good brandy with a good cigar after a good meal."

"You enjoy these things."

"Yes, sir, I do. I went too many years without them." He laughed bitterly. "Didn't we all. If we had never let that idiot come to power . . ." He stared out of the shadow at Bruno. "You're not a political man, are you?"

"Every man is political to some extent, especially when politics begins to touch him."

Komanski waved vaguely toward the East. "How have those people touched you?"

"They haven't."

"Then what's this business in my cellar? What is a man of your stature doing in there? It's damned nonsense."

"If I am to stand guilty of being aloof, you must confess to effrontery."

"I invented it, my dear Balderbach. It's the secret of my success. All one has to do is scare the fools to death and they'll do anything you ask."

"You don't frighten me."

"Of course I don't. You're not a fool."

Komanski stirred in his chair, adjusted his pillow and crossed his legs. There was only a trace of breeze wafting across the small balcony. It seemed oppressively hot compared with the air-conditioned room they had just left. Bruno felt perspiration accumulating in the small of his back.

"What brought you to the warehouse this morning?" Bruno inquired out of curiosity.

"It's my warehouse, isn't it?"

"Did someone tell you we were there?"

"No, no." He looked out over the city, to the north, as if seeking the warehouse from among the thousands of rooftops spreading to the horizon. "I always go there when I'm in Berlin. It's a ritual with me. I got started there, in 1948." He turned to Bruno. "Do you want to know how?"

"Yes."

"Making shovels, picks, wheelbarrows—anything useful in construction. Any fool could see that construction was going to be Berlin's biggest industry for many years to come. I got hold of some blacksmithing equipment and scavenged metal anywhere I could find it. In six months I had fifty people working for me in that old building. Now I make cranes, bulldozers, graders, tractors—all the big equipment. I'm in other things, too—chemicals, electronics, steel, publishing, real estate."

Bruno was impressed. "And it all started in that old building?"

"Yes."

"Interesting."

"Um." Komanski crossed his legs the other way. "What sort of picture will you paint for me?"

"What would you like?"

"My taste is eclectic. You decide."

"Very well."

He changed his position again. "Damn it all, Balderbach, you're a distressing man. You've got my conscience churning, and I don't like it one bit, not one bit."

Bruno acted astonished. "But what have I said?"

"It's not what you've said, it's what you haven't said. Why the devil aren't you beating my ears about how unpatriotic I am?"

"Are you unpatriotic?"

"And heartless."

"Heartless?"

"You've been thinking all evening, 'Why doesn't this rich old bird Komanski let those boys use his rotting building? Why must he exact a price? Doesn't he realize he's trading on human flesh?'" He gulped down his brandy and refilled his glass. "Yes, I've been aware of it. You haven't let me forget it, not for a minute."

"But I assure you—"

Komanski waved the cigar threateningly. "I won't have

you thinking that of me. I have some self-respect. I'm not so money-hungry as you think or unpatriotic or heartless. I know what it's like over there. I lived there. One can't live there without developing some compassion."

"Tell me, Herr Komanski—"

"Wilfred."

Bruno nodded. "Bruno."

"Bruno." He raised his glass. "To our friendship."

Bruno reciprocated, thinking the gesture premature. "Tell me, Wilfred, why did you leave the *Sektor?* Why did you come over here?"

"For the same reason everyone else did. What honest man can make money under communism? You've got to be a scoundrel and a conniver to make money over there. It's unnatural. It's stupid. Someday they'll wake up to the fact that man is not engineered to acquiesce to the group on every matter. There are certain aspects of life that demand competition. Economic activity is one of them."

"And you succeeded."

"Splendidly."

"You have your fine brandy and Havana cigars and French cuisine."

"As the Americans say, don't knock it, my friend."

Bruno had to laugh. "On the contrary. I'm not one of those sanctimonious, aesthetic snobs who sneer at the material side of life. I must say I enjoyed our dinner this evening as much as I would a good play or a well-written book."

"Money makes it possible—the play and the book as well."

"Agreed."

"I feel better."

"Good."

Komanski chuckled in his high-pitched way. "So you don't begrudge me my success."

"Do you begrudge me mine?"

The old man sat forward, letting the pillow slide down behind his back. His face came into the light, revealing a puzzled expression. "Have you made yours?"

"I am far from poor, my dear friend." The last he appended without forethought and, having said it, rather believed it might be true. He had to admit that he was taken by this little man with his gouty tastes and rigid opinions. Perhaps it was only that it was refreshing to hear someone speak so candidly, without equivocation, but he put himself on guard against the temptation to accept as truth something that was merely stated with conviction.

"So I don't impress you, either."

"Oh, you impress me, Wilfred." He grinned. "Do you feel the need to?"

The bony face darkened, then slowly, with humor that could come only from a basic good nature, it brightened into a smile of uncommon dimensions. "It's no wonder I like your painting!"

They had arrived at the moment Bruno had hoped for but had dared not expect. He was gratified that his acumen had not failed him. "You think we have much in common, then?"

"Yes, I believe we do."

"I tend to agree with you. That's why I think you will want to join me in a little enterprise I have in mind."

"Enterprise?" Komanski repeated the word tentatively, feeling its texture. "What sort of enterprise?"

"I am looking for a front man, so to speak, someone who will execute a piece of deception for me."

"If it's illegal, I'll have nothing to do with it."

"Wilfred, I'm surprised. Do you think a man of my 'stature' would suggest anything illegal?"

Komanski appeared suitably chagrined. "Proceed."

"If our tunnel succeeds, the people who escape will be arriving virtually penniless. You may say that they knew this before they made the decision to escape, that this is the price they must pay for their freedom."

"Bruno, my friend, do not put words into my mouth. I have a mind and a tongue of my own."

"Forgive me."

He waved him on.

"There will be a peasant family whose land was collectivized. Their wish will be to start again, on land of their own, somewhere in the Federal Republic. There will be a physician who will want to practice, in Berlin, perhaps. I don't know for sure. And there will be a bookkeeper."

"A bookkeeper?"

"Yes."

"I'm in need of a good bookkeeper at my plant in Erlangen."

"Ah, you are already in the spirit of my enterprise."

Komanski sat back, retreating into the safety of the shadows. "See here, Balderbach, I'm no philanthropist. Never have been, never plan to be. I had to work for every pfennig I ever got. No one ever gave me a hand-out."

"I'm not asking you to change."

The old man snorted. "Do you think I'm too old to change?"

"I don't think you're too old for anything. I don't even think of you as 'old.' How old are you, anyway?"

"None of your damned business."

Bruno laughed.

"So you think I am vain."

"Aren't you?"

"Maybe." He averted his eyes to the distant horizon, where the church spires of East Berlin standing in the night sky above the rooftops looked much like defiant individualists who refused to bow before a king. "A man should be allowed a little vanity," he said solemnly. "Vanity is the soul of pride. Without pride, a man is nothing."

"I find your vanity charming."

"You have no vanity, I suppose?" It was a challenge, a tactic to force Bruno into admitting that he was as fallibly human as the next man.

"Not so serious as yours."

"You make it sound like a disease." He again finished his brandy and refilled his glass. "Maybe it is. Frankly, I don't much care. I won't die of it. From this, maybe," he said, raising his glass, "but never from vanity." He snickered at some private thought, and Bruno had the distinct vision of the old devil ordering up a willing bed-mate as soon as he was rid of his guest. "Go on with your story. I am certain a man of your 'stature' has devised an ingenious plot."

"Not too ingenious, I fear, but suitably discreet. I am determined not only that these people escape, but that they have something more than a remote hope of renew-ing their lives. Each of them—the peasant, the doctor, the bookkeeper—is in his fifties. It will be difficult for them to start all over again, to find a place to live, to accumulate the paraphernalia of an entire lifetime."

"And you want to give it to them."

"Anonymously. I don't want them to feel obligated to me."

"You want to give it to them in my name."

"Yes."

"But, my dear Bruno, they will feel obligated to me."

"But, my dear Wilfred, think of what that will do for your vanity."

Komanski's bright eyes gazed at Bruno through the thick glasses, and a twinkle gathered in the corner.

"What kind of money are you talking about?"

Bruno recognized the businessman's tone of voice. "For the bookkeeper, five thousand and that job you have open."

"Five thousand?"

"For the doctor, ten thousand. He must be able to live according to his professional status."

"*Ten* thousand? You're mad."

"And for the peasant, fifteen thousand, to purchase a farm."

"*Fifteen?*"

"Twenty, then, if it can't be done for fifteen."

The old man groaned and drank his brandy. "Thirty, thirty-five thousand marks! You speak of it as if it were wastepaper." He shook his head solemnly. "I don't understand it. It's madness, madness."

Bruno beamed. "A wonderful madness."

Komanski eyed him curiously. "Does it really make you feel so good?"

"It does."

The old man grunted, poured himself another brandy, and sat back. He swirled the brandy in the glass and sniffed its bouquet. Satisfied, he drank. "I'll split it with you."

"Very well."

He grunted again. "You don't seem surprised."

"I'm not. I expected you to."

"Cheeky fellow, just like that boy—what's his name?"

"Sepp Bauer."

"Bauer. Cheeky fellow."

Bruno stood up and leaned back against the railing. From above, he could hear the music drifting down from the roof garden café. It was a waltz. He thought perhaps he would take Frieda there for an evening sometime soon. She liked to dance. How long had it been since they had been out for an evening, just the two of them?

"But you're going about this all wrong, my dear friend," Komanski said. "You can't just hand people such large sums. It smacks too much of charity. People don't take kindly to charity."

"You are concerned about their pride."

"Shouldn't we be?"

"We don't want to make them feel uncomfortable about it."

"What they need is a livelihood, not money. They'll want to be able to go on doing over here what they were doing in the *Sektor*."

"For the bookkeeper, that's no problem," Bruno said, "but the peasant needs land, a house and a barn, equipment, stock. And a doctor needs a practice. These things require money."

"And far more than you propose to give them. No, cash is not the answer."

"What do you suggest?"

The old man told him what he had in mind. Bruno listened with a growing appreciation of Wilfred Komanski. Although Bruno had shrewdly guessed that under his shell of avarice and arrogance there was some compassion, some generosity, he had misjudged the extent badly indeed. There was also a perspicacity about human nature that gave some insight into how this strange little man had built an industrial empire from virtually nothing.

They discussed their plans in some detail until Bruno had to leave.

"I'm afraid I shall not sleep well tonight," Komanski complained.

"On the contrary, I think you will sleep extremely well."

"You, my friend, are a sentimentalist."

"And so, my dear friend, are you."

Komanski grunted loudly. "That is without question the most cutting insult of all my seventy-six years." He got up with Bruno, grinning. "So, it is out. A little piece of my vanity has broken away from the main." He looked up at his guest. "Do I strike you as a man of seventy-six years?"

"Every year of it."

He seemed deeply touched. "Thank you," he murmured, "thank you."

He walked Bruno to the door. "Perhaps you will paint another picture of that woman for me. I would like that."

Bruno searched his memory. "Woman? What painting is that?"

"It's called *Oak Tree Number Nine*. I bought it here in Berlin in 1960. It was one of a series you'd done. *Oak Tree Number One, Oak Tree Number Two*, et cetera. Dreary titles." He smiled sheepishly. "I do remember the titles."

"I remember the painting well."

"Why did you call it *Oak Tree*?"

Bruno was confused. "Why, because it was a painting of an oak tree. The tree stands in my garden."

Komanski waved his frail white hands. "Yes, yes, the oak tree is there, all right—enormous—but it is the woman picking flowers that the painting is all about. It wouldn't be much without her. That's why I bought it. Her face fascinated me. There's a woman who's known a thing or two about life. Where did you dig her up? Or is she only in your imagination?"

Bruno was stunned. He fumbled for a reply. "Oh, she's a model, just a model. We use models, you know."

"Marvelous, marvelous. I hope you paid her well." He opened the door and extended his hand. "I can't recall when I've had such an expensive evening, Herr Balderbach. I think I'd have to go back ten years to the roulette table at the Lido casino."

Bruno managed a smile. "I should have thought you would be a lucky gambler."

"I usually am, but all gamblers must take their losses along with their winnings."

"Do you think I would be lucky at roulette?"

"Sentimentalists should never gamble. Good night, my dear friend."

"Good night, Wilfred."

The elevator came with a diminuendo rush of air. Bruno got in. Why did I tell him she was a model? he

wondered. The truth would have been an admission—but
an admission of what? Have I ever slighted Frieda's
importance to my success? Haven't I always told everyone
how well she bore up during all those years of seemingly
desperate hopelessness? Her loyalty, devotion, confidence
are renowned. They are etched in her face.

He stepped out into the lobby and moved with the
crowd to the doors. The heat fell on him like a wolf pack,
and he recoiled instinctively. A shudder rippled down his
back and arms.

Bruno parked on Marzstrasse, down the block from
the alley, and walked to the warehouse. In the dimly
lighted alley he saw that Emerich had taped an extension
to the exhaust hose of the generator. Its end disappeared
down a drain at the end of the alley, from where its sound
was barely audible, even at close range. He stood listening
for noise from inside the building. After a few seconds of
concentration he could just make out the whir of the
vacuum cleaner and the rhythmic turning of the generator.
He walked back up the alley and around to the front of
the warehouse, then crossed to the sidewalk running along
The Wall. Slowly he ambled down the walk, past the end
of the warehouse halfway past the plastics factory, stopping occasionally to listen. Once he heard the patrol on
the other side of The Wall talking in low voices, but there
was no sound at all from the warehouse. Satisfied, he re-
traced his steps, girding himself mentally for the grueling
hours ahead. There would be time for thinking, time he
needed badly.

29

CROWDED as ever, the little *Platz* had the air of an incipient political rally. The listeners were there—all that was lacking was the speaker. Sepp led Ilse to the island of grass under the young ash trees and found an unoccupied bench. He felt a little out of place in this sanctuary, which either by default or by ancient custom seemed populated solely by old people.

"What is your news?"

"The Knauers are impossible. I think we'll have to give them up."

"They wouldn't see you?"

"I spent two minutes arguing through a crack in the door. He's as stubborn and frightened as she is. What could I say, standing in the hallway with who knows how many ears listening behind closed doors?" She was dejected because of her failure, but her voice and manner were spirited. These days had revived much of what she had been a year ago, and it heartened him to see it. He was concerned that his news might weight the balance back the other way, but there was no helping it.

"I'll go there myself tonight. If they won't listen to me, then we'll give up on them."

"If only Georg could talk to them."

"I don't see how that's possible."

"Couldn't you get him some false papers?"

"I don't know how. I've never done anything like that. It might take days."

"We have a week."

He looked at the ground between his feet. "I'm afraid we don't. They're razing the houses on Vierickstrasse. Ours will be coming down soon. It's a matter of only a few days." He looked at her to see how she was taking it. She was staring at him in stunned disbelief. "I know. I couldn't believe it, either. But we're not licked. We're going to work straight through until we finish or they beat us to it." He took her chin in his hand and turned her head toward him. She looked as if she were about to break down. "We're not giving up, and neither are you. Is that clear?"

She nodded absently.

"This means you've got to do everything much sooner than we'd planned. We're counting on you. There's no one else. If you quit now, all our work will have been for nothing."

"I'm not quitting. It's just—"

"So infuriating, so unfair, so criminal that you want to scream."

She smiled meekly. "Yes."

He looked around at the groups of gray and white heads, some engrossed in animated conversation, some people watching, some fast asleep. "It would give them all a tale to take home if you did."

She shook her head. "Don't make fun of me, not yet. When it's all over, when I'm over there, I'll scream my head off."

He smiled. "We'll plan on it."

"When do you expect to finish?"

"That's the problem, especially with the Webers. We've got to get them to Berlin and keep them here until we're ready. The soonest we could be through would be this time on Wednesday."

"Two days?"

"If we're lucky, which we haven't been."

"Dr. Lentz will have to move quickly."

"Here's what I've decided. We'll operate on the assumption that the escape will take place at five after eleven on Wednesday night. That's late enough so that there won't be many people about, but early enough so that our people's movements won't be suspect."

"Why five after?"

"Because of the timing of the Vopo passing the house."
She remembered.

"The Lentzes and the Knauers—if they decide to join
us—are to go to the Edelweiss; the Lentzes at ten forty-
five, no earlier. Take separate tables. None of you is to
take any notice of the others. If that nuisance of a waiter,
Adolf, badgers you, just tell him you're waiting for me,
that I'm late. I'll be at Emerich's aunt's. So will the Webers,
I hope. We'll leave there in plenty of time to arrive at the
house at eleven five. As soon as we arrive, they'll go
straight into the house and into the tunnel. I'll go to the
Gasthaus. When I enter, that's the sign that it's all clear.
Everyone is to get up and leave immediately. Tell them
to hurry, not to run, but no dallying."

"If we all leave at once, won't someone—Adolf, perhaps—become suspicious?"

"Probably. But by the time he can do anything about
it, we'll all be away."

"You make it sound very easy."

"We must impress these people with the importance of
three things: One, they are to move quickly—no stopping
for reunions until they're safely on the other side; two,
there is to be no unnecessary talking until they are through
the tunnel; and three, they are to take no baggage. Another thing, the women should wear skirts they can move
in easily—and low heels. Do you have all that?"

"Yes."

"All right. Now, tonight, you have two assignments.
One, go to Dr. Lentz and tell him about the need for
haste. Tell him we leave it entirely up to him to make
certain the Webers get their travel permits in time to arrive in Berlin by Wednesday evening."

"Shouldn't someone meet them at the train? They'll
be terribly confused if they've never been to Berlin before."

"I could do that, I suppose. Or Emerich's aunt.

"What if they can't get here by Wednesday?"

"We'll delay as long as we can. But if the house is in
imminent danger of being razed, we'll have to go without
them."

"Oh." The prospect was painful to her.

"We have no choice."

"How are we going to contact them to tell them what we are doing?"

"That's your second assignment for tonight. Go to Emerich's aunt. She's to telephone them. At Wohner's *Gasthaus* in Überdreibrücken. There's a phone there."

"Isn't that terribly risky?"

"I don't think so. Tell her to use every device she can think of, but in some way convince Herr Weber that he's got to bring the whole family—every one of them—to Berlin. Tell her to say that Emerich wants them to come. Did she strike you as intelligent enough to pull it off?"

"I don't know."

"Well, it's up to her. Impress her with that. She'll rise to the occasion. People do."

"And what are you going to do?"

"I'm going to visit the Knauers. Maybe they'll trust me, being an American."

"Be prepared for a letdown."

"I am. I have another note from Georg. Maybe it will help."

"Are you coming over again tomorrow night?"

"Yes. I'll have to know what news you have. Tell Emerich's aunt to tell Herr Weber to let her know just as soon as possible when they'll be arriving in Berlin."

Ilse sighed. "Everything seems to be helter-skelter all of a sudden."

"It is. I'll know better tomorrow night what our chances are of finishing the tunnel by Wednesday. Let's meet here again at eight o'clock."

"All right."

He wondered if he had forgotten anything. To make certain she understood the plan, he went over it again with her. She answered all his questions correctly. She had a retentive mind—very useful in the circumstances—and he was grateful for it.

"Be careful," he warned her.

"I always am. And you, too."

"If all goes well, this will be behind us in about forty-eight hours."

She smiled. Her smile always brightened his mood. It was good to see that she could smile for him now. "I expect we'd better get going, darling."

"No time for pleasantries tonight."

They got up and crossed the *Platz* together. "No one followed me again. I think they've become bored by us."

"How lucky for us."

"We can use a little luck."

He had to knock twice before Georg's father opened the door.

"Yes?" He was a slim man, with blond hair thinning and receding into a widow's peak and going gray, dull gray eyes, a slightly hooked nose, and puffy cheeks covered with a road map of capillaries just under the skin.

"Herr Knauer?"

"Yes. What is it?" His gray eyes were as wary as his tone.

"I'm a friend of Georg's. Please let me talk to you."

His eyes narrowed and his thick lips thinned to a long crease of anger. "Why do you people continue to torment us? We don't want to see you. Go away." He started to close the door, but Sepp caught it, pushed it back, and entered the room. The man retreated, his anger giving way to fear. Sepp closed the door behind him.

"You're going to listen to me. I came here at great risk, not only to me but to others. Your son has been risking his life every day for the past week so that you and his mother can join him in West Berlin. Whether you want to go or not is up to you. Right now, either you choose to trust me, or you can stay here in this concentration camp and rot. Personally, Herr Knauer, I don't give a damn what you do."

Sepp took his passport and Georg's letter out of his pocket and tossed them to the man. He caught them both, fumbling them against his chest. "There's my passport. It tells you who I am—I'm an American. The other is a letter from Georg which he wrote today and gave me to give to you." He glanced at his watch. "I'll give you exactly five minutes to read the letter; another five minutes to decide whether or not you want to get out of here. Starting now.

"Oh, if you get any ideas about turning me over to the authorities, let me assure you that if I don't return to West Berlin safe and sound tonight, Georg will be dead by morning. But, then, you don't want to get involved with the authorities, do you, Herr Knauer."

The man slowly regained his composure. He flipped open the passport, looked at it, looked at Sepp, looked at the passport again. He closed it and stared at the imprint on the front for a moment. "How do I know this is genuine?"

"I guess you don't. But you do know that Georg is in West Berlin. A foreigner can cross over; a Berliner can't. That's why he asked me to come, because you wouldn't trust Fräulein—the young woman who was here to see you before."

"Can you describe my son?"

"Light hair, blue eyes, average height, small mouth, round face . . ."

"Why does he think we want to leave the *Sektor?*"

"I suppose he figures you're sane. Why don't you read the note?"

Sepp took back the passport and put it safely in his pocket. Herr Knauer unfolded the paper, glanced once at Sepp as if to make sure he was not planning a move against him, and began reading. The note was two pages long. He read it through without comment, with no sign of emotion. When he was finished, he folded it and put it in his pocket.

"It is very strange. Fräulein Dohr is released from prison. A week later, a woman comes to my wife saying she's come from Georg. Now you come, saying the same thing. How do we know this isn't some plot the Dohr girl has cooked up to get us in trouble, to take revenge on us, since she can't get at Georg?"

Sepp remembered that Ilse had mentioned a girl named Dohr. He had meant to ask Georg about her, but it had slipped his mind. "I don't know what you're talking about. Who is Fräulein Dohr? What did Georg do to her that she would want to avenge?"

The man turned away and walked slowly to the end of the small room. He stopped by a table where a family portrait stood—the father, the mother, the son. Georg appeared to be five or six in the picture. How little he had changed. There was no mistaking him, even from a distance.

"If you're concerned about getting a job over there, starting over again, I can understand that concern," Sepp said in a conciliatory gesture. "The government will help you, of course, and there is always a demand in Berlin and in the Federal Republic for skills like yours."

Sepp couldn't tell if he was listening. He seemed deep in thought, staring into space, his hands clasped behind his back, his shoulders hunched as though he were very tired. Sepp looked around the room for the first time. It might have been any of a million German living rooms. The furniture was sturdy, old, well cared for, drab in color, designed solely for comfort. Hand-crocheted doilies and antimacassars covered the arms and backs of all the chairs and the plump sofa. The tile space heater gleamed. Not a speck of dust was to be seen anywhere. He felt, as he always did in rooms like this, that he had been transported back thirty years in time.

"We are content here," Herr Knauer said suddenly, quietly, with an undisturbed calm that surprised Sepp. "The German Democratic Republic has been good to us. It was good to our son, but he was deluded by the daughter of a revisionist and chauvinist. We denounce him and disown him . . . his treason." He turned, his gray eyes now hard and dry with bitterness. "*Auf Wiedersehen,* Herr Bauer."

Sepp recognized his little speech for what it was—a confession of fear too awesome to be overcome—and he understood Georg a little better. "That is your final decision?"

"There was never any decision to be made."

Sepp nodded. "Very well. I'll tell Georg what you have told me." He started to leave, then had a thought. "Do you know where Fräulein Dohr lives?"

"You know as well as I do."

"I'm afraid I don't."

He hesitated. "In Pankow, Zimstergasse. I don't remember the number. It's a short street."

"Thank you."

As Sepp was going out the door, Herr Knauer came up behind him. "Is he well?"

"Yes, he's well. He's completed a year at the Free University."

"Give him . . . our love."

"All right."

"Tell him . . . tell him I'm sorry."

"About what?"

He made a vague gesture.

Sepp waited for him to go on, but he had nothing more to say. Or too much.

Zimstergasse was only a block long, a narrow arc of a street hidden away at the eastern end of Pankow. As he turned into it, Sepp wondered if he had been wise to come. His only concern had been that Georg might quit the tunnel now that his father had refused to make use of it. With no evidence to support his notion, Sepp had come more on intuition than from any reasonable hope. There might be a chance that Fräulein Dohr could tell him something that would change Herr Knauer's mind. He had no idea what her connection with Georg was, and if it was as sinister as his father had made it out to be, he was certain that Georg would not tell him about it if he asked him.

· Just around the corner he came upon a *Gasthaus* with a sidewalk window for outside beer sales. He rang the bell and waited. A woman slid the window up and stuck her head in the frame. "Yes, please?"

"Can you tell me where Fräulein Dohr lives?"

"Number eighteen, second floor."

"Thank you."

"Do you want something else?"

"No, thank you."

She was in a hurry, and the window came down with a bang. As he passed the *Gasthaus*, he saw her already threading her way between the filled tables with a tray of beers.

Eighteen Zimstergasse was a two-story building just at the center of the arc. Lights were burning in all the windows. The lock on the lower door was broken. Sepp pushed it open and, entering the hallway, mounted the dimly lighted stairs. The smell of pine filled the close air of the stairwell, an attempt on someone's part to overpower the more repugnant smell of years of decay. Her door was at the end of the hallway. A small, neatly handprinted card under the bell read simply: *G. Dohr*. He rang. The bell sounded loud inside. Footsteps approached the door, and through it a woman's voice asked who was there.

"An acquaintance of Georg Knauer."

There was a long, silent pause. Then he heard her sliding back a chain and snapping the lock. She opened the door slowly, peering out into the dim light of the hallway. "What do you want?"

"May I speak to you for a minute?"

She eyed him carefully—suspiciously—for a moment, and he felt a surge of weariness with the constant, predictable caution of these people. If dictatorship bred nothing but suspicion, it would still be evil. She opened the door halfway, still peering at him from behind it. He took it as an invitation to enter.

The room was surprisingly cheerful, furnished sparely in good, modern taste. Books were strewn about everywhere, art books mostly, and the walls were a profusion of cheap prints of the Masters, from an exquisite Botticelli drawing to a black-and-white nonobjective painting by Franz Kline. A long work table occupying one whole end wall was covered with notes and paper. A pencil lay across a pad. She had evidently been working there when he had interrupted her. She did not ask him to sit down.

He turned his attention to her. In contrast to the room, Greta Dohr looked far from cheerful. Thin and worn, she resembled a sparrow having a hard winter. Her cheeks were sunken, her arms and legs spindly. She might have been a beautiful girl once, and might be again if she put on some weight. Her blue eyes were lighted by a dull glow that held the potential for brightness.

"May I sit down?"

"What do you want?" She was not cold, only phlegmatic; willing to listen, but unprepared to care about what he had to say.

"I have to confess I'm not sure."

"I'm busy, Herr—"

"Bauer. Sepp Bauer." He smiled what he hoped was a warm, friendly smile. She did not respond in kind.

"I am busy, Herr Bauer."

"Yes, I see. You're a student of art, I gather. I can't say I know too much about it. I've a good friend who's an artist."

"Everyone has a good friend who is an artist."

"He's really an artist. Bruno Balderbach." She gave the first sign of interest. "He lives in West Berlin, you know."

Her interest heightened. She took her chair at the table and offered him a canvas folding chair by the window. She was a little more relaxed. "And you are a friend of Georg Knauer."

He corrected her. "An acquaintance."

"And you're from over there?"

"Yes."

"How is Georg?"

"As well as could be expected."

"Not well at all." She was not trying to be funny, but he could not help smiling. "It's nothing to smirk about, Herr Bauer."

"I wasn't smirking. You see, I don't know what the connection is between you two."

"How did you find me?"

"I didn't know you were hiding."

She was nonplussed for a moment. "I'm not . . . hiding. Who gave you my address?"

"Georg's father."

She made a face. "That imbecile. After meeting him, I think I understand Georg a little better."

"May I ask what happened? It's rather important to me. At least I think it might be. I can't tell you why I want to know about it."

"You're a mysterious character." She put her feet up on a rung of the chair and lighted a cigarette. "There's not much to tell. My father was once a deputy minister for defense of the DDR. He opposed the building of The Wall. He was arrested, and he was shot. Georg said he would help me escape. We drove my father's car through the border. The wire punctured a tire. The car turned over. Georg was thrown free and got across. I was trapped inside the car. I did not get across. I served eleven months in prison." She exhaled a stream of smoke. "Maybe I *am* hiding, Herr Bauer. . . ."

"Sepp."

She nodded. "Greta." She picked a bit of tobacco from her lips. "Maybe I am hiding. I'm not especially comfortable in that world out there. So I study. Art provides enduring beauty. Nothing can change it; nothing can destroy it. There are no problems of trust or loyalty, no politics, no disenchantment." She gave him a faintly ironic smile.

"I've never thought of myself as hiding. Escaping, perhaps, but not hiding."

"So you work."

She responded to his solicitude with a warm smile he thought might have been left over from better days. "I manage. It's kind of you to care."

"Are you sorry now you didn't make it across?"

"*That,* my dear man, is a most sensitive question. You may very well be from the Security Police, for all I know. Not that anyone can do much more to me now. I'm branded, so to speak."

He showed her his passport. She looked at it with interest, turning each page slowly before she handed it back. "So you're an American."

"Born, bred, and schooled."

"Zen you cahn shpeak English," she said in English with the British accent customary of German school English.

He replied in English, "Better than I speak German, I hope."

She laughed. "*Zat* is American English? I hahff nefer heard it before. Say somesing else."

"You know, it's impossible to think of something intelligent to say when someone asks you to," he said in English.

She giggled. "It is vonderful. I undershtand you perfectly, but it does not sound like English. It is vonderful."

"You speak very well," he said in German.

"Not as well as you speak German. You have no accent at all."

"I learned it at home, from my parents. I grew up speaking two languages, one as easily as the other."

"Wasn't it confusing?"

"It's somewhat like being ambidextrous, I suppose."

"Tell me, Herr Bauer. . . ."

"Sepp."

"Sepp. Tell me, is America as wonderful as they say?"

He had not intended to spend so much time with her, nor had he expected to be making small talk, but he lingered, becoming more and more captivated by her. For the first time in weeks, he felt completely relaxed; he could have sat there for hours. "How wonderful do they say it is?"

She laughed. "Better than this?"

"The DDR?"

"Yes."

"Much."

"Than the Federal Republic?"

"I only know Berlin. I usually feel very much at home in Berlin."

"Usually?"

"I'm not a German. I only speak like one."

She nodded toward the door. "In West Berlin is it so much better than here? Truly better?"

He did not hesitate. "It is truly much better."

She bit her lip. He studied her carefully, wondering what suffering she endured each day and whether she had really made her escape from the outside world as completely as she had given him to believe. He doubted she had. If she were a real sparrow, he knew, she would have flown over The Wall long ago, not because she was afraid any longer, as she had been the first time, with Georg, but because it was what she would consciously have chosen, had she had the choice. She put out her cigarette and immediately lighted another one. Then she remembered her manners and offered him one. He declined it.

"Did Georg send you to look me up?"

"He doesn't know that I know you exist."

"No, he would want to forget me."

"I don't think he's able to. I've known he was plagued by something, something that had affected him deeply. I didn't know what it was until now."

"It would have been foolish for him not to run. If he had come back for me, we would both have been sent to prison."

"I think he would have preferred that if he had known what it was going to do to him."

She threw him a look which could only have been fleeting contempt. "It is the responsibility of the human mind to recognize the consequences of one's actions."

"Quoth whom?"

"Quoth Fräulein Greta Dohr."

"Did you know that then, or have you learned it since?"

She thought for a moment before answering. "I suppose I must admit I've learned it since."

"Georg is still learning it—the hard way."

"I didn't learn it in church," she said acidly.

What had happened to the thread he had been winding from the ravel? He had dropped it somewhere in the peculiar concern he had so quickly developed for this girl. "If you were to see Georg again . . ."

"Oh, *the* question. A thousand different versions of just such a meeting have passed in and out of my mind. The only one that remains goes like this: 'Hello, Georg, how are you?' 'I'm fine, how are you?' 'I'm fine, how are you?' 'I'm fine, how are you?' Ad infinitum." She laughed. "You see?"

He nodded.

"But it will never come to pass."

"It might." He went further. "It could."

She looked at him with profound sadness. "Don't make rainbows."

"Maybe I can get you across. If it were possible, would you go?"

"Georg was going to get me across."

"I'm not Georg."

She turned away. "No, you're not."

He got up. "I have to go. Think about it. I'll stop by tomorrow night."

She got up with him, her lips forming a cynical smile. "Come tomorrow night if you wish. I'll be here. But you don't need to make empty gestures." Her smile suddenly lost its cynicism and radiated genuine cheer. "It's been nice talking to you. I haven't talked to anyone like this for a long, long time. Not since . . . Georg."

He was touched by her candor. "I'm not the sort to make empty gestures," he said gently.

She looked up at him with wondering, inquiring eyes, much like a child who for the first time has questioned the omnipotence of a parent. Impulsively, she rose on tiptoe and kissed his cheek. "Forgive me."

He smiled. "No need." He went to the door. "Until tomorrow night."

"Until tomorrow night."

He stood with one hand on the mailbox drop; the other held the letter, weighing it, much as if he were deciding whether or not he had put enough postage on it. It was a

short letter which he had no trouble remembering verba-
tim:

> Dear Konrad:
>   I've invited some friends over to my place to cele-
> brate my birthday on the 8th. Since I have been
> working the late shift recently, the festivities won't
> get under way until just after eleven o'clock. I hope
> you can join us. Don't be late!
>
>   Sepp
>
> P.S. In case I have to work overtime and don't show
> up, the party will be postponed until the 9th—
> same time, same place.

Would he be inviting protection or disaster?

Whether or not to mail the letter rested on the answers
to two questions, neither of which Sepp could give with
convincing assurance. One was: Is Konrad Möss to be
trusted? So far, he had reason to believe the border
guard had been true to his word, that he sincerely wanted
to escape from the *Sektor* and was counting on Sepp to
include him in his plans. Neither Sepp nor Ilse had detected anything unusual. At Checkpoint Charlie, Lieutenant Geller's attitude had not changed perceptibly. If he
was aware of what Sepp was up to, he was covering up
very well. Ilse was convinced she had never been followed on her visits to the Lentzes, the Knauers, and Emerich's aunt.

But had Möss informed on him? Were the authorities at
this moment keeping watch over the house on Vierickstrasse? Or did they think that by razing the house along
with the others they were aborting the escape in time?
If the authorities did know about the tunnel, they were
not acting true to previous form. They would not only
want to stop the tunnel from being used, they would also
want to catch the tunnelers and those who planned to
escape. The razing of the Vierickstrasse houses seemed
like reasonable evidence that they were ignorant of the
tunnel's existence.

The second question was: Did they really need Konrad
Möss? Sepp was far from satisfied with the plan he had
had to conceive so quickly. It was much as he had always

imagined it would be, but he had expected to have more time to work out the details carefully. The experience with the tunnel had not been lost on him; unforeseen circumstances could render the escape inordinately risky, or even impossible. The complicity of a border guard might very well be the deciding factor if unexpected obstacles should arise. Konrad Möss had already demonstrated his coolness in a trying situation; he would do it again if called upon.

Sepp dropped the letter through the slot.

It was past nine o'clock when he arrived at his room. His briefcase was packed with food, ready to go. He got the revolver from the wardrobe drawer, loaded the cylinder, set it on safety, and put it in his pocket. He looked to see if it showed. It did. He took it out and found room for it in the bulging briefcase. Then he decided to take the remaining box of ammunition. To get that in the briefcase, he had to sacrifice a square of cheese, which he crammed into his back pocket.

For a moment he stood wondering whether he had forgotten anything. He noticed Bruno's painting was hanging askew and straightened it. He wished he had time to clean up the room—his bed was unmade, and a pile of dirty laundry had accumulated in one corner; dust lay thick on every piece of furniture and had rolled like tiny tumbleweeds into every corner. It would give Ilse something to do. He smiled. It was hard to believe that, night after next, she would be back with him again—if everything went as he had planned.

When he arrived at the warehouse, Georg was alone in the cellar, gathering together pieces of lumber for a stretch of shoring. He searched Sepp's face anxiously.

"I talked to your father. He didn't say yes, and he didn't say no. I'll try again tomorrow night."

Georg gave a weak smile. "I knew you could do it."

"I don't know yet if I can."

"You will," he said confidently.

Sepp was having a hard time keeping his eyes on Georg's. He glanced at the hole where a pile of comforters muffled the sounds of the generator and the vacuum cleaner. He did not enjoy this kind of deception, but it would assure another twenty-four hours of work out of

Georg, and it would give Sepp time to think about what to do. "Where are Emerich and Bruno?"

Georg wasn't listening. "The police came looking for me." He made the announcement so casually that at first Sepp did not understand its implications.

"The police?"

"Two of them." He held up two fingers. "They won't find me here, though. I'm safe here." He seemed uncharacteristically calm.

"What did you tell them? What did they say?"

"Oh, I didn't see them," he said airily.

"You didn't see them?"

"I wasn't home!" He was pleased with himself for having had the sense not to be home.

"Well, how do you know they were looking for you?"

"Elsbeth told me."

"Who's Elsbeth?"

Georg was annoyed. "Don't you know Elsbeth?"

Sepp was becoming exasperated, but wary. Georg was acting most peculiar, but Sepp was not yet certain why.

"I don't know Elsbeth," he said evenly.

"She's my landlady's daughter. She told them I had moved out a month ago." He grinned inanely. "The people around here don't cooperate with the police much."

Sepp remembered a girl who answered the door when he had gone to tell Georg that they had taken care of Klaus. He couldn't recall what she looked like, though. He took up a splinter and cleaned between his teeth. "How do you figure the police got to you so fast?"

Georg shrugged. "I don't know."

"You don't seem worried."

He looked surprised. "Why should I be worried? I'm safe here."

"You aren't going to be here forever."

"When my parents cross over, we'll leave Berlin." He said it as if it solved everything.

Sepp did not like this new Georg. He was acting as if he hadn't a care in the world—whatever world he was living in. It was as if the pressure of his fears had become so intense that they had forced him out of the realm of reality into a sort of limbo where nothing could affect him, where he was insulated from the ghosts that had haunted him since his escape. Sepp thought of the delicate girl who must have loved Georg, and his conviction that she must be saved was reinforced. There are times when an individual has the opportunity to adjust the faulty balance of justice and injustice; this was one of those times for Sepp, and the more he thought about it, the more determined he became to make use of the opportunity. There was even a sense of ironic justice in using Georg, in deceiving him about his parents' intentions in order to give Greta Dohr a second chance. What was important now was to keep Georg working on the tunnel.

"What if your parents don't come over?"

"Oh, they'll come." He gathered his load of lumber into his arms.

"If the police do get to you, you have a perfect alibi."

"I know. I was home. Elsbeth was there. Besides, I didn't do it."

"You conspired with us. They can send you to prison for conspiracy."

He pondered this. Then he said, "They won't be seeing me. I'm leaving Berlin."

"Even if you leave Berlin, they may still get to you."

"I won't tell them anything."

"You're safe, and Emerich and I are safe, so long as you stick to the truth."

He grinned. "But not all the truth."

"No, not all the truth." Sepp was not satisfied that Georg could be trusted, but for now there was nothing he could do about it. "Where are Bruno and Emerich?"

"Bruno's in the tunnel. We're shoring." Georg headed for the tunnel.

"And Emerich?"

He stopped and puzzled over it. "I don't know."

"Tell Bruno I'd like to see him."

"All right." He went down the incline.

Sepp sat on a sawhorse and did some hard thinking. It was now imperative that Georg remain here in the warehouse so that Emerich and Sepp could keep an eye on him. What would he do if Sepp told him that his parents were not going to cross over? Could he reason with him? Could Georg be persuaded to stay and help finish the tunnel? Perhaps. But why take the chance? So long as he believes his parents are coming, Sepp decided, he will stay. It was the one sure way of keeping him here. Sepp realized that he would have to keep up his deception to the last moment, when it would be too late for Georg to do anything about it. But what about afterward? What then? Afterward will have to wait, he decided.

Bruno came out of the tunnel on his hands and knees. He came up the incline and went to the water can. Sepp joined him. Bits of earth clung to his thick eyebrows, making them look like bushes in bud. He filled the dipper and handed it to Sepp.

"How did your dinner with Herr Komanski go?"

"Splendidly." Bruno filled the dipper for himself. "You know, he's quite a fellow, all hammer and nails on the outside, as soft as down on the inside. I'm rather pleased to have him for a patron."

"A nonpaying patron."

"Oh, well, I suspect I will inveigle some money out of the old codger before I'm done with him." He smiled in a self-satisfied, secret way. It was the same sort of smug smile that Georg had given him. Sepp began to feel that things which he should have known about had been happening while he had been away. Bruno finished his drink and covered the water can carefully, quietly. "How is life in the concentration camp?"

"I won't know much until tomorrow night. Georg's parents are still not ready to risk coming over. Ilse is taking care of Emerich's people. At least I hope she is. That may prove to be sticky."

"I have confidence in her."

"How are things going here?"

"We did over a meter the first hour. Wolf was digging. Joachim is digging now." He took a piece of paper from his pocket and unfolded it. It was covered with dirty finger smudges. "We worked out a schedule. One man digs, three shore, one sleeps, one is on lookout. Every hour we change. The sleeping comes after the digging. Then two hours of shoring, then an hour on lookout, then another hour of shoring, then digging, et cetera. The shorers do the hauling when the sleds are filled. It's working out quite well, I think. We've had only two men shoring while you were gone."

"Where's the lookout?"

"At the window on the third floor. We didn't remove a board for fear of some light making its way up there, but there's a fair-sized crack between the boards through which one has a good view of the entire area." He looked at his watch. "It's almost ten. You'll be on the shoring crew for the next hour."

"Where's Emerich now?"

He consulted his paper again. "Sleeping. He brought a comforter along. We laid it up on the second floor. Everyone is to use it to take his hour's nap."

"I'll go up and talk to him."

"I suspect it's time to haul out the sleds." Bruno folded the paper and put it away in his pocket.

Sepp asked him, "Have you noticed anything strange about Georg?"

"No more than usual. Why?"

"I was just talking to him. He seemed . . . different, not his old reliable, trembling self. He was downright flippant."

"Georg flippant? That *is* strange. None of us has said ten words since we started work. I can't say I've noticed anything odd, but I'll keep an eye on him if you like."

"I'd appreciate it."

Bruno left, and Sepp went upstairs, where he found Emerich awake and just pulling on his trousers. A package wrapped in newspaper lay beside him. The comforter had been laid out near the stairs, where, with the door open, there was some light.

"Yon messenger bringeth tidings. If they be ill, I shall have his head."

Sepp smiled. "Do you think they really did that in those days? I've always doubted it."

"Certainly they did it. If rulers dared, they'd do it today."

"I bring neither good news nor bad. I left it in Ilse's hands."

"When will we know?" Emerich was serious now.

"I'm to see her again tomorrow night."

"Patience is a virtue. Not that virtue ever benefited anyone." He picked up the package and unwrapped it. It was the submachine gun. He held it up to the light for Sepp to see. "Ugly little bastard." It was dull gray, the color of death. Despite his time in the army, Sepp had never become accustomed to weapons. They were alien, they had nothing to do with anything he knew or understood or loved.

"Do you have any ammunition for it?"

"The magazine is full—thirty cartridges. I counted them." He set the weapon down. "Did you bring your revolver?"

Sepp nodded. He did not take it out, loath to resurrect the memory of the time when it was last used. He changed the subject. "Did Georg tell you his news?"

"Georg tells me nothing. I avoid him, and he avoids me."

"The police went to see him."

Emerich looked at Sepp and started lacing his boots. "And?"

"He wasn't home. He said his landlady's daughter told them he had moved out a month ago."

"What do you make of it?"

"The police must have found Georg's name in Klaus's effects. He probably kept a list of the people he had on his hook."

"How many were there, do you suppose?"

"Who knows? Maybe a dozen, maybe a hundred. But if the police were eager to talk to Georg, they would have checked the girl's story with the neighbors. When they found out she was lying, they would have become suspicious and waited around for Georg to come home. Since they didn't, I think we can assume that they have a long list to check out and are more concerned about talking to people they can get to now. They'll go back to Georg only after they've gotten nowhere with the others."

Emerich listened attentively, then smiled. "You're beginning to think like a criminal."

"Considering the source, I take that as a compliment. Which reminds me, do you intend to give me the money you saved by stealing the vacuum cleaner?"

Emerich's chin dropped. He recovered quickly. "The bastard."

"Who?"

"Joachim. Who else?"

"What's Joachim got to do with it?"

"He told you, didn't he?"

"He didn't tell me anything. I knew when you brought back a new one instead of a used one that you'd stolen it."

"Now you're thinking like a White Mouse."

"I play both sides of the board."

"Dishonorable."

"Necessary."

"I was going to give you the money after we're finished here. You can ask Joachim." He finished lacing his boots and got up.

"I believe you," Sepp said.

"Now you're thinking like a naive American again!" He took a wad of bills from his pocket and gave them to Sepp. "I had to pay for the hose."

"I won't tell anyone."

"What do we do about Georg?"

"There's nothing we can do, not just now, anyway. As long as he's in the tunnel, we're safe."

"You know he'll crack if the White Mice ever get to him."

"I don't think so. He'd only be implicating himself. He has an alibi—he was home that night. So was the land-lady's daughter. She was there when I went to see him afterward."

"Does he understand that?"

"I just told him as much. I can't guarantee what he'll do, though."

"You realize that the police must know what Klaus Schoenemann's real business was. They're probably not too eager to catch us."

Sepp hadn't thought of it in that way. "Do you think they're just going through the motions?"

"I wouldn't be surprised." Emerich grinned and rubbed the sleep from his eyes. "Besides, a West Berlin jury would never convict us." He put his arm around Sepp's shoulder in a rare display of affection. "Come on, *Ami*, let's forget our sins—or virtues, whichever they are—and finish this damned tunnel."

Every hour on the hour, they changed crews. Every hour through the night and early-morning darkness, they lengthened the tunnel by a meter—give or take a few centimeters. In the tunnel, no one spoke unless it was absolutely necessary, and then only in whispers. They went about their work like the veterans they had be-come, knowing what to do and when to do it. If any problem were to arise, Sepp thought, it would probably be boredom from the monotony of the routine.

Except for the comparative quiet, working in the tunnel at night was not very different from digging in the daytime. The heat lingered despite the air being blown in by the vacuum. The light was the same as during the day. The funky odors, the aching muscles, the sweat and grime, the taste of clay, the fatigue—all were the same. When it was his turn to sleep, Sepp was ready.

Upstairs, he awakened Joachim. He sat up slowly, rubbing his eyes and yawning.

"You don't want to sleep your life away, do you?"

Joachim gave him an annoyed look and started getting dressed. Sepp sat down on the comforter and began to take off his boots. Joachim moved slowly and said nothing.

"How do you feel?"

"Shitty."

Georg came down from the third floor, where he had been the lookout.

"How is it up there?"

"Spooky." He walked around them and went on down the stairs.

"He must have felt right at home," Joachim growled.

"Is this special, or do you always wake up so cheerful?"

"It's not special."

Sepp decided to leave him alone. He was lying down as Joachim was going out the door. He turned suddenly and said, "I had an interesting dream. I was under that pile of earth again, and I could hear you ask, 'Who's under there?' and Wolf answered, 'God.'"

Sepp waited for him to go on.

"What do you think you said to that?"

"God is dead."

"You're right, and I *died!*" He snickered. "Some dream, eh?"

"I don't believe a word of it."

Joachim smiled. "You're becoming wiser every day, *Ami.*" He left, remembering to tiptoe down the stairs.

Sepp closed his eyes and wondered whether Joachim had had any point in mind. He doubted it. More likely, it was a piece of absurdity his sleepy mind had conjured up for the fun of it. He mulled it over as he drifted off into a dreamless sleep.

⌐╥╥╥╥╥╥╥╥╥╥╥╥╥╥╥╥╥╥╥╥╥╥╥╥╥╥╥╥

30

I
T was ten minutes before seven the next morning when Emerich awoke from his second hour of sleep for the night. His first thought was of the hose on the generator exhaust in the alley and the cars which should be moved off the street. He quickly pulled on his trousers, slipped into his boots, and, without lacing them, hurried down the stairs. Joachim, Wolf, and Georg were in the cellar eating, Joachim sitting against a pillar, Wolf and Georg against the wall by the water can, with their briefcases tucked between their legs. Their hands and faces were washed clean.

"Breakfast time," Joachim said aloud. Emerich was immediately conscious of the freedom to talk aloud in the cellar once again.

"Where are Sepp and Bruno?"

"Sepp is taking up the hose. Bruno's gone for coffee."

The door opened, and Sepp came in carrying the hose wound into a coil. He dropped it over the rail to the cellar floor.

"Good morning, *mein Führer*."

"Good morning, peasant."

"Fifty meters exactly," Sepp told him. "Somebody goofed off."

Georg looked up. "What do you mean?" They all looked at him. His watery eyes flitted from one to another, expecting them to accuse him. Everyone laughed. Georg did not understand.

"I think we can forgive two-tenths of a meter," Sepp explained.

"How's the weather?" Emerich asked.

"Hot, hot, hot."

"No clouds?"

Sepp smiled. "Not a mare's tail." And to Joachim: "Throw me your keys, lover. I'll bring your car into the alley." Joachim threw him the keys. He caught them and left.

Emerich took a dipper of water. He rinsed his mouth and splashed some on his face. He should have known Sepp would have everything under control. He went upstairs to get his briefcase and, returning to the cellar, took a seat in the foothills of the mountains of earth.

Bruno and Sepp came back together, Bruno carrying a paper bag with the coffee.

"Fifty on the nose," Sepp was telling him. They came down the stairs.

"Spectacular." He handed him a paper container over his shoulder. "Have some coffee."

"We should be at fifty-point-two," Emerich said.

"I took a short snooze at one point. Old men do that, you know." He distributed the coffee, handing it out like an old-time peddler offering free samples of snakebite cure. "Italian coffee, gentlemen, guaranteed to keep you awake for twenty-four hours and clean out the large intestine as well."

Wolf took a sip. "Ugh!"

Bruno wheeled on him. "I heard that, young man!"

"I like mine with cream and sugar."

"With cream and sugar, only the small intestine is guaranteed to come clean."

"I have very clean intestines."

Bruno produced a container of cream and one of sugar. "For the fainthearted."

"Are you sure this is coffee?" Emerich asked.

"Although I am an old man, I try to keep up with the times, and since nowadays it is fashionable to be uncertain of everything, I assure you that I am not sure it is, indeed, coffee. But of course I can't be certain that I'm not sure."

"Would you mind going through that again?"

"I would."

The coffee was strong and hot, and Emerich had no doubt that it would do what Bruno advertised. He drank the coffee and ate some bread and wurst. He began to figure out loud. "If we keep up this pace, we should be through by this time tomorrow. But chances are, we'll slow down. It takes fifteen minutes to haul out the sleds now. Getting the shoring lumber into the tunnel is also taking longer."

"And we're getting tired," Joachim said. "We'll have to have more sleep."

"I'm for working straight through," Wolf said, "and sleeping when we're finished."

"It isn't wise to become too tired," Bruno said. "We could become careless, someone could get hurt, we could make noise inadvertently." He looked around. "I don't know how the rest of you feel, but I am already bone-weary. I'm operating on nervous energy."

"What is the other side doing?" Joachim asked.

"I was lookout the last hour," Wolf said. "The demolition crew hadn't started work yet."

"They probably start at seven," Sepp said. He turned to Bruno. "When do you sleep next?"

"As soon as I'm finished with my breakfast—until nine o'clock."

"Maybe you'll feel better then."

"I'm counting on it."

"Everyone else has had two hours, right?"

"I've had only one," Georg said.

"When are you scheduled to sleep again?"

"From nine to ten."

"Take it. You'll need it."

He nodded.

"We'll go back on our regular schedule starting at ten. We have to get enough flooring and joists ripped up and sawed for the night. That takes first priority."

"Isn't it time we gave some thought to a plan for the escape?" Bruno asked.

Sepp took a sip of the hot coffee and set it aside. "Last night, I told Ilse to tell your people that the escape will take place tomorrow night."

For a moment no one said anything. Even though they had talked about the possibility of carrying out the escape so soon, clearly they had not dared believe it could happen.

Emerich was skeptical. "That's pressing it, isn't it?"

"You yourself said we should be finished by tomorrow morning," Sepp said.

"That's if we keep up our present rate."

"Will Emerich's people be able to get to Berlin in time?" Bruno asked.

"I hope I'll know that tonight," Sepp said. "If they can't, we'll have time to tell the Lentzes and Georg's parents of the postponement."

"What is your plan?"

"It's relatively simple, but its simplicity is its greatest virtue. The Lentzes, the Knauers—if they decided to to come over—"

"They'll come over," Georg interrupted sharply.

"Why wouldn't they?" Wolf asked.

"Not everybody hates communism," Emerich observed maliciously.

Georg flushed. "My parents aren't Communists!"

"Maybe we ought to kidnap them—for their own good," Joachim suggested.

"They'll come over," Georg insisted. "They're not Communists, they aren't."

"We know they aren't," Bruno assured him. "Go on, Sepp."

Georg was about to protest some more, but Sepp cut him off.

"The Lentzes, the Knauers, and Ilse will go to the Edelweiss, the *Gasthaus* just across the street from the escape house, all at different times and separately. I'll be waiting at Emerich's aunt's house for his people. When they arrive, we'll leave his aunt's house in time to arrive at the escape house at just after eleven.

"On this end, there are things to be done. As soon as we break through, we must get some penetrating oil on the hinge pins of the door so that when it comes time to lift them we won't have any trouble.

"There is the Vopo to contend with. He walks a regular schedule up and down the street. All someone has to do is observe him from the window of the house and clock him. At the latest possible time before eleven o'clock, you'll lift the hinge pins, wait for the Vopo to

pass, overpower him, and take him into the house and
through the tunnel. We have two guns—Emerich's submachine gun and my revolver. With the Vopo's gun, we'll
have three if there's any trouble.

"As soon as I arrive with the Webers, they'll go through
the tunnel. I'll immediately go to the Edelweiss. When I
enter, Ilse, the Lentzes, and the Knauers will simply get
up and leave, cross over to the escape house, and
go through the tunnel. It should all take about five minutes."

"What about the captured Vopo?"

"Once everyone is safely through the tunnel, he can do
as he pleases."

"Poor chap," Emerich said, grinning.

Sepp looked around. "How does it strike you?"

"As you say, simple," Joachim said. "Too simple."

"What if there's more than one Vopo on guard?" Wolf
asked. "Maybe they've added some since they started
tearing down the buildings."

"I plan to go there tonight and have a look. If they've
added guards, we'll have to figure out what to do about
it."

"What happens if you and the Webers are delayed?"
Bruno asked. "We'll have a Vopo who is certain to be
missed. They'll come looking for him. We could have the
area swarming with guards just when we don't want any
around."

Emerich agreed. "We shouldn't take the Vopo until we
know you'll be there on time."

"I hadn't thought of that," Sepp admitted. "Any suggestions?"

"How do you plan to bring the Webers from Emerich's
aunt's to Vierickstrasse?"

"By subway."

"If there were a way to let Ilse know, at the Edelweiss,
that you were only a block or so away, she could signal
us in some way."

"He could telephone her," Wolf said.

"Why not?" Emerich said. "There's bound to be a telephone booth somewhere along the way. You can look
tonight when you go over."

Sepp thought about it. "All right. But how is she to
signal you?"

"Is she supposed to be waiting for you at the Edel-weiss?" Bruno asked.

"Yes."

"Well, then, she could go to the door and look out for you, as if impatient for your arrival. Somewhat unortho-dox behavior for a lady of Ilse's breeding, but in keeping with her role, nonetheless."

They agreed on this addition to Sepp's plan. Wolf wanted to know what his job would be during the escape.

"I haven't thought about who will do what yet. Let's wait until tomorrow before we decide that."

They went through it again, but no one could think of any changes. Unlike Joachim, Emerich liked a simple plan. Complexity invited something to go wrong, like a car with too many gadgets.

As they broke up and went back to work, Emerich wondered what the others were thinking. He was pessi-mistic. He didn't want to admit it, not even to himself, and he certainly would never show it. But in his heart he had a feeling they were going to lose. In his mind's eye he could see the steel ball hanging at the end of the cable, like a boxer in his corner waiting for the bell to ring; behind him, his trainer, the shovel, baring its teeth as if to frighten its opponent into submission before the fight began. And there were the trucks, lined up like ambu-lances to cart the pieces of the defeated off to the morgue.

There was no point in trying, but they were going to try. They were like an army set in motion, whose forward momentum, heavy fire and enormous casualties, could not be reversed. Only a totally impregnable position could stop them now. As long as there was any gap ahead, they would keep moving; and the gap was still there. Blindly, with instinctive resolution, they would go on, even knowing that their chances of succeeding were vir-tually nil.

31

"So you have returned, true to your word." She had prepared herself for the visit. She looked more alive, more vibrant than she had the night before. She had put on lipstick and rubbed some rouge into her cheeks. Her hair had been done, and she was wearing a fresh dress. She seemed less composed, though, as if she had been nervously awaiting his arrival.

"Did you think I wasn't coming?"

"One never knows anymore. Come in and sit down. Would you like something to drink?" She lighted a cigarette. "You don't smoke, do you."

"No." He closed the door behind him. "What do you have?"

"Beer and cognac."

"Cognac for me. I hope you didn't buy it especially for tonight."

"Why shouldn't I have?"

"Unless you can finish the bottle by tomorrow night, it will go to waste."

She did not say anything. She got out the cognac and glasses and poured. She handed him one—the glasses were as delicate as her hands.

"To rainbows," she said, her eyes too dark for the humor she intended.

"I won't drink to rainbows."

She explored his face with care. "You're quite serious, aren't you."

435

"Serious and pressed for time. Have you come to a decision?"

Her mouth slowly developed a smile. "Really, Herr Bauer, you're impossible. You walk into my life out of the blue and tell me you can get me to West Berlin. Now you tell me I'm to leave tomorrow night and you want my decision now."

"What's wrong with that?"

"I don't even know you, let alone trust you."

"Suppose I were from the SSD. What would my purpose be in trying to trap you? To find out if you're loyal? They already know you're not. To put you back in prison out of spite? They could have kept you there forever if they had wanted to. Besides, their prisons are crowded. They're short of manpower. They're not eager to put every citizen of questionable loyalty behind bars. Anyway, with The Wall, they've got them there already. And how would I know Georg unless I were from the West?"

"Why are you so eager to save me?"

"To say I'm eager is overstating it. This is a one-shot opportunity to get some people across. We have room for a few we hadn't planned on. It's my opinion you deserve the chance to go."

"I assume there's some risk involved."

"Some."

"And you won't tell me any more than I need to know, I'm sure."

"Would you, in my place?"

She laughed sardonically. "You see? You expect me to trust you completely, but you are willing to trust me only partway."

"I have nothing to lose; you have everything to lose."

"Including what little freedom I have, or even my life."

"We're all taking that chance."

She sat on the straight-backed chair at the table, her feet up on a rung. She smoked, contemplating her decision. It was getting late—he was to meet Ilse in half an hour, and before that, he had to look over the situation on Vierickstrasse.

"I'm planning to write a book on Stephan Lochner. Have you ever heard of him?"

He searched his memory. "Fifteenth Century. School of Cologne."

She smiled. "I'm impressed."

"You shouldn't be. That's all I know about him. I am a fount of superficial information."

"Could I take my notes? They represent a month's hard work."

"Will they fit in a briefcase?"

"I should think so."

"All right." He was making a concession, but he could see no harm in allowing her to take a briefcase along.

"That's all I have to lose, really. I was sitting here thinking about it. There is nothing else I care about, not even myself." She viewed him through a veil of smoke. "I'm not fit for a man anymore."

She was obviously expecting him to disagree. It surprised him. He had thought better of her. "I'd have to refute that," he said.

"Your gallant. Thank you. But you don't know me, not the *real* me."

Twice in succession she had disappointed him. "Oh, I suspect what little I know of you is real enough." He got up. "I'd like to go on talking with you, but I am pressed for time. There's still a lot to be done."

"You haven't touched your cognac."

"So I haven't." He took up the glass. "This is beautiful crystal."

"I managed to salvage a few things of my father's. The vultures took the rest."

He drank down half the cognac. It burned going down. It was cheap cognac, with the raw edge still on it. He set the glass back on the table. "What will it be?"

Her eyes were on his, luminous with the hope he had brought her, hope she dared believe in only because there was nothing else.

"Will I . . . will you be there in West Berlin?"

He had been expecting it, but the expectation did not lessen the disappointment. Perhaps it was his fault. He was in a hurry and tired. She was nervous, and he had put her on the spot. Still, he could not help thinking she was not quite the woman he had thought her the night before.

"I'll be leaving for the States soon."

She smiled to hide her feelings. "Lucky you."

"Lucky me."

"I suppose you think I'm dreadfully forward." She

made a gesture of helplessness. "I always make quick decisions about men."

"Did you with Georg?"

She laughed. "Ouch."

"I didn't mean to be cruel."

"I know."

"What about it? Will you go?"

She took a deep breath. "I'll go."

"Good."

"You must think me terribly ungrateful, too."

"Afraid, but not ungrateful."

"I am afraid. Why deny it? I can't convince myself that you're real."

He smiled and scratched his head. "I'm real, all right. At least the last time I checked, I was."

"You're making fun of me."

"I am."

"I deserve it."

Erase one black mark. "You do."

She laughed. "How could I possibly not trust you?"

"I'm a trustworthy fellow. Ask anyone."

"That is my intention, the first chance I get." She put out her cigarette and got up. Now that she had made her decision, she seemed more relaxed. "What do I do? Where do I go?"

"Do you know Vierickstrasse?"

"It's on the border, isn't it? A dozen or so streets west of here?"

"That's it. There's a *Gasthaus* there, the Edelweiss. It's number twenty. Go there tomorrow night around ten thirty. Order what you like and wait. I'll be along a little after eleven. As soon as I walk in, get up and go out. Pay for your drink when you get it so there won't be any problem about that."

She looked at him, expecting him to go on. "Is that all?"

"One other thing. Wear a loose-fitting skirt and flat-heeled shoes. And take nothing except the briefcase. No other luggage. Is that clear?"

"Quite."

"Twenty Vierickstrasse. The Edelweiss. Ten thirty."

"I'll be there."

"Under no circumstances should you leave until I get there."

"I understand." She finished her cognac.

He drew an arc around the room with his hand. "What are you going to do with all this?"

"The vultures will get it."

"I'm sorry you have to leave everything."

"I'm not leaving anything I care about." She folded her arms across her breast as if she were cold. "Will there be others there, at the Edelweiss?"

"Yes. Don't try to figure out who they are. Try to act as natural as possible."

"And I'll be seeing Georg."

"Most likely."

She smiled meekly. "I shall practice my lines. Will he know I'm coming?"

"I'd prefer not to tell him, not because I take any delight in the prospect of his unhappy surprise, but for another reason."

"I'll try to be understanding."

"That will help—more than you realize."

She put out her hand. "Until tomorrow night, then."

He took it. "Until tomorrow night."

She became very solemn. "Don't fail me, Sepp. I don't think I could bear going to prison again."

"I won't fail you," he promised.

The steel arm of the demolition crane rose high over the rooftops in the twilight, as if poised to come crashing down on them the moment its master gave the signal. It had already done its destructive work on the corner building and had decapitated the one next to it—its second story was gone. Only two houses remained untouched between the corner and the escape house. A crane with a claw scoop was stationed in the side street at the head of a line of four trucks. The light in the cab of the crane burned like a vigil candle in a window anticipating the return of someone dear. Plaster dust lay over the two cranes, the trucks, and in the street like the first finely powered snow of the season.

There was no steel in these old buildings, only brick and mortar, and the work was going fast. The exposed cellar of the corner house was filled to the ground level with rubble covered with plaster dust and scraps of lath. If any attempt was being made to salvage the materials, it was not evident. It seemed that all the Communists cared about was eliminating the buildings as fast as possible

He walked north along the east side of the street. It was two minutes before eight o'clock, and the two Vopos patrolling the opposite side of the street were converging on the telephone, the midpoint of the six-block length of Vierickstrasse. The guard on the south leg was just passing the escape house. There were no extra men on duty.

Sepp paused in front of the Edelweiss, pretending to study the menu posted in a glass-covered case by the door. The telephone number of the *Gasthaus* was printed at the top of the menu, under the name and address. He committed it to memory. At eight o'clock, right on the schedule, the Vopos met at the corner and telephoned in. It took them each only ten seconds. They chatted for another ten seconds, then started back, one heading north, one south. The Vopo going south passed the escape house two minutes and fifteen seconds after eight.

Satisfied that nothing in their routine had changed, Sepp went around the corner and headed east toward the streetcar stop two blocks away. At the first cross street he found what he was looking for—a telephone booth. He entered it, deposited twenty pfennigs, and dialed the number he had memorized.

"Edelweiss."

He hung up and left the booth in a hurry. He was five minutes late meeting Ilse.

Ilse was nowhere in sight. Sepp sat down on the same bench where they had met the night before. Although he was anxious about Ilse, he welcomed the chance to sit quietly. His fatigue had long since passed beyond mere physical discomfort. At times like this, when he found himself unoccupied, he fell into daydream. His mind wandered over an itinerary of disconnected remembrances and elusive aspirations. They would become lost in time, a sweet memory becoming an unfullfilled expectation, and a hoped-for moment being transposed into a recollection of what had been. He was aware that his mind was jumbling things, but he did not have the energy to sort them out.

After he had been there a few minutes, an old man arrived and sat next to him. He read his newspaper for a while, then folded it and tucked it under his arm. He was short and heavy, with a protruding beer belly. He was wearing bright red suspenders over his shirt. Sepp wondered whether this was a patriotic gesture.

He looked at his watch for the tenth time in as many minutes. It was eight nineteen.

"You are waiting for your woman," the old man said, grinning through false teeth. "I can tell."

Sepp nodded.

"Women are born to be late. They cannot tell time; they don't understand the value of time. My wife was always late. Thirty-seven years we were married. Not once was she ever on time. Women are like that."

"So it seems."

"Not *seems*. *Is*. I had thirty-seven years' experience. I know about such things."

"This is the first time she's been late."

"The first time?"

"The first time."

The old man made a face and muttered, "Remarkable." He inspected Sepp's face to see if he were telling the truth. "The first time?"

"The first time."

Clearly he was upset to have his theory so convincingly refuted. He unfolded his paper and scanned the headlines. *Neues Deutschland* was still impressively disturbed by the latest bombing of The Wall at Jerusalemerstrasse. It was but another excuse to threaten a separate peace treaty with the Russians. How boring it must be to read the same drivel day after day. Sepp thought of Konrad Möss. He had said he hated the boredom more than anything else. Sepp had assumed he had meant the boredom of life as a border guard, but there was also the greater boredom of communism itself. It seemed so well designed to bore.

"You're not married," the old man suddenly realized.

"No."

"*Ach!* That explains it! Of course she is on time! My

wife was always on time before we were married. Before they are married, they can tell time. Afterward—*pfft!*"

Sepp spied Ilse coming up the street. He got up. "Excuse me. *'Weidersehen.'*"

"Give her what for," the old man called after him. "If you let her off, she will always be late."

Sepp left the park and crossed the street to the sidewalk. Ilse saw him and waved. She ran a little but gave it up. She was out of breath. She looked beautiful coming up the street in her summer dress with her hair blowing slightly in the breeze. He felt proud knowing she was his woman. When they met, he took her hand and kept walking.

"The park is full."

"I'm terribly sorry to be late. It couldn't be helped."

"What happened?"

"Darling, they're coming! They're coming!" She was excited and was having a hard time speaking quietly. "Frau Halzapfel—Magda—was marvelous. You should have heard her. She's a very clever woman. Oh"—she remembered—"she's going over with us. That's all right, isn't it? They're all coming—isn't that splendid?"

"How did she do it? What did Dr. Lentz say?"

"Immediately after I told him, he was on the telephone to the authorities. He was magnificent. He badgered, threatened, and cajoled some poor bureaucrat. The fellow went to his office last night and got things moving."

They were out of the *Platz,* heading toward Schönhauser Allee, the main shopping street in the district. As always on hot nights, there were throngs of people in the streets; however, with little automobile traffic, it had none of the noise and bustle of West Berlin. There was, rather, a peculiarly rustic tranquillity about the street, an indolence that Sepp felt he could easily fall into.

He quickened his pace.

"Why were you late?"

"We had to telephone Emerich's father again, to find out whether everything was all right and when they would arrive in Berlin."

"When will they arrive?"

"Oh, I thought I'd told you. On the nine-thirty train. At the Ostbahnhof."

"That's cutting it close. I'd better plan to meet them."

"Frau Halzapfel told him they would be met."

"She'll have to come with me to identify them. Can you go to see her tomorrow?"

"Yes."

"Tell her I'll pick her up at her place at eight thirty. That should give us time."

"Will you take them directly from the station to the tunnel?"

"Yes. There's no point in going back to Frau Halzapfel's place."

"I'll tell her to be ready."

"Does Emerich's father understand what we're up to?"

"I'm sure he does. At least I'm sure Frau Halzapfel is sure he does."

He told her about the addition of the telephone call in their plans. "I'll have to know what color dress you'll be wearing, so that Emerich and Joachim will know for certain it's you."

She mulled it over. "Blue, I suppose. Yes, I'll wear the blue cotton. Do you remember it? I wore it the last day at Wannsee."

"I remember it well," he lied.

She smiled and squeezed his hand.

"When I telephone, I won't ask for you. It would look strange if you were called on the phone and then went to look out the door."

"Who will you ask for?"

"Any name will do—except Meyer. There may just be a Meyer there."

"Use my mother's name—Rosenkranz."

He smiled. "Do you think that will bring us luck?"

"A little divine intervention never hurts, does it?"

"Rosenkranz it is. I should be calling at about five minutes to eleven. After whoever answers the telephone pages Herr Rosenkranz, wait about a minute and then go to the door and look out. Stay there at least five seconds so they'll be sure to see you from the house."

"Are you certain there's a phone nearby?"

"I checked on it just a while ago. It's in working order." He laughed. "All those nights we went up and down that street on our way to the Edelweiss, and I was not certain until tonight that there was a phone there."

"Oh, darling, I'm so happy—happy for us, happy that the Webers are really coming."

"The whole family?"

"The whole family. Isn't it splendid?"

"Emerich will be pleased."

She stopped him and surveyed his face. Hers was alive with excitement. She looked more beautiful than ever. "What's the matter, darling? You don't seem very happy."

"I am. Really I am. I'm just too tired to show it."

She put her arm through his, and they walked on. "How stupid of me. You must be exhausted. And you've got to go back for more. Let's go someplace where we can sit down."

"I wouldn't dare. At times I thought I was going to fall asleep when I was sitting in the park waiting for you."

"How awful for you." She studied his face. "You do look ghastly tired, darling."

"Once this is finished, I plan to stay in bed for a week."

She clutched his arm and smiled brightly. "Make it two. It will take me that long to be sure I'm not dreaming."

"Do you think about it, much—I mean, being on the other side?"

"All the time. And I always end up in bed with you. Sometimes I wonder if I have a wholesome attitude about it. I'll start out dreaming about a day at Wannsee—remember?—when the sun made the sand so hot you couldn't walk on it, and we'd run on tiptoe, yipping like dogs, into the water."

"I never yipped like a dog."

"You did. You were outrageously demonstrative. How I laughed!" She laughed now as she used to laugh then, and he remembered that he really had been "outrageously demonstrative," but at the time it had seemed right.

"We never get to the water," she said. "We always end up leaping into bed." She brushed her hair back over her shoulders. "I can't even dream about going out for fresh rolls for your breakfast without being snatched back into bed before I'm halfway to the bakery. It's all terribly erotic."

"We must be telepathic. I have the same problem."

"Do you really?"

"I was afraid to admit it for fear you'd think I wanted you only for that."

"For two weeks that will be the only reason I'll want you. After that, it won't be so important, and my psyche will adjust itself, I'm sure."

"In two weeks we'll be starving, anyway."

She laughed. "I wish we were bears so we could store up food and not even have to bother eating."

"We are bears. We're a couple of Berlin bears."

She looked up at him. "It's true. I only think of you as being in Berlin. I don't know you anywhere else."

He did not miss the wistfulness in her voice.

"You'll like New York. It's an exciting city—like Berlin."

"I know." She looked up at him. "Don't worry about it. I'll adjust."

He laughed. "You'll be spending so much time adjusting, you'll forget I'm there."

"That will never happen. Don't ever say that."

"All right."

They went on a way without talking. Then he said, "Your mother will have to adjust, too."

"She'll get over it in a day. She's terribly well adjusted already."

"You're sure she won't go?"

"I'm sure, darling. There's no point in trying to persuade her. She's accepted it. She's very happy for me."

"*I'm* very happy for *me*."

"We're all very happy people." She was her old self again, and he felt a deep contentment. They were going to make it. She was going to be with him again as before, this time for the rest of his life. They had to make it.

32

A rat was perched on the covered water can, its tiny feet drawn together under its whiskery snout, gazing lazily into the light. Joachim approached it warily, expecting it to jump down and run off at any moment. It scented him, turned its dry eyes in his direction, and, with a furtive movement, shifted its bulky hindquarters around, aligning its defenses. Joachim stopped. The animal rose on its haunches, nose twitching, black eyes alert to danger.

"Go away," Joachim whispered.

The rat did not stir.

"I'd like a drink of water, Herr Rat. Be so good as to move your furry fanny."

With a squeak, it lowered itself to all fours, but budged no further.

"Come on, Herr Rat, you're holding up progress."

It made scratching noises with its claws on the metal lid. Keeping the rat in his field of vision, Joachim glanced around, looking for a weapon. He spied the spade standing up in the pile of earth and slowly backed away toward it. The rat's eyes followed him. At the edge of the pile, he pulled the spade loose from the earth. Feeling more secure, he scooped up a handful of damp clay, molded it into a ball, and flung it at the rat. The animal squeaked plaintively, leaped off the can, and scampered along the wall, disappearing behind the pile of scrap lumber. Joachim smiled to himself. He drove the spade back into place and went for his drink of water. He was rinsing the dirt from his face when Bruno came down the stairs, stretching and yawning. Joachim remembered the first day he had seen him there at the foot of the stairs, awesome, dignified even in work clothes, destined to be chronicled among the great of the art world. How long ago was that? A week? No, nine days. Lord, it seemed months ago. Odd how unimpressive the master artist seemed now. A tired old man—a dirty, unshaven, tired old man.

"You're up early," he whispered.

"What time is it?"

"Quarter to five. You still have fifteen minutes of sleep due you."

Bruno rubbed his face and came over to the water can. "I'm too exhausted to sleep, if that makes any sense. And the stench of Emerich's comforter has become absolutely unbearable. Next turn, I think I'll try that pile of earth." He cupped his hands. Joachim filled them. He splashed water on his face and wiped it off with his forearm. "I'll have a drink, too."

Joachim filled the dipper for him.

"Is this dipper sanitary?"

"It must be. Everybody uses it."

"Ah." He drank it down.

Emerich stuck his head out of the tunnel. "Joachim, we're ready to start hauling."

"Coming, peasant."

"What is the measurement?" Bruno asked. They had begun marking their progress on the tunnel wall and measuring after each hour.

"Seventy at four o'clock," Emerich said.

He reasoned, "Make it seventy-one now."

"Maybe. Georg is digging," Emerich said acidly.

"Was seventy meters on schedule?"

He grinned. "Only a meter behind."

"I'm glad to see you have the energy to smile."

"That wasn't a smile; that was an involuntary tic." He grinned again and disappeared back into the tunnel.

"He is a veritable lion since he heard the good news," Bruno said.

"He was always a lion."

Bruno looked surprised. "You two have come to an understanding?"

"We have respect for one another—at a safe distance."

Bruno smiled. "I have always contended that Christ made a strategic error when he admonished us to love one another. It is far more important that we respect one another."

"It's a more intellectual notion."

"You think that's why He chose love instead?"

"It figures."

"I think you may be right." He handed Joachim the dipper for a refill. "Seventy-one," he mused. "Four more that way"—he pointed East—"and one and a half up. That means, with an hour's break for breakfast, and one for lunch, we ought to be finished in eight or nine hours."

"Correction. Sepp brought it to our attention that it has to be seventy-six meters long before we can start the vertical shaft. That's to be a meter wide, too, so a meter of the tunnel has to be under it; otherwise, the shaft would be half in the cellar and half out."

"That would never do."

"Never."

"Perhaps we should make it seventy-seven to be on the safe side."

"We're going to bore a small hole first. If we see daylight, we'll go farther."

"So. Six and a half meters to go—nine or ten hours. Or am I being optimistic?" he laughed.

He mimicked Bruno, "I'm glad to see you have the energy to laugh."

"It's easier than crying, which I assure you I would do if I had the energy." He sighed. "It will be a relief just to talk normally again. This whispering is a damnable effort."

Sepp came out of the tunnel and picked up the rope. "Let's go," he said.

Joachim replaced the lid on the water can and hung the dipper on the handle. It clinked slightly. "It sounds like a Chinese gong in all this silence."

They hauled out the six sleds Georg had filled, and changed crews. Joachim started up the stairs to take over the lookout post from Wolf. Georg came up behind him on his way to sleep. His eyes were red and puffy, and he was working hard just to mount the stairs. It made Joachim feel better just to see him.

"So your parents are coming over," Joachim said affably.

Georg dropped his head without replying.

"You don't seem very excited."

They stopped on the first-floor landing. Georg glanced at him vacantly, then went ahead up the next flight of stairs. "I knew they would come."

"Not till last night, you didn't."

"I knew they would come," he repeated. "They had to come, you know."

The odor of Emerich's comforter filled the hot, humid air. Soaked with the sweat of six men, it smelled as bad as Bruno had said, but Joachim knew that when it came his turn to sleep again, he would suffer the stink without complaint. Georg did not seem to mind it. He dropped down onto the rumpled comforter and began unlacing his shoes. Joachim left him and went up to the third floor. Wolf was waiting for him.

"Is anything happening?"

"All quiet on the Eastern Front." Wolf moved away from the window so that Joachim could put his eye to the crack between the boards.

"This lookout job is the worst," Wolf said. "I can barely keep my eyes open."

"It's a chance to rest."

"I don't feel rested. I feel numb."

"So do I."

"How is it going down there?"

"A meter an hour, a meter an hour—or almost. The pace is slackening."

Wolf did not answer. He lingered, as if loath to abandon a dream from which he had been wakened. In the darkness Joachim could not see the features of his face, only its outline reflecting in a diaphanous aurora the thin sheet of moonlight that sliced through the crack between the boards. His breathing sounded fast and shallow, much as if he had been working instead of resting.

"Are you all right?"

Wolf sounded surprised at the question. "I'm not sick, if that's what you mean. Just tired."

"What do you do now?"

"Shoring."

"Watch out for rats in the lumber pile."

"Did you see any?"

"One. A cocky monster as big as a cat."

Wolf fell silent again. Joachim put an eye to the crack and peered out. The street below lay in the moonlight like a corpse set out for embalming. The silence was eerie. Like the heat of the day, it penetrated everything it touched, driving deep with its paralytic contagion.

Beyond the gray barrier of The Wall, nothing stirred. Barbs on the coils of concertina wire glittered like distant stars; the cumbersome tank obstacles arose from the dark earth like exotic shrubs from the surface of a strange and forbidding planet. Far off, beyond the string of doomed buildings along Vierickstrasse, beyond the rooftops of a score of succeeding streets of houses, the glow of East Berlin hovered over the land—the toxic atmosphere which had spawned these ugly plants.

"What are you going to do, Joachim?"

Joachim was perfectly aware of what his brother's question meant, but he did not want to answer it, so he did the next best thing. He delayed answering by feigning misunderstanding. "Do? When?"

"Afterward, when Mama and Papa are living here."

"They aren't here yet." Joachim was afraid he had sounded too hopeful, and quickly equivocated. "Don't worry, though. They'll make it, all right."

"Do you really think so?"

"I really think so."

He moved a few steps away, then stopped. Before he could speak, Joachim said, "I know, Wolf. This is something you have to work out yourself. Nobody can help you."

"I've already decided."

"Good. Indecision is the work of the Devil."

"It's been very confusing," Wolf said. "I never knew from one minute to the next how I felt or what I was going to think . . . or do. It's hard to believe now that I did it."

"Did what?"

Wolf was silent.

"Did what? What did you do?"

"I thought you knew . . . you acted as if you knew."

"Knew what?" As soon as he asked it, he realized what Wolf was telling him—that he was the one who had moved the struts in the cave-in hole out of line. Joachim could not grasp it. It was too incredible. Wolf— his little brother. Then he had another thought. "You didn't do it for *me*, did you?"

"For you?" Wolf sounded surprised. "No. No, I'm sorry, it wasn't for you."

Joachim stared at his brother's face, a face he could not see but whose features were undoubtedly no longer as he had always known them. He smiled an ironic smile. "Strange, isn't it."

"Yes," Wolf said, "strange," and he left.

Joachim listened until his footfalls were lost to hearing. He put his eyes to the crack. Nothing had changed. The great stillness held everything in view. I should have told him I'm leaving, he thought. It was the perfect opportunity. Why didn't I tell him? I'll have to tell him sometime, and damned soon. But I have to live with him until the tunnel is finished. Until tonight. Tonight. Lord, when is that? He yawned. His eyes burned with fatigue. Imagine it. Wolf! I ought to go now. Just walk out. He pictured himself doing it—going down the stairs, picking up his briefcase and street clothes from the nail by the door, inserting the key quietly, pushing open the door. He could almost feel the early-morning air on his face. The sun will be up soon. Sunrise—my time of day. My own. Wolf's now, too. He felt the ache of longing for those precious dawns when remembered ecstasy was often more fulfilling than its reality; and like an old man who feels a nostalgic stirring in his groin, he hated Walther Curzmann as much as old men hate old age.

33

━━━━━━━━━━━━━━━━━━━━━━━━━━━━━━━━━━━━━━

AS perceptible as the heat, the humidity, and the odor in the tunnel was the excitement in the air. Wolf first sensed it during his turn at digging from six to seven. It came like the first unseasonably warm day in early spring, charged with expectation and promise. He paused to consider it. There was no doubt of its presence, and he wondered if the others sensed it, too. Perhaps, he thought, it was only because he was younger, more susceptible to excitement, that he felt it. Perhaps it was his imagination.

As he emerged from the tunnel into the cellar, guiding his last sledful, he straightened up to see them all there waiting, staring anxiously: Georg holding the pulley rope, Bruno slumped in half-sleep against the wall, Emerich on the stairs, sleepy-eyed, his briefcase in one hand, ready to start breakfast, Sepp standing by the water can, the dipper poised halfway to his lips, Joachim with his foot on the spade at the base of the pile of earth. He knew then that they, too, felt it. He peeled away the dead skin of a torn callus.

"One and three-tenths," he said.

They broke into grins and looked at one another appreciatively.

"Seventy-three-point-five," Sepp said, his voice quavering slightly with the attempt to hold in his excitement.

That was all. They went back to what they were doing, each content to savor in his own way the satisfaction the announcement had given them. They were too weary to expend energy on demonstrations of their excitement.

At breakfast time they gulped their food and the hot coffee that Bruno again brought in, muttered restrained monologues about their progress, and fell into the shallow sleep of the exhausted.

As the morning hours wore on inexorably, as each report of progress was passed from mouth to ear in cryptic whispers, the excitement heightened. As it heightened, each one, when he took his turn at digging, was determined to match Wolf's record of one and three-tenths meters in an hour. Joachim fell short by one-tenth of a meter; the tunnel measured seventy-four and seven-tenths meters at nine o'clock. Sepp dug one and one-tenth meters, extending it to seventy-five and eight-tenths meters. He came out into the cellar and dropped down onto the bottom step. Wolf filled the dipper and took it over to him. He nodded his thanks and drank it down, dribbling water down his grimy chin.

"Tomorrow at this time," Wolf said, "we'll have forgotten how tired we are now."

"Tomorrow is everything," Sepp said. "Tomorrow is the resurrection and the life everlasting."

"Everything is tomorrow." Wolf remembered how he had waited for the tunnel, how he had longed for the day when it would begin. It seemed as if that were in another life and Wolf were someone else, much as if he had read about it rather than experienced it.

Georg came down the stairs, taking off his gloves. His face was flushed and dripping with sweat.

"It's hot up there," he complained. He had been on the second floor ripping up flooring. "What's the measurement?"

"Seventy-five-point-eight," Wolf told him.

"Then we're ready to go up."

"Almost," Sepp said. "After Bruno's turn. He'll put it past seventy-six. Then we'll start the vertical shaft." He got up and went back to work. Wolf could tell that he was avoiding Georg.

After Sepp had left, Georg said to Wolf, "He likes you. I can tell."

Wolf shrugged. "I never thought about it."

"I could tell by the look on his face."

Wolf felt uncomfortable, not so much because of what Georg was saying but because of the way he said it. He seemed half-witted, smiling inanely while he spoke, as if there were a secret meaning to his ordinary declaration.

"I'm very good at detecting things like that."

Wolf did not know what to say. He said, "Oh," and left, going for a load of shoring lumber. He laid out two struts, a crossbeam, and three pieces of overhead planking. Georg came across the cellar.

"I'll load you up," he offered.

Wolf nodded and held out his arms while Georg filled them.

"It's easier this way, isn't it?"

"A little." It was much easier, but Wolf felt strangely disinclined to agree. He didn't know what it was about Georg that made him feel that way. It was puzzling. "Thanks," he said, and headed down the incline.

When he reached the entrance, he dropped the load, took his rope out of his pocket, and tied it around one end of the lumber.

Emerich came out of the tunnel. "Bruno has started digging," he said. He looked feverish, his eyes glazed with fatigue, his lips dry and encrusted at the corners with coffee. A myriad pimples sprouted in the dark forest of whiskers on his face. He looked over Wolf's shoulder and saw Georg. His eyes narrowed, closing off the whites until only the black pupils were showing, glittering with contempt.

"Either you or Georg will make the breakthrough," Wolf said, hoping to distract him.

Emerich turned his eyes away from Georg to Wolf. "Probably." He seemed distracted. Suddenly he was gazing intently at Wolf's face, and he broke into a smile. "I didn't know you shaved, youngster."

"I didn't know there was anything you didn't know."

Emerich laughed. "You've found your balls in the past week—in more ways than one."

"Maybe it all happens together."

Emerich dissented vigorously. "Don't believe it, don't ever believe it. Millions of guys get laid and never grow up."

"I hear others grow up and never get laid." He had

never used the word *laid* before, and he felt awkward doing so.

Emerich did not seem to notice. He laughed again and, giving him a friendly pat on the shoulder, walked up the incline toward Georg. Wolf tied the rope to his belt and entered the tunnel, dragging the load of lumber behind him. Although all the excitement was now in the digging, there was still the shoring to be done.

Far ahead, where the tunnel dwindled in perspective, where the last of the lights fused together in a single glare of shimmering incandescence, the figures of Sepp and Joachim hid that of Bruno. Only the glint of the spade flashing behind them gave evidence that he was there, completing the final stretch of the tunnel. When he was finished, it would be Georg digging, then Emerich. If the vertical digging went faster than the horizontal, Emerich would probably make the breakthrough. That's all right, Wolf thought. He deserves it. Wouldn't it be something, though, to feel the spade cut through the earth and keep going out into thin air! That would be too much.

He passed under the high, dark cavity where the cave-in had occurred. He gave the struts a quick inspection to make certain they were still solidly in place. Doing so helped alleviate the sense of guilt he felt about what he had done. From this point on, lay the earth of East Berlin. There was always a slight apprehension, a subtle increase in tension when he passed this point. He wondered if the others felt the same. Beyond and above there were men who would, if called upon, kill him. They had tried once already. He knew they would try again if given the chance.

On occasion he would mull over the notion that it was all quite absurd. The man who had shot him in the Spree probably cared not at all if he chose to live in West Berlin. Those who beat the monotonous paths along The Wall above, weighted down with the transient power of their submachine guns, hardly cared whether his parents, or Georg's, or Emerich's, or Ilse wanted to live in West Berlin rather than in the *Sektor*. Yet, with just such a lack of care, they would kill to prevent the very thing they cared so little about. He knew the complexity of society and its political structure well enough to understand how it had come to this, but he could not grasp the reasons why.

He would like to have discussed it with someone. Maybe the reasons were more apparent than he realized.

They had shored as far as they could go, up to the file of filled sleds, when it came time to haul them out. Wolf crawled back through the tunnel to the cellar, took up the rope, and started pulling. He felt a surge of new strength when he realized that, except for the earth from the vertical shaft, these were the last sled loads they would have to haul out. How many times had he done this, his arms and back rebelling with pain at the effort his mind was forcing them to exert. Slowly, slowly, then faster, faster, as the momentum built up, the sled moved forward and the pressure of the rope slackened as, hand over hand, he drew it down through the sheave.

Six times he did this, as sled after sled emerged from the deepest point of the tunnel—the *end* of the tunnel. When Bruno came out, following the last sled, he was smiling broadly, his white teeth showing in his dirty face like unmelted snow in the dark crevice of a sunny slope. Wolf knew they were ready to start digging upward.

"Seventy-six-point-six," he said. "I regret it isn't more."

Sepp grinned. "It's enough. We've gone as far as we need to."

"What now?" Georg asked.

"Now the periscope," Sepp said cryptically. He went to the tool chest and took out a long, thin pipe. They gathered around him, curious to see what he was up to.

"This is our periscope." It was an ordinary lead pipe, narrow in diameter. Three-quarters of its length was in one piece; the fourth quarter was attached with a coupling. Sepp turned the pipe on end, and a solid steel rod slid out. He turned it up and the rod slid back into the pipe. A piece of tape across the other end prevented the rod from slipping out.

"Joachim and I measured the distance from here to the escape house, using triangulation. We both came up with approximately the same answer. Taking into account the thickness of the walls of the warehouse and the escape house, we figured the distance to be seventy-four-point-nine meters. We've now dug seven-six-point-six. We should be under the house." He held up the pipe. "This will tell us if we are."

Emerich asked the question Wolf had in mind. "What if it tells us we aren't?"

"There should be only a meter and a half of earth between the top of the tunnel and the floor of the cellar of the house. Remember, the cellar is sunk about a meter and a half below ground level. This part of the pipe"—he indicated the longer section—"is a meter long. This short section is about a third of a meter long. If we dig out a half meter, drive this up through the remaining earth as far as the coupling—that is, one meter—it should break out into the cellar. We can tell if it has because when we unscrew the coupling and take off the short section, we should be able to push the rod up into the pipe without effort."

"What if we're short of the house, though?" Georg asked.

"If we're short of the house, the thickness of the earth should be about three meters, so the pipe will not penetrate to the surface and the rod won't go beyond the end of the pipe because there will be earth blocking it."

"All this assumes there is no slope between here and the house."

"There's no observable slope," Sepp said. "If there is a slope, it's insignificant."

Wolf was impatient to get on with it, but he knew they had to shore the rest of the tunnel before they could start digging the vertical shaft. If their calculations were correct, the last meter and a half of the tunnel was under only a meter and a half of earth. Once they started digging the vertical shaft, the chances of a cave-in were considerably increased.

"Why not shore from the end back?" Joachim suggested. "That way, Georg can get started digging the vertical shaft."

"He'll need room to work."

"All he needs is the last meter, below where the shaft will be," Joachim argued. "We can start shoring from there."

Wolf was surprised at Joachim's apparent eagerness to get the tunnel finished. He recalled their exchange earlier that morning in the darkness of the third-floor room, and he wondered if he had come away with a mistaken impression of his brother's feelings. Thinking about it, he suffered qualms of guilt again. Somehow, he would work it out; he had a better hold on his life now, an understanding of what he wanted and what he was willing to do—and not do—to have it.

They accepted Joachim's idea with the modification that they shore a meter before Georg started digging. The last meter would not, of course, be shored, as that was where the vertical shaft would be dug. If Sepp and Joachim were right, the next to the last meter passed under the cellar wall of the house, so the first half was under three meters of earth, plus the wall, and the last half was under the cellar—a meter and a half of earth.

Sepp and Wolf had the meter of shoring installed by noon. Wolf was ravenously hungry and so tired he dared not dwell on it for fear he would surrender to fatigue and collapse into sleep. Following Sepp out of the tunnel, he nevertheless hoped they would not stop for lunch. He was too excited to eat, anyway, and impatient to find out if they were, indeed, under the house. When they reached the cellar they found the others sprawled around the base of the pile of earth. Bruno was already snoring. Wolf couldn't understand how he could sleep at a time like this. With an effort, Emerich pulled himself to a sitting position.

"Finished?"

"Finished."

"Who's for lunch?"

Bruno's snoring sputtered to a stop. He opened his eyes and, momentarily confused about his whereabouts, glanced around with bleary eyes, saw that he was among friends, and immediately fell back asleep. The snoring resumed.

Joachim chuckled. "There's one vote against."

"I'm for working," Emerich said. "Let's get it done. Then we can eat."

"I agree," Wolf said.

Georg yawned loudly. "I'm too tired to eat or work."

"I'll dig in your place," Wolf offered.

"What do you say, Joachim?"

"Let's get it over with. The sooner the better."

"Sorry, Georg," Sepp said. "It's four to one."

Georg groaned.

Joachim laughed. "Ah, the delights of democracy, eh?"

Georg gave him an annoyed glance. He got to his feet and stretched. "I don't see why we can't eat first. I'm starving."

"I'm too excited to eat," Wolf said. As soon as he had said it, he was afraid that it had sounded childish.

"So am I," Emerich said. "I want to take a look at that house. All these days we've been at this, I've built up an image of it in my mind. I want to see if it's close to the real thing."

"I just want to get it over with," Joachim said, "so I can *sleep*."

With this support, Wolf felt vindicated. "Let's get going," he urged.

Reluctantly, Georg put on his stocking cap and pulled on his gloves. "What about Bruno? Isn't he going to work?"

"Let him sleep," Sepp said.

"That's not fair."

Wolf looked at Emerich, expecting an immediate reaction. The peasant made a face but said nothing. It was Sepp who responded, with barely concealed exasperation. "Would you like us to vote on whether it's fair or not?"

Muttering to himself, Georg acquiesced and entered the tunnel. Wolf and Sepp followed, dragging the empty sleds behind them. Emerich and Joachim followed with lumber for the shoring.

At first it was hard going for Georg. As Wolf worked with Sepp on the shoring, he watched his progress. First he tried digging on his back as they had dug the rest of the tunnel. This worked all right up to the point where he had cut away about a fourth of a meter, but then he could no longer reach the earth with his spade. He tried digging on his knees. This was awkward because there was not enough headroom, so he had to keep his head down and cocked to one side of the shaft, then the other, letting the earth fall where it would. Usually a big clump fell between his legs into the sled, but the residue came in its wake in a shower, spewing bits all over him. He had to stop after each thrust of the spade to clear bits of clay and sand from his eyes.

By one o'clock, Sepp and Wolf had installed two meters of shoring and Georg had opened a half meter of the vertical shaft. Only a meter of the tunnel remained to be shored, and only a meter of earth separated them from the cellar of the escape house. Only a meter. If they had figured correctly.

When Wolf came into the cellar to haul out the first of the three sleds Georg had filled, Emerich and Joachim were there waiting. They had finished sawing the lumber for the last of the shoring. Bruno was awake, making water on the back slope of the first pile of earth.

"He dug about half a meter."

Joachim gave him a disgusted look. "Is that all?"

"It was hard to get at, at first," Wolf said. He looked at Emerich. "I guess you'll have the honors."

"How much did you get shored?"

"Two meters. There's only one left."

Bruno came out from behind the mound of earth. His face was haggard and lined with fatigue. With his stubble of grizzled beard and disheveled hair, his dirty overalls hanging on him like discarded clothes strung on a scarecrow, he might have been the legendary hermit stealing out of his cave to forage through his hostile surroundings for a bite to eat.

"Then I haven't slept through the finale?"

Wolf grinned. "It's just about to begin."

They helped him haul out the sleds. Sepp came out behind the first two, guiding them, and took the rope back in for the next. Georg came out with the third. As soon as it was clear of the entrance, he let it go, got to his feet, and headed for his briefcase. "Now I'm going to *eat*," he declared defiantly.

While, to Wolf's amazement, Georg ate, the rest of them crawled the length of the tunnel and crowded in at the end. There were no thoughts now of shoring the remaining meter. They could do that later. They crouched in enforced silence, although Wolf sensed that no one would have spoken, anyway. Emerich sat under the half-meter hole Georg had put in the ceiling, a sledgehammer, a spade, a pipe wrench, and the pipe-and-rod periscope Sepp had devised lying between his legs. Sepp and Wolf sat wedged shoulder-to-shoulder across the width of the tunnel. Behind them, on their knees, peering over their shoulders, were Bruno and Joachim. Joachim rested his chin on Wolf's shoulder.

Emerich took the pipe in one hand, raised it much like

a priest raising the Host to be blessed, and placed one
end up against the face of the earth. With the other he
began driving it home with the padded sledgehammer.
The sound was that of a muted tenor drum in the funeral
march.

When the pipe was lodged in the earth, he began
pounding it with both hands with the sledgehammer.
Slowly, with each stroke, the exposed end of the pipe became shorter and shorter, centimeter by centimeter. It
seemed to be taking forever. Wolf wanted to take
the sledgehammer away from Emerich and do it himself.
He was certain he could drive the pipe in faster. Emerich
continued with a steady, sure beat. It became almost
hypnotic.

Suddenly the pipe shot upward as far as the coupling.
At the same time, Emerich pitched forward, dropping the
sledgehammer on his foot. He stifled a groan. For a moment no one moved; then, as they realized all at once
what had happened, they looked at one another, grinning
with triumph.

Emerich righted himself. He brushed bits of loose earth
from his hands and peeled away the tape across the
open end of the pipe. The steel rod slid out. He let it slide
all the way. The sound it made scraping against the inside
of the pipe sounded like distant traffic. He got to his knees
and tried with the pipe wrench to loosen the short section of pipe from the coupling. Instead, the coupling
turned with it, turning the longer section of pipe as well.

Emerich laid aside the wrench and put his eye to the
pipe. He kept it there an agonizingly long time. Finally,
he looked at them and shrugged. "I can't see anything,"
he whispered.

"Good," Sepp said.

"I need another wrench. The threads must be stripped
from the pounding."

"I'll get it," Joachim offered and left.

"What does it look like up there?" Wolf asked.

Emerich gestured for him to take a look for himself.
"Be my guest."

Wolf got to his knees and put his eye to the pipe.
Nothing but blackness.

"Maybe it just struck softer earth," Sepp said. "The
soil up there would be softer from the rain."

Emerich shrugged. "Could be."

"But," Bruno reminded them, "if we are not under the house, the end of the pipe is still a meter and a half underground. It would not necessarily be softer at that depth."

"We'll know as soon as we get this coupling off," Emerich said

They waited for Joachim to return. Wolf looked up the pipe again, taking longer this time, but he still could not see anything. "Isn't there any light at all in the cellar?" he asked.

"Just from under the door upstairs," Sepp said. "You wouldn't be able to distinguish it through a hole that size."

"Thank God it isn't daylight," Bruno said.

"Misery," Emerich said at the mere thought.

Wolf stared down the long, receding shaft of the tunnel to the square of light at the end. The struts protruding from the sides made him think of the wrinkly muscles of a great prehistoric creature's intestine. Joachim appeared at the end and came crawling forward.

"Here he comes."

They looked down the tunnel, waiting.

Joachim arrived and handed the wrench to Wolf. Wolf cleared away the earth around the coupling and adjusted the wrench tightly. Emerich began turning the lower, shorter section of pipe.

It screeched loudly. He stopped.

"Shit," he said aloud.

No one else said anything. They listened in complete silence. No one moved. Only the sibilant hiss of the air hose intruded on the silence. Joachim reached back and put his hand over it. Instinctively Wolf looked up, as if that would help his hearing.

"Take the burlap off the sledgehammer," Sepp whispered, "and wrap it around the coupling."

Emerich did as he was told. They tried it again. It still screeched, but not so loudly. Emerich looked at Sepp inquiringly. Sepp gave him a go-ahead gesture.

After a few turns, the screeching diminished in volume, then ceased altogether, and Emerich was able to unscrew the pipe by hand. When he had it out, he gave it a cursory glance, much like a dentist quickly examining an extracted abscessed tooth that had caused the patient to

cry out with pain, and discarded it behind him. He inserted the end of the rod in the small hole afforded by
the coupling and slowly pushed it up the length of pipe.
It went up to the end without effort. He raised it and
lowered it with the tip of one finger, grinning with joy.
Suddenly everyone was shaking everyone's else's hand
and clapping each other on the shoulder. Emerich took
Wolf's hand and held it. He gestured upward. "It's all
yours, Wolf."

At first Wolf did not grasp what he meant. Then he
understood. Emerich was giving him the privilege of making the breakthrough.

Eagerly he picked up the spade and began chopping
away at the earth overhead. Emerich ducked and crawled
back out of the way, taking a ringside seat next to Sepp.
Sepp leaned forward and touched Wolf's shoulder. "Be
careful not to hit the pipe," he whispered.

Wolf nodded. With his fingers he cleared away the
earth around the pipe end, exposing it clearly so that
he would be sure not to hit it. He worked fast, faster than
he had ever worked before. The earth dropped away in
all directions. Clumps of it fell on his head, spewing bits
of clay over his face and down his back. He didn't
care. He let it fall where it would. He was too excited,
too impatient to care about anything except experiencing
the sensation of the spade slicing through the last barrier
of earth between him and the cellar above.

When he had dug out a quarter of a meter, he stopped
long enough to work the pipe out. Bits of earth dribbled
down behind it and dropped into the pile between his
legs. He glanced at the others. They were watching him
intently, the sweat standing in droplets on their faces like
new rain, each smiling in his own way: Joachim amused,
Bruno somewhat benign, Emerich smug, the smile of revenge satisfied. Only Sepp's smile eluded classification.
It was as if he were smiling about something else, recalling a sweet memory or projecting a happy thought into
the promise of the future. Wolf resumed his work,
wondering what it might be that occupied Sepp's mind.
Surely he must be feeling a great sense of satisfaction.
He was about to realize the fulfillment of *his* idea, *his*
organization, *his* leadership. This is Sepp's tunnel, he
thought. We helped him dig it, but it's his. If it weren't

for him, it would never have been started. And never finished. Wolf pondered this as he hacked away, deepening the hole to the point where he could stand in it. With each thrust of the spade, he expected to feel the earth give way, to surrender the last few centimeters to the relentless crusade they had launched back in the rat-infested cellar nine days ago. As he came closer and closer, as the gray clay dropped around him, filling the sled under his feet, spilling over the sides around the feet of Emerich and Sepp, he paused. He stood there, the spade poised for another thrust, accepting what to him was an important recognition of justice.

He squatted down and peered through the opening between the top of the tunnel and the top of the earth piled up to his knees. "Drag out the sled," he whispered.

"Are you through?" Sepp asked.

"Drag it out."

They did as he ordered. As the sled moved from under him, he lifted his feet out of the earth and stepped back. The sled drew away. He crouched down to watch. Joachim and Bruno were dragging it well back into the tunnel, out of the way. Sepp and Emerich were taking an empty one down off the tracks. They righted it and slid it forward. When it reached him, Wolf stepped into it, and they shoved it flush against the end of the tunnel under the vertical shaft. Joachim and Bruno returned. Wolf squatted and handed the spade to Sepp.

"I'm tired," he said.

Sepp looked momentarily surprised; then he understood. He took the spade and handed it to Emerich. Emerich refused it.

"I'm tired, too."

"And I," Bruno said.

"I'm lazy," Joachim said.

Sepp handed the spade back to Wolf. "Sorry. Tired or not, you'll have to finish. Your hour isn't up yet."

Wolf took the spade. He wanted to thank them, but he knew it would be inane. He also knew that nine days ago he would have thanked them without realizing it would have been inane. He stood up in the hole and, lowering the spade as far as his arms would reach, bending his knees, holding the spade rigidly upright, he thrust it upward, putting the full force of his strength behind it.

He felt the blade slice through the damp clay, the contact sending down the familiar scraping sound he had heard thousands of times since they had started the tunnel, the slight, almost unnoticeable recoil as the hilt struck home, then the sudden collapse of resistance. The hilt pased on through, then the shaft, sailing up through the thin crust of earth.

It's through! It's *through!*

He turned the handle and jerked the spade down out of its lodgement. Earth showered down after it, sprinkling his head and shoulders. He took bits in his fingers and gazed at them as if they were different from the tons they had dug out before. His excitement rose to a frantic pitch. He chopped away, opening the hole wider and wider. The earth came down in a torrent. He gloried in it. Inside, he was laughing with glee. How he ached to let it out, to laugh at the top of his voice, to laugh until he was hoarse. His hands and arms worked involuntarily, driving the spade up through the earth again and again. His arms were leaden with pain, but he ignored it. Eagerly, after each shower of earth, he glanced up at the hole he was making, measuring it for size. *My* size, he thought. I'm going up first. They've left it to me; now I'm going to take it all the way!

The next time he looked, he could make out the joists of the first floor lying naked to the cellar below like dried bones in the desert at night. As the hole widened, he could see, just to the left, the dark outline of a hand-rail rising up at an angle. He cut away in that direction, and when the hole was wide enough for him to get through, he could make out the wooden steps. He drove the spade into the earth piled up around his feet, crouched down, and told them to haul away.

When they had the sled out, they all wanted to look up through the hole. Wolf would not yield his ground, so they had to come in one at a time. As they stood up, gazing into the darkness, waiting for their eyes to adjust, he stood by, waiting patiently, expectantly. He felt as if he were letting each in on a secret he had been keeping all his life.

When they had all had their fill, Sepp wispered to him, "I'll boost you up. Take a look around, but don't go up the stairs yet. And above all, be quiet. Remember, a

Vopo passes right in front of the house, and the house is empty. Any loud noise will carry to the street."

Wolf understood. He nodded and stood to the side so that Sepp could crouch in the space under the shaft. He looked up.

"Ready?"

"Ready."

Wolf placed one foot on Sepp's shoulder, braced himself against the walls of the shaft, and raised the other foot up. Sepp's body wobbled, then steadied. Slowly, he rose. Wolf walked his hands up the shaft, directing his head and then his shoulders through the hole. When Sepp was standing, Wolf was through the hole up to his waist. He let himself go forward, fell on his hands, and pulled himself up into the cellar. He felt earth crumbling and falling behind him. On his feet, he brushed his hands against his leather shorts and looked around.

The only light came from a crack under the door at the head of the stairs. The light was diffused across the wall that extended halfway down the staircase. The steps were made of wood and were worn in the middle. There was nothing in the cellar but an old, battered floor lamp standing forlornly in a far corner.

They had come up just to the right of the steps and a meter or so from the back wall of the house. Wolf lay on his stomach and bent his head down into the hole. Sepp was still there, waiting anxiously.

"Well?" he whispered.

"It's a cellar, all right. There's nothing here but an old lamp."

Sepp's face broke into a grin. "A floor lamp? In one corner?"

"Yes."

"This is the place." He handed up the spade. "Finish it from up there."

Wolf took the spade. "With pleasure! With pleasure!"

PART III

卐 卐

THE ESCAPE

34

THE sun, high overhead, did not break through the windows in the vestibule. Two boards were nailed in an X across the outside of each window. Emerich crouched in the doorway to the cellar, waiting for the Vopo to pass. He could see the recessed overhang of the entrance, the sidewalk, the street, the houses across the street. The pavement was shimmering in the sun pouring down from above like liquid gold. Plaster dust from the demolition work hung suspended in its rays like gold dust. Every time the demolition ball struck a wall of the house only two buildings away, the windows rattled and the old floor shook under Emerich's feet. He gripped the oil can tightly and felt his hip pocket for the third time to make sure the pliers were there. Behind him, Joachim yawned. Emerich glanced over his shoulder at him. He was wedged across the third step, his back against the wall, his feet up against the side splashboard. The submachine gun lay cradled in his lap, both hands resting on it in serene repose. Emerich quickly returned his attention to the street.

"Not yet?" Joachim whispered.

Emerich shook his head. A woman carrying a net shopping bag full of apples passed on the opposite side of the street. She was dressed in black, like a peasant, and reminded him of his mother. Then the Vopo came into view. Instinctively, Emerich drew back into the stairwell. The Vopo strolled past at a leisurely pace, one hand gripping the sling of his weapon, the other tucked under his belt. His uniform and boots were covered with dust. Even though he was wearing sunglasses, he kept his head down out of the glare of the sun. Emerich recalled the pair of sunglasses he had bought the previous sum-

469

mer; they had cost nine marks. After he had worn them
awhile, he realized they were nothing but ineffectual
tinted glass. When he returned them and demanded his
money back, the clerk was indignant and threatened to
report him for disparaging the quality of Socialist manu-
facture. Emerich had let himself be cowed and had left
the store fuming and scared.

He waited one full minute by Sepp's watch, then got
up and darted across the vestibule to safety behind the
outer door. He looked back at Joachim. Joachim got to
his feet reluctantly and followed, leaving the door to the
cellar wide open. Emerich quickly closed it and returned,
cursing Joachim under his breath.

There were two hinges, one each at the top and the
bottom. Specks of rust crowded around the joints. He
squirted the penetration oil liberally over them and twisted
the pins with the pliers. The scratching noise they made
seemed uncommonly loud. He managed to raise the pins
a third of the way out and saturated their surfaces with
oil.

"Done yet?" Joachim asked.

"Almost." He looked at the watch. Only a minute and
ten seconds had passed. There was plenty of time. He
wanted to do a thorough job. He twisted the pins back in,
waited a few seconds, then raised them again. This time
they yielded quietly. He raised them halfway and applied
more oil. He raised and lowered each of them until he
was satisfied that they would easily come all the way out.
For good measure, he saturated each hinge again. Oil
was dripping from them and running down the door.

"Let's go," he said.

Joachim went first, opening the cellar door, and Emerich followed. He pulled the door closed behind him,
shutting out the light. They sat on the steps waiting for
their eyes to adjust to the darkness. Below, the dull
glimmer of the shaft to the tunnel lay like a pool of
water reflecting moonlight. Gradually, Emerich's pupils
opened wide enough so that he could see the steps
clearly.

"Ready?"

"Ready."

They went down. One of the ladders they had constructed to shore the cave-in hole was set up in the

vertical shaft. They climbed down and entered the tunnel. Sepp was there, waiting. Emerich made a circle of his thumb and forefinger. Sepp nodded and turned and they headed toward the cellar.

Sepp sat on the bottom step of the warehouse stairs. The others gathered in a semicircle around him: Bruno to his left, leaning against the wall; Wolf next, lying on his side with his head propped up in one hand; Joachim sprawled on his back on a tarpaulin lying on the slope of the mound of earth; Georg sitting with his arms wrapped around his legs, his chin on his knees. Emerich sat at Sepp's right, looking them over. A more disreputable-looking bunch he could not imagine. They were uniformly grimy, unshaven, haggard, red-eyed, ragged, and stinking. Once the breakthrough had been made, their strength had quickly dwindled away. Whatever nervous energy had kept them going was now dissipated. The excitement was over. Emerich felt much as he used to when the fields had been plowed and seeded. All that now remained was to wait for the first sprouts to poke through the surface. Then the work would resume, but there would be no excitement again until the harvest.

"I'll detail what I have in mind," Sepp began. "If you have questions or suggestions, let's have them as I go." He looked around to see that everyone was listening, that everyone understood. He was speaking slowly, with effort. He was as exhausted as the rest of them.

"All right, here's what we'll do. First, the Vopo patrolling the street has to be disarmed and taken to the cellar. That will be Emerich and Joachim's job. Emerich, you have the submachine gun. Joachim, you can use my revolver."

"I'm not much with guns." Joachim yawned, more from boredom, it seemed, than from fatigue. "Maybe you ought to have somebody else do that."

Emerich was not keen on having Joachim help him, but he preferred him to any of the others. Georg was too scared, Wolf too young, Bruno too old.

"I've given a lot of thought to all the things that have to be done," Sepp said, "and I have tried to place people where I think they're best suited."

"Can't Emerich take one Vopo alone?"

"There's more to it than just taking the Vopo. Once you have him, someone has to take him to the cellar, and another has to stand guard at the door until everyone is through the tunnel."

"And that's me, I suppose. Last one through."

"No, that's me," Emerich put in. "You can escort our guest to the cellar."

"How do we take this fellow?" Joachim questioned. "And what about the other Vopo down the street? He has eyes and ears, you know."

"The two Vopos meet at the corner and turn away from each other as they walk their posts. The other Vopo will have his back to you when you take our Vopo. You can do it quietly."

"What do we do, just invite him in?"

"Or he gets his head blown off," Emerich said.

"And if he chooses to get his head blown off?"

"He won't," Sepp assured him.

Joachim grunted skeptically. "I'm still not much with guns."

"I'll show you how to use my revolver. It's not hard."

Joachim raised his head and looked around. "I guess I don't have much choice, do I?"

"You have a choice," Sepp said evenly.

Joachim smiled wistfully and lay back. "I shall be a gunman. Bang. Bang."

"If you do it right, you won't have to shoot."

Suddenly Joachim sat up. "What happens when the other Vopo turns around on his way back and sees his buddy missing?"

"By that time it will all be over. Here's why. With unfailing regularity the Vopos report in on the telephone every hour on the hour. They *both* report in. The telephone is at the corner where they meet, which divides the length of the street in half, three blocks to each half, corresponding to the posts they walk.

"Our house is in the block nearest the telephone. It takes ten minutes—give or take half a minute—to walk the three blocks. The Vopo we're concerned about—our Vopo—will pass the escape house two minutes after calling in. The other Vopo, going in the opposite direction, will continue going that way for another eight minutes after our Vopo passes the house and is taken."

Joachim was still skeptical. "And you plan to get everyone into the house in eight minutes?"

"Five. Maybe less. If necessary, I'll keep the Webers on the move so that we arrive at Vierickstrasse at five minutes after eleven. That will allow three minutes' leeway for you to take the Vopo, and it still gives me five minutes to cross the street and get the others. That's more than enough time. And remember, even if the other Vopo turns around sooner—let's say, in four minutes— he'll be three and a half blocks away—well over two hundred meters. He can't see or hear much at that distance."

"You're quite certain," Bruno said, "that the Vopos report in on the hour."

"Ilse and I watched them almost every night for a month. They never failed. When I was there last night, they called in at eight o'clock, right on schedule."

"If they don't," Joachim observed wryly, "we're in trouble."

"I can't devise a course of action to cover every possible contingency," Sepp said hotly. "You and Emerich will have to use your heads. Remember, if we don't make it tonight, we may never make it. They're tearing down the second house from ours already. Tonight is probably our only chance."

He looked from Joachim to Emerich to make sure the point was made.

"Timing is terribly important. You must be in the vestibule where you can observe the Vopo and the Edelweiss. Ilse should show herself at about five or four minutes to eleven. By the way, she has blond hair and will be wearing a blue dress."

"What are her measurements?" Joachim asked. "I'm not too good on colors at a distance."

"Classic."

"I'll try to control myself."

"When the Vopo makes his last pass before eleven o'clock—which should be about two minutes to eleven— give him one minute, then take the door off the hinges and wait in the entryway on his side—that is, the left side. He won't be able to see you on his way back. You can grab him before he knows what's happening."

"I have the picture," Emerich said.

"Joachim?"

"I, too, have the picture," he said dryly. "It is *not* one of Bruno's masterpieces."

"Perhaps," Bruno suggested, "it is your visual acuity that is faulty, and not Sepp's workmanship."

Joachim nodded. "I am open-minded in these matters."

Emerich smiled to himself. Joachim knew how to retreat gracefully. He could learn much from Joachim. He felt somewhat wistful knowing that their friendship, such as it was, was coming to an end.

"Wolf, you'll be in the cellar of the escape house," Sepp went on. "When Joachim brings the Vopo down, he'll give you the revolver. Joachim?"

He raised his head—"Check"—and lowered it again.

"Have you ever used a revolver, Wolf?"

"No."

"I'll show you how later, you and Joachim."

"What do I do with the Vopo?"

"Take him through the tunnel and keep him here in the cellar. Don't take your eyes off him for a minute. And keep the gun on him."

"I guess I'm supposed to shoot him if he tries to get away."

"I doubt very much that he'll try, but if he does, yes, shoot him."

"Even if we're still on the other side?" Joachim asked.

"Even then."

"People will hear the shot."

"We'll just have to take that chance. Remember, we're not helpless. We'll have two submachine guns on our side."

Wolf nodded hesitantly. Then he said, "I've never shot anyone."

Sepp regarded him with an empathy only Emerich could appreciate. "You can do it if you have to."

Georg raised his head off his knees. "What about me? What do I do?"

"I'm coming to you," Sepp retorted with unusual curtness. Perhaps, Emerich thought, it was because of his bit of hypocrisy with Wolf. Once again, the memory of the moment in the Grunewald returned, bringing with it an uneasy apprehension about Sepp. Somewhere in his character there was lodged a peculiar incongruity, a contradiction that eluded Emerich's insight. It was as if a small part of Sepp were not Sepp at all but a separate entity, a symbiotic creature sharing his life by mutual agreement, willing for the most part to accept whatever Sepp decided, only occasionally overpowering Sepp's will with its own.

"Isn't that right, Emerich?" Sepp was asking.

Emerich looked at him blankly. He had not been listening.

"There are four children in your family."

"Four. Yes, four."

Sepp stared at Emerich for a moment, then turned back to Bruno. "I'll hand the two younger ones and Emerich's grandfather down to you, and you set them in the sled. Their father—what's his name, Emerich?"

"Dietrich."

"Dietrich will guide the sled through the tunnel. It's important that he be with them so they won't be afraid."

"One is only a baby," Emerich said. "Little Dietrich. He's only six months old . . . no, that was a year ago, almost. He's a year and a half now." He felt a little embarrassed and gave a nervous laugh. "I remember them as they were when I left."

No one said anything for a minute. They were watching him in a curious way. Even Joachim had raised his head to look at him.

Bruno broke the silence. "I take it, then, that I am to remain at the foot of the ladder, helping people down and sending them on their way through the tunnel."

"Yes. The older children will go next, then the women, and the men last."

"Perhaps some candy for the children will take their minds off their fears."

"That's not a bad idea."

"I'll get some."

"Georg, you'll haul the sled with the children and the old man out. Post yourself at the entrance to the tunnel. When Bruno gives you the signal, haul away."

Georg lifted his head from his knees. The loose flesh under his eyes was dark and puffy from lack of sleep. "What is the signal?"

"Any signal will do."

"Have the rope in your hands," Bruno told him. "I'll give it a tug when we're ready."

"When the people get here to the cellar, Georg, they may be frightened, and they certainly will be dirty. Try to calm them down, remind them they are safe in West Berlin, and show them to the water so they can clean themselves up a bit if they want."

"When will my parents come through?"

"In the second group from the Edelweiss."

"I want to be over in the escape house."

"Your job is here."

"I want to be over there."

"There's nothing for you to do over there."

Georg was insistent. "I want to be there."

Sepp lost his patience and became stern. "You're to stay here and do as I told you."

Georg just looked at him and said nothing. He put his chin back down on his knees. Sepp looked around. "Any questions?"

Emerich suddenly remembered that he had not made arrangements for a place for his family to stay. "I'll have to get hotel rooms for my people."

Bruno made a diffident gesture. "My wife and I would like them to stay with us." He looked around at the others. "We extend the invitation to all. It may be a little crowded, but our house is quite large."

Emerich thought of Bruno's wife, of his house. He had not seen either, but a man of Bruno's stature would have a sophisticated wife, a beautiful house. He pictured her dressed in a long silk gown, wearing diamonds, serving cocktails to the elite of Berlin society, surrounded by elegant, expensive furniture, antiques, porcelain, and ivory. The talk would be witty, cultivated, esoteric.

Joachim answered first. "Thanks, Bruno, but we have room in our apartment for our parents."

"What about you, Georg?"

"I guess it's all right. All I have is a rented room. They can't stay there."

"Sepp, I suspect you've made arrangements for Ilse."

Emerich smiled. How tactful he is. Papa would never have thought to say it just that way.

Sepp nodded. "Yes, I have."

"Well, then, it's settled. Emerich's and Georg's people will stay with us."

Emerich made a hesitant protest. "There are ten in my family."

"I know. As I say, we will be a little cramped, but we will manage. My wife is very clever about such things."

"They are. . . ." He did not know how to say it. He did not want to appear ashamed of his family, and he did not want to hurt Bruno's feelings. But he had under-estimated Bruno. The artist looked at him with an af-fectionate understanding that told Emerich he knew what he was trying to say.

"Perhaps," he said with some amusement, "we will be able to demonstrate to your people that we city slickers are not so far removed from the soil as they might think." He ran his hand over his filthy belly. "Certainly this one isn't."

Emerich was chagrined that he had not realized that Bruno had understood perfectly well what he was think-ing, that he knew Emerich's people were peasants and what peasants were like. It made no difference to him. If Bruno were that kind of man, he would not be here.

"Thank you." Emerich wanted to say more, but it would have been superfluous.

Joachim sat up. "Are we finished?"

"I don't have anything else," Sepp said.

"Good. I'm going home to bed." He stretched. "You do remember what that is."

"Seems I recall vaguely."

Everyone but Georg got up.

"What time are you crossing over?" Bruno asked Sepp.

"I have to pick up Emerich's aunt at eight thirty, so I'll be crossing over about an hour before."

"When should we return here?"

"Ten thirty will be soon enough."

"I'm not leaving," Georg said.

"Don't you want to get cleaned up?" Wolf asked him.

"I'll just get dirty again."

"I'm staying, too," Emerich said. "Half of my bed is here, anyway. And somebody reliable has to put on the exhaust extension at six o'clock."

"Not me," Wolf said. "I've been dreaming of a hot shower and my bed for two days."

"You'll have to race me for the shower," Joachim said.

"I couldn't race a turtle."

Bruno, Joachim, and Wolf started up the stairs to wash
up and change their clothes.

Sepp came over to Emerich and took him by the arm.
"Take a look at these tools, will you?" He walked him
across the room to the tool chest.

"What about them?"

"There's something I have to tell you," he said in a
quiet, confidential voice. "I don't want the others to hear
me." He glanced over his shoulder at Georg, who had not
moved. He looked as if he were asleep. "You may condemn me for this. You have a right to. I hope you'll understand. I'm counting on you to understand." He seemed
distressed, but calm nonetheless.

"What is it?"

"The night I went to check out the house . . . I didn't
tell you the whole truth about it. In fact, I was caught."

Emerich did not understand. The apprehension he had
felt before returned, a shapeless, insidious presence that
pried at his fear. Questions poured into his mind, but he
held them there, waiting while Sepp told him what had
happened. As Emerich listened, his apprehension evolved
into despair. From the point when he realized that Sepp
had let Konrad Möss go, he knew they were finished.
Sepp's shipload of intelligence, industry, ingenuity, and
determination had been wrecked on the shoals of his
incredible naiveté. But Sepp was not the only one who
would go down. The hopes of all those who had signed
on, who had trusted to his leadership, would suffer with
him. Emerich wondered why he felt no anger, only a
terrible, unrelenting sadness. *Maybe I'm too tired to be
angry, or maybe I've mellowed.* He let himself down onto
the edge of the tool box and put his head in his hands.

"It's *kaputt*," he said quietly.

"What?"

"I said, it's *kaputt*. Done. Finished."

"No, it's not."

Emerich looked up at him. "You're a fool, *Ami*. You're
a wonderful fool."

Sepp's mouth drew itself into a thin line, and his eyes
darkened. "I thought you would understand."

"I understand. I understand very well. I understand
all this has been for nothing." He listened to the word
echo through his head. "For nothing because of your

idiotic compulsion to be a nice guy, to trust everyone as if he were your brother. People are weak and destructive; they're cowardly, suspicious, equivocating, selfish, stupid, mean and destructive. They're especially destructive of themselves. What better evidence do you need than The Wall itself? Why are we here among the rats, digging in the earth like animals, if it is not because of the baseness of men?" He sighed, more from resignation to defeat than from fatigue. "Men are not angels, Sepp. They are not angels."

Sepp did not speak for a moment. He raised his head as if listening to the garbled conversation dropping down from the floor above, where the others were washing up. Emerich looked across the room and saw that Georg had joined them. How small the cellar seemed now, intimidated by the two huge piles of gray earth rising to the ceiling.

"Remember that day in my room," Sepp began, "when you questioned me about Joachim and Georg and Bruno? You were very skeptical about them, you didn't think they could do the job. I asked you to trust my judgment then. I'm asking you now to trust it again."

"I trusted you then, yes. But you were wrong about Georg, and I was right."

"I wasn't wrong about Georg's doing the job. He's done it. He may be a weakling and a coward, but he did the job, he kept up with us right to the end. You have to grant me that. I told you then, as you're telling me now, men are not angels. Bruno and Georg, Joachim and Wolf, you and I—we're not angels. But we're not what you said we are, either. There's a part of each of us that is base—I'll grant you that—but only a part. What about the other part? What was it that gave us the strength and determination—and, yes, the courage—to do what we've done? This was no mean feat, peasant. The Wall may be a monument to the baseness in men, but this tunnel is a monument to man's will to be something else. Men aren't angels, but there is something of the angels in them."

"Which part do you think Konrad Möss listened to? Do you really believe he didn't hightail it to the SSD as fast as his legs would take him?"

"I have every reason to believe he didn't. Why

shouldn't he want to get out of that Hell just as much as you did? He was not fifty meters from a direct telephone to his superiors. He could have called them as soon as he discovered the door latch had been tampered with. He could have gone after the other Vopo for help. He could have turned me in before I crossed back into West Berlin. Everything he did points to his sincerity about wanting to escape."

For the first time, Emerich was moved by Sepp's argument. It was true that plenty of Vopos had escaped over The Wall. Just because they were there to prevent others from getting across did not mean that they themselves did not want to escape.

"Maybe he did inform on you, and they're waiting until tonight to bag the whole lot of us."

"I thought of that. But then why would they be planning to tear down our house?"

"They haven't torn it down yet," Emerich replied skeptically.

"I keep going back to the first point. Why did Möss go down into that cellar alone unless he had a hunch about what I was up to? There's no other explanation."

"Maybe he's stupid."

"He didn't strike me as stupid. He's a gutsy little kid, sort of a wiseacre. You'd like him."

"But would I trust him?"

"I think you would have, if you had been in my place."

Emerich's despair was waning. He was not certain whether it was because Sepp was beginning to convince him that Möss was trustworthy or because he could not bear to accept defeat at this late hour. "You should have told us before we began."

"Would you have gone ahead with the tunnel? Would Joachim, who, you claim, would have welcomed any excuse to get out of it? Would Georg have been too afraid? Would Bruno have thought it wise?"

Emerich suddenly knew he had underestimated Sepp, after all. It was funny, it was all very funny. He laughed. The more he thought about it, the harder he laughed. He only wished the laughter had some joy in it.

35

THE long claws of the animal's paw dug into his shoulder. Its leather pads scratched his skin. The animal became Walther Curzmann with a hairy paw for a hand. The claws dug deeper and shook him violently. Walther Curzmann's lips mouthed his name over and over —Joachim, Joachim, Joachim—but they emitted no sound. Then, as if echoing back from a distance, the sound came louder and louder until it shattered sleep.

He opened his eyes. It was Wolf's hand on his shoulder. He put his hand to his eyes to shade them from the lamp.

"Telephone, Joachim."

"What time is it?"

"Almost seven."

He sat up and rubbed his face. It had healed. He ran his fingers over his chest and arms. Not a scab; a few scars of pinched skin on his chest, but not a scab.

"Man or woman?"

"Man."

Curzmann! He bolted out of bed and raced into the living room. "Make some coffee," he called over his shoulder as he picked up the receiver.

"Hello."

"Herr Lentz?" It was Curzmann's man, Otto.

"Yes."

"*Herr Direktor* Curzmann wishes to speak to you."

481

The line went dead for a moment. Wolf passed through and went into the kitchen.

Curzmann came on, his voice clear and ringing as if he were reciting lines from the stage of an empty theater. "Joachim, where in the devil's creation have you been? I've been trying to raise you for three days."

"I've been working, Herr Curzmann."

"Working?! I told you you were through with Karl Buhlen. When I tell you a thing—"

"I wasn't working for Karl, I was working on the tunnel."

"Oh, that." His temper cooled.

"I'm sorry you had so much trouble."

"I called nights, too," he remembered. "What were you doing, enjoying the last rights of a condemned man?" He chuckled obscenely. "It won't be so bad, my boy. You'll get used to it. It won't exactly be servitude, you know."

"We've been working the past two nights," Joachim said evenly.

Curzmann was suddenly all business. "Well, your tunneling days—and nights—are over. You can start earning that six hundred I gave you. Pack your bags. We're off to Munich. We'll pick you up at nine sharp."

"Tonight?"

"Certainly tonight."

"You said it would be a couple of weeks."

"The film business is a most erratic, most chaotic affair. You'll get used to it, just as you'll get used to other things."

"It doesn't give me much time."

Curzmann was not listening. "The plane leaves at ten." There was a pause. Joachim's brain refused to function. He felt himself once again riding with destiny. No matter what he decided now, what he said, it had all been determined long ago.

"Joachim?"

"Yes?"

"What's the matter? Not backing out, are you?"

"No, I'm not backing out."

"Be ready at nine, then. Don't keep me waiting. I don't like to be kept waiting."

"Could I . . . could I follow you tomorrow?"

Curzmann's voice became heavy with restrained anger.

"I thought I made myself clear the night we met. There will be no bargaining, no hesitation, no cajolery, no finagling. You will do *as* I say, *when* I say. Is that quite clear, my boy?"

"It's clear enough."

"I do not expect to have to say it again. Ever. Do you understand?"

"I understand."

"Until nine o'clock then."

"Nine o'clock."

Joachim set the receiver on the cradle and sat down.

Wolf came in, yawning. "There're still a couple of hours left to sleep. Why do you want coffee?"

"Coffee?"

"You told me to make some coffee?"

He had forgotten.

"Is something wrong?"

Joachim shook his head. "There's nothing wrong." He looked up at his brother. His blue eyes reflected sympathetic concern. "Go back to bed if you want."

"I guess I'm not tired. I probably am, but I'd never get back to sleep." He was as excited now as in the days before the tunnel.

Joachim looked him over carefully. "Did you really do it? Did you really try to knock down the shoring in the cave-in hole?"

Wolf's eyes narrowed, and he set his jaw firmly.

"Don't worry, I'm not going to tell anyone."

"I know it."

"And now you're excited about Papa and Mama coming over."

He nodded.

"It doesn't make sense."

"It makes sense to me. It would have been worse for me than for them."

Joachim knew what he meant, but he could not accept it, not for himself. He would tell him now that he was not going back with him to the tunnel. He looked across the room to the windows, but the drapes were closed. Tell him now, he thought. But instead, he got up. "I'm going to get dressed."

Wolf laughed. "We'll have to change our ways. We're

so used to running around here naked, we're apt to do it when Papa and Mama are here."

Joachim did not answer. In his bedroom, he put on clean underwear. *This is the safety catch. When it's up, it's on, which means you can't pull the trigger. When it's down, it's off, and the trigger is free.* He took a clean white shirt from his wardrobe, unfolded it, unbuttoned the collar, and put his arm through one sleeve. *The plane leaves at ten. You're not backing out, are you? The plane leaves. . . .* He took off the shirt and threw it onto the bed. Wolf was shouting something from his room. "What did you say?"

"I said, where are we all going to sleep tonight?"

"Oh." Joachim looked down at the floor. *When you fire, keep your arm extended like this and bring your target into the line of these two sights.* He lifted a foot. The lines in the sole were still dirty. It will take a month of scrubbing to get clean again, he thought. "I'll sleep with you. Papa and Mama can have my room."

"I'll change the linen," Wolf said, appearing in the doorway. He was putting on a clean work shirt. "Do you think they'll wonder why you have a king-size bed?"

"They'll know, but they won't say anything."

"It's good I don't have one. Mama would probably faint."

Joachim recalled the way his mother had taken his side when he wanted to swim the Spree. "Mama's tougher than you think."

Wolf tucked his shirt into his trousers, zipped them, and buckled his belt. "Do you think she'll be able to tell about me?"

"I don't know. Maybe. Mothers are shrewd people."

"Did she know about you?"

Joachim had never thought about it. "Maybe. If she did, she never let on."

"I think I'd feel odd if she knew. With Papa, it's different. He'd probably be sore as a blister, but Mama. . . ." He went back into his room without expressing the rest of his thought.

Joachim remained standing for a moment, then went to the bed and lay down. *The plane leaves at ten. . . . It fires six shots semiautomatically. . . . Not backing out, are you? Not backing out, are you? . . . There's a slight*

*kick that raises the piece in your hand. . . . It would
have been worse for me than for them. . . . Until nine
o'clock, then. . . .* He heard Wolf cross the living room
and go into the kitchen. He got up. *If I put on my suit
and tie instead of work clothes, he'll ask why, and then
I'll have to tell him. They can make out all right at the
tunnel. Sepp is a genius at innovation. He'll think of
something.*

"Coffee's ready!"

*Sepp won't be there! He'll be in the Sektor! Damn.
If anything goes wrong over there, if I'm caught, call
Lieutenant Wayne, will you? He's the same one you
would have called if I hadn't made it the other time. . . .*
Joachim put on a pair of old slacks and his slippers. A
compromise.

Wolf was pouring the coffee. He was wide awake now,
moving briskly about, his eyes as bright as cornflowers
in the sun. "I've decided to get a job," he announced.

"A job? What for? What kind of job?"

"Papa won't have any money for a while. He'll need
time to get started again. I can work until school starts,
and then after school hours."

"I make enough. You don't have to get a job." Joachim
thought of the check for six hundred marks still in his
wallet in his suit coat pocket. And as of today, Curzmann owed him another six hundred.

"I think I'll get a job in construction. It pays good
money, and I'm in shape for it."

"I told you, you don't have to get a job."

"I ought to have money of my own, anyway. I'll be
going out more now."

"Don't I give you enough?"

Wolf hesitated. "That's just it. You *give* it to me. I'd
like to earn it myself. It's not the same when—" He broke
off and looked down at his cup.

"It's all right, go ahead."

"I appreciate what you've done for me. I don't want
you to think I'm not grateful. I am. But it's not healthy
to be too dependent on somebody else. It's sort of like—"

"Servitude?"

Wolf drank some coffee. "I guess so." He felt bad
about it and would not look at Joachim. Joachim drank
the coffee. Wolf always made good coffee. Whatever Wolf

did, he did well. He was superb in the tunnel, the most productive digger of the lot, and never a problem to anyone.

"It's hard to believe, isn't it. I keep thinking we have to go back and dig some more." Wolf shook his head. "It's really hard to believe."

"The hardest part is yet to come."

Wolf's excitement waned, but only momentarily, like the moon passing behind a small cloud. "I guess you're right. Maybe something will go wrong. I sure hope I don't have to shoot that Vopo. You don't think I'll have to shoot him, do you?"

"You won't have to shoot him. Think of what you would do in his place."

"It would depend on whether I wanted to get out of the *Sektor*."

"He may try to get you to relax your guard by telling you that. Don't listen to him. Keep that gun on him every second."

Wolf nodded.

"Just remember, they tried to kill you once. They'll do it again if you give them the chance."

Wolf gave this some thought. Then he said, "Do you think the Vopos really care if Papa and Mama want to live over here instead of over there?"

It was an odd question. Joachim had never thought much about it. "I suppose some of them do. Why do you ask?"

"I was just thinking today while I was working. I don't believe most of those fellows care one way or another where people live. I'll bet ninety-nine percent of those people in East Germany, even the party members, don't really care."

"Somebody cares; otherwise, why The Wall?"

"Do you think the men who built The Wall—I mean the men who actually piled up the bricks and mortar and put in the barbed wire—do you think they wanted The Wall?"

"Probably most of them didn't care one way or the other. There were undoubtedly some who were in favor of it and some who were against it."

"That's what I mean. It's all so stupid. It's all so absurd."

Joachim realized that Wolf was just coming to understand something that he himself felt he had always understood. "If the Vopos didn't shoot escapees, or if the workmen didn't build The Wall, they would be put in jail."

"Not if the other Vopos wouldn't arrest them."

"They have to arrest them; otherwise, *they* would be put in jail."

"What if everybody refuses to arrest anybody?"

"There's always somebody who will do the arresting, either because he figures he'll have more power, more wealth, by doing what the authorities want him to, or because he's scared of what will happen to him if he doesn't. Most Vopos and wall builders are of the latter type. That's how governments stay in power. People are scared to death of what will happen to them if they get out of line."

Wolf mulled this over, then said, "I wonder which are worse, the ones who will be slaves for power and wealth or the ones who are too scared to do anything."

"The former, because they make a positive choice, and if it weren't for them, the others would have no one to fear."

Finishing his coffee, Wolf sat back and smiled. "I'm glad you weren't either type. We wouldn't be here now if you were."

The cuckoo clock bird cuckooed nine times. Joachim looked at the check once more. I could keep it, he thought. There isn't much he could do about it. He might stop payment on it, but not if I cash it—after all, he got a free thrill. I wonder if that would hold up in court—six hundred marks in consideration of a moment's look at Joachim Lentz's extraordinarily exciting body. He'd never take it to court. He wouldn't dare. Maybe he has henchmen who take care of people like me. No, he's not the type. He'd take his loss philosophically.

The bell rang. It was not the insistent, long ring he had expected, but a moderate, polite ring. Otto, of course, Curzmann wouldn't do his own doorbell ringing.

"I'll get it," he called and went to the door. He opened it and went down the stairs to the outer door. He felt surprisingly buoyant. Otto was there, dressed in a chauffeur's uniform. Beyond, in the street, a long black Mercedes stood idling at the curb. Curzmann's profile put a jagged line in the rear window. Joachim brushed past Otto and went to the car. He leaned over and rapped on the window. Curzmann looked out and rolled it down. He was a perfect picture of consternation.

"Good evening, *Herr Direktor* Curzmann."

"You are not properly dressed, Joachim. And where is your luggage?"

Joachim smiled. "I've changed my mind. We would have compatiblity problems. I'm ugly when I wake up. I have an independent streak. I laugh when I shouldn't, especially at pomposity. And I like girls." Behind him, he felt the presence of Otto, but he did not look around.

"And you are a fool."

Joachim shrugged. "Perhaps. I'll never know, will I."

"You already know." Curzmann gestured over Joachim's shoulder. "Otto! Tempelhof!" Otto sprang to the driver's door and got in behind the wheel. "Wait!" And to Joachim: "My check, please."

"Sorry, I cashed it today."

"The money, then."

"I'm keeping that as payment for services rendered."

Curzmann's consternation had developed to a well-controlled fury. He was breathing heavily and spitting out his words between his teeth like cleanly sucked grape seeds. "Do you think I'm going to let a cheap little con artist like you take me for six hundred marks without having your ass?"

"Consider yourself lucky. I could have gone with you to Munich and made off with another six hundred before you'd even laid your nervous little hands on me."

Curzmann's rage was reduced to a glare of hatred and frustration. He slammed his fist on the control button, and the window started up. Joachim retrieved his fingers just in time. The motor made barely a sound as the car left the curb. It gathered speed and was around the corner in a remarkably short time. Joachim stood there in the quiet, his hands stuffed into his pockets, wondering how much a car like that cost.

36

"EVENIN', Lieutenant."

If Sepp were to pass through Checkpoint Charlie every night for the rest of his life and if Sergeant Eddie Doyle were on duty every one of those nights, he would still be addressing Sepp as "Lieutenant" on the last night.

"Good evening, Sergeant."

Corporal Armstrong stuck his head out of the shack. "Evening, sir."

"Evening, Corporal."

"Not so hot tonight, sir."

"No, it's cooled off a bit."

True to his word, Sergeant Doyle had straightened Armstrong out. He now had the snap of a good soldier and the courtesy to leave two friends to their own devices. He went back into the shack and picked up the book he was reading.

"He seems to be shaping up."

"Smart kid. He's gonna reenlist. I told him there ain't no better life than the Army, 'specially for a kid like him. He's smart, but he quit school and got into a few scrapes. I got him workin' on his schoolbooks again. No more comic books."

"I wish you luck."

"Somebody else'll need it. I'm about to rotate."

"Back to the States?"

"My tour's up in eight days. This here's my last night at ol' Checkpoint Charlie." He patted the doorjamb affectionately. "I'll miss the place. Kinda like home."

"That's great—going back to the States."

"For my last tour. I'll have twenty years in, then."

"You'll join up again."

"Not me. The Army's for smart young kids like Armstrong there. It ain't the same, not like it used to be." He tapped his head. "If you ain't got it here, you ain't got it."

"What are you going to do?"

"I'll get half pay. That ain't bad. Maybe I'll settle down in a little cabin up in the mountains in West Virginia and just hunt an' fish." He laughed self-consciously. "Maybe I'll run for sheriff."

"You'd make a good sheriff."

"You think so?"

"I'd vote for you."

Doyle rubbed his chin and smiled. "Maybe I will. I guess I got the experience, all right—twenty years in the MP's—when I get out, that is." He looked down the street toward the East Berlin side, where the barrier rested across the roadway like a fallen tree. "You goin' over?"

Sepp nodded.

"I reckon you'll just keep goin' over till The Wall comes tumblin' down."

Sepp laughed. "We could use a Joshua."

"Now *there* was a soldier, Lieutenant. I figure if he'd of been commander in chief, we'd of never of let them Commies build The Wall in the first place. Yes, sir, he was a *real* soldier."

"He had a little help from Upstairs."

"I reckon he deserved it."

"I suppose so." He put out his hand. "I'd better go. All the best to you, Eddie. I hope you do run for sheriff someday."

"Maybe I will. Take care now, Lieutenant." Doyle threw him a smart salute.

"You too, Sergeant."

The distance from the western to the eastern side was not great. He could walk it in less than a minute, but tonight it seemed like a mile. He felt refreshed after five hours of precious sleep. As he approached the barrier in East Berlin, he was thinking hard about making it seem like any other night. The realization that this was the last time he would walk this piece of earth, this no-man's-land, this stretch of Friedrichstrasse where no one stopped to chat or while away the time, was so acute that he could scarcely believe that everyone else did not know it, too. He had passed the test with Sergeant Doyle; only Lieutenant Geller was left.

The Vopo raised the barrier and let him pass without comment. He had been on duty there the past week and had come to recognize Sepp. In the customs shack, Lieutenant Geller rose to meet him, dropping his booted feet from the desk with a thump and folding the newspaper he had been reading. The inevitable cigarette dangled jauntily from his lips. There were two Vopos behind desks, both doing some kind of clerical work. They looked up, gave him uniformly blank stares, and returned to their work.

"Herr Bauer, how nice to see you. Pleasant evening we're having for a change. The heat has been unbearable, eh?"

"It's been beautiful in West Berlin all summer—cool and clear, just like spring."

Geller laughed. "Always the humorist, always full of jokes and wisecracks. You Americans are wonderful people. It's too bad you have such misguided leaders."

Sepp was not in the mood to trade sarcasm and insults, but he reminded himself again that tonight he must appear no different from any other night. "Did you know that there are more people in the United States who think our leaders are misguided than there are people in East Germany who think it?"

"But everyone in the DDR thinks so."

"Almost half the people in the United States think so."

Geller leaned back and eyed Sepp suspiciously. "You are joking again."

Sepp raised three fingers. "Scouts honor."

"What is this 'scout's honor'?"

"It's . . . it's not important. Let's get the formalities out of the way. I'll be late again, and it doesn't help matters when I'm late." He handed over his passport. Geller placed a currency form on the counter and took the passport.

Sepp started filling out the form.

"Half the people?"

"Yes."

"It's hard to believe. No government can survive with so many disloyal citizens."

"That's what I keep telling you."

Geller retorted heatedly, "All the traitors are on the other side of The Wall. Good riddance." He did not like to talk about The Wall and closed off the conversation by browsing carelessly through Sepp's passport. The attention he gave to the passport changed from night to night. Sometimes he scrutinized each page as if searching for a secret code written in invisible ink; other times he scarcely looked at it. He handed it back, and Sepp slid the currency form across the counter. Geller looked it over and placed it in a basket on the nearest desk.

"So, enjoy yourself, Herr Bauer, spend money, and return safely home."

"I shall do all three, I promise."

" 'Wiedersehen, Herr Bauer."

" 'Wiedersehen, Lieutenant."

Sepp went out into the cool night air and breathed deeply. Through the screen he could hear Geller muttering to himself about "half the people, it's hard to believe." He smiled and headed toward the subway station.

"What time is it now?"

"Nine twenty." It was the fifth time in as many minutes that Frau Halzapfel had asked the same question. She was very nervous, and she was beginning to make him nervous, too.

"It won't be on time. The trains never run on time, not since *they* took over." They were sitting in the waiting room of the Ostbahnhof. It was not crowded and they had a bench to themselves, but Sepp was becoming concerned that she might say something out of line loud enough to attract attention. To prove her right, a voice came over the loudspeaker announcing that the nine-thirty train from Leipzig would be fifteen minutes late.

She jabbed him with her elbow. "I told you. Let's go have some beer. You've got money, ain't you? My nerves are up around my ears." She got up without waiting for an answer, and he followed.

To the casual observer, Magda Halzapfel looked like a

typical, gentle German grandmother, basking in the warmth of tender memories, anticipating the next opportunity to spend the day spoiling her grandchildren with presents, kisses, and an overabundance of love. She had quickly disabused Sepp of that impression.

She strode into the shabby *Bierstube* off the station's waiting room and plunked herself down in a chair, jamming her big purse between her legs. Sepp sat across the table from her. Two workmen were seated nearby, drinking beer and eating sandwiches. They looked like trainmen. She reached down and, taking off a shoe, rubbed her foot. "Corns."

"Oh."

"Putting corns in new shoes is like putting a rat down a snake hole." He had to laugh. Thirty years in Berlin had not weathered the peasant stone from which she was wrought. "I'll have light beer. A stein. You have to get it yourself here. No waiters."

Sepp went to the counter and bought two steins of light beer. When he returned to the table, he saw that she had both shoes off and her feet planted flat on the floor.

"You smoke?"

"No."

She made a face. "I could use a smoke. My nerves are playing Gypsy music in my stomach."

"What kind do you like?"

"Any kind. I'm not particular."

He bought her some cigarettes. She opened the package with nervous fingers. He lighted one for her. She took a long draw and exhaled loudly. "Ahhhh. That's better." Her beer was half gone. "You know it's been thirty years since I've seen Konstanz? And *Papa*. Papa has never forgiven me. What will Papa say? Maybe I won't recognize them."

"People don't change that much."

"Peasants do. They die early, even before their time comes."

"They'll be in a group. It's not likely there will be another group of ten people traveling together."

"Why'd you want me along if you're so sure about that?"

"Insurance."

She drank another quarter of the stein and drew long

and hard on the cigarette. Her hands were shaking. "I don't know if I'm more nervous about . . . you know, or about seeing Konstanz after all these years. He probably thinks I'm a rich widow. People get strange ideas like that, 'specially peasants. Peasants get the strangest notions. What time is it now?"

He looked at his watch. "Nine twenty-seven."

"You going to drink that beer?"

He slid it over to her. She finished hers off and started on his. At nine forty the loudspeaker informed them that the train would not arrive until ten five. Sepp cursed under his breath.

"You better get yourself a beer."

He decided he would. He drank a quarter of it in one go. It was not good beer, but it felt good going down. He recalculated the time it would take them to get to Vierickstrasse. It was seven stops away on the subway. That shouldn't take more than fifteen or twenty minutes. He had thought of using taxis, but he did not like the idea of separating. And it would be just his luck that one of the taxis would have a flat tire on the way.

Getting out of the station, explaining to them what they were going to do, then getting them to the subway station would take another fifteen minutes.

From the subway to Vierickstrasse, ten minutes.

Altogether, forty minutes, forty-five at the outside. He felt better. If the train arrived at ten five, they would still make it. If.

"Maybe they're not on this train," she said. "Maybe they missed it or changed their minds. Peasants are strange people. They'll change their minds just to be contrary."

Her abrupt siege of foreboding annoyed him. "They'll be on it." He wondered where Ilse was at this moment. There was an hour yet before she was due at the Edelweiss. The Lentzes were already on their way— if *they* hadn't changed *their* minds. I wonder if Konrad Möss will show up, he thought. And Greta Dohr. She's still at home, waiting. God, waiting is hard.

"What time is it?" she asked.

"There's a clock on the wall." It was nine forty-five.

"I feel better." She had finished both beers and was smoking her fourth cigarette.

He thought about Konrad Möss. Maybe Emerich was right. Maybe he was a fool. He began to have visions of truckloads of shouting, clattering Vopos swooping down on them from all directions; of plainclothes SSD men appearing out of the dark doorways of the old buildings on Vierickstrasse, converging on them with quiet, deadly intent. His hands began to sweat.

At nine fifty the loudspeaker announced that the Leipzig train was now scheduled to arrive at ten fifteen.

"You see how it is? The whole system is rotten." She was talking too loudly. The two trainmen at the next table glanced at her and then at Sepp. He leaned across the table. "For God's sake, keep your voice down."

She hunched her head into her shoulders and gave the room a furtive inspection. "You'd better get me another beer."

"Not a chance."

She gave him an indignant look but kept quiet. Sepp took short sips of his beer. He put his hands around the stein to cool them off. Frau Halzapfel lighted her fifth cigarette. The two trainmen finished their beer and left. The table looked forlorn with the empty, foam-specked steins standing on it, the chairs pulled away as if avoiding it. A porter staggered hurriedly past the plate-glass windows carrying two huge suitcases slung over his shoulder on a strap. A woman and her son came in and sat down at the table vacated by the trainmen. She took off a close-fitting hat she was wearing and tucked in the strands of hair that had come loose. Sepp looked at the clock. Nine fifty-seven. He could not sit there any longer.

"Let's go," he said curtly.

They went into the waiting room. At any moment he expected the loudspeaker to announce a further delay in the train's arrival. People were on their feet, waiting huddled in groups, looking dully at one another, muttering expressions of impatience.

At ten o'clock the loudspeaker informed them that the train was arriving on track three. Sepp felt his body relax. Frau Halzapfel chortled. "You see! They say it will arrive at ten fifteen, now it comes at ten o'clock. It has probably been here since nine thirty all the time."

Sepp was too nervous about it to answer her. People

began milling toward the gate to track three. Sepp and Frau Halzapfel joined them.

"Let's go down the platform."

"No, we may miss them. We'll wait right here."

"I can't see anything."

"They have to come through here."

"How do I look? Not too rich, I hope."

"You look fine."

"Thirty years. Can you imagine it? I was just a girl then. What do you think they'll say? Should I give them a kiss?" She stood on tiptoe to see better, then remembered her corns.

The first of the passengers began coming through the gate. The people waiting made a path for them. They came carrying suitcases, boxes tied with rope, baskets, bags, satchels, and briefcases. Brief scenes of greeting took place, some quiet, some loud, some tearful. The area was quickly disintegrating into mayhem, the original restraint and courtesy forgotten as more and more passengers crowded through the gate.

Suddenly, despite her corns, she was jumping up and down, waving her arms, sweeping an arc clear of people around her with her purse, and shouting, "Papa! Papa! Konstanz! Konstanz! Here I am! Here's Magda! Over here!" She began elbowing her way forward, using the points of her new shoes expertly against the unsuspecting ankles of people in her way. Sepp stayed close behind her, suffering the indignant stares and muttered curses of her victims. Her arms spread wide and came together like a giant pincer around the frail black figure of an old man. He let out a squeak and his hat fell off, a black felt hat so old it bounced like cardboard when it struck the floor. Sepp reached for it, but another hand had it before his. He rose, looking into a pair of eyes exactly like Emerich Weber's.

"Herr Weber?"

"I am Konstanz Weber."

"Josep Bauer, a friend of Emerich's."

They shook hands. The man's skin felt like the bark of a tree. His free hand gripped a large black leather suitcase tied neatly with coarse rope. Behind him in a tight group came his family: his wife, a stocky, dark-haired woman holding the hand of the oldest child, a girl of about ten or eleven, his son Dietrich carrying the baby and a battered rattan suitcase; Dietrich's wife, holding the hands of the two other children, boys, one about seven, the other about four of five. Emerich's younger brother, Ulrich, stood aside, close to his grandfather, as if to be there to catch him when Madga let him go.

They all had an air of imperturbability, even the children, much as if they were stoically resigned to whatever fate was leading them to. All the adults were dressed in black. The men, including Ulrich, wore starched white shirts, black ties, black hats, and black shoes that gleamed with a high polish. With their weathered faces, their thick black hair laboriously forced into place, and their rough hands and broken nails, they looked much like children reluctantly dressed up for church.

Sobbing, near hysteria, Frau Halzapfel began running from one to the other and back again, scattering tears, hugs, and kisses indiscriminately among children and adults alike. They bore it with dignity, without responding. None of them except Konstanz Weber and her father knew her, and Sepp had the feeling that even if they had, they would not have approved of such an undisciplined display of emotion in public.

Herr Weber let her indulge herself for half a minute more, than, as if correcting a child he knew would obey him instantly, told her dully, "That will be enough, Magda. There will be time for that later."

She immediately got control of herself and, nodding vigorously, wiping the seemingly endless stream of tears from her eyes, fell in behind the group, clutching her purse as ardently as she had each of the children.

Taking Herr Weber's arm, Sepp steered him out of the crowd toward the exit. The others followed, keeping close together.

" 'Surely, He shall deliver thee from the snare of the fouler, and from the noisome pestilence.' " Sepp looked back over his shoulder at the old man trudging feebly with the help of a cane on one side and Ulrich's arm on the other.

"My father is very old," Herr Weber said, explaining, not apologizing. "He finds comfort in the words of God."

"Does he understand where he's going?"

"No more than the children."

"What did you tell the children?"

"They will do as they are told and keep quiet." He looked at Sepp with unexpected sympathy. "You do not need to worry about the children. They will behave."

"Didn't Frau Halzapfel tell you not bring luggage?"

"If you were a policeman, Herr Bauer, and came across a family of ten traveling from Überdreibrücken to Berlin, would you not be suspicious if they had no baggage?"

Sepp smiled to himself. It was the sort of thing Emerich would have said. "We'll have to get rid of it. I'm sorry."

Herr Weber nodded. "I know. I have thought about it. Could we not check it in the baggage room?"

Sepp had no better idea. Three minutes were used up getting rid of the bags. When they were outside the terminal, Sepp led them off to one side, away from the traffic of people going in and out of the building. "I want to speak to the adults."

Emerich's father nodded and turned to his family. "Dietrich, Herr Bauer wishes to speak to the adults." He turned to Ulrich, who Sepp judged to be about Wolf's age. "You will hear, too, Ulrich." The boy nodded but expressed no emotion. He helped his grandfather to a bench and sat him down with great care. Unlike Emerich or his father, Ulrich was fair, but he had the same black eyes.

Dietrich said a few words to the children; then he, his wife, Emerich's mother, Magda, and Ulrich stepped forward and huddled around Sepp. "This is Josep Bauer," Herr Weber told them, "a friend of Emerich's. He will tell us what we are to do." He turned them over to Sepp.

"I want you to know what you are going to do, what to expect. We do not anticipate any trouble, but it is important that you do what I say and do it promptly and quietly." He looked around at the faces gazing at his, six sets of black eyes giving no sign of emotion, no reflection of the thoughts that lay behind them. He felt a deep admiration for them and wondered if he would have been able to remain so calm under the circumstances. "From here, we are going to the subway station, only a short walk. We will ride seven stops on the subway. Our stop is Schönhauser Allee. From there, we will walk one block. We will stop then, while I make a telephone call. We will then walk three more blocks. Our destination is an apartment house. When we arrive at the street in which the house is situated, it will be necessary to move quickly and quietly. The children and Grandfather Weber must be carried, except for the older girl."

"Roslyn," her father told him.

"I will carry Grandfather Weber. Herr Weber, you take the older boy. Dietrich, you take the baby. Ulrich, you take the younger boy."

He nodded. "Little Emerich."

"We will cross the street to the house and enter. It will not be necessary to run unless I tell you to. In the house there will be people who will take you to the cellar." He smiled for the first time since they had arrived. "One of them will be Emerich." A smile flickered over Ulrich's face, but there was no reaction from the others. "Do not stop, no matter how much you may want to. The stairwell will be badly lighted, so be careful going down the steps. There are handrails on both sides. There are twelve steps."

Herr Weber repeated the number to them, making certain they remembered.

"In the cellar is the entrance to a tunnel that goes under The Wall to a building in West Berlin." Sepp detected a barely perceptible reaction to this. Frau Weber's lips curled inward involuntarily. Dietrich's dark eyes narrowed and seemed to draw back under the protective overhang of his thick black eyebrows. His wife slipped her hand into his. "The entrance to the tunnel is a hole straight down, only two and a half meters to the bottom. There will be a ladder in the hole and a man to help you down.

"The two younger children and Grandfather Weber will go first. They will be put on a sled of sorts and pulled through the tunnel, so they will not have to crawl. The two older children can crawl, can't they?"

"Like monkeys," their father said fondly.

"Good. They will go directly behind you. I suggest—"

Sepp stopped abruptly as a man came out of the terminal and wandered slowly toward them, lighting a cigarette. He looked them over, shook the match out and threw it away, and continued on his way. Sepp's imagination took hold, and he had to fight it back. He had thought of all the faces he would imagine watching them. He had prepared himself to realize that he would be seeing SSD men everywhere. The man had obviously not been looking where he was going, lighting his cigarette. It was no more than that. When he was gone, Sepp went on.

"I suggest that you, Ernestine, go behind them to comfort them in case they become frightened."

"They will think it is a game." Her voice was surprisingly soft and melodious. Sepp thought she must sing beautifully, and he imagined her singing softly to her children.

"Dietrich, as soon as the two children and your grandfather are all in the tunnel, go after them and stay with them, crawling behind the sled. Is that clear?"

He nodded. "How big is the tunnel?"

"A meter square, seventy-six meters long. It will take about two minutes to crawl the length."

"Is it lighted?"

"Yes."

Dietrich's eyes widened in frank admiration, but he did not say anything.

"After the children, the women; then Ulrich; then you, Herr Weber."

"I want to be last," he said.

"After you, there are others to follow, so it is important to get through as quickly as possible."

Herr Weber looked around at his family to make sure they understood. He did not need to say anything. They all nodded, including his sister, Magda. Sepp was amused at how readily she fit in with the others. He looked at his watch. It was already ten fifteen. "We must hurry now. Are there any questions?"

He looked from Herr Weber to his wife, to Dietrich, to Dietrich's wife, to Ulrich, to Frau Halzapfel. As he scanned each face, he tried to understand the anxiety and fear that each of them must be feeling, and he tried to think of something to say that would help. All he could say was, "Put your trust in us. Everything will be all right." Then he remembered that he had not told them what to do in case anything went wrong. It was a harsh way to end his speech, but it had to be done.

"If for some reason we cannot use the tunnel, if there are police about, just follow me. Do as I say and you will be safe." He glanced at them once more and, hoping they all understood, said, "All right, let's go."

37

"WHAT time is it?"

"Ten fifty."

Bruno was standing in the shadow near the door to the downstairs apartment. Through the narrow window to the left of the door he could see up the street from where the Vopo would be coming back. Joachim was across the vestibule from him, crammed into a dark corner next to the other window, where he commanded a good view of the Edelweiss. Emerich should be in the corner, Bruno thought. Joachim is too broad. Emerich would fade into the plaster. But it might crumble and fall from the smell. Having showered and shaved himself, Bruno was keenly sensitive to Emerich's smell. In the closeness of the small hallway it had quickly pervaded the air. It was not much different from the stench of Bruno's compost heap in the dead heat of summer.

"Anything yet?" Emerich was directly behind the door to the street, a gray figure against the black wood, an ascetic Gothic saint cast in concrete set in front of a church entrance no longer in use. He was holding the submachine gun. Bruno had suggested that he keep it slung until it was needed, but Emerich would have no part of the idea. "I want it handy," he had said with dramatic foreboding.

"Take it easy," Joachim whispered. "There's still plenty of time."

A noise came from below. Emerich turned like a cat. Bruno could imagine his long hair on end.

"It's only Wolf," he told him.

Slowly, he turned back. His gun rattled mutely, like a train far off in the night. Bruno held his watch up to the light from the window. Ten fifty-one. They had been there since ten thirty. The Vopo had passed them at ten thirty-seven and a half and at ten forty-two. At ten fifty he should have turned and started back. He was due to pass again at ten fifty-eight.

Across the street a man came into Bruno's view. He watched him dispassionately. He was walking along in a leisurely way, looking straight ahead. He had a destination and knew the way. Bruno could sense when he came into Joachim's view. Joachim did not move, but there was a slight shift upward in the level of tension. He could feel it on his skin. When Joachim said nothing, Bruno knew the man had gone on down the street.

Bruno wiped his brow. It was not particularly hot, but he was sweating. The sweat was trickling down his spine. He rubbed his back gently, carefully against the door-jamb.

"What time is it now?" Emerich asked.

Bruno held his watch to the light. "Ten fifty-two."

"Nothing," Joachim intoned, anticipating his question. "Misery."

Bruno was surprised at his own calm. He had thought that he would be very nervous, not from fear that he might be harmed but from concern that he might do something stupid or fail in some way to do his appointed task. He had had no conception of what form that failure might take. He was pleased to find that his fears had been groundless. Perhaps a little sleep made the difference, he thought. I wonder how many medals are presented for bravery to men who had a little more sleep than their comrades. Fatigue, like hunger, can reduce a man's concern for his soul.

"What time is it?" Emerich again.

"Ten fifty-three."

"Misery, time goes slow."

38

"'AND the Lord said unto Satan, Whence cometh thou? Then Satan answered the Lord, and said, From going to and from in the earth, and from walking up and down in it.'"

Sepp wondered if the old man's quotations were always so apt. They were gathered together on the sidewalk outside the subway station in front of a store window. Even on this important shopping thoroughfare there were few people in the street. A light breeze lifted a piece of paper out of the gutter and sent it dancing down the sidewalk.

During the ride, the old man had sat rigidly in his seat, looking neither to the right nor the left, not speaking a word. The others had been frightened, especially Ernestine, Dietrich's wife. She had sat clutching her husband's arm until her fingers turned white. Sepp had dreaded the approach of each stop, afraid that they would all of one mind decide that they had had enough and get off. Only the children had seemed to enjoy it; Ulrich had been thrilled and had looked at everything his eyes could take in, grinning and gaping the entire time. Now they all looked relieved, much as if a storm had passed without the lightning striking their house. Ernestine even glanced at the dresses displayed in the store window.

Sepp looked at his watch and smiled. "Everyone here?"

"We are all here," Herr Weber said.

They started down the side street from Schönhauser Allee toward Vierickstrasse, moving only as fast as the old man could go. From there, The Wall was clearly visible, the white facade like a frozen waterfall in the night. Somebody murmured, and they all took it up.

503

"Is that—"

"The Wall."

It was the first sign of emotion Sepp had detected in Emerich's father. His face reflected the shame that Sepp had seen so often on the faces of tourists when they first saw The Wall. It was a shame that reached deep into a man's spirit and made him consider, if only briefly, whether his other works were grand enough to hide this ugly piece of architecture.

"Do we go so far?"

"No, not so far. Only to the second street. We turn north a block first, though."

Herr Weber gave him a sad, curious look, and Sepp realized he had misunderstood him. He was embarrassed and would have liked to explain, but his mind was narrowly occupied with the immediate task.

They came to the first street, where the telephone booth was located. He looked at his watch. It was ten fifty-seven. Up ahead, all was quiet. The street lamp at Vierickstrasse glowed in the silence like a question too private to be answered.

"Wait here," he said, and entered the booth. They stood in a clutch, not moving, not speaking. Herr Weber stood gazing at The Wall in the distance. Then he turned to the baby in Dietrich's arms and chucked him under the chin with his rough finger. The baby's eyes lit up, and he giggled.

Someone answered after the second ring. It sounded like the waiter Adolf, but Sepp couldn't be sure. "Edelweiss." The sound of laughter and clinking glasses revived the memory he had of the place.

"Would you ask if Herr Rosenkranz in there, please?"

"Rosenkranz?"

"Yes."

"One moment, please." He took the receiver away from his mouth, and Sepp could hear him paging Herr Rosenkranz. He called the name three times, then came back on. "There is no Rosenkranz here."

"All right. Thank you. *'Wiedersehen.*"

"*'Wiedersehen.*"

Sepp hung up and left the booth. Herr Weber gave him an inquiring look.

"Everything is in order."

39

"HERE he comes," Bruno whispered. "Right on time."

"Anything, Joachim?"

"Nothing."

Emerich slung the submachine gun on his back. "Tell me when he's out of sight."

"Shhh!"

Emerich held his breath. He could hear the Vopo's boots on the sidewalk. They sounded close enough to tread on his toes. Involuntarily, he curled his toes under Then the sound began to retreat off to the left, to fade, and then it was gone. He reached a hand up to the top hinge. It felt oily.

"One full minute yet," Bruno warned him.

Joachim stirred. "There's Ilse." He was not excited, only relieved.

Emerich grinned.

"She's gone back in."

"You're sure it was Ilse?"

"No, I'm not sure. I've never seen her, remember?"

"Well, did she look like Sepp's description?"

"Long blond hair, blue eyes, nice teeth, terrific figure. She has a little mole just under her left cheekbone."

Emerich transferred his impatience with time to Joachim. "Damn you," he snarled.

Joachim laughed quietly. "She had on a blue dress," he added reassuringly.

505

"Thirty seconds," Bruno announced.

"From what I could see," Joachim remarked, "it's no wonder Sepp wanted to get her out."

Emerich tried the hinge pin. It was loose and turned easily.

"You'd be better off taking out the bottom one first," Joachim suggested.

Emerich considered this and decided he was right. He bent down and tried the lower pin. It would not turn. Panic swept through him—and departed when he remembered the pliers in his hip pocket. He got them out.

"Fifteen seconds."

"Anyone in the street?"

"No one in my direction," Bruno said.

"All clear," Joachim said.

"Ten seconds."

Emerich fitted the jaws of the pliers around the hinge pin. Joachim got out the revolver, turned it over in his hand, and put it back in his pocket.

"Five seconds."

Joachim started counting, "Four . . . three . . . two . . . one . . . blast off."

"Very funny." Emerich twisted the pliers and pulled. The pin came put without a whimper. He put his weight against the door to keep it in place and pulled at the pin in the upper hinge. It came out three-quarters of the way by hand. He had to use the pliers to get it all the way out. Bruno and Joachim put their hands up to the door while Emerich began prying it off the hinges with the pliers. When it was partway free, Joachim got his fingers under the bottom of it.

"Make it fast," he said. "This is going to be heavy."

Emerich pried it off the rest of the way. Joachim grunted as the weight of the door shifted from the hinges to him. Emerich quickly got a grip under the hinge and, together, they opened it inward, far enough to get it out, and set it down noiselessly. Joachim got up, squeezing and shaking his fingers.

Bruno left for the cellar, taking care to leave the cellar door open.

Emerich unslung his weapon, and he and Joachim went out onto the stoop under the overhang. The night air was cool, with a breeze dusting the street. Emerich pressed himself up against the wall, his back in the direction from which the Vopo would come. Joachim stood against the window facing the street. He took the revolver out of his pocket and released the safety. The click seemed unjustly loud. In the distance Emerich could hear the night sounds of the city, a muted pulsation that seemed only to emphasize the poignancy of his loneliness. Not even Joachim's measured breathing gave him comfort.

If they know, Emerich thought, if Konrad Möss has informed, will they come now, or will they wait for Sepp and the others? They could be hiding anywhere—in those dark doorways like us, on the rooftops, inside the apartments across the street. Why are all the lights out in those apartments? *Someone* living there must stay up this late.

How much time had passed? A minute? Two? Two certainly. The urge to look around the corner of the recess was strong, and as time dragged its cumbrous bag of seconds up the steep hill of each minute, it became compulsive. Not able to see, Emerich strained to hear, trying to filter out the secret whisperings between the breeze and the cobbles, the thrum of the city, Joachim's exhalations; to concentrate solely on detecting the languid scrape of jackboots coming up the sidewalk. Joachim held his watch close to his face, tilted to catch the fine gauze of light that hung over the darkness. He held up one finger. What did that mean? One minute has passed or one to go? It must mean one to go. Misery, how long a minute can be!

It's too quiet. Everything has been too easy.

You haven't done anything yet.

The door came open too easily, not a squeak, not a hitch. I know they're here, I can feel them, like humidity in the air. Misery, where *is* that Vopo?

It might have been only harsh whispering, an argument with the wind, perhaps footsteps in another street, the wind lifting the sound over the rooftops. It might have been either, but he knew it was the Vopo coming back. The sound emerged from the debris of sounds like a rat sticking its nose out of a trash heap. Emerich's stomach muscles contracted. He moved to grip the gun more tightly and found he was already holding it as tighlty as he could. The footsteps came more loudly, enumerating the seconds like a pendulum. Emerich looked at Joachim to see

whether he was ready. His arm was cocked and held close
against his body, the revolver poking out of his ribs like
a mutated appendage. His thumb curled over the cylinder
in a sinewy caress.

Emerich pressed against the wall. The stone abraded
his shoulder blades. His body seemed like one great ear,
vibrating with the sound of the boots coming closer and
closer, analyzing each component—the insulated thud of
the rubber heel, the grinding of minute particles of dirt
under the leather sole, the dragging scuff as the toe
reluctantly lost its contact with the concrete. Then he was
there, directly before him.

Joachim's hand shot through the air, and the Vopo was
suddenly up off the ground and under the overhang.
Emerich jammed the base of his gun under his chin. It
was a very white chin. "One word and you're dead."

Joachim's hand was clasped firmly across the Vopo's
mouth. His eyes bulged like marbles ready to pop out
of a boy's shooting hold. Emerich took his weapon.
Joachim jerked him around and pushed him through the
open door, across the vestibule, and through the open
cellar door. Emerich slung the Vopo's weapon with one
hand, keeping his weapon trained on him with the other.
Joachim jabbed the Vopo in the back with the revolver
and, holding his other hand over his mouth, started him
down the steps. Wolf was waiting at the bottom.

Emerich stood watching until he was halfway down,
then closed the cellar door behind them.

40

JOACHIM passed the revolver to Wolf. "He's all yours. If he doesn't do as you say instantly, shoot him. He's only in the way, as it is."

The Vopo was only a couple of years older than Wolf, of average size, about half a head shorter. His uniform was too big for him; the trousers bagged at the knees too much, and the sleeves of the jacket came down almost to his knuckles. He looked pale and frightened. His eyes darted back and forth between the two of them.

"You won't give me any trouble, will you."

He tried to speak, but his words stuck in his throat. He shook his head emphatically.

Joachim gave Wolf's shoulder a reassuring squeeze and bounded up the stairs two at a time. Bruno stuck his head over the edge of the vertical shaft. He studied the Vopo for a minute. "Come peacefully and nothing will happen to you."

Wolf motioned toward the hole, and the Vopo virtually sprang across the room.

"Move slowly!" Wolf hissed. His heart was everywhere in his body all at once. He swallowed hard.

Bruno went down the ladder. The Vopo turned around and started climbing down. Wolf stood over the hole watching him, the revolver trained on him. When he was down, Bruno motioned him into the tunnel, and he did as he was told. Wolf hurriedly climbed down the ladder and squatted next to Bruno, who was gripping the Vopo's

509

coattails. It struck Wolf as funny, and he smiled. Bruno
let go, and Wolf poked the Vopo's seat with the gun. He
crawled gingerly over the sled, as if he were afraid to
touch it, and started forward.

As they emerged at the other end, Georg got up out
of the way and pressed himself against the wall of the
incline. He stared at the Vopo as he and Wolf got to their
feet and passed by him up the incline. Wolf gave Georg
a big smile. "One through, sixteen to go."

Georg smiled weakly and quickly resumed his vigil just
inside the tunnel entrance.

Wolf directed the Vopo to the second pile of earth.
"Sit down."

The Vopo obeyed quickly. He glanced up at Wolf like
a punished dog. Wolf noticed for the first time that the
fellow was shaking uncontrollably and there were tears
in his eyes.

"We aren't going to hurt you," he assured him. "Just
don't move from there and you'll be safe. But I'm warning
you, if you do move, I'll shoot you. One of you shot me
once, so I won't hesitate to shoot you."

"I . . . I won't move. I promise. Just don't shoot me.
Please don't shoot me."

"I said I wouldn't—if you don't move."

"I won't move. I won't move. See? I'm not moving."

Wolf backed away, holding the gun pointed at him,
reaching his arm out behind him until he felt the hand-
rail of the stairs. He moved along it, felt the first step with
his foot and sat down.

"Are we in West Berlin?"

"And don't talk, either!"

He put his hand over his mouth to show he would
obey.

"Yes," Wolf said, "we're in West Berlin."

The Vopo dropped his hand away, revealing a big
smile.

41

"**W**HERE *are* they? Misery, where *are* they?"

Joachim gave Emerich's arm a sympathetic squeeze. He kept his eyes on the retreating figure of the other Vopo. He was just coming to the end of the first block. It was the longest of the three. He stopped at the curb, glanced off to the left where he could probably see The Wall, then stepped down into the street and continued on his ambling gait. Joachim looked away long enough to glance in the opposite direction, toward the corner on the other side of the street around which Sepp was supposed to come with Emerich's family. There was no sign of them. He scanned the dark buildings across the street, down as far as the light of the *Gasthaus*. They're in there now. It made him feel odd. He tried to visualize them, but their faces would not come into focus. He could imagine his father cleaning his glasses, breathing on them and rubbing each lens carefully, thoroughly, with a clean handkerchief. What are they drinking? Cognac, probably. Mama would have it with water; Papa, straight.

Lord, I think I'm excited.

Emerich shifted his weapon to the other hand. "They should have been here by now."

"They'll come."

"What time is it?"

"Four minutes after."

"Six minutes left."

511

Joachim returned to his observation of the Vopo. He was well along in the second block. *If Sepp doesn't move his tail, we'll never make it. I wouldn't want to have to fire this contraption.*

Down the street, a man came around the corner on the opposite side, a block away. He was walking fast, moving in their direction. As he passed the window of the Edelweiss, the light fell on him.

Joachim's heart stopped. A Vopo. For a moment he could only stare at the telltale visored cap, Sam Browne belt, and jackboots. As he came closer, sometimes breaking into a dogtrot, he unslung his weapon and held it ready at port arms. Joachim nudged Emerich and pointed with his head. Instinctively, they drew back into the shadows.

Joachim raised his gun.

"Don't fire!" Emerich whispered. "Misery, don't fire."

The Vopo stopped directly across the street from them. A voice from the right startled him. He jumped backward into the entryway of the apartment building. Joachim looked toward the noise. "It's Sepp."

Emerich did not say anthing.

"Let's shoot the son of a bitch."

"Wait."

"They'll get Sepp."

He could see them clearly now, Sepp out in front, carrying someone, the others strung out behind, three men, three women, and a child. The men were carrying children.

"Konrad Möss." Emerich's voice floated into the air, neither a shout nor a whisper. Sepp halted. The others froze behind him.

"Konrad Möss."

Joachim's nerves stood on end. "What the hell's going on?"

"Don't shoot, damn you," Emerich hissed. "Don't shoot unless I do."

The Vopo stepped out onto the sidewalk. He glanced once toward Joachim and Emerich, then turned toward Sepp and the Webers. They were only five meters apart.

Emerich raised his gun.

Joachim fingered the trigger nervously. *God, don't make me fire this thing.*

The Vopo started across the street, and Sepp followed. The others came in their tracks. The Vopo was the first to reach the house. He was grinning. Gingerly, he reached out and turned away the bore of Joachim's gun. "Stolen property?"

Sepp came, breathing noisily, carrying Emerich's grandfather. Without stopping, he sidled through the door. Then came the three women, a boy, the three men, each carrying a child. Not one paused to speak to Emerich, to touch him, even to nod. They moved like phantoms hurrying back to their sepulchers lest the enemy dawn find them still about.

The Vopo eyed Joachim and Emerich with amused curiosity. Joachim eyed him back. Skinny little kid. Who the hell was he, anyway? He stepped back onto the sidewalk and gazed down the street toward the other Vopo. Joachim put his head around the corner.

"He'll be turning around in a couple of minutes," Konrad Möss said. "Let's get out of here."

"More to come," Emerich said.

Joachim looked at Emerich. He wondered how he felt. "How did you know this character was on our side?"

"Sepp. Sepp told me."

"Why didn't somebody tell *me?*"

"Later, Joachim." He put a hand to his eyes. Joachim saw that there were tears there and turned away.

Footsteps sounded behind them, and Sepp came out. He quickly put his hand in Konrad Möss's and without a word hurried across the street. Joachim watched him until he entered the Edelweiss; then he looked down the street. The Vopo was too far away to tell how much farther he had to go. Joachim looked at his watch. "Lord, it's ten after."

"He'll be turning," Konrad Möss said.

No one said anything. Joachim squinted through the veil of light and shadow, trying to discern the second when the Vopo turned.

Konrad Möss slung his weapon. "I'll be with you. Don't leave me behind. And stay put, no matter what I do." He raced up the street to the right, stopped at the corner, turned, and then, as if he were out for a Sunday stroll, started ambling back toward them.

Joachim started breathing again. He understood. When

the other Vopo turned, he would see what he thought was his partner coming toward him as usual. "That fellow has a brain," he said.

Emerich said nothing.

The door to the Edelweiss opened. Sepp came out, then Ilse. Joachim peered around the corner. The Vopo had turned. A woman came out next, carrying a briefcase. At first Joachim thought it must be Georg's mother, but she looked too young for that. Then he saw his own mother and father. He stared at them curiously, as if he were seeing them for the first time. His father drew the door closed behind him. Joachim knew something was wrong, but he could not bring his mind to bear on what it was. As they passed in front of the *Gasthaus* window, the light was reflected from his father's glasses. Joachim smiled.

Sepp stopped. He was looking up the street at Konrad Möss. He glanced in the opposite direction. For a moment, consternation was clear on his face, then he understood. Instead of coming across the street on a diagonal, he led them straight up the sidewalk until he was directly across from the house. Konrad Möss appeared from the right. As they started to cross the street, he went toward them unslinging his weapon.

"Don't run! Walk fast!"

They obeyed him, coming toward the entryway at a fast walk. Konrad Möss walked beside them like a guard escorting prisoners. Just as they reached the curb, Joachim heard a noise behind him. He and Emerich wheeled at the same time. Georg came out.

"What are you doing here?" Emerich hissed.

He was gasping for breath.

Sepp gained the shelter of the entryway. He saw Georg but said nothing and kept on going. Ilse followed, then the woman with the briefcase.

Georg moaned and fell back against the wall. Emerich put out a hand and caught him before he fell. Joachim was staring in astonishment when he felt a hand on his face. His mother's eyes met his—sad, proud eyes. Then she was gone. His father nodded to him and followed her.

"Is that all?" Konrad Möss was no longer smiling.

Joachim nodded vaguely.

"Let's get out of here. That fellow down there is getting nervous." He started toward the door.

"No!" It was Georg.

"Who's this?" Konrad Möss muttered impatiently.

"My mother and father! Where are my mother and father?" Georg jabbed a finger toward the inside. "*She* wasn't supposed to come! My mother and father!"

Joachim suddenly realized what had been wrong. "What happened?"

Sepp appeared in the doorway. "Come on! Hurry!"

Georg seized his arm. "Where are my mother and father? Where are my mother and father? Where are they?"

Sepp pried his hands away. "They aren't coming," he said quietly, "I couldn't convince them."

Konrad Möss stepped in under the overhang. "That Vopo's on the run."

"Let's go," Emerich said. He darted into the vestibule. Konrad Möss went after him.

Georg wrenched his hands free and backed out onto the sidewalk. "No! I'm not going until my mother and father come. You said they were coming! You tricked me. You brought *her* instead." His face was streaming with tears, and he kept bending over, clasping his hands between his legs as if he were in terrible pain. "You said they were coming! You said it!" He screamed, "*Where are they?*"

Sepp leaped forward. He got one hand on Georg's arm, but Georg was too fast for him. He twisted away and ran out into the middle of the street. Sepp started after him, but Joachim caught hold of him and pulled him back into the doorway. "For God's sake, come on!"

From inside, Bruno called out. "Sepp! Joachim!"

Joachim put his head around the corner. The Vopo was running toward them, coming fast, only half a block away, carrying his gun at the ready.

"Come *on*, Georg!" Sepp cried.

Georg stood his ground, trembling like a frightened animal, panting, his fingers clawing at his shirt.

Joachim brought the gun up to eye level, sighted several meters in front of the Vopo, and fired.

"Sepp! Joachim!"

He opened his eyes. The Vopo was gone.

Georg stood staring with terror. The sound of the shots

went echoing through Joachim's head. The world was a
great hall filled with their stentorian rattle.

Georg turned and raced up the street.

"Georg! Come back! Georg!"

He kept running, his arms flailing wildly. He stumbled,
got up, stumbled again, then got up and kept running.

"Gee-oorg! *Geeeooorrrg!*"

42

"**H**OW old do you judge this tree to be, Papa?"

Konstanz Weber pushed his felt hat back on his head
and studied it with the eyes of a man who had a sixth
sense about things that grow in the earth. "Sixty years."

"Bruno thinks it's older. He talked about it as if it
were a hundred years old."

"He has a feeling for trees," his father said cryptically.
Wilfred Komanski came out onto the patio and saw
them. "I thought I would be the only one up."

"God's greetings."

"Good morning," Emerich said politely, only because
his father was there.

He came down the steps into the garden, taking short,
stiff-legged steps, as if his knees had trouble bending.
"People sleep too much. Can't understand it. Life is too
short; there's too much to do."

Emerich's father nodded.

"What are you two up to?"

Emerich did not like Herr Komanski. He had not
liked him the day he met him in the warehouse, and he
had no reason to feel different about him now. He was
disappointed that Bruno had apparently become friends
with the old buzzard.

"How old do you think this tree is?" Konstanz Weber
asked him.

Komanski seemed startled by the question, but inter-

ested. He walked around it twice, examining the bark,
its girth, the branches.

"Fifty, perhaps sixty years."

Emerich was impressed.

"You are not a city man, Herr Komanski."

"Half and half."

His father grunted, whether approvingly or disapprov-
ingly, Emerich was not sure. Herr Komanski did not feel
obliged to explain what he meant by "half and half,"
and Emerich's father did not seem to need an explanation. Emerich wondered if all old men were like these
two.

The three of them strolled down the path to the end
of the garden without speaking. His father stopped to
turn up a rose. Dew lay on its petals like crystal on
velvet.

"What are you going to do?" Komanski asked him.

"Do?"

"You and your family. How are you going to live?"

"We'll get along," Emerich said.

"I asked your father."

"My son answered well."

"Go to work in a factory, I suppose," Komanski concluded with ill-concealed distaste.

"Perhaps that. Until we can save enough to buy land."
He let the rose go and looked at Komanski. "We will
have land again."

The sun broke over the garden wall and fell in among
the flowers. They continued to stroll.

"Would you be interested in working land while you
pay for it?"

Even though his father showed no sign of emotion,
Emerich knew him well enough to recognize that he was
interested.

"I have some land," Komanski continued. "A hundred
hectares in Franconia."

"A hundred hectares!" Emerich blurted out.

His father gave him an admonishing glance.

"That's a big piece of land," Komanski said defensively.
"That's not a piece of land to sneer at."

"He was not sneering, Herr Komanski."

The old man grunted. "Well, what do you say?"

Konstanz Weber stopped and looked at the man. Emerich was surprised to notice that they were the same height. He had never thought of his father as being so short.

"What do I say to what?"

"Damnation. I thought I said what! Would you be interested in farming my land?"

"You mentioned buying it, too," Emerich reminded him.

"We have no money, Herr Komanski. Our wealth was our land."

He waved a frail hand impatiently. "I know all that. I said you could buy it by working it. It's lying fallow, nobody to work it. Can't find competent people these days. It's been a while since I worked on a farm. The you, naturally. I wouldn't want you to farm my land if I thought you were a fool."

Emerich was becoming interested, too. He did not trust Herr Komanski—not a bit—but he knew his father was a match for any man in a business transaction.

"To farm, one must have equipment, seed, animals, a house and barn."

"All that's there—except the animals and seed. There's a fine house in the village—biggest one of the lot. Twelve rooms. A barn, too. What's a farmhouse without a barn? There's trees on it—an oak as big as this one, with the branches hanging over the roof like it was in love with that old house."

Emerich thought of the two thousand marks he had saved. With two thousand marks they could buy seed, some geese, a few piglets, even a milk cow.

"There's a tractor—only two years old. All the rigging —plow, planter, harrow, whatever else they use nowadays. It's been awhile since I worked on a farm. The last tenants I had—last season, it was—bought the things." He snorted with disgust. "*They* weren't peasants. Passed themselves off as such, but, damnation, they didn't know wheat from oats. Had to get rid of them."

"Planting time is long past," Konstanz Weber said.

"I know, I know. Lost a whole year because I couldn't find competent people. That's the big problem in business today—finding competent people. Oh, there are a million people looking for a paycheck, but only a fraction of them looking for work."

"We would have no income from the land for over a year."

"I figured that out, too. I could advance you money to live on and to buy seed and stock. Then, when you harvest next year, you can pay me back—not all in one year, of course. You'd never get ahead that way, but let's say in five years."

Emerich's excitement was opening like the roses to the warmth of the sun. He had forgotten his antipathy toward the old man and could see only the beauty of the vision he was unfolding for them.

"A hundred hectares of land," his father mused. "It would take my sons' lifetimes to pay for that much land."

Komanski performed a nervous little step, scattering pebbles into the flower beds. "I told you, you pay for the land by working it."

"Sharing the profits with you."

"No, no, no. Just by working it. That's what I told you."

Konstanz Weber looked at his son, his black eyes as big as the buttons on his suit coat. He dared not look back at the old man. In a dry, almost distracted tone, he said, "Do you mean to say, Herr Komanski, that as long as we work the land, it is ours?"

"Now isn't that what I said at the start?" He shook his head. "Maybe I'm getting old and don't make myself clear anymore, or maybe you aren't the man I thought you were."

The black eyes narrowed, then a rare smile widened Konstanz Weber's thick lips. He turned to the old man, still smiling. "You understand what you are doing." It was a statement, not a question.

"Perfectly."

There was moment of silence, the kind of silence Emerich's mother always called the voice of God.

"Why, Herr Komanski? Why do you want to do this?"

At first he waved it off, did not want to discuss it. Then, as they strolled back toward the patio, he said, "I was born in that house, brought up on the land, in the way of the land. We didn't own it all; no, we had a big mortgage on it. Lost it in 1930. You remember those years, Herr Weber."

Emerich's father nodded gravely. "Much was lost in those years, Herr Komanski."

"The family broke up, fell apart, scattered around in the grimy factory neighborhoods of a dozen cities. I headed north to Berlin. It killed my father. He died of a broken heart. I believe it." He glanced at them to see if they were scoffing at the notion. They were not. "I watched him die, day by day, like a plant dies if you don't water it. There's no worse way to die, I tell you."

He had to stop to keep his anguish from getting out of control. Emerich felt a strange, detached compassion for the man. He could not yet allow himself to admit that the source of the feeling was within himself; rather, it was as if it had been transplanted to him and was trying to take root.

"I vowed one day I would have that land." Komanski gave them a faint smile. "Nothing fires ambition like poverty and suffering once you've known the good life."

"You fulfilled your vow," Emerich said.

He nodded vigorously, his ample shock of white hair jouncing like a skirt in the wind. "I did, my boy, I did. I have the land, the house, the tree that stands beside it. . . . Oh," he remembered excitedly, "there's a stream with trout, beautiful trout, plentiful and delicious. It meanders through the land like it owned the place." He looked a little sheepish. "If you don't mind, I'd like to be able to do a little fishing there once in a while. There's a brake of willows in a bend where I used to play when I was a boy. I go there now to fish." He looked inquiringly into Konstanz Weber's eyes, the sun glinting on his glasses. "You fish." It was more a statement than a question.

"When there is time."

"Good. You'll go fishing with me. Don't like to fish alone. Usually take Clemnitz with me, but he hates it. Oh, he pretends he likes it, but he hates it. City fellow, down to the marrow." He folded his hands behind his narrow back and considered the configuration of the pebbles in the path.

"The house is furnished—best furniture I could find in Erlangen. Maybe not your wife's taste. She can change what she doesn't want. I just didn't like the old place standing empty. Ghosts take over an empty house."

"You have no sons, Herr Komanski?"

"Daughters, only daughters. Married to city fellows. Can't even get one of 'em to go fishing. Now I ask you, what kind of man is it who doesn't like to fish?"

They had reached the patio and were standing at the confluence of the paths at the foot of the steps. Moss roses were blooming along the patio retaining wall. Komanski bent over with considerable effort, singled one out with his shaking fingers, plucked it, and stuck in it his lapel buttonhole. "Well?"

When his father did not answer immediately, Emerich's heart sank like a rock in water.

"You are a generous man, Herr Komanski."

"Nothing generous about it," he snapped. "Can't stand to see the land neglected. Land needs discipline; it needs a man who understands how to control it, make it do what it was meant to do—produce and look proud doing it."

"And you think I am that kind of man?"

"Don't you?"

For the second time that morning, Emerich saw his father smile. "I will visit your land, Herr Komanski."

"Good! That's good sense. Can't buy land without rubbing a little between your fingers, getting the smell of it."

"My sons, my wife . . ."

Komanski took an envelope out of his inner pocket. "Here's tickets to Nuremberg for everybody. Plane leaves at one o'clock. I got one-way tickets. When you see the place, you won't want to come back. Soil like ground velvet. My assistant will meet us, and we'll drive to the airport. He's got the papers all drawn up—at least, he better have. Has two days and six lawyers to do it. A man can't pull his ear nowadays without checking with a lawyer. Damned nuisance. More laws than people."

Bruno came out tying his bathrobe. "Wilfred, you chatter like a bluejay. The whole house is up because of you."

"Time they were getting up, anyway. Why aren't you working on my painting?"

"I am accustomed to having breakfast before I start work." He smiled. "Good morning, Herr Weber, Emerich. Forgive my discourtesy. This man brings out my worst nature. I hope you slept well." He breathed deeply. "Ah! It looks as though it will be a glorious day. Glorious."

Emerich's father looked up into the sky. The sun was well above the garden wall and was flickering through the branches of the tree. "God gives us glorious days, Herr Balderbach. Good men fill them with kindness."

43

SUNLIGHT poked through the windows cautiously, bringing with it the song of Frau Meizner's canaries. Joachim looked up at the clock on Wolf's table. It was just past six. His arm was hanging over one side of the bed, and he suddenly realized it was asleep. He raised it awkwardly and began rubbing it. Slowly the blood began to circulate. Through the door came the sound of dishes being placed on the table, and he remembered that it was not Wolf out there, but his mother. He sat up. A crick in his back made him groan. He felt as though he had just finished a wrestling match, not a night's sleep—and had lost, at that.

Wolf was sprawled out over three-quarters of the bed, still deep in sleep. A smile kept trying to insinuate itself on his lips, but something in his dream was preventing it. Joachim shook him. He opened one eye, then closed it.

"Get up, you bed hog."

He grunted.

Joachim swatted his buttocks. He jumped and scuttled over to the far side of the bed.

"You are a swine of a capitalist, little brother."

Wolf yawned. "What time is it?" His voice sounded far off under the sheet.

"Six o'clock."

Wolf groaned. Then he said, "Why am I a swine of a capitalist?"

"You have an overdeveloped sense of ownership."

Wolf pulled the sheet away from his face. "In what way?"

"I considered myself fortunate at three o'clock this morning when I woke up and found I had a quarter of the bed—and again at four o'clock, and at five o'clock. . . ."

Wolf pulled the sheet back over his face and said something. Joachim didn't understand.

"What did you say?"

He uncovered again. "I said, Uschi never complained."

"She probably didn't have the energy by the time you got through with her." He got up and stretched. "Oh, I have more aches than a constipated elephant."

Wolf snickered.

Joachim noticed his pajama bottoms were loose around the waist. It was months since he had worn them. "I lost weight in that damned tunnel."

"You were getting too fat, anyway."

"There's not a gram of fat on my bones."

"It's all settled between your ears."

Joachim sighed. The docile, obsequious Wolf he had once known was no more. Maybe it's good Mama and Papa crossed over, after all, he thought. I'd probably be doing the cooking and housekeeping in a matter of days if they hadn't.

"Joachim! Come! Breakfast is ready." His mother's voice sounded extraordinarily normal, as if the past seven months had never been, or, at best, had been a long, exciting dream.

"Coming!" He finished combing his hair and looked himself over in the mirror. His face was free of blemishes. The tunnel had not changed his good looks, nor his satisfaction with them. He smiled for himself and winked at his reflection.

Wolf and his father were already seated at the table. Joachim kissed his mother and sat down. "Like old times."

"Yes," his father said without enthusiasm, "like old times."

"Papa, you promised me last night you wouldn't worry anymore. Wolf and I will work. We'll manage."

"Yes, yes, I know. All you have said is good, and I am proud of you both for having such an attitude."

"You'll have your new practice going in no time."

"It takes years to build a practice."

"You're exaggerating, and you know it."

"I am not exaggerating," his father said sternly. "I did it once, before you were born, mind you. I believe I know better than you what it takes to build a practice."

Frau Lentz sat down and poured Joachim's coffee. "Let's not argue, not now."

"We are not arguing, Mama," Dr. Lentz said. "We are discussing. There is a difference."

"I'm going to get a construction job," Wolf said. "It pays very well."

"You both must return to school. That is the most important thing. I will start investigating today. I am certain I will find a position—not a regular practice; that is out of the question, I know, but some kind of work. The sick are always with us. Isn't that what the Bible says?"

"That's the poor, Papa," Wolf said.

"The poor, too. The sick and the poor. Mama, more coffee."

"Anyway," Wolf said hesitantly, "I'll be needing some money for myself."

"For yourself? What for?"

Wolf looked to Joachim for help and, as he did, decided he didn't need it. "I have a friend . . . a new friend. . . ."

"A girl friend," Frau Lentz realized.

"Her name is Uschi," Wolf said.

Dr. Lentz sat back and looked his younger son over. "Her father's a banker," Joachim put in.

Dr. Lentz looked at Joachim with growing curiosity. "Wolf has a girl friend?"

"And you and Mama need some clothes," Wolf added quickly.

"Clothes? Why do we need clothes? We have clothes."

"You can't wear the same clothes every day."

"This is my best suit. Perhaps we will buy Mama a dress or two."

"I will manage until Papa is situated," she said.

"Mama, I have almost a thousand marks saved. Surely we can get you a few things."

"A toothbrush," his father agreed, "and a comb."

"At least some underwear—and socks."

Dr. Lentz wavered. "Perhaps underwear and socks—for the sake of proper hygiene."

Joachim was becoming exasperated. "You are letting your pride interfere with good sense, Papa."

"Mama, listen to your son. Seven months out of the nest, not yet twenty-one years old, and he is counseling his father about pride and good sense."

Frau Lentz spoke in her unaltered, quiet, conciliatory way. "Joachim, you must understand that Papa and I do not intend to let you and Wolf support us."

"But you supported us all these years. Why can't we help out now for a while?"

"Yes, yes, of course you will help. You have already provided us with a temporary home. We are grateful."

"We are grateful," Dr. Lentz said, "but we are not the kind of people who can live off their children's labor and feel comfortable. It is not our way. And as we have said, you both must finish your schooling."

Joachim was about to retort when the doorbell rang.

"Who can that be at this hour of the morning?"

"Bad news," his mother surmised, "only bad news comes at odd hours."

"Mama," Joachim said admonishingly. He got up and went to answer it. Going down the stairs, he wondered whether his mother might not be right. Maybe Curzmann . . . He opened the street door. A man in his fifties carrying a physician's bag was there.

"Is Dr. Lentz at home?"

"Dr. Lentz? Yes, he's here."

"May I speak with him? I am Dr. Frey."

"Yes, of course. Come in." Joachim opened the door wide and let him in. "How did you know Dr. Lentz was here?" He looked the man over. He seemed nervous and in a hurry.

"That probably does surprise you. I was told two days ago that he was to cross over."

"Oh? Who told you that?"

"The Foundation for Refugee Assistance. You've heard of it, I'm sure."

"I can't say that I have." They went up stairs together. "Do you have some identification, Doctor?"

"Ah, you are cautious. It's only natural, of course." He took out his wallet and showed Joachim his identity card and a card showing his membership in the medical association. "You can call the association if you like."

"No. I'm satisfied. I hope I didn't insult you."

"Not at all. In your position you must be cautious. You're the doctor's son, I take it?"

"Yes. I'm Joachim." They shook hands and entered the apartment. "Papa, this is Dr. Frey. He wants to talk to you. Dr. Frey, may I present my mother, my father, and my brother, Wolfgang."

Wolf and his father got up and shook hands. His father gave Joachim an inquiring look. Joachim hunched his shoulders to show he had no idea what the man wanted.

"I am sorry to disturb you at breakfast, but I had instructions to come as early as feasible." Dr. Frey looked around. "May I sit down?"

"Won't you have coffee with us, Doctor?"

"That would be splendid. I ran off so early I haven't had any yet. It is not good to ignore dietary habits at our age, eh, Dr. Lentz?"

"I quite agree, Dr. Frey."

"You must consider it rude of me to call at such an early hour, but, as I said, I had instructions to do so."

Frau Lentz returned from the kitchen with a cup and saucer and poured coffee for him.

"I take it black, thank you." He sipped it. "Ah. I was afraid I would have to make my rounds without my coffee. It ruins my bedside manner to go without my coffee." He chuckled.

"Dr. Frey represents the Foundation for—"

"Refugee Assistance. You've heard of it, I'm sure."

"We have been in the *Sektor*."

"Yes, yes. Stupid of me."

"Are we refugees?" Dr. Lentz spoke the word as if it were pejorative.

"Oh, yes you are definitely refugees. The foundation would not have sent me if you were not classified as refugees." He took an envelope out of his pocket and handed it to Dr. Lentz. "I am to give you this. You must understand that it is not a gift in the usual sense, not at all. It is compensation for the loss you suffered by crossing into West Berlin."

"What is it?" Wolf asked.

The doctor looked surprised. "Why, money, of course. To get you on your feet. To live with until your fees start coming in."

"Fees? What fees? I don't have a practice."

"Open it, Papa."

Dr. Lentz slit the flap and pulled a check out of the envelope. He stared at it for a moment, then slipped it back into the envelope and handed it back to Dr. Frey. "I cannot accept this."

"But why not?"

"It is charity."

"It is not charity. I am to make that quite clear. It is compensation."

"It is charity."

"You do not believe in charity?"

"Not when I am the recipient."

"Then I suppose you will not accept a practice, either."

"A practice?"

"A very good practice. Dr. Erwin Teitz, a most respected physician in Spandau, died last week. God rest his soul. His practice is available."

Dr. Lentz showed hesitant interest. "Internal medicine?"

"Internal medicine."

"In Spandau?"

"You know Spandau?"

"From before the war." He was distracted. "Internal medicine, you say."

"Yes, yes, internal medicine."

"In Spandau."

Frau Lentz put her hand on her husband's arm. "Don't say no, Papa."

"I would be able to look into it a little?"

"As much as you like. I can make the arrangements today if you wish."

Dr. Lentz looked from his wife to Wolf and Joachim. Joachim gave him a smile and nodded vigorously.

"Very well, I will look into it."

"Good, good. I think you will find it a very interesting situation. I will make the arrangements and telephone you this afternoon. Will that be convenient for you?"

"That will be fine."

"Excellent." Dr. Frey glanced at his watch. "I must hurry." He quickly gulped some coffee. "You really ought to take the money, Dr. Lentz. The foundation will be distressed."

"I don't need the money, Doctor." He looked at Wolf and Joachim and winked. "I have two sons who are quite able to help me out until I am, as you say, back on my feet."

Dr. Frey got up. Dr. Lentz rose and shook his hand. "You must thank the foundation for its kindness."

"Of course. However, they will be distressed about the money."

"I am sure they will be able to put it to good use."

Dr. Frey took up his bag. "I'm sorry to rush like this— in and out—but you know very well what a doctor's life is like. Until this afternoon, Dr. Lentz."

"Until this afternoon."

When he was gone, they all sat down again. Joachim looked at his father and saw that the fear that had been lingering with him was gone.

"Well," Dr. Lentz said. He took off his glasses and began cleaning them.

"Why didn't you take the money, Papa?" Wolf asked.

"How much was it?" Joachim asked.

"Ten thousand marks, and I did not take it because, as I told Dr. Frey, I have two sons. What does a man need with ten thousand marks when he has two fine sons to help him out?"

Joachim swallowed hard. Ten tousand marks! he thought. What a glorious time I could have along the Kudamm with ten thousand marks!

"Papa," Wolf said, "if you're going to have a practice, there is something we ought to buy today, if we can."

"What's that?"

"A bed for Joachim."

Joachim laughed. His mother and father did not know why he was laughing, but they began to laugh, too. Soon all four of them were laughing as none of them had laughed in a long time.

44

BEFORE the last of the good light was gone, Bruno was able to finish the shadowing on the arms. He stood back, wiping the brush clean, studying the result. The painting looked half-done, which meant that it was three-quarters done. The conception, the studies, the sketches—all were behind him.

The door opened and Frieda came in. She was wearing a yellow dress. He could not recall the last time he had seen her in yellow. It made her look younger, somehow. She stood beside him and contemplated it. There was the smell of spring about her.

"What do you think?"

She looked up at him, a look of mild astonishment on her face.

"What's wrong with it?"

"Do you know this is the first time you have ever asked my opinion of your work?"

He grunted. "Nonsense." He wondered if it were true. "Well?"

She turned back to the painting. "You know it's good."

"Only 'good'?"

She smiled. "You're not going to become an egotist after all these years?"

"Oh, I might. I'll need some bad traits so I can mellow properly in my old age."

She laughed. "Dear Bruno, you'll never grow old. I'm not altogether certain you've ever advanced to middle age."

"Oh, I have, I have," he said wistfully. "No young man could make a painting as great as this one is going to be."

She clasped her hands together. "Oh, my. Oh, *my*."

He laughed and put his brush in the rack. "Come along. Is there brandy in the garden?" He put his arm around her, gingerly at first, but when she leaned her head against him, he held her firmly around the shoulder. "Your lazy days will be over for a while—as soon as I'm finished with this." They went through the house with their arms around each other.

"My lazy days?"

"You'll be sitting for me. I'm going to do some portraits of you."

"But you've never done portraits before. And why me?"

"What's a better reason to do portraits? And why not you? You have a marvelous face. It shows you know a thing or two about life. I have it on good authority."

They went out into the garden. The sun was just dropping over the wall, leaving the flowers in shadow. The oak tree was there to see, as always. He fingered the thick wrinkles of bark. "Emerich told me his father judged this tree to be only sixty years old." She was not listening. She was staring over the top of the wall into the brittle blue of the late-afternoon sky. "I always thought it was much older than that." He looked at her, wondering what she was thinking. She broke away from the dream that had held her attention.

"Sixty years. Yes, I would have thought it was about that old."

A light breeze came up, ruffling the leaves.

"I'll pour the brandy," she said.

"Should I get your sweater?"

"I'm not chilly. If anything, I'm a little warm." She went to the table and turned the glasses up. "Do you really want to paint my portrait?"

"Yes."

She poured the brandy. He went to the table and took a glass. She turned away from him with hers, out toward the garden.

"Don't you like the idea?"

She did not answer. He cupped her chin in his hand

and turned her face toward him. Tears were standing in her eyes. "What is it? What's wrong?"

She shook her head and turned away. He set down his glass and put his arms around her. She was trembling, but she would not cry. He held her in his arms for a long while until he could feel her relax. She wiped her eyes. He kissed her hair and turned her face up to his. "Finished?"

She smiled a faltering smile and nodded. The remaining tears made her eyes shine.

"I want to paint you so the world will always know what a good woman I had."

"Oh, don't, don't." She laughed nervously. "I'll start all over again."

"Happy tears?"

She smiled with vigor. "Very, very happy tears."

They sat in silence, watching the day fade, listening for the first cricket. Bruno wondered what they all were doing at that moment—Sepp, Joachim, Wolf, Emerich . . . Georg.

"Do you think you'll ever see any of them again?" she asked.

He smiled. How well she knew him. "I was wondering the same thing," he said.

"It would never be the same."

She was probably right. The tunnel was finished, and with it the friendships he had made. Except for Sepp, of course, and Wilfred. "I think Wilfred Komanski will be popping in and out from time to time."

"He's a wonderful man."

"Unique."

"He's somewhat like Alfred, don't you think?"

"Cut from the same stone," he agreed. He sipped the warm brandy. "I think I'll call Grupmann tomorrow, tell him to set up a show in January sometime."

"He'll be pleased," she said, doing a bad job of hiding her own pleasure.

A swallow darted into the tree. Bruno wondered if it had a nest up there. He studied the oak tree standing stolidly in the center of the garden. "I can't understand why I ever thought that tree was so special. It looks very ordinary to me now."

45

"IT'S starting to rain."

She said something under the sheet.

He picked up the sheet and looked at her. "What did you say?"

"I said it doesn't exist."

"What's that?"

"*It*—where it's starting to rain."

He smiled and bent down and kissed her hair. He was sitting up looking out at the steeple of the church, at the gray sky, at the rain spattering the windows. She was lying next to him, as close as she could get. He had the feeling she was not yet convinced they were actually, irretrievably back together again in his room on Neuestrasse. He turned back the sheet and ran his fingertip down the center line of her face, down her forehead, nose, mouth, and chin, catching a quick kiss as it crossed her lips. They laughed.

"I'm so happy!" she said.

"Are you?"

She looked up at him. "Aren't you?"

"Of course."

She kept looking at him to see what was bothering him, and he felt constrained to look away. The rain was coming down steadily, a quiet, serious rain, unruffled by wind or the clangor of thunder and lightning. "You are happy, Sepp?"

He smiled and wrapped a lock of her hair about his finger. It unraveled into a ringlet. "I've never been happier. That's God's truth."

"What is it, darling? Is it Georg?"

He had been weighing how much he could tell her. He knew there were some things that should never pass between two people in love. True love is like tempered steel —it is very strong, but under certain kinds of stress it cracks easily.

"Listen," he said, "I wouldn't do anything differently if I had it to do over again. I'd deceive them all about Konrad Möss. I'd lie to Georg about his parents. I'd ask Greta Dohr to use the tunnel to escape. I'd. . . ." He stopped, sensing that telling her about the Klaus affair would be going too far. Besides, there was Emerich to protect. "I'd do it all again," he said. "I would."

"But that doesn't make you feel any better about having done it."

"No."

She looked away without saying anything. At length, she said, "I have a feeling Georg is better off this way."

He couldn't fathom that.

"Yes, really I do. He would never have found the proper expiation for his sin. He would have gone through life feeling horribly guilty, unable to enjoy his freedom knowing that Greta was still behind The Wall, perhaps in prison. This way, at least he knows she is free. If he comes to want freedom badly enough, he'll find a way to get out. Then he will be truly free."

Sepp thought about it. Maybe she was right. He would have liked to think so. But she had reminded him of his own expiation. What would he have to do to cleanse himself of his own cowardice—a cowardice no different from Georg's, really, except that the consequences had not been so dire. He rather thought there was not going to be an easy way out. He was just going to have to live with it, he supposed, and work at overcoming it. The main thing he was concerned about was not letting it get in the way of their happiness, as it was at this moment. Then he had the thought that living with it and not letting it ruin his life was something he could do, something he had been learning how to do. He understood that realizing he was not yet quite the man he had hoped to be gave him the capacity to become that man. What he did from this moment forward was what mattered.

She moved.

"Don't move," he said.

"I won't leave you. I'll never leave you again."

He caressed her and slid down next to her and was about to begin making love to her again when someone knocked at the door. They both froze.

"Who can it be?" she whispered.

He shrugged. He had no idea.

Whoever it was knocked again, more insistently.

He called out, "Who is it?"

A man's voice said something he couldn't understand.

He got out of bed and pulled on his pants and, opening the door a crack, peered out. It was a man with a package.

"Package for Herr Bauer."

"I'm Herr Bauer."

The deliveryman set the package down and got a pad of delivery slips from his pocket, and handed it to Sepp. There was a pen clipped to it. "You have to sign first."

Sepp opened the door a little wider, signed, and handed the pad back. When he looked up, he saw the man looking through the open door at the bed. When the man realized that Sepp had caught him, he didn't even blink. He was used to that sort of thing. He gave Sepp the package. It was large and heavy.

"Who's it from?"

The man shrugged. "Maybe it says inside. *'Wiedersehen.'* And he was off down the echoing stairwell.

Sepp closed the door and took the package to the bed. "What is it?"

"I don't know." He unwrapped it. She sat up with the sheet around her, watching him. Under the outer wrapper, the box was wrapped in white tissue paper and tied with a ribbon. They looked carefully but could find no card attached.

"Who do you suppose it's from?"

"I have no idea."

He told her to open it. She was all thumbs. When she had the paper almost off, he suddenly realized what it was.

She opened the box. "A vacuum cleaner!"

"A *stolen* vacuum cleaner."

"Stolen?" She was puzzled. "How nice."

"We used it to pump air into the tunnel while we were digging."

"Oh."

"It's a wedding present from the troop," he said.

She brightened. "What a marvelous gift." She caressed it as if it were something precious. Then she gave him a solemn look. "It's rather presumptuous of them, isn't it?"

"Presumptuous?"

"You've never asked me to marry you."

"Good Lord! Are you sure?"

"Of course I'm sure. I'd never forget something like that."

"I've been very busy."

"Excuses, excuses."

He sat up on the bed, propped his chin in his hands, on his knees, and looked into her eyes. "Yes or no?"

She remembered and smiled. Then she started to laugh. He didn't move a muscle.

"Has anyone actually said yes?"

"Of course."

"Who?"

"You."

"I? When?"

"You were just about to."

She threw back her head and laughed with joy. "Yes! Yes! Yes! yes yes yes yes!"

46

K ONRAD pulled his collar up around his neck and pulled Greta closer to him. The rain was coming down in a steady drizzle. His hair was wet and the water was running down the back of his neck, but he didn't mind the rain. He didn't mind anything today. Life was too good to let anything like a little rain bother him.

"Why do you want to see The Wall?"

"I just do," he said.

"I would have thought you had seen enough of it."

"I've never seen it from this side."

"I'm sure it looks the same." She had a plastic rain hat on and a new raincoat she had bought with some of the money Bruno had lent them. She seemed tiny under the rain hat, like a little girl.

They turned east at the canal and walked along it until they came to Potsdamerstrasse. The rain falling on the water made a comforting sound.

"I'm still not used to it," he said.

She smiled with the rain on her face. "Neither am I. I keep wanting to look over my shoulder. Do you think we'll ever get used to it?"

"Yes, but we'll never forget what it was like over there."

She shook her head. "No."

Ahead, Potsdamer Platz was deserted in the rain. They could see the top of a watchtower in the distance. The sight made Greta shudder, and she pressed closer to Konrad.

The little souvenir stand was open, but there was no one about. Rain dripped from the worn wooden steps of the observation platform. The man in the stand looked at them indifferently, convinced they were not going to buy anything on a day like this.

"Would you like something to drink?" Konrad asked.

"No, not now."

They stopped in front of The Wall and looked at it. "You're right. It does look the same on this side." He sounded almost disappointed.

They mounted the steps. Konrad felt his heart beating hard and fast. At the top they stopped and looked out over the Death Zone, at the steel tank traps standing ominously, yet somehow forlornly, in the rain, at the concertina wire stretched in rusting coils in both directions as far as they could see. The vacant fields lay wet and yellow under the gray sky. Konrad lifted his eyes to the horizon, to the rooftops of East Berlin. He felt a strange sense of relief, as if not until now had he been convinced that he was truly on the other side of The Wall.

He glanced up at the watchtower and spied the Vopo looking at them through binoculars. "Poor, stupid pig slopper."

"Who?"

"That Vopo up there—all the Vopos walking their posts in the rain. Up and down, up and down . . . Poor potato diggers."

She was looking along the length of The Wall, where it became lost in the trees of the Tiergarten. "Maybe," she said, "maybe there are people over there somewhere digging another tunnel under The Wall." She looked at him with her newfound hope. "Do you think there are?"

"I think there are, Greta."

"I would like to believe that."

"And there's a Vopo over there somewhere," he said, "walking his post in the rain, bored beyond endurance, dreaming of the day when he'll be over here on the other side of The Wall, standing with his arm around a beautiful girl, thinking about some poor Vopo over there, walking his post in the rain, dreaming. . . ."

She smiled. "Will his dream come true?"

Tentatively, he put his arm around her. "I think it will, Greta, I really think it will."

AFTERWORD

The following is an excerpt from *A Documented History of Escapes and Attempted Escapes from East Berlin, Volume II, 1962*, published by the Escape Coordinating Committee of the Federal Republic of West Germany, Frankfurt-am-Main, 1963.

Chapter IV: Tunnels

Tunnel No. 21—Precis
Beginning date: July 31, 1962
Completion date: August 8, 1962
Troop members: B. Balderbach, J. Bauer, G. Knauer, J. Lentz, W. Lentz, E. Weber
Work site: Abandoned warehouse, 74 Koenigstrasse, Wedding
Terminating point: Abandoned private residence, 25 Vierickstrasse, Pankow (Demolished)
Dimensions: One meter square, 75 meters long
Times used: One
Number of escapees: 17 (Includes one Volkspolizei, J. H. Moelter, who was abducted during the operation and elected to remain in West Berlin.)
Disposition of refugees: Five remained in W. Berlin, eleven settled in the Federal Republic, and one emigrated to America
Status of tunnel: Flooded
Remarks: Three escapees, G. Dohr, J. H. Moelter, and K. Möss and two members of Tunnel No. 21 troop, J. Lentz and W. Lentz were also members of Tunnel No. 30 troop. (See P. 57ff.)